The Hand of Providence

PRELUDE TO GLORY

Prelude to Glory

VOLUME 4

The
Hand of
Providence

A NOVEL BY
RON CARTER

BOOKCRAFT
SALT LAKE CITY

Library of Congress Cataloging-in-Publication Data

Carter, Ron, 1932–
    The hand of providence / Ron Carter.
       p.   cm. — (Prelude to glory ; 4)
    ISBN 1057345-783-3
    I. United States—History—Revolution, 1775–1783—Fiction.   I. Title.
PS3553.A7833   H36   2000
813'.54—dc21   00-037943

Printed in the United States of America   72082-6674

10   9   8   7   6   5   4   3   2

This series is dedicated to the common people
of long ago who paid the price.

For Melvin W. Carter
and Birdie Ione Thueson Carter.
My parents.

The Hand of Providence

"Writing home?" Billy asked.

"To Mother. How does this sound? 'It was a glorious sight to see the haughty Brittons march out and surrender their arms to an army which but a little before thay despised and called paltroons.'"

Men slowed and stopped, listening in the firelight as Boardman read on.

"Surely the hand of Providence work'd wonderfully in favour of America."

More than fifty men had gathered to listen as Boardman concluded.

"I hope every heart will be affected by the wonderful goodness of God in delivering so many of our enemy into our hands, with so little loss on our side."

Boardman raised his eyes back to Billy, and for the first time realized he was surrounded. The men peered down at him, sitting beside his campfire. They wiped at their eyes, then nodded to him as they moved on.

Boardman watched them go, then turned back to Billy. "Was it too much? Did I say it too strong?"

Billy stared at the fire for a moment. "No, it wasn't too strong. It was fine. It was fitting. The hand of Providence was with us."

PREFACE

· The reader will be greatly assisted in following the *Prelude to Glory* series if the author's overall approach is understood.

The volumes do not present the critical events of the Revolutionary War in chronological, month-by-month, year-by-year order. The reason is simple. At all times during the eight years of the conflict, the tremendous events that shaped the war and decided the final result were happening simultaneously in two, and sometimes three, different geographical areas. This being true, it became obvious that moving back and forth, from one battle front to another, would be extremely confusing.

Thus, the decision was made to follow each major event through to its conclusion, as seen through the eyes of selected characters, and then go back and pick up the thread of other great events that were happening at the same time in other places, through the eyes of characters caught up in those events.

The reader will recall that volume I, *Our Sacred Honor*, followed the fictional family of John Phelps Dunson from the beginning of hostilities between the British and the Americans in April 1775, through the Lexington and Concord battles, and then moved into the experiences of Matthew Dunson, John's eldest son, who was a navigator in the sea battles that occurred later in the war. In volume II, *The Times That Try Men's Souls*, Billy Weems, Matthew's dearest friend, survived the terrible defeats suffered by the Americans around New York and the disastrous American retreat to the wintry banks of the Delaware River. In volume III, *To Decide Our Destiny*, Billy and his friend Eli Stroud followed General Washington back across the Delaware on Christmas night, 1776, to storm and miraculously take the town of Trenton, and then Princeton.

Volume IV, *The Hand of Providence*, addresses the tremendous, inspiring events of the campaign for possession of the Lake Champlain–Hudson

River corridor, wherein British General John Burgoyne, with an army of eight thousand, is sent by King George III to take Fort Ticonderoga, proceed to Albany, and in conjunction with the forces of General William Howe and Colonel Barry St. Leger, cut the New England states off from the southern states, and defeat them one at a time. To oppose Burgoyne, the United States sends General Arthur St. Clair, with less than half the army commanded by General Burgoyne. The heroics of men on both sides, the battles, the unbelievable tricks, the startling performance of General Benedict Arnold, all seen through the eyes of Billy and Eli, are probably among the most gripping stories in the entire Revolution. Historians have long since included the events of the summer of 1777 in the single term, *Saratoga,* and it is clear that this battle changed the history of the world.

Volume V will also address the events of the summer of 1777, following General George Washington as he seeks a way to stop General William Howe on the eastern seaboard. Caleb Dunson, age sixteen, the rebellious runaway son of John Dunson, has already joined Washington's army and is rapidly learning the brutalities of camp life and war. Mary Flint, the beautiful, plucky widow of wealthy Marcus Flint, now destitute and seeking a new life, is desperately trying to find Eli and Billy, the only two persons she can look to for help and understanding.

And, reader, be patient. Matthew and Kathleen are going to be reunited, and the wait will make it all the sweeter. Mary Flint has realized her strong feelings for Eli, feelings he shares for her. Billy has given his heart to Brigitte; however, she sees him only as a dear friend of the family. These wonderful young people are going through that painful but exciting time of finding each other and experiencing the blossoming of young love into mature love. It's all yet to come.

CHRONOLOGY OF IMPORTANT EVENTS RELATED TO THIS VOLUME

1775

April 19. The first shot is fired at Lexington, Massachusetts, and the Revolutionary War begins. (*See volume 1*)

June 15. The Continental Congress appoints George Washington of Virginia to be commander in chief of the Continental army.

June 17. The Battle of Bunker Hill and Breed's Hill is fought, which the British win at great cost, suffering numerous casualties before the colonial forces abandon the hills due to lack of ammunition. (*See volume 1*)

September. King George III of England and his cabinet agree upon a strategy for putting down the rebellion in the American colonies, as well as the British officers who shall command and the armed forces that will be necessary.

1776

February–March. Commodore Esek Hopkins leads eight small colonial ships to the Bahamas to obtain munitions from two British forts, Nassau and Montague. (*See volume 1*)

March 17. General Sir William Howe evacuates his British command from Boston. (*See volume 1*)

July 9. On orders from General Washington, the Declaration of Independence (adopted by the Continental Congress on July fourth) is read publicly to the entire American command in the New York area, as well as the citizens. *(See volume 2)*

Late August–Early December. The British and American armies clash in a series of battles at Long Island, Kip's Bay, Harlem Heights, White Plains, and Fort Washington. Though the Americans make occasional gains in the battles, the British effectively decimate the Continental army to the point that Washington has no choice but to begin a retreat across the length of New Jersey. He crosses the Delaware River into Pennsylvania and establishes a camp at McKonkey's Ferry, nine miles north of Trenton. *(See volume 2)*

September 21. An accidental fire burns about one-fourth of the city of New York.

October 11. General Benedict Arnold leads a tiny fleet of fifteen hastily constructed ships to stall the British fleet of twenty-five ships on Lake Champlain. The hope is that Arnold's forces can at least delay the movement of thirteen thousand British troops south until the spring of 1777 and thus save George Washington's Continental army. *(See volume 1)*

December 10. Benjamin Franklin travels to France to persuade the French government to support America in the Revolution.

December 14. General William Howe closes the winter campaign, and the British troops retire into winter quarters. Howe stations General James Grant at Princeton with a small force of British soldiers. Colonel Carl Emil Kurt von Donop is given command of three thousand Hessians along the Delaware River opposite the American camp, and he quarters fourteen hundred of his men in Trenton under the command of Colonel Johann Gottlieb Rall.

December 22. John Honeyman, an American spy posing as a British loyalist, is under orders from General Washington and makes a reconnaissance journey to Trenton, is later "captured" by the Americans, and reports his findings to Washington directly.

December 25. Washington's three-point attack of Trenton begins as he and his army cross the Delaware River at McKonkey's Ferry at night and during a raging blizzard. General James Ewing attempts a crossing at the Trenton Ferry, and General John Cadwalader moves into position at Dunk's Ferry.

December 26. The Battle of Trenton is fought to a dramatic conclusion.

December 29. Benjamin Franklin meets with Comte de Vergennes to discuss French aid for the Americans.

December 31. Enlistments for the majority of soldiers in the Continental army are due to expire at midnight.

1777

January 2. General Charles Cornwallis leads a British force of 8,000 men out of Princeton with orders to destroy what is left of Washington's army. Colonel Edward Hand and a small force of 600 Pennsylvanian riflemen are dispatched to stop the British before they can reach Trenton.

January 3. Washington and his army of over four thousand men endure a midnight march out of Trenton and into Princeton, where they surprise British colonel Charles Mawhood's command shortly after sunrise. The Battle of Princeton is fought with surprising results.

January 7. The Continental army establishes winter quarters in Morristown, New Jersey.

February 25. As the political relationships between England, France, and America tighten, Comte de Vergennes receives news regarding the outcome of the battles of Trenton and Princeton and plans a course of action for France.

May 6. British General John Burgoyne arrives in Canada to begin his campaign down the Champlain–Hudson region.

June 12. General Arthur St. Clair arrives at Fort Ticonderoga to take command of the American forces.

July 4. The British scale Mt. Defiance to mount cannon that are within range of Fort Ticonderoga.

July 5. The Americans discover the presence of the cannon and recognize that the British are now capable of destroying the fort at will, together with the men therein.

July 5–6. General St. Clair abandons Fort Ticonderoga to the British and retreats with his men, part of them moving south in boats to Skenesborough, the balance marching toward Hubbardton, intending to join the boats at Skenesborough.

July 6. The British fleet sinks every American boat at Skenesborough and scatters the Americans.

July 7. The Battle of Hubbardton is fought, in which the Americans make a good accounting until British reinforcements arrive, driving them from the field.

August 16. General John Stark leads his American New Hampshire militia against German Colonel Friedrich Baum in the Battle of Bennington and soundly defeats the German column and their reinforcements.

August 19. General Horatio Gates arrives at Stillwater to replace generals Philip Schuyler and Arthur St. Clair as American commander of the Northern Army. Congress has ordered Schuyler and St. Clair to explain their actions in abandoning Fort Ticonderoga, and they are to report to General Washington, ostensibly to face courts-martial.

September 19. The American and British forces clash at Bemis Heights, and the Battle of Freeman's Farm is fought. Neither side claims victory.

October 7. The Battle of Barber's Wheat Field is fought near Bemis Heights. General Benedict Arnold, against orders from General Horatio Gates and with spectacular leadership on the battlefield, leads the Americans to victory.

October 17. General John Burgoyne surrenders his army to General Horatio Gates.

December 2. King George III is informed of the surrender of Burgoyne's army, and Horace Walpole reports that "the king fell into agonies."

December 12. Benjamin Franklin, American ambassador to France, meets with Comte de Vergennes, French foreign minister, to persuade him, and eventually King Louis XVI, to enter the war on the side of the Americans.

1779

September 23. Commodore John Paul Jones, aboard the *Bonhomme Richard*, engages the larger British man-of-war *Serapis* off the east coast of England in the much-celebrated night battle in which Jones utters the now-famous cry, "I have not yet begun to fight!" (*See volume 1*)

Boston

May 24, 1777

CHAPTER I

★ ★ ★

*H*is strong, square, homely face with the sandy red beard was suddenly there in the swirling sea mists, hovering just beyond her fingertips, and her heart leaped as she thrust her hand toward him. He was dressed in his seaman's jacket with his first mate's cap pulled low over eyes that, at the sight of her, were soft and yearning.

"Bartholomew," she exclaimed, "you've come!"

Dorothy Weems tried to move her feet, but it was as though they were mired in something that would not let go. She reached for him with both hands, and he reached toward her with those thick wrists and strong, blocky hands, and she heard him murmur, "Dorothy. Dorothy."

"Four o'clock. Fair weather. Four o'clock."

The faint call came from behind, and Dorothy turned to look, but there was no one. She turned back to Bartholomew, who was drawing away from her, fading into the fog, his hands still reaching.

"Bartholomew," she cried, and tried to follow him, but she could not make her feet move.

"Four o'clock. Fair weather. Four o'clock." The voice was closer. Again she turned to look, but saw nothing. When she turned back, there was only the swirling mist and the fog and deepening gloom.

"Bartholomew," she shouted, and lunged wide-eyed. Instantly she was plunged into blackness, and then she was sitting upright, her feet snarled in something. She felt the beads of perspiration cold on her face, and she flailed her hands outward, but could feel nothing. Her hands dropped to her side, and the soft warmth of the great comforter of her bed was there. She clutched at it while her mind slowly came back to her small, sparse bedroom. Her shoulders slumped as she understood where she was.

Slowly her head tipped forward, and the tears came welling up. Her mouth formed the word *Bartholomew* before she fell silent, and the warm salt tears trickled. For a time her shoulders shook with her silent sobbing before a timid rap came at her door, and then it opened. The shape of her daughter was framed in the dim light, and then the nine-year-old voice came softly.

"Mama?"

Quickly she wiped at her eyes. "Trudy. Come, get in with me."

The slender body bounded across the room and the thin arms circled Dorothy's neck, clinging.

Dorothy held her close and smoothed her hair.

"Child, you're shaking."

"I heard something."

"It was me. I had a dream and made a noise. Everything is all right."

"A *bad* dream?"

"No, a good one."

"Can I stay here with you?"

"Of course. Let me smooth the covers." With a mother's practiced hand, Dorothy quickly adjusted the comforter while Trudy curled into a ball, her back toward her mother as she waited for the sure, strong arm to circle her and draw her close. She smiled in the darkness, and her shivering stopped.

"What did you dream?"

For a moment Dorothy hesitated. "Your father."

"Did you see him?"

"Yes."

"Did you talk to him?"

"He called my name, and I called his."

"What did he look like?"

"Like always. Strong. Gentle."

"Do you love him?"

"Always."

"Did he talk about me?"

"In a way. He came to see his family."

"Was Billy with him?"

"No. Your father is in heaven with God and the angels. Billy is just away for a while, with the army."

"When is Billy coming back?"

"As soon as he can. Now you hush and go to sleep."

From the street came the call, much closer, louder. "Half past four. Fair weather. Half past four."

Trudy twisted her face toward Dorothy. "What is that?"

"The bellman. You've heard him before."

"But I didn't know."

"The bellman walks the streets at night. A man, and a boy, with a lantern on a long pole. They call out the time and tell the weather. They're our friends. They watch for bad men and keep us safe at night. Now you go back to sleep."

In the warmth of the bed, curled against her mother, Trudy closed her eyes, and Dorothy waited until the girl's breathing became slow and regular before she allowed herself to drift into a dreamless sleep.

She started at the voice of the bellman once more. "Half past five o'clock. Fair weather. Half past five o'clock."

Gently she slipped her arm from her daughter and sat up silently in the bed. The first faint light of the quiet time between full darkness and sunrise showed through the window curtains. She swung her feet to the oval rag rug that she had patiently braided with her dark-eyed daughter, teaching her, watching her earnest face as she worked with the heavy, wooden hook to pull the corded rags through the succeeding loops. She stood in the darkness and then walked barefoot, out of her bedroom, down the chilly, polished hardwood floor of the hall, past Trudy's door, into the parlor.

The coals banked last night in the fireplace still glowed under a layer of ash. Exposing the coals with a poker and sprinkling a handful of fine shavings of dried pine on them, she used an aged leather bellow to coax a finger of flame from the smoking heap. She added a few sticks of larger kindling and after they caught, some bigger pieces of chopped wood. With the fire lighting the room, she straightened to look at the clock on the mantel, and for a moment admired the delicate oak-leaf design worked into the polished wood. It was a Dunson clock, crafted by John Dunson, and given to her as a gift by his family many years before. The clock read forty minutes past five o'clock.

With the thought of John Dunson, the pain of that dread day—April 19, 1775—rose searing in her breast. That was the day the Americans had met the British on the green at Lexington, and then at the North Bridge in Concord, eighteen miles west of Boston, and turned them, driving the redcoats in a panic back to Boston. The day Tom Sievers had brought John Dunson home, shot through the lung by a .75-caliber ball from a British Brown Bess musket. The day John died in his home. The day her Billy was shot in the side by the redcoats, then bayoneted and left for dead. The day that changed the world forever.

"Three quarters past five o'clock. Fair weather. Three quarters past five o'clock." The call came from the street again, much closer.

She stood silent for a moment, waiting to see if the bellman's call would waken Trudy. There was no sound, and she drew and released a great sigh. Unexpectedly, in the twilight of the room, she was seeing the round, plain face, sandy red hair, and square, strong build of her only son, a copy of his father. Her breath came short at the familiar, sudden clutch of fear. Her eyes opened wide as the thoughts came flooding.

Is Billy safe? Well? Still in Morristown with General Washington? Or has there been another battle? Is he wounded? Dying? Dead?

Images of torn, dead bodies on distant battlefields came rushing, and she could no longer stand still with the torment. She set her jaw and drove the terrifying scenes away, murmuring, "This isn't getting the work done." The relentless, grinding business of living left little time for a widow to ponder her pain, her wounds of life, when she had a household to manage and a nine-year-old daughter to raise.

Today candles had to be made from tallow she had carefully saved from every piece of meat she had cooked through the long, cold months of winter. She had boiled the fat and tallow, carefully strained it twice through cheesecloth, then stored it in the cool of the vegetable cellar in the backyard beside the waxy residue she had cooked and skimmed from the wild bayberries gathered last fall and saved in pewter jars. She could not afford to pay the itinerant candlemaker to spend a day at her home with the heavy iron kettles, and the fires, pouring the smoking wax and tallow into the molds. If she were careful, she could sell most of her spring candles at the beginning of the fall season.

She straightened and walked silently to the window and pushed the curtain aside to peer out at the rose colors rising in the eastern sky. To the north, nearly to the corner of the street, a single lantern carried on a pole cast faint, long shadows on the cobblestones of two figures, bellmen, walking side by side—one large, one smaller. They were two of the thirteen "sober, honest men and householders" selected by the citizens of Boston to walk the streets at night in pairs, watching for thieves, and calling out the hour and the weather for those who were awake to hear.

Dorothy squared her shoulders and turned back toward her bedroom. *Fair weather. Cool enough to dip them out of doors and warm enough to let them set up without cracking. A good day for candlemaking. Time to start the fires.*

With the growing firelight sifting down the hall and into her bedroom, Dorothy silently collected the clothing she needed, paused for a moment to bend and lightly kiss the hair of her sleeping child, then walked from the room, quietly latching the door behind. She went into Trudy's bedroom, where she laid her work clothes on the bed, then went to her knees, hands clasped, head bowed.

"Almighty and merciful God, hallowed be Thy name. Thy will be done. In humility I beseech Thee, spare and protect my Billy in his adversity. Bless Bartholomew. Bless and protect Trudy and all who enter this household this day. For all good things I thank Thee. Amen."

She rose and quickly straightened the bed, changed from her nightshirt into a plain gray cotton work dress, slipped into her heavy shoes, tied her hair back with a white bandanna, and tiptoed down the hall, through the kitchen, out into the small backyard, quiet in the growing light of a new day in Boston Town. A faint, cool, salty seabreeze came off the harbor and for a moment the old, familiar ache rose inside as memories of Bartholomew came, and she paused.

Square, powerful, homely, first-mate on a fishing boat, he had met her when his boat was nearly sunk in a hurricane off the Grand Banks and had limped into Gloucester harbor for repairs. She had lived there, and he had seen her at church. The second Sunday he had stopped her, and with downcast eyes and awkward words had asked if she would allow him to write. They exchanged letters, and within weeks he reappeared. Would she consider marriage to such a man as he?

Dorothy held no illusions about herself. Stocky, plain, round-faced, friend to many, sweetheart to none, she had been courted by no other man—never asked for her hand. Yes, she would marry him. The reverend in Gloucester wed them that very day, and she joined Bartholomew on his boat back to Boston.

He had loved her with all his heart, and she had loved him, oblivious to the rough, direct ways of a man whose life had been spent at sea. They had lost one child, then came Billy: barrel-chested, sandy haired, plain—the image of his father. Their daughter, Trudy, was born years later, and then one day Dorothy answered a knock on her door. She knew the instant she saw the man standing on the doorstep, working his seaman's cap in his hands, refusing to look her in the eye. Her Bartholomew had been lost at sea.

For a time, her sole reason for living was the children. Stoically, as though detached from all feeling, all reality, she kept an austere house and took in laundry, braided rugs, learned to be a midwife, baked for neighbors, did needlepoint—anything to honorably scrape together enough money to pay the cost of maintaining her small family. Through it all, the Dunson family had been there to bring in food, help during times of sickness, and Margaret to talk. Matthew, Margaret's eldest son, was the brother Billy never had. The boys grew, and through the years became inseparable.

Then came the day when her adolescent Billy had faced her in his bedroom. With trembling lip he had said, "Mother, father died a long time ago, and it seems that some of you died with him."

White-hot pain had gone through her like a sword as she realized that in sealing her grief away from her heart, she had sealed the children away as well. She had flung her arms about Billy and buried her face in his shoulder as the inner wall crumbled, and they stood there alone, clinging to each other while racking sobs shook them both as they vented their festered sorrow. From that day, the healing began.

Dorothy heaved a sigh. *The fires won't start themselves.*

She took a determined breath as she peered at the two black cast iron cooking pots turned over against the back wall of the house, inside the small wood yard, where she had placed them after dragging them out of the root cellar in the late afternoon of yesterday. Two heavy metal tripods leaned against the wall beside the pots. She moved them away from the wall and spread the tripod legs wide, with the center chain and the hook dangling low. She slipped the handle of the nearest pot over the tripod hook, then began working the tripod legs closer together, one at a time, until the pot was nearly two feet off the ground. Then she turned to the other pot and hooked it up to the second tripod.

She crouched to pile pine shavings and small sticks beneath each pot, then went back into the house to the fireplace, where she scooped glowing coals into a long-handled brass scoop, then hastened outside to spread them on the shavings. She watched until small yellow flames came licking, then added kindling.

While the flames grew and the pots heated, she went to the well for four dripping buckets of cold water and emptied them hissing into the two heated pots. Then she walked to the root cellar, lifted the heavy pine door, descended the five steps, and opened the second door into the chill, damp darkness. With the doors open for light, she carried the first two jars of clean, strained tallow outside and set them close to the fire. She had made the third trip to the vegetable cellar before the hard tallow in the first two jars had softened around the sides enough for her to lift them with thick burlap pads and turn them upside down above each pot, waiting for the hard lumps of tallow to slide out, splashing into the hot water. She set the empty jars on the ground, then waited for the tallow in the other jars to soften around the edges before she emptied them into the pots. She watched and waited while the large lumps of floating tallow slowly heated, and wisps of steam began to rise as they melted and spread on the water.

She leaned over one pot to smell the thick, animal odor, made her judgment, then returned to the cellar for four smaller jars of clear, light-green wax, cooked down last fall from wild bayberries she and Trudy had gathered along the shores of the Boston peninsula. Together they had skimmed the dirty green residue from the pots to strain and refine it into a clear, sweet-smelling wax, and then stored it for spring candlemaking. When mixed with the tallow, the pungent bayberry wax gave the candles a pleasant scent instead of the malodorous smell of animal tallow. She warmed the jars, emptied two into each pot of tallow, and watched them bob before they began to melt.

That should be enough. She straightened and turned to look toward the east, where the risen sun had turned the tops of the trees to fire, shot through with the gold and rose colors of a warm, spectacular Boston May morning. For a moment she stood still, breathing the clear, clean air, savoring the salt tang, caught up in the revival of the earth after a hard, gray winter. She reveled in the renewal of the earth, and the promise of the goodness it would bring. She filled her lungs and caught the sweetness of pink peach and white apple blossoms and red and yellow tulips just opening. Her elderly neighbor, Florence McIvers, hair bound back by a sky-blue bandanna, called a cheery "Good morning" over the white picket fence, and Dorothy brightened as she waved and returned the greeting. A smile came, and she realized she was humming as she walked back into the kitchen.

She found Trudy sitting on the polished hardwood floor before the fireplace in the parlor, arms wrapped about her knees, which were drawn to her chin, watching the dancing flames and the glowing coals. The French braid of her long dark hair hung far down her back. She turned her head as Dorothy walked from the kitchen through the archway.

"I couldn't find you when I got up. Then I heard you in the backyard."

"You forgot. We make candles today. They'll bring in a few dollars for meat."

"Are we going to have breakfast?"

"Soft-boiled eggs on bread and milk. Get washed and put on your work clothes. If you hurry we might have some honey on bread."

Dorothy transferred hot coals from the fireplace to the fire box in the small, black cast iron stove in the kitchen to start the fire before she went to the root cellar for two eggs and a pat of butter. She dipped water from the kitchen water bucket into a small pewter pan and set the eggs to heat, then went quickly to her room to wash, brush her hair, and tie it back with the white bandanna once again.

"Trudy! Don't dawdle."

Hurrying feet sounded in the hall. "I'm here, mother. Help me with my hair. I've brushed it."

"I've showed you how."

"It's hard when I can't see it . . ."

"Feel and go slow. You can do it."

Trudy plumped herself down on her breakfast chair, mouth clamped shut in disgust, and slowly divided her hair into three long locks. "I can't start it."

"Yes, you can." Dorothy opened the cupboard to lift out two pewter plates and cups and did not look at Trudy.

Working with her hands behind her head, Trudy slowly lifted one lock over the next one, then the third lock back over the two, and was soon working more rapidly. She finished the long French braid, tied the end with a small white ribbon, and walked to her mother for approval. Dorothy diverted her eyes to look for a moment, then reached to touch the braid.

"Fine. Not too tight." She looked her daughter in the eye and gave her a five-second New England lecture. "Don't ask for help you don't need. It wastes time and makes lazy hands."

Trudy shrugged. "Do we get honey?"

"Fetch it from the root cellar. And bring some buttermilk."

Trudy brightened and trotted from the room.

They blessed the bounties of their table and cracked their soft eggs on the sliced bread before Dorothy carefully poured steaming milk over it. Trudy broke the yellow yolk of her egg with her fork and watched it spread to make designs in the white milk and on the soggy bread. Eyes wide in anticipation, the young girl spread butter high on a separate slice of bread and smeared honey deep while Dorothy poured thick buttermilk into their pewter mugs. Trudy said nothing as she spooned the bread and egg and hot milk and stuffed her mouth with the bread and honey, to wash it all down with buttermilk.

Dorothy covertly watched, finding a mother's joy in watching her child take pleasure in eating what she had been able to provide.

"Eat slowly. It will taste better, and your stomach will appreciate it."

Trudy neither slowed nor chewed longer. She finished and raised smiling eyes to Dorothy. "More bread and honey?"

Dorothy nodded.

They cleared the table and put the dishes into the wooden dishpan in the kitchen. All dirty dishes were placed there until after supper, when the two of them would boil the water to fill the dishpan and rinse pan, add the brown soap they had made from ashes and lye last fall, and alternate in washing and drying.

Dorothy wasted no time. "Go to my room and fetch the candle wicks we made last fall. They're in the bottom drawer in the chest of drawers, wrapped in brown paper. Remember?"

Trudy turned on her heel and was gone, while Dorothy pulled a chair to the center of the kitchen floor and stepped up onto it. Wooden pegs were set in the side of the massive, low overhead beams, on which long wooden poles were placed, along with many shorter, thin iron rods. Carefully she reached high to lift down two of the long poles, and eight of the metal rods, and took them outside where she laid them in the grass close to the woodyard while Trudy returned with the bundle of wicks.

"Put them there," Dorothy said, pointing, and Trudy laid the brown paper bundle on the grass. Together they carried four sawhorses out of the small woodyard to a place near the kettles and arranged them in pairs with the ends touching, one pair facing the other eight feet away, and then laid the two long poles on them, parallel, about four feet apart.

"Good. Now open the bundle of wicks, and I'll show you how to double them and put them on the rods. It's time you learned."

"I've watched you before."

"But you've never done it. Watch closely."

Trudy watched Dorothy open the brown paper, and as Dorothy reached for the first long, thin wick, Trudy was remembering the afternoons the two of them had spent during the previous fall, walking in the open fields and along the roadsides, the banks of the streams around Boston, and past The Neck on the mainland, gathering the silky down from the milkweed that grew in wild abundance. They gathered it in their aprons and put it in sacks to carry home. Dorothy taught her how to gently roll the silky fibers between her hands to start it, and then draw it with one hand while she twisted it with the other into a long thread. When they were finished, they had cut the strands into thirty-six-inch lengths, soaked them for two days in water laced with saltpeter, dried them, and carefully wrapped them for their spring candlemaking.

Bostonian custom was to make candles in the fall, but Dorothy Weems had discovered that if she would mix bayberry wax with the tallow to improve the smell, make them in the springtime, and store them in a cool place so they would retain their pleasing, clear color, and not crack, she could sell them to half a dozen regular wealthy customers for fourpence, or fivepence, at the beginning of candlemaking season. It brought in enough money to buy ham, and perhaps salted beef, to be stored in the cool root cellar for the worst of the winter months.

Dorothy seized both ends of one, thirty-six-inch thread and began twisting the ends in opposite directions until it was wound tightly. Then she brought the two ends together to tie them. She inserted a finger at each end of the loop and again she twisted, this time in the opposite direction, until the doubled thread was tight and stiff.

She looked at Trudy. "Twist it, double it, tie it, twist the other way."

Trudy nodded, and Dorothy continued. She picked up one of the thin metal rods and inserted it through the loop left by her finger at the knotted end, held the rod firmly in one hand, then pulled on the string until it was hanging straight down, stiff, a fully formed wick. She looked at it with satisfaction and spoke to Trudy.

"There. Now you make one."

For a moment Trudy's brow furrowed as she went over the steps in her mind. Then she picked up one of the long threads and began twisting it under Dorothy's critical, approving eye.

While Trudy twisted wicks and strung them on the metal rod, Dorothy watched the two pots, waiting for the tallow and bayberry wax to become molten. She stirred the mixture with a long, clean stick from the wood yard until it was mixed, then skimmed it twice with cheesecloth. When the mixture began to emit tiny wisps of steam, she used a brass shovel to pull the fire from beneath the pots, stirred the steaming mix once more, and turned to Trudy.

"It has to cool to just the right temperature before we dip the wicks. Not too hot, not too cool. Let's finish twisting wicks while we wait."

With six wicks dangling from each of eight metal rods, Dorothy dipped a small amount of the mix in a cup, then slowly poured it back into the pot, watching intently to gauge how it was thickening.

"It's ready. Do what I do, and we'll start the dipping."

Dorothy grasped one end of a metal rod, and Trudy picked up the other. They lifted it high, and positioned the six twisted wicks above the nearest pot. Slowly, being careful not to dip so quickly that the wicks would bend, they lowered the rod, watching the wicks sink into the soft tallow and bayberry wax mix. They held the rod steady for ten seconds, then slowly drew it straight up and held it above the pot while one or two drops from each wick fell back into the pot, waiting while the mix began to harden. Carefully they carried it to the two long poles set on the sawhorses, and each lowered their end of the metal rods onto one of the wooden poles. They stepped back to look at their handiwork, smiled in satisfaction, and picked up the next rod.

With all eight rods through the first dip, Dorothy used the brass shovel to push the coals back under the pots and then added a few sticks of kindling. "Getting just a bit cool. Needs a little more heat," she explained to Trudy.

While she waited for the pots to warm, she took Trudy to the rack and leaned over to examine the wicks. "See how they are starting to show a clear, light green color? That's from the bayberry wax. If they were all tallow, they would be a brownish color, and they'd smell like animal fat, not sweet. You've got to let them cool and harden slowly. If the day was too cold, they'd harden too fast and crack. If it was too warm, they'd harden too slowly and lose their shape. Today's a good day. If it weren't, we'd have to do this inside, and that always makes a mess on the floors."

She raised her head to glance at the sun and the sky. "The weather is going to hold. We'll be all right."

They dipped all eight rods again, replaced them on the poles, waited, and then dipped them a third time before Dorothy shaded her eyes to look at the sun and turned to Trudy.

"Hungry?"

Trudy nodded, and they walked into the kitchen where they ate some boiled cabbage with mutton and bread and drank cold well water.

By midafternoon they had finished the eighth dipping, and Dorothy stood back to examine their handiwork. The candles were curing to a light, clear green, twelve inches in length, about one inch in diameter, and hardening perfectly. None had cracked. She scattered the coals to put out the fires and turned to Trudy. "We'll let the pots cool. What's left of the wax will be hard by Monday. We'll break it off the top of the water and save it for fall before we clean the pots. We'd better go in and finish the house work. Tomorrow's the Sabbath and we . . . ."

Movement at the corner of the house caught her eye, and she turned to look, then brightened as she spoke.

"Reverend Olmsted! What a surprise." She glanced down at her stained apron, and her face reddened. "We didn't expect . . . I'm sorry for how we look."

Thin, hunch-shouldered, hawk-faced, with graying hair and beard,

Reverend Silas Olmsted picked his way through the sawhorses and tripods, speaking in his high, nasal voice.

"You look fine, Dorothy. And, Trudy, you're just about grown up. Look at you. A young lady." He smiled at her, and Trudy grinned and blushed and dropped her eyes.

Dorothy spoke. "We just finished dipping candles, Reverend. Won't you come in for coffee?"

"Thank you, but I need to get back to help Mattie get ready for the Sabbath. I was just down at the market getting my mail, and there was a letter from Billy to you. I thought I'd bring it over."

Dorothy caught her breath, and her hand flew to her breast. "From Billy?"

"Right here." He thrust it forward, and Dorothy reached with trembling fingers. "Mind if I stay while you read it? I'd like to know if he's all right."

Her hands were shaking as she broke the seal and unfolded the brief writing. She stood still while her eyes flew over the words, and then her shoulders slumped in relief. "He's all right. Let me read it to you."

The reverend nodded and listened intently.

> May 5, 1777
>
> Morristown, New Jersey
>
> My Dear Mother and Sister:
>
> I first assure you I am well in mind and body. Since I wrote last, I have enjoyed good food and a warm log hut. The army remains camped here at Morristown, where we are safe. Spring has arrived and the mountains here are green—the weather generally warm.
>
> I am obliged to inform you that I am being sent north with my friend, Eli Stroud. We are to join the militia in the region of Lake Champlain where it is thought Eli can be of help in fighting the British, since he knows the country and the language of the Indian people up there. I do not

know when I will return, or when I will be able to write again. You are not to worry. We are in the right cause, and the Almighty favors us, as I have seen many times.

I think of you often. Trudy, I will try to bring you a surprise from the north country when I return. Obey Mother and help her in every way. You are a fine daughter and sister.

I am sorry I do not have more time. I think of you every day, and you are in my prayers always. I look forward to the day when I can return. I'll have much to tell. Please let Margaret and Brigitte read this letter, and ask them to inform Matthew about me when they write to him next.

I place you all in the hands of the Almighty.

> Your loving and ob'dt son and brother,
> Billy Weems

She paused for a moment, studying the neatly formed words, treasuring them, until Silas spoke.

"He's going north?"

"That's what he says."

"I heard the British are sending General John Burgoyne and an army down from Canada on Lake Champlain to try to cut off the New England states. If that's true, they'll be coming right through the Iroquois country. Has Billy told you how his friend comes to know the Indian language and customs?"

"He wrote about Mr. Stroud earlier. It seems Eli was taken by the Iroquois as a baby and raised by them. Billy says he's a good man." Dorothy's face clouded. "Will they be in among the Indians?"

Silas reached to thoughtfully scratch at his beard. "Sounds like it." He placed his hand on Dorothy's shoulder. "Now, you're not to worry. We'll have soldiers up there, and Billy will be all right. He's a good boy. God will look after him."

Dorothy nodded, but the fear did not leave her heart. "I hope so."

Silas gave her a reassuring pat on the shoulder, then stood for a moment examining the candles. "You've done a good day's work. They should bring a good price this fall. Will you and Trudy be at church in the morning?"

"Yes."

"Good. If you need help trimming those candles, just say so. Mattie and I can come."

"Thank you, Trudy and I can do it."

"I know, but a little company now and then won't hurt." He turned to walk back out to the street. "See you in the morning."

"Thank you for bringing the letter."

He nodded and waved and was gone.

For a moment Dorothy stood in the afternoon sunlight, holding the letter. *North, into Iroquois Indian country.* She struggled while horrifying images flitted in her mind of families and entire villages where the savage Iroquois Indians had struck, leaving behind only dead, scalped, mutilated bodies. She shuddered, then shook herself and squared her shoulders. *He will be all right. The Almighty is watching over him. He will be all right.* She repeated it to herself silently and pushed away the heart-rending scenes before she turned to Trudy.

"Billy wants us to take this letter down to Margaret to read. Would you like to visit the twins for a while?"

Trudy's eyes widened in surprise. "Now?"

"Yes."

The girl turned on her heel and dashed to her room to change, with Dorothy following. It would not do for a mother and daughter to be seen walking the streets of Boston in candlemaking garb.

A few minutes later, wearing their long-skirted dresses with wrist-length sleeves, they tied on their bonnets, inspected each other, and walked out into the beauty of the late afternoon of a warm spring day, petticoats and skirts swishing. Side-by-side they passed the white picket fences and manicured yards, calling greetings to friends and acquaintances. High-stepping horses in well-oiled and ornamented harnesses, pulling shiny buggies and coaches, clattered by on the tree-lined cobblestone streets while the drivers and those in the vans nodded sedately to those they knew. A man wearing a leather cap and an old threadbare coat, leading a huge dog hitched to a rickety milk-cart, made his way homeward after a day of delivering milk to his customers. A chimney sweep, black from head to toe except for the whites of his eyes, walked briskly up the far side of the street, carrying his whisks, scoop, and broom, whistling as he made his way to his last chimney for the day.

They pushed through the gate in a white fence where a five-foot sign stood in the yard with a large clock carved in the top and *JOHN DUNSON, MASTER CLOCKMAKER, GUNSMITH* neatly carved below. As the gate closed behind them, the door to the house burst open, and the twins, Adam and Priscilla, came bounding out, shouting to Trudy as they ran down the brick walkway. Trudy shrieked with joy as she threw her arms around Prissy, and the children turned to go into the house as Margaret Dunson came through the doorway into the bright sunlight. Average height, well-built, a handsome woman, Margaret threw open her arms, and the two women embraced warmly before Margaret linked her arm through Dorothy's and led her into the house, smiling, chattering.

"Well," Margaret exclaimed, "what an unexpected pleasure. Take off your bonnet and come into the kitchen. We'll fix coffee."

Dorothy hung her bonnet on a peg by the door and followed Margaret into the kitchen, where Margaret stirred the coals in the stove firebox, added two sticks of kindling, and set the coffeepot to heat. She gestured to a chair, and the two women sat down to wait. Margaret spoke.

"Have you gotten to your candlemaking yet, Dorothy?"

"Today."

"How many?"

"Forty-eight."

"My. A good day's work. Did Trudy help?"

Dorothy's eyes brightened with pride. "She helped twist the wicks, and we did the dipping together."

Margaret smiled. "Wonderful. I'll start training Prissy and Adam this fall when we make our winter candles. How are the blossoms on the apple and peach trees?"

"Good. We should have plenty for winter."

Margaret hesitated for a moment, watching Dorothy keenly before asking, "Heard from Billy lately?"

From earliest childhood, Margaret's son Matthew, and Billy, had been inseparable. They were a contrast, with Billy stocky, sandy-haired, strong as a bull, and Matthew tall, slender, dark-eyed. Billy, plain, homely, open, loud, laughing, fun, while Matthew was handsome, serious, intense, tending to withhold. But somehow the two seemed to complement each other. They had shared everything while growing up. When Billy lost his father, it was Matthew who had come to his house and slept on the floor beside Billy's bed for a week, never leaving his side. School bullies soon discovered they could not pick a fight with just one of them, and with Billy's strength, there were few who tried. Those who did quickly regretted their mistake. Each boy barged into the home of the other as though they belonged, and if either mother found both boys at their home at supper time, they simply set another plate.

The coffeepot came to a boil, and Margaret reached for the coffee can.

As Margaret busied herself at the stove, Dorothy plucked the letter from the pocket in the folds of her dress and laid it on the table. "Silas brought this today. Billy asked that I share it with you."

Margaret's breath came short. "He's all right, isn't he?"

Dorothy nodded. "For now. But he's going north, into Iroquois country."

Margaret stared at her friend, her eyes intense. "North? I thought the army was still at Morristown."

"It is. Billy and his friend are apparently going up there alone."

Quickly Margaret measured coffee into the steaming pot and set the lid on it to let it steep, then wiped her hands and reached for the letter. She read it slowly, then laid it back on the table, deep in thought.

Dorothy spoke. "Silas said the British are sending an army down from Canada, through the Iroquois country."

A look of puzzlement crossed Margaret's face. "From Canada? Why?"

Dorothy shrugged. "Silas didn't say."

Margaret's words came slowly. "They're probably after Fort Ticonderoga. If they come down the Hudson River, they'll have an army in New York and another one west of us, and they'll also hold Fort Ti." She rounded her mouth and blew air for a moment, then quietly murmured, "They'll be on both sides of us, and they'll control the river."

Dorothy nodded. "It frightens me." She raised one hand as though to protest. "What can two boys do against a British army?"

Margaret took two cups and saucers from the cupboard. Proper Bostonians served coffee to their guests in the parlor, but the rare friendship of twenty years that bound these two women together rose far above Boston's stiff rules. Margaret served Dorothy in the kitchen, on the small table near the stove. Carefully she poured the steaming brown coffee and set out milk and sugar while she spoke.

"Maybe General Washington will take his army north, or at least part of it."

"Maybe. Maybe they'll have to order out the militia."

Margaret nodded. "I hadn't thought of that. Either way, don't worry about Billy. He's old enough, and he's seen enough battles to take care of himself." She locked eyes with Dorothy, trying to reassure her. "He has good judgment and a strong measure of common sense. He'll be all right."

The sound of feet running down the hallway from the bedroom wing brought both women up short as the three children burst through the archway into the kitchen.

"Mother, can Trudy wear some of my clothes? We want to play hoops in the backyard, and her dress is too nice."

"Of course." Margaret raised a warning finger. "Adam, you be fair, and don't tease!"

Both women smiled as they watched the children turn on their heels and run back through the parlor and down the hall. The mothers both squinted against the heat as they raised their steaming coffee cups and gingerly sipped. Dorothy set her cup down as an involuntary shudder ran through her body. Margaret looked at her friend, silently questioning, waiting for Dorothy to speak.

"For a moment I saw images of people the Indians had killed." She shuddered again. "It's horrible, what they do. I can hardly think of Billy going up among them."

Margaret set her coffee cup on her saucer, and for long seconds the two remained silent, each working with her own thoughts. After a moment, Margaret spoke quietly.

"It seems the Almighty has given the women to do most of the suffering in this life. I watched and I worried and I prayed for you when you lost Bartholomew. You wasted away for a long time—got so thin I thought you would die. I wept for the pain in your heart." She paused and her eyes dropped. "Now, every day when I wake, the first thing I see is John, in bed, dying from that musketball. I doubt any man will ever understand what it does to a woman to lose her husband." She shook her head. "Sometimes I wish I could join him."

For a time they sat in silence until the children came clambering through the parlor and out the back door, each with a wooden hoop and a long, thin stick to guide it as they rolled them around the yard, racing. The two mothers watched the back door slam shut, and they listened to the children's loud talk as they made the rules for the hoop race. Then the yard was filled with shrieks and shouts, accusations and exclamations, as the children pushed and guided their hoops around the racecourse in the backyard.

Margaret turned back to Dorothy. "I received a letter not long ago, written by Matthew clear last October. He was in the battle on Lake Champlain when Benedict Arnold and Philip Schuyler met the British fleet coming down to attack General Washington from the west. Matthew was cut badly on the cheek—over an inch long, and deep." She bowed her head and stared at her hands as she worked them together on the table. "My Matthew, with a deep scar on his face." She shook her head sadly. "Your Billy with the wounds in his side, and on his back." Her lip trembled and she waited until it stopped.

"And now, both boys gone, we don't know where, or for how long.

We don't even know if they're still alive. We may never see them again. The men may do the fighting, but the women bear all the heartbreak. The Almighty must know what it does to a woman's heart. Why does he let it happen?" She drew a great breath and let it out slowly, shaking her head. "All we can do is keep faith in Him that no matter how it turns out, it is His will. If I didn't have that, I doubt I could stand it."

Dorothy swallowed hard and leaned forward. "Have you any news of Kathleen?"

Margaret's shoulders slumped, and her face clouded. Kathleen Thorpe. Tall, strong, gentle, dark-haired, dark-eyed, beautiful, decent, a born mother. Raised not four blocks from the Dunson home. She had loved Matthew since they were in grade school together, and Matthew had loved her. In their thirteenth year, Matthew had spent weeks with his father's woodworking tools to carve a little snow owl from white pine, and two more weeks painting on the eyes and the veins on the feathers—perfect—for Kathleen. And she had secretly spent months with hoops and needles creating a delicate needlepoint watch fob of royal blue silk, with Matthew's initials embroidered in a gold scroll above a tiny heart in the lower corner.

They could not wait to exchange the gifts, and stood facing each other, shy, unsure, red-faced, loving the misery of every moment of it, casting their eyes at the ground, or the ceiling, anywhere but at each other. They stammered, not knowing what to say or do, aware only that their young hearts were forever entwined.

No one could know that Kathleen's father, Doctor Henry Thorpe, a pillar in the community, a member of the critically important Committee of Safety, would become a spy for the British, passing coded messages to the British general Thomas Gage. He had secretly revealed the names of the patriots and the plans they made in secret meetings in the night, in dimly lighted rooms behind drawn curtains, to rise and throw off the British tyranny. The patriots knew someone had become a traitor to the cause, but none suspected it was Henry Thorpe, with his burgeoning medical practice, his wife from the highest social circles in the colonies, and his family of beautiful children, the eldest of which was Kathleen.

When Tom Sievers set the trap that flushed the truth out into the open, the shock rocked the patriots in Boston Town, stunned them, left them silent, wide-eyed, staggering to believe. The trial of Henry Thorpe in the Massachusetts court was brief, the verdict quick in coming, and the sentence severe. Henry Thorpe was banished from the colonies forever, to leave immediately and never return. He was never heard from again.

Reeling from disbelief, heartbreak, shock, and shame, Kathleen had found it impossible to face their family friends and acquaintances. She went to Matthew to tell him she could not, and would not, disgrace him further. He was not to see her again. He had rebelled; her father's infamy had nothing to do with their love. She stared him straight in the eye as she firmly shook her head. No, she would not bring the shame of the Thorpes down on the Dunsons.

The Thorpe family fortune disappeared as if by magic, and Kathleen had taken control of the family affairs. She took work wherever she could find it, finally doing the backbreaking work of cleaning fish alongside the rough men who worked the Boston docks. At last she was given work at the British garrison in Boston, laboring at the big, brass washtubs twelve hours a day, scrubbing British army uniforms on a corrugated washboard with brown lye soap.

A British officer, a Major McMullen, cast hot eyes on her and approached her with an offer of "work more appropriate to her status." Insulted and infuriated, she called him an animal and stalked out of his office. At midnight of that day, in a horrendous rain and thunderstorm, Tom Sievers had kicked open the locked door of Major McMullen's quarters. In a black room that shook with thunderclaps, lighted only by lightning flashes, with Tom's knife at his throat, Major McMullen had been only too willing to agree he would never talk to Kathleen Thorpe again.

The scandal utterly destroyed Kathleen's mother, Phoebe. Her mind never worked correctly again. She wrote a letter to King George III, asking asylum for herself and her children in England, with a yearly stipend to support her family. To the utter amazement of everyone, the king granted her request. Kathleen exploded, but when Phoebe announced she would take the children, Charles and Faith, and go to England without Kathleen, there was little that could be done. Nothing could have been more clear than the hard fact that Phoebe was not mentally capable of caring for either herself, or the children.

On the darkest day of her life, eyes vacant and dead, beyond tears, Kathleen boarded the British ship *Britannia* with Phoebe and the children and stood at the ship's rail for a last look at her beloved Boston Town— the only place she had ever lived. Inside, the devastation was total and complete. There was no light, no hope—only desolation and blackness. For a moment she remembered the utter sweetness and joy of the warm spring evening only weeks before, when Matthew had impulsively asked for her hand in marriage, and then drawn her inside his arms, and kissed her. She remembered throwing her arms about his neck, and the smell of him, and the feel of his embrace as she said yes.

She swallowed as she gazed at Boston Town once more, then bade good-bye to the only life she had known, and to the man who would own her heart forever.

Margaret shook her head. "Nothing." She lowered her eyes to stare unseeing at her coffee cup and saucer as she repeated the sad word. "Nothing. I can hardly bear the thought. Her in England—Phoebe and the children. Her heart broken—Matthew nearly lost his mind. The love they had . . . " Her voice trailed off, and her chin trembled.

Dorothy reached to touch her friend's hand as the first silent tears trickled down Margaret's cheeks. Margaret grasped Dorothy's hand, and tears rimmed in Dorothy's eyes and then ran warm down her own cheeks as the two women sat in silence, shoulders shaking, as they wept.

Finally Margaret released Dorothy's hand and reached unashamedly to wipe at her eyes with the heels of her hands. She shook her head as a cryptic chuckle surged up. "Would you look at us? Sitting here crying like babies. The Almighty knows this isn't going to churn the butter." She laughed again, then pulled her apron up to wipe at her face, then reached for a towel and handed it to Dorothy.

Dorothy chuckled, then laughed as she wiped her face and the tear-stained front of her dress. "We must look a sight," she said, "sitting here red-eyed."

Margaret looked at her. "I don't know about me, but you do."

Dorothy pointed at Margaret, and they threw back their heads and laughed.

It was enough. They had emptied their hearts of their innermost fears and pain as only good friends can. They had wept together and laughed at themselves, and it had worked its magic. They could once again pick up the crushing burdens of life that are known only to the soul of a woman, and move on.

Dorothy folded the towel and laid it on the table, then leaned forward inquiringly. "Where's Brigitte? I nearly forgot about her. And Caleb?"

Margaret shook her head. "At a meeting. The Patriots Group is planning to send medicine and clothes to Washington's army in Morristown. They think Brigitte and Caleb can help."

"After that awful thing last year? They were nearly killed!"

"I know, I know. Who can account for good sense when people get excited about these things? I've told them they can't go, but they won't listen. Brigitte wants to redeem herself, and Caleb wants to get out of Boston." She exhaled a great breath. "I'm so worried about Caleb. He's struggling. He has a lot of hate for what this war has done to our family. John gone, Matthew at sea. In a way I can't blame him."

"I'm sorry."

Suddenly Dorothy leaned forward, eyes bright. "Have you heard what they're saying about our bonnets in church?"

Margaret's eyebrows arched. "No."

"You heard about the law they passed in Abington? Women have to hang their bonnets on pegs by the church door because it's wrong to wear them during worship? Well, there's a rumor they're going to pass the same law here in Boston."

Margaret gaped. "What? Take off our bonnets in church? Absurd!"

"I know, but that's what I heard."

Margaret shook her head as Dorothy continued.

"Sally Von Steinman says that if they do it, she's going to march right in wearing her new pumpkin hood and sit in the front row!" She bobbed her head for emphasis.

"Sally Von Steinman? A new pumpkin hood? I'll bet it's orange, too. Have you noticed she's starting to wear those broad borders on her skirts again?" Margaret shook her head. "What some women won't do, just to draw attention and shock people. Imagine. An eight-inch border on a church dress. Why, next thing, she'll be going without petticoats!"

Dorothy straightened. "She wouldn't dare!"

Margaret tilted her head and raised a finger. "She might. There's no telling what some of these young women will do."

The back door banged open, and the children came tumbling in, Prissy wailing. "Mother, Adam's being mean! Just mean. He won't play fair. He just keeps hitting our hoops so we can't win, and he pushes us. Make him stop."

Margaret fixed her son with a glare. "Adam, are you tormenting the girls again?"

Adam was vociferous. "No, I am not. Girls just don't know how to play. If they can't win, they just make up lies."

Trudy stood to one side, silent, waiting to see who won and who lost.

"Adam, you tell me the truth. Did you hit their hoops?"

"Once. Just once. Because Prissy hit mine."

"Prissy?"

"That's not true." She caught herself, and her eyes fell. "Well, it was an accident."

Margaret shook her head. "Put the hoops away. If you can't get along and have fun, you lose the privilege of playing."

Prissy turned on Adam, hands on hips, pouting. "See! Now we can't play at all. It's your fault."

Margaret pointed, and the children stalked out of the room to put the hoops away. Margaret shook her head. "Some days those two just wear a body out."

"Be thankful you've got them. You don't now how Trudy treasures having someone to play with once in a while."

Margaret looked at her. "You're right. Help me. I'm going out to the root cellar for some milk. You fetch the cookie jar and some cups from the cupboard right over there. Oatmeal cookies and milk ought to settle their nonsense."

Dorothy stood, and as she did, she noticed the letter lying on the table. She folded it carefully, and as she tucked it into the pocket of her dress, her thoughts reached out to her son.

Is he safe today? Will he be all right? Please, Dear God, watch over my Billy.

She set her chin, squared her shoulders, and reached for the knob on the cupboard door.

Notes

The following facts are taken from Earle, *Home Life in Colonial Days.*

Early colonists provided light for their homes by burning pine knots, which left a sticky tar residue. Tar was a valuable commercial product. In time, lamps and lanterns were used, with a wick that burned fish oil or beef tallow. Candles became popular. Colonists strained all the animal fat from their meat through the winter and saved it in jars in root cellars. They also gathered bayberries, which grew wild along the eastern coast and could be gathered at will. The bayberries were boiled down, producing a waxy substance that was light green in color and had a pleasant smell when burned. It was strained until it was clear, then stored in jars in the root cellar. By mixing animal tallow with bayberry wax, the animal smell was eliminated. The description of the equipment used by Dorothy and Trudy in making their candles is accurate. They twisted their own wicks from hemp, tow, milkweed, or other materials; mounted them on iron rods; dipped them; and set them between sawhorses to harden, indoors or outdoors, depending on the weather. They often stored their candlemaking apparatus in their kitchen rafters (pp. 32–42).

In most New England towns, men and boys shared the responsibility of walking the streets at night to watch for thieves, fire, and the weather, and to call out the time and weather conditions at regular intervals. They were often sent out in pairs—an adult and a boy. In Boston, they were called "bellmen" (p. 363).

Dress styles for both men and women were closely watched. The early pilgrims were "deeply disturbed over the dress of their minister's wife, Madam Johnson, who wore lawn coives, and busks, and a velvet hood, and whalebones in her petticoat bodice, and worst of all, a topish hat." Roger Williams instructed the women in his Salem parish to wear veils in public; however, John Cotton preached against it. In 1769, the church at Andover voted to disapprove the "female sex sitting with their hats on in the meetinghouse in time of Divine service," this practice being considered indecent. In 1775, in the town of Abington, it was voted that the women were to hang their hats on pegs during church services. The law was not enforced (pp. 285–86).

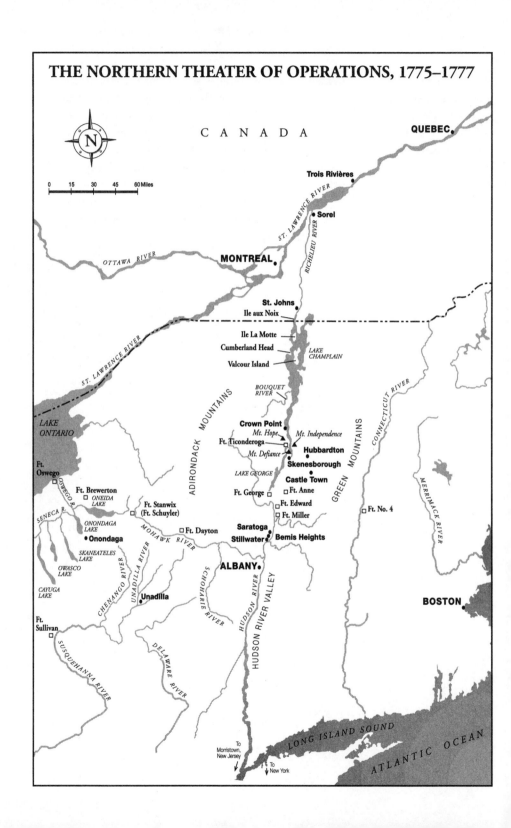

THE NORTHERN THEATER OF OPERATIONS, 1775–1777

CANADA

QUEBEC

Trois Rivières

Sorel

ST. LAWRENCE RIVER

RICHELIEU RIVER

OTTAWA RIVER

MONTREAL

St. Johns

Ile aux Noix

Ile La Motte

Cumberland Head

Valcour Island

LAKE CHAMPLAIN

ST. LAWRENCE RIVER

BOUQUET RIVER

CONNECTICUT RIVER

LAKE ONTARIO

ADIRONDACK MOUNTAINS

Crown Point

Mt. Hope   Mt. Independence

Ft. Ticonderoga

Mt. Defiance   Hubbardton

Skenesborough

GREEN MOUNTAINS

Ft. Oswego

OSWEGO R.

Ft. Brewerton

ONEIDA LAKE

Ft. Stanwix (Ft. Schuyler)

LAKE GEORGE

Castle Town

Ft. Anne

MERRIMACK RIVER

SENECA R.

ONONDAGA LAKE

Onondaga

SKANEATELES LAKE

OWASCO LAKE

CAYUGA LAKE

Ft. Dayton

MOHAWK RIVER

Ft. George

Ft. Edward

Ft. Miller

Ft. No. 4

Saratoga

Stillwater   Bemis Heights

CHENANGO RIVER

UNADILLA RIVER

ALBANY

SCHOHARIE RIVER

HUDSON RIVER

BOSTON

Ft. Sullivan

Unadilla

DELAWARE RIVER

HUDSON RIVER VALLEY

SUSQUEHANNA RIVER

To Morristown, New Jersey

To New York

LONG ISLAND SOUND

ATLANTIC OCEAN

0   15   30   45   60 Miles

Hudson River valley, south of Albany

Mid-May 1777

CHAPTER II

*I*t came swift and brutal, in the strange twilight time between sunset and full darkness, when purple shadows turn the great trees, and the rotting trunks of fallen giants, and the thick ferns of the deep forest into vague shadows, and for a moment the world is suspended between the real and the surreal.

Eli Stroud, tall, clad in Iroquois buckskins, stopped dead in his tracks and stood slightly crouched, eyes narrowed, knees flexed, ready to move. Six feet behind him, Billy Weems, shorter, barrel-chested, thick in the neck and shoulders and legs, stopped and stood perfectly still, silent, barely breathing, every sense focused on Eli. Six hundred yards eastward, to their right, the mighty Hudson River, invisible through the trees, silently rolled south through the great valley, while mosquitoes swarmed from the marshy bogs to hum incessantly.

Suddenly, one hundred yards to the north, straight ahead in the forested twilight, the birds—huge, black ravens—cawed, their raucous protest ringing through the gloom as they rose from tree tops on glossy wings to disappear, and once again silence settled. Soundlessly, without looking back, Eli slowly retreated to Billy's side, and Billy was aware that once again Eli was an Iroquois warrior, seeing, hearing, feeling, sensing things that the forest shared only with those who had learned her secrets. Every fiber of Eli's being was fiercely alive, reaching for something he felt out in the twilight. His eyes were glittering slits as his head slowly turned from side to side, testing every sound, every scent, every shadow, every movement against some inner source. He hooked his thumb over the hammer of his long Pennsylvania rifle and drew it to full cock, the two clicks sounding loud in the silence. Billy also cocked his musket while Eli silently drew his black-handled, iron-headed tomahawk from his weapons belt and slipped the leather thong over his wrist to let it dangle free as he stood still, testing the air, watching every shadow.

Eli tensed, then raised his right hand only far enough to motion to Billy to follow, and they started back through the heavy undergrowth, Eli leading at a trot. The only sounds were the hum of mosquitoes and the whisper of the ferns and bushes that brushed at their legs as they dodged through roots and trees, and over the decaying, crumbling trunks of ancient windfalls, and around clusters of great boulders left behind in distant eons of time, when ice two miles thick had crept slowly southward to gouge and sculpt lakes and mountains and valleys before melting to form the oceans.

Without sound or warning, a shadow flickered in the trees to their right, and in that instant Eli twisted, swinging his rifle to meet the dusky figure that came leaping, naked to the waist, face painted black from the nose down, hair roached, carrying a spiked war club high above his head, swinging downward. The man's chest was only two feet from the muzzle of his rifle when Eli pulled the trigger. The crack of the rifle rang through the forest as flame leaped to burn the man's chest and light the awful surprise in his face as the .60-caliber ball tore through his chest and cracked his spine. Eli dodged to his left to let the dead body fall headlong as a second sprinting figure came hurtling in the dwindling light, and Billy's musket blasted. A tongue of orange flame spurted as the huge musketball spun the man twisting, to drop, rolling in the foliage, dead at their feet.

With the sounds of the two shots still ringing through the forest, Eli pivoted, crouched, ready, as three more half-naked, painted shadows erupted from behind them, two with war clubs, one with a tomahawk, raised, swinging as they came. Eli dropped his rifle as he swept his tomahawk above his head in both hands to take the downstroke of the war club and turn it, and in the moment it turned, Eli slashed his tomahawk downward with both hands. The blade struck deep, and the man's eyes widened as he dropped to his knees and toppled.

Six feet to Eli's right, Billy faced the charge of a second man with raised war club. With his feet set, Billy jammed his musket muzzle violently forward into the pit of the man's stomach, and he heard the grunt as the man stopped in his tracks to grab his ruptured mid-section and buckle over. Billy dropped his musket and was a blur as he closed with the man to grasp him by the braid of hair at the back of his head and by his buckskin leggings, and throw him headlong into the trunk of a giant pine. He heard the crack of the neck, and the body slumped to the ground.

Eli's desperate, shouted warning came, and it flashed in Billy's mind—*the third one.* Instinctively he crouched and moved quickly to his right. From the corner of his eye, he saw the raised tomahawk plunging and in the next instant took the electric shock of the numbing blow on his left shoulder blade as he drove his right shoulder into the naked, painted chest to knock the scrambling man onto his back, and then Billy was sitting on top of him. He saw the tomahawk coming upward as he smashed his doubled fist into the snarling face and the man stopped struggling. Twice more Billy drove his fist into the face with all his strength, and the body went limp.

Eli swept up his rifle and Billy's musket, and Billy heard the urgency in his voice as he hissed, "He's finished! Let's go!"

Billy sprang to his feet as Eli tossed his musket to him and he caught it and they sprinted. All caution was thrown aside as they tore through the undergrowth, south, back the way they had come, leaping fallen trees, dodging among the trunks of those standing, hunched forward to avoid branches. The only sounds they heard were their footfalls and the gasping of their own breath as they plunged on—two hundred yards—three hundred—past a gigantic outcropping of worn granite boulders, over the remains of an ancient, decayed tree, then another, when Eli stopped abruptly, spun around, and dived onto his stomach behind the huge, rotting trunk of the fallen forest giant and uttered a single whispered word.

"Load!"

Billy grabbed a paper cartridge from the leather case on his hip, ripped the bottom open with his teeth, flipped the frizzen from the pan, sprinkled powder, slapped the frizzen shut, poured the remainder of the powder down the bore of his musket, jammed the paper with the ball into the muzzle, and tamped it down onto the powder with the ramrod. At the same time, Eli tapped powder from his powder horn into his pan, closed the frizzen, held the patch over the muzzle, seated the ball, and drove it down the barrel with the hickory ramrod.

Weapons loaded, both men thrust the muzzles over the log, cocked the hammers, and waited. The twilight deepened before they heard the first faint sound of ferns brushing buckskin leggings somewhere in front of them. Eli tensed and held up one finger, then another, another, and finally four, with Billy counting. Without a sound Eli laid his tomahawk on the log next to his rifle, then tapped Billy's arm and touched the handle of his belt knife. Silently Billy drew the knife and laid it on the log beside his musket, then settled, unmoving, battling to breathe silently as he peered into the darkness, waiting, every nerve singing tight. A deep ache throbbed through his shoulder as the sticky warmth spread on his left shoulder blade, down his left side, to his shirtfront. Gritting his teeth against the pain, he said nothing and remained motionless, waiting, forefinger lightly on the trigger of his musket, tense, ready, mouth dry.

Time lost meaning. Billy licked dry lips as his thoughts ran, and he let them go. *Brigitte—the hazel eyes and brown hair—will she ever know what happened—why we never returned—Mother and Trudy—Matthew, on the sea—who will tell them—who will find the letters—who will deliver them to Brigitte—she'll never know—I wish somehow the letters could reach her—I wish she could know.*

Silently Eli held up three more fingers, and Billy counted.

Seven—seven of them out there—they know where we are—how much time left?—five more minutes?—ten?—how long before they come at us all at one time?—we'll get the first two and maybe the second two, but in this dark we can't get all of them—how will Mother ever know—Matthew—I wish Brigitte could see the letters.

A hint of sound reached them in the darkness and instantly Billy was focused, ready, waiting. Seconds became a minute, and then two minutes, and there was nothing—no movement, no sound, no dark shapes rising from the thick foliage with raised war clubs or tomahawks. The great muscle on Billy's shoulder blade throbbed, and he flexed the fingers of his left hand then moved his left arm slightly to be certain he could control them. A three-quarter waxing moon rose in the west to cast deceptive silvery light on the crowns of trees so thick that only random shafts of pale light filtered through to cast small flecks on the forest floor.

Minutes became half an hour, then an hour, while the moon climbed steadily above the mountains to the west. The hum of the mosquitoes quieted and gave way to the rhythmic, rasping chirp of crickets. From marshes and bogs near the streams came the steady belching croak of giant bullfrogs. Overhead, the night birds silently performed their nocturnal ballet as they took small, invisible flying insects. From a distance came the sharp, high bark of a fox.

One hour became two, and then Eli silently worked his way closer to Billy and spoke in a whisper. "It's over for now. They won't come into this place to get us."

Billy's forehead wrinkled in puzzlement. "They won't come here? Why?"

"Indian burial ground." Eli tilted his head back and pointed upward.

Billy turned on his right elbow to peer into the overhead canopy of trees, and in the sparse moonlight he saw it. Suspended in the lower branches of the trees were platforms of poles tied together with rawhide, and he understood that on the platforms were the wrapped, decaying bodies of the dead. A strange, eerie sensation that he and Eli were not alone crept over him as he stared. "How did you know?" he whispered.

"Saw it at sunset, when we were going north."

"They won't come in here to fight?"

"No. Respect for their ancestors. They believe their spirits are free to roam and come to this place often. Might be here now."

Billy's breathing slowed at the thought, and for a time he remained motionless, silent, somehow expecting a sound or a manifestation from the dead, but there was nothing. He licked dry lips and asked, "What happens at daylight?"

"Nothing. Daylight or dark, they won't attack here. By morning I think they'll be gone. They don't have much patience. They made their try and lost four or five men. Sometime tonight they'll take their wounded and dead and go back to wherever they came from. They'll tell how they attacked an enemy party and killed many. They'll say they didn't have time to take scalps. Just before dawn, I'll go see if they're gone."

Billy moved his left arm, and Eli heard the sharp intake of breath.

"You hurt?" he hissed.

"My back. Left shoulder. That third one, with the tomahawk."

Eli reached for Billy's left hand and laid two fingers in the palm. "Squeeze hard."

Billy bore down, and Eli noted the raw power of Billy's grip. "Grip seems all right. Can you raise your arm above your head?"

Billy winced but raised his arm high, feeling the crusted blood crack and the warm, sticky flow begin again.

There was relief in Eli's voice as he spoke. "I think it struck with the grain of the great muscle—not cross-grain. How bad? Can you tell?"

"I think pretty deep."

"Let me feel."

"There's blood."

"No matter." Gently Eli worked his fingertips over Billy's shoulder blade. He found the place where the sodden shirt had been cut through and gently parted the cloth to tenderly probe the sticky cloth, while Billy gritted his teeth.

"Deep. Nearly an inch." He fell silent for a moment. "We'll have to close it somehow. You walk with it that way, you'll keep it open. It won't heal."

"Close it now?"

"No. Can't strike a light. They won't attack us here, but they might shoot at a light. We'll have to wait for daylight. Can you stand it that long?"

"I'll be all right."

"Don't move that arm again. Lay on your right side while I go get some spider web."

"Spider web?"

"To stop the bleeding."

Eli disappeared to return after several minutes with the fine web of great catspiders dangling from his hand. Carefully he raised the edges of the cut in Billy's shirt and packed the sticky web into the gaping wound.

"That should do it. Get some rest. I'll watch."

Eli helped Billy slip out of the straps of his canteen, cartridge case, utensils pouch, and blanket roll, and Billy folded the blanket beneath his head and curled up on his right side. Eli pulled the musket over next to his rifle, then Billy's knife beside his tomahawk, and settled beside Billy to watch and listen.

The moon reached its apex, then began to dip back toward the skyline. The chirping of the crickets droned on, punctuated by the incessant croaking of the frogs. At two o'clock, a chill breeze from the Hudson River stirred the leaves for a time, and Billy groaned in his sleep and awakened. Eli unrolled his own blanket and spread it over him, then resumed his vigil. The distant, haunting call of an owl came floating, and Eli froze for a moment, waiting, while Billy held his breath. A nearby owl answered, and Eli relaxed. "Authentic," he whispered, and Billy began breathing again.

A little after three o'clock, Billy cried out and jerked awake. Instantly Eli reached to steady him, so that he wouldn't roll over onto his wounded shoulder. Billy flinched at his touch and stared upward in the dark while his mind came back to reality.

"What happened," he asked.

"You fell asleep. Cried out. Must have dreamed."

Billy nodded and reached to wipe the sweat from his face. "I was back at the fight. That tomahawk." He waited for a time while the vivid images of painted men with weapons in their hands, leaping at him from hidden places, faded and vanished. Then he turned his face to Eli.

"Who were they? What tribe?"

"Mohawk."

"How do you know?"

"Their hair. Paint. Leggings. The way they came at us."

"War party?"

"Not likely. Probably Joseph Brant's scouts, with the British." Eli's voice intensified. "If they *were* Brant's scouts, it means they were sent out to find someone, or something. Most likely to find out where the American army's gathering. If that was what they were doing, it means the British army's on its way down here."

Seconds passed while Billy reflected, and Eli sensed his need to talk, to pass the hard hours of waiting in the dark of night. He waited, and Billy finally spoke.

"If Brant's a Mohawk, how did he get the name Joseph Brant?"

"That's his baptized Christian name. Got it from a man he lived with for a while. His Mohawk name is Thayendangea. His older sister's Christian name is Mary Brant, but her Mohawk name is Gonwatsijayenni. She has much power among the Mohawks."

Billy's eyes widened. "A woman?"

Eli nodded. "The women have strong standing in their villages— sometimes more than the men."

"How powerful is Joseph Brant?"

"Probably the most powerful Mohawk living. Speaks all six Iroquois languages, as well as French and English. Been to England and met the king. They made him a Freemason. He's translating the white man's Bible into Mohawk. Been a warrior since he was thirteen. He's the one who led the British when they came through the Jamaica Pass. Nearly ended the Revolution."

"The Iroquois have six languages?"

"Five main ones. Six if you count the Tuscaroras. There's some other smaller tribes, too. A couple of hundred years ago, the main ones got together and formed a sort of league or a confederation, to unite for peace."

"Who were the five?"

"Mohawk, Oneida, Onondaga, Cayuga, Seneca."

Confused, Billy asked, "There was no tribe named Iroquois?"

"No. Together they're called the Iroquois confederation."

"Who formed the confederation?"

"A Huron named Deganawida and a Onondaga named Hiawatha got the other tribes to bury the hatchet. Deganawida was not a good speaker, so he got Hiawatha to do the talking. Uniting the tribes had never been attempted before."

"Bury the hatchet?"

"Stop fighting. You take up the hatchet when you declare war, and when you stop fighting, you bury it beneath a tree."

"Did Hiawatha have a white name?"

"No."

"What does Hiawatha mean in English?"

For a moment Eli pondered. "It would translate, 'He was awake.'"

For a moment they fell silent, each aware of an odd, unexpected feeling that had come over them. Billy lying injured in an Indian burial ground in the black hours after midnight, Mohawk Indians somewhere near in a primeval forest waiting to kill them. And yet, Billy wanted to know, and Eli needed to tell, of the life and customs of the people who had murdered most of Eli's family eighteen years earlier and then raised Eli as one of their own.

"What tribe were you with?"

"In the beginning, Seneca. Then with the Onondaga."

"Where?"

Eli lowered his face while he gathered his thoughts. "Six or seven miles north of Albany, the Mohawk River empties into the Hudson from the west. About seventy miles up the Mohawk River is a settlement called Oriskany, and about five miles past that, Fort Stanwix. West of there is Lake Oneida, and beyond that is Fort Brewerton, located on the Oswego River. South of Fort Brewerton is Lake Onondaga, and the village of Onondaga is on the tip of the lake. West of there is the Seneca River with three lakes—Skaneateles, Owasco, and Cayuga—all draining from the south into Seneca River. Northwest, the village of Oswego is right where the Oswego River drains into Lake Ontario. Northeast is Lake George and Lake Champlain, which drain into the Richelieu River, and it runs north into the St. Lawrence."

Eli stopped for a moment to arrange his thoughts. "The five big lakes are west of Oswego. I was raised mostly by the Onondaga, in the country between the Hudson River and those five big lakes. The Onondaga are the keepers of the records for the whole Iroquois confederation. When I was thirteen, I left to fight my first battle against the French and the Huron. They had joined to fight the British. It was in one of those battles that I met Joseph Brant."

"The Onondaga keep records? What records?"

"Not like whites. They keep wampum belts, or sometimes strings of wampum beads, one belt or string for each thing they want to remember. Treaties, visions, councils, loss of great chiefs, sachems, battles—all the things that mean something to them."

"Sachems?"

"Medicine men—the spiritual leaders."

"Are there a lot of these wampum belts at Onondaga?"

"Thousands. They have men whose duty is to remember what each one means. Put them all together, and there's a pretty good record of the history of the Iroquois, going back a long way."

"I thought wampum was Indian money."

Eli shook his head. "Not money. Iroquois history."

"You served with the British?"

"Right. After that first battle, I lived wherever I was sent, to help the British drive out the French. That's when I first heard of George Washington. I heard what that old chief said about him, and I heard other things. I spent some time with the Jesuits, too, and learned English and French and read their Bible twice. The second time I went into the forest alone for over sixty days and studied it. Something happened inside of me. I had a desire to know more about Jesus and the whites and George Washington. I purified myself, and my thoughts settled, and I knew I had to leave the Iroquois and find out those things for myself."

"What to do you mean 'Purified yourself'?"

"Built a sweat lodge. Fasted and sweated and prayed for three days. Then the answer came."

"A revelation?"

"Not like a vision or an angel or a voice in the night. A feeling in my heart that I knew was right."

"From God?"

"It was Him I prayed to. I've never questioned it."

"What's His name? You told me once, but I've forgotten."

"In Iroquois, Taronhiawagon."

"What does that mean in English?"

Eli paused for a moment, searching for words. "'He who bears the heavens on his shoulders.' There are lesser Gods. He is the one who is over all others."

"He gives revelations then?"

"He can. Dreams, visions—about what will happen in the future. He knows all."

"When did the Iroquois side with the French against the British?"

Eli shrugged. "Maybe thirty years ago. An Englishman named William Johnson took Indian wives and learned Indian ways. One of his wives was Mary Brant, Joseph Brant's older sister. Johnson became the spokesman for the British and helped drive out the French, and then when the Americans rebelled he tried to put them down. He's dead, but his son Guy Johnson took his place. It was Guy Johnson who traveled to England with Joseph Brant and met the king. Now his son John Johnson has taken over."

Eli paused, and Billy watched him peer over the log, into the darkness for a time before he spoke again. "A second white missionary named Samuel Kirkland has tried to keep the Indians friendly to the Americans. With Johnson pulling them to the British, and Kirkland pulling them to the Americans, things have become pretty mixed up among the Iroquois tribes. It seems like white men only use the Indians for what they want, and never see what they're doing to the Indians. The conflict is pulling the Confederacy apart. If it keeps up, everything Deganawida and Hiawatha did will be gone."

"Why is Joseph Brant against Americans?"

"When the British first came, they promised to protect the Mohawk if they would let them come onto their lands. Later on, when the French came to trap furs, the British kept their promise and drove them out. No one ever thought some of the British would call themselves Americans and turn on their own mother country, and when they did, the Mohawk didn't know what else to do but join with the British again, against the Americans."

Eli stopped for a moment, and then his voice became intense. "Indians don't like to lose. They stayed with the British because they figured the French would lose. Now they think the Americans will lose, so they're still with the British. The day they see the British losing, I expect they'll walk away and be gone."

Billy shifted to ease set muscles, and suddenly Eli raised a warning hand. He closed his eyes and turned his head and neither moved nor spoke in his deep concentration. A full minute passed before he whispered to Billy.

"Did you hear it?"

"Hear what?"

"The frogs. They quieted over to the right, toward the river."

"Trouble?"

"No. I think the Mohawk left that way. The frogs quit talking while they passed through. Just before dawn, I'll go find out."

Billy glanced at the eastern sky, which remained black, showing no definition between earth and sky. The moon was touching the western rim. Dawn was yet a little time away. He settled his head back onto his own folded blanket as a shiver shook him. He pulled Eli's blanket up to his chin and lay in thoughtful silence, aware that the strange need in both men—one to talk, the other to listen—had passed. He moved his left arm, and it awakened the throbbing, and he lay still. He did not know when he passed into a restless sleep with Eli beside him to be certain he did not roll on his left shoulder.

He wakened in the darkness to the soft touch of Eli's hand on his chest. "Dawn's coming," Eli whispered. "I'll be back. If anything goes wrong, work your way to the Hudson and set a log in the water. Keep your good arm over the log, and it'll take you downstream. There's half a dozen settlements where you can get help."

Billy nodded, understanding, as Eli rose, picked up his rifle, slipped his hand through the leather loop on his tomahawk handle, and stepped over the log. Guided by senses and instincts long since lost by white men, he moved soundlessly north through the lush undergrowth, missing no shadow, no movement, instantly recognizing every noise in a primeval forest moving from night toward day. The chirping of the crickets had ceased with the onset of the chill of night, and the frogs had fallen silent an hour earlier. The near owl spoke again, and to the west another answered, but Eli did not pause. Authentic. He moved on as the light of the coming sun gradually separated the earth from the sky, and the first gray came filtering through the forest.

The birds were awakening, moving in the trees to call out their territorial claims. Eli slowed to allow a porcupine to stop and stare up at him with two beady eyes before he waddled on, contemptuous of anything that had only two legs. To his left, a mother raccoon with the black mask of a bandit over her eyes and three white rings on her bushy tail paused by a tiny stream while she studied him. He was harmless, and she grasped one of her two young and thrust its face into the water, then rubbed it vigorously. The little one had to learn he could not eat until he washed both the food, and his face.

Suddenly Eli dropped to one knee. A large, lacy fern leaf showed a slight bruise, and he gently pushed it aside. Beneath it was a moccasin track, then another. He studied them for a moment, then rose, moved on, and again dropped to his knee. The tracks continued, moving north. He moved twenty feet to his left, to where he and Billy had plunged wildly south in their desperate run to the burial grounds, and turned north once more, following their trail through the disturbed undergrowth as easily as if it were a beaten path. He slowed as he approached the place of the ambush and dropped to his haunches for several moments, listening, testing every scent on the air.

Nothing.

After a time, he rose and cautiously walked to the place where the fight had taken place. The underbrush was crushed, twisted, broken. The dead and wounded were gone. He studied the dark splotches where blood had stained the green, and he studied the moccasin tracks. Then he moved on north, and forty yards later once again dropped to one knee to read the sign on the ground.

The Mohawk had stopped to study the tracks left by his moccasins and Billy's shoes. They now knew Eli was from the Onondaga tribe, his height, weight, stride, and that he was a white man, knowledgeable enough of Indian ways to take refuge in a burial ground to save himself. They knew he carried a rifle and was skillful in the use of a tomahawk. They knew, too, that Billy was white, shorter, built square, carried a musket, was powerful enough to throw a man against a tree with sufficient force to break his neck, and hit hard enough with his fist to break a man's jaw and knock him unconscious with one blow. Perhaps fracture his skull.

Eli made a broad circle to his right, moving slowly until he again cut their trail, and for yet another time, went to one knee. The moccasin prints were deeper here—they were carrying their dead and wounded. He counted seven sets of tracks, followed them half a mile north, until he was satisfied they had left no one behind to set an ambush. Then he turned and trotted back to Billy, who was sitting with his blanket around his shoulders, his musket lying across his legs.

"They're gone. Took their dead and wounded north."

"Sure?"

"Sure."

"I've been thinking," Billy said, "did they have muskets?"

"Yes."

"Why didn't they shoot us instead of what they did?"

"They prefer to fight hand-to-hand if they can. They think it shows their bravery, courage." Eli worked the corncob stopper from Billy's wooden canteen. "Thirsty?"

Billy raised the canteen and drank long before he handed it back. Eli held it in his hand as he spoke. "Want to eat anything before I look at that shoulder?"

Billy shook his head and pulled the blanket from his back. "Let's get at it."

Eli knelt behind Billy and carefully tugged at the slit in Billy's shirt. "Shirt's stuck to your shoulder. We'll have to soak it off."

Billy gasped as Eli poured cold canteen water onto the crown of his shoulder and waited for it to soak into the shirt, then poured more and waited again. Gradually the stiffness in the blood-soaked fabric softened, and he poured more, then stood with the canteen in his hand and reached for his own. "While that loosens, I'm going for more water. We'll need it before we're through."

Minutes later he returned with both canteens wet, dripping clean water taken from one of the hundreds of small brooks that worked their way to the Hudson. He set the canteens on the blanket beside Billy, dropped to his knees, and tugged at the slit in the shirt. A corner of the crimson-black cotton cloth broke away, and a bubble of thick blood rose in the wound. Again he poured, waited, pulled, and the shirt came away from the wound.

"Raise your hands," he said, and pulled the shirt over Billy's head, dripping blood-stained water. He folded it with the clean side showing, poured water, and patiently used the cloth to swab the dried blood from Billy's back, side, and belly, while Billy shivered in the cool morning air. Eli draped his blanket over Billy's right shoulder and gathered it beneath his left arm. Then he carefully soaked the five-inch cut and wiped it as clean as he could before he spoke quietly in a matter-of-fact voice.

"That's about an inch deep, and it's going to break open and bleed every time you move your arm." There was a pause before he finished. "I think we'd better close it."

"Burn it?"

"Can you stand it?"

"Get on with it."

"After, it ought to be sewed shut."

"There's needle and thread in my pouch."

Grimacing against the pain of the open wound, Billy watched as Eli gathered twigs, then larger sticks of gray, dead branches from an ancient windfall pine tree, cleared the soft, decaying matter from the forest floor behind Billy, shaved a handful of thin shavings, and struck flint to steel.

While he waited for the flames to catch the larger sticks, Eli worked the point of the needle on a piece of granite shale until it was as sharp as he could make it. Then he laid the needle aside, wordlessly drew his knife from his belt, and held it in the flame. The iron blade began to glow, then turned orange.

"Ready?"

"Yes."

"Bullet or leather strap?"

"Leather strap."

Eli doubled the leather shoulder strap of Billy's pouch and handed it to him. Billy seized it in his teeth.

"Lean a little forward."

Billy settled forward, head bowed, teeth clenched on the leather strap.

In one smooth stroke, Eli raised the knife, carefully lowered the blade into the gaping wound, and pressed it against the raw, bleeding flesh, first one side, then the other. Smoke curled, and the sound of burning flesh crackled for a moment as the orange-hot blade seared and sealed the bleeding. The muscles in Billy's jaw stood out like ridges as he bit down on the leather strap. His eyes were clenched shut, sweat dripping. He made no sound, nor did he move.

Eli jerked the knife back and blew to clear the smoke, then leaned forward to carefully study the gray, burned flesh. Most of the bleeding had stopped.

"I think it's enough," he said. "You all right?"

Billy spat the leather strap from his mouth. "So far."

"Want to wait for the stitching?"

"No. Get it over with."

Eli laid the knife aside and heated the heavy iron needle in the fire, then waited for it to cool before he doubled the cotton thread and forced it through the eye.

"This is going to take some time."

"Go ahead." Billy shoved the strap back between his teeth.

For forty minutes Eli worked, using the handle of his knife to drive the needle through the tough, stubborn flesh, pulling the two sides of the wound together into a ridge. One stitch at a time, the gaping wound closed. He tied each of the eighteen stitches tight, knotted them twice, and left more than an inch of thread hanging from each one to make it easy when he clipped them out.

He set the knife and needle on his blanket and drew and released a great breath. "Finished."

Billy took the belt from his mouth; the tooth marks in the leather were deep. He used the corner of his blanket to wipe at the sweat dripping from his nose and chin. "How many?"

"Eighteen."

"Think they'll hold?"

"When we finish they will."

"I thought you said you were finished."

"With the stitching. We've got to pack it, and tie down your arm."

"Pack it with what?"

Eli ignored the question, rose to his feet, and laid Billy's pouch and canteen by his side. "There's food and water. Sit quiet and don't move. Keep the blanket around yourself, but not on the stitches. If you hear one rifle shot, that will be me. If there's more than one, get ready for anything. I'll be back, but it might be a while." He took the wet, bloody shirt, slipped his tomahawk through his belt, picked up his rifle, and stepped over the log to disappear silently into the forest.

Billy reached for his canteen, locked it between his knees, and worked the stopper out. He drank long, reset the stopper, and laid the canteen back on the blanket. He pushed himself backward, close to the log, then leaned back. The deep, throbbing ache in his left shoulder held, and he could count his heartbeat in the gash where Eli had laid the smoking knife blade and then driven the needle through, eighteen times.

A giddy, light-headedness came. He waited for it to pass, and then he felt the fierce tension begin to drain from his entire body. He knew he was fevered and for a time felt so weak he feared he could not stand if the Mohawk returned. He sipped from the canteen once more and knew he could no longer fight off the demand of his body to sleep. He laid his musket across his legs and let his head fall forward. His last thought before he dropped into the dreamless blackness was, *I can't tip over onto my shoulder.*

Something moved. Something whispered. The message reached from his inner springs to his brain, and Billy jerked awake. For a moment he could not remember where he was, and then awareness came jolting. Only his eyes moved as he scanned the forest, and there was nothing. Then, six feet from his right side, he sensed movement and turned his head far enough to see.

A mother raccoon with two tiny balls of fur by her side stared back at him. Her nose was working, testing, and her eyes stared from her mask to reach to the depths of Billy's being. In that instant he sensed the mother was probing him with one clear question. *Friend or enemy?* As though it were as natural as the primeval forest all around him, he felt his own silent answer reach out. *Have no fear.* As he watched, she cautiously made her way toward him, her young following.

Slowly he moved his hand to his pouch and carefully raised the flap. He drew out a wrapped oil cloth and unfolded it to break off a piece of dried salt fish. He set the packet on the ground with the piece of broken fish on top and drew his hand back. The mother slowly approached the offering and carefully reached to seize the piece of dried fish. She drew it to her nose and sniffed at the strange scent while the two balls of fur remained at her side, watching her every move. She raised her eyes to Billy, turned, and calmly walked away, carrying the piece of fish to the nearest stream where she washed it, then tasted it, then broke portions of it with her forepaws for her young.

Billy watched until she disappeared with her two babies. Half a minute passed while Billy marveled at what had happened.

We understood each other. Me and a raccoon!

He raised startled eyes. It seemed a veil had been lifted, and he was seeing the forest and all within it for the first time. He saw the jays scolding from the branches of the trees, and the finches darting, and the raucous ravens perched in the tree tops, watching all below. Red and gray squirrels scurried with lightning moves, stopping with their bushed tails arched up their backs, curled over their heads, while they surveyed the forest with large, round eyes before they disappeared into holes in the trunks of ancient trees. A huge porcupine sat undisturbed in the upper branches of a nearby young pine tree, stripping the tender new bark to stuff in his mouth.

These creatures all see—feel—know something I don't know—things they can tell me. The feeling washed over him, left him stunned, wide-eyed. *Not just the creatures—the forest—all of it has its message—its story to tell—if one can only learn to hear it!*

He marveled at the growing feeling of oneness with the beasts, the birds, the creeping things, and the great pristine forest. With it came a strong sense of his own infinite smallness beneath the great vaulted heavens. He was diminished and expanded in the same grain of time—only one man, but part of it all. He did not know how long he remained transfixed; he only knew that he had been changed, added upon.

The distant crack of a rifle came echoing from the north, and Billy blinked as his mind came back to the reality of being wounded, sitting in an Indian burial ground in Mohawk territory. He opened his mouth to breath silently while he waited for a second shot, and a third, but none came.

Eli? Or Mohawk? Eli.

He settled in to wait, listening intently to every sound, sensitive to every movement. Minutes rolled into half an hour. The ravens came to perch in the high branches of the pines and oaks, cawing as they gathered, then falling silent. Billy studied them, and realized they had been drawn to the blood on the blanket, and on his back. Scavengers that had sensed something wounded on the forest floor and had come to do the work to which nature had ordained them: clean all that died from the forest floor. He marveled at how they had known he was there, wounded. Scent? Could they scent blood that far?

Mosquitoes, the first of the annual generation, rose from the swamps and bogs to swarm where they could find sunlight. Bees came seeking the wildflowers that grew at random—small, delicate bursts of blue, yellow, red in the earth, or growing from the rich, decayed pulp of trees that had toppled a thousand years before. Billy drank again from his canteen, then broke off dried salt fish and put it in his mouth to soften before he chewed it down.

He glanced upward at the burial platforms suspended in the trees and was not prepared for the thoughts that came. He could see tattered, ragged edges of blankets hanging from the poles, where the years and the birds had frayed them. He saw some of the weapons and pottery, left by the living to be used by the dead in the invisible world to which they had traveled as they moved from this life to the next. Yesterday he had wondered about the spirit world, and about the power of Taronhiawagon, the Iroquois God of Gods, to send dreams to answer prayers, and to provide visions in which He foretold things yet to come. Today he wondered no more. The spirit in all things did not die. The remains of the dead on the platforms above his head were not the end of those who had once lived in the bodies. They were somewhere, moving on.

John Dunson is there. My father is there. Bartholomew. Sometime I'll see him again, and he'll know me.

His thoughts ran on. *Those bodies on the platforms—are their spirits nearby? If I can't see them, can they see me?* Strangely the thought that the spirits of those who had died could be in his presence did not frighten him. Rather, he found a sense of relief that one of the mysteries of life had at least in part lifted from his mind.

What's happening? I've read the Bible—know about Jesus—the spirit—heaven— why are these things suddenly new to me?—powerful—as if I've never heard of them?

"Coming in."

Jolted, Billy stared straight ahead before his mind came back to the forest, and he twisted his head to look north. Eli came striding through the trees and the undergrowth, the body of a small, spike buck deer wrapped about his shoulders, holding the four legs to his chest with his left hand, rifle in his right. He stepped over the log and lowered the carcass to the ground.

He looked at Billy. "Are you all right?"

"Yes."

"Any trouble?"

Billy hesitated, then said, "A raccoon paid a visit. With her young."

A rare, wry smile passed over Eli's face. "I said hello to her earlier."

Billy answered, "She said hello to me. I returned it."

Eli sensed something he had never heard before in Billy's voice. He stopped and looked into Billy's face. "Something happened." It was not a question.

Billy nodded and remained silent. For two seconds each man stared at the other without a word, and in that moment they knew much needed to be said, but the time was not yet. Eli broke it off and turned to the carcass of the young buck deer.

"I've got work to do."

Billy did not question him.

Eli shaved more pinewood into the cold ashes of the fire, struck flint to steel, and within minutes had flames curling. With practiced efficiency he dragged the deer carcass a short distance, turned it on its back, and opened it from vent to throat. He emptied the entrails from the carcass, sorted out the liver, carefully cut the gall bladder away from it, then laid both the liver and the gall bladder aside. Minutes later the deer hide was spread hair side down flat on the ground with the skinned carcass on top of it. Carefully Eli cut deep into the liver and checked the large artery to be certain there were no flukes. He sliced thick chunks of meat from the loin, then gathered up the liver and gall bladder, and walked back to Billy.

He cut a branch from a nearby live maple, quickly peeled away the bark, and drove the slick, white stick through the center of two chunks of venison. Within two minutes he had driven forked sticks into the ground on either side of the fire and suspended the meat above the flames, where it began sizzling, dripping fat and juices sputtering into the fire. He sliced off a piece of raw liver, rinsed it with canteen water, and knelt beside Billy.

"Eat this."

Billy looked at him, inquiring. "Raw?"

"Raw. You've lost a lot of blood. Liver will replace it."

Billy shuddered, but took the dark, slippery morsel and gingerly put it in his mouth. By force of will he chewed and swallowed. Eli picked up the gall bladder. "I'm going to wash the wound."

"With gall?"

"It cleans anything and will start the healing. It will sting a little, but no pain."

He removed the blanket from Billy's shoulder, then punctured the gall sack with the point of his knife. Kneeling behind Billy, he squeezed a small amount of the thick, green, malodorous liquid into his cupped hand, then used his fingers to gently rub it onto the eighteen stitches on Billy's shoulder blade.

Eli rose. "Let that dry in the open air." He reached for the liver. "Can you stand more?"

Billy grimaced.

"Think you can get some venison down?"

"Yes."

Eli plucked the stick from above the fire. The two chunks of loin were seared on the outside, but the inside was red, raw, dripping blood. "Eat all you can. Especially the blood. You need it." He took salt from his own pouch and pinched some onto each of the two pieces.

Billy was ravenous. He blew on the meat to cool it, then tore pieces with his teeth. He drank cool water from his canteen and did not stop until he had finished both pieces of smoking venison. While Billy ate, Eli sliced two more pieces and set them broiling over the fire, then reached inside his buckskin shirt to draw out Billy's shirt, washed clean in a stream. He unfolded it, shook it, and rummaged in Billy's pouch for the needle and thread. After lifting the stick with the second two chunks of sizzling venison from the cross-arms, he handed them to Billy, then sat down with the needle and thread. Ten minutes later he had sewn the slit in the back closed, and again his smile came and went.

"It isn't pretty, but it will hold." Billy looked and grinned. The shirt was white, the thread black. Eli draped the damp shirt on the branches of a nearby bush and spoke once more. "I'll be back in quarter of an hour."

Billy had finished one more piece of venison when Eli's voice came from the forest, "Coming in." In one hand he carried a gathering of fronds cut from growth in the forest, and in the other, a lily pad. Without a word he laid the fronds on a large, flat stone, and with a smaller rock, began to crush them to a pulp. Finished, he lifted Billy's shirt from the bush.

"Lift your right arm."

The two of them worked Billy's shirt over his right arm, then his head, and straightened it.

"I'm going to put this poultice on the stitches and the lily pad over it to hold it in place."

"What's the poultice?"

"Jimson."

"That will help?"

"Draws poison. Helps heal. Lean forward."

He lifted Billy's shirt, carefully mounded the pulp over the stitches, then laid the lily pad over the poultice. He pulled the shirt down, then draped Billy's pouch over his left shoulder with the strap holding the poultice in place.

"Sit still for a while. I have to make a strip to tie down your arm."

Fascinated, Billy watched him spread the deer hide on the ground, then start with his knife. He began at the neck and made but one continuous cut, round and round the hide to the center, creating a single strip of rawhide half an inch wide, twenty-five feet long. He tied a loop in one end and came back to Billy.

"Put your left arm across your body and raise your right arm."

He tightened the loop around Billy's mid-section just below his left arm, then began winding it around and around, working upward. He brought the end of the strip over Billy's left shoulder and tied it off. Billy could not move his left arm, and the poultice was firmly in place.

"Too tight?"

Billy shook his head.

"When you can, get on your feet and walk around a little. I'm going to cook as much of the venison as I can, and then move what's left of the deer away from camp."

"Are the Mohawk likely to return?"

"Not those we met yesterday. I think they were sent down here by the British on a scout. We might meet some others, but I doubt it. This is pretty far south for them to be here by accident. I'll take a look a little later on." He paused, then spoke with quiet deliberation. "Listen to the birds. Study the squirrels. Watch whatever comes to feed on the remains of the deer. They'll tell you when something is moving in the forest. Try to feel what's going on around you."

Farther from Billy, Eli built a second, larger fire, and as the afternoon wore on, cut thick strips of meat from the deer—the loins, hams, then shoulders, and set the pieces to broil. While the meat was cooking, he gathered the deer entrails and was gone for a time. When he returned, the intestines had been slit open, washed clean, and wound around a section of tree limb, and the paunch had been opened, emptied, and also washed. He set the limb with the intestines on a rock near the fire, then hung the open paunch on a bush to dry.

Billy rose, and spread his feet while the lightheaded dizziness passed, then walked to Eli. "Anything I can help with?"

Eli shook his head. "Get some sleep. We're going to have to move on, and for what's coming, you'll need your strength."

With the sun halfway to the western rim, Eli set the last of the meat to cook, then gathered the remains of the deer and walked fifty yards south, where he scattered the offal in the foliage. When he returned, Billy was leaning against the log, awake, and Eli spoke.

"Can you eat some more venison?"

"Yes."

As Eli stepped over the log, he said, "Wait. I'll be back soon." Ten minutes later he returned, carrying a dripping bundle of green growth in his hands. Both sleeves of his buckskin hunting shirt were soaked past the elbows.

"Watercress. Tasty." He dropped the tangle of wet stems and leaves on his blanket and went to his haunches beside Billy. "Feeling any better?"

As he spoke, the westering sun dimmed, then disappeared. Instantly the forest darkened, and there was a strange, loud rushing sound overhead. What had been bright one instant was cast in shadows the next.

Billy peered upward but could not see through the tree tops. He looked at Eli in question.

"Carrier pigeons. Millions of them. Once when I was young they covered the sun for more than two hours. We had twilight twice that day." For more than ten minutes they sat quietly in the queer mid-afternoon shadow before the rushing sound overhead faded and the light once again filtered into the green of the forest.

Eli brought cooked venison, and they sat cross-legged on their blankets, eating the meat and watercress and drinking sweet, cold water from their canteens until they had their fill. Finished, Eli gathered the remainder of the cooked meat and the watercress onto a flat rock and covered it with ferns against the gathering flies, then walked back to Billy.

"I'm going to walk a circle about half a mile out, to be sure we're alone. You should be all right. Watch the place I took the last of the deer. The birds will gather first, then others. They'll tell you if anyone's coming from the south."

Within seconds Eli had disappeared, and the sounds of the forest quietly returned beneath the green cathedral dome overhead. To the south, where the remains of the deer carcass were scattered, one great black raven circled, then settled in the top of the trees to study the forest floor. Another joined him, and another, and then they came flocking, calling among themselves.

Billy remained motionless, leaning against the log, watching intently. Soon one raven tucked its wings and dropped eighty feet like a bullet before it spread them. Billy heard the whisper as the glossy black feathers caught the air, and the bird settled lightly to the soft forest floor. An instant later the air was filled with black bodies dropping and the rush of flared wings catching the air as they came to rest. Billy remained still and made no sound as he watched their every move.

Most of them vanished in the thick foliage. Some reappeared, heads held high, carrying strips of meat or hide locked in their strong black beaks. A sleek, dark marten came slinking through the ground cover to seize a bone and was gone. Squirrels darted about, scolding, furious at the invasion of their domain. A rabbit stopped to watch, and was gone, uninterested in meat and bone. A horned owl silently perched on a pine branch thirty feet above the scramble beneath, head swiveling, patiently watching, waiting its opportunity.

Suddenly, for a moment, all movement ceased. In a twinkling the ravens rose to the lower branches of the trees, and the squirrels disappeared. Billy reached for his musket and waited, breath coming short as he waited for shadows slipping toward him among the trees, and the dreaded rush of painted men with spiked war clubs and tomahawks.

There were no shadows. Billy saw instead a slight movement in the foliage, then heard a purring sound from deep in the throat of something large. Without warning, the head and shoulders of a great, yellow-gray cat reared upward from the ferns with the neck of the deer carcass clutched in its mouth. Holding its head high, the huge panther effortlessly dragged the carcass of the deer away through the forest, while all living things made way. The tawny animal was gone as quickly as it had appeared, while Billy gaped. From what he had seen, he estimated the cat was twelve feet long, tip of nose to tip of tail. As soon as the great beast vanished, the ravens dropped back to the ground to scavenge the scraps, the squirrels reappeared scolding, and the sights and the sounds of the forest resumed.

The last arc of the sun was setting the treetops on fire when Billy heard Eli's voice from the north, with his familiar, "Coming in." Moments later Eli stepped over the log, and Billy turned his head, musket still across his knees.

Eli glanced at the musket. "Someone came?"

"No. A panther came to the deer carcass."

"Big?"

"About twelve feet long, nose to tail."

"Fairly good size. I didn't hear a shot."

"I didn't shoot."

"Good. Anything else?"

"No. Just the birds and squirrels. Anything happen where you were?"

"No Mohawk. We're safe for now." He leaned his rifle against the log. "I'll have something to eat in a few minutes. Then we'll have to put out the fire. It draws too many things in the dark."

Eli set about warming some of the cooked venison over the small fire, with Billy watching until he could stand it no longer.

"Let me help. There's something I can do."

Eli turned to face him. "You got hurt this time. Next time it could be me, and you'll have to tend me. For now, the biggest help you can be is to rest, gather strength. We have to move on soon." Billy nodded, and Eli turned back to the work of getting their evening food ready and settling in for the night.

They ate warmed-over meat and finished the watercress, then drank from their canteens. Eli repacked the remainder of the cooked meat in ferns, shook both blankets, then settled them onto the ground next to the log, with the rifle and musket nearby. With purple-gray gathering around them, he banked the fire while Billy sat down on his own blanket and leaned gingerly back against the log, taking care to keep the wound on his shoulder from touching the rough bark. Eli settled onto his own blanket, cross-legged, before he spoke.

"We'll repack your shoulder in the morning. Any pain?"

"It aches a bit. No real pain."

A few moments passed before Billy continued. "Earlier, when the raccoon came, something happened."

Eli sensed the time for talk had arrived. He remained motionless, silent, while he waited, eyes locked onto the dying fire.

"She studied me, and I looked at her, and it was like she understood I wouldn't hurt her. I put some fish on my pouch, and she came and took it and left." Billy paused for a moment. "Almost like we were talking."

Eli studied Billy's face for a moment. "Anything else? The birds? Squirrels?"

Billy shrugged. "No. But something opened up inside of me."

"What?"

Billy cleared his throat, hesitant, afraid he could not find the words he needed.

"It was like the birds and animals all have thoughts—like they could tell me if I could learn how to listen. Like the whole forest has things to tell."

At that moment, movement to the south caught the eye of both men, and they turned to see the horned owl that had been patiently sitting in the tree above the remains of the deer plummet downward and set her wings in a silent glide. At the right instant her legs swung forward, and the black, needle-sharp talons plucked an unsuspecting squirrel from atop a log, frantically squirming to escape. With strong strokes of its powerful wings, the owl ascended up through the trees into the twilight and was gone.

Eli turned back to Billy. "Anything else?"

"I don't see anything quite like it was before, even things I knew." Billy stopped, waiting, and saw that Eli was working with his thoughts. He gave him time.

Slowly, choosing his words carefully, Eli spoke. "The Indians have lived in the forest for thousands of years. It's their school, their food, clothing, religion—their life. They've learned the lessons the forest can teach. They know that everything in the forest has a spirit."

Billy's eyes narrowed. "Everything?"

Eli nodded.

In the gathering twilight he waited for Billy to speak, but Billy remained silent. Eli continued. "Maybe the whole earth is a living thing."

Billy did not try to speak, or move.

"The Indians think it is. All they think, all they do, is built on that understanding. To them, death is only the passing of the spirit from the body. Those left behind mourn, but they know the spirit goes on. They'll join it later."

He paused, choosing his thoughts. "Taronhiawagon—their God—created it all. Carries the heavens on his shoulders. He can talk with all of it—animals, birds, mountains, streams, clouds—and they can talk back, each its own way according to how he created them. Every thing has its place, its purpose. Every thing obeys his voice, his laws."

Eli stopped and drew a great breath and slowly released it. "Everything except man. Man is special. He gave man the power to know right from wrong." Eli raised his eyes to Billy's. "And he gave man—only man—the power to choose which one he will follow."

He dropped his eyes once more. "To force man to choose, he sent the twin boys, Good and Evil, like the Devil and Jesus. Choose evil, bad things happen. Choose good, and you feel peace. Joy."

Eli stopped again and looked into the purple gloom of the forest, and Billy saw a faraway look steal into his eyes.

"God gave man dominion over the earth, and that was the beginning of trouble. White men think that means cut out the forests, change the streams, kill the birds and animals, take the land from the Indians, make them live on small sections like white men, or die. Send missionaries to change the Indian religion."

A great sadness stole over Eli as he continued. "The Indians believe that all those things are bad—no one should do those things. They believe all things are a gift, to be honored and revered. Not changed, destroyed."

Again he turned serious eyes to Billy. "They believe all things were made to work together. They think God intended that man would learn his place in the great plan, and that he would fulfill it if he was given the choice. For Indians, happiness occurs when all things are working together, just as God meant them to, including man. The yearly cycle of the Indian—the seasons, the ceremonies, the planting, the harvest— everything is guided by this great plan. Right now the Iroquois are preparing for the Green Corn ceremony. For two or three days they will gather, and dance, and pray, and they will thank God for the green corn that he has sent once again to feed them through the hard winter. They will have another ceremony when they harvest it. They will have their midwinter ceremony. And many, many more. For all things they thank Taronhiawagon, who is the creator."

Eli gestured to the south, where he had left the remains of the deer. "When I shot the deer, I went to him. I told him he had fulfilled his purpose, that I needed his body to make you well. He had been brave, and had great speed and strength, which I honored. I told him that God was pleased with his sacrifice, that you could live and be healthy. I told him that God would accept him in heaven, where he would be at peace forever. I poured clear water over his head to wash him. I used every part of his body I needed for you, and then I gave the rest of it to other creatures who needed it. The deer is honored, happy where he is. You are getting well. It is God's plan."

Billy swallowed, his mind laboring with thoughts and feelings he had never known, as Eli continued.

"It is evil to take more than you need. It is evil to insult the forests by cutting them where you do not need to cut them. It is evil to kill what you do not need or cannot use."

Eli stopped and his words came low, powerful, spaced. "But most of all, it is evil not to thank God for his great plan of harmony, and to not try to understand how man was meant to take his part."

The shadows were deep before Billy moved, and Eli spoke once again.

"Most white men have never thought that for them to live, something must die—that for anything to live, another thing must die." He gestured south, to where the great owl had swept down to seize the squirrel. "For the owl to live, he had to take the squirrel. For the squirrel to live, it had to take the nuts. For one thing to live, another must die." He exhaled and seconds passed. "It seems a harsh thing to us, but I do not think it seems harsh to God. I do not think other creatures see death as we see it. It frightens us, and we fear it. But once we understand that death is a part of life, and that as with all things God has provided, it is meant for our good, it is no longer a fearsome thing."

Eli fell silent, and for a long time the two men studied the last of the glowing embers of their small fire as twilight deepened and their thoughts ran. Then Eli spoke once more.

"To choose between the twin boys, Good and Evil, a man must be free. If another forces him to act, it is not a choice at all. I think that is what the Americans are fighting for right now. Freedom—liberty—their right to choose what they will be. I think that is what God wants us to do."

He stopped for a moment, then finished. "That is why I came to join in the war. Inside, I know God means men to be free to choose. I have to be part of that. That's why I'm going north. Somehow, Joseph Brant and his Mohawk must be stopped from bringing the British down on us." For a moment he paused, face clouded, and he spoke as though by afterthought. "We've got to find him, and stop him."

"How are we going to stop a Mohawk army?"

Eli shook his head. "I don't know. Brant's smart, and a fighter, and likely he will have Cornplanter and Red Jacket somewhere close by. We've got to find our army up there and help them get ready for what those Mohawk can do. They're fierce."

Billy looked at him. "Why do they do such cruel things? Scalping? Mutilating?"

Eli looked him in the eye. "It isn't just the Indians. They learned some of it from the white men. Whole Indian villages have been slaughtered and scalped and mutilated by the whites."

Billy's eyes widened. "I didn't know."

Eli shrugged. "No one seems to want to talk about that. About seventy or eighty years ago, the whites killed a hunting party of Indians, so the Indians raided a white settlement. Killed a lot of people and took others captive. One captive was a woman named Hannah Duston. Out in the forest, she got free, and she killed and scalped ten Indians, then walked back to the whites. Became a hero overnight. The legislature gave her twenty-five pounds of English money for the scalps, and it didn't seem to matter that six of those scalps were from children. The story is still told around Indian campfires. One side is about as bad as the other when it comes to being cruel."

Billy fell silent for a time, struggling to accept the ugly truth. He raised his eyes back to Eli. "How do you plan to stop Brant and his Indians?"

Eli shook his head and released a weary breath. "I don't know. I do know that if he has gathered a fighting force of Mohawk, there's no end to the misery he can bring down on our people. I doubt our army can stop him out there in the forest. Most white men don't know how to fight out there." He stopped to study the fire for a moment. "Someone will have to stop him. I'll have to try. Maybe I can do something if I can get to Brant, but getting past his Indians won't be easy."

"Get to Brant? Kill him?"

Eli thought for a long time. "I hope not."

Lost in their thoughts, neither man noticed when the crickets began their scratchy nightly work and the frogs in the marshes commenced sending their staccato message. The last embers of the fire winked and then died. The moon rose, and the silvery light filtered through the great dome of trees overhead to once again make lacy patterns on the forest floor.

Eli stood. "I don't think I ever said so much at one time. Tomorrow is going to be a long day. I have to cut the deer entrails into strips to dry, and make a carrying pouch out of the empty paunch for the cooked meat. We'll also have to change the poultice on your shoulder."

Billy looked at him in the darkness and knew the powerful moment had passed. "When will we leave here?"

Eli shrugged. "When you're able. Maybe tomorrow late."

"I have some questions."

"We'll have time."

Billy pointed to his bullet pouch. "Those letters I wrote to Brigitte Dunson are in there. Things can happen. Will you see that she gets them if I don't get back?"

Eli nodded. "I will. If I don't make it, will you find Mary Flint for me? Tell her I surely hope life brings her some happiness." For a moment he stared at the ground, remembering the soft brown eyes and the brave face that masked a broken heart that had lost everything she treasured in life—newborn child, husband, family.

"I'll find her. I'll tell her."

Eli reached for the blankets. "We'd better get some rest. You sleep. I'll watch for a while."

Notes

Unless otherwise noted, the following facts are taken from Graymont, *The Iroquois in the American Revolution*, on the pages indicated.

Musket "cartridges" were made of paper and carried by soldiers in a cartridge case. For details on how they were made, see Wilbur, *The Revolutionary Soldier, 1775–1783*.

Anesthetics, other than liquor and opium, were unknown in colonial days. To help manage pain, patients often took a lead rifleball between their teeth, or a leather belt, to bite on during surgeries. Surgeons often cauterized wounds, either by applying hot tar or a heated piece of iron such as a knife blade (see Wilbur, *The Revolutionary Soldier, 1775–1783*).

The Mohawk leader known as Joseph Brant was named Thayendangea in his native Iroquois language. His baptized Christian name was Joseph Brant. An accurate and detailed description of his early history and remarkable achievements with language with his people is given (pp. 52–53).

Wampum belts played a critically important part in the society of the Iroquois. They served as the "archives" of their history, and the keeping of them, and the remembering of what each belt represented was assigned to the Onondaga tribe, one of the six tribes of the Iroquois confederation. The belts numbered in the thousands. They were created to commemorate most of the important occasions in the history of the Iroquois. They were often exchanged between the Iroquois and white men, e.g. from the American Congress, and from General Philip Schuyler. No formal message was acceptable without an accompanying wampum belt (pp. 16, 32, 69–79, 90–91, 109, III, 158–59).

The name of the highest god in the Iroquois religion is Taronhiawagon, which means "The holder of the heavens" or "He who carries the heavens on his shoulders" (see Hale, *The Iroquois Book of Rites*, p. 74).

The Iroquois word for fox is *skuhnaksu* (p. 8).

The mighty Iroquois confederation was founded by Deganawida and Hiawatha. Historians differ on the date, some claiming its origin as early as A.D. 1450, others as late as A.D. 1660. The Confederation included five tribes, with a sixth often added. They were Mohawk, Seneca, Onondaga, Oneida, and Cayuga, the sixth being the Tuscarora. The name Hiawatha (nothing to do with Longfellow's famous poem) means, "He was awake" (p. 14).

Sir William Johnson, who played a critical role in the Revolutionary War in behalf of the British, married Mary Brant. Her Iroquois name was Gonwatsijayenni. She was the granddaughter of Chief Hendrick and, apparently, the sister of Joseph Brant. She became a very powerful figure in the politics of the Iroquois and enjoyed the status of sachem or spiritual leader. Sir William Johnson's son, Guy, and his grandson, John, carried on for the British after Sir William's death. It was Guy Johnson who accompanied Joseph Brant on his historic voyage to England to meet King George III (pp. 13, 29–30, 52, 79, 157–61).

The great Christian missionary Samuel Kirkland was of immeasurable help to the Americans. It was Kirkland who challenged Sir William Johnson for control of the Iroquois (pp. 34–61).

The Iroquois described the process of declaring war as "taking up the hatchet," and of ceasing war as "burying the hatchet." The process included formalities, which are described (pp. 104–56).

The personages known as the Good Twin and the Evil Twin are critically important figures in the Iroquois story of the creation and the affairs of this earth. The Good Twin brings all that is good, the Evil Twin all that is evil (p. 9; see also Graymont, *The Iroquois*, pp. 16–17).

The story told by Eli to Billy concerning the taking of scalps by an American woman is true. In 1697, following an attack by the Iroquois on the New Hampshire hamlet known as Haverhill, Hanna Duston, five days after delivering a baby, assisted by Mary Neff and a boy named Samuel Lennardson, followed the Indians into the forest for one hundred miles and killed and scalped ten of them. Six of the scalps were those of children. She became famous. The Great and General Court of New Hampshire awarded her twenty-five pounds, English sterling (see Ulrich, *Goodwives*, pp. 167–68).

The Iroquois built platforms for their dead and placed them in trees or on high poles, where they left them. The Iroquois believed the spirit left the body at death and lingered nearby for at least one year, perhaps longer, revisiting the body it had inhabited on the earth. Burial grounds were therefore sacred, as related by Eli to Billy (see Morgan, *League of the Ho-de-no-sau-nee, or Iroquois*, Volume I, pp. 166–70).

For an excellent map of the home grounds of the Iroquois and other tribes, see Graymont, *The Iroquois in the American Revolution*, p. xii.

CHAPTER III

★ ★ ★

*I*n a time beyond memory, red men from the west ventured into the dark, vast, primeval forests of the Northeast wilderness. Those who came first, perished. Those who followed, suffered. An unforgiving nature taught the survivors the great secret: among all living things, the strong, who learned their place in this harsh land, lived; all others died.

Nature became the core of their existence. Their year was reckoned by the seasons—planting, cultivating, harvesting, the running of the salmon, the bugling of the mating elk, the deep sleeping of the bear in the frozen winter, the awakening warmth of spring. They looked at the earth, with its bounty, and they gazed into the heavens and beheld the sun, the moon, and stars, and they thanked the Great Spirit—Taronhiawagon—who had given them these inestimable treasures. They thanked the lesser gods that controlled the planting of their squash, corn, and beans and the growing of them, and the harvest. They recognized the twin boys, the Good Twin and the Evil Twin, and they followed the teachings of the Good Twin.

They learned the deep lessons of the rhythm and balance of nature. Where one thing perished, another grew. Good could come of bad. Nature seldom took something without giving something. Famine would be followed by times of plenty. They watched the eagle take the salmon, the hawk take the rabbit, the panther take the deer, and they learned the lesson. Every creature on the earth, or in the waters, or in the air, and every growing thing, and all that was in and on the earth, had been given by Taronhiawagon. Each had its place, and its use. The greatest joy came with the using of all things as intended. It pleased Him when, with thankfulness, they partook of His great gifts according to their need. To take what they did not need, or to take without thankfulness, was evil. Such a thing would bring sorrow.

They prospered, and divided, and pushed their way southward into new lands. They created structures of poles and bark, large enough for many families, and called them *kanonses*—longhouses—and the people called themselves by new names: Huron, Mohawk, Onondaga, Oneida, Cayuga, Seneca, Tuscarora, Abanaki, Mohican. Each adopted their own new ways of life and dialect. In time, Hiawatha and Deganawida did their work. The great Iroquois Confederacy was formed and became strong.

Then, from a distant land across the great water, came a new breed of men, down from the frozen north country. White, with a strange language on their tongue, and wondrous weapons in their hands that made smoke and thunder, and killed far, and tools made of brass and iron, superior to anything ever seen before. They called themselves *French*, and the red men they called *Indians*, and they offered peace. They took red women for wives, and they traded their iron tools and their weapons to the Indians for furs. They worked their way ever southward, following the great rivers and the streams and the lakes in their unending quest for the furs of the beaver, marten, mink, and otter.

From the east came more of the white men under different flags, calling themselves *Dutch* and *English*. They landed on the shores of the great eastern water to establish their small, tenuous villages, and they suffered. The red men saw it, and came in peace to teach them how to live in the land, and the white men learned, and survived. The white men saw the riches in the red men's raw, sprawling land, and they desired to have it, and they began to take it.

In shock, the red men struck back in the only way they understood. From the forest, quick, silent, deadly, they destroyed entire villages, but where they destroyed one, another sprang up. Finally, the red men accepted what they could not change, and they made peace, and the white men came on.

The inevitable collision—between the white men from the north and the white men from the east—came in the wilderness. Where they met, they warred to possess the land. Soldiers came to build great forts, and more soldiers came with cannon to destroy them. From both sides, ever more soldiers, ever more cannon. In this war, the Huron took up the hatchet on the side of the French, while the Mohawk joined the English. Other tribes of the great confederacy were confused, some joining one side, some the other, and some refusing to fight on either side. For seven years the war waged, and in the end, the English were victorious. The French withdrew.

Then, to the utter bewilderment of the red men, the victorious Englishmen, who had built their towns and settlements on the east, near the great water, declared themselves free, divided themselves away from their mother country, called themselves *Americans*, and took up the hatchet against their mother country. Again the red men took sides, the Mohawk remaining strong with the English, whom they were certain would win, while others joined with the Americans in their fight for independence. Each side knew the red men were masters of the forests. They could move in the primeval wilderness like none other, covering great distances quickly, with unerring accuracy, to strike with the ferocity of the panther and the wolf. The attack of the red man became a thing most feared. Both sides used the Indians as their eyes and ears in the trackless forests, and to terrorize the hearts and minds of their enemies.

And the great Iroquois Confederacy trembled. Divided against itself, allowing the white men to control their destiny, they fought on in the white man's war, one tribe against another, while the great work wrought by Hiawatha and Deganawida began to slowly crumble.

In the brilliant warmth of May sunshine, the shuddering thunder of half a billion tons of mountainous ice floes in violent collision rang off the mountains and echoed inland for miles as the great floes relentlessly ground their way northeast, through the great granite cliffs, and the boulders, and the banks of the mighty St. Lawrence River, ripping, jamming, flooding—swept onward by the heavy spring runoff. Behind the monstrous floes, southwest, were the five Great Lakes, from whence the ice had come. Ahead, to the northeast, were the open waters of St. Lawrence Bay and the North Atlantic.

On the north bank of the river, west of the place it widened to lead to the Gulf of St. Lawrence, the cold, brooding Quebec Castle, built by the French to protect their rich fur trade, stood high and square and stubborn. All who chose to venture on the St. Lawrence must come under the muzzles of her deadly cannon, mounted in gunports cut in the thick, gray, granite walls.

Where once the French had decided which vessels passed, and which would not, it was now British officers and ten thousand regulars garrisoned in the historic old castle, who sent up the flags granting or denying passage, and it was British gunners who manned the cannon that settled any disputes. Such had been the misfortune of the French when they capitulated to the British in 1763, ending the Seven Years' War for the northeast section of the continent. The treaty required France to relinquish all claims. Quebec, and all other French possessions, became the property of England. While France seethed inwardly and yearned for a day of redemption, England wallowed in her victory and clutched the newly won land and treasure to her breast.

Warm sunlight streamed through twelve tall, narrow windows in the east wing of the spacious, high-ceilinged governor's office on the main floor, to make an orderly pattern of rectangles on the chill stone floor. The roar of the rampaging river reached inside, into every corner, a constant reminder that in the end, all mankind must humble itself before the raw power of this country. A massive stone fireplace with a heavy, dark oak mantel formed the north end of the room, where three large pine logs burned to drive out the chill. Above the mantel hung a portrait of King George III, with the Union Jack proud on one side and the gold-on-blue English lion on the other. A large, plain desk of Canadian maple stood on the only carpet in the room, before the fireplace, facing the high, thick, double doors with the heavy, wrought iron strap hinges and the brass studs.

Sir Guy Carleton, major general, British army, sat hunched forward in the straight-backed chair, staring unseeing at his hands as he slowly worked them together on the desktop. His eyes were narrowed, face drawn, brooding with a dark premonition that had insidiously crept into his consciousness to grow and fester until it clouded his every moment, every thought. He had been notified by General John Burgoyne that Burgoyne was to arrive on the ship *Apollo* and present himself at Carleton's office as soon as the ice conditions on the St. Lawrence River would allow. *Major* General John Burgoyne. Not lieutenant general, or brigadier general, as Burgoyne had been when he was second in command to Carleton only months before. *Major* General Burgoyne—equal now in military rank to Sir Guy Carleton.

What Burgoyne had *not* said was the *purpose* of the meeting. Why? All rules of protocol demanded that a visiting general at least identify the purpose for which he had come. Just passing through? Reporting for duty?

Instantly Carleton had recognized the implication. If Burgoyne were scheduled to arrive in Quebec, it was the duty of Lord George Germain, and not Burgoyne, to notify Carleton of both the visit, and the purpose. Lord George Germain had been Secretary of State for the American colonies in the cabinet of King George III since November 1775, and Germain, pudgy, thick-lipped, protruding eyes, plagued with a lisp, was nothing if not a master politician, whose well-honed skills included giving and taking rank and status among the high and mighty, both in government and the military, with deadly efficiency.

Germain had been in office when Carleton had made his heroic stand at the gates of Quebec on December 31, 1775, and defeated Montgomery and his beleaguered American command in a raging blizzard. Germain had participated in the decision that such conspicuous bravery should receive its reward, and shortly after, King George had tapped Carleton on each shoulder with his sword and bestowed the status of Knight of the Realm upon him.

Then, abruptly, with Germain prominent in the decision, King George had handpicked Major General Sir Guy Carleton to serve as governor of the gigantic, wild, sprawling Dominion of Canada, in command of the ten thousand regulars sent by the king to enforce English rule in what had been a French nation. Knighthood and governor, all within months! The fortunes of Sir Guy Carleton in the British Empire had indeed spiraled upward with dizzying velocity. His second in command was Brigadier General John Burgoyne, who had served as second in command to General Thomas Gage through that humiliating affair at Lexington and Concord, followed by the disaster at Bunker Hill sixty days later. Burgoyne's transfer to the Northern Army had been instant, where he had received both experience and training in the ways of the Canadian frontier under Carleton's leadership.

Carleton drew and slowly released a great breath while he fought to control his growing perception that the colossal breach of protocol by Germain, coupled with the terse notice from Burgoyne that he was coming for reasons not stated, were not merely odd coincidences, but were harbingers that bode ill for Carleton. Perhaps catastrophic.

The massive door yawed open, and Carleton started, jolted from the black abyss of his fears to the realities of the arrival of the spring ice breakup, and along with it Major General John Burgoyne. Carleton stood, portly, average height, rounded, unremarkable features. He straightened his tunic, waiting while Colonel Bruce Thornton strode to the front of his desk.

"Suh, Major General John Burgoyne is here for his appointment."

Thornton, Carleton's aide-de-camp, stood straight in his sparkling crimson and white uniform, chin tucked in, his huge, meticulously trimmed mustache bristling. The sunlight through the windows reflected off the shine on his knee-length black boots as he waited for orders.

Carleton's voice cracked as he spoke, and he stopped to start again. "Is the general alone?"

"He is, sir."

Carleton felt the grab in the pit of his stomach. *Alone! No one to witness. He's bringing trouble.*

"Show him in."

"Yes, suh."

Carleton glanced at the clock on the heavy mantel above the massive stone fireplace—nine o'clock—and watched Thornton's ramrod-straight back as he strode to the two, ten-foot-tall oak doors, heels clicking a determined cadence. The colonel pushed one of the massive doors open and disappeared. As it thumped closed, Carleton clamped his jaw closed and braced himself. His thoughts and memories reached back, and for a few moments he let them run unchecked.

Major General John Burgoyne—Gentleman Johnny, the dashing bon vivant of London and Paris—Burgoyne, the gambler—Burgoyne, the lady's man—Burgoyne of the Light Horse.

He heard the steady staccato tapping of two sets of boots approaching in the vacuous waiting room, and his thoughts continued unbridled.

Rumored to be illegitimate—joined the army at age fifteen—captain at age twenty-two—Burgoyne, the playwright—theatrical Johnny, wrote several successful satires for the stage—married Lady Charlotte, daughter of the Earl of Derby—eloped because the Earl was furious about the match—gambled away everything—defected to France for six years to avoid the mortification of bankruptcy—returned only when the Earl made peace with them and set them up with enough money to once again enter English aristocracy.

Thornton rapped sharply at the door and Carleton called, "Enter!"

The door swung open and Carleton held his breath as Thornton paced three steps into the room, halted, turned, and announced, "Suh, Major General John Burgoyne."

Without realizing it, Carleton's back straightened, his shoulders squared, and his heels came together. In that instant, Major General John Burgoyne swept smartly into the room, tall, slender, charismatic, dark-haired and dark-eyed, handsome in his own way, smiling superbly, hat under one arm, and a thin leather folder with his seal stamped in gold clutched in his other hand. His uniform was that of a British major general, with one exception that set Burgoyne apart from any other officer in the British army. He had paid handsomely to have the best tailor in London create his tunic with a tiny gold piping gilding the lapels. A small thing, but one correctly calculated by Burgoyne to catch every eye, to draw glances, and flutters and guarded whispers among the ladies, and envious disgust from his peer officers in high London society.

Burgoyne strode briskly to the front of Carleton's desk and thrust his hand forward to the man who had been his superior officer but short months earlier. There was no hint of military protocol, no salute, no compliments, no statement of purpose, no stiff formal bow. Only Gentleman Johnny Burgoyne at his dashing best.

"General, sir, how good to see you again," Burgoyne said.

Carleton shook his hand briefly. "It is my pleasure to welcome you back." He glanced at the leather folder, then locked eyes with Burgoyne, waiting for the traditional statement by Burgoyne of the purpose of his visit.

Burgoyne ignored the protocol. "You are looking well. And I have heard nothing but compliments of your conduct from the king and cabinet."

King and cabinet! He's had audience with king and cabinet, who address only matters of international importance. Instantly Carleton recognized the implication and knew that beneath the warm greeting and overpowering smile, he had just heard the opening of a terrifying floodgate.

Carleton gestured. "Would you care to be seated?"

Burgoyne drew the leather-bound, straight-backed chair to the front edge of the desk and sat down. "Thank you."

Carleton settled onto the leading edge of his chair and waited. Burgoyne plowed straight in.

"General, I am under orders to deliver this to you. You will note that it bears the seal of Lord George Germain."

Germain! He who creates or destroys careers on his own whims! Carleton reached into the core of his being to find the control necessary to maintain a calm, disciplined exterior. He accepted the document.

"Thank you. Am I to read this immediately?"

Burgoyne leaned back and for the first time his eyes were direct, his voice paced. "May I explain." His eyebrows peaked, and an unexpected intensity came into his voice. "General Howe crushed the rebel resistance in and around New York and is now well in control there. He experienced minor setbacks when General Washington's army recrossed the Delaware and took Trenton, and then Princeton, before going into winter quarters at Morristown."

Carleton interrupted. "I learned those facts from a letter I intercepted that was written by Washington to Benedict Arnold, and from a prisoner captured by a scouting party. General Howe has communicated none of that to me, and I am sore pressed to understand why not, since it seems to me I should know these things as commander of the Northern Army." Carleton dropped his eyes for a moment. "Nonetheless, proceed."

Burgoyne leaned forward. "General Howe has full control of the New York entrance to the Hudson River. It is now thought by the king, and by Lord Germain, and the cabinet, that the rebellion can be stopped most expeditiously by sending the Northern Army up the Richelieu River to Lake Champlain, then on up Lake George, and down the Hudson River to effect a junction with Howe's army at Albany. Divide the colonies, north from south, by seizing the Lake Champlain–Hudson Valley waterway. Since the hotbed of the rebellion is in the New England states, once we have restored our control of the waterway, and isolated the north from the south, the rebellion will die." Burgoyne stopped, eyes narrowed, waiting.

The two words that had leaped out at Carleton were *Northern Army.* *His* army. *His* command. The king and Germain. *They* thought. Never a word, never an inquiry, never a letter from any of them seeking his advice about the most critically important assignment the Northern Army would ever have. Why? For what reason had they dealt so deviously with him? He spoke in even, civil tones.

"May I now read the message from Lord Germain?"

Burgoyne nodded and leaned back, watching Carleton's every move, every expression. Carleton leaped past the wordy salutation to the first paragraph.

"Whenever an army leaves the province in which it has been standing, the governor of the province shall not have the command over it outside his gubernatorial district, even if he had previously commanded the army as commander in chief, but shall surrender its command to the senior general under him."

In shock, his mouth slowly fell open, and he raised vacant eyes to Burgoyne. He closed his mouth and swallowed.

"Who wrote this?"

Burgoyne answered quietly. "The king."

"The king? When?"

"In the past ninety days."

"I have never heard of such a thing."

"Nor had I."

"If I interpret this correctly, I am to remain here, and I lose command of the Northern Army to my next senior officer. That would be you, I presume."

"So says the king, and Lord Germain."

Carleton's brain went numb with the realization that he had just been delivered the most colossal, unbelievable insult he had ever heard of in the annals of the British military. Deny a major general command of his own army when it leaves the province in which the same major general is also governor? Ridiculous! Utterly insane! For seconds that seemed an eternity, the only sound in the room was the unending roar of the ice in the distant river, while Carleton battled hot rage that welled up inside him. His face reddened, and his mouth narrowed to a slit as he stared into Burgoyne's eyes. His hands trembled as his thoughts ran wild.

You saw it coming just as I did—but you were the one that persuaded me to give you permission to return to England to mourn the loss of your wife! And to conduct other business. Other business! You never mentioned that the 'other business' was to give you almost exclusive entree to King George through Germain so you could persuade the king that you are the man to lead my army down the Lake Champlain—Hudson River corridor! You! Not me! Five months! December of last year until now! In London, consorting with Germain, gaining audience with the king. What truths did you distort? What lies did you tell? About whom? What papers did you use? What part of my military career have you used against me, to destroy me? How did you persuade Germain to draft this hideous paragraph, and then obtain the king's signature to it? How? Why?

Carleton felt tiny beads of perspiration on his forehead, and did not care, as his thoughts continued with a fury of their own. *It was I who stood at the gates of Quebec in that blizzard and turned the Americans. It was I who was knighted, and made governor! It was I who achieved what no other could in settling the entire country of Canada, setting up the laws, courts, commerce, settlements, preparing the Canadians to be valuable allies. It was I who remained here, devoted to my duties, while you were in London for five long months, whispering to the king through Germain. And it is I who should now lead my Northern Army down the corridor to meet General Howe! It is MY name that should go down in the annals of history as the one who led the Northern Army in the conquest of the colonies. Carleton.* Not *Burgoyne.*

Carleton dropped his eyes to the paper, and Burgoyne's breathing slowed as Carleton read on.

"I reluctantly recall your supineness in regards the opportunity that fell into your hands last October to attack and invest Fort Ticonderoga following your skirmish with the inferior American fleet on Lake Champlain. You were victorious, and that critically important prize was yours for the taking, yet you turned your back on Fort Ticonderoga and returned to Quebec. I trust you are cognizant that had Fort Ticonderoga been taken, we would have been spared that humiliating affair at Trenton on December twenty-sixth, last."

Only his lifelong commitment to unyielding discipline saved Carleton from slamming down the document and shouting his white-hot defiance in Burgoyne's face. He could no longer remain seated, and he stood, choking on his rage as he spoke.

"You will excuse me for a few moments while I attempt to grasp this . . . writing."

"Of course." Like a hawk, Burgoyne was watching Carleton's every move, every expression, knowing exactly what Germain had written, knowing that never had he seen such an outrageous document.

Shaking, Carleton walked to the lead-paned windows to peer unseeing southward, toward the river.

How did he do it? How did he convince Germain he was the man to command this campaign, and not me? Did he use that skirmish down in Portugal fifteen years ago? The Valencia de Alcantara business, and then that Villa Velha fuss? They were absolutely of no consequence. Oh, Burgoyne had been brave enough, and had led his three thousand troops well enough, but he was always certain to be spectacular when others were watching. Took some prisoners and some cannon, and the entire affair came to nothing! But not for Burgoyne! Oh, no! He wrote a report of his own, and saw to it that people in high places got it, while one of his well-positioned, politically positioned friends, who owned some tiny boroughs, got him elected to the House of Commons! In absentia, no less! And then he formed his Light Horse command, and saw to it they were the showpiece of the cavalry. Light horse! Wait until he leads his light horse into this wilderness!

Still trembling, Carleton ground his teeth together and continued to stare out the window with his back to Burgoyne.

And now I know how he destroyed me. Failure to take Fort Ticonderoga? The fools! The fools! It would have been easy to take the fort, but suicidal to think of wintering there without supplies. I made the right decision—return to Quebec, refit my fleet, provision my army, and take Fort Ti when the spring thaws came. My decision was right! But I was not there in London to defend myself while he destroyed me! For long moments seething rage welled up. His entire body was trembling, and he feared his legs would buckle.

Behind him, Burgoyne leaned forward, every nerve, every feeling reaching out as he waited to see how Carleton would accept the insult he had received and terrible things that had been done to him. He sensed the white-hot pain that had pierced Carleton's heart, and he despised Germain for requiring that he hand deliver the evil document to Carleton, when it was clearly the moral and ethical duty of Germain to do his own hatchet work. He had protested, but Germain would have it no other way. To have an inferior officer bear the message to his superior that he was to take his command was inhuman. Burgoyne felt the suffering Carleton was enduring. He watched, and he waited.

Carleton took a deep breath and reached deep into the wells of discipline and his own innate humanity to take charge of himself. Slowly he straightened and raised his chin, and he shook himself before he turned back to Burgoyne. He walked back to his desk, picked up the document, and read the balance of the terse message.

Major General John Burgoyne will take command of seven thousand of the regulars of the Northern Army and proceed south, up the

Richelieu River, thence to Lake Champlain, on to Lake George, reduce Fort Ticonderoga to British control, then proceed to the Hudson River. Two thousand Canadians will be employed for transportation. One thousand Mohawk Indians will be employed as scouts and advance skirmishers. A second command will be led by Lieutenant Colonel Barry St. Leger, under orders of General Burgoyne, to proceed from Niagara east to take Fort Stanwix on the Mohawk River and then continue east. General William Howe will proceed up the Hudson River, all three commands to meet at Albany, thus taking control of the waterway, isolating the northern colonies, which shall then be reduced to British control. Major General Carleton is to remain in Quebec with a small remainder of the Northern Army, and of course, give all assistance to General Burgoyne.

A three-pronged campaign. Burgoyne from the north. St. Leger from the west. Howe from the south. Isolate the northern colonies and pick them off one at a time.

Carleton raised his eyes. He was now under control. He spoke evenly, earnestly. "Would you care for tea? Chocolate?"

The unbearable crisis was past. Relief surged through Burgoyne as he realized Carleton had risen above the pettiness, the insult, the professional wounds, the destructive machinations of Germain, and had taken the high ground expected of an excellent British major general, and a superior human being.

"Thank you, no."

Carleton drew and released a great breath and settled down. "How may I be of service?"

Burgoyne opened the scarred leather cover of his folder, picked up the top document, unfolded it, then flattened it on the desktop. It was a map of the northeast section of the continent, nearly four feet square. He scanned it briefly, turned it to lay true with the compass, then selected a sheaf of papers from the folder.

"Yes, here we are." He raised his eyes to Carleton. "I thought it wise to review the entire campaign with you in some detail, then seek your advice on some matters. I presume that is agreeable." It was a statement, not a question. Burgoyne continued with studied deliberation. "As you know, the overall plan was carefully worked out in London between myself and Lord Germain months ago. As you have seen, it now carries his written approval." He paused for three seconds before adding, "as well as the signature and seal of the king."

Burgoyne raised his face and locked eyes with Carleton to be certain Carleton had clearly understood. The plan was Burgoyne's and carried the force of the king's seal. It was the sacred instrument by which Burgoyne would loose the lightning bolt that would defeat the colonists and put an end to the American rebellion. But infinitely transcending the subjection of the rebellious Americans, the plan would enshrine the name Burgoyne through all time as one of the brightest shining stars in the history of the British military.

Carleton understood perfectly.

Burgoyne lowered his eyes to the map and tapped it with a forefinger. "We are here, at Quebec." His finger moved as he spoke. "I shall proceed southwest, up the St. Lawrence River from here, past Trois-Rivieres to Sorel, here. There we turn due south, up the Richelieu River. We continue to St. Johns, here, then move on south on the west side of Lake Champlain, past Ile aux Noix, Ile la Motte, Cumberland Head, past the Bouquet River, Crown Point, Mount Hope, to Ticonderoga, here."

He stopped as a look of overpowering anticipation crept into his face. He continued. "The plan has two objectives. First, seize Fort Ticonderoga."

Fort Ticonderoga! A Mohawk word meaning "Between two great waters"—Lake George and Lake Champlain. Five hundred thirty feet in width, built by the French in the 1750s to stop the British in their push to the north. First named Fort Carillon after a French fur trader, Philippe de Carrion du Fresnoy. The French pronunciation of Carrion became Carillon in English, and it was he who had established the strategically important fur trading center on a tiny peninsula that juts into Lake Champlain, at the place where a narrow, three-and-one-half-mile chute descends two hundred feet, draining Lake George into the south end of Lake Champlain. All nations intimate with the vast, primitive North American continent held the opinion that the interior could be reached most easily by the great St. Lawrence—Lake Champlain—Lake George—Hudson River corridor, and that the cannon of Fort Ticonderoga controlled the great water highway. Whoever held Fort Ticonderoga, held the key to the continent.

Burgoyne nodded his head in silent approval as he went on. "Second, proceed with my forces south, down the Hudson River valley to meet an army led by General Howe, here."

Oddly, in the dawn of time, the continental plates deep beneath the surface of the northeastern section of the country had shifted, causing a rise on an east-west line, creating a watershed. The lakes drained to the north, while the Hudson River, located but a short distance from Lake George, drained south. Burgoyne's finger traced the course of the Hudson, past a mountain named Sugar Hill, then Lake George, Fort George, Fort Edward, Fort Miller, Saratoga, Stillwater, and Half Moon, all on the west bank of the Hudson River. His finger stopped at the word *Albany*.

Established by the French fur trappers as they worked the lakes and rivers south from Canada, Albany had become a major trade center where Canadian furs were exchanged for traps, muskets, knives, axes, lead, gunpowder, trinkets, sugar, rum. Strategically located on the Hudson, it was the southern anchor for the great north-south waterway, stretching between Albany and Montreal, two hundred miles north.

Burgoyne continued. "General Howe will leave from Manhattan Island at New York, here," he pointed, "and proceed up the Hudson by boat to effect a junction of our forces. With that accomplished, we will have cut off the entire northern half of the American colonies. We can do with them as we will."

He tapped his finger on the long, slender strip of island that divided the Hudson River from the East River. Manhattan—a name derived from Manahata, an Indian word meaning "The place encircled by many swift tides and joyous, sparkling waters"—on which New York harbor had grown to become the busiest seaport on the New England coast, and the most strategic harbor in the British effort to subdue the fledgling United States.

Burgoyne moved his finger to the easternmost of the Great Lakes. "The third prong of our campaign will originate here on Lake Ontario." His finger moved as he spoke. "A force of our Mohawk Indian allies gathered by Chief Joseph Brant will assemble with a contingent of our forces—British and German—under the command of Lieutenant Colonel Barry St. Leger, at the Niagara River on the west end of the lake, and then move east to here—Oswego. From Oswego they shall travel inland, take Fort Stanwix, here, and continue east along the Mohawk River past Oriskany, here. Then, on to the confluence of the Mohawk and the Hudson rivers, here, just below Half Moon, a few miles north of Albany, and then south to join us."

Burgoyne's eyes were narrowed, alive, glittering. In his mind he was seeing the simple, brilliant campaign unfold with cold British precision. Take the Lake Champlain–Hudson River corridor; remove Fort Stanwix from the west; meet St. Leger's forces and Howe's command at Albany; then, with the combined, irresistible power of the three armies, crush the states, one at a time. Simple. Straightforward. Quick. Conclusive. How many of the states would fall before the remainder understood their ridiculous rebellion was finished, beaten, crushed? Two? Three? Five? No matter. With the northern half of the colonies cut off from the southern half, it would only be a question of how many men the Americans would be willing to sacrifice before coming to their senses.

Burgoyne straightened and for a moment looked at Carleton, who silently raised his eyes from the map as Burgoyne continued.

"To accomplish these objectives, I will have just under four thousand British regulars, and just over three thousand Germans from Brunswick and Hesse-Hanau under my direct command. Chief Joseph Brant, also under my command, will provide about one thousand Mohawk Indians to help take Fort Stanwix and then serve as guides and a small advance group for fighting. With wives, children, and camp followers, there will be about ten thousand in my column."

Carleton's eyes rounded, and he blew air, choosing to hold his thoughts in silence while Burgoyne continued.

"Major General William Phillips will be artillery commander, and my second in command."

Carleton's eyebrows arched. Phillips, a member of the House of Commons with Burgoyne, was widely recognized as probably the best commander of cannon in the entire British army. Big, strong, fiery-tempered, proud, fearless, it was said of Phillips that the word *failure* was not in his vocabulary. Artillery officers and engineers, usually far removed from the fierce heat of head-on battle, were held in low regard by the line officers, upon whose shoulders fell the wrenching duty of ordering men to march into musket and cannon fire, there to see them maimed and killed. The standing rule in the British army was that artillery officers and engineers were not to be given command of rank and file infantry. That Burgoyne had been able to coax reluctant and temporary approval from the king's cabinet for Phillips to receive such a commission was an indication of the high regard in which Phillips was held by the entire army.

"In command of the British regulars will be Brigadier General Simon Fraser. Major General Baron Frederich Adolph von Riedesel will command the Germans."

Burgoyne paused to collect his thoughts, then once again placed his forefinger on the map. "I plan to move my command south by sending designated companies from here on daily intervals, so that each night, the next company will use the campground of those who went before. Those in the lead will bivouac and wait here, at Cumberland Head, below St. Johns, until all companies are reassembled. At that time, we will continue south as one command, on up Lake Champlain. We will travel by water, using the fleet now in place, some of which is the result of your foresight following the battle on Lake Champlain with Arnold's and Schuyler's fleet last October."

Burgoyne picked a sheet of paper from his leather flat. "Yes, here it is. At present the fleet consists of the *Royal George, Thunderer, Inflexible, Maria, Carleton, Loyal Convert, Washington, Lee,* and *Jersey.* About ninety guns among them. In addition, there are several hundred bateaux. From all reports, the Americans have no vessels on the lake to oppose us."

Burgoyne stopped, waiting for comment from Carleton, who again chose to remain silent. After a moment, Burgoyne moved on.

"I am advised that the colonials surrounding the lakes and along the Hudson are loyal to the Crown, and that I can count on them for assistance—food, lodging, and when necessary, information."

Again Burgoyne paused, waiting for Carleton to comment. Again, Carleton deferred.

"I plan to begin the movement south as soon as the spring runoff has finished, probably early in June. I expect to be in Albany the last week in August."

Burgoyne selected another document from his leather folder. "Standard military procedures indicate there are three ways to take a fort such as Ticonderoga: tunnel underneath and set mines, breach the walls with heavy artillery, or place it under siege. Considering the time element, I do not consider a siege to be practical." He glanced at the document he was holding. "General Phillips will command one hundred thirty-eight artillery pieces, ranging from twenty-four-pounders down to 4.4-inch mortars. I am told his artillery train is probably the best of its kind ever allotted to support an army. I am not going to repeat the Abercromby disaster."

Burgoyne was remembering the assault made by British General James Abercromby with fifteen thousand regulars on Fort Ti in 1758, when he attempted to take it from thirty-five hundred French defenders, without waiting for his artillery to arrive. Attacking with only infantry and small arms, Abercromby watched wave after wave of his men cut down by the French from behind the thick walls in what was one of the most horrendous British disasters of the Seven Years' War. For years afterward, the soldiers who garrisoned Fort Ti used the skulls of Abercromby's dead for drinking cups, and their shinbones for tent pegs.

For a moment Burgoyne's eyes glittered with anticipation. In his mind he was seeing the glorious sight of Fort Ticonderoga surrounded by his army, splendid in their crimson and white uniforms, and he was hearing the continuous thunder of his artillery systematically blasting the fort to rubble.

He studied the map for a moment longer, then straightened. "I think I've covered the fundamentals. I believe the plan is consistent with those of a soldier of sanguine temper and whose personal interest and fame depend upon a timely departure." He raised his eyes to Carleton. "I would value any advice you might care to give."

Carleton's eyes dropped to the map for a few seconds while he weighed his thoughts. *Personal interest and fame! This man is lost in himself! What do I tell him? What he wants to hear? Or the truth?*

Carleton made his decision. He locked eyes with Burgoyne, and his voice was unemotional, steady.

"General, the fundamental plan to take Fort Ti, and establish dominance of the waterway from Montreal to New York is sound." He began shaking his head slowly. "But the detail of what you have just told me is shot through with dangers that could defeat the plan entirely."

Burgoyne slowly straightened, his eyes flat, dead, as he stared.

Carleton did not wait for him to speak. "To take a command of ten thousand from Montreal to Albany will require a secure supply line that can provide a prodigious amount of food, medicine, blankets, munitions. And you must remember, the supply line on which you are totally dependent is not two hundred miles long; it is three thousand two hundred miles long. It runs from England across the Atlantic, to this wilderness. Do you have any idea what a horrendous logistics problem that is going to be? If for any reason that supply line fails, there is absolutely no way you can live off the land. Your days would be numbered."

Carleton paused. Burgoyne's face was a mask. Carleton continued.

"To my recollection, you have been down the waterway, but you have had almost no exposure to the forests on both sides of the lakes, and along the Hudson River. Believe me, they are nearly impenetrable. No roads. Rivers, streams, gorges, swamps, snakes, insects, animals—there are places a column cannot go. There are places where you will be fortunate to make one mile in one day, with every available man in your command sweating to cut a roadway. There are places you will have to build causeways, bridges—up to one mile in length, in stagnant water swarming with every conceivable insect. You can presume you will be moving through country the like of which you have never seen before, and which can beat you without you ever firing a shot."

Burgoyne swallowed.

"You mentioned two thousand Canadians to assist with transporting your wagon train. You will be fortunate indeed to get one thousand. Maybe five hundred. These Canadians are good in the wilderness, but are not as warm toward England as you may have been led to believe. They might help with the wagons, and the ships and bateau, but they will not fight. They will leave first."

Carleton paused to order his thoughts. "You mentioned one thousand Indians. At this moment, here where we are, I doubt you can get half that number. And if you proceed south without Indians to serve as your eyes and ears, expecting them to be an advance strike force, you will be in fatal trouble almost from the day you leave."

Burgoyne slowly sat down.

"You must understand that the basic nature of most Indians is a mystery to almost all whites. They fight for two things: plunder, and scalps. They will remain with you as long as they believe they will gain plunder, and be allowed to massacre and scalp. But if they once believe you are going to lose the battle, they will leave. If they obtain liquor, they lose all sense of civilization, and will butcher and scalp your soldiers as quickly as they will the enemy. Lose control of them, and they can become the worst devils you will ever know. I need not remind you what they did at Deerfield, and Albany, and during the raids on Schenectady and Saratoga years ago."

Burgoyne dropped his eyes, probing his memory. Deerfield, Massachusetts. Burned to the ground. Men, women, children, all dead, scalped, mutilated. Albany. Burned, all dead. Schenectady and Saratoga. Burned. Nearly all dead.

Carleton gestured to his desk drawer. "I have a letter from General Howe, written sixty days ago. In it he states his intention to take Philadelphia during the 1777 campaign. To do so, he intends being in Pennsylvania about the time you will be arriving in Albany. He briefly mentions a 'diversion' up the Hudson, but not one word about joining you to complete the conquest of the waterway. The word *Albany* is conspicuously absent. Certainly he mentions nothing to compare with the plan you have laid before me. In my opinion it is utter nonsense for General Howe to think he can take Philadelphia at the same time he is meeting you in Albany. I have no idea why this was all determined without a word from either Germain or Howe to me, nor is that for me to ponder. I only know that as of this minute, it is my opinion that General Howe has no intention of meeting you at Albany. I leave that matter to yourself, and Germain, and Howe."

Burgoyne licked dry lips, and Carleton didn't stop.

"Apparently, you have been led to believe the regions bordering the waterway are filled with colonials loyal to the Crown, who will rally to support you. May I remind you, it was rebels from this very region who gathered to humiliate generals Gage and Howe at the Battle of Bunker Hill and to drive them out of Boston to New York. And do not forget, those men dress in buckskins and carry the deadliest rifles on the continent. They learned their forest skills, and fighting style, from the Indians. Among them are men called the Long Hunters, who can disappear into the forest today, strike with deadly effect eighty miles from here tomorrow, and be back the next day. They can live off the land indefinitely. They move like shadows. They terrified one company of Germans by suddenly appearing in the middle of their camp without a single German picket or soldier having seen them. Last year, one of them, Benjamin Whitcomb, shot and killed Brigadier General Patrick Gordon from ambush near Chambly. I have offered a reward of fifty guineas for Whitcomb, dead or alive, and I would much prefer him alive since nothing would be more satisfying than to hang him publicly. But we will never catch him."

Burgoyne sat silent, unmoving, as Carleton went on.

"To move a column of ten thousand to Albany will require more than a thousand horses or oxen. They will not be able to forage in the forests. You will have to carry their fodder. That alone will require hundreds of wagons. If for any reason the animals or wagons break down, your column will be absolutely stopped in its tracks."

Carleton cleared his throat before continuing.

"Your fighting force will be about evenly divided, British and German. Do the Germans speak English?"

Burgoyne broke his silence. "No. Only one or two officers can speak it, and then only a very few words."

"How do you communicate with them?"

"Their officers speak French, as do I and a few of my officers."

"Do you all speak it fluently?"

"No. Limited."

"English and German officers intend communicating in broken French?"

"Yes."

"Can you see the latent problems that could develop?"

"I believe we can handle it."

"What if the Germans are required to communicate with the colonial loyalists, who speak neither German or French?"

"We will have to provide an interpreter."

Carleton nodded before he went on. "You surely recognize that once you start down the waterway, the colonial rebel militia will come to meet you, and when they do, they will do all they can to harass you. Run off your stock, block your path with trees, shoot your officers over long distances with those accursed rifles, burn your wagons, cut your supply line, capture your messengers, give you no sleep, no rest. Their concept of war in this wilderness is altogether different from anything you have ever known."

Burgoyne interrupted the flow. "I believe I have studied their style of warfare enough to understand it. With Indians to assist, I believe we can withstand them."

Carleton moved on. "You must also remember, if you take Fort Ti, you will have to leave close to one thousand of your regulars there to garrison it. That will reduce your fighting capabilities as you move further south. And I tell you frankly, every fort on the waterway—Ti, Edward, George, Miller—has been essentially abandoned for years. They're in deplorable condition. My decision last October to return to Quebec after defeating General Arnold on Lake Champlain was based in part on the fact that if we did take Fort Ticonderoga that late in the season, trying to keep it supplied and garrisoned through the winter would be a nearly impossible task."

"I understand. I have prepared to garrison Fort Ti."

Carleton fell silent for a time, studying the map, before he once again raised his face to Burgoyne. His expression changed. A smile slowly spread, and the flat look left his eyes.

"I'm afraid I've disappointed your expectations by my rather gloomy observations and opinions. May I remind you, you're leading one of the finest armies on the continent. Your troops admire you, as well they should. Your staff of officers is exceptional. You have an enviable array of artillery, and you will be traveling in the best season of the year. If you are prudent and cautious, I can see no real reason you cannot avoid all the calamities I have pointed out. You should enjoy resounding success in this vital effort."

Burgoyne visibly brightened as Carleton finished.

"I offer you the fullest cooperation of my office to assist you in your preparations and departure, General Burgoyne. You have but to ask, and I shall do all possible."

Visibly moved, Burgoyne slowly rose from the chair. He thrust out his hand and shook that of Carleton warmly. "I thank you for your candid advice, sir. I could not ask more from you. Rest assured, your demeanor today will be in my first report to Germain."

Carleton bowed slightly. "If there is nothing else today, may I invite you to remain for a refreshment? Lunch?"

"Would that I could." Burgoyne quickly gathered his papers and placed them inside his leather folder. "There is simply too much to be done. But I assure you, we shall talk again, and we shall dine together before I leave, you and I, at which time I shall consider it a privilege to express my appreciation for all you have done."

Carleton came from behind his desk and called, "Aide." The door opened immediately and Thornton stepped into the room, a model of military perfection.

"Yes, suh."

"Colonel Thornton, would you show General Burgoyne to his carriage? And should you receive any message from him, at any time, would you see to it that it is delivered to me at once, day or night?"

Thornton saluted smartly. "Yes, suh."

Burgoyne nodded to Carleton and turned on his heel. Carleton watched as the heavy door closed behind him and listened until the echo of the clicking heels had quieted. Then he turned back to his desk and settled onto his chair, his forehead drawn in deep reflection. He sat thus for a long time, with the constant roar of the distant river sounding loud in the great, austere, stone-walled room.

In the late twilight of that same beautiful spring day, Carleton made his way from his quarters back to his office, and once again sat unmoving, heedless of the unending sound from the river. Dusk settled, and Thornton rapped, then entered the room. Without a word he lighted the six large candles on the desk, turned on his heel, and marched out.

Minutes passed before Carleton reached for his inkwell and his quill. Thoughtfully he began making notes, the scratch of the pen lost in the roar of the river.

Lord Germain—I herewith tender my resignation as governor of the Province of Canada—for reasons unknown to me you have treated me with slight, disregard, and censure—it has disabled me from further functioning effectively as governor—having been apprised of the plan for conquest of the colonies I can only render my humble opinion—it is the highest folly to think Canadians will respond to bear the burden of transport—the hope of employing Indians is ludicrous—that you have failed to consult me in these matters—failed to afford me my right to respond and defend myself—is an offense that I will not endure. I retain my military rank of major general and my command of whatever minuscule portion of my Northern Army that will remain here with me in Quebec. I have afforded and will continue to afford Major General John Burgoyne every possible assistance in his campaign.

Carleton stopped and carefully laid his quill back on its tray. He read his notes, then leaned back to stare at the steadily burning wick on the nearest candle. He started when the large clock on the mantel sounded its gong, and he counted nine as it continued to toll the hour.

He stared at the clock for a moment, in deep thought. *I cannot endure what Germain has done. I must resign as governor. I will remain faithful to my military duties, but I will not accept his unforgivable treatment of me as governor. I will compose the letter tomorrow morning, and it will go out on the first ship bound for England.* A brief, ironic smile flickered for a moment. *Perhaps on the* Apollo—*the ship that brought Burgoyne here today. How appropriate.*

In the west wing of the castle, in his own private office, Major General John Burgoyne sat at the elaborately carved desk in one corner of the large room. A fire danced in the fireplace, and two candles in engraved silver candlesticks gave light to the desk. Burgoyne plucked his quill from its tray, dipped its point in the inkwell, and began scratching notes.

Delivered the sealed letter to Carleton—seriously affronted—recovered immediately—received me and the orders I brought in a manner that, in my opinion, does infinite honour to his public and private character—the soul of cooperation—I believe he shall be of immeasurable assistance.

He read what he had written, then dated the notes and closed them inside the blank pages of a bound book in which he intended keeping memoirs of his entire campaign. Perhaps he would share the notes with others at the appropriate time. He put the book to one side, then reached for his leather folder, drew out the map, and was soon lost in the endless details that are the plague of every military commander.

It was well past one o'clock in the morning when he blew out the candles and wearily sought the comfort of his bed.

Notes

The Iroquois longhouses are well described in Graymont, *The Iroquois in the American Revolution*, p. 9.

General Carleton's description of the changeable, undependable, rather child-like nature of the Iroquois is somewhat explained in Graymont, *The Iroquois in the American Revolution*, pp. 17–37. This is consistent with General Burgoyne's opinion of the Indians (see Ketchum, *Saratoga*, p. 230). For an excellent explanation of the vast difference between the world of the Iroquois and that of the white men, see Ketchum, *Saratoga*, pp. 95–96. For a description of how the Europeans were frightened by the Indians, see pp. 98–99. Many, perhaps most of the Indians who came to support General Burgoyne, came for scalps and booty or plunder (see pp. III, 144).

Unless otherwise indicated, references hereunder are taken from Ketchum, *Saratoga*, and identified by page number only.

Burgoyne's history as a soldier is chronicled, as well as his five-month visit to London, where he persuaded Lord Germain that he, Burgoyne, and not Carleton, was the proper general to lead the expeditionary force south from Quebec to take the Hudson River valley and meet General Howe in Albany. He bolstered his petition by reminding Germain of Carleton's decision the previous summer to return to Quebec without taking Fort Ticonderoga. Carleton turned back due to the lateness of the season and his belief that he did not have sufficient men to hold the fort through the winter (pp. 41–42, 64, 72–79).

Major General Sir Guy Carleton was knighted, serving as governor of Canada, and commander of the Northern Army stationed at Quebec at the time General John Burgoyne arrived May 6, 1777, aboard the *Apollo*. The ice on the St. Lawrence River was breaking up in thunderous clashes, and it was the first day navigation on the river was possible. General Burgoyne was given the extraordinarily distasteful assignment of delivering the letter from Lord Germain to General Carleton, informing him that he, General Burgoyne, was to take about two-thirds of Carleton's command and lead the expeditionary force south. It was an almost unheard of insult to General Carleton. It was only because of General Carleton's extraordinary character that he did not lash out at Burgoyne and Germain on the spot. Rather, he cooperated with General Burgoyne to the fullest extent possible. However, he promptly wrote a stinging letter to Lord Germain, resigning his position as governor, while roundly criticizing Germain for thinking they could rely on Canadians, Indians, and Tories to support General Burgoyne. General Carleton did not resign his commission as major general but remained commander of what was left of the British army in Quebec. Part of the language used in this chapter in the letter of resignation by Carleton is quoted from historical documents (pp. 41, 87–88, 101–3).

The letter written by Lord Germain, explaining to General Carleton the new policy which supported General Burgoyne taking two-thirds of General Carleton's command, is quoted verbatim in this chapter. In said letter, Germain reasoned that Carleton's refusal to capture Fort Ticonderoga was part of the cause of the catastrophic defeats of the British forces at Trenton and Princeton. Lord Germain's letter and reasoning were seen by all who knew about it as "hogwash" (p. 103).

Neither Lord Germain nor General William Howe had informed General Carleton of events in London or in and about New York. General Carleton learned of the defeat of the Americans in and around Long Island and the subsequent events at Trenton and Princeton through a letter he intercepted from a prisoner (pp. 103–4).

The plan proposed by General Burgoyne, and approved by Lord Germain and the king himself, provided that the eight-thousand-man army under command of General Burgoyne was to be divided into two sections. Colonel Barry St. Leger would take one force west to Oswego, capture Fort Stanwix, then come east down the Mohawk River Valley to Albany, to meet General Burgoyne. General Burgoyne would take the second section and proceed south on Lake Champlain, capture Fort Ticonderoga, then continue south on the Hudson River, to meet with Colonel St. Leger at Albany. General William Howe was to move from the New York area up the Hudson and rendezvous with Colonel St. Leger and General Burgoyne at Albany, where the three forces combined would proceed to cut off the New England states and defeat them (pp. 82–85, 102–5).

Through a monumental lack of communication between Lord Germain, General William Howe, and General John Burgoyne, General Howe never did commit to join General Burgoyne in Albany; rather, he devoted his attentions to taking Philadelphia and left General Burgoyne without his support. General Carleton received but a single letter from General Howe in which Howe mentioned the Hudson River valley campaign, and in said letter, Howe only briefly alluded to "a diversion occasionally up Hudson's River" (pp. 103–5).

British General Clinton is described (p. 82).

The ongoing, volcanic rivalry between American generals Philip Schuyler and Horatio Gates, which played a critical part in the Saratoga campaign, is very well described, as are the generals (pp. 52–55).

The peculiar geological phenomenon of lakes George and Champlain draining to the north, into the St. Lawrence River, while twelve miles to the south of the two lakes, the Hudson River drains south, is explained. It resulted when great continental plates far below the surface shifted and a gigantic block of bedrock dropped into place (pp. 24–26).

The naming, and subsequent renaming, of Fort Ticonderoga is explained. Ticonderoga is an Iroquois word meaning "Between two great waters"—in this case, Lake George and Lake Champlain. Lake George drains into Lake Champlain through a narrow, three-and-a-half-mile-long gorge called "the chute." Lake George is two hundred feet higher in elevation than Lake Champlain. The chute has several waterfalls and required that the bateaux be portaged around the falls and rapids. The flat-bottomed bateaux are described. Fort Ticonderoga was built by the French on a peninsula in the 1750s, between the two lakes, George and Champlain. It was five hundred fifty feet in width, with walls sixteen feet thick. It was considered the "jewel" of the forts in the Hudson River valley, capable of controlling all who passed on the great river, hence, of highest strategic importance. In the Seven Years' War, British General Abercromby attempted to storm it with eleven thousand ground troops, unsupported by cannon. The French, with only three thousand five hundred troops inside the fort, stopped him with tremendous losses to the British. When American Colonel Anthony Wayne saw the fort in 1776, he reported it to be in deplorable condition, with the soldiers using the skulls and shinbones of Abercromby's troops, long dead, for drinking cups and tent pegs (pp. 28–29).

General Carleton's attempt to explain to General Burgoyne the tremendous problems related to moving an army through the American forest is detailed (pp. 106–8).

The American scouts, called long hunters were noted as being among the best frontiersmen. One of their leaders, Benjamin Whitcomb, shot British General Patrick Gordon from ambush. Upon hearing of it, General Carleton issued a reward of twenty-five guineas for the capture of Whitcomb, dead or alive. It was the same Benjamin Whitcomb who suddenly appeared in the center of a German camp. The Germans were terrified at how he had reached the heart of their camp with five men, without being detected by anyone (pp. 161–62).

General Burgoyne's staff officers were General Fraser, close confidant and friend, General William Phillips, excellent gunnery officer, and General Baron Frederich Adolph von Riedesel, in command of all German forces. The number of men they commanded was three thousand nine hundred eighty-one British troops and three thousand one hundred sixteen German troops. The fleet of ships Burgoyne had on the lakes consisted of the *Royal George, Thunderer, Inflexible, Maria, Carleton, Loyal Convert, Washington, Lee, Jersey,* and more than two hundred bateaux (pp. 127–37).

In general support of the above, see Higginbotham, *The War of American Independence,* pp. 175–79; Mackesy, *The War for America 1775–1783,* pp. 130–31; Leckie, *George Washington's War,* pp. 367–77.

CHAPTER IV

★ ★ ★

*S*pring had once again wakened the world from its chill, gray, winter sleep. The warm sun had reached its zenith and was settling toward the western rim of the world, across the Boston back bay. On the mainland, the rolling hills of the Lachmere farms were a checkerboard of orderly fruit orchards, spectacular with white blossoms smothering green trees while bees swarmed. On the Boston peninsula, the faint, sweet scent of flowers rode gentle in the streets and homes and shops. Renewal was in the air—a lift in spirits, a spring in the step, people calling greetings across the cobblestones, laughing, waving.

On the docks, sailmakers and riggers wore their knit caps far back on their heads and had the sleeves of their ancient, worn sweaters pushed above their elbows as they worked on the mountains of canvas that must be mended and remounted on the yards and spars of the forest of masts undulating in the harbor. Grinning longshoremen lustily cursed all officers of all ships of all flags as they loaded and unloaded the freight that was the lifeblood of the world. Sweating blacksmiths pounded orange-hot iron into the fittings that held ships together.

Near the Charlestown ferry landing, bearded men in gum rubber boots slowed, and their eyes narrowed at the sight of a handsome, dark-eyed, dark-haired, well-dressed young woman picking her way through the barrels and crates, piled canvas, coiled hawsers, and fish-cleaning tables on the great, black timbers that formed the waterfront docks. An old sailmaker sitting on a bench, legs covered with layers of sail canvas, raised startled eyes and shifted his ancient pipe in his yellowed teeth, then squinted at the sun. *She better be thinkin' of goin' home.* He drove his large sailmaker's needle through the double-layered canvas, pulled it through, set the head of the needle against the thick leather pad tied to his right palm, and drove the point through again. *Lookin' like that, she better be careful.* He eyed her as, shoulders squared, chin up, she approached the first ship's officer she saw.

"Sir, I'm Mary Flint. I was told by the harbormaster that I could find these two offices on the docks, close by the Charlestown ferry landing. Could you help me, please?" She coughed as she held out a folded piece of paper.

First mate Nels Dahlgren, round-shouldered, his beard white from thirty-four years at sea, took the paper while he studied Mary. Her skin was sallow, eyes sunken, cheeks hollow, and he had heard the rattle in her quick, hacking cough. He read the two written lines, then spoke with a heavy Swedish accent as he turned to point at two weathered, brown brick buildings.

"The office of Hamburton Company is there, and the office of the Tordenskjold Company is further, over there." Watching Mary intently, he handed the paper back to her.

"Thank you, sir." She bowed slightly and turned toward the building with a sign above the door that once read "Hamburton & Company" but which years of salt air and weather had reduced to an unreadable series of peeling, faded marks.

Dahlgren spoke and she stopped. "Ma'am, you should leave the docks before dark. Things happen. You do not look or sound well."

She nodded. "I understand. I will leave as soon as my business here is finished. I do thank you for your concern."

Dahlgren touched the bill of his leather officer's cap and nodded to her as she walked to the door of the Hamburton office and entered. Inside the small, plain office, a short, plump, balding man in a rumpled white shirt was seated behind a battered desk, poring over columns of entries and figures in a large, scarred, leather-bound ledger. His sagging jowls jiggled as he raised puzzled eyes and leaned back in his chair. "Ma'am, you have business here?"

"Yes. I was told by the harbormaster that occasionally you have ships coming here to Boston from New York City."

His eyes narrowed as he studied her, aware of the thick fabric purse that dangled from her right hand on two embroidered straps. He shook his head. "We're not taking passengers right now."

"Oh, I am not seeking passage. I believe you were taking passengers in December of last year, and January of this year."

He nodded, suspicious, noncommittal. "Maybe. Who are you? Why do you want to know?"

"I'm Mary Flint, from New York. My father told me he intended moving his residence to Boston, and that he would leave information at the Boston mayor's office as to where I could find him when I came to join him. The Boston mayor's office knows of no such message but said some companies have ships sailing here from New York. The harbormaster gave me the name of this company. Did you have ships arrive here from New York last January?"

"You're looking for your father?" The man pursed his mouth and shook his head. "Can't help you with that."

"If he came here on one of your ships, you should have a record, shouldn't you?"

An irritated frown crossed his face. "Ma'am, New York is under British blockade. Things happen. Sometimes no one keeps records. Sometimes they get lost."

"I arrived on a ship from New York two days ago without trouble."

"Then she was flying a foreign flag. Our ships don't. We fly American colors, and we have to run the British blockade out of New York at night."

"Could you look in your records for January?"

His eyes flickered to her purse once again, and he shook his head. "Come back later. Maybe Monday, or Tuesday. Maybe I'll have time then."

"Could I have your name, please?"

His eyes slid over her purse once more. "Ma'am, I've got to finish checking the manifest of a ship that docked six days ago and it won't wait. She's loading now to sail out. Come back later."

Mary placed her hand over her mouth to stifle a cough, then leaned forward, hands on the edge of the desk. "Sir, it's urgent that I find my father as soon as possible. He's elderly. Hours are important."

He recoiled from her. "What's that cough? Tuberculosis? Smallpox? Plague? We've got enough trouble on these docks without an epidemic."

"No. I had pneumonia. It's nearly gone."

"Nearly?"

Mary's eyebrows peaked. "Sir, if you could just look for one name in the records of the ships that arrived here last December and January, I'll be gone. There couldn't have been more than two or three of them."

The man shook his head and started to speak when Mary cut him off. "I can pay." She settled her purse on the desk before him.

The man eyed the heavy purse. "You've got money?"

"How much is your demand?"

He reached thick fingers to scratch a jowl. "Well, if I look right now I won't get out of here until maybe nine o'clock tonight, maybe ten. Three, four hours late. Considering the load of work, that ought to be worth, shall we say, ten pounds sterling."

Mary straightened in shock. "Ten pounds?"

He leaned forward and thrust a finger toward her. "You want to know about your father or not? It makes no difference to me."

Mary loosened the drawstring on her purse and quickly counted the money, then held it clutched tightly in her hand as she spoke. "When you have finished your search, I will give you the money. Not before."

He waved a hand as though to brush the matter from his mind. "Now, or leave."

She stepped back from the desk. "No."

He dropped his hand. "Feisty, eh. All right, we'll see. What's your father's name?"

"Rufus Broadhead. He probably had two people with him."

"What names?"

"Sarah and Michael."

"Last names?"

"No last names. They are servants."

The man drew open a large desk drawer and lifted out a worn leather-bound ledger with the words *ARRIVALS—DEPARTURES* stamped on the cover, laid it on the desk, and opened it. He turned pages until he came to one with the date of January 22, 1777, scrolled in ink at the top. Beneath the date was the word *Orpha.* He mumbled to himself, reading, as he traced the entries with his finger. His finger stopped, and he blanched as he raised his face, his eyes locking with Mary's.

"Rufus Broadhead?"

Mary's breath came short. "Yes."

Slowly he closed the book. "Rufus Broadhead and two unnamed persons with him were on the *Orpha.* She sailed out of New York at twenty minutes past one o'clock A.M., on January ninth, this year. The British saw her as she cleared the blockade. Two gunboats followed her and ordered her to heave to. She refused, and they opened fire. They left her burning and sinking with the captain dead and half the crew dead or wounded. The first mate got the fires out and brought her here. We salvaged some of her cargo, but the ship was beyond repair. We towed her out three miles and scuttled her. There is an insurance claim pending."

Mary's voice cracked as she asked, "My father?"

The man shook his head. "All passengers were killed by British gunfire. Your father is dead." His face softened. "I'm sorry."

Mary gasped and grabbed the front of the desk for support. "Dead? That can't be."

"Regrettably, it is true. There was no one to claim the body, so it was delivered for burial in the pauper's cemetery."

Mary gasped and took a step backwards. "Father? In the pauper's cemetery? He had money!" She clamped her mouth shut, and her body shook as she battled to hold back the tears.

"Everything he had with him was lost when the ship caught fire."

For long moments Mary stared, chin trembling. Then, without a word she dropped the ten-pound note on the desk, turned on her heel, and walked out of the office, west, into the setting sun. Hardened dock hands stopped to look as she walked past, eyes straight ahead, mouth set. Dark was gathering as she left the waterfront, walked steadily toward the Bluebell Inn, and went directly to her room.

Inside she collapsed on the bed while tears flowed, and her heart-wrenching sobs filled the room. It was dark before she rose and lighted the lamp on the table beside the bed, then sat down in the rocking chair in the corner to begin a slow rocking, still fully dressed, her spring bonnet tied beneath her chin. Sometime after one o'clock, her chin slowly settled on her chest, and the rocking slowed and stopped as she nodded into an exhausted sleep.

With the lamp glowing yellow in the gray dawn light of the room, she jerked awake and for a moment could not recall where she was or how she got there. Then the remembrance came welling up, and she laid her head back and let the tears flow. After a time she rose and pushed the window curtains aside to peer out at a sun half-risen, turning the underside of a high skiff of clouds gold and rose-pink in another beautiful spring day in Boston Town. Slowly she untied her bonnet and dropped it in the chair, then sat on her bed, staring at her hands in her lap while trying to form a plan.

I will find father, and I will have him buried in New York beside mother. And then what? There's no one. Father and mother, their estate, all gone. Marcus—my husband—gone, my baby, gone. Marcus's family, all gone, the house burned. Doctor Purcell, gone. Left me with some money, but where do I go? To whom? What do I do?

The sharp hacking cough came for a moment, and she covered her mouth until it stopped.

Doctor Purcell taught me much about nursing. I can find work in a hospital. Perhaps a military hospital, helping our wounded soldiers.

From the recesses of her mind came two images, sharp and clear. Her breathing constricted, and she clasped a trembling hand to her breast.

Eli! Billy and Eli!

She saw Billy's square, blocky face. Solid, plain, dependable Billy, and she yearned to be near him, to feel his quiet strength and his innate goodness.

Then she saw the face of Eli—the hawk nose, the cleft in his chin, and the look in his eyes of one who had long known unutterable pain. She felt once more the deep, disturbing fascination of something wild and untamed in him, something as native to him as the vast primeval forest from whence he had come.

"Eli," she whispered, and for the first time she understood that somehow her heart, that of a woman raised in wealth and high social status in New York City, had become entwined with his—he a man raised wild and free by Iroquois Indians in the wilderness. She stiffened at the thought. A New York socialite woman raised in a mansion, dressed in silks and satins, and a man from the forest, raised in an Indian wigwam or longhouse, dressed in buckskins and moccasins, carrying a tomahawk, knife, and rifle. She could not force the two worlds to come together in her mind.

Suddenly the implications of her thoughts struck into her consciousness, and she sat bolt upright, eyes wide in shock. *My world and his? Myself and Eli? Had Doctor Purcell been right? Had he seen what I could not see? Am I in love with Eli? Am I?*

Forgotten things came flooding with a force of their own, and she let them come. *That day in August last year when Eli and Billy unloaded the ammunition from my wagon into the Manhattan Island magazine—something different—I thought it was the buckskin hunting shirt and the beaded moccasins. The night we moved the army from Manhattan to Long Island with the dead man tied behind us on the wagon— how right it seemed to tell him about the death of my husband and my baby—learning of him watching his family killed when he was two years old—taken by the Iroquois— raised by them—my tears—his gentle arm about my shoulders while I wept—so natural, so natural. The day at Fort Washington when I learned Josephus Tanner had heard of an orphaned girl taken in by a minister eighteen years ago—perhaps his sister—the leap of hope in his eyes when I told him—and the night on the ship in New York harbor when I learned the minister was named Cyrus Fielding—I could not wait to have Doctor Purcell write to Eli—tell him—and the hope that sprang in my heart that perhaps I had done something to help him find what was left of his family—my prayers for him—all so natural.*

She reined in her thoughts and her feelings and slowly faced the question that she had refused to articulate until now.

Love? Do I love him? Me, from my world, and he, raised by savages? Can it be true?

It was as though the facing of the question tapped into a wellspring of emotions that had been hidden from her, and they came flooding to overwhelm her, leaving her stunned, silent, uncomprehending. She saw his face and suddenly knew she yearned to see him, talk with him, feel his strong arm about her shoulder once again, feel his inner strength as she buried her face in his shoulder to sob out her pain, share her innermost joys and fears with him, touch his face, and assure him they would find his sister, make his life complete once more.

She did not know nor care how long she sat on her bed, mesmerized by the soul-shaking realization that had changed her forever. All questions of where she belonged, and what she would do with the years remaining in her life, were gone in the brilliant light of knowing who she was and where she was going.

She stood. *I must move father to be beside mother in New York. And then I will find out where General Washington is camped with the army. Surely he has a hospital there, where I can work. I will go there, and if Eli is alive, I will find him.*

Notes

Mary Flint, as she appears herein, is a fictional person, although the name is taken from a woman whose true name was Mary Flint. She lived in the hamlet of Lincoln, near Lexington and Concord, and upon the request of Paul Revere, she left her children with a servant and rode to warn her neighbors of the approach of the British regulars on the night of April 18, 1775 (see Flint and Flint, *Flint Family History of the Adventuresome Seven*, pp. 87–91).

In this book, her father, Rufus Broadhead, is also fictional, as is Doctor Otis Purcell.

Quebec, Canada

June 7, 1777

CHAPTER V

★ ★ ★

I expected one thousand Indians, mostly Mohawk, for the Albany campaign. I am informed this morning that I will be fortunate to get four hundred."

With sober, narrowed eyes, Burgoyne, dashing, resplendent in his fresh uniform with gold piping gilding the lapels, shifted his weight on the woven leather-strap seat of the straight-backed chair facing General Carleton's desk, while his words echoed in the cavernous office. His face a blank, Carleton leaned back in his upholstered chair, saying nothing, giving Burgoyne free rein to continue. From outside the great, brooding Quebec Castle came the first distant rumble of thunder from the southwest, where thick, purple, June storm clouds were sweeping down the St. Lawrence River. Burgoyne waited until the sound faded and Carleton's office was silent once again.

"My understanding was that the Chevalier St. Luc de la Corne and Charles Langlade were capable of bringing in one thousand Indians." He paused, eyes locked with Carleton, whose face was expressionless while he remained silent. Burgoyne forced the issue.

"Was I misinformed about St. Luc and Langlade?"

Carleton leaned forward, resting his elbows on his desk. "I have no idea who suggested they could raise one thousand Indians. I believe my advice was, if anyone can raise Indians to be scouts and guides for your campaign, it would be St. Luc and Langlade. I have never presumed to tell you how many, certainly not one thousand. I recall advising that white men simply do not understand how to control and handle Indians."

He paused, eyes boring into Burgoyne's. "And I repeat that advice. Call it a warning. The foundations of Indian thought have little to do with those of white men. That which is acceptable, reasonable, logical to them, is all too often a mystery to us. Their value to you will be as your eyes and ears in the forest, guides, and advance skirmishers. Restrict them to those services, and they will be of great help. If you are not able to do that, you will very likely wish you had never brought them along."

Carleton leaned back in his chair, watching Burgoyne's eyes for reaction, and he saw little that suggested Burgoyne understood or accepted the hard warning. He felt a growing sense of apprehension, nearly fear, for Burgoyne. He leaned forward once more.

"Let me tell you about St. Luc and Langlade. Langlade is a Frenchman, and one of the most skilled forest fighters and interpreters in the area. It was Langlade who made and executed the plan that totally destroyed General Edward Braddock's army near the Ohio River in 1755. Need I recall to you that massacre?"

Burgoyne said nothing but slowly leaned back in his chair. Carleton continued. "As for St. Luc, he is now about sixty-six years old, but is as capable as a man half his age. He was twenty-one when he left his wealthy, privileged family here in Quebec to go fight the Sauk and Fox Indians. He was one of the leaders in the attack on Saratoga when they burned every building at the garrison and took one hundred captives. He was with the party that attacked Deerfield—burned the entire settlement to the ground—massacred everyone there. He raided Albany and Schenectady. It was St. Luc who ambushed a British wagon train and took eighty scalps and sixty-four prisoners. In 1757, with the Marquis de Montcalm's army, he led eighteen hundred Indians, who took a great number of English prisoners. He was in charge of escorting them when his Indians found liquor in a fort they destroyed. They got drunk and went wild. When they finished the butchering, sixty-nine of the prisoners were dead, scalped, mutilated."

Carleton paused to let Burgoyne ponder the horrors of the story, then continued. "He has become wealthy dealing in furs and in the slave trade. He speaks at least five Indian languages, as well as French and English, and is an excellent interpreter. There is no atrocity he does not know, and he has been generous in exercising all of them at his pleasure. He is the devil incarnate when it comes to scalping and mutilations. He is known on both sides of the Atlantic, and is the white man most capable of gathering Indian war parties, simply because the Indians have learned he will indulge them with plunder, scalps, and liquor, if they find it. Be warned, it is not money or loyalty that will bring in the Indians and hold them in line. It is the hope of scalps, plunder, and all too often, liquor. If you were to ask your regulars, particularly your Germans, who they fear the most, the rebellious Americans or the Indians, their honest answer would be the Indians."

"Do you include the Indians we have recruited? The ones who are serving with *our* army?"

"Most emphatically. Ask your troops. Watch them. When your Indians are close by, your regulars will never be far from their weapons, and their eyes will never leave the Indians until they have gone. Mark my words!"

The sky had darkened, and three miles up the river, jagged lightning tore through the thick, black rain clouds. Moments later, rolling thunder drowned out all sounds. Burgoyne remained still, and Carleton gathered his thoughts until it quieted.

Carleton went on "I now repeat to you what I said previously. If anyone can raise the one thousand Indians you desire, it will be St. Luc and Langlade. If they cannot do it, then it cannot be done." He cleared his throat. "I believe I have said enough to provoke some sense of the realities of dealing with our red brothers."

Burgoyne slowly sat upright in his chair. "Indeed. Indeed. Do the Americans share this morbid fear of the Indians?"

Carleton nodded his head vigorously. "They do, and rightfully so."

Burgoyne glanced down at a small document on which he had

written notes, and Carleton settled back, studying Burgoyne, waiting for him to move on.

Burgoyne cleared his throat. "I was advised by Philip Skene that there were large numbers of Canadians in this area, loyal to the Crown, who would be eager to sign up for duty as freighters and cartdrivers and to repair the forts at Sorel, St. Johns, and Ile aux Noix. Mr. Skene served as a brigade major with General Amherst, and has extensive land holdings at the south end of Lake Champlain. I presumed he would be of sound judgment, so I commissioned two men, John Peters and Ebenezer Jessup, to recruit two thousand of Mr. Skene's loyalists."

Burgoyne glanced again at his notes, then continued. "Peters and Jessup appeared to have the credentials and the desire for the job, but I am now told they have assembled only three companies, one hundred men to the company, under the command of three officers: a Major Samuel McKay, Captain Rene Boucherville, and Captain David Monin, and I understand that at least thirty of those men have deserted. If Mr. Skene was correct in his judgment, why are we facing a critical shortage of necessary labor?" His expression was very close to being accusatory.

Carleton shook his head. "The truth is, the question of how many loyalists are available is one thing, and the question of how willing they are to forsake their villages and their families to join your campaign is another. There are many who feel strong ties to England, but when it comes to taking up your cause against their homeland and some of their neighbors, loyalty to king and crown fades rather quickly. Last winter they moved hundreds of tons of supplies to St. Johns to prepare for your campaign, and last month they interrupted their critical spring planting to haul more supplies to St. Johns. They know this campaign will continue through the summer, and they have no enthusiasm for anything that will take them away from their farms and crops during the growing months. They depend on the corn, oats, wheat, rye, and barley. If their crops fail, next winter will be a disaster for them. I'm afraid Mr. Skene could have been swayed in his judgment by the fact that he has a fortune in landholdings around the south end of the lake, which will be in jeopardy if you fail in this campaign."

Burgoyne swallowed. "Let me be clear on this. I can expect less than half the Indians called for, and only three hundred of the two thousand loyalist Canadians who are needed?"

Carleton's words were conclusive. "From all appearances, that is true."

For a moment Burgoyne pursed his mouth, then asked the heavy question. "As Governor of Canada, is there any power you have to force them?"

Carleton studied him. *He's asking me to declare martial law, so that he can take what he wants at bayonet point. I will not do it.* He shook his head emphatically. "Canada is under no immediate threat of attack, and in my judgment there is absolutely nothing to justify declaring martial law. Quite the contrary, it is we who are attacking them." Carleton paused and his voice lost its brittleness. "I have done all I can. I invoked a corvée, which is tantamount to forcing them into slave labor. They deserted about as fast as I conscripted them. I refuse to hunt them down and throw them in prison, or worse, have them shot."

Burgoyne compressed his lips for a moment, and his eyes narrowed as he accepted Carleton's reply. *He won't declare martial law. All right, so be it.*

Without warning, high winds came whistling, moaning at the windows, and seconds later the torrential rains of a spring cloudburst passed over the great castle, driving giant hailstones pounding at the windows, bending the trees to the northeast, tearing at the new leaves, ripping small branches to send them flying. Hailstones quickly piled on the windowsills and against the west wall of the old stone building, and in minutes turned the ground white as far as the eye could see. A lightning flash suddenly illuminated the castle, and an instant later a thunderclap shook the room. For a time, the men sat still, silent, humbled, caught up in the realization of how diminished men and their dreams are in the face of the unfathomable power of nature.

The storm front passed on down the river, and the wind and driving rain and hail dwindled and died as quickly as they had come. The flashes of lightning and the booming of thunder became more distant, and then golden shafts of sunlight pierced the purple clouds overhead. Full sunshine followed, flooding the white, rain-drenched world strewn with shredded tree branches and leaves in brilliant light.

Burgoyne continued. "I'm in desperate need of uniforms. The men have had to cut the tails from their tunics to make patches. Their breeches are badly worn, as are their shoes."

Carleton replied, "A few months ago an American privateer intercepted one of our supply ships. We lost sixteen thousand uniforms and thirty thousand shirts, pairs of shoes, and socks. There's little we can do about it, other than make do as best we can. I thought you knew."

Carleton studied Burgoyne, who shifted in his chair and hesitated for a moment, and in that instant Carleton knew. *He's sparring—hasn't yet stated his greatest reason for coming.*

Burgoyne spoke with studied casualness. "I find I will need more transport and more draft animals."

There it is—that's what brought him here! Carleton remained calm. "Specifically?"

"Four hundred more horses or oxen for General Phillips's cannon, and five hundred more carts with teams for hauling supplies."

Carleton's expression did not change. "You're leaving when?"

"We'll leave in stages, beginning about June thirteenth. We rendezvous at St. Johns and leave from there in total force on June twentieth."

Carleton's eyes dropped to his desk for a moment while he made calculations. "I believe we can provide both the draft animals and the carts, but you must understand a few things. On this short notice, the carts will be made of green, uncured wood. They will be the standard Canadian two-wheeled affairs, because the four-wheeled wagons you are used to will not survive on the forest roads you will have to travel. Many of the wheels will not have iron rims. You will be fortunate indeed if they remain in service for the entire campaign."

Burgoyne licked dry lips before he spoke. "I rather expected you would have anticipated the need for more carts months ago."

Carleton's expression remained controlled, masked. "The question came into my mind, but you will remember, I was not informed of the facts of this campaign until you arrived here May sixth, thirty-one days ago. Lord Germain sought my advice on absolutely nothing, nor did anyone else in London. It is difficult for me to prepare for such an expedition without being privy to the hard facts. Lacking any intelligence to the contrary, I assumed you intended making the journey by water. I'm sure you understand."

The barbed statement cut into Burgoyne, and he started to speak when Carleton cut him off. Carleton's expression was still unchanged, conversational, congenial as he continued. "May I ask, are the extra carts needed to transport the . . . uh . . . rather sizable stock of champagne and clothing and food delicacies I have heard about? How many cases of champagne was it? One hundred fifty? And how many carts filled with clothing? Forty? How many of the carts are needed for the camp-followers and wives and civilians? How many such persons are there going to be? Two thousand? Three? With your regulars, that exceeds ten thousand souls, and more than two thousand draft animals. Sustaining such a command in that wilderness will be a monumental task." Carleton's expression remained cordial, but there was no mistaking the intent of his words. They called into question Burgoyne's competence and his ability as a commander, and they cut deep.

For one instant Burgoyne's face flushed while he battled with an overwhelming need to slam his fist on the desk and rip into Carleton. Only the fact that Carleton had spoken the embarrassing truth restrained him. After a struggle, he brought himself under control, and his charming smile once more crossed his face. He was once again the dashing, enigmatic Gentleman Johnny, spectacular, captivating.

Burgoyne's eyes crinkled with his smile. "I did not anticipate that so many men, or so many officers, were going to bring their wives. General Von Riedesel is expecting his wife, Frederika, from Germany, along with three small children and a staff of servants, not to mention trunks of clothing and food. Major Acland will bring his wife, as well as two servants and their dog. Major Harnage is also bringing his wife. A great many other officers and enlisted men are doing the same. There is no way I know to avoid it. We have to provide for them."

Carleton smiled back. "I understand." He fell silent, waiting to see if Burgoyne had completed what he came to say and do.

Burgoyne stood. "Well, thank you for your advice, and your cooperation. I trust the carts and draft animals will be timely available."

Carleton nodded. "I'm certain that can be arranged."

Burgoyne started for the door. "If the storm's passed, I'll be on my way."

Carleton walked with him to the tall, black double doors. Major Thornton was on his feet to meet them as they walked out, Carleton nodding to Burgoyne and Burgoyne flashing his most devastating smile.

Back at his desk, Carleton slumped into his chair, fingers interlaced across his paunch, lost in thought.

I am unable to make him understand anything that might detract from his vision of a quick, easy campaign, and instant glory. He has no comprehension of how to handle Indians, nor of what will happen when he fails to control them. He does not see that the failure of the Canadians to turn out in force to help him is a clear signal there is little support in the civilian populace for him. He intends taking more than two thousand women and camp followers, and now, may the Almighty help them, servants and children. Gentleman Johnny. Commander of the Light Horse. One quick cavalry charge, cut down the enemy, and retire from the field in bright, eternal glory. I cannot convince him otherwise. May the Almighty provide that learning his lesson will not kill him.

Carleton drew a great breath and released it slowly. *Vanity. His vanity will be his undoing.*

He stepped to the windows on the east side of the room and looked out at the dark, heavy storm clouds on the horizon, watching the lightning bolts flash and listening to the grumbling thunder as the storm passed on eastward. He looked at the full sunlight, dazzling on the piled hailstones, and at the leaves and branches strewn about in the brilliant, newly washed world.

The storm came, fierce, and it did its work, but it changed nothing. We're still here. New leaves and branches will come on the trees. The hail will melt. The crops and the grass and the forests will grow. Tomorrow, we'll hardly remember any of its fury.

For a time he stood at the window, watching the people continue the business of living. He clasped his hands behind his back and once more cast thoughtful eyes out at the world.

Burgoyne will sweep down the lakes, toward Albany, and it will be spectacular. But when it is over, and he has finished, will anything be changed? Will it?

Outside, picking his way through the piled hailstones as he walked down the stone walkway to his waiting carriage, Burgoyne also cast an eye into the bright blue, sun-washed heavens and grinned his infectious grin.

Unbelievable country, this. Big. Strong. Powerful. Invigorating. Beautiful.

His aide held the door while he climbed into the carriage and slammed the door. He stared outside as the driver clucked the wet, steaming horses to a trot, and the carriage swayed on its way back to his officers' quarters for a conference. A smile remained as he worked with his thoughts.

So the Americans are terrified of the Indians. Excellent. Their fear will become one of my greatest weapons. An open letter will do it. Hundreds of copies, distributed to all the villages and settlements on the east side of the lakes as we move south. How best to word it? Stretch. That might do it. If they don't cooperate with us, I'll give "stretch" to my Indians, who will inflict depredations and horrors on them as never before. Let them see a few of those half-naked savages decked out in their feathers and paint, carrying tomahawks and scalping knives, and the letter will just about finish any thoughts of resistance. It will work. It will work.

He craned his head out the window to gaze once more at the sparkling, clean world.

Beautiful country, this. Marvelous.

Notes

Unless otherwise indicated, the following facts are from Ketchum, *Saratoga*, on the pages indicated.

On June 7, 1777, General Burgoyne complained to General Carleton that he had not received the horses and oxen, carts, wagons, tents, uniforms, food, equipment, and additional troops he needed and expected. Neither Carleton nor Burgoyne had paid proper attention to the shortage of animals and carts, perhaps thinking the expedition to the south would be conducted mostly on water—on the lakes and Hudson River. They enlisted the aid of John Peters and Ebenzer Jessup, two Canadians, to enlist men. To enlist one thousand Indians, they turned to Chevalier St. Luc de la Corne and Charles Langlade, two of the worst cutthroats on the frontier. Peters and Jessup got less than half the requested number of Canadians, and St. Luc and Langlade raised only five hundred of the desired one thousand Indians. The histories and general character of Peters, Jessup, St. Luc, and Langlade are defined. Burgoyne requested five hundred more two-wheeled Canadian carts with teams to pull them and four hundred more oxen and horses for pulling other wagons. Unfortunately the carts were built of green, uncured lumber, without iron rims for the wheels (pp. 105–12).

Burgoyne suggested Carleton could raise the desired number of Canadian troops by declaring martial law, which Carleton refused. He had previously attempted the use of a corvée, a form of forced labor, which failed among the Canadians (p. 108).

Carleton was short of uniforms, shoes, socks, and shirts for his men because months earlier an American privateer had seized a ship with uniforms for sixteen thousand men, plus thirty thousand shirts, and thirty thousand pairs of shoes and socks (p. 131).

Burgoyne wrote a proclamation, or document, to be delivered to Americans on the east side of the lakes and Hudson river, advising that their cooperation would be rewarded, but their refusal to cooperate would be punished by Burgoyne giving "stretch" to his Indians, who would bring "devastation, famine, and every concomitant horror" down upon them. The document was intended to frighten the Americans into submission; however, it provoked the exact opposite reaction (pp. 141–42; see also Leckie, *George Washington's War,* p. 378).

Most of the German soldiers under Burgoyne's command could not speak English, although officers on both sides had a vague working knowledge of French. The result was the British and German officers spoke in a sort of pidgin French (p. 137).

Burgoyne had personal baggage, including uniforms and champagne, to fill at least thirty carts and was known to have a relationship with the wife of one of his commissaries during the Saratoga campaign (see Leckie, *George Washington's War,* p. 376; Marvin L. Brown, ed., *Baroness von Riedesel and the American Revolution,* pp. 55–56; Higginbotham, *The War of American Independence,* p. 188).

In addition to his force of about eight thousand soldiers, Burgoyne brought along nearly two thousand women and children, with their baggage, which created an enormous need for wagons and horses (p. 108).

Burgoyne had made his reputation as leader of a light cavalry regiment, and the American forest was no place for a light cavalryman (see Higginbotham, *The War of American Independence,* p. 176).

CHAPTER VI

★ ★ ★

*E*li dug the pit in the gray light of daybreak and set lengths of dry logs in it, then rocks on top, before setting fire to the wood. While the rocks were heating, Eli swung his tomahawk to cut small stripling pines. He sank the larger ends of the slender trees in the ground in a six-foot-wide circle around the pit, then pulled their limber tops together and lashed them to form a crude, round, domed framework. While Eli worked, Billy gathered branches and heavy undergrowth into a pile, patiently working with his right hand, stopping occasionally to adjust the deer hide straps that held his left arm and hand tightly against his body. The eighteen stitches in his left shoulder were holding, and the flesh was knitting, but it was still too pink, too tender. He could not risk reopening the long, deep wound.

With the afternoon sun still three hours high, Eli nodded to Billy. "It will do."

The small, round, domed sweat lodge was covered with eighteen inches of pine and maple boughs, mixed with large lily pads and heavy ferns to hold the heat in and the cool air out. The opening, large enough to crawl through, was draped with a blanket to close it. Inside the lodge, the rocks in the pit were hot enough that a few were beginning to split, while beneath the rocks, the logs still smoldered, as they would for another day. Two short logs provided a place to sit next to the fire. The crude structure was shielded on three sides by gigantic formations of granite rock and could only be seen from the south. A clear, cold stream, twenty feet to the west, wound its way to Lake George, three hundred yards to the north.

Eli wiped the sweat from his face, then picked up his rifle. "I'll be back about sunset."

"See something?"

Eli shook his head. "Going to make a big circle to be sure we're alone."

Billy nodded and again marveled at how quickly Eli could soundlessly disappear in the forest. He picked up both canteens and walked to the stream to sink them and watch the bubbles cascade out, then stop. He poured enough from each to accommodate the stoppers, then smacked them in with the palm of his hand. He returned to the sweat lodge, dropped the canteens near his musket and pouches and their bedrolls, and sat down on a large, smooth rock twenty feet away. Cautiously, he worked his left arm against the leather thongs, gently working muscles that had been too long unused. For a few moments he watched the sun as it reached for the trees on its downward path on the distant rim.

Sunset, maybe three hours.

He glanced at the sweat lodge, then lowered his eyes as thoughts came in random disorder.

After the fight he was unsettled—not like himself. Found tracks of two more Mohawk scouting parties—both came from the north, both returned to the north. Something big going on up there. Probably Burgoyne's army gathering. How many? Where will they strike?

A long-tailed, beautifully marked black and white magpie set up a raucous scolding from a gnarled oak tree, and Billy smiled back.

You think I don't belong here. You're probably right. I'll be gone soon. Forgive me this time, and I'll try not to bother you again.

The magpie shifted to a lower branch and kept up its complaint. Billy watched for a moment, then ignored the impertinent bird. He glanced at his bullet pouch, where he kept the letters he had written to

Brigitte, and for a moment he saw her face, her brown hair, hazel eyes, and felt the rise in his breast.

Brigitte. I wonder if she will ever see those letters. I wonder if anyone will. Things happen so fast in this forest—one second they weren't there, and the next second we had killed four of them. It could have been me instead of them. He shook his head in thoughtful regret. *For one thing to live, another must die. But that ought not be the rule between men. Men can rise above that. It can be done. I've killed men, and it's a sad thing. Will the Almighty punish me for it? When is killing justified? Is it justified when one man tries to rob another of his liberty? Is it? It must be. It has to be. It is in a man to be free, and it is the Almighty who put that determination there. It has to be right.*

The magpie rose to a higher branch, perched, and thrust its large head forward, its beady eyes fixed on Billy and its oversized black bill opened wide as it cawed its continuing argument at him. A gray squirrel darted from nowhere onto a lower branch to stop, fix its white-rimmed eyes on Billy, and chatter its quick, abrupt warning. It scampered farther out on the branch, then turned and leaped, all four feet extended, bushy tail straight out behind, to a branch in a neighboring tree, and was gone as quickly as it had appeared.

The magpie made its final statement, then suddenly spread its wings, rose to the tops of the trees, and was gone in the approaching sunset.

Billy watched it disappear, and an unexpected echo rose in his memory. *Watch the birds and the small animals. They'll tell you.* The thought passed without notice, and then it came back again. *Watch. They'll tell you.* For a moment he saw Eli's eyes, intense as he had spoken those words while Billy was weak from loss of blood, battling the fever from the tomahawk wound.

Billy did not know whether it was the remembrance of Eli's words, or a sound, or an instinct, but suddenly he was intensely aware of an unknown presence. The hair on his arms rose as he slowly turned his head to his left and then stopped all movement. Not thirty feet away a mother brown bear and two cubs stood immobile, fixing him with small, black eyes that were too weak to distinguish detail far away. She was out berrying, to replace the heavy fat that had sustained her through her long winter sleep, and to gain milk to nurse her young cubs. The big sow raised her head, and Billy saw her nostrils move, testing the air to determine what the strange scent was. Her eyes might deceive her, but her nose—never.

Without moving, Billy glanced at his musket, lying by the bedrolls twenty feet away—judging how long it would take to cover the distance, cock it with one hand, and fire. *Too far? Maybe. It will be close.* He tried to remember if it was loaded. It was.

In one fluid, easy move, the bear that had appeared so clumsy and incapable, reared onto her hind legs, her nose still working, and small, grunting sounds coming from deep in her throat. The two cubs instantly disappeared behind her, then peeked back to study Billy.

His breath came short as he judged her nose to be nine feet from the ground and her weight to be eight hundred pounds. Never had he considered the power that must be in an animal that size. A rank, musty odor reached him, and he understood he was scenting a bear that was at that moment scenting him. Having seen the effortless grace of her rise to stand on her hind legs, he knew he might reach the musket before she reached him, but with his left arm tied and useless, he would clearly never get it cocked in time, bring it up, fire it. And the thought struck him, that a single musketball hitting that immense body would likely do nothing more than enrage the bear. *Where do you shoot a bear to stop it? Head? Heart?*

The mother bear dropped to all fours, and with her head swinging from side to side while her nose continued to test the air, she started toward Billy, walking in the deliberate toed-in stride common to her genus.

An unlikely calm came over Billy. He did not move, nor did he make a sound or change his breathing. He remained seated on the large stone, intently looking into the small, pig-like eyes of the huge sow bear and listening to the guttural grunts that ordered her cubs to stay close. They were on either side of her, jammed against her so tightly they were nearly invisible as she continued in her slow, ambling gait. When she was three yards away she stopped. Her head lowered and her eyes locked onto Billy, while her nose continued probing the strange scent of a man. Billy saw the scars on her nose—from striking sharp, buried rocks as she rooted for grubs and herbs and roots—and her drooping left ear, from a three-inch tear taken in some forgotten battle. He saw the long, black, curved claws extending from the huge paws, and could only guess at the ease with which they could rip apart a rotted tree trunk to reach a store of grubs or colonies of ants.

The impression came clearly and strong to Billy. *Friend or enemy? She wants to know.*

He did nothing, said nothing. He sat still on the rock, staring at her as intently as she was staring at him. He watched the small, pointed snouts of the cubs appear from behind the massive front legs of the mother, then quickly draw back, only to appear once more. For ten full seconds they faced each other at nine feet, the bear's nose twitching, her eyes locked onto Billy, while her cubs dared not come out from the protection of those thick legs and huge paws. Then she made her decision.

With an indifferent toss of her head she turned toward the bedrolls and Billy's musket and pouches, then slouched over to them where she lowered her nose to touch them, blowing and inhaling hard. The moisture from her nose and muzzle smeared on the musket stock and the leather bullet pouch. She cuffed the bedroll with one paw and sent it rolling, then turned her back on the small camp and walked directly away from Billy, her hindquarters switching from side to side as she disappeared in the forest growth. One cub stopped for a moment to turn and look back at Billy. A single grunt from its mother brought the cub scampering, and they were gone.

Billy sat still for thirty seconds before a blue jay glided in on silent wings to perch on a tree and begin the raucous calls that declared its territorial rights. A raven came cawing, and then three magpies. Two tiny chipmunks with the three light stripes prominent on their backs darted from nowhere onto a tree limb, flitted their tails, and commenced their squeaking chatter at Billy. The bear was gone, and once again the forest was safe.

Billy stepped to the place where the bear had stood, nine feet from him, staring at him, scenting him, concluding he was no threat. He knelt and placed his right hand in the faint track left by her front paws in the soft cushion of the forest floor. The track was nearly double the size of his spread fingers. He shook his head in wonder, then walked to the bedroll and returned it to its place. *Odd that I felt no real fear. Somehow I knew she only wanted to be certain her cubs were safe. Somehow she knew I only wanted to let her pass in peace. Strange.*

He sat cross-legged on the bedroll to open his bullet pouch and remove the small piece of cotton cloth he used to clean his musket, and wiped the bear smear from the musket stock and the leather pouch. As he tucked the cloth back into the pouch, he touched the packet of letters to Brigitte, wrapped in their oilskin. *If I told her about the fight, and the tomahawk cut, and the bear, would she believe it? A boy from the city of Boston?* He smiled ruefully. *I doubt I'd believe it if someone told me.*

He closed the flap on the pouch and tossed it beside the musket, then glanced at the sun, gauging time. *Late afternoon. Mother's getting supper for Trudy. Boston is beautiful right now—trees and yards greening up, things growing. I wonder when I'll get back to see it all again.* He sobered. *Maybe the question is whether I'll get back to see it at all.*

He picked a sliver of wood from the chips strewn on the ground where Eli had cut the logs to feed the sweat lodge fire and slipped it into his mouth to thoughtfully chew. *I wonder if we'll find Eli's sister up there. Eighteen years. Is she still alive? Married? Children? What would Eli think if he had nieces and nephews? Uncle Eli.* Billy smiled at the thought. *I hope we find her. Part of him would be at peace if we did.*

For a little time the tops of the trees were golden in the setting sun, and the forest was cast in a dim golden glow. Birds began going to nest, and squirrels and chipmunks moved closer to their burrows, glancing upward, watching for owls and hawks. The sun slipped below the horizon, and the shadows deepened. The patient, quick eyes of a red fox peered out from a growth of heavy ferns, judging whether it was yet dark enough to begin its unending nocturnal search for food.

Eli appeared from the south as silently as the creeping shadows and walked directly into their small, sparse camp. He did not slow his stride as he studied the ground coming in, reading the tracks as if they were an open book.

"No one out there for more than two miles," he said quietly. "We're alone."

Billy nodded.

Eli laid his rifle beside Billy's musket, then set two large fish that had been cleaned and hung on a forked stick beside them before he sat down and pointed at the fish.

"Pike. Good white meat, for after the sweat lodge."

He gestured toward the tracks of the mother bear and cubs. "The bear. Did she cause any trouble?"

Billy shook his head, and Eli continued.

"Good sized. Maybe eight hundred pounds, with two cubs. She got close."

"About nine feet."

"What did you do?"

Billy shrugged. "Talked it over with her. She paid her respects and left."

Eli smiled. "Scared?"

Billy's eyes widened in mock surprise. "Me or the bear?"

Eli chuckled his rare chuckle, then sobered. "Remember one thing. If you see the cubs and not the mother, find out quick where the mother is, and get out from between her and her cubs. They ask no questions, and they move fast and hit hard when they fear for their cubs. They may look slow and clumsy, but on flat, open ground a bear can catch a horse, and one as big as that one can break the neck of an ox with one blow."

For a moment Billy reflected on it, then nodded, but said nothing.

Eli walked to the sweat lodge, dropped to one knee, and thrust a hand inside, then bent to peer into the darkness. He returned to Billy to sit on the forest floor with his feet apart, elbows on his raised knees, fingers laced loosely together. His face was downcast as he gathered his thoughts.

"The lodge is ready. I'm going in tonight. Do you still want to come in?"

"Yes."

"Once we're in, we come out only to get more water for the rocks, and maybe take a sip. No food. We stay until our minds are clear."

Billy nodded but remained silent, and Eli continued slowly, thoughtfully.

"I need to know what to do about Joseph Brant and his Mohawk. Without them, I doubt the British will make it very far in the forest. There's a chance I could get close enough to shoot Brant, but I doubt I would get away afterwards. Maybe, maybe not. But that's not what bothers me most. What bothers me is I have a feeling that if I could find a way to talk to him, he might quit the British, and if he did, most of the Indians would quit with him. If I kill him, the whole Iroquois Confederacy will likely take up the hatchet against every American they can find, soldier or not, all across the frontier. Mohawk, Onondaga, Cayuga, all six tribes. Blood would flow like a river."

He raised pained eyes to Billy. "It's hard to know what to do. The only thing I can think of is to purify ourselves in the sweat lodge until our minds are clear on it. When we come out, I will need to make a prayer to ask if my thoughts are right."

Billy nodded. "I'm ready."

Eli took the fish to the stream to wash them. Then, in the gathering darkness, they carried their weapons, bedrolls, and belongings to the sweat lodge and laid them against the outside north wall, closest to the high granite boulders. Eli carefully unlaced the deerhide binding, and with Billy gritting his teeth against the pain, worked his shirt over his head. He replaced the binding, then removed Billy's shoes and stockings.

Clad only in their breeches, they picked up their canteens, and with Eli bringing the fish, the two men approached the low, rounded opening. Eli dropped to his hands and knees and crawled inside the small, circular enclosure and sat down on one of the logs next to the pit filled with hot rocks bedded in flickering, glowing coals. Billy followed to sit opposite him, and Eli reached to pull the blanket over the opening. The sweat lodge was plunged into darkness, save for the dim light from the firepit. It turned their bare torsos into ghostly apparitions and their faces into a study of ghoulish shadows. Eli reached to lay the fish on the edge of one of the heated rocks.

The heat inside the enclosure was stifling, but there was little smoke from the low fire and glowing embers. Eli jerked the stopper from his canteen and carefully dripped some water onto the rocks. The loud hiss of steam was followed by two sharp pops as two rocks split under the cold water. Eli waited for thirty seconds, then patiently dripped more water until the air inside the tiny structure was filled with tiny, invisible water particles. It clung to their bodies and hair and the inside of the sweat lodge and began to trickle down their chests and backs. Their loose hair became sodden, and sweat poured from every pore on their bodies, dripping from their noses and chins onto their breeches and running down their legs to soak their bare feet. For a time they labored to breathe, and then it became easier. They leaned forward, knees on elbows to take the weight off their backs, and settled in for the long, quiet time ahead.

The passing of time began to lose meaning. From time to time they poured water from their canteens onto the heated rocks and watched the steam cloud billow. They sat patiently in the darkness and sweltering heat with sweat running in rivulets to soak the logs on which they sat and make tiny puddles on the dirt floor. Sometime after midnight, when their canteens were empty, Eli took both of them, pushed aside the blanket, crawled out into the cool night lighted by an eternity of stars, and refilled them at the small stream. He reentered the sweat lodge, and each took a small sip of the sweet, cold water, then poured more onto the heated rocks. They knew it was dawn when the blanket showed light around the edges, and still they remained. With the sun two hours high, their canteens were again empty, and Billy left the lodge to refill them. Returning, he and Eli each took a small sip of water, poured some steaming on the rocks, and settled back again.

Their stomachs were empty, and with the fierce, unrelenting heat steadily draining their strength, their bodies clamored for food in the growing inner struggle between their mortal needs and their determination to bring them into subjection. They denied the demands of their bodies, and slowly their resolve and their will rose above them. By midafternoon it seemed that the spirit in each of them had defined itself from the physical and had conquered the demands of the flesh. With their minds uncluttered by the dictates of the natural man, the clouds and shadows that obscured their reasoning vanished in the pure light of clear, unfettered vision.

Thoughts from a level higher than mortality began to come, quietly, surely. They seemed at first common, unremarkable, but they grew and expanded, one leading to another until in their minds they saw and understood with the sure conviction of those who have perceived truth and know it in their hearts. They heard no voices, nor did they see surreal visitors, nor did they wish to.

With a sureness not of the mortal world, the soul-wrenching question of the course they should take in the days to come began to order itself in their minds. With no conscious effort from either man, the core of it became clear, simple, and then each man silently reached for the peace that would come when the light of understanding opened in their minds, and they would know what to do. They sat silent, unmoving, while they struggled. One minute became ten, then fifteen, before their minds, and their hearts, settled, and they knew.

Eli stirred, then raised his head and spoke softly. "It is enough for me. My mind is clear, as far as it can be."

Billy nodded. "I'm ready."

Eli plucked the cooked fish from the rocks, Billy picked up the two canteens, and they worked their way out of the tiny structure into a setting sun that had streaked the western sky with reds and yellows and brushed the domed trees with gold. Drenched with sweat, they walked to the stream and waded in, then went to their knees to cup water in their hands and wash themselves with the chill water until the sweat had stopped and they were clean. They wrung out their breeches, and Eli helped Billy with his shirt, then his shoes and stockings before he put on his own. They tied back their hair, and Billy refilled the canteens.

Eli laid the fish on a flat rock near the sweat lodge, and they sat down on either side, weak, glowing from their bath in the cold creek water. With their stomachs shrunk, they felt little desire for food. Eli gestured toward the fish.

"Eat just a little, then wait for a while. We'll leave most of it until morning, but we have to get back our strength. We have to be moving tomorrow."

Billy nodded, and they broke chunks of the broiled fish with their fingers and began to work it in their mouths.

Eli broke the silence. "My mind is clear. We have to find a way to talk with Joseph Brant. We cannot kill him." He brought his eyes to Billy's.

"It came to me the same way."

Eli nodded. "I don't know yet how we're going to do it, but I do know one thing. If we are clear that's what we must do, then there is a way to do it."

Billy answered softly. "We'll find it."

They ate sparingly and drank cold water before Billy wrapped the remainder of the fish in ferns and lily pads and placed it just inside the sweat lodge entrance. The sun was gone and deep dusk was settling as he untied his bedroll and spread his blanket near his musket. When he turned back, he saw Eli just beyond the far edge of their little clearing. He was standing straight, face lifted to the north, arm raised high, hand pointing toward the north star, faint in the dusky light. Eli's words came with a quiet reverence, and Billy realized they were Iroquois. Eli turned to the east, face still upward, hand extended, pointing, then to the south, then the west, and finally back to the north, where he ended his spoken words. He lowered his arm, then his face, and for a time stood straight and silent, face cast downward. Then he walked back to work with his bedroll.

Billy did not speak to him of what he had seen. While Eli untied and spread his blankets, Billy bowed his head for a few moments, and silently repeated, "Almighty God, for my blessings I thank thee. In thy tender mercy protect my loved ones this night. We pray thy will to guide us. Amen."

They were wrapped in their blankets before Billy turned toward Eli in the dark. "If one Iroquois tribe is at war with another and wants to end it, how do they tell the other tribe?"

There was silence for a moment. "Send a messenger."

"Under a white flag?"

"No. Most often with a wampum belt."

"Who makes—"

Billy got no further. Suddenly Eli sat bolt upright, and Billy stared at him in puzzlement. Eli spoke with an intensity Billy had not heard from him.

"Joseph Brant would honor a wampum belt. We can make one—you and I."

Notes

Billy and Eli are fictional characters, hence the sequences in this chapter are fictional. However, the Iroquois often used sweat lodges for religious and spiritual purposes (see Trigger, *The Children of Aataentsic,* p. 81).

Fort Ticonderoga

June 12, 1777

CHAPTER VII

★ ★ ★

*W*eariness lined his face. It showed in his eyes and in his two-day beard stubble and the sag of his shoulders and his wilted uniform. Arthur St. Clair, lately commissioned major general in the Continental army of the United States, hung his tricorn officers' hat and cape on the pegs behind the door, walked past the old, scarred pinewood desk and slowly settled onto the straight-backed, rough-hewn chair facing the door. The chair groaned, and St. Clair let it take his weight gradually, waiting for it to crack. It held. For a time he sat in silence, critically studying the detail of the low-ceilinged office reserved for the commanding officer of Fort Ticonderoga.

The best of the French engineers had used trees and stones from the forest when they built the large, five-sided, thick-walled fort. The ravages of time had taken their toll, and the scars left by cannon and musketfire were grim evidence of the battles the aging structure had survived as the British took it from the French and the Americans took it from the British.

The office walls were of deteriorating pine logs, chinked with mud, lime, and straw. The floor and ceiling were of rough-sawed pine planks that had shrunk since being nailed to their log underpinnings, and slight gaps had appeared between the boards. Tiny crumbs of chinking had sifted from the walls to the floor to leave a dusting of fine white powder around the perimeter of the room. A small stone fireplace divided the south wall, and a narrow cot and blanket occupied one of the corners next to it. Two small windows on either side of the door in the north wall provided light during the day, sufficient only to cast into the room an atmosphere of perpetual gloom. A five-foot bench made of unfinished pine stood beneath one window, and a small American flag graced the west wall, its red and white stripes and blue field with thirteen circled stars the only splash of color in an otherwise colorless room. Two pine chairs, neither sanded nor finished, both with cracked seats, faced the battered desk. A faint, musty odor tainted the air.

Two small north-facing windows provided a narrow view into the large parade ground and the mess halls for officers and enlisted men, barracks, hospital, commissary, and armory built into the thick, crumbling stone walls that surrounded a forty-foot flagpole in the center. Two lamps stood on the desk, one on the plain mantel above the fireplace, and two others hung on the east and west walls. There was no clock in the room.

St. Clair drew his watch from its pocket in his tunic. Twenty minutes past eleven o'clock. He thrust it back and pulled his orders from inside his tunic to read them once more.

Born forty years earlier in Scotland to the clan St. Clair, pronounced Sinclair, that had emigrated from Normandy to Scotland in the eleventh century, he had early devoted himself to the life of a soldier. He came to America with the Royal American Regiment, where he fought with distinction at Louisbourg, under the command of William Howe when General Wolfe took Quebec during the Seven Years' War, which ended in 1763. With the fighting finished, he had shocked his family, and the British army, by siding with the upstart colonies in their rise against English domination. Using inherited money and his wife's fortune, he bought four thousand acres in the beautiful Ligonier Valley in Pennsylvania, to become the largest landowner west of the Appalachian Mountains. When the rebellious Americans chose to stand against the British at the North Bridge in Concord, St. Clair made his services available as a colonel in the militia, then in the Second Pennsylvania Battalion, where he was with those who reached the gates of Quebec on December

30, 1775, before they were turned back by a blizzard and a determined stand at the city gates by the British under General Sir Guy Carleton.

Despite the failure at Quebec, St. Clair's leadership and uncommon judgment were noticed, and he was with General Washington when the tattered remains of the Continental army struck the feared Hessians garrisoned at Trenton the morning of December 26, 1776, and killed or captured the entire command. It was St. Clair who cornered and demanded, and received, the surrender of the last Hessian regiment near Assunpink Creek. Six days later the American army found itself pinned against the Delaware River by British General Charles Cornwallis and four thousand angry British regulars, whose sole ambition in life was to avenge their humiliation at Trenton and utterly destroy the upstart Americans.

St. Clair had sat at the table of General Washington's hastily convened war council, and siding with General Washington against some of the other officers, provided critical suggestions that resulted in the daring, unheard of strategy adopted by Washington, by which the Americans circled the entrenched Cornwallis in a forced night march to take Princeton, while Cornwallis prepared his army to storm empty American trenches on the Delaware River the following morning.

Handsome, with steel-blue eyes, deep brown hair, and a granite jaw and chin, St. Clair had proven his tough, brilliant thinking, his unflinching loyalty to Washington and the American cause, and fierce courage under fire, and had been promoted by Congress to the rank of major general. Shortly thereafter he received a letter from Pennsylvania Congressman James Wilson informing him with flowery accolades that " . . . the important Command of Ticonderoga is destined for your next campaign. I presage it a Theater of Glory."

St. Clair unfolded his written orders, glanced at the signature at the bottom—Major General Philip Schuyler—and read them once more. He had long since learned that orders written in the confines of the elegant office of a commanding general, or of the president of the Continental Congress, in the comfort and security of a city, are not the same orders when they are read in the field, where men are every minute facing the harsh realities of camp life and living with the daily threat of the horrors of war.

Proceed with all haste—Fort Ticonderoga—take command—bring the fort and environs to a state of readiness earliest—send a written report of conditions upon arrival.

St. Clair slowed to read what he considered the most critical words in the document: "You have the strongest assurances from Congress that the king's troops were all ordered round to New York, leaving only a sufficient number to garrison their forts in Canada."

He raised his eyes to stare at the north wall, remembering the last words spoken to him by John Hancock, president of the Continental Congress, before St. Clair left Philadelphia for his journey up the Hudson. Hancock had been firm, unequivocal, when he told him "there is absolutely no probability of an active campaign by British forces from Quebec." Rather, Hancock had said, all British soldiers now gathered there were to be boarded on troop ships, to sail east down the St. Lawrence River, thence south down the Atlantic coast to New York.

Hancock sitting in Philadelphia, Schuyler sitting in Albany—from there, they can afford the luxury of absolute certainty that Fort Ti will not be attacked. Sitting here, in this forsaken wilderness, with a fort and men that are destitute and an angry army of the best trained soldiers in the world gathering within striking distance to the north, is a very nervous thing. If they're right, so much the better. But if they're wrong . . .

At the thought, a slight shudder ran through him. He again read the painstakingly flourished signature of Major General Philip Schuyler, and a cynical frown passed over his face as he remembered.

Generals Schuyler and Gates at each other's throats—Gates adamant that Washington was wrong about the Trenton plan—abandoned Washington while we were loading the boats to cross the Delaware to attack—went to Philadelphia to inform Congress of Washington's folly in thinking he could take Trenton—Gates, a politician, paper-shuffler, but no field commander, no fighter. Schuyler, given command of Fort Ti—me his second in command, while the two of them sit in Albany, so they can keep an eye on the other while they continue their ridiculous squabble over who will command the entire western army—and Congress finally deciding to give Gates command of the southern half—Schuyler command of the northern—stupidity beyond belief! I hope some day to understand the process by which the Continental Congress comes up with the insanity of splitting what plainly should be a single command, half to one general, half to another, when the two generals are locked in a feud born of vanity and lust for power.

A brisk rap at the door broke St. Clair's thoughts.

"Enter."

The door squeaked on its rusty iron strap hinges as it swung open and Major Isaac Dunn, St. Clair's aide-de-camp and trusted confidant, strode into the room, balancing a plain pewter tray with a napkin cover. Average build, strong, balding, Dunn had been with him for months, and St. Clair had requested him as his personal aide when he received his orders to take command of Fort Ticonderoga.

Urgency had driven St. Clair to push his entourage relentlessly from Philadelphia north, eighteen hours a day. They had traveled through the night of June 11th to arrive at the gates of the fort just after ten o'clock this morning. They had not slept for twenty-nine hours when they arrived. Nonetheless, St. Clair had perfunctorily executed the formalities of assuming command of the fort, politely but firmly refused the offer to rest and enjoy an officers' banquet in the evening to celebrate his arrival, and sought out Colonel Jeduthan Baldwin, who had previously been ordered to Fort Ti to begin repairs to bring it up to fighting capability. St. Clair had stunned both Baldwin and the highly qualified Polish engineer, Colonel Thaddeus Kosciuszko, who was assisting Baldwin, when he requested that Baldwin appear in St. Clair's office at twelve o'clock noon to make a verbal report on conditions at the fort, after which Baldwin was to take St. Clair on a complete tour of the fort and its surrounding defenses, for St. Clair to make his own appraisal of its state of readiness. St. Clair had not bathed, nor shaved, nor changed his uniform. He intended conducting the inspection just as he was.

Dunn strode across the room. "Sir, I've brought some refreshment. You need to keep up your strength." He set the tray down on the scarred desktop and waited while St. Clair removed the napkin and examined smoking coffee and the plate of hardtack and honey, broiled trout, and steamed potatoes.

"Thank you, Major."

"Not at all, sir." Dunn bobbed his head, turned on his heel, and strode to the door, his boots thumping hollow on the weathered, stained floor planks.

St. Clair's voice stopped him in the door frame. "Major, have you eaten?"

"Yes, sir, while I was at the officers' mess, waiting for your tray."

"Very good. Carry on."

Fish bones and skin were all that remained on the gray metal plate when the sound of boots outside the office brought St. Clair up short. He reached for his napkin as a rap came at the door, and he called, "Enter." The door squeaked open and Dunn stepped inside.

"Sir, Colonel Baldwin is here."

St. Clair stood. "Bring him in."

Well-built, square-faced, slightly hunched in his shoulders from countless hours spent poring over engineering books and making scale drawings of structures of every description, Baldwin had been a prominent figure in his hometown of Brookfield, Massachusetts. Feeling a duty to serve his country, he had become a captain in the British militia that in 1755 attacked the French-held position at Crown Point on the west shores of Lake George in the Seven Years' War and plunged into the thick of the heaviest fighting. He took a severe wound to his leg, and when the doctors said amputate, he hauled himself upright on his cot, seized his bayonet, pointed it at the surgeons, and declared he would run through the first man who tried to hold him down. Looking into his face, the surgeons backed up, and the leg stayed on.

With the British ever tightening their stranglehold on the colonies, Baldwin had slowly come to realize that the rights the Americans held so dear could be preserved only by breaking from the mother country. He rebelled at the tea tax and was elected to the Provincial Congress. He was with the leaders at the Battle of Bunker Hill, who stopped General Howe and his vaunted British regulars dead in their tracks three times before the Americans ran out of ammunition and withdrew. As he left the breastworks, he gathered up the body of his brother, Isaac, who had been killed by his side, and from that moment, the die was forever cast for Jeduthan Baldwin. Through the worst of it, and the best of it, he gave everything in him for the revolution and the cause of liberty. There was no patriot more respected than he.

St. Clair extended his hand, and Baldwin took two steps to grasp it firmly, shake it warmly.

"General, may I welcome you here. I stand at your service in anything you may wish." It was genuine, sincere—not solicitous, not political.

St. Clair nodded. "It is my great honor to meet you, sir. Please, be seated." He gestured to the chairs in front of the desk and glanced at Dunn. "Major, would you remain with us?"

Baldwin and Dunn sat in chairs in front of the desk as St. Clair sat down facing them. St. Clair's eyes swept Baldwin for a moment before he spoke.

"I trust you will forgive my rough appearance. Duty sometimes interferes with protocol."

Baldwin's answer was firm, strong. "Sir, your appearance is excellent."

St. Clair had not expected the reply. In that moment something between the men slipped into place, and by instinct alone they knew there was little need for pretense or maintaining a respectful distance. St. Clair sensed he could ask this man anything, and the answer would be the precise truth as best Baldwin understood it, let the chips fall where they may.

"I was advised your health began to fail some time ago. Are you fit now? Am I imposing on your comfort to ask you here?"

"Not at all," Baldwin answered. "I went home for a time. I got well and returned here February eleventh. Been here since. I'm fine."

"February eleventh? In the winter?"

"By sled, sir. Across the lake." Baldwin smiled. "Passed over some cracks in the ice that were quite . . . interesting."

St. Clair smiled with him, then moved on. "Colonel, I have written assurances from both John Hancock and General Schuyler that there is no possibility of the British proceeding down Lake Champlain to attack this fort. They are firm on the idea that the British army around Quebec is going to move by boat down the St. Lawrence to the Atlantic, and then south to New York to join Howe. Do you have an opinion about that?"

Baldwin did not hesitate. "With all due respect, our scouts are telling us the British and some German mercenaries are beginning to gather at St. Johns, and that Indian patrols are coming south in larger numbers every day. I believe they are being sent by the British to feel out our strength and the condition of this fort. It's nonsense to think the British would send their troops that far south on the Richelieu River, if they mean to turn them right around and send them back to Quebec to get on boats to go down the St. Lawrence."

"Are our scouts reliable?"

"The best, sir. Major Benjamin Whitcomb's Rangers. Long Hunters. Raised in this wilderness. They know all the Indians know about the forest."

St. Clair continued. "If an attack comes, when would you expect it?"

"Soon. Whitcomb says they're gathering boats up north on the Richelieu River."

Baldwin's words struck deep, and St. Clair rounded his lips to blow softly as he accepted them. He moved on.

"My orders are to bring this fort to battle readiness for two reasons. First, so Congress can assure the Americans we hold the key to the western frontier, and second, to stop the British in the event they ever decide to come up the lakes."

Baldwin remained silent, listening intently. Dunn leaned forward, elbows on knees, waiting. St. Clair spoke with measured words.

"This fort was built by the French, who held the ground to the north, to stop the British who held the ground to the south."

He paused, and Baldwin's head began to nod as understanding of where St. Clair was going broke clear in his mind.

"The result is, the three heavy walls and the great share of the heavy cannon face south. The fort is exactly backwards to stop an attack from the north."

Baldwin answered. "I am aware of that, sir. It will be a distinct disadvantage should we ever have to face a determined attack from the north."

"Precisely. To change it all around will take time, which I do not think we have."

Dunn straightened as the first faint feeling of tension crept into the room. St. Clair leaned forward, elbows on the desktop, forearms extended, palms lying flat. His eyes were like flecks of blue flint.

"I understand that last July you and Lieutenant Colonel John Trumbull made a written report to General Gates that considering the condition of this fort, it would be easier to defend East Point, across the lake, where cannon could reach enemy vessels coming south through the narrow neck, as well as cover this fort. Your report stated this fort was an 'Old Fort & Redoubts, out of Repair.' Is that correct?"

"Yes, sir."

"Was anything done to build defenses on East Point?"

"Nothing, sir."

St. Clair leaned back and dug thumb and finger into weary eyes, then straightened. "I was told that at about the same time, Trumbull was at an officer's dinner with General Gates, Colonel Anthony Wayne, General Benedict Arnold, and some others, when Trumbull stated that in his opinion, cannon placed on top of Mount Defiance, just south of here, could reach both the fort, and East Point. Was I correctly informed of Trumbull's opinion regarding the cannon?"

"You were."

"Gates and some others rejected the idea, but they gave Trumbull permission to fire our cannon toward the top of Mount Defiance to see how far up the balls would strike?"

"Correct. Permission was granted."

"And Trumbull did it. I was told the cannonballs almost reached the top."

"Correct."

St. Clair shook his head in astonishment. "If a cannon fired upward from here could put a ball nearly at the top of the mountain, a cannon fired from up there would reach us easily, and East Point, too."

Baldwin replied, "True, however, General Gates and a few others did not think cannon could be transported to the top of Mount Defiance."

St. Clair shook his head. "I was told that General Arnold and Colonel Wayne climbed the mountain and reported they could move cannon up there."

"That is correct."

St. Clair interlaced his fingers on the desk and leaned forward. He paused before he put the next question to Baldwin.

"Was anything done to construct defenses on top of Mount Defiance?"

Baldwin shook his head firmly. "No, sir. No orders were ever given."

"Do you know why?"

"No, sir. No one ever said."

Slowly St. Clair straightened, staring at his interlaced fingers. He sat thus for a long time before he finally raised his eyes to Baldwin, then to Dunn. The room was filled with thick silence as all three men recoiled at the horror of what exploding cannonballs and raining grapeshot would do to the fort, and the American defenders, if heavy cannon commenced a continuous bombardment from above while British regulars and German mercenaries surrounded the fort to shoot those who tried to escape to the woods. The Americans would be caught inside the thick walls like animals in a trap, helpless, unable to either hide or defend themselves. Slaughter of the entire command, and total destruction of the fort would only be a matter of time, probably less than forty-eight hours. They stared at each other, and shuddered.

And then it hit them. Should the unthinkable happen—should the British get big guns on top of Mt. Defiance—General Arthur St. Clair would find himself in the one decision that is the purgatory waiting for all good men who bear the white heat of combat command. Would he allow the murder of his helpless command to provide the commanding generals and the politicians in Congress with the lie of singing praises and heaping laurels on St. Clair and his dead command for their glorious but vain defense of the fort, to hide their own sin of having failed to occupy Mt. Defiance when it was so clear that their failure, and their failure alone, was the cause? Should the decision be forced on St. Clair, what would his answer be? Would his command become a bloody sacrifice to the stupidity of vain commanding generals and politicians?

Would it? Would it?

St. Clair moved and broke the tension. Baldwin wiped at his mouth while Dunn shifted his weight on his chair. When he spoke, St. Clair's voice sounded too loud in the dead silence.

"Let's begin the inspection. Colonel Baldwin, would you lead? Major Dunn, bring writing paper and something to write with, to keep notes."

Baldwin led them out of the small office, across the shaded boardwalk, and stepped into the dust of the parade ground. They squinted in the brilliant June sunlight, and for a moment St. Clair was caught up in the wild beauty of the endless forest. The deep emerald blue-green of the towering pines caught the sunlight, and the air was sparkling fresh with the scent of green growing things. St. Clair marveled, but he had not forgotten the first rule of this primeval country, learned from hard experience when he passed through it going to Quebec, and returning. With all its breathtaking grandeur, this wilderness knew a thousand ways to kill a man, or an army, as though they were nothing.

"Sir, what is your wish? What do you want to see first?"

"Where do you keep your ordnance?"

"This way." Baldwin strode out with the energy of a man who was never still, always active, in both mind and body. He led the small group across the parade ground, with soldiers in unkempt uniforms pausing at a distance to watch them pass. The troops wore no hats, some wore no shoes, many wore their hair loose, tangled, most had untrimmed beards. They did not come to attention, nor salute as the small group passed them. Baldwin stopped at a heavy oak door in the north wall with a faded wooden sign nailed to it declaring their weaponry was stored inside. He unlocked the big lock, opened the hasp, and pushed the door open. Sunlight from the door partially illuminated the large, dank room, and the men entered.

St. Clair walked slowly down the center aisle, expertly scanning the muskets, bayonets, swords, pikes, spontoons, and stores of musketballs, cannonballs, and spare parts. He stopped at the far end of the armory and made some mental calculations, then turned to Baldwin.

"There aren't enough muskets for the troops."

The answer was immediate. "No, sir. We lost some muskets when a boat bringing them in capsized and sank. Tories have also stolen many. One-third of our fighting force must carry pikes and spontoons and spears. We have only enough bayonets for one fifth of our serviceable muskets. Many muskets here are unusable because we have no spare parts for repairs."

St. Clair's eyes narrowed, and he glanced at Dunn to be certain he was taking notes.

"Where's your gunpowder stored?"

They stepped out of the armory, Baldwin locked the door, and led them to the east corner of the north wall, where he unlocked and opened a door bearing a large sign, *GUNPOWDER—NO ENTRY.* Inside the small room, St. Clair quickly counted the kegs and turned to Dunn, who had finished his count and recorded the figures. St. Clair spoke to Baldwin.

"It seems raw in here. Too damp for gunpowder."

"It is, sir. After five weeks in here, we have to crack open each keg and take the gunpowder out to dry it."

"You must have more gunpowder buried somewhere. There's hardly enough here to fire the cannon more than once each."

"We have about ten tons buried just outside the wall. There is a tunnel leading to it."

"Is the buried powder serviceable?"

"It appears so, sir. We check it twice a month."

"Where's your equipment storage room?"

Again Baldwin led them out into the parade ground, to the east wall, where he unlocked a pair of double doors into a huge room with a low ceiling. And again St. Clair walked through it, stopping from time to time to inspect tools and equipment. He silently gestured to Dunn to record the number of bins that were empty, and the number of tools that were broken, rusted, neglected, out of repair and out of use. He turned to Baldwin.

"You don't have half enough shovels, picks, and axes, and half of the store is not fit for use. Awls, drills, saws, and you're nearly out of nails, bolts, screws. Who's responsible for this?"

"I don't know, sir. I've requested more of everything in writing every month since February, and nothing's happened. The generals or the Congress seem to consider other places more important than this one."

"Your infirmary? Where is it?"

"Follow me."

The stench hit them twenty feet before they reached the double doors in the west wall, and they began to breathe shallow. Baldwin stopped them just inside the room. Every cot was filled. Blankets had been spread on the floor beneath the cots, and men lay on them. The smell of carbolics and alcohol made them blink their eyes, and the moans of the men were a constant undercurrent throughout the room.

"Sir, I think you can see what you wish from here. I highly recommend you not go in. We have measles and dysentery."

"How many men are in here?"

"Nearly three hundred fifty."

"The design was for how many?"

"One hundred fifty."

St. Clair's face clouded. "Vermin?"

"Pervasive. Lice everywhere."

"May I see the enlisted men's mess, and then the officers' mess?"

The kitchens smelled of mold and filth, with rat droppings in the corners and along the walls. In the cavernous mess halls, the rough-hewn tables showed unwashed spills from the breakfast and midday meals, and bits of dried food and black coffee stains soiled every table.

"Uniforms? Tents?" St. Clair waited.

"There's a storage room, sir, but there's nearly nothing in it. We've been asking for uniforms for months with no results. Same with tents. Every tent we have is in use, ragged, torn. If it rains, every soldier and blanket in a tent gets soaked."

"What is the status of your stores of food?"

"Follow me, sir."

The commissary was nearly empty. There were limp, wilted carrots and soft potatoes with four-inch sprouts growing from the eyes from winter storage, fourteen barrels of dried beans, twelve barrels of rice, fifteen barrels of flour shot through with weevil, and eighteen barrels of salted beef.

"You've got salted meat for about fifty days, and enough of the rest of it for less than a month. There's weevil, and mold."

"We'll lose a lot of what's left, sir. The men bring in deer and fish for fresh meat when they can."

"Your latrines?"

"Against the south wall, sir. In poor condition, I'm afraid. Flies, stench."

St. Clair drew a deep, troubled breath. "I need to see your defensive works outside the fort."

"I've asked to have saddled horses waiting."

The ponderous gates in the west wall swung open, and the three men cantered their mounts out toward the distant tree line. The gap between the fort and the forest was filled with the stumps of trees taken to build the fort, and for fuel.

"Where are your abatis?"

Baldwin led, and St. Clair and Dunn followed. St. Clair pulled his horse to a halt in disbelief as the first abatis came into sight. It was one hundred yards from the southwest corner of the fort, facing south. Designed to have sixty sharpened pine logs embedded in rock and dirt, and pointed outward to impale invaders, it was nothing more than a neglected pile of stones and dirt. Not one log remained.

St. Clair pointed and demanded, "What happened?"

"The soldiers cut the logs for fuel last winter."

They moved on to the nearest redoubt, with its breastworks and cannon emplacement. The breastworks were sagging, and the wooden ramp on which the cannon was wheeled into place was largely missing;

what was left was broken, splintered, useless. The rusted cannon was on its carriage, but the carriage wheels were no longer in their grooves.

Gesturing to the crumbling structure, St. Clair demanded, "Are the other redoubts in similar condition?"

"Yes. The ramps were pulled up for fuel. The cannon were neglected during the winter."

"On all the redoubts?"

"All of them, sir."

St. Clair thrust his chin forward. "You mean there are no functional outer defenses for this fort?"

"That is correct, sir."

"Where's your woodyard? Don't you have two months supply of wood cut and stacked?"

"No, sir."

"Why not?"

"Too far to go to get the wood. The timber next to the lake shore has been cut for three miles in both directions."

St. Clair sat his horse in silence for a time, studying the exterior of the fort, working to accept the harsh truth that it was an old, decaying, dilapidated ruin that had outlived its time. He reined his horse around, and Baldwin came in on his left side, Dunn on his right. St. Clair spoke to Baldwin without turning his head.

"In what condition are the timbers supporting the barracks, the mess halls, the offices?"

"Not good. Termites. Dry rot."

St. Clair fell silent for a moment, then continued. "I've heard no laughter, not one argument, not even one word of loud talk among the troops since I got here. How would you describe morale? Both officers and enlisted?"

"Nonexistent. The men haven't seen mail from home in months. We're isolated out here. No visitors, no travelers. These men don't know if we're winning or losing the war, or even whether their families are alive. We have no more powdered ink or paper to spare for them to write home. Every man here is concerned about hearth and home, and their worries are reaching proportions that are beginning to cripple the entire command with melancholy and homesickness."

"I was told you've done some construction since your return. I need to see it."

"On the south side of the fort, sir. I'll show you." Baldwin spurred his horse to a gentle lope and rounded the southeast corner of the fort before he reined it in. St. Clair pulled his mount up beside him, Dunn beside St. Clair. Baldwin pointed as he spoke.

"A big storehouse over there for supplies we hope to get, and a bakery over there. Two guardhouses further, over there by the wall. The larger building beyond the guardhouses is the new hospital, nearly finished. It will relieve conditions at the infirmary inside the fort."

He tapped spur to his horse and turned left, toward the lake. "We've built a wharf at the lake to make handling boats easier." He paused to point. "And there, we've built a bridge across the narrows to the other side of the lake. We call it our 'Great Bridge.'"

St. Clair's eyes widened. A bridge more than twelve feet wide—wide enough to accommodate wagons and cannon, as well as horses—reached from shore to shore. He turned to Baldwin. "How did you do it?"

"Built twenty-two caissons twenty-four feet square and thirty feet high and filled them with rock. Skidded them out onto the ice and spaced them in a line, then cut the ice from under them and they sank. Then we set those floats you see—fifty feet long and twelve feet wide— between the caissons to connect them. We tied it all together with heavy chains and bolts and rivets. Crossing the lake is simple, and we can keep a constant communication with our forces over there. We expect it will also slow down any British ships that try to get past."

St. Clair looked Baldwin in the face. "Remarkable." He gestured back toward the hospital and other buildings newly built. "You've done some good things in the past four months."

The late afternoon sun was beginning to cast shadows eastward when they dismounted their horses in front of St. Clair's office and handed the reins to the waiting stable sergeant. He led their mounts away as the three men pushed through the door, and St. Clair hung his hat back on its peg. He sat down behind his desk while Baldwin and Dunn took their places opposite him. St. Clair sighed, ran his hand over his head to smooth his hair, and faced Baldwin.

"Thank you for your assistance. I have to write all this up in a report. When I'm finished, I would like you to read it to make necessary corrections before I send it back to General Schuyler."

He turned to Dunn. "Leave your notes here on my desk. I'll start on that report now. Is there anything else?"

Dunn raised one hand. "Do you wish to take dinner with your staff of officers at their mess, or here?"

St. Clair pursed his mouth for a moment while he reflected. "Tonight, probably here. I'll take my meals with them tomorrow."

"Very good, sir. I'll bring your supper here."

St. Clair bobbed his head and stood. "If that's all, then, you're both excused for now, with my thanks."

With the closing of the door, St. Clair reached for Dunn's notes, then writing paper and his inkwell and quill.

At ten minutes past six o'clock, Dunn interrupted to leave a tray of boiled salt beef, rice, boiled carrots, scalding coffee, and brown bread. At six-thirty St. Clair lighted the lamps on his desk, then picked up his quill and continued writing, slowly, selecting his words with great care. At seven o'clock he paused to listen to the long drumroll as a patrol of six soldiers retired the colors from the flagpole. At seven-thirty, Dunn interrupted again to remove the tray and utensils. At ten minutes past eight, Dunn again rapped on the door with an unusual insistence. St. Clair raised his head in the lamplight.

"Come."

Dunn stepped inside. "Sir, something unusual. Two men have arrived, claiming to be American soldiers with orders from George Washington to report to you. They brought two other men with them at rifle point, under suspicion of being British agents."

St. Clair laid his quill on the paperwork. "What? What's this about?"

"I don't know, sir."

"Is it an emergency? Are we under threat of attack?"

"No, sir. No one suggested that."

"Did they give names?"

"The Americans did. Corporal Billy Weems and Private Eli Stroud."

"Recognize them? Or their names?"

"No, sir."

"Any reason this won't wait until morning?"

"None that I know of, sir."

"Tell them I'm unable to see them tonight, unless it's a dire emergency. If they're hungry, get them something from the enlisted men's kitchen, and bed them for the night. I'll see them in the morning."

"Very good, sir." Dunn turned on his heel and closed the door as he left. For a moment St. Clair sat still, puzzled, then continued with the careful drafting of his lengthy report. At half past nine he drew a great breath, let it out slowly, and rose to stretch cramping muscles. He walked to the door and out into the warm, starry night. A light breeze brought in the smell of the lake, and from a long distance to the west a wolf pointed its nose at the newly risen half-moon and sent its haunting call floating through the night. At ten o'clock the drummer rattled taps, and the lights in the tents and sleeping quarters winked out. At eleven-thirty St. Clair buried his face in his hands for a moment, then stretched. At ten minutes before one o'clock he jerked awake and raised his head from his arm, folded on his desk, unable to remember where he was.

He could no longer order his thoughts, and with a weariness that touched every fiber of his being, he pulled off his boots, removed his tunic, and laid down on the cot against the south wall. The tension began to drain, and five seconds later he was breathing slowly and deeply in an exhausted, dreamless sleep.

The roll of the reveille drum jolted him and he jerked, then opened his eyes to stare for a moment at the aging wall, struggling to recognize where he was. It came to him at first in bits and pieces, then in a rush. He rolled over, swung his legs off the cot, and sat for a moment while he rubbed bloodshot eyes and grimaced at the sour taste in his mouth. On his feet, he glanced down at his badly rumpled breeches and shirt, then walked to his desk and sat down to gather his nine-page report for review.

Fort oriented south, not north—in deplorable condition—exterior defenses worthless—weapons in poor repair—one-third of what is needed—gunpowder damp and in critically short supply—rations rotting and nearly gone—sanitation terrible— disease rampant—uniforms and tents in tatters—melancholy and homesickness destroy- ing morale—Baldwin exerting heroic effort to rebuild, restore—has built new hospital, bakery, dock, storage building, excellent bridge spanning lake, large enough for wagons— restored sawmill, workshop—if we are to survive we must absolutely have more troops, weapons, gunpowder, food, uniforms, tools of every kind, regular mail service—detailed list attached.

He pushed the paperwork away, then padded softly in his stockinged feet across the floor to draw aside the curtain and peer out at the parade ground, bright now in the golden glow of a sun half risen, where the cooks in rumpled uniforms were crossing to the mess hall to prepare oats and boil weak coffee for morning mess.

He clasped his hands behind his back, silently watching the fort come to life. The drums sounded assembly, the regulars fell into rank and file around the flagpole, the long drumroll began, and two soldiers set the hooks through the brass-studded eyes of the American colors to slowly raise them, shining brilliant in the sunlight. For a time St. Clair studied the flag through narrowed eyes, recalling the peculiar, soul- stirring emotion that arose when he had stood at attention beneath those colors on July 18, 1776, and with tears running down his cheeks had lis- tened with the entire Continental army in New York to the reading of the Declaration of Independence. Standing now in Fort Ticonderoga, remembering, it seemed only a lingering memory of a time long, long ago. As he peered upward, remembering, the thought came to him.

How long will it wave?—can we win?—can we?

He turned back to his desk as a rap came at the door.

"Major Dunn?"

"Yes, sir."

"Enter."

Major Dunn entered, carrying a pewter tray draped with a linen cloth. "Breakfast, sir."

St. Clair gestured to his desk, and Dunn set the tray down, then turned to the general. "Sir, there's the matter of those two scouts and the two men they brought in last night. You wanted to see them early this morning."

For a moment St. Clair struggled to remember. Six hours of sleep in two days had dulled him. "Yes. Take them to the enlisted men's mess for breakfast, then have them here in half an hour. I have to wash and change."

St. Clair wolfed down his coffee, brown bread, and fried mush, wiped his mouth on the plain cotton napkin, and strode to his chambers. He washed and shaved in cold water, donned a fresh uniform, then paced back to his office. Two minutes later Dunn returned.

"The four men are here, sir."

"What are their names again?"

"The Americans are Private Stroud and Corporal Weems. The other two are Amsbury and Adams, as I recall."

"You say that Stroud and Weems claim to be sent by General Washington?"

"They do, sir. They're suspicious the other two men are British agents."

St. Clair pondered for a moment. "Bring Stroud and Weems in first, together."

"Yes, sir." Dunn turned on his heel and returned in a moment, Billy following, Eli behind.

"Sir, Corporal Billy Weems and Private Eli Stroud." Billy stood at rigid attention, Eli straight, but loose and easy. Dunn stepped aside, and St. Clair's eyes narrowed slightly as he carefully studied them. Neither man was armed, nor did they change expression under St. Clair's withering stare.

St. Clair spoke. "Major Dunn, that will be all for now."

"Yes, sir." Dunn stepped out, and the door thumped shut. St. Clair gestured. "Be seated."

The two men sat down on the two rough-finished chairs facing the desk and remained silent, waiting.

"I'm sorry I couldn't see you last night. Too much to do since I arrived." His eyes never stopped probing. "Did I understand you to say you were sent by General George Washington?"

Billy answered. "Yes, sir."

"I presume you have written orders."

"Yes, sir." Billy drew the document from inside his shirt and laid it on the old desk. St. Clair unfolded it and settled back in his chair while he studied the even, disciplined penmanship, and the signature. His chair creaked as he leaned forward. "This appears to be the handwriting and signature of General Washington. How did you get it?"

Billy glanced at Eli, then back at St. Clair. "General Washington gave that to us the day we left and said to deliver it to the commander of this fort. He said that would be either General Schuyler or General Gates."

St. Clair lowered his face for a moment to cover a cryptic smile that flickered. *Schuyler or Gates. The two generals who have been in a fools' battle over command of the entire western army for a year.* He raised his head to continue. "This fort is under command of General Schuyler. I am his second in command. I'm here, he's in Albany, with General Gates." He stopped to stare intensely at the signature on Washington's written orders.

Eli leaned back in his chair. *He isn't sure—thinks maybe we're spies.* Eli spoke, "I remember your command and your cannon at Trenton. Billy and I were with Glover's regiment when you demanded the surrender of that last bunch of Hessians down by Assunpink Creek. You told that officer that if he didn't surrender right then, you'd blow them all to pieces."

Eli paused, and St. Clair leaned back, startled, intensely focused, silently waiting for Eli to finish.

"I've always wondered. If they hadn't surrendered, would you have done it?"

St. Clair leaned forward, elbows on his desk, hands clasped, chin set like a bulldog. "Right where they stood!"

"That's what I thought."

The concern that had clouded St. Clair's face vanished, and he spoke eagerly. "Were you at Princeton?"

Billy replied, "Yes, sir. We were with Hand's command when they slowed down Cornwallis the night we marched out, and we were there at the end when Captain Alexander and Captain Moulder opened up Nassau Hall with their cannon."

Suddenly St. Clair thrust his head forward. "Wait a moment. Were you the two that went in the front doors of that building after the cannon blew them open?"

Billy's expression did not change. "Yes, sir."

"Alone?"

Eli glanced at Billy. "Billy charged right on in and started throwing redcoats around like sacks of oats. I followed to try to get him out before he got himself killed."

Startled, Billy turned questioning eyes to Eli as a deep laugh rolled out of St. Clair, and then Eli began chuckling and Billy grinned.

St. Clair broke in, his voice rising, excited as he spoke to Eli. "I heard something about a tomahawk. Frightened some of our men, but terrified the British. Was that you?"

Eli nodded.

St. Clair leaned back, shaking his head slightly. "So you're the ones." He sobered and took charge of himself.

"General Washington says you are to have a free hand. Move about pretty much as you see fit." He looked at Eli, dressed in buckskins with beadwork on the breast of his hunting shirt and on his moccasins. "I presume you're the one who has had experience in the forest?"

Eli nodded. "Seventeen years. I was taken by the Iroquois when I was two and left them when I was nineteen. I fought on their side with the English in a lot of battles against the French. Speak their language, know their habits, their trails, and I've been in the forest."

"Taken when you were two? From whom?"

"My family. They were white. Mother and father killed, sister disappeared."

"You're white then? Not a half-blood?"

"White."

"You know the British are using Indians against us?"

"Yes. I expect Joseph Brant is among them, and maybe Cornplanter and Red Jacket. If they are, this army has trouble. Maybe I can find a way to avoid some of it."

St. Clair settled back in his chair, hands across his midsection, fingers entwined. For a time he studied Eli while his thoughts ran, and then he leaned forward once more. "If it's Brant, what do you propose doing?"

"I'm not sure yet. I think I'll have to talk with him."

Incredulous, St. Clair straightened. "Talk with Brant? Where? How?"

"Probably in his camp."

"You two intend walking into his camp alone?"

Eli shrugged. "Maybe."

St. Clair pulled his thoughts together. "I leave that to you. You brought in two men you suspect of being connected with the British?"

Billy answered. "Yes, sir."

"Where did you find them?"

Eli spoke. "On the Onion River, near a settlement. Colchester."

"What makes you think they're with the British?"

Billy cut in. "They have British passes, and a lot of gold and silver, and Continental paper money. The bigger one is carrying several letters from Canadians to Americans."

St. Clair's eyebrows arched. "What are their names?"

"One says he's Amsbury, the other Adams."

"Did they say what they were doing out in the wilderness, alone?"

"Not yet."

St. Clair pursed his mouth. "It's time I talked with them. I want you two present." He pointed to the bench. "Sit over there and listen."

Billy and Eli moved, and St. Clair called, "Major Dunn."

The door opened and Dunn stood at attention. "Yes, sir?"

"Bring in the two prisoners."

Dunn stepped back out the door, gestured, and two men dressed in worn colonial homespun entered the room, each carrying a wide-brimmed, brown felt hat, their faces noncommittal, eyes darting everywhere. One was short, thin, bearded, with hands that were constantly working with his hat. The other was taller, well-built, square-faced, clean-shaven, clearly the leader of the two. They stopped, and the two armed guards stepped behind them, muskets at the ready. The two prisoners faced St. Clair in silence, waiting for his orders.

"Thank you, Major Dunn. That will be all."

Dunn bobbed his head, motioned to the guards, and the three men withdrew. When the door closed, St. Clair pointed. "Be seated," and the two sat on the chairs facing his desk. The larger one turned to study Billy and Eli for a moment, the question plain on his face as to why they were there. Seated opposite them, St. Clair ignored it. The men remained silent as he spoke. His words were measured, precise, his voice quiet, intense.

"I am Major General Arthur St. Clair of the American Continental army. I am commander of this fort. You are here under suspicion of being agents for the British army. Do you understand?"

The smaller man swallowed and blanched. The larger one spoke evenly. "Yes."

St. Clair leaned slightly forward, blue-gray eyes narrowed, cutting into the two men. "What are your names?"

The larger glanced at the smaller before he spoke. "I'm Kevin Amsbury. He's Franklin Adams."

St. Clair fixed his stare on the smaller man. "Adams, do you speak?"

The man's voice cracked as he tried to answer. He cleared his throat, then stammered, "Yes, sir."

St. Clair shifted back to Amsbury. "You were found near Colchester. What was your business there?"

"Visiting relatives."

"Their names?"

"DeVere Amsbury. My uncle. Three miles from Colchester."

St. Clair straightened for a moment, then leaned forward intently. "With British passes?"

Amsbury hesitated for a split second, and St. Clair, Eli, and Billy all caught it before Amsbury replied, "Yes."

St. Clair paused for a moment, and his next question was flat, harsh. "Why?"

Amsbury swallowed. "I was sent to Montreal to claim some family money held in the Bank of Montreal. We had to have British passes to go in and come out. I was to deliver the money to DeVere, my uncle. Up in Montreal, the authorities asked me to carry some family letters back down, from Canadians who have relatives down here. I agreed."

"Why did you need Adams along?"

"Safer for two traveling than one."

"In what currency did the Bank of Montreal deliver the money?"

"Gold. Silver. I requested it. Took two days to get it."

"Then why were you carrying a large amount of Continental paper currency?"

"I exchanged for some of it."

St. Clair's hand dropped slapping to his desk top. "*What!*" he exclaimed. "Exchanged gold and silver for Continental paper? Gold and silver have value, Continental paper very nearly does not." He recovered, and his eyes bored into Amsbury. "You said you were visiting relatives near Colchester. Where do you live?"

"Belleville."

"Where is Belleville?"

"New Hampshire, north of the Connecticut River."

St. Clair turned to Eli. "You familiar with that country?"

"Yes."

"Ever hear of Belleville?"

Eli shook his head. "No."

Tension was beginning to fill the room like something tangible as St. Clair continued, his voice controlled, intense.

"Where are the letters they asked you to carry?"

"With my things. Your soldiers took them," Amsbury answered.

"Any to your family?"

"No. I don't know the families the letters are for. Some in Boston. I did it because it's hard to get mail from the British down to here, and it seemed a good thing to do for the American families who hadn't heard from their people in Canada."

St. Clair moved on. "What route did you take going north, and then coming south?"

"West to St. Johns, then north down the Richelieu River. Came back the same way."

"Tell me, what did you see when you passed through British-held territory, and what did you hear in your two days at Montreal?" He did not move as he waited.

Amsbury reached to wipe at his mouth, and for the first time St. Clair saw the slightest tremble in his hand before he leaned forward and spoke, wide-eyed, too loud.

"There's a British general named Burgoyne up there. He's got most of Carleton's soldiers, and a lot of others, gathered into a big army at St. Johns. We saw it. We heard Burgoyne figures to put that army on ships and come on up Lake Champlain and take this fort. Maybe go on further south. Already got some soldiers as far as Pointe au Fer."

Startled, St. Clair straightened, and his breathing came short for a moment. "Did you see ships up there?"

Amsbury nodded vigorously. "Many."

St. Clair brought his racing thoughts under control. "What else did you hear or see?"

Amsbury's forehead wrinkled in an attitude of remembering. "They're sending someone named Johnson—Sir John Johnson—that's it—east from Oswego with a bunch of Iroquois Indians to meet Burgoyne at Albany. From there I think they're all coming south, right on down the Hudson."

"Who said all this?"

Amsbury shrugged. "Soldiers at the inn. People in the pubs, the bank. The bankers. It's no secret up there."

Billy was watching Amsbury, listening to the inflection of his voice, watching his gestures, mannerisms, as he spoke. *Too smooth. Too practiced.*

Eli was scarcely breathing as he studied Amsbury, every inner sense singing tight, probing. *He's holding back—something's wrong.*

St. Clair straightened in his chair and placed both palms flat on his desktop. For long moments he sat thus, eyes boring into Amsbury. *Too coherent—professional.* He broke off and said, "Thank you. That will be all for now." He called, "Major!"

The door opened immediately, and Dunn stepped into the room, eyes sweeping everyone in an instant before he relaxed. "Yes, sir?"

"Take these men back to their confinement until further notice."

Amsbury and Adams stood, Adams's moves quick, jerky, nervous, Amsbury wiping at his mouth as he covertly watched St. Clair's face, looking for anything that would tell him St. Clair's thoughts. There was nothing. Dunn took each man by an arm and walked them out of the room to the waiting guards. St. Clair waited until the sounds of their boots on the boardwalk planking ended, then turned to Billy and Eli.

"Sit over here."

The two moved to the chairs in front of the desk and sat, silent, waiting.

St. Clair looked at Billy. "Was he telling the truth?"

Billy shook his head. "I doubt it. Too smooth."

St. Clair shifted his gaze to Eli. "The truth?"

"Only part. He's holding back."

"I agree. I think his story was rehearsed. I think he's probably a spy."

Billy and Eli neither moved nor responded.

"I don't know what their mission is, but I have a suspicion they wanted to be caught. And if that's true, the question is, why? The only thing I can think of is so they could get a good look at this fort, inside and out, and report its condition to Burgoyne. If Burgoyne finds out the shape this fort is in, he won't hesitate. He'll be here as fast as he can move, and I doubt we'll have a chance. Especially if he realizes he can get cannon to the top of Mount Defiance."

Eli and Billy both started, then settled back.

St. Clair stood, clasped his hands behind his back, and began to pace, his boot heels sounding hollow on the floor. "The last spy they brought in here escaped. The officer responsible was court-martialed but acquitted. I don't intend that happening again, and I don't intend risking either of these men escaping to get back to Burgoyne with a report about our condition." He walked back to his chair, speaking as he sat down.

"I'm sending those men on down to Albany to be questioned by General Schuyler. He needs to make his own judgment on them." He stopped long enough to consider his next words carefully. "I *must know* how much of what they said is true. If Burgoyne has a large army and intends coming down to take this fort, I have to know it now. Both his numbers, and his timing. This fort is in desperate condition, and we do not have enough men to withstand a heavy attack."

He stopped, rounded his lips to exhale, and looked at both men. "That brings me to you. Will you go up there, locate Burgoyne, get a count on his numbers, and determine whether he has boats enough to carry his army down here? Report back to me as soon as possible."

Billy glanced at Eli, then spoke for both of them. "Yes, sir."

"I must warn you, my scouts are from Whitcomb's Rangers. The Long Hunters. They're good, and they've returned talking about many Indian patrols north of us. They haven't been able to get far enough up there to make an accurate report. I tell you this so you'll know what to expect."

Eli nodded. "When do you want us to go?"

"When can you?"

"Soon. I'll need two things. A cup of alcohol and someone here to gather about a peck of seashells from the lake and drill a tiny hole in the middle of each while we're gone."

St. Clair's eyes narrowed in surprise. "Alcohol?"

Eli gestured to Billy. "I've got to take eighteen stitches out of his shoulder, and I'll need the alcohol to wash it when I'm finished. I'll need the seashells to make a wampum belt when I get back."

St. Clair raised his eyebrows. "Eighteen stitches? What happened?"

"A fight on the way here."

"Where? With who? How many?"

"Just south of Albany. About eleven, twelve Mohawk."

St. Clair was incredulous. "You engaged eleven or twelve of them, and only Mr. Weems was injured?"

"Tomahawk. Shoulder blade. We stitched it shut."

"I have surgeons here."

Eli shook his head. "No need. The cut's healed tight. We just need to pull the stitches. Won't take five minutes."

"The seashells? A wampum belt?"

"They're usually made out of shells. It might be a way to get into Joseph Brant's camp to parley with him."

St. Clair stood, stunned. "You mean a wampum belt would get you in?"

Eli shrugged. "It might."

"And if it doesn't?"

"Then we made a mistake."

Billy interrupted. "We'll also need two telescopes."

St. Clair settled back onto his chair. "Major!"

Dunn opened the door. "Yes, sir?"

"Get a pint of alcohol from the infirmary, and return with it at once, along with two officer's telescopes. Then assign two men to go to the lake and gather a peck of seashells, take them to our artisans, and have them drill a small hole in the center of each one. I'll need them in the next few days."

Dunn's mouth dropped open, and he thrust his head forward two inches. "Beg pardon, sir. Alcohol? Seashells? Holes?"

"I'll explain later."

"Yes, sir." Dunn walked out of the room shaking his head.

St. Clair turned back to Billy and Eli. "How many days will it take?"

Eli considered, then answered. "St. Johns is at the other end of Lake Champlain, on the Richelieu River. We can cover most of it on water. Maybe three days up, three days back. How long we're there will depend on what we run into. Maybe ten, twelve days in all."

"On the water? One hundred forty miles in three days?"

"Canoe. There are a few tied to your dock on the lake. We can cover fifty, sixty miles a day without much trouble, mostly at night. In daylight we'll stay close to the east shore of the lake, away from the British."

"They'll have scouts out."

"We'll have to handle that when it happens."

St. Clair stopped to think. "Need food? Ammunition?"

"Maybe some hardtack and smoked fish. Coffee. Sugar. A little gunpowder."

Quickly St. Clair wrote half a dozen lines on a piece of paper, folded it, and handed it to Billy. "They'll give you whatever you require at the commissary."

"Thank you, sir."

Dunn rapped on the door.

"Enter."

Dunn walked in and laid two telescopes in battered leather cases on the desk, followed by a pewter jar with a lid clamped on. "The telescopes and alcohol, sir. May I know the use of the alcohol?"

"To wash Mr. Weems's shoulder after Mr. Stroud takes out the stitches."

"Stitches?"

"Eighteen stitches. From a battle with Indians."

Dunn's eyebrows arched. "Oh. Anything else, sir?"

"Not right now. Thank you, Major Dunn."

"Not at all, sir."

Billy and Eli each picked up a telescope, and Eli lifted the jar. "We'll return this in a few minutes."

"Good. You plan to leave now?"

"As soon as we pick up some things from the commissary and pull Billy's stitches. We need our weapons."

"Dunn will get them."

Eli and Billy had started for the door when St. Clair's voice stopped them, and he raised a pointed finger. "You two be careful. I've got to know what we're facing from the north. Good luck, and Godspeed."

Billy and Eli walked across the dusty parade ground toward the infirmary, Eli carrying the small flask of alcohol. The strong stench of antiseptic and too many bodies in a small room stopped them at the door. Billy entered long enough to persuade one of the men on duty to give him a patch of clean cotton bandage, then walked back out to Eli.

He gave a head gesture, and they walked to a stack of rough-sawed planks near where a crew of men were repairing a roof. Billy pulled his shirt over his head, then sat on the stacked lumber and leaned forward with the sunlight on his back, the line of eighteen black stitches showing prominently on the white skin.

Eli drew his belt knife and stuck the point into the lumber, opened the jar, soaked the cotton cloth, and washed Billy's left shoulder. The repair crew slowed and stopped, staring, fascinated. Eli held his knife away to pour alcohol on the blade and let it drip into the dust, then turned to Billy.

"Ready?"

"Pull 'em."

Eli tugged at the slack in the first stitch, cut the thread with the heel of his knife blade, then applied pressure until Billy flinched and the thread broke free. He dropped it onto the planking next to Billy as a small bead of blood appeared at each hole. Seventeen more times he tugged and cut, and dropped the stitches onto the small, growing pile. Then he slipped his knife back into its leather sheath, decorated with Iroquois fringe and beadwork.

"You all right?"

Billy raised his head. "Yes."

Eli soaked the cloth again to wash away the beads of blood, then sat down beside Billy. "Let's wait for that to dry in the sun."

The small knot of men took one last look at the long, straight, pink scar, wishing they could hear the story of how it came to be. Reluctantly they went back to their work, buzzing, quietly creating thrilling fictions of how Billy got the scar, while Billy and Eli sat without speaking in the warm June sunlight.

After a time, Billy asked, "The scar look all right?"

Eli nodded. "Good. Knitted tight."

"If we get caught up there, dressed like we are, they'll hang us for spies."

Eli rubbed the palms of his hands together, studying them. "If we get caught, I doubt it will make much difference how we're dressed. The trick is, don't get caught. We better return this jar and get our things and go."

Notes

Unless otherwise indicated, the following facts are taken from Ketchum, *Saratoga*, on the pages indicated.

In mid-June of 1777, General Arthur St. Clair arrived at Fort Ticonderoga to take command. General St. Clair's history and character are described. The terrible condition of Fort Ti is described, as well as the fact that it was built to defend against invaders coming from the south, and Burgoyne was coming down from the north. The facts related to the very poor morale and condition of the men at the fort are accurate. The powdered ink mentioned was commonly called iron gall ink and was made of ferrous sulfate, or copperas, and galls from the bark of oak trees, which contain both tannic and gallic acids. These two elements were mixed with gum arabic from the Middle East and reduced to a fine powder. The user then added rainwater or white wine or beer to restore it to a usable liquid.

Colonel Jeduthan Baldwin, a great and energetic patriot engineer, was in charge of bringing Fort Ti up to fighting condition, assisted by Polish immigrant engineer Colonel Thaddeus Kosciuszko. Together they had built a new bakery, hospital, breastworks, defenses, a bridge, and other improvements. St. Clair had strong assurances from John Hancock, president of the Second Continental Congess, as well as from General Horatio Gates, that the British were not intending to come down the Lake Champlain–Hudson River waterway, rather, they intended moving their army down the St. Lawrence River to the Atlantic Ocean, then south to New York. The ongoing acrimony between generals Gates and Schuyler has been explained in prior chapters of this book, as have the facts concerning Whitcomb's Rangers.

Sugar Hill was renamed Mt. Defiance, and Rattlesnake Hill was renamed Mt. Independence. Lieutenant Colonel John Trumbull proved cannon on top of Mt. Defiance could bombard Fort Ti, as well as Mt. Independence. General Benedict Arnold and Colonel Anthony Wayne scaled the mountain from the backside to prove cannon could be taken to the top. Despite this critical knowledge, no general issued orders to occupy Mt. Defiance. The two spies, Amsbury and Adams, captured near Colchester, led to information that was important to General St. Clair; their canteen had a false bottom in which was discovered the letter from Peter Livius, of the highest court in Canada, to American Major

General John Sullivan, soliciting Sullivan to join the British. Billy and Eli are fictional characters (pp. 113–26).

Gayentwahga, or Cornplanter, was a Mohawk war chief who fought with the British against the Americans (see Graymont, *The Iroquois in the American Revolution*, p. 123).

In general support, see also Leckie, *George Washington's War*, pp. 382–88; Higginbotham, *The War of American Independence*, pp. 188–90.

New York

June 17, 1777

CHAPTER VIII

★ ★ ★

A light rain that had fallen in the early morning hours left the tall maples and spreading oaks that graced the grounds of the grand Broadhead estate on the northern fringe of New York City shrouded in misty fog. The moisture clung to the trees and the grass and the June flowers, sparkling like minuscule diamonds in the rising morning sun. But by nine o'clock, the mists had cleared to leave a cool, crystal-clear morning, with the promise of a hot day to come.

The driver pulled the coach to a stop and quickly climbed from the box to the cobblestone street to unfold the two-step departure from the coach. Opening the carriage door, he grasped Mary Flint's hand to steady her as she stepped to the ground. She placed two coins in his hand and said, "I'll be here for a little time. Then I must go to the London–New York Bank on Broadway in town. Would you wait?"

The driver bowed slightly, then walked to the horse to drop a round, four-pound iron tether weight to the street and check the leather straps that connected the weight to the bit chain of the bridle. Satisfied, he climbed back into the driver's box for the wait.

Dressed in black, her face veiled, Mary turned toward the mansion and for a moment stopped, as though seeing it for the first time. Massive, three-storied, with its sixty-two windows and six-column portico towering above two dark, heavy oak doors, the mansion dominated the twenty-acre estate from the low hill on which Rufus Broadhead had built it thirty years earlier. To the west, one could see the three hundred foot, sheer granite cliffs of the Palisades on the New Jersey side of the Hudson River. To the south, most of the trees and rooftops of New York were visible. It was the only home Mary Broadhead had known before her marriage to Marcus Flint, son of the wealthy and powerful Flint family, whose grand estate was less than half a mile from that of her father.

When war had erupted between the Americans and the British in the small village of Concord eighteen miles west of Boston, both families had become leaders in the patriot cause of liberty. None could have then known that sixteen months later, British regulars, commanded by General William Howe, would shatter the Continental army under General George Washington in and around New York, then drive them across the state of New Jersey in blind panic and over the Delaware River to hide on the Pennsylvania side, devastated, scattered, beaten.

Nor could anyone have known that Mary Flint's first child would be stillborn, or that her husband, a volunteer officer in the Continental army, would be crushed to death on the New York docks when the hawsers cradling a cannon being unloaded from a ship on the Catherine Street docks snapped, sending the two-ton gun smashing down on him. White-faced patriots who lifted the gun from his crushed body said the hawsers had been cut, and blamed British loyalists, but the murder of Captain Marcus Flint was lost in the ravages and frantic pace of the war.

Nor could anyone know that with the strategic seaport of New York in their control, the British would seize the Flint mansion and estate for a hospital, and the Broadhead mansion for their headquarters. And no one could have predicted that within one year, the Flint and Broadhead fortunes would be gone, vanished, and the last of both families would be dead, save for Mary alone.

Steadily she paced up the wide brick walkway to the broad porch, where a pair of British regulars in crimson tunics and white breeches stood, one on either side of the doors with their ten-pound Brown Bess muskets held stiffly upright at their sides, nothing moving but their eyes. She had taken her second step on the porch before the regular with the three chevrons on his sleeve brought his musket up and stepped in front of the door.

"This building is occupied by British officers, ma'am. Please move on."

She faced the sergeant and opened her purse. "I'm aware of that. My name is Mary Flint. This was my home until I was nineteen years old. I have come to bury my father in the family burial plot behind the house." She reached into her purse. "I have permission from Colonel Albert Cochran to do so." She thrust a written document toward the sergeant. He unfolded it, read the terse message, returned it to her, then stepped aside.

"You may pass."

She reached for the familiar door handle and walked into the spacious, high-ceilinged reception room, unprepared for the shock. Costly carpets imported from China were gone from the hardwood floors, and the treading of military boots had dulled and cut into the polish. The great family coat of arms was missing from its place high above the carved maple fireplace mantel, on the huge sandstone chimney. The eighteen-foot mural of the birthplace of the Broadhead clan in Ireland, which had graced the east wall, was gone. The music room and the drawing room were both stripped to accommodate desks and cots for officers. Uniformed British soldiers, both officers and enlisted, marched about, each preoccupied, paying her no attention other than a surprised glance at seeing a beautiful young woman with her face veiled, dressed in black, obviously going to, or coming from, a funeral. Wars resulted in funerals; they had long since lost meaning.

A wave of nostalgia swept through Mary as memories came flooding. She saw the great home as it had been—a place famous for hospitality, graciousness and beauty, loved, cared for, with rooms where a little girl could run and beds to jump on and secret places to hide. She saw her mother, who kissed bumps better, and she sensed the smell of sweet pipe tobacco, and of musty, old volumes in the library, where her father would take her on his knee and read to her from large books with pictures of thrilling and mysterious places, where people had eyes and skins that were different and dressed in strange robes.

The French doors into the library swung open and a uniformed officer strode to face her indifferently.

"I am Major Farthington. May I ask your purpose in being here, ma'am?"

"Yes." She handed him the written message.

He nodded. "I see." He raised his eyes to hers and paused, startled by her youth and beauty. "I take it your father's remains were previously interred in New York, then disinterred to be delivered here. The casket arrived late yesterday. Our men have prepared a grave in the family plot, and the casket is there waiting. Do you wish an escort?"

"No, thank you. I know the place."

"Will anyone be attending your service? Family?"

"I am the last of my family. There will be no one else."

The officer's eyes widened. "You will bury your father alone? Deliver the eulogy?"

"I will say what needs to be said."

"Very well. When you finish, the gravediggers will lower the casket and take care of the grave."

Mary took a deep breath. "I want to thank you for your understanding and consideration. May I pay you?"

The officer glanced around the room. "If this was your home, I think you've paid enough."

Mary bowed slightly. "I do thank you. I'll be on my way." She turned on her heel and walked back outside into the sunlight, past the guards at the door, and down the three steps to the brick walkway. To her right was a narrower brick path, leading west, past the house, angling north to the family burial plot. She walked steadily to the tall, black, wrought-iron gate, opened it, and made her way to the mound of freshly turned earth with her father's lead-lined, sealed casket resting above the open grave on two large planks, with the heavy ropes waiting. A granite tombstone stood at the head of the grave, with her father's name, dates of birth and death, and the names of his wife and Mary engraved. Beneath was a

delicate engraving of a single dove. Two gravediggers stood at a respectful distance, shovels in hand, waiting until they could lower the casket
and complete the burial.

There were no tears left in Mary. Dry-eyed, she walked to the head
of the casket and for a long time stood in silence, remembering what had
been. Then she lowered her face and spoke quietly.

"Dust thou art, and unto dust shalt thou return. I commend the soul
of this good man to the care and keep of the Almighty. I love you,
Daddy. We shall meet again, with Mother, and Marcus, and the family.
Until then, rest in the peace of the Lord Jesus."

She raised her face to the beauty of a rare New York June morning.
A blue jay scolded lustily in the great oak that stood at the head of the
plot. A robin scurried through the grass and stopped, head tipped to
catch the vibrations of something beneath her feet. White seagulls with
yellow bills and black eyes soared overhead. The quiet hum of bees doing
their annual work among the blossoms on the trees and the myriad of
flower beds on the rolling green hills of the estate reached her, and she
turned to look at the reds and golds of tulips and rosebuds unfolding.
With the sights and sounds of eternal life all around her, Mary felt a
presence, and she smiled. *I know, Daddy. It's beautiful. You'll be at peace here, with
Mother. Until we meet again, I thank you with all my heart.*

She nodded to the grave diggers, who came to the sides of the heavy
casket, looped the ropes over their shoulders to remove the planks, then
slowly lowered the casket into its final resting place in the womb of
Mother Earth. They drew the ropes from the grave, coiled them, and
waited for the signal from Mary. She walked to each of them to press a
gold coin in their hand. As they silently bowed their thanks, Mary
stepped to the head of the grave and waited for them to cast the first
shovel of fresh earth onto the casket.

Without a word Mary turned and walked back down the brick path
to the front of the mansion and on to the waiting carriage. The driver
held the door while she mounted the steps, closed it when she was
settled, climbed back into the box, and clucked the horse to a trot. Mary
did not look back.

The outskirts of the city of New York passed by the carriage window as the steady clacking of the horseshoes moved them ever further away from the great estates on the northern fringe, toward the center of the city with its rows of square, painted houses mixed with small shops and family businesses. The driver reined the horse east on Vesey Street, then south again on Broadway, to pull the buggy to a stop in front of a low brick building, located two blocks from the huge Fort George battery on the southern tip of Manhattan Island, with its cannon aimed south, covering New York harbor. Wall Street was two blocks further east. The sign above the door into the old, weathered building read *LONDON–NEW YORK BANK, LTD.*

When the driver opened her door to assist her to the ground, Mary again gave him two coins. "I will be a short time here, and then I must go to the docks on Catherine Street. I have passage on a small boat up the Raritan River and then by wagon on to Morristown in New Jersey. Would you wait?"

"Beg pardon, ma'am. Did you say Morristown? Where General Washington has the Continental army?"

"Yes. I have people there I must see."

"Yes, ma'am." The driver dropped the coins into an old leather purse, snapped it shut, and climbed back to his box. Mary walked to the bank door and entered. She blinked to adjust to the lack of light in the plain, sparse room, then walked to the nearest desk. A balding man with a heavy double chin marked his place on a ledger with a finger, raised his eyes to her, and asked, "Is there something I can do for you?"

"I'm Mary Flint. Two days ago I arranged with the manager to withdraw some money from my account here. I would like to do so now."

The man swallowed, placed a ruler in the ledger to hold his place, then leaned back in his chair. He licked his lips, then cleared his throat, while his eyes avoided her. A chill ran through Mary as she waited.

"Uh, ma'am, you will have to talk with the manager. His office is there, in the corner." He pointed. "You can just—"

Mary cut him off, her voice soft, low. "I know where his office is. What's wrong? Is something wrong?"

"That's for him to say, ma'am."

"Would you please get him?"

"Uh . . . knock on his door, ma'am. He'll want to talk in his office."

The dark premonition grew in Mary, and her breathing constricted. She turned and quickly strode to the corner of the room where there was a door with fading sign over it that said *CHARLES PARTRIDGE, MGR.* She knocked firmly and listened to the sound of muffled footsteps behind the door before it opened. Partridge, average height, elderly, thick gray hair, and lipless, dressed in an ancient gray suit with black tie, dropped his chin to stare over the bifocals perched on his nose. He recognized Mary instantly, pursed his mouth while he studied her for a moment, then stepped back.

"Come in, Mrs. Flint." His voice was high, tired, scratchy. He walked to his side of a square, plain desk and sat down on a chair upholstered with cracking leather. He motioned Mary to sit opposite him on a wooden chair. She remained standing.

"I have come to withdraw the money I arranged for two days ago. Eight hundred pounds."

The sparse man leaned forward, forearms on the desk, fingers interlaced, and for a time peered upward at her before he broke the strained silence. "I'm afraid there is a problem."

Mary stiffened. "What problem?"

"This bank has been served with an order from the British army to impound all moneys that have come from the estate of Otis Purcell. Apparently he was a colonel in the British army who—"

Mary cut him off. "I know about Dr. Purcell."

"Let me finish. Apparently he was a colonel in the British army who died unexpectedly. He was a widower at the time, childless, thought to be without kin. With his body was a handwritten document that said he was giving all of his estate to you. I'm told the document found its way to you. You presented it to the British authorities, and they honored it." He stopped for a moment, then continued. "At the time, his assets were mostly in an account in this bank. With no wife or children, he had invested his money wisely, and when they added in his pension, the account was just over thirty-two thousand pounds. The British army let you transfer it to an account you opened, and you have been drawing against it since, maybe six hundred pounds, total."

He paused and leaned back while Mary stood stock-still, white-faced, silently waiting.

He cleared his throat. "The impound order I got yesterday says someone named Alfonso Eddington from Liverpool claims to be a distant cousin, and the only living blood kin of Otis Purcell. He filed his claim in court there and got an order to hold the money here until his claim is heard."

Shaking her head, Mary said, "Why wasn't I notified?"

"He says he couldn't find you."

"I was in a hospital for months, with pneumonia. May I see the order?"

Partridge opened the center drawer of his desk and handed two documents to her. "The one with the blue seal is the official court document. The other is a copy for you."

Mary scanned it, handed the original back, and folded the copy for her purse.

"I don't understand. The paper Dr. Purcell left was legal. On what basis does Mr. Eddington claim it is not valid?"

"Two things, so far as I can tell. First, he claims the document you have is a forgery. He says the handwriting and the signature aren't genuine, and to prove it he compares it to other documents known to have been written by the deceased." He raised his eyebrows. "Apparently there's a wide difference between the handwriting on his will, when compared to other things he wrote."

"Of course there is," Mary exclaimed. "He was dying. It is surprising he could write at all. The general who discovered the body signed an affidavit stating the circumstances and giving his firm opinion that the document and the signature were genuine."

"I know all that. But the claim of a blood relative as against that of a rather beautiful young woman raises enough question that it must be heard."

"Heard where?"

Partridge swallowed. "Here, in New York, if you can get the court in Liverpool to send it."

"He didn't have to make his claim here?"

He shook his head. "England has not been in a hurry to recognize the United States as a foreign country. In many ways they still think of us as their colonies. With the relative living over there, that's where the case sits until you get legal counsel to obtain an order sending it here, where it should be."

"You said this relative made two claims. What is the second one?"

Partridge wiped at his mouth for a moment, searching for words. "Otis Purcell was aging, and was alone for years after the death of his wife." He hesitated and pursed his mouth before he went on. "Lonely men who are feeling their own mortality sometimes seek the company of . . . uh . . . younger women. And they make, shall we say, arrangements for the pleasure of their company." He dropped his eyes and did not look at Mary for a few seconds.

Mary gasped and recoiled backwards one step. Her hand flew to her mouth, and she stared at Partridge in stunned disbelief. For five seconds they faced each other before Partridge raised his eyes to stare over his bifocals at Mary, and Mary stared back. She began to tremble, dropped her hand, and exclaimed, "He accuses me of being Dr. Purcell's consort for money?"

Partridge slowly nodded his head, but remained silent.

Shaking with outrage, Mary stood silent until she could bring her wild anger under control and trust herself to speak. She squared her shoulders, raised her chin, and said, "I did not know a man could sink so low, to get money. He accuses me falsely, and he also accuses Dr. Purcell of such filth." A look of sadness crossed her face. "Dr. Purcell was one of the kindliest and truest gentlemen I have ever known. What this man is doing is a sin in the sight of the Almighty."

For a time neither Partridge nor Mary moved in the silence. Then Mary drew a weary breath to speak. "What should I do?"

Partridge shrugged. "Hire a barrister."

"Here?"

"Unless you travel to Liverpool."

"And what do I do in Liverpool, with all the witnesses here, scattered by the war?"

Partridge shook his head. "I don't know. Perhaps a barrister would. Do you know any barristers?"

Mary's forehead creased in thought. "My father used one. Lawrence Weatherby."

Partridge nodded. "Over on Wall Street? I know of him. Go see him."

Mary paused a moment to consider. "I will. Thank you." She turned to leave, and Partridge called to her.

"Tell Mr. Weatherby to contact me."

"I will."

With her brain struggling to emerge from the numbing shock of finding herself penniless, and the unthinkable outrage of having been accused of being the hired mistress of Dr. Otis Purcell, the carriage ride east to Wall Street and then north two blocks was but a blur. The carriage rocked to a halt before a two-storied brown brick building, with *YARBRO INVESTMENTS* neatly lettered on the ground floor window. On the door were the words, *WEATHERBY AND ASSOC., BARRISTERS, SECOND FLOOR.*

The driver assisted Mary from the coach, and she again placed two coins in his hand.

"Should I wait, ma'am?"

She reflected for a moment. "No. I don't know when I will be finished."

He tipped his hat. "As you wish, ma'am." He climbed back into the driver's box, and the carriage rolled away, the horseshoes clacking on the cobblestones.

A sick, hollow feeling welled up inside her as she watched the carriage disappear in the midmorning traffic. She stood on the brick sidewalk and carefully counted the money remaining in her purse—thirteen pounds, twelve pence. For a moment she stared into the faces of those walking past. They hurried on, preoccupied with their own affairs, their own troubles, paying her no attention, not knowing or caring that she was standing there in the shambles of a life suddenly stripped of everything. As if in a dream, she walked to the door of the building and pushed inside, then climbed the stairs to the second floor and through the door of the Weatherby office.

"Is there something I can do for you?"

Mary blinked, then turned to a plump, middle-aged woman with a round, pleasant face, seated at a desk to the right of the door. It took Mary a moment to order her thoughts.

"Yes, my name is Mary Broadhead Flint. Rufus Broadhead was my father. I believe he had business with Mr. Lawrence Weatherby while he was alive."

"Yes, I remember Mr. Broadhead."

"Is it possible for me to see Mr. Weatherby?"

"Does it have to do with your father's business?"

"No. My own."

"May I tell Mr. Weatherby the purpose of your visit?"

Mary pulled her thoughts together. "Thirty-two thousand English pounds."

"I see. Mr. Weatherby has a client with him. They should finish within the hour. Would you care to wait?"

"Yes. Thank you."

Mary sat on a chair against the wall, purse clutched in her lap, staring unseeing at the three doors on the far side of the room that opened into offices, while she battled to control the blind panic that had seized her at the realization that she was alone, penniless, in a city divided by war and a world gone insane.

She started at the sound of a door opening, and watched as a portly man with a high-topped beaver hat, a polished walking stick, immaculate suit, and a huge gold chain stretching across his paunch, emerged. The man who walked him to the door was tall, thin, sallow-skinned, hawk-nosed, with a face pitted by smallpox. His hair was thinning, and he walked slightly hunched forward.

The two men stopped at the office door, and the thin man reached for the handle. "I'll finish the first draft by Friday. Come back Monday, eleven o'clock." He turned to the woman at the desk. "Ellen, schedule Waldo back on Monday, eleven o'clock." The woman turned three pages in an open ledger, wrote with a quill, nodded, and smiled.

"Till then." Waldo nodded, tipped his hat to Ellen, and walked out onto the landing, where Mary heard him begin to descend the stairs. The thin man hooked a thumb in his vest pocket and turned back toward the room from whence he had come. Ellen rose to follow him, and the door closed behind them. A moment later Ellen emerged and motioned to Mary.

"Mrs. Flint, Mr. Weatherby will see you now."

The room was unpretentious. Square, fairly large, one wall was lined with bookshelves holding books of every description. A worktable stood in one corner with a dozen books laid out, helter-skelter, some open, others not. A faded painting of a four-masted ship in full sail hung on one wall, with windows looking out onto Wall Street on the other. Lawrence Weatherby cast a shrewd eye on Mary as she entered.

"I'm Lawrence Weatherby," he said. "I understand you're Mary Flint. Rufus Broadhead was your father."

"Yes, I'm Mary Flint. I want to thank you for seeing me without an appointment."

Weatherby shrugged. "I knew your father. Please have a seat. What can I help you with?"

For ten minutes the story tumbled out of Mary, while the thin-faced Weatherby watched her like a hawk. He heard every word, but more than that, he caught the expressions and the changes that flitted across her face, the timbre and intensity of her voice, the movement of her hands as they worked with her purse, the twitch at the corners of her mouth as she refused to break into tears. Finally she stopped, raised her eyes to his, and waited.

"That's quite a story. Remarkable. I take it you need help in contesting the claim of this man in Liverpool. Alfonso Eddington? Was that it?"

"Yes."

"I'll need to ask you a few questions."

"Ask."

He leaned forward, intense, focused. "You worked long hours with Dr. Purcell, over an extended period. Was there ever anything improper between the two of you?"

Her answer was firm, immediate. "Never!"

"Did he ever give you any indication he intended giving his estate to you?"

"Never."

"Where were you when he died?"

"In the big freight room on the Catherine Street docks where they took all the patients when the Flint mansion burned. The British had been using the mansion for a hospital. I was on the third floor, with pneumonia. The smoke nearly killed both of us when Dr. Purcell came to get me. He saved my life."

"What was the name of the general who found his body?"

"General Hollins. Jarom Hollins."

"You talked with Hollins?"

"Yes. Later. He told me how he had found Dr. Purcell, and he gave me the paper written by the doctor. He also gave me an affidavit Hollins had made and signed that day."

"Do you still have it?"

"Yes. Both documents."

"Where?"

"Packed in my luggage on Catherine Street. I'm leaving on a boat later today." She told him of her plans to get to Morristown.

"Can you get those documents back here before you go?"

"Yes."

Weatherby reached for his pipe, packed it, then struck spark to tinder and lit it. His cheeks hollowed as he drew on it, eyes narrowed in thought, while a cloud of smoke rose to the ceiling and dissipated. He turned back to Mary.

"How long were you in the hospital with pneumonia and smoke asphyxiation after the fire?"

"Thirteen weeks. Until the middle of April."

"Did Purcell ever express anything akin to affection for you?"

"He saw me as a daughter. And I saw him much like a father. Nothing more."

Weatherby drew on his pipe, then laid it on a round pipe holder on his desk and stood. He thrust his hands into his pockets and began to slowly pace, speaking while his mind worked.

"I'll have to tell you this as clearly as I can. This is precisely the wrong time for all this to pop up. Purcell was British. Eddington is British. We're at war with the British. In the middle of all this, we find you, the American woman accused by the British man of using her womanly charms and a forged document to swindle him out of thirty-two thousand English pounds that he swears ought to be his as the only blood kin of the deceased Purcell."

Weatherby paused to study Mary for a moment, gauging how she was receiving his summary. Then he continued pacing.

"You say you have the Purcell document as well as the Hollins affidavit supporting your story. That poses two questions: first, just what does Eddington have to support his claim? And second, even if Eddington has nothing, will that make any difference in a court hearing?"

"Why wouldn't it?"

Weatherby turned to face Mary, his eyes boring into hers. He spoke sharply. "Think! Eddington's British. The thirty-two thousand British pounds in question are from a dead British officer. This will be heard in a British court, by British judges, or a British jury. Perhaps in Britain." He paused and pointed a thin finger at her. "You're an American. A rebel. An enemy of the Crown and all that is British." He reached for his pipe. "Need I say more?"

"I thought courts were to give justice, on facts."

Weatherby shook his head violently. "In theory. But in truth, all too often human weakness tilts the scales. In this case, I am giving you my best professional advice when I tell you, I don't think a British court will ever get to the facts. It will be enough for them when they are told you're an American, trying to wrest a small fortune from a deceased British officer, at the expense of a British subject, who claims forgery and seduction on your part. I apologize for using the word *seduction*, but I must tell you, if it comes to a court hearing, you will hear that word bandied about until you will wish you had never heard of either the doctor or his estate. And I promise you, every newspaper in every major seaport will pounce on it. Your name will become commonplace, and it will be forever connected with the term *seduction.* I am truly sorry, but I would not be serving you well if I did not state all this as plainly as I can. I only hope you understand."

Mary's shoulders sagged, and she lowered her face. Weatherby sat back down, relit his pipe, and drew on it while he waited.

Her words came quietly, with her eyes downcast. "Me. A paid seductress." She shook her head slowly, unable to force her mind to accept the thought. "What shall I do?"

Weatherby sighed. "You had better decide whether fighting for thirty-two thousand English pounds is worth going through the humiliation of being portrayed in newspapers as a seductress and a fraud."

"Must I decide now?"

"Soon."

"Is there no other way?"

Weatherby shrugged. "At this point, no one knows, but you had better presume it will happen, if that helps in your decision."

Suddenly Mary straightened. "You will need money. I no longer have money."

Weatherby leaned back in his chair. "Yes, I will. Quite a bit of it."

"How much?"

"One thousand dollars for my retainer fee, more as the case progresses. And costs."

"How much for costs?"

"Probably fifteen hundred dollars to begin with, more later."

"Two thousand five hundred dollars to begin? I have thirteen English pounds in my purse, and no more. It's out of the question. I should have thought of that first. I'm sorry I took your time."

She stood to go when his voice stopped her. "Go get those two documents and bring them to me."

"Why? I can't pay you."

He tapped the top of his desk with a bony finger. "Bring them here before you go on your trip."

In the late afternoon, Lawrence Weatherby reread the document written by Otis Purcell and laid it on his desk, then picked up the affidavit signed by General Jarom Hollins. For twenty minutes he studied every word with fierce intensity before he laid it back on his desk. He sat in his chair for a time, sucking his cold pipe in deep thought before he rose and walked to open his office door.

"Ellen, would you send a messenger over to the London–New York Bank on Broadway. You know the one. Charles Partridge is the manager. Tell him I'd like to see him sometime tomorrow."

He returned to his desk and eased onto his chair, then turned to gaze out the windows at the long shadows and bright sunlight of a sun setting on Wall Street. In his mind he was seeing Mary Flint on the Catherine Street docks, boarding a small boat for her journey up the Raritan to disembark and board a freight wagon. She would wait, perhaps through the night, for the two wagons that were leaving for Morristown, and she would ride one of them over the rough roads carved through the forests, through canyons that girdled and shielded the small mountain town, in her quest to find the Continental army.

Thirteen pounds in her purse. Almost penniless. Is it enough to pay her fare? Food? What will she do when the money's gone? Is there danger? Soldiers? Highwaymen? Swindlers? Men who would take advantage?

Weatherby broke off the thoughts and ran bony fingers through his hair. He looked at the two documents once more, glanced at the clock on the worktable, and rose from his chair. It was past six o'clock. His day was ended.

As he opened his office door, a thought flickered through his mind. *What about Mary Flint's day? Is it ending, or just beginning?*

Notes

Mary Flint as she appears in this book is a fictional character, as are the events and other persons described in this chapter.

CHAPTER IX

★ ★ ★

*J*ames MacIntosh squinted at the golden glow in the western sky, left by a sun that had set ten minutes earlier. He lowered his eyes to watch the lights of Fort Ticonderoga wink on, four hundred yards east of his ancient, weathered cabin. With the coming of spring, the eighteen inches of dirt on the cabin roof had brought forth the usual stand of grass, flowers, and weeds, and in the twilight it appeared the old, one-room structure was growing hair.

Adrift after his wife died many years before, MacIntosh had built his cabin in the shadow of the fort to live out his years alone in the wilderness. He occasionally worked at the fort for what little money he needed; all else he provided with his own hands, preferring the solitude of his small place to the noise and bother of civilization. He was not aware that sometime in the past he had begun talking to himself.

MacIntosh reached to scratch at his scraggly gray beard before he closed and latched the gate on the ramshackle pen and hutch that held his brood sow and her eight weaner pigs. He paused a moment to watch the little ones rooting headlong at their mother as she lay on her side, head thrown back, eyes closed. A grin crossed his wrinkled face at their grunts and high-pitched squeals as they jostled for position and the muffled sounds of bliss as they drew their life sustenance from her. "If they all make it through the summer," he muttered, "there'll be ham 'n bacon 'n lard 'n sausage for winter, and some to sell to the soldier boys at the fort." His speech had a slight Scottish burr to it.

Average height, longsince retired from the British army, and gray from years in the wilderness, MacIntosh tossed the round, battered pan he used to carry his table scraps to the wooden feed trough, into the old wooden wheelbarrow next to the pen. Years before he had made a deal with the cooks at the enlisted men's mess inside the fort. He would bring his wheelbarrow to their back door, they would toss their wet garbage into it until it was full, and he would wheel it back to his place for pig feed. In return, twice a year, he would deliver to them a gallon jug of chokecherry wine. Over the years the wood in the wheelbarrow had swelled, discolored to a dirty black, and acquired a permanent stench. The wooden wheel had worn slightly lopsided, which caused the heavy, handmade contraption to rise and fall rhythmically when he pushed it.

"Got to fix that wheel one of these days," he mused as he walked past it. He continued on to the weathered shed and pen where he kept his mule and stopped to throw an armful of dried grass into a wooden box. The tired old animal lowered its head, and MacIntosh listened as its teeth began their grinding. He glanced to be sure there was water for the mule in the wooden half-barrel, then continued on the worn path toward his cabin. On the way, he passed the crude garden he and the mule had plowed and he had planted, and slowed to peer at the rows of green sprouts crowding upward through the soil, reaching for sun and water. Carrots, squash, corn, beans, potatoes. "Keep a-comin,'" he mumbled. "Just keep a-comin.'"

He walked on to the door of his cabin, and it opened soundlessly on its leather hinges. Once inside, he lighted a lamp and set it on the table. He was reaching into the kindling box beside the stove when he heard the mule stamping its feet in its pen.

The thought flashed in his mind—*bear*—and he moved quickly to the door, reached above it to jerk his musket from its pegs, pulled the door open, and stopped dead in his tracks, stunned, wide-eyed. Filling the door frame was an apparition that struck terror into the hearts of all who dared challenge the wilderness. A Mohawk warrior faced him, stripped to the waist, hair roached high, face painted vermilion from the hair to below the nose, then black to the throat. A tomahawk dangled on a leather cord from his left wrist, and in his right hand he grasped a bone-handled scalping knife. MacIntosh opened his mouth to speak, and in that instant the Indian was on him. He swatted the musket to the floor, then clutched the front of MacIntosh's coat with his left hand while his right hand flashed upward to hold the tip of the knife against his throat. Without a word the Indian dragged MacIntosh out through the door, onto the dirt path. He released his hold and pointed west, toward the mule and pigpens.

MacIntosh nodded his understanding and began walking, the Indian four feet behind, knife and tomahawk ready. MacIntosh slowed at the mule pen to open the gate and leave it standing. The mule watched with detached disinterest and continued working on the dried grass. At the pigpen, MacIntosh caught the gate and swung it open as he walked past.

In gathering dusk they reached the tree line and were instantly into the gloom of the forest, walking west, then angling right in a circle to the east. MacIntosh did not know when the second Indian came in behind them. He only knew that when he broke clear of the trees on the shores of Lake Champlain, there were two of them, each stripped to the waist, painted for war, and armed. They pointed to a light birch-bark canoe tied in the foliage on the shoreline, MacIntosh stepped in, moved to the center and knelt, waiting. One of the Indians moved past him, then the other one launched the canoe into the black waters before he leaped inside and took his position in the other end. Each leaned a musket against the gunwales, then picked up a paddle, and dug the blade into the water. In the deep shadows, MacIntosh saw the fur-trimmed quivers filled with arrows, and the short, powerful war bows at each end of the canoe. The trim, lightweight watercraft leaped forward, creating a slight hissing sound as the high back-curve of the graceful bow raised a white curl in the gathering darkness.

From long experience, MacIntosh knew they had come to capture him, not kill him. Had they been on a raid, he would already be dead on the floor of his cabin, and his buildings would be smoldering ruins, his animals slaughtered. Having been taken captive, he would remain alive only so long as he remained silent and did what he was told. On the lake, a cough, a whistle, a spoken word would reach for miles, and if he made a sound that could draw pursuit, he would be dead in seconds, his scalp-less body floating face down in the lake while the canoe sped on.

He silently shifted off his knees to sit cross-legged while the two Indians settled into a rhythm, soundlessly dipping their paddles in the glassy, smooth water, driving the canoe with powerful strokes steadily north. The moon rose to cast the lake in silvery shadows and send a shimmering path across the still waters to the canoe. MacIntosh sat quietly, listening to the loons laugh near the shore, the occasional bark of a fox, and the howl of a distant wolf. Sometime in the night he nod-ded off to sleep, to awaken with gray showing in the eastern sky. They sped on, with MacIntosh watching the shore, counting the familiar landmarks.

They passed The Narrows in the gray of dawn, then the Bouquet River, then Split Rock, where the lake widened, from less than two miles across, to more than ten. With the sun directly overhead, they slowed the canoe and turned it toward the eastern shore. Thirty yards from the rocks, the Indian in front strung his bow, nocked an arrow, and rose to a crouching position, studying the dark waters intently. Strangely, MacIntosh noticed the buckskin leggings, fringed, and the beautiful beadwork on his moccasins in the bright sunlight.

A white underbelly flashed beneath the calm surface of the lake, and the Indian instantly drew the arrow to its iron head and released it. It hardly made a ripple as it sliced deep, out of sight. There was a roiling in the water, and a huge brown trout came writhing to the surface, impaled on the arrow. Its struggling slowed, then stopped, and it rolled belly up in the water. The Indian in front reached with his paddle to pull it closer before it could sink, then raised it dripping from the water. He raised it at arm's length toward the heavens, incanted his thanks, then laid it in the bottom of the canoe. He resumed his position in the prow, and once again they settled into their rhythm with the paddles.

They had passed Valcour Island in the middle of the lake, then

Cumberland Head, and were approaching Ile la Motte before they once again turned toward the eastern shore. With the sun setting, they beached the canoe and kindled a small fire. When the sun reached the western skyline, the trout was roasted. The two Indians ate their fill, then pointed, and MacIntosh ate what he wanted. Nearly half the great fish remained, and one Indian wrapped it in green ferns, then laid it on a flat rock, and covered it with another flat rock. With dusk now fully upon them, they spread a blanket, and MacIntosh lay down. They did not tie him, but he knew. He would never be able to sneak away in the night unnoticed, and the penalty for trying would be death.

By the time the sun rose the next morning, they were already gliding north in the canoe, and by midmorning had passed Ile aux Noix. It was only then that MacIntosh understood they were taking him to St. Johns, located twelve miles down the Richelieu River. His eyes narrowed as he searched his memory. Hadn't there been word at Fort Ticonderoga that the British were gathering at St. Johns? Perhaps intending to come south to attack Fort Ti?

The lake narrowed to empty into the Richelieu, and the current picked up. The canoe raced forward, light and easy on the running water. It was not yet noon when MacIntosh saw the first orderly rows of military tents and the bright red and white uniforms of thousands of British soldiers on the east riverbank, and then, flying over the settlement of St. Johns, the British Union Jack, rippling high and bright and proud in the sparkling morning sunlight.

The Indians skillfully brought the canoe to the wharf that extended into the river, with a crowd of their own kind gathering, and half a dozen British soldiers coming in from behind. They climbed onto the dock, waited for MacIntosh, then turned to face the gathering. With their heads high, chins thrust out, scowling in bravado, they made their abrupt, dramatic declaration of their feat in capturing and bringing in a white prisoner from the very gates of Fort Ticonderoga. No matter he was not an American officer, or even an American soldier, but a civilian. Only the bravest and strongest and most skillful could penetrate the enemy's defenses to the center, and return with a prisoner.

Their vanity satisfied, they marched their prize through the throng, faces fierce, looking neither left nor right, into the cluster of buildings that were called St. Johns, stopping before a large, frame home in which General Burgoyne had established his headquarters. Only then did they stop, waiting for a British officer to open the door and step out to face them. Neither Indian spoke English, and the officer spoke no Mohawk. The Indians pointed at MacIntosh, then turned indifferently to walk away, leaving the British officer to do the easy work, after they had done the impossible.

The officer surveyed MacIntosh, dressed in his coarse, threadbare colonial garb, while MacIntosh squinted back at him, dressed in his immaculate crimson tunic, white breeches, black boots, and gold-trimmed tricorn hat.

The officer's nose wrinkled slightly as he spoke. "I am Major Richard Darby, aide to General John Burgoyne," he declared. He gave a head motion to the building behind him. "What, sir, is your name?"

"James MacIntosh."

"From where?"

"Fort Ti."

Darby's eyes widened in surprise. "Military?"

"No. Civilian. Retired from the military years ago."

"Which military?"

"British. Seventy-eighth Foot."

For a moment Darby lost his superior bearing. "You served with the Seventy-eighth?"

"While you were just a pup." The insolence was calculated.

Darby stiffened, and his lip curled. "Come with me. General Burgoyne will want to interrogate you."

MacIntosh shrugged indifferently. Darby turned on his heel and entered the building, MacIntosh following. The anteroom of the home had been the parlor, and the paintings on the walls remained, along with the parlor table and chairs. Darby turned to MacIntosh. "You will remain here for a moment while I announce you to the general." MacIntosh waited while Darby disappeared through an archway and down a short hall. He glanced about the room, remembering the constricting feel of a home and polished hardwood floors and walls with paintings and windows with curtains. He heard a door open and close, then after a moment, open and close again. Boot heels thumped on the floor until Darby reappeared in the archway.

"The general will see you immediately. You will follow me."

You will follow me. Humph. He could have asked, not ordered. A sour look crossed MacIntosh's face as he followed Darby down the hall to a door. As Darby raised his hand to rap, the door behind them opened, and Brigadier General Simon Fraser, a member of Burgoyne's staff, commander of one wing of the Burgoyne army, brilliant, admired, liked, stepped into the hall. Darby instantly clacked his heels together as he came to attention.

Fraser's smile was genuine. "Major, how are you this morning?" He eyed MacIntosh, still smiling.

"Excellent, sir. And yourself?"

"In good health, thank you."

MacIntosh's eyes narrowed in shocked disbelief. His head thrust forward for a moment while he recovered sufficiently to come to full military attention and speak. "Is that you, sir? Colonel Simon Fraser of the Seventy-eighth Foot?"

Fraser looked full into MacIntosh's face while he studied him for a moment. "Yes. I was with the Seventy-eighth Foot."

"Sergeant James MacIntosh, sir. With the Seventy-eighth Foot, under your command for four years. I must say, sir, I'm surprised and very much pleased to see you again."

For a moment Fraser stood silent while he searched his memory. "Sergeant MacIntosh? I believe I do remember a Sergeant MacIntosh. Scotland. Am I correct?"

MacIntosh grinned. "Yes, sir."

Fraser spontaneously thrust out his hand to the old Scot, and MacIntosh reached to grasp it as the two former comrades in arms shook hands warmly. Then Fraser glanced at Darby.

"What is Sergeant MacIntosh doing here?"

Darby cleared his throat. "Sir, he was brought in by the Mohawk for interrogation."

Fraser's eyebrows arched. "A prisoner? Enemy?"

"I don't know, sir. I only know that General Burgoyne issued orders to have someone brought in who is knowledgeable about Fort Ti."

Fraser turned back to MacIntosh. "Are you lately with the American forces at Fort Ti?"

MacIntosh shook his head. "I am lately making it my business to live my own life in peace. My place is near the fort, but I take no sides in the trouble between the Americans and British."

"Would you be willing to answer some questions about Fort Ti?"

MacIntosh shrugged. "Yes, but there's not much to tell."

Fraser turned back to Darby. "May I come with you to see General Burgoyne?"

"Certainly, sir."

Darby rapped on the door, which bore gold, black-edged lettering: *MAJOR GENERAL JOHN BURGOYNE*. It was immediately opened by an eager young lieutenant who snapped to attention, then stepped aside to allow the three men to enter the small waiting room. "I'll inform the general you're here," he said, turned on his heel, and marched to a door to the left of his desk. He rapped, they heard the word "Enter" from inside, and he disappeared inside the room, to reemerge almost immediately.

"The general will see Major Darby."

Darby disappeared through the door to reappear in ten seconds. "The general will see us all."

Fraser led MacIntosh into the moderately-sized room with large French doors in the wall to the left. A colorful mural of a lake filled the wall opposite. A polished desk with delicately styled designs carved into the four legs faced the door. A worktable stood in one corner, covered with folded maps, an inkwell, and quill. As the men entered, General John Burgoyne stood. He wore no wig, but had his dark hair tied neatly behind his head with a black bow. His tailored uniform sparkled. His smile was sincere, and MacIntosh caught the aura of charisma that drew people to the man. It was Gentleman Johnny Burgoyne, the toast of London and Paris, at his best.

"General Fraser," he said warmly as he came from behind his desk, "how good to see you." He did not wait for the reply, but turned to Darby and gestured to MacIntosh. "Is this the man of whom you spoke?"

"It is, sir."

The smile never left Burgoyne's face as he turned shrewd eyes to the Scot. "I trust you were not mistreated by the Indians."

"I was treated well."

"I'm told you are an old acquaintance of General Fraser."

"I served under him in the Seventy-eighth Foot."

Burgoyne shook his head. "Remarkable. After all these years." He turned to Fraser. "Did you remember this soldier?"

"I did, sir."

"Extraordinary! You asked permission to remain while he and I have a talk?"

"I did, sir."

"You're welcome to stay." He turned to Darby. "Thank you, Major, that will be all."

As Darby closed the door, Burgoyne gestured to two upholstered chairs facing his desk. "Be seated, gentlemen."

They sat facing his desk while Burgoyne took a seat in a high-backed, blue velvet upholstered chair. In the back of the chair the golden English lion had been carefully set in tiny needlepoint. Burgoyne sat nonchalantly cocked to one side.

"Mr. MacIntosh, I understand you live near Fort Ticonderoga."

"For many years."

"Ever been inside the fort?"

"Many times. I've worked on it."

"Good. I hope you will not be reluctant to talk about it."

MacIntosh shook his head. "I told General Fraser, I haven't taken sides in the British and American troubles. I choose to live in peace."

Burgoyne thrust a finger upward. "Ah! Excellent. Do you need anything? Coffee? Food?"

"I'm all right."

"May we begin, then?"

"Anytime."

Burgoyne began. He wanted to know, where are the cannon—what is the condition of the abatis outside the fort—the redoubts, blockhouses, and redans—the trenches, breastworks—how many officers—soldiers—artisans—workmen—wagoneers—the number of boats—ships—gondolas—bateaux—their armament—their stock of food—the position of their powder magazines—are they bombproof—how are they protected—where inside the fort are the officers' quarters, enlisted quarters, food stores, musket and cannon stores—outside the fort where is the sawmill—hospital?

The answers MacIntosh gave were freely given and genuine. The fort is a wreck—the abatis stripped of all wood—the redoubts and redans totally inoperable—the trenches without breastworks—the total force at the fort, including working civilians, is under four thousand—morale is nonexistent—the navy has but two galleys with twelve, six-pound cannon each, a gondola with two nine-pound guns, a sloop named *Betsey* with two guns, and seventy bateaux, half of which are unusable because there was no pitch to caulk the hulls—less than eight weeks' food stores.

A rap at the door interrupted, and on invitation, Darby entered. "Do you wish to take lunch in here, sir?"

Startled, Burgoyne looked at the clock on the corner of his desk. "Lunchtime already? Yes. For three."

Darby left, and Burgoyne flashed his charming smile as he spoke. "I lost track of time. I apologize. Stand if you wish." Rising himself, he stretched set muscles, then walked to the windows to peer out at the bright sunshine and the bustle of soldiers and civilians in the streets of St. Johns. He turned back to Fraser and MacIntosh, who had also risen to stretch.

"General, any thoughts on all this?"

"Yes, sir. Do you have a map of the Fort Ticonderoga area?"

"Excellent idea! Of course." He quickly stepped to the worktable, selected a folded map, and returned to his desk. He was unfolding it when Darby rapped again at the door.

"Lunch, sir."

Burgoyne set the map aside as Darby placed a large tray on the desk, excused himself, and left the room. The three men ate hot sliced ham, boiled vegetables, boiled apple slices covered with cinnamon, fresh bread, elderberry wine, and plum pudding. Darby reappeared to remove the tray, Burgoyne spread the map, and they took their places again.

Burgoyne spoke to Fraser. "Was there something on the map you had in mind?"

Fraser studied it for a moment, turned it to lay true to the compass, and pointed at the outline of Fort Ticonderoga on the small peninsula where Lake George joined Lake Champlain. He turned to MacIntosh. "Where is your home?"

MacIntosh located the fort, then moved his finger due west. "There."

"How far from the fort?"

"Maybe four hundred yards."

"What defenses lie between your home and the fort?"

MacIntosh shook his head. "None. Trenches, but no breastworks. No cannon. The Americans think they can defend that stretch with muskets."

Burgoyne leaned forward, eyes narrowed, intense. "There are no cannon covering the approach from the west?"

"None. Not one."

Fraser tapped his finger on Mt. Defiance and continued. "Tell me about this mountain. I've heard things."

MacIntosh raised his eyes from the map. "Sugar Hill?"

"I thought they renamed the mountain a year ago."

"They did. Mount Defiance. I can't get used to it." He moved his finger to the east side of the lake, directly opposite Fort Ticonderoga. They also changed the name of this one, from Rattlesnake Hill to Mount Independence." He shook his head in disgust.

"Did I hear something about getting cannon up onto Mount Defiance?"

"Yes. Last summer. Some engineer—Trumbull, I think—figured cannon on top of Mount Defiance could blow the fort to pieces. Gates didn't agree, but let him shoot from the fort at the mountaintop. The cannonballs nearly made it to the top. I was there—saw it. If someone gets a few heavy guns up there, the fort can probably be taken without an infantry attack."

"Didn't someone take a look to see if guns could be taken up there?"

"Arnold and someone else, maybe Trumbull. They said it can."

"Do you think it can be done?"

"From the back side. It won't be easy, but it can be done."

"You've been there?"

"I've been all over that country."

Burgoyne raised startled eyes to Fraser, but remained silent. Fraser went on.

"When reinforcements arrive at the fort, from which direction do they come?"

MacIntosh pondered for a moment. "Depends. Either through the Grants, here, or Skenesborough, here."

"I see. How many have been coming at any one time?"

"Not enough. Bunches of ten or twenty, mostly. Once in a while maybe a hundred. Never more."

"Do you think, then, the fort is undermanned?"

"Yes. Bad."

"If the Americans were forced into a retreat, which way would they go?"

MacIntosh pursed his lips, then moved his finger on the map. "I think, either through Castle Town, or Skenesborough. Probably Skenesborough."

"Who is in command at the fort now?"

"St. Clair. A general."

Fraser nodded. "I know him. I think he's Scot, too."

"That he is."

Fraser turned to Burgoyne. "I think that's all I have."

Burgoyne straightened. "Mr. MacIntosh, you've been most helpful. I thank you. I'll have Darby find suitable quarters for you for a day or two. Then we'll find a way to get you back to your home." He turned and called, "Darby!"

After the door closed behind Darby and MacIntosh, Fraser turned to Burgoyne. "I believe MacIntosh told the truth. May I recommend we have our cartographers make detailed drawings of everything MacIntosh told us, hold a war council and show it to your staff of officers, then make plans to get down there as soon as possible. St. Clair's a good general. Every day we give him to bring Fort Ti up to readiness will cost us when we make our attack. Get there quick, cut off their supply lines from Castle Town and Skenesborough, hit them where they're weakest, and take the fort while they're still in such a deplorable condition. If you can get cannon on top of Mount Defiance, the engagement should be much reduced."

Burgoyne seized his quill, dipped the tip in the inkwell, and hastily scrawled notes on a piece of paper. "We start today. I'll have Darby get the cartographers over here the minute he's back."

Then Burgoyne sat down in his chair and gestured for Fraser to also sit down. For several seconds Burgoyne stroked his chin in thought while Fraser sat silent, waiting.

"Simon, about these Indians. It's a thorny thing. They're unpredictable and often unreliable, but they're incomparable out there in the forest as eyes and ears, and for mounting bloody, lightning attacks. They strike a particular terror into the hearts of whites, on either side." A cynical smile flitted across Burgoyne's face. "Our men are more afraid of our own Indians than of the Americans." He leaned forward and came to the point. "It strikes me that this element of fear could work to our advantage. I'm thinking of sending a written warning to the Americans on the other side of the lake, telling them that if they do not cooperate with us, we will visit them with our Indians."

Burgoyne paused to consider what he had said, then asked, "What do you think?"

Fraser leaned back in his chair and for a moment stared at the ceiling, lips rounded, blowing air, quickly calculating the words he would use to tell Burgoyne that his flair for high rhetoric and theatrical dramatics could do more harm than good in such a written document. He leveled his gaze at Burgoyne. "The truth?"

"From you? Always."

"There's risk if it's done wrong."

"Risk?"

"These New England Yankees are hardheaded, common sense people, and I don't think they scare very easily. Plain, sensible talk might appeal to them, but I doubt they would be impressed with anything that departs very far from it. Gets too flowery. Maybe it would be better to not call it a warning. Call it an appeal to good sense. Something like that."

Burgoyne picked up his quill and added to his notes. "Simon, as always I am indebted to you. You handled MacIntosh beautifully. I'll remember what you said about how to reach the Americans across the lake."

He stood and hunched his shoulders to relieve tension. "The first of the boats leaves tomorrow for the gathering at Cumberland Head. Some of your command will be with them. Have I taken you away from them too long?"

Fraser spoke as he stood. "No. They have good officers."

"Go back to your command with my thanks. I'll start work on a draft of something for the Americans across the lake." Burgoyne walked him to the door. "If you see Darby, tell him to report to me soon."

Fraser nodded and walked out the front door, squinting into the late afternoon sunshine, struggling with foreboding thoughts. *I failed—I did it wrong—I should have told him to not write a warning to the Americans east of the river—he'll wax too dramatic—too dramatic.*

Inside his office, Burgoyne sat down at his desk and picked up his quill. Deep in thought, he twisted it slowly between his hands, then opened his desk drawer and drew out a leather folder. He opened it on his desk and sorted down through the dozens of pages of meticulous notes he had made as he had pieced his master plan together for the campaign. He paused, then drew out a sheet of paper with his handwriting on both sides, then spoke aloud.

"Ah. Here it is. *Stretch.* That's the word. *Stretch.* I will give *stretch* to my Indians." He repeated it to himself thoughtfully, then smiled. "Good. Very good. That sounds entirely civil, but very subtly conveys the thought. Either they cooperate, or my Indians will descend upon them like a river of fiends."

He laid the leather folder and its precious notes back in the drawer, closed it, and pulled his inkwell and fresh paper into position, eyes glistening with anticipation as he scratched the first lines of the warning that would certainly bring the full cooperation of the Americans across the lake.

Notes

James MacIntosh was taken captive by two Indians, from the shadow of the walls of Fort Ticonderoga where he lived, and transported north to be interrogated by General Burgoyne concerning MacIntosh's knowledge of the fort. While there, by purest coincidence, he recognized General Simon Fraser, who had been his commanding officer when he served as an enlisted man in the Seventy-eighth Regiment of Foot years earlier. MacIntosh knew most of the intimate details of the Fort Ti and also the defenses on Mt. Independence, their condition, and the men and their condition, and gave a full report to General Burgoyne in a four-hour interview. Based on his information, Fraser had a drawing made of the area and urged an immediate siege (see Ketchum, *Saratoga*, pp. 143–44).

CHAPTER X

★ ★ ★

hey got about a minute to show their colors—then the Indian in the rear goes down. The tall man in the fringed buckskin hunting shirt, leather breeches, and moccasins, shifted his weight in the fork of a great, ancient oak tree, and laid the long barrel of his Pennsylvania rifle over a gnarled limb. He brought the muzzle to bear loosely on the Iroquois war canoe, three hundred fifty yards from the west shore of Lake Champlain, less than two miles north of Fort Ticonderoga. Hidden, he peered intently between the tree leaves at the two men, one in the stern, one in the bow. They were kneeling in the fashion of Indians, throwing their weight into each rhythmic stroke of their paddles, driving the light craft south fast enough to leave a wake forty feet behind. The man in front wore nondescript colonial homespun; the one in the rear was dressed in what was clearly an Iroquois buckskin hunting shirt with beadwork on the breast.

Without conscious thought the hidden rifleman began making calculations of distance, canoe speed, and bullet drop. He brought the rifle to his shoulder, laid his cheek against the smooth, worn stock, and began moving the muzzle, tracking the speeding canoe. *Thirty seconds—if they're ours they know to show it, this close to the fort.*

In the canoe, Eli was matching Billy stroke for stroke, Billy digging his paddle in on the left side of the bow, Eli on the right side of the stern, keeping their course in a line parallel with the lake shore. The brilliant early morning sun had risen on a world caught in a hush. The air

187

was dead—not a breath of breeze, not a leaf stirred. By lifelong habit Eli's head was moving slightly from side to side, with every sense reaching to feel what was around him, on the lake, in the forest. In the moment the hidden rifle muzzle on the west bank came to bear on him, the sun from the east caught the gunmetal, and a flash of reflected light blinked in the shadowed branches of the tree. Instantly Eli turned his head to peer, and he called to Billy, voice low, urgent. "Stop. There's something in the trees." Billy lifted his paddle, and the canoe began to slow.

On shore, the hidden rifleman drew back the big hammer clicking on his rifle, refining his bead on the distant figure of Eli as his rifle muzzle continued to swing steadily with the canoe.

Eli caught the movement. "There!" Eli's arm shot up to point. "In that oak tree!" He dropped his paddle and seized his rifle to bring it above his head, arms stretched high, hands spread wide apart, grasping the rifle near each end. He turned broadside to the shore and continued to hold the weapon high, while Billy grasped his musket in a similar fashion and hoisted it above his head.

The canoe slowed, then stopped, then began to drift slowly backward in the current created as the waters from Lake George drained thundering through the Chute into the southern tip of Lake Champlain. The two men continued to hold their weapons high, permitting the canoe to drift.

On shore, the hidden rifleman raised his head from the rifle stock, startled when the Indian in the rear of the canoe suddenly pointed directly at him, then instantly raised his rifle over his head—the universal sign of peace. A second later, the man in the bow of the canoe also had his weapon above his head, and the canoe was slowing to a dead stop in the water. Then it began drifting backward with the current.

Quickly the sentinel eased the rifle hammer forward, drew his rifle back, and waited in silence for any sign, any sound, that other eyes might have seen his movements or heard the click of the cocking of his rifle hammer. There was nothing, and he remained still, silent, watching for a silent shadow slipping through the forest, listening for anything that might betray a Mohawk patrol passing. There was only the quiet buzzing of the insects.

"Keep your musket high," Eli said to Billy. He laid his rifle back in the canoe, took up his paddle, and began stroking again, dragging his paddle for a moment after each third stroke to keep the canoe on course. One mile from the fort they turned to within one hundred yards of the shoreline, and a four-man patrol stepped from the forest into the sunlight on the shore to study them, then wave, and half a mile from the fort another patrol hailed them. Eli brought the canoe into Baldwin's newly finished wharf, jutting into the dark waters. Billy stepped out of the canoe onto the pale, rough-finished split-log planks, tied up the craft, and the two men, weapons held loosely in their right hands, walked toward the dozen men gathering on shore.

A captain met them, eyes narrowed in question as they approached and stopped. Billy saluted and spoke. "Corporal Billy Weems and Private Eli Stroud returning from scout to report to General St. Clair."

The captain eyed them both for a moment, then turned. "I'll take you in. Hand me your weapons."

Crews of men stripped to the waist, digging a trench in the rocky soil, paused to watch them pass, and carpenters working with saws and hammers on the walls of a crumbling abatis raised their heads to look as the knot of men walked through the heavy gates into the parade ground of the fort. They stopped before the door into St. Clair's office, the picket nodded, the captain knocked, and Major Isaac Dunn opened the door.

"Captain Arnold Telford, sir. These two men docked in an Iroquois war canoe and claim to be scouts coming back to report to General St. Clair."

Looking past Telford at Eli and Billy, a look of relief crossed Dunn's face. "Thank you, Captain. I recognize them. Return their weapons and let them pass." Billy and Eli followed Dunn into the office, feeling confined in the smallness of the room after spending thirteen days with the heavens for a ceiling and the endless wilderness for walls.

Dunn spoke. "The general's with Colonel Baldwin right now,

inspecting progress on the northeast blockhouse. Should be back momentarily. Stand your weapons in the corner and take a seat." In the poor light from the two small windows on either side of the door, he watched them put their weapons in the corner, then lay the two telescopes on the general's desk. It was then he noticed three slender sticks thrust through Eli's weapon belt. Puzzled, he asked, "What are the sticks?"

Eli glanced down, then spoke. "Didn't have a pencil or paper. Kept the count on the sticks."

"Count of what?"

"Their troops, cannon, horses."

Dunn passed it off. "Are you both all right? Any trouble?"

Eli shook his head while Billy answered, "No real trouble."

"What do you mean, *real* trouble?"

"They had patrols and scouts out everywhere up there. We had to stay hidden. Ran into one patrol near Valcour Island. They left."

"What are you not telling me?" Dunn pressed.

"We had trouble with two Indians in that patrol. It was them or us. We hid the bodies."

Dunn studied the look in Billy's eyes as he spoke and read the sense of regret that they had to kill two more men. He saw in the young man's face the sadness, the anger, that people were unable to rise above the horrors of war to settle their differences. For a moment Dunn stared at the floor in somber reflection.

Boots sounded on the board walkway in front of the building, and the door opened. A shaft of sunlight flooded the room as General Arthur St. Clair strode in, removing his hat, eyes opened wide in the shadowy room, seeing only silhouettes for a moment.

Billy and Eli stood as Dunn came to attention. "Sir, scouts Weems and Stroud have returned."

St. Clair stopped for a moment, then hung his hat on its peg. "Glad you're back alive. I was getting worried. Are you all right?" He walked to his side of the scarred old desk.

"Yes, sir," Billy said.

"Good. Be seated. Do you need anything? Food? Medicine? Rest?"

"No, sir. We're fine."

"Any reason I can't take your verbal report now?"

"None, sir."

"Major Dunn, stay with us." He turned to face Billy. "All right. First things first. General Schuyler got my report, and eight days ago he came up from Albany for an inspection. He was appalled. He held an officers' council and left. I don't know what he intends to do, but now he knows what we're facing."

He paused for a moment, and his demeanor sharpened. "Let's move on to the critical question. Are the British gathering a major force up there?"

"Yes, sir."

"Where?"

"Many of them gathered at St. Johns, then moved on down to Cumberland Bay to meet more. The entire force sailed out of Cumberland Bay in the morning, two days ago, coming south."

"How many total?"

Billy turned to Eli, who drew one of the wooden sticks from his belt, followed by his knife. On the stick were a series of consecutive notches. Eli ran his knife blade down the notches, counting the clicks. There were ten, and Eli answered.

"Counting British, Germans, Indians, Canadians, camp followers, close to ten thousand."

St. Clair reared up in his chair. "Ten thousand! How many British regulars and Germans?"

Eli turned the stick to fresh notches and again ran his knife blade down the stick. There were four clicks, followed by three more, then one. "About four thousand British, and three thousand, one hundred Germans."

"Over seven thousand troops?"

"Yes."

"How do you know?"

"Counted them."

"From where? How close?"

"From the top of a tree about two hundred yards from their camp, with the telescopes." He pointed at the desk where the two borrowed telescopes lay in their scarred, stiff leather cases.

St. Clair's jaw dropped for a moment in astonishment. "You were that close? Right in among them?"

"Yes."

"How? One of our best scouts, Sergeant Heath from Whitcomb's Rangers—the Long Hunters—reported that Indians are so thick in the woods up there they can't get within six miles of the main camp. If he couldn't get in, how did you?"

Billy turned to Eli, who answered. "Waited for a rainy night. Came in through one of the horse herds. The horses and rain took care of our tracks. Not many think to look up eighty feet at the tops of the trees without a reason."

"How did you get out?"

"Stayed in the tree all day, counting. About two the next morning, we went out in the dark through the same horse herd. Stopped only long enough to stampede 'em."

"Stampede them? How?"

Billy answered. "When we were right in among them, Eli started barking like a fox. The pickets thought it was real. Scattered the horses all through camp. They spent the rest of the night gathering them. When they finished, no one was thinking about looking for our tracks, and if they had, I doubt they could have found them after the horses and half their camp had run over them."

"How many horses do they have?"

Eli drew out the next stick and once more ran his knife blade downward, counting the clicks. "About fifteen hundred."

"Oxen?"

More clicks. "Eight hundred."

St. Clair exclaimed, "What! Twenty-three hundred draft animals? How many wagons and carts?"

Eli drew the last stick and counted the clicks. "Thirteen hundred."

St. Clair was incredulous. "Is Burgoyne insane? Trying to move thirteen hundred wagons through this wilderness?"

Eli remained calm. "Looks that way."

St. Clair brought his racing thoughts under control and asked the single question that weighed heaviest. "How many cannon?"

Eli turned the stick and ran his knife blade one more time, counting. "One hundred thirty-eight."

Silence gripped the room for a full five seconds while St. Clair's mind reeled and Dunn sat transfixed. St. Clair licked dry lips and asked, "You're sure? You counted?"

Billy answered. "We both counted. Twice. One hundred thirty-eight."

"What size?"

Billy answered. "A lot of big ones I estimate to be twenty-four-pounders. From there on down to some mortars, maybe four or six inchers."

St. Clair clasped his hands on his desktop and studied them for a time, then spoke quietly, as though to himself. "Enough guns to put us under siege." He raised his eyes. "You say you saw this army moving south? They're coming here?"

Billy nodded. "Yes, sir. We tracked them from St. Johns on down to Cumberland Bay. You should have seen it. Like something out of a storybook. They sailed out of the bay and turned south in the early morning, the Green Mountains to the east, the Adirondacks to the west, all in shadows. About twenty Indian war canoes led, with as many as forty warriors each, all painted and feathered and dressed for war. Behind came heavier ships and boats, then bateaux, all filled with British in red and white and Germans in blue, sails up, the Union Jack and regimental flags flying—I never saw anything like it."

St. Clair shook his head. "John Burgoyne. Had to stage it like a great drama in a London theater. When did you last see them?"

"Two days ago when they sailed. We got ahead of them and came here as fast as we could."

"Any idea how close they are?"

"No. Would you like us to go back up and find out?"

St. Clair set his jaw and shook his head. "No. I have heavier work than that for you. But first, is there anything else you have to report?"

Eli answered. "Yes. I'm sure I saw St. Luc and Langlade in their camp up there. Know who they are?"

"By reputation only."

"Two of the bloodiest cutthroats in the northeast. Things could get bad if they lead those Indians on a few raids down here."

"Anything else?"

Billy pulled a folded sheet of paper from his shirt. "General Burgoyne had a lot of these handed out to the Americans on the east side of the lake. Might want to read it."

St. Clair's face clouded in puzzlement as he took the crumpled paper, smoothed it on his desk, and read it. His eyes began to widen as he went on.

"A PROCLAMATION to the harden'd Enemies of Great Britain. We offer open arms, restoration of their rights, and security to loyal subjects of the king, however, to those harden'd criminals who have inflicted grievous and arbitrary imprisonment upon the loyalists, confiscation of their property, persecution, and unspeakable tortures, we give solemn warning. To consummate these shocking proceedings, the profanation of Religion is added to the most profligate prostitution of common reason, the consciences of Men are set at naught, and multitudes are compelled not only to bear Arms, but also to swear subjection to an usurpation they abhor. In consciousness of Christianity, my Royal Master's clemency, and the honor of Soldiership, I have but to give stretch to the Indian Forces under my direction, and they amount to Thousands, and the king's enemies could then expect to meet the messengers of justice and of wrath, devastation, famine, and every concommitant horror. Signed, Major General John Burgoyne."

In silence St. Clair lowered the paper, struggling to believe a British major general of the stature of John Burgoyne had drafted such a thing. Playwright or not, theatrically talented or not, writing the costly and complex *The Maid of the Oaks* play for his nephew's London wedding, or the well-received farce *Blockade of Boston,* ridiculing the American rebels was one thing. Writing the sophisticated, lofty language in the proclamation before him, with the bald-faced threat of turning his Indians loose to wreak "wrath, devastation, famine and every concommitant horror" on the tough, no-nonsense American Yankees across the lake, was altogether another.

He spoke quietly to Billy. "Where did you get this?"

"From a settler east of the lake."

"What did he think of it?"

"The same as most of the others who got it. Anger at the British. He was ready to fight."

St. Clair shook his head. "I think Burgoyne's made a mistake. Maybe a bad one. Time will tell."

Eli broke in. "Was there something else you wanted us to do?"

St. Clair drew in a great draught of air and exhaled it slowly, foreboding surrounding him like a pall. "Yes. I put it to you not as an order, but as a request. If you go, it will be as volunteers."

Billy settled back in his chair. *Volunteers! He doubts we'll return.* Billy said nothing and waited in silence.

St. Clair addressed Eli. "I'll have to give you some background. You mentioned seeing St. Luc and Langlade. I think they're up here because Burgoyne's Indians have been coming closer to the fort every day. Nine days ago, two of our men named Whiting and Batty left the fort to go to the sawmill. We found them killed and scalped and mutilated by Indians within sight of the fort. Since then the woods to the north have been so full of Indians close to the fort that we've stopped sending out small parties. We've got three of Whitcomb's best rangers out right now, two days overdue. I have a premonition that St. Luc or Langlade's Indians got them. It confirms what you said about them."

He paused to order his thoughts. "You recall the two men you brought in just before you left? Amsbury and Adams?"

Both Billy and Eli nodded.

A hard, flat look came into St. Clair's eyes. "You knew I sent them on down to General Schuyler in Albany for full interrogation. He sent me a detailed message by special messenger."

St. Clair slowed, and a sense of tension came creeping.

"They found a note on Amsbury written by one of Burgoyne's brigade majors declaring Amsbury was on secret service for Burgoyne and stating he was not to be searched or interfered with. His canteen had a false bottom, and in it was a letter written by a New Hampshire Tory named Peter Livius, who is right now the Chief Justice of the Canadian courts. The letter was for General John Sullivan, begging Sullivan to recant his loyalty to the American cause and exert himself for king and crown."

Billy gaped. "John Sullivan? You mean *our* General John Sullivan, the one who had a command at Trenton and Princeton?"

"Yes. Our General John Sullivan."

Billy slowly shook his head as St. Clair continued.

"Amsbury told us that Sir John Johnson was leading a command of Iroquois Indians from Oswego to meet Burgoyne at Albany. Remember? What he didn't tell us, but did tell Schuyler, was that the regulars and Germans are led by British Lieutenant Colonel Barry St. Leger, and that the Indians are being led by Joseph Brant. St. Leger has about two hundred British regulars, one hundred Hesse-Hanau mercenaries, some Canadians, and loyalists. Brant has nearly a thousand Indians. About two thousand troops, all told."

St. Clair paused to watch the blank expression come into the faces of both Billy and Eli before he continued. His voice was soft, acrid. "And he didn't tell us that St. Leger and Brant are under orders to wipe out Fort Stanwix on the way."

Billy sucked air sharply. Eli started, straightened on his chair, and then leaned back, wide-eyed. *There it is. Brant's going to close off the western side of the lakes.*

St. Clair plowed on. "Amsbury also said Burgoyne had ordered hundreds of new carts and all the horses he could get to move his army down the west side of the lake. He intends cutting off our communications with just about everybody, isolate us, and take the fort with his cannon. He has about eight thousand troops to our four thousand. The report you made today confirms it all. Then he's moving on down to Albany to meet General William Howe coming from the east—New York—and St. Leger and Brant coming from the west. Those three combined forces intend cutting off all the New England states and taking them one at a time."

For a few seconds the only sound in the room was the spring flies buzzing at the windows. St. Clair continued, "Congress and most of the country believe this fort is the key to the western defense. What they've never been told is that if the British get their big guns up on top of Mount Defiance, this fort and most of the men in it will be gone in less than two days."

He paused, and his eyes took on a flinty look. "Fate has given me the choice of two ways to destroy myself: sacrifice four thousand men to hold a fort that cannot be held, and enter history as a butcher; or, abandon Fort Ti, and enter history as a coward."

He looked down, and Billy and Eli saw the man writhing within as he contemplated the terrible choice. "I can only hope that decision never has to be made."

For a time the four men sat in silence, struggling to grasp the enormity of what was happening, hating the white heat of the decision St. Clair might have to make. Billy broke the silence.

"Do your men know what's coming down on them?"

"Pretty much."

"What's their attitude?"

Deep sadness filled St. Clair's face. "They're mostly young, raw, barefoot, green militia who still think this is a great adventure. They're anticipating a great battle in which they will hold the fort and live to tell their grandchildren."

Eli leaned forward to interrupt. "What's your plan? Is there something you have for us to do?"

St. Clair nodded. "The best plan I can conceive is to try to stop St. Leger and Brant before they come in from the west, and hope that General Howe doesn't come in from the east. I know Howe believes taking Philadelphia is critical to ending the war. If we can stop Brant, and if Howe decides to take Philadelphia this season, or if General Washington can engage him and hold him in New York, or around Philadelphia, there's a chance we can draw Burgoyne into pursuing us as we move south. If he does follow us, our knowledge of the terrain, and of the people, might be enough to slow him down. Maybe force him to return to this fort."

Eli responded. "A lot of 'ifs,' but it sounds like the best you can do. I gather you want us to go west to try to slow down Brant and his Mohawk."

St. Clair swung his face directly to Eli's, and his response was curt, direct. "Yes."

"Who's in command at Stanwix?" Eli asked.

"Stanwix is now called Fort Schuyler, but I know it as Stanwix and will call it that. You've seen it?"

"Many times. The last time it was a wreck."

"Colonel Peter Gansevoort is in command. Dutch. Good officer. He has five hundred fifty of his own New York continentals. They've been doing everything they can to bring the fort to fighting condition."

"Five hundred fifty men inside the fort, against two thousand? And one thousand of those are Indians?" Eli pursed his mouth for a moment, making calculations. "At best, that will be a close thing."

St. Clair delayed responding for ten full seconds before he put the question directly to Eli. "The question is, is there any way you can slow down or stop Brant and St. Leger?"

Eli shrugged. "Maybe. Won't know 'til we get there."

St. Clair caught it. "You're volunteering?"

Eli looked at Billy, and Billy gave him the slightest nod.

"Looks that way."

"When will you leave?"

"Tonight."

"What will you need?"

"A little sleep. A bath. Food. Some clothes for Billy. Gunpowder.

Ammunition. I'll also need the seashells you were going to get, and I'll need an artisan to make a small handloom."

"Handloom?"

"To weave a wampum belt. I'll show them how to make the loom. I'll weave the belt."

"The shells are ready. Do you need string for the loom?"

"No, it has to be gut to be right. Can't chance Brant taking insult from string. I have some gut with my things."

"I leave it to you. What's your line of travel?"

"Do you have a map?"

St. Clair quickly unfolded a map and spread it on his desk. Billy and Eli came to it, and Eli traced with his finger as he spoke.

"Down Lake George in the canoe, portage the twelve miles on south to the Hudson River, south on the Hudson to where the Mohawk River comes in, and west on the Mohawk River to Fort Stanwix."

For the first time, St. Clair turned to Dunn, who had sat totally absorbed through the entire meeting. "Major, go with these men. Get them anything they want. Bath, clothes, food, ammunition. Find a good carpenter for them, and get the basket of shells you had drilled for them. Also provide them a quiet place to sleep."

The three walked out squinting into the bright June sunlight, and Dunn turned to Billy. "Where do you want to start?"

Eli glanced at Billy, who spoke. "Sleep. We were in the canoe since yesterday morning."

Dunn turned toward the enlisted men's barracks, and Eli spoke. "Could you bring a carpenter over? I'll show him about the loom and maybe he can make it while we sleep."

In early twilight, Eli sat hunched over a small table beneath a window in the corner of the enlisted men's barracks, a section of board in front of him on the tabletop. On one corner of the table were the clean, dried intestines of the deer he had shot to feed and heal Billy after the combat far to the south. He had honed his knife on a whetstone, and was now carefully slicing the lengths of intestines into long, very thin strips. Billy sat on the other side of the table, carefully selecting seashells of the same color from the basket and threading the strip of intestine through the hole.

Eli glanced at him. "About a foot long. I'll need ten. Two have to have mixed colors. The others, all one color."

With daylight fading, they lighted a lamp and worked on. They had slept five hours, bathed in a wooden tub with hot water, shaved their two-week beards, gotten their supplies, new clothes for Billy, and had mess with the enlisted men.

Patiently Eli began stringing shells on a strip of gut. Carefully he tied a loose knot six inches from the end, then began the selecting of shells, considering their shape and color. He threaded them on, loosely, until the shells were more than twice the length of the loom. Then he untied the knot, took one wrap around the headless tack in the upper left corner of the loom, brought the string down to the other end, caught it on the first tack in the lower left corner, brought the string to the next tack to the right, caught it, and brought the string back up to loop it around the second tack in the upper arm of the rectangular loom. He worked on, threading, adding string after string loosely on the loom, while Billy continued threading shells.

One hour became two as the pattern of colors appeared on Eli's work. With the loom filled, Eli began working strips of gut from side to side, over, under, over, under, until all strings were laced together and could not separate. Finally he began to tighten all the strings, round and round the loom, pulling them a little tighter each round, until the strings were all locked tightly into place. Then he tied them all off, one at a time. Finished, he cut the wampum belt from the loom and trimmed the excess gut with his knife.

He had not been aware that half a dozen enlisted men had silently gathered, fascinated as the wampum belt took form and substance before their eyes. They murmured in admiration, and Eli turned to look at them in surprise while they pointed and commented.

Eli raised his hands to shake his cramped fingers for a moment, then reached for the first of the ten strings Billy had finished and laid at the head of the table. Five minutes later he raised the finished wampum belt. Fifteen inches long, eight inches wide, with five strings of shells dangling from each end. He held it up for Billy to see.

The design in the belt was clear—a circle in the center, formed by light-colored shells, with light lines radiating outward, surrounded by shells of other colors. On each end, the strings of mixed colors were in the center, with two strings of all light-colored shells on either side. For a moment the two of them admired their work before Eli laid it on the table.

Billy asked, "Is there meaning to the design?"

"If that old Indian was right a long time ago, Washington will become the father of a great nation. The sun represents that nation—the United States."

He fell silent, and for a moment a strange, sure feeling stole over both men as they stared at the belt. Neither spoke of it, and it began to fade, and was gone.

Eli broke the spell. "Anything else we need to do before we leave?"

Billy reflected. "I'd like to take a few minutes to write a letter."

Ten minutes later Billy folded the letter, wrapped it carefully in the oilskin with the others, and slipped it into his bullet pouch. He turned to Eli. "I'm ready when you are."

Eli was sitting on a chair, hunched over the small, battered, leather-bound Bible he carried in his pouch. "That letter to the Boston girl? Brigitte?"

"Yes."

Eli laid his open Bible down to carefully wrap the wampum belt in oilskin, then work it into his pouch. While he worked, Billy reached for the Bible, suddenly intensely interested in what Eli would be reading just before leaving on an assignment from which St. Clair thought they might not return. Eli turned to reach for the Bible, unaware Billy had lifted it.

Billy handed the book to him, eyebrows raised in question. "Joshua? The battle of Jericho?"

Eli nodded as he slipped the small book back into its place in his pouch.

Billy watched him, deep in thought. "The shouts and trumpets brought down the walls?"

Eli didn't answer, waiting.

Billy continued quietly. "Trumpets, or the Almighty?"

Eli answered. "They were doing His work, not theirs. I think it was Him." For a moment the two men stood thus, and in that moment a quiet assurance rose in the heart of each of them.

Billy reached for his bedroll. "Let's go."

Notes

Unless otherwise indicated, the facts herein set forth are from Ketchum, *Saratoga*, on the pages indicated.

Billy and Eli are fictional, however, the facts reported by them to General St. Clair are historical. The British did set sail out of Cumberland Bay as described herein, moving south on Lake Champlain, cradled between the Adirondack Mountains on one side and the Green Mountains on the other. The colorful Indian war canoes came first, and the other regiments and soldiers in the sequence set forth. It made a most interesting, exciting spectacle (p. 140–41).

The PROCLAMATION appearing in this chapter, drafted by General Burgoyne, by which he intended frightening the Americans into submission, is nearly a verbatim reproduction of the language he actually used. Rather than frightening the Americans, it raised in them resentment and anger (pp. 142). General Burgoyne did write theatrical productions for the London stage, two of which were *The Maid of the Oaks*, for his nephew's wedding, and a farce titled *The Siege of Boston*. His PROCLAMATION was far too theatrical for its intended purpose. As a result of the document, most Americans drove their livestock away to avoid the British taking it (pp. 145–46).

Lieutenant Colonel Barry St. Leger was assigned to lead a force west to Oswego, then back east to capture Fort Stanwix from its American commander, Colonel Peter Gansevoort, then proceed on east through the Mohawk Valley to arrive at Albany and join generals Burgoyne and Howe (pp. 102–3).

John Whiting and John Batty were American tent mates, who walked out of camp about mid-June, were attacked by Indians less than one mile from Fort Ti, shot, stabbed, and scalped (p. 157).

In general support, see Leckie, *George Washington's War*, pp. 375–80.

CHAPTER XI

★ ★ ★

*A*ncient and dark, shrouded in legends and tales of monsters and apparitions, and of the brave men and the cowards who had gone before, and of their spirits that lingered to drift and whisper in the shadows of the great primeval forest, the mysterious Adirondack Mountains rose from the banks of the mighty Hudson River and Lake Champlain westward, piled tier upon purple tier, beyond the horizon.

The red men who came seeking, found sanctuary in the valleys of the rolling mountains. A thousand unnamed streams, winding through the jumbled hills, worked their way to rivers, forming the mighty waterways that drained north and south, teeming with fish. The rich soil sustained thick forests filled with boundless wildlife, great and small. Birds of every description flitted beneath an overhead canopy, so thick it blocked the sun.

With men came war. Hate, fear, territory, wealth, prejudice, jealousy, wrongs imagined, wrongs real—the causes were those that have divided men from the dawn of creation. It was only a matter of time until the Adirondacks rang with the warbling battle cry of warriors from one village, intent on spilling the blood of those from another.

And with war came those few men who abhorred the evil and the devastation. They rose from among their people, and they met, and they sought and found common ground. Slowly they led their people to the council fires where they sat in peace, talking, seeking. In time they reached an accord, and he who was chief among them, Deganawida, with Hiawatha, wrote it, and the leaders of all tribes at the council fire signed it.

"I, Deganawida, and the union lords now uproot the tallest pine tree and into the cavity thereby made we cast all weapons of war. Into the depths of the earth, down into the deep underneath currents of water flowing to unknown regions, we cast all the weapons of strife. We bury them from sight, and we plant again the tree. Thus shall the Great Peace, Kayenarhekowa, be established."

It was done. The five nations had buried the hatchet beneath the pine tree, in waters that would carry it far away, and had bound themselves together in the mighty Iroquois confederation, sworn to stand united forever in peace, and to defend the confederation from all who would seek to divide or destroy. The eternal council fire of peace was lighted at the village of Onondaga, their capitol.

With the union of the five nations came the need to organize, define, delineate. To set boundaries, they turned to the mountains and valleys, the rivers and forests, which for them were the source of all things in their lives—their schoolmaster, provider of food, clothing, dwellings, religion, ceremonies—their all.

Far to the east were the two long lakes, Champlain and George. Below was the mighty Hudson River, flowing south. To the west and parallel to the Hudson, were other rivers—the Schoharie, the Delaware, and the Susquehanna. Also the Unadilla, the Chenango, and much further west, the Seneca, with the four Finger Lakes, Cayuga, Owasco, Onondaga, and Skaneateles, draining into it, thence further west into the Oswego River that emptied into the great lake, Ontario.

Flowing from the west to empty into the Hudson, just above Albany, was the Mohawk River, the northernmost boundary of the Iroquois territories. The southernmost portions of the Susquehanna, and the headwaters of the Delaware, marked the southern boundaries of their domain.

By common consent the tribes each occupied their own lands. The Mohawk dwelt to the north of the Mohawk River, reaching east to the

Hudson. They were the eyes and ears of the Confederation, watching for invaders from the north and east. The Oneida were further west, on the lands bordered by the Chenango River on the east and by Lake Oneida and the Oswego River on the north. Farther west, the Onondaga lands were bordered by Onondaga Lake on the east, Lake Ontario on the north, and Owasco Lake on the west. To the Onondaga were trusted the sacred wampum belts—more than two thousand in number—that held the record of the nations spanning hundreds of years. The Cayuga were furthest west, bordered by Lake Cayuga and the Seneca River. The Tuscarora, not a signatory to the constitution of the Confederacy, were south, near the junction of the Unadilla and Susquehanna rivers.

The five nations, along with the Tuscarora, thrived. Each welcomed the other into their own territory with food and lodging. They joined together in times of trouble for their common defense; for outsiders, to war with one was to war with them all. In times of need or famine, they shared. Strangers were made welcome, fed, clothed, and sent on their way. Soon none dared confront the mighty Iroquois confederation.

Then came men with white skins—French from the north, English from the east—who brought government and religion, which were strange and incomprehensible to the red men. The white men were not prepared to survive in the forest, and the religion and the treaty between the five nations required the red men to save them, nurture them, teach them. Slowly the white men learned, and they flourished, and they brought to the red men new and wonderful things from their society—iron traps, axes and hatchets, gunpowder, muskets that could kill far, glass trinkets, woven cloth, sugar, and rum, which made the red men into fools. And they brought new and dreaded diseases that killed entire villages. The white settlements grew, and more came, and then they poured, as numerous as locusts, into the territories of the Great Confederation.

The five nations inquired and learned that the white men did not intend to return to their homeland beyond the sea. Rather, they challenged the five nations for their territory. The Iroquois took up the hatchet against them to drive them out, only to discover they could not sustain war against the weapons and the numbers of the white men. The red men had unwittingly become dependent on the muskets, gunpowder, iron axes and hatches, traps, sugar, cloth, trinkets, and the rum. Their trusting innocence had led them into a fatal trap.

In the midst of their sporadic attacks on the white men, the French and the English went to war for control of the entire northeast section of the continent, south of the great St. Lawrence River, far to the north. Confused, frightened, fragmented in how to face the deadly threat, most of the five nations took up the hatchet once again to defend what was theirs—the Huron, far to the north, fighting for the French, the Iroquois nations for the British. The British prevailed, and the French abandoned their claims, to disappear back to their homelands. Peace returned for a time to the lands of the Iroquois confederation.

Then, to the utter confusion of the Iroquois, rebellion divided the British. A faction calling themselves Americans rose against their mother country, demanding independence and freedom. With which side should the Iroquois cast their lot? The British, who came from far across the sea, or with the Americans, who lived among them and traded with them? There was but one solution: declare neutrality. Let the British and their rebellious children settle their family differences, after which the Iroquois could once again resume their peaceful stance. The Iroquois confederation agreed. Remain neutral. Do not take up the hatchet for, or against, either side.

The clouds of war gathered, and the storm finally burst between the red-coated British soldiers and the Americans, at places called Lexington and Concord, far to the east. Cannon and muskets were going to decide the outcome of the conflict.

From the five nations came a few rare men with a vision: survival of the Iroquois confederation depended on peaceful coexistence with the whites. Perhaps the greatest among those few men was Thayendangea, who dedicated himself to finding a way to save his people. He proved his selfless bravery and courage in battle as a boy, then mastered all five dialects of the five nations, then the English language, and the French. He studied the Jesuit Bible, graduated from a white school in Connecticut, and was baptized under the Christian name Joseph Brant.

He sought and courted the friendship of William Johnson and others who were faithful to England, then other white leaders in his own territory, always watching, listening, studying, learning the new and strange thoughts of the whites. He rose steadily in the councils of his people and then became recognized as a leader by the whites.

To solidify his leadership among the Iroquois, Brant, with the British Superintendent of Indian Affairs, Sir Guy Johnson, and a Mohawk companion, John Hill Oteronyente, sailed the great waters to England, where he was courted by King George III. Amid great fanfare he was introduced to the high and powerful in the English government and society. He held council with Lord George Germain, where he was assured the British would resolve his complaints against the Americans, who were encroaching on the territory of the Iroquois confederation, as soon as the troublesome American rebellion was put down. And when Germain told him the Mohawk nation was capable of being a great ally to the British in quelling the Americans, Brant committed to lend all assistance possible.

He was initiated into the Falcon Lodge of the Freemasons and interviewed by reporters of the great newspapers. Much was said when the king presented him with a gift of a silver, engraved gorget, or throat collar, a token of the bonds and promises existing between the two peoples—English and Mohawk.

Bedecked with laurels and finery, Brant returned to America in the summer of 1776, the most famous and honored red man on the continent. He found the British and Americans locked in war, their opposing forces gathering around New York for the battle each side thought would be decisive. Either the Americans would win their freedom, or the British would subdue and reclaim them.

Brant sought out General William Howe and offered his services. It was his Mohawk warriors who led the night march of ten thousand British regulars eastward on Long Island, then north through the Jamaica Pass, then back to the west to come in behind George Washington's Continental army, inflicting a catastrophic defeat upon the Americans that left them trapped in Brooklyn with their backs against the East

River. Only the unbelievable skill and bravery of Colonel John Glover and his Marblehead fishermen in transporting the American survivors across the river to Manhattan Island, in one night, and a providential fog that covered them in the early hours of the morning, saved the shattered remains of the American rebellion.

Impatient, anxious to quickly end the war, certain in his heart the British would conquer the rebellious Americans, Brant again sought out General Howe, as well as Sir Guy Johnson, to propose a plan. He volunteered to go north through the American lines, then east into the heart of the Five Nations country to rally his Mohawk brothers and others of the Iroquois confederation to take up the hatchet against the rebels. Howe reluctantly agreed, Colonel Johnson advised him to make a wampum belt to dignify the mission, and Captain Gilbert Tice volunteered to go with Brant. Disguised, moving at night, hiding during the day, they moved north up Manhattan Island, crossed to the New Jersey mainland near King's Bridge, and veered left into the Catskill and then the Adirondack Mountains.

Brant made his wampum belt, and sent messengers ahead to proclaim his coming. The Great Joseph Brant is coming with a wampum belt! He has counseled with the good and kindly Father across the great waters and received honors and gifts and laurels! He now returns to share with you his knowledge and wisdom. Come. Gather to hear him.

Dressed in his British finery, with a silver chain holding the heavy silver gorget inscribed by King George III about his throat, he struck awe into those who came. He stopped at the Onoquaga village in an elbow of the Susquehanna River and gave a great oration to the Oneida, Tuscarora, Mohawk, and Mohicans gathered there. "I am sent by the Great Father in England, and by his General William Howe and Colonel Johnson. The rebellious Americans are threatening their Father in England, and they are threatening you, your villages, your families, all you hold sacred from your ancestors. Rise. Unite. Join the Great Father in bringing his rebellious children, the Americans, into subjection, and we will once again live in peace under the Great Iroquois Constitution and Confederation."

The sachems—the medicine men and spiritual leaders in the village—reminded the people of their pledge to take neither side. Let the Great Father bring his own children back into his fold. But so powerful was Brant in appearance and speech that some of the Iroquois broke from the time-honored rule of following their spiritual leaders, the sachems, and chose to follow instead a warrior, Brant. He continued to the west branch of the Susquehanna and gathered the Delawares, then proceeded on north to the Seneca village of Chenussio to persuade those gathered there.

With winter upon them, he made snowshoes and continued on to the large village at Niagara. There he met and reported his orders from General William Howe and his journey since leaving New York to a distrustful and antagonistic Major John Butler, then continued on to deliver his message to the smaller villages as he made his way to the great village of Onondaga. There, he spoke to large gatherings. His message always the same: the Americans are threatening not only their Great Father over the waters, but they are threatening the Iroquois confederation. Arise. Assist the great and good Father in restoring peace.

He left his wampum belt with the Onondaga sachems to become part of the great collection of Iroquois history. Then, with spring in the air, he sent word to the four great leaders of the Tuscarora and Oneidas: I am coming to the village of Ganaghsaraga, west of the headwaters of the Chenango River. Meet me there.

He received word back. No, they preferred not to come. If Brant had a message for them, let him come to them to deliver it. Then, with the days growing longer and the buds swelling in the trees, they recanted, and came to meet with him.

He appeared before them in all his splendid finery, with the sun reflecting off the king's large, silver gorget about his neck. He reached deep inside to deliver his message with power. They listened, then met in their own council, and returned to him. No, they would not take up the hatchet against the Americans. They had long ago given their pledge to remain neutral, and they intended honoring it. If the Great Father was as powerful as Brant had claimed, he did not need help from the Iroquois confederation to discipline his disobedient children. Brant moved on, stopping in the villages of the Cayugas to gather support for the British cause.

Word of Brant's journey through the heart of the Iroquois confederation, and of his stirring the warriors against the Americans, spread rapidly through the mountains and valleys by that mystical process known only to the Indians. It was whispered in Albany and heard by General Philip Schuyler, recently commissioned commander of the American northern army, who had a long history of living in the wilderness.

Schuyler had no illusions. To have a man of the heroic stature and tremendous influence of Brant systematically turning the Iroquois confederation from its pledge of neutrality to take up the hatchet against the Americans struck terror into his heart and that of his staff. If the Americans were to retain control of the Lake Champlain–Hudson River waterway, they must either neutralize the Indians in the western mountains, or conquer them. It was not a question of choice. It was a question of do-or-die necessity.

One hundred ten miles north of Schuyler, at Cumberland Head, General John Burgoyne and his staff had reached the same conclusion. Either gain the support of the Iroquois confederation, or fail in their expedition down the great waterway.

Thus the issue resolved itself into a single proposition, on which victory would stand or fall. Control the Iroquois, and consequently the waterway, or lose the war. And while the saying of it was easy, the doing of it was not. No white man on either side fully understood the simple innocence, the childlike mind of the Iroquois, whose world was grounded on the fundamental lessons life had taught them over centuries of surviving in the forest. They were not prepared to deal with the intrigues, the hidden motives, the latent manipulations, and the subversive, brutal politics of the white man. With a naive faith, they believed what they were told by the white men simply because it did not enter their minds to do otherwise. When treachery was discovered, the fury of their revenge knew no limits, and the bewildered white men could only accuse them of being ignorant savages when they came with scalping knife and tomahawk.

Feeling the beginnings of desperation, and knowing the weakness of the red men for the goods of the whites, Schuyler ordered the hasty construction of a trading post at Fort Stanwix, far to the west in Iroquois territory, and stocked it with an abundance of muskets, axes, hatchets, glass trinkets, looking glasses, traps, blankets, cloth, sugar, and salt. Samuel Kirkland, a lifelong missionary to the Indians, watched them flock to the new treasure, then loaded six barrels of rum into a wagon and traveled long distances to report to the Iroquois villages the unbelievable news of the great victories achieved by General Washington at Trenton and Princeton. With a barrel of free rum to assist him in the telling, Kirkland found ready audiences in each of the villages.

Electrified by the news that the Americans had beaten the feared redcoats and Hessians, the Iroquois celebrated, shooting off their village cannon, and drinking themselves senseless on the rum that was slowly making devastating inroads into their society.

Then came disheartening news from the west. An unknown white man's disease had swept through Onondaga, the Iroquois capitol, killing great numbers of the people and three of their sachems. Onondaga had taken a nearly fatal blow. The great council fire, a symbol of peace, that was to burn forever, died, and with heavy hearts the message was sent: we cannot keep the fire burning, and it is extinguished. We will support peace as best we can, but the Great Fire is gone.

Kirkland well understood that the catastrophe at Onondaga could be the beginning of the unraveling of the great Iroquois confederation. He quickly advised Schuyler that if the Confederation was to be saved, Schuyler must go to Onondaga and there perform the Ceremony of Condolence with all speed, replace the lost sachems, stabilize the Iroquois government, and rekindle the Great Fire of the Iroquois nations. Hurriedly Schuyler sent men to conduct the condolence ceremony and instructed them to extend to all Iroquois nations an invitation to a great celebration to be held at Onondaga on July 15, 1777. It was to be a glorious event, with a wealth of gifts from the Americans for their red brothers, at which the Iroquois would solemnly renew their pledge to remain neutral and friendly to their great neighbors and benefactors, the Americans.

The condolence ceremony succeeded. The Council fire was lighted again, once more burning as a symbol of the eternal flame of peace among the Iroquois nations. But the invitation to a grand council of July fifteenth reached Brant, and he and Butler set out once again in their insidious work of stirring up the Iroquois, dividing them, preparing them to breach their pledge of neutrality and take up the hatchet against the Americans.

Suddenly the heartland of the Iroquois nations was alive with the hotly divisive conflict between those who followed Brant and those who did not. Whispers became rumbles, then open disputes. Tomahawks and muskets that had long been wrapped in deerskin and buried began to appear. Because their history had not prepared them to cope with being manipulated by the hidden intrigues, promises, lies, and political sophistication of the British and Americans, the inevitable process of taking sides began among the Iroquois nations.

With his intimate knowledge of his own people, Brant knew when and where he should go next to solidify his leadership among those who had committed to take up the hatchet and follow him in an alliance with the British. In early June he once again visited the strategically critical village of Unadilla, located in the angle where the Susquehanna and the Tienaderha Rivers joined. He sent William Johnson Jr. ahead to assure the nervous residents of Brant's peaceful intentions. Upon his arrival he counseled with the village minister and his son, entreating them that they had used him and his men poorly, requesting that they soften their opposition to his mission. He asked for supplies for his continued journey, which they provided. He thanked them and departed in peace, but he knew he had accomplished his intentions when his scouts brought him the news. Many of the families who favored the Americans had packed what belongings they could, and on the day Brant left Unadilla, they had fled to the east. They did not want to be in Unadilla for the massacre, should Brant return with his warriors.

War was in the wind. Schuyler ordered Colonel Van Schaick to take one hundred fifty armed soldiers and move instantly into the Iroquois country to protect American interests. Brant's spies and scouts brought the news to him the day they saw uniformed Americans marching through the green valleys, and he thoughtfully considered it. It was good, he concluded. He had spent the entire winter and spring preparing as many of the Iroquois as he could to take up the British cause, which was clearly the wise course if he intended saving his own people. His work of preparation was done. The time for them to make their decision was fast approaching.

When the news of Schuyler's proposed July fifteenth grand council at Onondaga reached British Major John Butler at Fort Niagara, his reaction was instant and decisive. With a body of Seneca and western warriors he sailed to Irondequoit, where a great assembly of Senecas, including warriors, sachems, women, and children were gathered. The British showered them with gifts of every description, declaring over and over again how generous and kind their great friend and father in England was to see to their every need. Rum flowed like a river. After two days, the British suggested the Senecas hold a council and reconsider their pledge of neutrality. They were reminded that nothing could be more clear than the fact the British had the power to protect and provide for their red brothers, while the poor Americans could do nothing for them. The Senecas returned from their council and announced their decision. They had pledged neutrality to the Americans, and they would not break their pledge.

Again, Butler showered them with gifts, and all but drowned them with rum. Once more he requested they meet in council to consider who could best protect and provide for them. Their council lasted one day, and was carried over into the next. Slowly the men became divided, and the women and children entered into the fiery debate.

In the midst of the argument, a second ship ordered by Butler arrived, loaded to the gunwales with gifts. With the entire Seneca delegation watching, the British unloaded the ship and broke open the wooden crates. Tens of thousands of colored glass beads, small bells that jingled, and ostrich feathers were handed out to the silent Senecas, who stood transfixed with things they had never seen before, nor had ever supposed. Their silence turned to buzzing talk, then to open shouts of glee and joy. Never had they been so delighted with the gifts that could adorn their necks, wrists, clothing. Surely, surely, the Great Father across the waters in England would protect and provide for them forever.

Shrewdly, Butler waited until the Seneca council reconvened, and then he approached them as they sat before the council fire. In his hands were two wampum belts. One was the ancient Great Old Covenant Chain, remembered by the elders, new to the young, by which the Seneca had in times long past sworn eternal allegiance to the king of England. The elders exclaimed, it is true! Many years ago we made the promise! The second belt was confirmation of the covenant. Surrounded by the gifts and awash in rum, it became clear to the Seneca. They were honor bound to reaffirm their allegiance to the good and generous father in England. They all agreed. Warriors, sachems, even the women and children.

To solidify and celebrate the reaffirmation, the British threw a lavish feast that evening. To the astonishment and utter delight of the Indians, they presented still more gifts. New suits of clothing were handed out to everyone, and brass cooking kettles, guns, ammunition, tomahawks, scalping knives, and money was given to the chiefs.

Watching for the right moment, Butler made two final announcements: there would be a reward for every scalp taken from an American, and, the Seneca were entitled to name two war chiefs to lead them into the great battles yet to come. The Senecas met once more in council to make their selection, then returned to Butler to inform the British.

They had selected Sayehqueragha of the Turtle Clan, and Gayentwahga of the Wolf Clan. The name Sayehqueragha translated to "He who is lost in the smoke," or, "Smoke revanishes." Gayentwahga translated to "Cornplanter." It was never known whether the Senecas had remembered that Thayendanagea, or Joseph Brant, was also from the Wolf Clan. It was only known that the two great war chiefs, Joseph Brant and Cornplanter, both from the mighty Wolf Clan, were among those designated to lead their Iroquois followers into battle against the Americans.

Few of the Iroquois seemed to comprehend the momentous, heartrending truth that had come to pass. The mighty Iroquois confederation, which was to last forever, was undone. The British and Americans? The fate of the Iroquois was of little consequence to either. The single question that burned in both of their minds was, which side will the Iroquois follow?

With the heartland of the great Iroquois confederation a seething cauldron of division and conflict, news of what Butler and Brant had done at Irondequoit, and of the resulting sudden shift of the Senecas from the Americans to the British, reached veteran militia Brigadier General Nicholas Herkimer. He and his command of the Tryon County, New York state militia were stationed at Fort Dayton, on the north bank of the Mohawk River, just east of Canada Creek.

"Repeat that."

"Brant and Cornplanter was right there at Irondequoit with Butler and a lot of other British. They unloaded one boat of guns and a lot of other things for war, and a second boat with baubles and trinkets, and handed it all out to the Seneca. Then they gave out maybe thirty barrels of rum, and when the Seneca was falling-down drunk, Butler brought out those two old wampum belts the Indians got so much faith in, and Brant got 'em to swear to help the British. Men, women, kids, sachems— all of 'em. I was there. I seen it."

General Nicholas Herkimer's eyes narrowed. "What were you doing at Irondequoit?"

Johann Pedersen, a short, young, wide-eyed American settler, sweaty, dirty, and unshaved from his flight to Fort Dayton, wiped at his mouth. "My cabin's a mile and a half from Irondequoit, and right up to then the Senecas was on our side. When things got bad with Brant's warriors sneakin' around the woods, I figured the best place to be was right there in the village with the friendly Seneca, and I went. I didn't know Brant and Butler could sway 'em from our side to the British so easy. As soon as I could, I run and come here."

"Your wife and family are still at your cabin?"

The man's eyes dropped. "Wife's dead. When the smallpox come through from Onondaga, it took her. Lost our first baby afore that, to the whooping cough."

"Brant still at Irondequoit?"

"No. I heard he left for Unadilla."

Herkimer, tall, craggy face, receding brown hair, strongly built, stood behind his desk and called, "Bates!"

The door into his crude office opened and a colonial dressed in homespun, except for a tunic with a captain's epaulets on his shoulders, stepped inside. "Yes?"

"Get this man some food and a bath and a bed. Then report back here."

Bates, a shorter man than Herkimer, husky, round-faced, long blond hair tied back, nodded, and gestured to the young man, then followed him out the door, through the tiny anteroom, into the small parade ground of Fort Dayton, toward the first long, low enlisted men's barracks. Alone, his face clouded, Herkimer slowly settled back onto his chair and pondered and weighed the news.

Brant's been agitating among the Iroquois all winter—got them all stirred up—his own Mohawk, and the Cayuga, Onondaga, and Oneida, and now it's the Seneca—Butler with him.

He stood and walked to the small window in the east wall of the log building to peer up at the bulging underbelly of thick, purple rain clouds.

Is this the time we go after him shooting? Start a war here while Burgoyne and St. Clair are getting ready for one over in the Hudson River valley? Can't start a war here without St. Clair's consent—St. Clair and Washington. Maybe I should send out six riflemen to find Brant and kill him from ambush? No. Can't do that—it would unite the Iroquois, and they'd come down on us like fiends from the infernal pit.

He moved his feet, nervous, not liking the thorny thing that had just been thrust upon him, uninvited.

What do I do? Forget it? And let them think we're afraid? Make them bolder? No—must make them understand—it has to stop.

He clasped his hands behind his back and began pacing the rough-finished plank floor as his thoughts deepened.

Shooting is coming—do I let them pick the time and place? No. Can't let them take control.

He was seated at his desk before the thought struck him. *Parley! Send Brant a messenger. Ask him to meet me on neutral ground and parley. Find out his intentions. He'll have to come or risk being branded a coward, unfit to lead.*

Bates rapped on his door and entered without invitation. "Reporting back."

Herkimer pursed his mouth for a moment. "Get Colonel Brownley and Major Whetten in here as soon as you can."

Bates wiped at his mouth. "We're going to have a cloudburst out there."

"They've been wet before."

Bates shrugged and walked back out the door, peering up at the roiling clouds, gauging the minutes until the storm would break. He broke into a trot down to a second door and rapped sharply.

"Enter."

"General Herkimer wants you in his office as soon as you can."

Brownley rose from the table that served as his desk as well as for dining, his face suddenly pensive. "What's happened?"

"Looks like Butler and Joseph Brant have gone too far."

Brownley reached for his tunic. "I'll be right there."

Bates stepped quickly to the next door, rapped, and repeated his message. Major Whetten followed him out, still working with his tunic, one eye squinting upward at the boiling clouds. Bates was reaching for the latch on the door of Herkimer's office when a gigantic bolt of lightning turned the purple clouds white, and the first clap of thunder boomed overhead. In that instant the wind swept through, splatting great drops of rain against the door as he slammed it closed.

Brownley was already seated on a plain wooden chair facing Herkimer's desk. Herkimer, seated at the desk, gestured, and Whetten sat down in a chair beside Brownley, watching the general for some indication of the extent of the emergency. Bates sat on a stool in the corner.

Herkimer drew a great breath. "It looks like we're finally going to have to do something about Brant."

At the mention of the name, both Brownley and Whetten stopped moving, and for several seconds the only sound was the rain pelting at the front wall and windows. Herkimer continued.

"He and Butler were just at Irondequoit. They gave two shiploads of trade goods to the Seneca and served up about thirty barrels of rum. It took them three days, but when they finished, the Seneca had abandoned us and sworn loyalty to the British. Until that moment, the Seneca had been among our best allies."

Brownley glanced at Whetten, who was sitting in white-faced silence. Herkimer went on.

"I don't have to tell you men, Brant's been out in those mountains all winter, dividing the Iroquois confederation. For all practical purposes, the Confederation is dead as of right now. Split. Divided. Ready to go to war with each other according to which side they favor, the British or us."

He paused to shake his head, and a look of deep sadness came into his eyes. He quietly murmured, "What have we done to them?" He shook off the melancholy moment and went on. "Let me come straight to it. What are we going to do?"

Brownley tilted his head forward and closed his eyes for a few seconds in deep thought before he spoke. "The whole Hudson Valley and the Adirondacks are an open powder keg waiting for a spark. Hadn't we better consult with General Washington, or at least Schuyler or St. Clair before we risk setting it all off at the wrong time?"

"I thought about that. Whetten, what are your thoughts?"

Whetten reached to scratch under his chin. "It's going to happen, and probably sooner than later. I don't know if there's a right time or a right place. I do know it concerns me if we let Brant go very much farther before we stop him. Maybe it would be enough to make a show of strength, like marching a regiment right through the middle of Iroquois country to Irondequoit, and sending ten men to find him and deliver a written warning."

Herkimer shook his head. "I thought about that, too. It's hard to know what to do." He leaned forward intently. "It occurs to me there's a way to check him without shooting." He paused, and both Brownley and Whetten fell silent, waiting.

"Invite Brant to parley with us. Meet him face to face. Hear him out. Try to persuade him to stop what he's doing." He stopped and waited for a reaction.

Brownley spoke. "There's risk. He might become belligerent. Start something. With Indians, you never know."

"Take along enough men that he wouldn't dare," Herkimer said.

Whetten cut in. "You think he'd come to a parley with a large force of militia?"

"Probably. It would likely cause some ridicule from his own warriors if he refuses. He'd lose face. He wouldn't let that happen if he could avoid it."

Whetten fell silent, weighing the proposal against the dangers. "It might work."

Herkimer looked at Brownley, waiting, and Brownley spoke.

"We pick the time, the place, and the conditions. Give him a chance to be heard." He began a slight nodding of his head. "Probably better than a head-on confrontation. Might work. May be the best we can do for right now."

Herkimer spoke. "I'll send a written message to him to meet us at Unadilla for a peaceful parley. Brownley, do you have three or four Iroquois scouts you can trust to deliver it?"

"Yes."

"Are we agreed?"

"Yes."

Herkimer bobbed his head. "Your two commands together are three hundred eighty men. Have them ready to march out at six o'clock in the morning." He turned to Bates. "Draft orders for the men to draw rations for fourteen days, and half a pound of gunpowder and thirty rounds of ammunition each. Arrange wagons to carry it. Two, twelve-pound cannon and thirty rounds each, plus two kegs of grapeshot each. I'll sign the order when you're finished."

"Yes, sir."

Bates led the two officers through the anteroom and opened the outside door. The steady drumming of heavy rain filled a world blurred with a torrential cloudburst. The dirt parade ground was a sea of mud with great raindrops pounding the surface to a froth and rivulets of muddy water running to make small lakes in the low places. Brownley and Whetten both looked sour as they stepped out to make a run for their quarters. They were drenched to the skin and muddy to the knees within the first thirty yards.

Bates sat at his desk for more than an hour using an eagle feather quill and paper, laboring over the drafting of orders that would provision three hundred eighty men for fourteen days and arm them for a heavy battle should one occur. Finished, he opened the outside door to look. The cloudburst had dwindled to a steady rain, and he closed the door, irritation plain on his round face. He rapped on Herkimer's door twice, then walked on in.

"Here's the orders you wanted."

"Good." Herkimer quickly read the three documents, signed them with a bold flourish, then pushed them back to Bates. "Get those delivered as soon as you can, then come back. I'll have a rough draft of the message for Brant to meet and parley with us. You'll finalize it for my signature and get it to Brownley. He'll know what to do with it." He glanced at the signed orders. "Don't get those wet."

Bates folded the papers twice, paused in his office to wrap them in oilskin, then opened the outside door. The rain was slacking off, and the first breaks were appearing in the solid bank of blue-black clouds scudding eastward. The parade ground was a swamp of mud, and Bates reached to strip off his shoes and socks and set them on his desk. It was much easier to wash feet than to clean square-toed leather shoes with brass buckles, and knee-length white cotton socks.

The startled sergeant at the commissary read the food order and stared back at Bates in disbelief. "Supplies for three hundred eighty men by morning? Who lost their mind?" His scraggly, six-days' stubble of whiskers moved as he spoke.

"General Herkimer. Read the signature," Bates growled.

At the ordnance building, the fat little sergeant gaped. "Thirty rounds of ammunition each for three hundred eighty men, plus officers? By morning? That's . . uh . . let's see . . . near twelve thousand rounds." He set his jaw belligerently. "I'm not going to count out thirty rounds, three hundred eighty times. I'll just send about twenty kegs of musketballs, and the officers can do their own counting."

"General Herkimer signed the order. Suit yourself."

"Then let Herkimer count 'em out."

Bates shrugged. "Go tell him."

"I will!"

A wry grin crossed Bates's face as he slogged back to his tiny office. In his mind he was seeing the chubby little ordnance sergeant, hands on his hips, looking upward at the tall, angular Herkimer, loudly telling him to go count the bloody musketballs himself. Inside his office, Bates dipped drinking water from the wooden bucket in the corner and held his feet out the door to rinse them, then walked to the door into Herkimer's office to stand with water puddling at his feet.

"You have a rough draft of the invitation for Brant?"

Herkimer pointed to a paper on the leading edge of his desk, then looked at Bates's wet, bare feet. "Bad out there?"

"If the rain holds, we'll need an ark to get to Irondequoit."

Herkimer shook his head. "Just a late spring storm. It'll be gone within the hour."

Bates picked up the document from Herkimer's desk and walked back out to his desk, mouth moving as he silently read the scratchings and the words that had been crossed out and replaced in the margins. With fresh paper and his quill, he began the painstaking labor of abiding all the frills and requirements of an official military document. Finished, he sighed his relief, then glanced at the small clock on the corner of his desk. Fifteen minutes past five o'clock. He rose, knocked once on Herkimer's door, and walked in.

"Ready for your signature." He sat down while Herkimer read it carefully, nodded approval, and reached for his quill to scratch his signature beneath the "Your obd't servant" at the foot of the page.

"Get that to Brownley for delivery to Brant."

"Think we can find him?"

"Brownley's Iroquois scouts can."

"What if he finds us first, and thinks we've come to attack him?"

Herkimer shrugged. "He'll do whatever he thinks he should, but that's one Indian who's smart enough to know he better not launch an attack on a United States column without first talking it over with Butler, and probably Carleton up in Quebec. If he triggered a war before they're ready, they'd likely haul him in and hang him."

"I hope he's as smart as you think." Bates jerked a thumb to point over his shoulder. "Nearly time for mess. Want your supper here?"

"No, I'll go with the officers."

Bates turned and walked back through his office to open the outside door. The rain had stopped, and shafts of golden sunlight reached through the clouds to turn Fort Dayton and the fresh, wet, emerald green of the Adirondacks to a spectacular, shifting kaleidoscope of sun and shadow. He eyed the muddy, steaming morass that lay between himself and the officers' mess, one hundred fifty yards to the west, and reached to tuck his shoes and socks under his arm. He would arrive at the mess hall barefooted and muddy to his knees, but his shoes and socks would be clean and dry.

Soft, warm rain fell for a time in the middle of the night. The trees and shrubs were dripping when the camp drummer pounded out reveille in the gray dawn. At six o'clock General Herkimer mounted his bay horse, looked over his column, called out his orders, and turned his mount due south toward the Mohawk River, a winding, shining ribbon in the morning sun, just south of the fort. They crossed the river in boats, then pushed on through the forest toward the headwaters of the Tienaderha River.

Strung out in single file for nearly half a mile, the column bore little resemblance to a regimented, disciplined army. Most of the men were barefooted, their shoes and socks, or moccasins, or rarely boots, tied around their necks as they slogged through the fresh, warm mud of the crooked trail that wound like a gigantic snake through the tall pines and maples and the spreading oak trees and thick undergrowth. There was not a uniform among them. Rather, they were dressed in loose home-spun shirts and breeches. They carried their muskets and rifles loosely, some over a shoulder, some in their hand, with their powder horn and bullet pouch dangling, one on one side, one on the other. Their bedrolls were slung across their backs by a cord looped over their shoulders. A few wore battered tricornered hats, most had their long hair tied back with a piece of string or buckskin. Altogether the column would have drawn cutting derision and scornful disgust from the uniformed, disciplined, haughty British soldiers.

But as they moved silently onward, the eyes of every man were con-stantly moving, peering into the shadows of the forest, identifying every-thing that moved, danger or no danger, friend or foe. They heard and instantly catalogued every sound, waiting for the slight whisper of ferns on buckskin that warned of an enemy hidden in the shadows. Within seconds of an alarm, not one man would remain exposed on the trail. They would be hidden on either side, crouched, silent, ready, waiting. Only the two wagons with supplies and ammunition, and the two, twelve-pound cannon would remain in sight. In a fight the men would become shadows in the forest, firing, moving, firing, moving. And they would be silently contemptuous of the British, standing in rank and file like trained animals, wearing red tunics with white belts crossed over their chests—the best targets the Americans had ever seen—fully exposed, shouting obscenities at the cowardly Americans while the Americans chopped down their ranks—officers first—with relentless, hidden gunfire.

At days' end they posted pickets and boiled strong coffee and crisped sowbelly over low campfires scattered in the trees, then went to their blankets beneath the black forest canopy overhead, and the stars, to rise at dawn and march out as the first arc of the rising sun broke clear and bright above the eastern rim. The afternoon of the second day they were four miles north of the junction of the Tienaderha River and Butternut Creek when suddenly the two flanker scouts stopped dead, then dropped to disappear in the foliage while they identified three incoming shadows slipping silently through the trees.

"Ours," said one of the flankers, and they waited for a moment before they suddenly stood, musket muzzles held loosely on the three Indians coming in. One flanker held his position two hundred yards from the side of the column while the other one led the three Iroquois to the column, calling out "friendly" as they came in. The four of them trotted to the head of the column, where General Herkimer ordered a halt, beckoned to his interpreter, and dismounted.

The Indians stood facing him and the interpreter, one in front, two behind, hands clasped over the muzzles of their upright muskets, silent, waiting.

He spoke to the one leading. "Did you find Brant?"

The interpreter started to translate when the Indian spoke. "Yes."

"Did you deliver the paper with the writing?"

The Indian bobbed his head deeply, once.

"Did Brant send back a message to me?"

Again the Indian bobbed his head, then spoke. "Brant say he come Unadilla, two, three day, no musket, no rifle, no cannon."

Herkimer's forehead knitted. "He'll come if there are no guns?" He turned to his interpreter. The man raised one hand to sign while he spoke to the Indian. The Indian spoke back, and the interpreter turned to Herkimer.

"Brant is afraid of a trap. He says you are an honorable man. He will come to Unadilla for a council if you send him a writing with your signature, pledging no guns, no ambush. Only peace."

Herkimer turned to the Indian. "Is he waiting for you to come back with a writing on paper from me?"

The Indian bobbed his head.

"How far from here?"

"One day. Chenango River."

Herkimer glanced west toward where the Chenango flowed south parallel to the Tienaderha to join the Susquehanna. "One day," he said thoughtfully, then turned to Brownley and Whetten, who stood holding their horses' reins, concentrating intently on every word. "I think we should be in Unadilla in two days. I propose we accept his terms. Are we agreed?"

"Yes."

He turned to Bates, standing off his left elbow. "Can you get quill and ink and paper? I'll make the answer now."

Fifteen minutes later, with young lieutenants trotting up to see what had stalled the column, Herkimer handed the folded document back to the Indian. "Can you take that back to Brant?"

The Indian's face had not changed expression since his arrival. Stoically he once again bobbed his head and reached for the folded paper. He slipped it inside his shot pouch and waited for orders to leave.

Herkimer asked, "Do you need rest? Food? Anything?"

For the first time a smile flickered on the Indian's face, but was just as quickly gone. "No food. No rest. We go." For a moment the Indian wondered if the white men would ever understand that the forest was their home. All they needed could be found there. The inability of most white men to flourish in the wilderness was a profound mystery to the red men. Without a word the three Indians turned on their heels, and within moments had disappeared.

At noon the second day Herkimer called the midday halt, and while the column was hastily setting up the black iron cook kettles, the three Indians returned to stand stiffly before him and make their report.

"Brant will come." The message was delivered. They turned and were gone.

At mid-afternoon the advance scouts came trotting back into camp to report. "Road's clear to Unadilla, about three miles ahead. No sign of Brant or his men."

With the sun still three hours high, Herkimer rounded a gentle bend, then crested a rise in the trail, and before him spread a wide, shallow valley. To his left, a line of trees in the forest marked the hidden Susquehanna River, and to his right, a second line of trees marked the course of the Tienaderha. Where the two rivers met, a church steeple thrust upward, white in the emerald green forest, to mark the tiny village of Unadilla. Herkimer's horse sensed the end of the trail and began to toss its head, chewing the bit, wanting to be finished. Herkimer held it in check while he intently studied the valley floor, looking for a telltale wisp of campfire smoke that would identify Brant and his men. There was none, and Herkimer kept his column moving. He called a halt in a clearing two hundred yards from the scattering of buildings on the northern fringe of Unadilla and gave orders to set up camp. Then he sent Bates for Brownley and Whetten. Sitting their horses while the soldiers began the chores of erecting tents for the officers and starting the supper process, the four men gathered twenty yards distant from the nearest troops.

"I think we better go to town and tell the mayor, or whoever's in charge, what this is all about."

The four of them cantered their horses through the crude, crooked streets, past low, log homes with dirt roofs, watching for anything to move. A spotted dog came barking, nipping at the heels of the nervous horses, then retreated. A few people emerged from their homes to stand silently, watching them pass, one or two raising a hand in a half-hearted waving gesture, but none called or spoke. Curtains stirred at windows, and vague faces appeared to stare. They rounded a building with a full rain barrel standing at the corner and reined to their right. Forty yards further along the rutted dirt street was an old trading post, weathered black, with an array of black iron traps hung on pegs driven in the side-wall, and the hide of a great tawny panther pegged against the logs to dry. There was an open area before the old trading post, with a flagpole in the center, but no flag. The buildings stopped, and the forest began one hundred yards to both the east and west.

Herkimer and his three men pulled their horses to a stop and dismounted, looking around at the few people who ventured into the street to stand at a distance, silent, staring. He walked to the plank door of the trading post, pulled the latch string, and stepped inside the dark room, Brownley and Whetten following, eyes wide as they left the bright sunshine outside. The sharp odor of rum and smoked meat hit them as they looked about the low-ceilinged room at the shapes of the few men inside the building, who stood motionless, waiting.

"I'm General Herkimer, Tryon County militia. Can you tell me where to find the mayor?"

A bearded man in a fringed buckskin hunting shirt answered "No mayor. Reverend Belnap usually takes charge."

"Where might I find him?"

"Right there." The man pointed beyond a small counting table to a corner, and Herkimer turned. "Reverend Belnap?"

Reverend Herman Belnap, middle-aged, portly rose from a stool. "Yes."

"I thought I better let you know what's happening."

"That your army setting up camp just north of town?"

"Part of it. We've come here to parley with Joseph Brant. Try to talk some sense into him."

The reverend started. "Humph. You think you can bargain with the devil?"

"No. I think if we make a strong enough showing we might get him to leave here. Go back to Onondaga and quit stirring up trouble for you people."

Belnap suddenly leaned forward. "You intend meeting Brant here? In town?"

"Yes."

The reverend's voice rose in anger. "Half the people left town the last time he was here. Most haven't come back yet. Likely the rest will be gone the minute they hear he's coming back."

Herkimer shook his head. "Tell your people there will be no trouble. I've brought three hundred eighty seasoned soldiers. Brant won't start anything."

The reverend's reply was instant, hot. "Not while you're here. But when you're gone, what do we do if he comes back with his warriors and takes revenge? The whole town could be burned to the ground and all of us dead. Scalped."

"We'll watch him. That won't happen. Tell your people so they won't do something foolish."

"I'll tell them. But they'll do what they think best."

Herkimer moved on. "He'll likely be in late tonight, or early morning. We'll hold a council with him. I need you and three or four more from town to come with me to parley with him, out near the flagpole."

"I doubt any of us want to be any part of it."

Herkimer ignored it. "I'll also need four cattle. I'll pay."

"Cattle for what? Your men?"

"No. Gifts for Brant."

Belnap snorted. "Gifts to him? The gift he has in mind for you isn't cattle."

Low laughter sounded from around the room, then stopped, and Herkimer continued. "He'll expect gifts." The general dug inside his tunic for a small leather purse, unsnapped the clasp, and quickly sorted out four gold coins. "That's a fair price for four cattle. Pay whoever owns them and have them ready in the morning. I'll need you and your people ready about two hours after sunup. Agreed?"

Belnap shrugged. "I'll tell them. They'll do what they decide."

"I'll see you in the morning."

Herkimer and his two officers walked back out to Bates, who was holding the horses. Without a word they remounted, and Herkimer led them back north to the camp. His command tent was pegged down, and he spoke quietly to the other three.

"Come inside with me."

Inside he gestured to the plain, wooden plank table and benches. "Sit down."

His face was clouded, drawn as he spoke in low tones. "This is not to leave this tent, except for the three riflemen we pick."

Instantly all three men across from him froze.

Herkimer lowered his voice even more. "With us at the north end of town, it seems natural for Brant to camp his men at the south end, which puts their backs against one of the two rivers down there. That means if anyone starts shooting, we can fall back, but he can't. So I doubt he'll be inclined to provoke a fight. But when it comes to Indians, who knows?"

He paused, then went on. "I think it would be a mistake to send out men to scout Brant when he comes in. If they were caught, he'd declare a breach of our agreement, and there might be shooting." He stopped to shift his weight and collect his thoughts. "And I think Brant will reach the same conclusion. I doubt he'll try to scout us. But if he does, and our men catch his warriors snooping around here, I want them brought in. I'll put them in chains and march them to Brant's camp with every man I've got behind me, armed and ready to fight, and let Brant know he's a liar and can't be trusted, and then I'll hang 'em in public."

Brownley reached to scratch his beard, then settled. Herkimer's narrowed eyes were points of light beneath his shaggy brows. "Brownley, name the three best riflemen in your command."

Bates recoiled, and Whetten's head jerked forward. For a moment the tent was locked in dead silence, then Brownley swallowed hard and answered.

"Phelps, Attenborough, and Briscoe."

Herkimer tapped an index finger on the table. Still speaking in soft tones, he said, "Now listen close, because if this goes wrong, there'll be the devil to pay. I intend to hold the council down in that open area around the flagpole, in front of the trading post. To the east and west, the forest comes within about one hundred yards of the flagpole. An easy shot for a good rifleman."

Brownley stiffened as it broke in his mind where Herkimer was going.

"Tonight, send those three riflemen out, two west, one east, a mile or two. Have them spend the night in the forest. In the morning while we're gathering with Brant, have them come in toward the clearing where we'll parley. They are to stay hidden and be ready. If Brant does anything that provokes a breach of the peace, they're to shoot him. No matter who else gets hurt, they're to kill Brant. Do you understand?" He glared at the officers.

Brownley's voice cracked as he spoke. "Yes, sir."

"I know how that sounds, but let me tell you the reason. When the war starts between Burgoyne and St. Clair over on the Hudson, Brant's going to become a factor in how it turns out. He's agreed to meet and council with us in peace. He can avoid those three riflemen if he keeps his word. If he doesn't, I don't have the slightest reservation about shooting him. Him being gone will likely save hundreds of lives. If any of you have a quarrel with that, now is the time to settle it."

Herkimer fell silent and waited. He looked at each man in succession, and none of them made a sound. Herkimer slapped the table with the palm of his hand.

"Then it's settled. Let's get back to our command."

With the western rim hiding half the sun, the Americans gathered around their steaming cookpots, and the company cooks doled out the beef stew. Talk was subdued as each of the soldiers sought a rock, or a log to sit on while he held the steaming plate in one hand and worked his fork or spoon with the other, blowing to cool the hot mix. From time to time all eyes glanced nervously to the south, past the tiny village, for the first flicker of campfires in the trees, but none came. Finally, in full darkness, the regimental drummer rattled out taps, and the soldiers sought their blankets, to lie in silence, facing south, still waiting, watching, wondering.

No one knew when they came in the night. The Americans only knew that when the reveille drum sounded at dawn, the Indians were camped two hundred yards into the woods at the south end of town. Herkimer walked among his men, carrying his plate of fried mush and sowbelly, talking, settling them. "Eat your breakfast and roll up your bedrolls. Just stand easy, and all will go well." In his walking, Herkimer sought out Brownley sitting on a rock with his plate and asked quietly, "Did your three riflemen go out?" Brownley nodded without looking up.

With their morning camp chores done, Herkimer gave orders. "Have your men fall into ranks for marching. Brownley, circle around the west side of town, Whetten, you to the east, and meet at the flagpole. Bates, you come with me. We go straight in and get Belnap and his men and the cattle just before the two commands meet."

The militiamen fell into marching ranks, quiet, subdued, thoughts reaching ahead to the moment they would catch their first glimpse of Joseph Brant and his band of Mohawk warriors. *Joseph Brant. Thyendanagea. Heroic warrior in battle. Educated, with six Indian dialects and two foreign languages on his tongue. Bound by treaty with King George III in London—dined in his palace—received gifts from him—inducted into the Falcon Freemasons' Lodge—wooed by the London aristocracy. How would he be dressed? What would he say? What magic did he possess?*

The thoughts rode them heavy, preoccupied them, held them silent, would not let go as they fell into marching ranks. Brownley barked his orders and led his men west, while Whetten's command followed him east. Their soldiers circled the town in silence, heads turned, watching every shadow, hearing every sound, knowing Brant was still to the south of them, but nonetheless they were seeing one of his painted, feathered warriors in every movement of a leaf, every sound in the forest.

As his men disappeared from either side of him, Herkimer spurred his horse forward, Bates beside him, to pick their way through the crooked street while the shoes of their horses picked up large clods of firm mud left from the cloudburst a few days earlier, to throw them behind as they moved on. They passed the rain barrel and Herkimer turned to look west. Belnap was standing in front of the old trading post, three men with him, all four of them grasping the leadrope of a spotted steer or cow. Herkimer and Bates reined over to them and stopped, but remained mounted.

"Ready?"

Belnap answered sarcastically. "As ready as we'll ever be."

Herkimer spoke to the three men beside Belnap. "You're coming as witnesses to what happens. You'll be safe as long as you remember what I tell you. Brant's no fool. Don't anger him. I knew him a long time ago when we both lived in the Mohawk Valley. He'll say some things to purposely provoke me, and I'll handle it. When I say so, lead the cattle to him and give him the lead ropes. It'll all be over soon."

Gesturing to one of the townsmen, Belnap said, "Ebenezer here lived in the Mohawk Valley for a while."

Herkimer looked at the other three men, studying them, and one spoke. "I'm Ebenezer Cox. Used to be a colonel in the militia."

"You know Brant? Or more important, does he know you?"

"Might. I married the daughter of George Klock—"

Herkimer started and cut him off. "Wasn't Klock the one who accused Brant of stealing cattle? Tracked him down and humiliated him at musket point in front of his own people? Hated Brant?"

Cox's head bobbed. "The same."

Herkimer's eyes narrowed. "You share the same feelings?"

"I don't like Brant."

Herkimer looked at Belnap, then back at Cox. "If you can't control yourself, maybe you shouldn't be out there with us."

"I'll be all right. I'm going."

Belnap bobbed his head with finality. "If any of us goes, Cox goes with us."

Herkimer leaned slightly forward to speak to Belnap. "Then you're responsible for him. See to it."

Brownley and Whetten brought the two bodies of marching men together to form a semicircle on the north side of the village flagpole. Herkimer and Bates sat motionless on their horses in front of the trading post with Belnap and his men behind them, holding the lead ropes to the cattle, while a few other Unadilla citizens stood at random behind them. Their eyes were all wide in surprise. There was not an Indian in sight. Herkimer called orders to Brownley and Whetten.

"Have your men open a path for us to come through, then stand at ease. We wait."

Orders were given, the rank and file of the two commands separated to make a ten-foot opening, then broke from attention to remain standing silently in ranks, watching, waiting. Herkimer remained still, facing south, sitting with his shoulders hunched slightly forward, every nerve focused on the tree line dead ahead.

Ninety seconds later a hushed murmur swept through the Americans at the first movement in the shadows of the forest south of them, and a moment later Joseph Brant walked out into the clearing. Close around him were but twenty Mohawk warriors. All were dressed in buckskin hunting shirts with bead and quill work on the breasts, buckskin breeches, and decorated moccasins. The single mark that set Brant apart from any of his warriors was the large, silver gorget slung around his neck on a silver chain, delicately engraved with the British lion, unicorn, shield, and other emblems. None were armed.

Herkimer turned and gave orders. "Belnap, you and your men follow me. Bring the cattle." Unarmed, the six of them moved through the opening in the semicircle of militia, out toward the flagpole, while Brant and his twenty warriors walked steadily to meet them. The two opposing groups stopped ten feet from each other, eighty yards from the rank and file of American soldiers. Brownley and Whetten came to join Herkimer and Bates as they dismounted and stood their ground. Belnap and his men, with the cattle, were behind. When both groups had come to a halt, Brant took two steps forward and stopped.

Larger than average, solidly built, Brant exuded the impression that inside was a coiled steel spring, ready to unleash a feral energy that would be terrible and deadly. His unpainted face was remarkably handsome. The aura that moved with him was peaceful, even humble, but his dark eyes appeared to miss nothing, and in them was a chilling light. He spoke to Herkimer in perfect English, his voice soft, purring.

"I see many of your soldiers behind you, carrying arms. I have your paper and signature saying this was not to be. I am surprised to be treated thus by an old friend and neighbor."

For a moment Herkimer's startled surprise showed in his face. Brant had purposely seized control of the parley by speaking first, and had tipped Herkimer off balance with an accusation that Herkimer had treacherously broken his own signed word and brought soldiers against an old neighbor. Herkimer tried to recover.

"My soldiers are far behind, and they are under orders not to raise their muskets. They will not harm you."

"I see they are many. Perhaps four hundred. I have brought but twenty with me to meet you in open council, but I have many in my camp to the south. They are also under orders to leave their weapons untouched. Only if they hear the sounds of battle will they come here, in a great swarm, like the locusts. I intend you no harm. I have come to parley with you in peace concerning that which divides us. I tell you of my warriors in the forest because I do not wish to deceive you."

Herkimer's eyes never left Brant. "I have come for the same purpose. Do you wish to council here, or in a building where we can sit to parley?"

"Here. I have brought blankets." Brant glanced at one of his warriors and in an instant, blankets appeared. The Indians spread them on the ground, and Herkimer and his small knot of men sat facing Brant and his warriors.

Herkimer continued. "It has been said that Brant has spent many months among the Iroquois, from Onoquaga to Oriskany, and from Schoharie to the lake Ontario, talking against the Americans, seeking to unite all Indians with the British. Is it true?" Herkimer's eyes narrowed.

Brant nodded once, but his facial expression did not change. "It is so."

"What is the reason?"

Brant did not hesitate. "It is not hard to understand. The Americans have ever diminished our lands. They have restricted our travel. Our sachems and ministers are not allowed to come to Canajoharie. The Americans have been industrious to build forts on the lands guaranteed to us in the Treaty of 1768, nine years ago. I have a copy of that treaty and of the line that was drawn and the location of the three forts with me. Would you care to see it?"

Herkimer's eyes dropped. It was true. The Fort Stanwix Treaty of 1768 had established a north-south line near the Tienaderha River, with the firm agreement that the Mohawk were to have the territory to the west of the line without interference from the Americans. Nonetheless,

Fort Oswego, Fort Brewerton, and Fort Sullivan remained within the lands reserved to the Mohawk. There was nothing Herkimer could do about it. He raised his face to Brant.

"I know of the forts, and I regret they remain on your land. I have no power to correct it. I would if I could. But it is not the forts I have come to discuss. There is the greater matter of the trouble that has developed between the Americans and the British. That is for the white men to resolve, not the Indians. The great Mohawk, and the Iroquois confederation, gave their solemn pledge that they would not take up the hatchet in this matter. They would leave it for the Americans and the British to settle. I remind you of your pledge, and I ask you now to honor it."

There it was. Herkimer had brought the deadly question out in the open and put it squarely before Brant. Much of the fate of the oncoming battle of the Lake Champlain–Hudson River corridor hung on the answer. Brownley, Whetten, and Bates were holding their breath. Belnap's face was a ghostly white. Cox's face was a blank.

"I cannot. I have treated with the king in London. He has sworn to drive all Americans from our lands and close the forts. He has sent us great gifts and promised to deliver more. The British have the power to keep their commitments and humble the rebels from Boston. I will honor my treaty with the king."

For five seconds the air was charged. No one moved as the hair raised on their necks. The only sounds were the birds and insects busy doing their spring work. Then, out of the silence, Ebenezer Cox spoke directly to Brant, his voice thick with acrimony.

"Fergot already the pledge you and the Iroquois made to remain neutral? What happened? Did the British offer you more rum than the Americans?"

Herkimer recoiled in shocked horror and opened his mouth to speak, but Cox continued, his voice booming, insulting.

"This trouble between the Americans and the British has nothing to do with you. It's for them to settle. Take your warriors and get back to your own—"

He got no further. Brant turned his face slightly to his left, and the twenty warriors behind him were instantly on their feet. The American soldiers eighty yards to the north swung their muskets up, waiting for orders. In the forest west of the flagpole, the two hidden riflemen, Attenborough and Briscoe, laid the barrels of their Pennsylvania rifles over a branch of the oak tree in which they were hidden, and eared back the big hammers, while to the east, Phelps, twenty feet up an ancient pine, did the same. All three men laid their cheeks against the stocks of their rifles and buried the stubby foresight at the end of the long barrel in the center of Brant's chest while they began taking up the slack in the triggers.

Herkimer bolted to his feet and raised his hands, signaling no further action from the Americans. It seemed the world stopped for a time before eighteen of the Iroquois warriors turned on their heels and ran south to disappear into the trees. Moments later, out of sight in the forest where they had gone, came the sustained firing of muskets. North of the flagpole the Americans cocked their muskets and raised them to the ready while the three hidden riflemen began to take up the last one-eighth inch in the pull of their rifle triggers.

"Stop!" shouted Herkimer. "They're not shooting at us. It's a show of strength. Uncock those muskets and lower them. Now! Do it!"

Confused, the American militiamen uncocked their muskets and peered at their officers, waiting, not knowing what to do. In disbelief, the three hidden riflemen jerked their heads from their rifles and peered through narrowed eyes, trying to understand what was happening in the clearing, one hundred yards away. Slowly, carefully, they uncocked their weapons and waited, not knowing whether they had failed in their assignment to shoot Brant dead if he broke the peace. From their position, they could not tell if the Indian muskets blasting in the trees was, or was not, the beginning of the war on the Hudson River. They remained unmoving, focused, frustrated, hating what they did not know.

Infuriated, face red, neck veins extended, Herkimer turned to Brant. "You promised peace at this parley. When did Joseph Brant cease keeping

his word? Order your warriors to stop, now!" Herkimer knew the terrible risk he was taking in giving Brant a direct order.

Still seated, Brant stoically raised his right hand high above his head, fist clenched, and two seconds later the rattling blasts of gunfire ceased. He raised his eyes to Herkimer. "You promised peace if I would come to this parley, yet you bring along this man Cox who does not want peace, and you allow him to insult me and my people to provoke us. My warriors fired their weapons as a warning. We will accept no more insults. We will talk as brothers, or not at all."

Herkimer's hot answer came instantly. "I came in peace. Cox speaks for himself." He turned to look at Cox, eyes flashing, jaw set, chin thrust out. Cox swallowed and dropped his gaze. Herkimer turned to the rank and file of militia eighty yards north and gave them a hand signal. The butts of their muskets and rifles were to be on the ground. In the trees to the east and west, the hidden riflemen stared in puzzlement, but remained silent, motionless.

Slowly Herkimer regained control of himself and sat back down on his blanket facing Brant, and spoke with restraint.

"You complained that your minister, Mr. Stuart, cannot visit you. I will see to it he can come to Canajoharie, and that he can bring with him the wife of John Butler."

Brant reflected for a moment, then bobbed his head slightly in acknowledgment while Herkimer continued.

"I cannot cause the militia to leave the three forts in Mohawk territory, but I can promise that the Tories who support the king will not be molested."

Again Brant thought for a moment before he nodded. Herkimer turned and with a great flourish, pointed at the four cattle. "I offer these to you as a gift showing our good faith."

Brant nodded once again, then waited, knowing that the concessions made by Herkimer, and the gift of the four cattle, were but a preparation for a demand that Herkimer was about to make, and there was no doubt in Brant's mind what it was to be.

Herkimer spoke slowly, firmly. "In return I will expect you to keep your pledge to let the Americans and British settle their differences and to influence your people to do the same."

Brant's expression did not change as he rose to his feet. "I will take the cattle, and I will go to counsel with Colonel Butler at Oswego."

Brant had been taught well the subversive art of the white men. He had extracted from Herkimer the concessions he wanted, and four cattle besides, then instantly concluded the parley without saying yes or no to the single, critical demand of Herkimer.

He said no more as he gave abrupt hand signs to the two warriors who had remained with him. They gathered the lead ropes of the four cattle, then followed Brant to walk steadily away, not looking back.

Stunned, livid with anger, Herkimer opened his mouth to call after him, then clamped it shut, teeth grinding as he watched Brant's back moving calmly toward the safety of the forest. *I can't call after him without showing everyone that he is in control, and I won't give him the satisfaction of having me beg. I'll fight him first.*

A hush held for a moment before murmuring erupted among the rank and file, and then the explosive moment was over. Herkimer slowly brought his outrage under control and forced his mind to make a judgment of what he had gained, and what he had lost, and to plan the next step. He turned to Reverend Belnap, who shrugged and turned away. In restrained anger, Herkimer turned to Ebenezer Cox, who shook his head in sour disgust and followed Belnap before the general could say a word.

Herkimer stood with head tilted forward, mouth pursed for several seconds, pondering, pulling his thoughts together. Then he turned to Brownley and Whetten. Neither man would look him in the eye. Herkimer's shoulders slumped as bitter thoughts cut into his heart. *I failed. All I did was give him what he wanted, and I got nothing in return—no promise that he would stay out of the war.* The unbearable humiliation rose to choke him for a moment. *What will Schuyler say? St. Clair?*

Teeth clenched, he raised his face to stare south at the trees where Brant had disappeared. *What will he do? When the battle starts that will decide who controls the Hudson River and Fort Ticonderoga, what will Brant do?*

Notes

The history of the Iroquois as well as the other Indian tribes of the northeastern section of the United States, which the author thought helpful to the reader in understanding the conduct of the Indians in the revolution, is set out in the following references: Graymont, *The Iroquois;* Hale, *The Iroquois Book of Rites,* pp. 18–38; Graymont, *The Iroquois in the American Revolution,* pp. 1–26.

In addition, specific facts set forth hereafter are taken from Graymont, *The Iroquois in the American Revolution* on the pages indicated.

Joseph Brant, in concert with British Major John Butler, Daniel Claus, and others, used the winter of 1776–77 to circulate widely through the territory of the Iroquois and other Indian tribes, seeking support for the British. He gained access to their councils by use of a wampum belt, eventually depositing it at Onondaga, the repository of thousands of such belts. Brant, with a few warriors, circulated from Lake Ontario in the Great Lakes, to the Hudson River.

Eventually he invited most of the tribal leaders to a great conference at Ganaghsaraga, a short distance south of Lake Oneida. Brant's efforts tended to stir division among the various tribes, some taking sides with the British, others wishing to remain neutral and let the white men settle their own wars, and yet others favoring the Americans.

With unrest rising, General Philip Schuyler sought to gain favor with the Indians by opening a large trading post at Oswego, and the Indians came in droves to trade. Samuel Kirkland, a powerful Christian missionary who favored the Americans, came to make speeches to the Indians, describing the great success of General Washington at Trenton and Princeton, at which time Schuyler provided six barrels of rum, all of which were well received by the Indians. It was then the sad news came from the Onondaga tribe that a disease had swept through their villages, killing many. Their council fire was extinguished, and only by a herculean effort was Samuel Kirkland able to persuade them to rekindle it and carry on. A proposed Grand Meeting at Onondaga was poorly attended; nevertheless, Brant and others continued their work, aimed at stirring up the Indians against the Americans.

In May 1777, Colonel Peter Gansevoort replaced Colonel Elmore as commander of Fort Stanwix, near the headwaters of the Mohawk River. In June 1777, Brant visited the village of Unadilla at the junction of the Susquehanna River and Butternut Creek, and the meeting was reported to General Schuyler and the Committee of Safety. When General Nicholas Herkimer of the militia heard of it, he, with three hundred eighty soldiers, went to Unadilla to investigate and requested Brant to meet him for a conference. Brant came. Herkimer met him in the village, bringing with him four local leaders, including Ebenezer Cox, who despised Brant. Herkimer, who had known Brant for years, and been a neighbor of his, had three riflemen hide nearby with orders to shoot Brant and his lieutenants if they started trouble.

The conference went reasonably well until Ebenezer Cox interrupted with harsh criticism of Brant, whereupon Brant gave a signal and his warriors, at their camp in the trees, fired their muskets. For a moment it seemed a battle was imminent, but Herkimer ordered his men to refrain, then made several concessions to Brant to console him, including a gift of four cattle. The conference ended with Brant leaving, having obtained the concessions he wanted, and four cattle for food besides. Herkimer was largely unsuccessful in gaining any commitments from Brant.

See Graymont, *The Iroquois in the American Revolution*, pp. 110–17.

CHAPTER XII

★ ★ ★

Something's wrong with him—different—he's too quiet, preoccupied— something's happened. Margaret Dunson glanced from the kitchen to the dining table at one end of the parlor, where Caleb sat with the other children—Adam, Priscilla, and Brigitte—just finishing their supper of broiled salmon, baked potato, and garden greens. He was seated at the end of the table, where his father, John Dunson, had presided over his family, until Tom Sievers brought him home at dusk on April 19, 1775, shot in the back, with a huge British musketball lodged in his right lung. The two men, along with Matthew, the eldest of the Dunson children, and Billy Weems, a lifelong friend, had been with those who met the British at Concord, turned them, humiliated them, shattered them, drove them back the eighteen miles to Charlestown and Boston. In a bewildering dream world, Caleb had watched his father die the next day, making Matthew the man of the family, until he received a request to use his skills as an oceangoing navigator on American ships, working to intercept British vessels on the high seas. At age fourteen, the weight of being the eldest man in the Dunson home had then fallen on Caleb's young shoulders.

The leap from angry words against the king to the deadly shooting had happened too fast, caught too many unprepared. Still just a boy in the awkward beginnings of the awakening of manhood, Caleb had struggled to understand a world gone mad. At the time in his life when he most needed the strong, steadying hand of a father to guide him through the strange, confusing, bittersweet, ever-shifting, ever-changing world of a boy becoming a man, Caleb had no one.

With the people in the colonies divided in their loyalties between England and America, and with the best of men shaken, vacillating, uncertain, young Caleb faced questions that rolled over him like a tidal wave, swamping his mind, numbing his heart. If the American cause of freedom was God's work, then why had God allowed his father, one of the leaders, to be killed? And why had He then taken Matthew and Tom Sievers away from the family? Why had his mother been left a widow, heartbroken, grieving, with five children to raise and support? Why had Billy Weems been all but killed by musket and bayonet, when he was fighting for the right? Why had God let the British smash George Washington's army on Long Island, and then drive the remnants running in desperate panic clear to Pennsylvania, across the Delaware River, to save anything they could?

True, this great and omnipotent God had allowed Washington to retake Trenton, and then Princeton, but why, with those two victories won, had they come to nothing? The British remained. They continued to crush the rebellious Americans. And now they were coming down the Hudson River, to divide the states and take them one at a time.

If this great, righteous, omnipotent, Almighty God was using the colonists to accomplish His work, then why were these chosen people being killed, beaten, massacred at every turn? When He needed them, they were there. But when they needed Him, where was He? Why was He indifferent to their suffering, their pleading, their cries, their prayers? Was He hiding? Or maybe He simply didn't exist at all. Caleb's young mind spiraled ever downward into a black, abysmal fog that led first to criticism, then bitterness, then rebellion against God.

Terrified, Margaret had pled, prayed, begged. Old Silas Olmsted, who had been the family reverend since John had courted and won Margaret's hand, had tried to reach across the growing abyss that lay between Caleb and the Almighty, but Caleb had refused him and silently turned his face away from God.

Sick in her heart, Margaret had prayed long and fervently every day, begging God for a miracle, then pled with Caleb, and given the last ounce of her strength to try to reach him, but he was deaf and blind to it all. Secretly, he resolved he would leave home to join the fight against the British, but for one reason only. Not for freedom, not for his country, not for the Almighty, but because the British had killed his father. He would make them pay. He would have his revenge. Vengeance is mine, said this Almighty God, but Caleb only smiled. You take your vengeance. I'll take mine.

With his resolve fresh in his heart, he now sat quietly at the supper table, subdued, head bowed, shoulders hunched forward, his mind leaping ahead, making a plan of how he would leave home in the dark of night. At sixteen years of age, he had no concept of what the instinct of his mother's heart was telling her as she watched him. Everything within her sensed a decision and resolve in him, but she had no way of knowing what it was.

Using a thick pad, Margaret drew a sweet-smelling raisin custard from the kitchen oven, raised and locked the door, then walked to the dining table. She set it steaming on the table, then went back to the kitchen for bowls while Prissy reached to feel the rising steam and Adam grasped his spoon, waiting.

"Brigitte, how much milk is left?" Margaret called.

Brigitte tilted the pitcher to peer inside. "Enough."

"Good." Margaret returned to set the bowls on the table, then began portioning out the rich, creamy custard, speckled with large, plump, dark raisins.

Adam's eyebrows peaked as he raised his voice in protest. "That's not enough. You always give more than that."

"It's enough to start. If you want more, we'll talk about it."

"I want more now," he complained.

Margaret shook her head. "Brigitte, pour the milk. Adam, you wait until the custard is cool."

Brigitte poured the rich milk onto the custard, and Adam instantly thrust in his spoon to draw out the first heaping load, sticking out his tongue to gingerly test for heat. He jerked back, sucking his tongue furiously. Margaret shook her head. "When will you learn to listen?"

She set Caleb's bowl before him, and for a moment he did not stir or give any recognition that it was there. "There's your custard," she said, and paused for a moment when he did not move.

"Caleb, what's wrong? You've been too quiet. Something happen today? Was there trouble at the print shop?"

Caleb raised his head. "No. Nothing's wrong. Just thinking."

"About what?" She waited, intently watching his downcast eyes.

He shrugged. "Nothing. Work. Got a heavy load tomorrow."

"Sure it's work? Not something else?"

He shook his head and reached for the milk. "Just work."

With supper finished, Brigitte washed the dishes while Margaret dried, listening to the twins playing in the backyard as the long, warm, beautiful June day came to a close. There was a hush in the air, and from the distance came the clanging of ship's bells in the bay and the squawking of seagulls as they settled the question of which one would get the greater share of the scraps of fish and food on the beaches. As the shadows of dusk deepened, Margaret lighted the lamps, and Brigitte sat in an upholstered chair, legs drawn up beneath her, reading a book. Caleb wandered out the front door to stand near the front gate, watching the street traffic thin.

Margaret sat down beside Brigitte and asked, "Notice anything about Caleb?"

Brigitte put her finger on her place in the book and for a moment went back over the events of supper and the evening. "Not especially. He seemed quiet, but that happens."

"Not like tonight," Margaret said. "His mind was somewhere else."

"He said he has a lot to do at work."

"He's had a lot at work before, but it never kept him quiet the whole evening. We didn't get ten words from him. Look at him now. Outside, just standing by the gate. He never goes out there to just stand by the gate watching Boston go by."

Brigitte shrugged. "Who knows? Maybe he's growing up."

Margaret rose. "I hope that's all it is." She walked to the great stone fireplace, with its four iron arms for hanging cooking pots, and using a brass shovel carefully banked the glowing coals for the night. She replaced the shovel and walked to the front door.

"Caleb," she called, "we need kindling wood."

"I'm coming."

She watched him walk through the house, looking neither right nor left, and out the back door. There was rustling in the wood yard, and he came back, arms loaded with split sticks of pine firewood. It took him two trips to fill the wood boxes in the kitchen and beside the parlor fireplace. Finished with his chore, he sauntered out the front door once again.

Margaret shook her head. "Something's wrong."

Brigitte raised her head from her book, glanced at the front door, then resumed reading.

Lights were coming on behind window curtains all up and down the street when Margaret went to the back door. "Adam, Prissy, time for bed. Tomorrow we've got to iron and fold all the clothes we washed today, and you both need to help."

With the family wearing their long nightshirts, and Brigitte with her long, honey-brown hair brushed and wound beneath her night cap, Margaret called them all to their places around her bed, where the stiff clothes from the day's wash were stacked, waiting to be sprinkled tomorrow, packed in a wicker basket, then ironed. John's pillow was still beside her own; she could not bring herself to store it on the top shelf of the closet. At times she reached to touch it in the night. More than once she had drawn it to her, to hold it tightly to her breast while she buried her face in it and sobbed her heart out.

For a moment she looked at Caleb, wanting desperately to call on him to offer the evening prayer, but for months, he had offered prayers that were devoid of spirit or reverence toward God and then had begun asking that someone else to do it. The twins had come to her wide-eyed, asking why Caleb no longer took his turn, and with a heart that was breaking, she had told them he was working too hard, first at school, then at the print shop as school ceased for the summer and he went on with his work. She knew she could not let Caleb's rebellion infect the twins, and quietly ceased calling on him to pray.

"Brigitte," she said, and they all closed their eyes, hands clasped before their faces, as Brigitte offered the nightly family prayer.

Later, with the house silent, Margaret turned all the lamps down and sat in the rocking chair before the dull glow of the banked coals, watching them, deep in her own thoughts.

John, I don't know what to do. It was too much for him. Too much for any boy his age. I'm losing him. Something's happened inside him—he's made some decision that he will not tell me about. I can only pray it is not to leave. If he leaves, I don't know what will become of him. I can accept him going to the fighting, and I can accept it if he doesn't come back. But I cannot accept him turning his back on the Almighty. Oh, John! What would I do if he were not allowed to be with us in heaven? What would I do? What would I do?

In the deep shadows of the parlor, silent tears welled up and rolled down her cheeks to wet the front of her nightshirt. It was midnight before she wiped at her eyes with her sleeve, then rose to silently pad through the archway and into her own bedroom. She dropped to her knees beside her bed and with bowed head poured out her pain to the Almighty. Then she moved the day's wash to the far side of the bed and silently slipped between the cool sheets.

She did not go to sleep. With an intuition known only to a mother whose life is her children, she lay staring at the ceiling in the darkness, listening to every sound, waiting. At one o'clock she heard the call of the bellmen as the pair walked the streets, watching for thieves, calling out the time and the weather. At two o'clock their call came again: "Two o'clock. Fair weather," and still she forced herself to rise above the weariness of the heavy day of washing, hanging, and gathering clothes, to remain awake, alert.

At three o'clock their call came once again, and moments later she heard the first faint sound of a footfall in the hallway. She knew instantly who it was. She did not move, nor did she cry out. She listened to the soft click of a door opening, and a moment later closing, then a second door opening and closing, and she knew. He had silently gone into the twins' bedroom, then into Brigitte's, to look at them before he left. She waited, but he did not open her door to enter for one last, silent look at his mother. At sixteen he knew mothers seldom sleep deeply enough to fail to hear sounds from their children.

With her heart and mind racing, she listened to the creaking floor boards leading through the archway into the parlor.

He's going. That is what possessed him at supper—through the whole evening. He's leaving. Do I let him go? Do I try to stop him? John, John, what do I do?

She heard the squeak of a chair as he sat to tie on his shoes, and suddenly she did not care what wisdom or reason would require of her. She only knew the soul-wrenching grab in her mother's heart. Her boy was leaving! She lunged out of bed, opened her door, and ran silently down the hall, through the archway, and across the parlor to the front door as he swung it open. In the soft, warm June night, she saw the silhouette of Caleb stop and turn as she ran to him.

Without a word she threw her arms about him and held him close, clung to him, then buried her face in his chest as the tears came. He dropped his bedroll and raised his arms to wrap her inside, his cheek against her hair, feeling her shake as she sobbed. Neither of them knew how long they stood in the door frame, the boy holding his mother, while she clung to him with all her strength. After a time, her sobbing slowed, then stopped, and she tipped her head back to look into his face in the light of the stars and the full moon. He started to speak, and could not. She remained silent, studying him, memorizing every line of his young face.

Finally she released him and stepped back. Again Caleb tried to speak, but was unable to choke out a word. Margaret picked up the bedroll that held his blanket, a change of clothes, and a leather purse with money he had saved from work and handed it to him. He took it and held it loosely in his hands, not knowing what he should do next.

She stepped back and nodded to him. "I love you. God bless you, son. I'll be waiting."

He looked into her face for a long time, then raised his hand to gently touch the familiar softness before turning and walking into the night. She did not move as she watched him reach the front gate, where he stopped and turned to look one more time. He opened the gate, and in her bare feet she walked to the white picket fence to watch him disappear in the blackness.

Notes

The Dunson family is a fictional family, hence, the ongoing story of the various family members, including Caleb, is fictional.

The custom of having bellmen patrolling the Boston streets at night, calling out the weather and the time, is set forth in Chapter I.

CHAPTER XIII

$\mathcal{T}$he noon sun was a ball of brass that bore down relentlessly to turn the world into a sweltering, oppressive oven of dead, wet air that lay heavy on the rolling New Jersey hills and valleys. The wild flowers and lush foliage that lined the banks of the Raritan River hung limp, drooping, while the brown-black water flowed south, twisting and turning until the river suddenly veered due east to empty into the Atlantic at the southern tip of Staten Island.

River traffic labored in both directions—the southbound moving with paddles and the current, and the northbound being driven upstream with long poles. The men moving the northbound boats and barges had long since stripped off their sweat-soaked shirts and draped them to dry on barrels or shipping crates or on the roof of the tiny, low cabins on the small, squat freight boats and barges, while they continued to walk the narrow planks along the inside of the gunwales. They jammed their long poles into the mud on the river bottom, then threw their weight against them, legs driving, as they walked from the bow to the stern, bucking the current to move the boat and its load of freight another few yards upriver. Muscles stood out like cords while sweat ran shining to soak their rough, homespun trousers, and dripped from elbows and chins and noses.

Amos Jennings, owner of the *River Belle*, sat slumped on a plank bench in the stern of the small, aging freight boat, arm draped over the tiller, intently watching ahead for sandbars, shallows, and submerged logs. He clamped his cold clay pipe between his teeth and squinted one-eyed at the sun. *Noon, and we got no time to spare. We miss the freight wagons at the pier and we might be three, four days getting some more.* He drew a determined breath and watched his six-man crew continue their steady rotation, silent, heads down, sweat running as they set their poles and drove the boat and its thirteen tons of flour, blankets, shoes, and dried beef wallowing up the river, the gunwales a scant eight inches above the water line.

He removed his pipe long enough to wipe the sweat from his face and beard with his sleeve, then clenched it grimly back between his teeth. *Three days lost waiting in New York for the shoes from Boston—lost another day when that storm come through from the Adirondacks—can't make up no time going upstream—if we miss those wagons at the pier, the army in Morristown's not going to like it—can't lose the hauling contract—got to protect it somehow.*

At the pier, newly built to unload river freight bound for the Continental army in Morristown, contract wagons waited to make the two-day haul due east on a rutted dirt road that wound its way through the forest, to the depot on the fringes of the army encampment. The wagons ran on a schedule. To miss them at the pier meant waiting, sometimes four days, for them to return for the next load.

He glanced to his right at the young, attractive woman who had paid him ten pounds British for passage from New York to the pier. She had said her name was Mary Flint and that she had an urgent need to see someone in the Continental army. With the British swarming in New York and New Jersey, she had been forced to seek passage on freight boats and wagons whose operators were willing to chance getting stopped by the British. The delay in New York forced her to pay for food and lodging at an inn for three extra days, and left her with almost nothing after she paid Jennings for passage up the river.

He had warned her about robbers and thieves who preyed on the riverboats and freight wagons, and the chance that British soldiers might intercept and confiscate the entire load, as well as the boat. She listened but said nothing. He also told her she would have to pay to ride the freight wagons to Morristown, and she said she was aware of it, since she had made the arrangements with the teamsters herself, but the cost of the three extra days in New York had left her without enough money. She looked Jennings in the eye and said she would find a way. She would sell her luggage if necessary. Jennings was puzzled. Her manners and speech bespoke cultured breeding, and her clothing and baggage were of high quality. He wondered at the dichotomy of expensive clothing, high breeding, and no money, but staid New England custom would not allow him to inquire into the private affairs of a young woman. He could only wonder in silence.

The dark-eyed, dark-haired woman sat on an empty upside-down keg with her two large leather suitcases, one on either side. She had untied her bonnet strings but left the bonnet in place to shade her eyes and face. Jennings studied her as she leaned to her right to drench her handkerchief in the river, then squeeze it tightly, shake it out, fold it, and wipe at the beads of perspiration on her face. She repeated it to wipe at her neck, then her wrists and hands. She had taken her meals with the men, and with the boat tied to the shore at night, she had slept aboard while the men all slept on the river bank. She had asked no privilege, nor did she complain.

Jennings shifted his gaze back to his crew, watching for the first signs of heat exhaustion. They could endure the backbreaking work of poling the boat under the fierce midday sun for a time, but not all day. When their legs began to quiver and their hands to shake on their poles, it was time to either get them off the boat and into the shade of the forest for a time, or lose one or two of them for two or three days, or worse, dig a shallow grave and move on.

He grasped the tiller with both hands, hauled it to the right, and the boat nosed over toward the east bank. "Get ashore. I'll bring food."

The men tied the boat, set the gangplank, and walked down to the thick green growth, into the dank shade of the forest, to lay down on their backs, arms flung wide. They closed their eyes and did not move until Jennings brought cheese, bread, and ham in a sack, and Mary carried two canteens of fresh water. They ate in silence, then once again lay down on the forest floor, closed their eyes, and did not move. One hour after stopping, Jennings called, "Back to the *Belle*. Miles to go before we sleep."

They pushed steadily northward until darkness hid the sandbars and shallows and the submerged logs and snags. They tied up once again to the east bank and shared their simple meal, then the men slipped into their dry shirts with the sweat rings showing around the neck and sleeves before they sought their blankets among the trees on shore. Mary remained aboard the gently undulating boat. One hour later, certain the men were asleep, Mary quietly dipped a wooden bucket of water from the river, lowered herself into the cramped hold of the small boat, washed herself in the darkness, put on dry clothing, then went back up on deck. She dipped her sweat-stained dress in the river, then carefully wrung it out and draped it over the edge of the cabin to dry. Minutes later she spread her blanket on the deck near the tiller, and for a time sat with her back propped against the side of the boat, arms wrapped about her drawn-up knees, listening to the quiet murmur of the river, the croak of the bullfrogs, and the chirping song of the crickets.

A night breeze arose fresh and cool on her face. She turned her eyes upward to the countless stars in the black velvet dome, and as the weariness and tension began to slowly drain, she let her thoughts run.

Alone—so far from home. Home? I have no home—or family—all gone—money gone—husband gone—baby gone—war all around—how did it happen—what grand design in heaven took everything—left me on a riverbank with strangers, trying to find two men—one from Boston—one raised Iroquois—am I foolish to be looking for them—no—they will help—Eli will understand—what do I expect from Eli—what will he think—what will he think?

She jerked awake at a sudden shuddering of the boat and the sound of pounding and twisted to peer at the gangplank. Jennings stepped off onto the deck and started back toward the tiller, followed by five of the crew, who picked up their long poles and took their positions on the sides of the boat. Mary stood and waited for Jennings to take his seat beside the tiller. He called, "All clear!" and the sixth man, still on shore, cast off the line and trotted up the gangplank as the boat began to drift backward with the current. On deck, the man grasped the gangplank and pulled it on board, then picked up the last pole and took his place.

With the mosquitoes rising from the marshes and the river, and the sun one hour high, Jennings passed out hardtack and cold, fried sowbelly, and the men ate while continuing their rotation. Mary kept her place near the tiller and ate when the men did. When they finished, Jennings rationed out one cup of rum each, and the men took turns to stop and savor it. Mary drank from a water canteen. At one o'clock, with the sun pounding down, they tied up for their midday meal, and the men again sought shade to escape the withering heat.

At half-past three, with the crew running sweat, Jennings stood, hand on the tiller. His arm shot up, pointing. "Around the next bend, two hundred yards. The pier. The wagons have got to be there."

Mary stood, balanced against the rocking of the boat in the current, watching as the crew slowly drove the boat onward. They passed the bend, and Jennings pushed the tiller to the right. The nose of the boat swung eastward, and suddenly the pier was there, dead ahead. The only sound was the lapping of the river against the boat as all eyes counted the wagons.

There were four, with sixteen thick-necked, heavy-legged horses hobbled nearby, muzzles thrust into the grass. Jennings's pulse quickened. "We made it! They left four wagons for this load!"

But while he watched, the wagoneers, who had been sitting in the shade of the great freighters, rose to come to the pier, and Jennings counted but three. His face fell, and he counted again. There were only three.

The boat bumped the pier, two of the crew jumped to tie it fore and aft to the pilings, and Jennings climbed over the gunwales onto the rough planking and trotted to meet the wagoneers. He spoke to one of the men.

"You the wagonmaster?"

"Yes. Name's Gerhardt."

"You only got three drivers?"

Gerhardt nodded. "We waited for you, but this morning one driver pulled out. Said he had to get home. Left a wife and sick baby six days ago. I told him to wait, but he wouldn't."

"Four wagons and three drivers. How're you going to get that fourth wagon to Morristown?"

"We aren't, at least not this trip. We could try to rig it behind one of the others, but the Morristown road has eight or ten turns too tight to let them both pass. We're going to have to leave it and come back for it."

Jennings's voice raised in fear and anger. "Four days? It won't be here when you get back."

Gerhardt asked, "Can one of your men stay?"

"No. We've got the next load waiting."

The leader shrugged. "Then we leave it."

"Who stands the loss of the freight if it's gone?"

"You. You were late getting here. I stand the loss of the wagon, but I got insurance."

Pain showed in Jennings's face as he glanced at his crew, then back at Gerhardt. "You can't load heavy? Get it all on three wagons?"

Gerhardt shook his head vigorously. "A storm hit and turn the road to mud, we'd mire to the axles. Have to sit there 'til the roads dried out. Can't risk it."

Jennings's shoulders sagged in resignation. "Let's get at it. We can have you loaded by dark if we start now."

The men hit a pace, a rhythm, and the crates and barrels in the hold of the boat steadily moved up and out, down the pier, to the wagons, where two men loaded them, packed tight. The sun set, and they stopped to drink cold water, wipe the sweat, and then continue. It was fully dark when the last of the freight was in the wagons, covered with heavy tarps, tied down so the loads could not shift. Their work finished, the men boiled coffee over a small fire and warmed strips of salt beef on sticks, ate it with stale bread and cheese, and chewed on dried apple slices. Jennings brought out a small keg of rum, and they took their rations in wooden cups, sitting cross-legged around the fire, silent, each with his own thoughts while they sipped at it, nursing it, savoring it. They rinsed their utensils in the river, spread their blankets, and then laid down facing the fire. Within minutes they were breathing deeply, and Mary could hear the snoring from her place on board the *River Belle*.

She let an hour pass before she dipped a bucket of river water, washed herself, tugged on fresh clothing, and sought the quiet solitude of sitting alone on the gently undulating deck. *Tomorrow, and then the next day, and we'll be there—two more days—two more days.* It repeated in her head like a chant. Everything inside her was gathered in anticipation. Eli. Billy. They understand. Things will be all right. Her head slowly settled forward and she slept.

She was up and waiting before the morning star began to fade, standing on the deck beside the gangplank, luggage packed. She watched the spark struck in the pitch black of the forest to light the morning campfire, and watched the dim shape come to the river to scoop water for coffee and mush. Jennings brought her a wooden bowl of oatmeal, sweetened with brown sugar, and strong, steaming coffee, and she ate. She peered into the darkness as the wagoneers hooked up twelve horses to three wagons, puzzled that four horses were left hobbled to graze, and one loaded wagon still stood with its tongue on the ground. She walked to the gunwales and turned her head to listen.

Jennings voice was raised. "There's three thousand dollars worth of flour and blankets in that wagon. Sure you can't rig it to another wagon and hook up the last four horses to pull the double load?"

The wagonmaster shook his head violently. "There's no hope of getting both wagons around some of the bends in that road. There's two places it's hard getting one wagon through—takes good drivers to make it. I hate the risk of losing the load and the wagon to thieves, but I don't know what else to do."

Jennings shook his head. "I'd leave one of my crew, but five men can't handle this boat. I've got another load waiting in New York in two days, and I can't be late without taking a chance on losing the contract." He pulled off his narrow-brimmed, battered felt hat and nervously scratched his head, then his beard. "Never lost a load in my life, and now here I sit, about to walk away from one." He shook his head. "Well, I'll help your passenger get loaded. I better tell you, she's without money—can't pay her fare. Says she'll have to sell her luggage at Morristown to pay you. She's been a good passenger. I think she'll do it."

The wagonmaster blew air through rounded lips. "Another one that can't pay? That's four so far this summer." Disgust was plain on his face as he looked toward the boat. "All right. Let's move. We can be gone by sunrise."

The men started to move their separate directions, then stopped at the sound of firm footsteps rattling the gangplank, and turned to look. Mary strode down, onto the riverbank, and over to the surprised group of men. They stood without speaking, startled at her sudden appearance in the gray of morning. Mary stopped six feet in front of Gerhardt.

"Sir, do I understand you lack a driver for the fourth wagon?"

Gerhardt glanced at Jennings before answering. "Yes, ma'am. That's a fact. Left to tend a sick wife and baby."

"You will have to leave the fourth wagon and the freight here for a few days until you return?"

"Looks that way."

Mary's expression did not change as she said firmly, "I'll drive it. I have no money to pay you for my passage, so I'll expect teamster's pay. That way I can pay you and maybe have a little left."

Gerhardt's mouth dropped open for a split second before he clacked it shut and blurted, "You? You're going to drive that wagon?" His eyes worked up and down Mary and her expensive clothing. "You ever drive a wagon before? A loaded freight wagon that size?"

Mary's answer was firm, measured. "Many times. Six-horse teams, eight-horse teams. Twelve tons of ammunition one time to the magazine on Manhattan Island. A seventeen-ton load from Manhattan Island to Long Island the night General Washington crossed the East River to prepare for the battle he lost. I can drive those four horses and that wagon easily." She pointed at the wagon without looking.

Every man gaped. Buzzing broke out, then subsided.

Gerhardt looked at Jennings in bewilderment. "Want to trust your freight to this woman?"

Jennings wiped his sleeve across his mouth and looked at Mary. "Yes, I do."

Gerhardt shrugged. "I'm good for it if you are." He looked at Mary. "We'll get the horses hooked up."

Mary bobbed her head. "I'll help."

The man froze. "You'll what?"

Mary did not answer. She walked to the horses, talking softly as she came in from the side where they could see her. She touched the neck of the nearest one, then rubbed it, then reached to handle its ears briefly. She worked her hand down, onto its near front leg, and to the buckles of the leather hobbles. Gerhardt stood in dumbstruck silence as she deftly removed the hobbles and moved to the next horse. Then he hurried to help her.

The light wisp of clouds in the eastern sky were shot through with color when Mary and Gerhardt snapped the last traces to the double-trees and wound the eight, long leather ribbons around the brake pole. Mary didn't hesitate. She pulled her skirts high enough to reach the front wheel hub with her right foot, grasped the wheel, and pulled herself up, then reached with her foot for the cleat and stepped into the driver's seat. She unwound the reins, sorted them out, and threaded them through her fingers, four to each hand. She took up the slack, adjusted them for even tension, then slapped the long leather ribbons down on the rumps of the horses and called, "Giddap."

The four horses leaned into their collars, and their iron shoes dug into the earth as they started the load moving. Mary threw her weight against the reins in her left hand, and the horses started into their turn with the wagon complaining all the way. Her jaw was set, feet spread and planted, and her eyes shining in the sunrise as she kept the pressure on the left reins. She swung them in a half circle and brought the leaders up behind the wagon in the rear of the column before she leaned back and seesawed on the reins as she called, "Whoa," and the horses came back against the load. The wagon came to a rocking stop with the noses of the lead team ten feet behind the next wagon, lined up perfectly.

She turned to call to Gerhardt and the other two grinning teamsters, "Ready when you are."

All ten men came at a high trot. The three teamsters climbed to the boxes of their wagons, while Jennings and his six rivermen loaded Mary's luggage in the driver's box next to her and gathered around, looking up at her. Jennings had his hat in his hand.

"Ma'am, you are sure full of surprises. I don't know how to thank you. I will not forget you, Mary Flint. I hope you find whoever it is you're looking for."

"I'm happy I could help. Thank you for everything. All of you."

The other six rivermen nodded up to her, suddenly feeling awkward, self-conscious. Gerhardt gigged his team into motion, and then the two wagons ahead of Mary creaked forward. She waited a few moments, then slapped the reins down on the rumps of her team and clucked them ahead. Mary turned to look over the top of her load once, to see Jennings and his crew waving, and then the forest closed in.

Midmorning they stopped at a stream to water the horses. At one o'clock they pulled their wagons in while they drank canteen water and Gerhardt doled out bread and meat. They each took their ration and climbed back to the wagon boxes to set it on the seat, and the little column moved on, the teamsters eating as they drove.

Twice in the late afternoon they came to switchbacks in the narrow, rutted, dirt road, lined with trees, stumps, and boulders. Each time, Mary slowed her team long enough to make calculations, then swung them wide into the turn, to bring them back sharply while she watched the inside rear wheel to be sure it cleared the rocks and stumps at the edge of the road. Both times she straightened her team and looked ahead to see the other three drivers all turned, watching her, grinning.

With coffee boiling over a low campfire and mutton slices sizzling in a big, black, cast-iron frying pan, Gerhardt came to her, seated in the grass near her horses. He pulled his ragged hat from his head. "Ma'am, it would be good if you'd come take supper with us. I'll bring it to you if you want, but the men and me talked it over, and it seems right you ought to be with us, since you sure done your share today. You needn't have any fears about us, ma'am. Not after what you done today."

He stopped and worked his hat with his hands for a moment, not knowing what to say or do next. Mary looked up at him, then rose to her feet. He turned and walked back to the fire while she followed.

The teams were hitched up and the teamsters were in their wagon boxes before the morning star had faded. At one o'clock, beneath an overcast sky, they hauled the wagons to a halt to let the horses water from a wide, shallow stream. They climbed down to get their ration of tough brown bread, cheese, and dried peach slices, and to drink from a big, two-gallon canteen before they remounted to gather up and sort their reins once more. The sun was two hours past its zenith before the wagon-master pointed, then turned his head to call back above the creaking of the wagons and the steady, muffled rhythm of the horses' hooves.

"Morristown dead ahead. Watch for American patrols."

Ten minutes later movement in the trees to her right brought Mary's head around, and she saw indistinct forms moving in the forest. Two minutes later they broke into the roadbed, and Gerhardt came back on his reins to stop the column.

Mary heard muffled words, then Gerhardt said, "We're bringing contract supplies in for General Washington's army." Seconds later, the lead wagons moved on, and Mary stirred her team to keep her interval. She passed four men with muskets, standing on the right side of the roadbed. They wore the clothes of common colonials, and each had a musket with bayonet mounted.

Her breathing quickened. *American patrol—we're getting close—will they be here?*

They did not reach Morristown. They drove their wagons into the sprawling American camp, one quarter mile from the edge of the neatly built village, and soldiers waved them in to the freight depot, half of them stopping to stare at the beautiful, dark-eyed woman, wearing a dress and bonnet, sitting straight in the last wagon box, handling a four-up as though she were born to it. Gerhardt stopped the column and waited while the quartermaster strode quickly to the lead wagon. The man wore a New York militia tunic, a tricorn hat, and carried a sheaf of papers in one hand. He faced Gerhardt.

"I'm Quartermaster Buttars. You're bringing freight from who?"

"From Jennings. *River Belle.* Got a contract for flour, shoes, blankets, salt beef."

The officer scanned his papers and then pointed. "Flour and blankets over there, salt beef and shoes over there."

The other two teamsters came to Mary's wagon and helped her to the ground, then set her suitcases beside her and waited while Gerhardt came striding and pointed. "We unload over there." He looked at Mary, then reached inside his shirt for a sweat-stained leather purse. He drew out four gold coins and dropped them into her hand. "That's standard teamsters wages for two days. Take it with our thanks."

Mary reached to extend two coins back to him. "That's for my passage."

Gerhardt shook his head. "No, ma'am. There's no way you can get me to take it. Me and the boys don't pay for our passage, and it's sure you aren't going to either. What you done was worth more than the pay. Take it, and our thanks."

Mary accepted the coins, then thrust her hand out to Gerhardt. "Thank you. Good luck to each of you."

The men all mumbled their thanks, then turned to begin the work of unloading thirteen tons of army supplies. Mary stood long enough to locate the quartermaster, then moved quickly to catch him.

"Sir, I'm looking for two of your soldiers. Who should I talk to?"

"What regiment?"

"I suppose Boston, if there is such a thing."

"There's a Massachusetts battalion." He studied Mary. "Aren't you the one who was driving that last wagon that just came in?"

"Yes."

His eyebrows arched for a moment. "The Massachusetts camp is about two hundred yards to the west, over there." He pointed. "Stop and ask."

"Thank you." She walked back to her luggage, lifted one bag in each hand, and started west, working her way through the mix of soldiers and civilians. She stopped every fifty yards to set the heavy luggage down and give her hands and arms a rest. Soldiers slowed to covertly stare at her as she moved on. She came abreast of two young officers, set her suitcases down, and spoke.

"Sir, is the Massachusetts camp close by?"

"Yes, ma'am. You're in it. Can we be of help?"

"Yes. I'm looking for two soldiers."

"Do you know their names?"

"Billy Weems and Eli Stroud. Would you know where I might find either one of them?" Her breathing slowed and her heart pounded as she waited for the answer. *They have to be here. Must be here!*

"No, ma'am, but we might be able to find someone who does." The young lieutenant turned to look about, then called, "Sergeant, would you come here for a moment?"

A bandy-legged, hawk-nosed little man left a crew of men loading sacks of oats onto a slip and walked over. He eyed Mary before he spoke. "Yes, sir?"

"This young lady is looking for two soldiers—Billy Weems and Eli Stroud. Would you know where they might be?"

The sergeant peered out from beneath shaggy brows. "Yes. Gone."

Mary gasped and recoiled as though struck. She steadied herself before she tried to speak, but her voice was barely audible. "Gone?"

"Yes, ma'am. Up north on the Hudson to fight Burgoyne. Special orders from General Washington."

"Not dead?" It was as though her life hung on the answer.

"Oh, no, ma'am. Didn't mean to give you a start. I suspect they'll be back soon as the battle's finished over there."

Hope leaped as Mary's breath came with a rush. "Do you know them?"

"Yes, ma'am. Fought alongside 'em from Long Island on."

"Are they both all right?"

"They was fit last time I saw 'em. I wouldn't worry. They know how to take care of themselves."

Mary let out all her breath. "Thank you, Sergeant."

"Glad to oblige, ma'am." The sergeant started to turn back to the officer, then stopped to stare at Mary for a long moment. "Uh, ma'am, not meanin' to step out of place, but don't I know you? Have we met before?"

For the first time Mary focused on the wiry little man. "Something . . . it's possible. Yes."

"Might I know your name, ma'am?"

"Mary Flint. From New York."

The sergeant's craggy brows lifted as he exclaimed, "New York! Manhattan Island. Last summer did you deliver a load of ammunition with a wagon and team to the magazine there on the west side of the island?"

"Yes, I did."

"Billy and Eli was there. I was the sergeant. Name's Turlock. Alvin Turlock."

Mary's hand flew to her mouth in surprise. "Of course! I remember. Sergeant, how good to see you again. Have you been with Billy and Eli since then? Are they all right?"

Turlock saw the fear in her face and heard it in her voice. "I been with 'em 'cept for some time I spent in a British prison camp. Ma'am, there's no sense you worryin' over those two. They'll be back."

For a moment Mary's chin quivered. "Thank you. Thank you."

"I'll tell them you was here. Let me know where you'll be." Turlock turned back to the officer. "Anything else, sir?"

"No. Better return to your men."

"Yes, sir." Turlock turned and marched back to his crew, calling loudly, "All right, you lovelies, put your backs into it. Oat sacks don't load theirselves. Hear?"

The officer turned to Mary. "Sorry you were disappointed, ma'am. Are the men family?"

"No. Friends." For a moment Mary's head dropped forward, then she raised it to look directly into his face. "Sir, I need to find employment. Do you have a camp hospital? I'm a trained nurse, and qualified to keep medical records."

Notes

Mary Flint as she appears herein is a fictional character, as are all other persons in this chapter.

General George Washington did winter his army in Morristown in 1776–77 and left to pursue General Howe in the spring of 1777 (see Ketchum, *The Winter Soldiers*, pp. 319–31).

The Raritan River runs near Morristown and served as a waterway for transporting supplies to the American army stationed there (see Leckie, *George Washington's War*, p. 46).

CHAPTER XIV

★ ★ ★

*G*ood morning, gentlemen." Resplendent in his fresh uniform, gold lapel piping bright on his crimson tunic, Major General John Burgoyne smiled broadly at the three officers who had just entered the British command tent under orders to assemble for a war council. Each nodded a silent greeting, then waited for Burgoyne's hand gesture before walking to the upholstered chairs surrounding the polished table in the huge tent that dominated the camp. They remained standing beside their chairs while Burgoyne proceeded to the head of the table.

Behind Burgoyne was his private rolltop desk and chair. Against one tent wall was a bed, replete with mattress and pillows. A painting of King George III hung on another canvas wall, and the red, white, and blue of the Union Jack on another. Two poles, thirty feet high, supported the massive canvas ceiling. Outside, half a dozen large, colorful pennants fluttered in the morning sun from each of the tent's two peaks. Another red, white, and blue pennant hung from the place where each of the sixty-four peg-down ropes connected to the tent's rounded canvas dome. Unloading the tent from the four wagons it took to transport it, erecting it, or striking it to repack in the wagons took an entire company of men half a day each time they made camp.

Outside the great tent the raucous, boisterous morning business of a bivouacked army of ten thousand human beings pressed on, with officers calling orders and sergeants bellowing their companies into obeying them. Two thousand wives, children, and civilian camp followers noisily carried on the necessary business of washing, ironing, mending, stripping bedding to air on lines strung among the trees, tending fires, cooking, and cleaning up, all amid the unending buzzing of insects, larger and more numerous than any of them had ever seen in Europe. Occasionally the yelp of a surprised soldier, or the shriek of a terrified woman rang throughout the camp as one of them came face to face with an angry rattlesnake or copperhead, coiled and prepared to defend its territory.

Tall, dark, charismatic, hair pulled back and tied with a small black bow, Gentleman Johnny bowed to his officers with a graceful, theatrical flourish. "Thank you for coming. It is good to be here with you." To his left was his large, upholstered master chair. Before him several documents lay on the table in two neat stacks

Baron Frederich Adolph von Riedesel, German general in command of the Hanau-Hessians in Burgoyne's army, stood at rigid attention beside the chair immediately to Burgoyne's right. In February of 1776, von Riedesel had marched two thousand, two hundred, and twenty-two Brunswick mercenary troops out of Wolfenbuttel, Germany, lustily singing one of their hymns, bound for America to fight for the British for pay in the amount of seven pounds, four shillings, four and one-half pence each. He was followed to America by his petite, charming, and stunningly beautiful wife, Baroness Frederika Charlotte Louise von Massow, daughter of a Prussian general, now Baroness von Riedesel, with whom von Riedesel was deeply in love, and she with him. With her came their three daughters, the youngest an infant in arms.

Next to von Riedesel stood British Brigadier General Simon Fraser, youngest in the council. Cool, clear-headed, respected, Fraser was loved by those under his command and favored by his peers. Burgoyne had found in him exactly what he wanted to help lead the expedition. He had entreated the king, then Lord Germain, that he must have Fraser, and they had consented. Fraser had only lately arrived from England.

Opposite von Riedesel stood Major General William Phillips, reputed to be the toughest artillery officer in the British empire, likely the world, and in whose vocabulary the word "retreat" did not appear. If

Phillips was involved in a campaign, the entire British military knew they could depend on spit and polish discipline, military maneuvers by the book, precision in execution of every detail, and the infliction of massive damage on the enemy. Phillips had his jaw set like a bulldog's while he waited.

Burgoyne's eyes flitted from man to man. "I believe we're all here. Be seated." He remained standing while his officers took their seats, all eyes turned toward the general. His cordial demeanor changed in an instant. Suddenly he was all business, efficient, decisive. He drew a great breath and began.

"Gentlemen, for what is to come, I invite you to examine some maps. Since we made our plan at Crown Point and moved on south to where we are today, developments require this meeting. Each of you will be asked for an opinion regarding how we should now proceed, based on the facts now before us, so I request that you give serious consideration to the positions of our forces and theirs, and the geography separating us." He picked up the top document from the nearest stack and unfolded it, smoothing it on the tabletop, turning it slightly to lie true with the compass. He reached to tap it with his finger, which he moved as he spoke.

"As you know, we are now here, three miles north of Fort Ticonderoga. The southern reaches of Lake Champlain are here. Our morning reports show that we have just over seven thousand men fit for duty today. Well armed, well rested. Morale high." He shifted his finger south a short distance. "General St. Clair commands about twenty-five hundred American militia here at Fort Ticonderoga, three miles south. Reports have it that they are lately suffering from dysentery and measles. Most of their troops are young and have never been under fire. They delude themselves that they can hold Ticonderoga. I believe it is fair to say their morale will plummet soon after our cannon commence. Uniforms are nearly nonexistent among them. They are low on rations, and very poorly armed. Some of their companies carry nothing more than spears and spontoons." He paused to turn to Phillips. "Not entirely effective against grapeshot, would you say, General?"

Phillips cracked the slightest vestige of a smile but remained silent while the other two officers moved and chuckled briefly.

Burgoyne continued. "Between where we are now and Fort Ticonderoga, is Mount Hope, here. The Americans have a small advance post there, and it is garrisoned. Here, just south of the garrison, they have a sawmill, and a bridge that spans a sizable stream. Here, about one mile from the fort, are what are called the French Lines—old breastworks built by the French. The Americans have improved them and have men stationed there."

He paused for a moment to let them track with him, then moved his finger east. "Here, across the lake, on the east side, is Rattlesnake Hill, recently renamed Mount Independence. The Americans are constructing some defensive positions there. I believe it is their intent to cross to the east side of the lake in the event they cannot hold the west side." A smile flashed and was gone. "They renamed it in honor of that document they concocted last year—what was it about?—independence?"

The other officers quietly snorted and shook their heads. The Declaration of Independence had incited momentous celebration in America, but high hilarity in Whitehall and Buckingham and in the British Parliament in London.

He glanced at von Riedesel, then moved his finger back to the west side of the lake. "Here is the fort, and here, just south, is Sugar Hill. The rebels now call it Mount Defiance."

Burgoyne's speech slowed, and his voice lowered with new intensity as he continued with the map. He shifted his finger to the east side of the lake once again. "South of Mount Independence, here, is Skenesborough, and to the east is Hubbardton, here. The Americans have built a bridge running generally north and south, across the narrows of the lake, here, from the area of Fort Ticonderoga to the foot of Mount Independence, here. The bridge is wide enough and strong enough to support horses and cannon. Should the Americans retreat from the east side of the lake, it is possible they will do so through either Skenesborough or Hubbardton. If they retreat from the west side, they will likely cross the bridge and follow the same route. However, the bridge is vulnerable to our cannon. I believe we can destroy it quickly if we get guns close enough."

He straightened for a moment, then went on. "General von Riedesel and his command have proceeded south on the east side of the lake, here, and are easily within striking distance of Mount Independence." He moved his finger again. "General Fraser and his command have moved south on the west side of the lake, to here, within one and one-half miles of the outer defenses of Fort Ticonderoga."

He shifted his finger to a point in the waters of Lake Champlain, one and one-half miles north of Fort Ticonderoga. "The *Royal George* is anchored here, the *Inflexible,* here. Together, they have about forty-five heavy guns. In addition, we have twelve bateaux carrying two or three heavy guns each, spaced between the two heavy gunboats. Between the gunboats and the two lake shores, east and west, is the boom we had constructed of massive logs, chained together, which will prevent any American fire boats from reaching the bateaux."

He paused to straighten. "Gentlemen, we have blockaded the lake. We control it. Nothing moves on it without our consent." The expression on his face was that of a man who had conceived a master plan, acquired the power and the men to put it in place, and executed it perfectly. For a moment his eyes passed from one officer to another, holding each long enough to be certain he understood the genius of what he was explaining, and the source of it all. Satisfied he had made his point, he returned to the map.

"Thus we have all our forces in place in a line, here, east to west, one and one-half miles north of Fort Ticonderoga. General von Riedesel and his forces on the east side of the lake, the gunboats and bateaux across the lake, and General Fraser and his forces on the west side. We have the advantage of Indian scouts capable of keeping us informed of enemy troop movements almost hourly, and you will recall, I have ordered that while they will be allowed to take various spoils from the fallen enemies on the battlefields, they are absolutely forbidden to engage in scalping and mutilating."

He paused to gather his thoughts, and in that moment the officers looked down at the table, or their hands, refusing to meet his eyes. They remembered the great, theatrical speech he had delivered to the bewildered Indians, by which he intended giving them permission to plunder the enemy dead, and at the same time stop them from taking scalps. While none of the officers professed intimate knowledge of the working of the Indian mind, neither did any of them have any illusion that a flamboyant speech impressive to white men would persuade a red one to quit an ancient and sacred right of battle. For Burgoyne to have given them permission to plunder in the same breath he denied them their right to scalp and mutilate was sheer insanity. None of them had talked of the speech openly, but in their hearts, each knew it had been made to provide Burgoyne with a perfect defense in the event he was ever criticized for atrocities committed by Indians under his command. With his speech having been heard by hundreds of Indians and thousands of British soldiers and officers, he could indignantly point out to the king, or his cabinet, or Parliament, that he had ordered them to cease; done all in his power to prevent the butchery.

Burgoyne drew a great breath. "There is nothing I can see that has the faintest chance of stopping us once we move south against the fort." Again he straightened and waited while the three officers leaned forward to study the map. Each in turn satisfied their questions, then leaned back in their chairs while they tested the facts before them against all they knew of the accepted, proven, basic principles of successful warfare. Slowly their minds settled. Every element of success was present. Numerical superiority, arms superiority, position superiority, officer superiority, experience, supply lines, morale. The sole question, and the most critical one, remaining unresolved was how they intended using their advantage to take Fort Ticonderoga from the Americans.

Burgoyne didn't hesitate. "I would like your opinions on how to take the fort in the least time and with the fewest casualties."

He sat down, waiting as silence held. Then Phillips cleared his throat. All eyes turned to him, and with his usual blunt, caustic style he had his say.

"It's obvious. The only tactic to reduce Ticonderoga is by siege.

Encircle it, put it in a box, cut off all communication and supplies, and place it under constant bombardment. One hundred thirty-eight cannon will convince them soon enough."

Burgoyne pursed his mouth and nodded. "That is one method. Any other opinions?"

Fraser turned to Burgoyne. "Considering the terrain, I doubt we have enough troops to sustain a prolonged siege. We would be spread too thin. A relief column could penetrate our lines easily enough, if they scouted us well and waited for a weakness or an opening. In executing the final infantry charge to finish a siege, there's the chance they would repel us."

Phillips's nose came up. "Humph. If it is done properly, there would be no infantry charge. Our infantry would simply walk in."

Fraser shook his head. "I doubt cannon will reduce the walls of that fort very rapidly, and perhaps not at all. Some of those walls are sixteen feet thick."

Burgoyne interrupted to once again refer to the map, finger pointing. "I have had it in mind to order a corps of Germans across the lake, east into the interior, to cut off any hope of a major relief column reaching the Americans. By taking and holding the great road that reaches from Fort No. Four on the Connecticut River, here, to Mount Independence, here, we will have seriously reduced their chances of getting relief to the fort, overland. They could still come up from the south, but it would have to be on the Hudson, and then on Lake George. That would take too long. They would never arrive in time. As I see it, the great road from the east is critical. We must seize and hold it."

Again Fraser shook his head. "The Germans are neither trained to operations in heavily wooded, swampy country, nor are they inclined to it, and the terrain just north of Mount Independence is a morass of forest and swamp. They will have to move sixteen miles north to get around it, and if they do, they will lose both their line of supply and any real hope of reinforcements should they encounter trouble. I would not send Germans, and I doubt if I would send anyone at all. If we take Fort Ti, we must do it quickly enough that the question of a relief column reaching the Americans is never a factor."

Burgoyne's eyebrows raised in surprise. "Any other opinions?"

Fraser went on. "Yes. I would like permission to reconnoiter the ground on the west side of the lake, near the fort. As I recall, Mr. MacIntosh led us to believe there is a weakness in the defenses at a point on the west side of the fort, where the Americans have no cannon. They apparently believe that section of the fort can be defended by infantry behind breastworks alone. I would like to know more about it. It seems to me possible that if we work it to our advantage, we may be able to persuade the Americans to evacuate the fort without a fight."

Phillips shook his head. "We're wasting time. And we're forgetting the principles that have been so dearly bought and paid for over the last two hundred years." He thrust his chin forward, emphasizing every word. "Follow the rules. Dig in. Save our strength. Wait while we build roads that will accommodate our artillery. Bring in our heavy guns. Put the fort under siege and starve the Americans out. I see neither need nor benefit to any other scheme."

Von Riedesel remained silent. Fraser interlaced his fingers and stared at them while he resolved to say no more. Phillips sat ramrod straight, certain he had delivered the final word.

Burgoyne reached to run a hand lightly over his carefully combed hair. For a time he sat with his hands before him on the table, eyes half closed, while he weighed all that had been said. Then he drew a great breath and spoke.

"We will proceed to prepare for a siege." He turned to Fraser. "Starting this afternoon, have any of your troops still remaining on boats or bateaux wade ashore. Tomorrow morning, order your Canadians and Indians, with six hundred men of your advanced corps, to move around the American left. Take the sawmill and the garrison at Mount Hope, then the French Lines, and then move on down to the place MacIntosh described, where the Americans have no cannon covering an approach to the fort. Fire two or three volleys, then wait and hold them in place. We will move our heavy artillery in as soon as we can."

Fraser unwaveringly nodded. "Yes, sir."

"I'll have the orders in writing for you before nightfall." Burgoyne stood, once again his old engaging self. "Well, then, gentlemen. Thank you all for coming. Your counsel is invaluable to me."

They all stood and proceeded toward the entrance to the tent. Burgoyne himself held the flap open for them and stood waving as they walked out into the noise and clutter of the camp.

Twenty minutes before the officers were to gather for their evening mess, a young captain cantered his tall sorrel horse to the front of General Fraser's quarters and dismounted. Responding to the picket's challenge, the captain showed the sealed document and said, "Sealed orders from General Burgoyne for General Fraser."

Minutes later, alone inside his tent, Fraser broke the wax seal and spread the beautifully scrolled document on his table. The orders were in strict conformance with the verbal instruction given by Burgoyne at the council. Thoughtfully, Fraser pushed the document to one side, then reached for quill and ink. He opened his daily journal, and under the date of July 1, 1777, slowly began to write.

"Rec'd orders from General Burgoyne to move south from Three Mile tomorrow morning, take the American sawmill, their garrison at Mount Hope, and engage them at the west side of Fort Ticonderoga. It seems clear that if the rebels were to voluntarily evacuate the fort without a battle, the conquest would not be sufficiently brilliant when news of it reached London, since there is little glory in capturing only a large store of supplies and a body of soldiers who would rather be prisoners than fight."

Fraser read what he had written and wondered if he had been unfairly judgmental of his commanding officer. *Gentleman Johnny. Ambitious Johnny. Wants immortality by winning the great battle at Fort Ticonderoga. If St. Clair knows he cannot defend the fort, will he abandon it? And if he tries, will Burgoyne let him go without a battle?*

Fraser leaned back in his chair, lost for a time in thought. Finally, he roused himself and stood. *We'll see. We'll see. Time will tell.* He turned and ducked through the tent flap, angling toward the officers' mess tent.

Notes

Unless otherwise indicated, the following is taken from Ketchum, *Saratoga,* on the pages identified.

General Burgoyne held a war council prior to proceeding south to begin the shooting war with General St. Clair. The council was held at Three Mile Point, three miles north of Fort Ticonderoga, and attended by generals von Riedesel, Fraser, and Phillips. The use of the British ships *Royal George* and *Inflexible* was discussed.

The British had constructed a large boom and floated it south to stop any American vessels from coming north to fire upon the British bateaux. General von Riedesel's troops were to cross Lake Champlain and proceed south to take Mt. Independence, formerly Rattlesnake Hill. Fraser was to lead a second force south on the west side of the lake to attack the French Lines and drive the Americans from Mt. Hope, back to Fort Ti.

Burgoyne wanted to use a large force of Germans to seize the major road going east from the lake to cut off any incoming reinforcements for the Americans, but General Fraser argued against it, claiming the German soldiers were "a helpless kind of troops in the woods."

General Phillips proposed a siege of Fort Ti, with the opposing argument from General Fraser that Burgoyne did not have enough troops to conduct a proper siege. Burgoyne decided on a siege, and Fraser wrote in his journal that if the Americans decided to abandon Fort Ti rather than fight, he feared that from Burgoyne's point of view, "the conquest would not have been sufficiently brilliant by capturing a great number of prisoners or a large quantity of stores." In short, Fraser was of the opinion that Burgoyne, ever mindful of the politics in London, wanted to capture Fort Ti only after a glorious battle in which he would heroically lead his men on to victory (see pp. 164–65).

The pay by the British for one German soldier for one year's service was seven pounds, four shillings, and four and one-halfpence, payable whether the soldier was dead or alive at the end of the year (p. 95).

The entire British expedition was ill-suited to John Burgoyne, who was by training and experience a light cavalryman and badly prepared for the daily grind of moving ten thousand people through thick forests, building roads, providing food, handling sickness and enemy harassment (see Higginbotham, *The War of American Independence,* p. 176; Leckie, *George Washington's War,* p. 376).

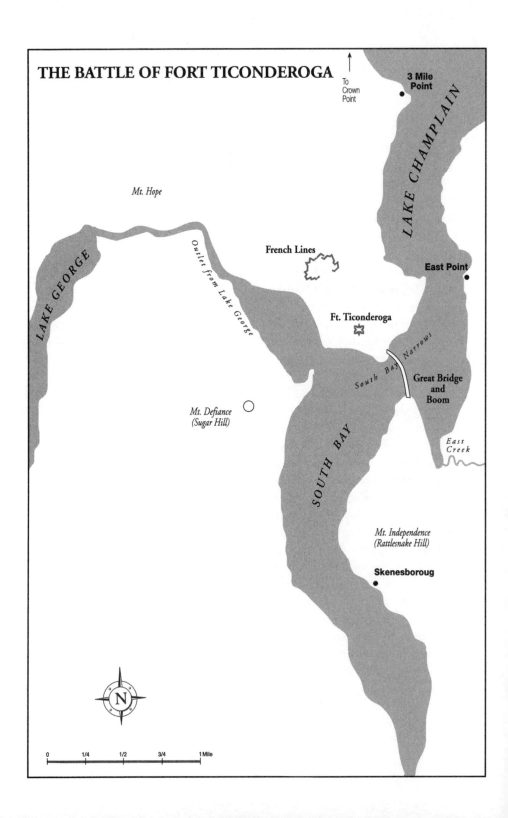

THE BATTLE OF FORT TICONDEROGA

To Crown Point

3 Mile Point

LAKE CHAMPLAIN

Mt. Hope

French Lines

East Point

LAKE GEORGE

Outlet from Lake George

Ft. Ticonderoga

South Bay Narrows

Great Bridge and Boom

Mt. Defiance (Sugar Hill)

East Creek

SOUTH BAY

Mt. Independence (Rattlesnake Hill)

Skenesboroug

N

0   1/4   1/2   3/4   1 Mile

Mt. Hope, northwest of Fort Ticonderoga

July 2, 1777

CHAPTER XV

★ ★ ★

*M*ajor General Arthur St. Clair flinched at the sudden, urgent rap at his office door. He quickly glanced at his pocket watch— twenty minutes past seven on a hot, sultry July morning—then called, "Enter."

Major Isaac Dunn, his aide-de-camp, pushed through the door to stand before his desk in the small, crude, poorly lit office, breathing heavily, eyes alive, beads of sweat on his forehead from his sprint across the parade ground of Fort Ticonderoga. He had left the door flung wide, and sunlight cast an irregular rectangle of light on the rough floor planking. Dunn did not wait for St. Clair to acknowledge him.

"There's a private on his way over here, says he was on scout up north, just this side of Three Mile. Says he saw Germans coming ashore—a lot of them. Says he's got to see you. He ran most of the way here and was staggering when they let him through the gates. I had a corporal take him to the enlisted men's mess to get some water and settle him down before one of them brings him here."

Seated at his desk, St. Clair stiffened. "Germans coming ashore? When?"

"Daybreak this morning."

"How many?"

"This man says hundreds, maybe thousands!"

"Is he wounded? Out of his head?"

"Not wounded. Excited. Badly frightened."

"When is he coming to—"

Footsteps pounded on the wooden walkway outside the office and Dunn stepped aside. Two enlisted men stopped at the open door and came to attention.

St. Clair stood. "Enter."

The two men took four steps forward and stopped before St. Clair's desk. One of them spoke. "Sir, I'm Corporal Wylie Pitkin. Major Dunn ordered me to get this man some water and then bring him here."

Dunn interrupted. "Thank you, Corporal. Wait outside, and close the door."

Pitkin walked back out into the sunlight and closed the door while St. Clair studied the man for a moment. His plain homespun shirt was sweated out, and his dark cotton trousers were ragged. His square-toed shoes were worn, battered. St. Clair spoke. "Your name?"

The man's voice was high, strained, and his words came tumbling in a torrent. "Private Calvin O'Donnell, sir. Pennsylvania Second. I was assigned scout duty along the lake at Three Mile, and this morning when it was still dark I seen these big boats out there and then there was these men getting out—"

St. Clair raised a hand, stopping O'Donnell. "Be calm, Private. Sit down." The general gestured to one of the plain, rough-cut wooden chairs facing his desk. "Just start at the beginning and tell us about it one step at a time." St. Clair also sat, leaning forward in his seat, focused, intense.

O'Donnell sat down and took charge of himself. He took a deep breath and wiped at his mouth, then dropped his hand. "Yes, sir. Like I was tellin', before dawn I seen these two big ships out on the lake under the stars, one near, one far, and then when it got light enough I seen little boats all over. Square, flat bottoms, full of troops, flags flyin' everywhere, even a band playin' music. I knew they was Germans because they was dressed in blue and had those tall copper hats. Soon as it got light enough, they started unloadin' over the sides of those flat boats and walkin' ashore. There was hundreds, more like thousands. Then after a while I seen some British, redcoats."

"Did you count the square boats?"

"There was so many they got in each other's way, and I couldn't see 'em all. I counted maybe fifty."

"How many men in each boat?"

"I counted forty got out of one, fifty-five from another. Different amounts."

"What did they do?"

"Waded ashore and formed up in ranks and then started marchin' south, and some of 'em east."

"What did you do?"

"Waited 'til it was certain they figured to stay ashore, and then I come here."

"Did they see you?"

"No, sir. I was hid in the woods."

"Was there any fighting? Shooting?"

"None I know of. No one was there but me. I waited 'til I knew they was startin' their big push south, and then I come here. They're comin,' sir. Thousands. They figger to take this fort, sure as sure."

"Did you see any cannon?"

O'Donnell stopped to search his memory. "No, sir. But that don't mean they don't got 'em. When they get here, they'll have cannon, an' that's certain."

"Did you see their officers?"

"Plenty."

"German, or British?"

For a moment O'Donnell's eyes narrowed in thought. "German. Blue coats."

"Were there any Indians?"

"None got out of the boats."

St. Clair turned to Dunn. "Anything you want to ask?"

"Where's the rest of your company?" Dunn asked.

"There was ten of us set up in a line, east to west, maybe five hundred yards apart, watchin'. When I seen the Germans comin' so thick, I figgered there wasn't much use in wastin' time tryin' to find the rest of the scouts, so I come back to report."

Dunn fell silent, and St. Clair said, "Take him back out and have Corporal Pitkin get him something to eat from the enlisted men's mess. Let him stay with Pitkin's command for further orders. Then come back here."

Dunn nodded and followed O'Donnell back out the door. After they were gone, St. Clair sat down on his chair, leaned forward, arms on his desk, palms flat, mind racing. *Congress and Hancock and Gates—assuring me over and over again that the British are not going to come south on the lakes and the Hudson—going to send their army down the St. Lawrence, then south to New York by boat. Do not concern yourself with extensive defenses—you will not need to defend Ticonderoga against a major force!*

St. Clair straightened, eyes flashing. *Stupidity! Sheer stupidity! I told them my fears, and I requested men and munitions and supplies to defend this fort against a major force, and they sent almost nothing. They were told that cannon on top of Mt. Defiance could cut this fort to pieces in hours, and yet they did nothing. And now their stupidity has placed me where I must defend this fort with too few men and too little armament and supplies. If Burgoyne discovers he can get cannon to the top of Mt. Defiance . . .* He shuddered and stood as Dunn strode back into the room. St. Clair was giving orders before Dunn came to a halt.

"I have no confirmation of O'Donnell's story, but I can't take a chance. I must presume it is true. Tell Colonel Pierce Long to take his command down to the Lake George landing and get those provisions and stores hauled back within our lines. Order the bateaumen down there to stand ready to move their crafts on a moment's notice. Sleep in their boats until this is over, if necessary. If for any reason it appears the British might get those stores, load them into the bateaux at once and move them down to the south end of Lake George, to Fort George. We can't let the British take them."

"Yes, sir." Dunn pivoted and was gone at a trot.

St. Clair smacked one fist into the other palm as he paced, slowing his mind, forcing reason. *A large force of Germans coming ashore two miles north—moving this way—Burgoyne wouldn't send Germans alone—they have to be part of a larger operation—British troops have to be coming with them—with Burgoyne in command there will be troops moving down on us from every quadrant to the north— both sides of the lake, east and west.*

He stopped short as his thoughts reached their inevitable conclusion. *Mt. Hope! The garrison there—the bridge—sawmill. Are they under attack? Have they fallen? Are the French Lines under attack?*

In two great strides, St. Clair was at the door. He threw it open to hurry out into the heat and dust of the parade ground and stand, facing northwest, eyes narrowed, as he searched for signs of telltale smoke that would signal the burning of the Mt. Hope outpost, or the sawmill. There were no dark smudges staining the azure blue sky. He turned his head and closed his eyes, concentrating to hear the distant rattle of muskets or the deep-throated boom of cannon that would tell of a battle at the French Lines. He heard only the sounds of the fort entering another hot, sticky day. He turned and strode quickly back into his office and slammed the door. Time had suddenly become his most precious commodity if he was to make and execute a plan that would save Fort Ticonderoga.

Sergeant Arne Olsen wrinkled his nose in disgust as he picked at his piece of tough, boiled salt fish. "Don't seem right, servin' salt fish for breakfast every day." He thrust the last piece into his mouth, set his heavy pewter plate on top of the breastworks just north of the Mount Hope garrison, and reached for his wooden cup of lukewarm coffee. While drinking, he glanced over the top of the wood and earthen structure for a moment, looking for movement in the distant trees. There was none.

Private Peter Johannesen hunkered down next to him, forked a mouthful of the fish and chewed. "Maybe some day they'll call us to a breakfast in a big hall somewhere and serve us pink ham and fried eggs and sweet tarts and hot spiced cider." He reached for his coffee to wash the fish down and cut the thick salt taste from his mouth.

Olsen snorted and shook his head. "Not if the officers hear about it.

They hear about it, there won't be no pink ham or fried eggs or sweet tarts or cider left when we get there. They'll have it all et." Olsen reached to set his coffee down, and as he did, he once again studied the distant woods. He suddenly froze, coffee cup poised, eyes narrowed as he concentrated.

Johannesen glanced at him, puzzled. "See something?"

Olsen pointed north, out over the breastworks, and Johannesen rose far enough to peer over the barrier of dirt and logs. For five long seconds the young men stared before Olsen murmured, "What is that in there among the trees? Must be a big herd of deer, but that don't make sense."

Suddenly Johannesen's head jerked forward, and his face blanched. His arm shot up, pointing, and his mouth fell open. "Indians! Hundreds of 'em. And some redcoats with 'em." Olsen spun to his right and shouted to the next two pickets lounging in the shallow trench behind the breastworks, "Do you see 'em?"

The two startled pickets stood and followed his point and then immediately lunged for their muskets.

Olsen's arm shot up, pointing further west. "Look over there! Must be five hundred redcoats workin' their way around our left! They're tryin' to get around behind us, cut us off. They're comin'! The whole British army!" He stood bolt upright and shouted up and down the trenched breastwork, "Get back to the garrison! Get back! Get back!"

Within seconds, the fifty men in the breastworks north of the small fortress that dominated a low hill bordering Mt. Hope were sprinting south toward the cover of the fortress walls. They leaped over logs and plunged through the underbrush and lush ferns, shouting to the pickets on the ramparts inside the fortress, "They're coming! They're coming!"

The northern gates of the small structure swung wide, and the men streamed through, fighting for breath, sweating, pointing, exclaiming. Up on the ramparts, Lieutenant Ambrose Thurston stood stock-still, steadily sweeping his telescope from right to left, watching everything that moved in the north trees. He was facing due west when he stopped. He jammed his telescope closed and then leaped the nine feet from the rampart to the ground inside the fortress, sprinting for the small office of the commanding officer the moment he hit. The door of the office burst open when Thurston was yet thirty feet distant, and Brigadier General Daniel McPhee strode out, still buttoning his tunic.

"What's happening?" he demanded.

Thurston stopped, facing him. "Sir, there's a major force of Indians and British regulars coming from the north and circling around our left. I think they're trying to cut off our escape route."

McPhee's eyes opened wide. "Is this the major assault we've been expecting? Are they coming after Fort Ti?"

"My opinion, yes, sir, they are."

"Give me that telescope." McPhee grabbed it, ran to the nearest ladder and scrambled up to the wooden walkway that overlooked the northern approach to his garrison. He jerked the telescope full length, then steadied it as he began his sweep, east to west, mumbling numbers as he went.

"At least twelve hundred, maybe more, and they're circling our left." He exhaled heavily and his forehead drew down in a frown as he struggled with the decision that all commanding officers dread in the face of a superior force—abandon his post, or fight a hopeless battle? He shouted down to Thurston, who stood waiting on the ground below him.

"I don't know if they have cannon, but I must assume they do. Four heavy guns can cut this stockade to pieces in half an hour. We'd be overrun and gone within one hour. I won't do that. I'll save these men to help defend Fort Ti before I sacrifice them here."

He slammed the telescope closed and barked his orders. "Have fifty men set fire to this place immediately! Tell all the officers to get their men out of here now! Stop for nothing but their muskets and ammunition! Head for the French Lines! We'll hold there if we can, then fall back to Fort Ti if we have to! Have the same fifty men set fire to the sawmill when we pass it, and then the bridge when we're all south of it! Do you understand?"

Thurston bobbed his head emphatically. "Yes, sir."

"Move!"

Thurston turned on his heel and sprinted toward the officers' quarters, shouting orders as he ran. Two minutes later, flames were rising from the dry, weathered roof shingles on the buildings, and black smoke was billowing into the clear blue sky. The south gates swung open, and the officers led their men through the smoke and fires at a run, down the incline, southeast toward the French Lines. Lieutenant Thurston waited until General McPhee was clear of the gates before he sprinted to the powder magazine, kicked open the door, threw a burning firebrand inside, and ran for his life out the south gate. He had covered one hundred fifty yards before the horrendous blast blew flame and wood two hundred feet into the bright July sky and leveled half the north and east walls. Thurston involuntarily ducked his head and hunched his shoulders, and then, for a moment, the entire American command turned to watch the great column of black smoke boil upward, and the bits and pieces of their fortress, some of them still burning, leaving black smoke trails, drift back to Mother Earth. Then they turned and resumed their headlong run downhill, across the bridge, on to the French Lines.

The regiment assigned to hold the French Lines was waiting, muskets laid across the breastworks, taking aim as the Americans broke out of the trees and brush into the cleared area between the forest and the fort. The officer in charge turned and shouted to his men, "Hold your fire! Hold your fire! They're ours!"

Behind the wave of oncoming Americans, the fifty men assigned stopped at the sawmill long enough to set fire to the stacked lumber and the shed covering the huge band saw and the great pile of sawdust, then sprinted over the bridge, and once again paused long enough to set the undergirdings on fire. They arrived at the French Lines fifteen minutes behind the main body, sweated out, fighting for breath. With McPhee's command from the fortress, the lines were filled, and each man had taken a place, shoulder to shoulder, behind the breastworks. They waited in tense silence for the first of the British, or the Indians, or the Hessians, to make their charge across the open ground between the French Lines and the burning bridge. Minutes became half an hour, then an hour, with the men wiping sweat from their eyes, waiting, nerves fraying, inventing ways to make sunlight filtering through the distant trees into the dreaded Hessians or Indians. The only sounds were the clicking of grasshoppers in flight and the undercurrent of the buzz of unnumbered, swarming insects.

Brigadier General McPhee wiped his sleeve across his eyes and suddenly stood upright to walk out in front of the lines. "Lieutenant Thurston," he called out, "take the fifty men who set the fires and proceed north toward the bridge. Take cover and wait there. At first sign of the British coming in force, fire at them, and then conduct an orderly retreat here. We want all the warning we can get."

"Yes, sir!" McPhee's breathing came short as Thurston called out his men, formed them into a skirmish line, and led them forward at a run, hunched low, back to within two hundred yards of the burning bridge. On Thurston's command they dispersed, disappearing, crouching behind anything they could find for cover and began their vigil, watching everything to the north that moved. McPhee began to breathe again, relieved to know that he had not sent them into an ambush.

The distant blast and then the shock wave rolled over General Fraser's British command tent at Three Mile. He laid down his quill and rose from his desk to walk outside to look south at the black cloud billowing into the clear sky just to the left of Mt. Hope, and at some pieces of the fortress as they began their fall back to earth.

Our forces got there. He glanced at his pocket watch. *Nine o'clock. Right on time. The rebels have set fire to their own fortress and blown the magazine. Our men will have possession of both the fortress—what's left of it—and the sawmill, and be at the bridge in about four hours. They'll wait at the bridge for the other regiments to take up their positions, and then move on down to take the French Lines and then Fort Ti. The siege is about to begin.*

He walked back into his tent, resumed his place at his desk, and again picked up his quill to sign his name to the document he had just finished writing. He paused a moment to skim it.

Commanding Officer at Crown Point—possible we will need reinforcements for operations at Three Mile. Bring one regiment south—join us for further orders should you be needed—your ob'dnt s'rvnt, General Simon Fraser.

He carefully folded it, melted the tip of a blue wax stick in a candle flame, dropped a tiny mound onto the flap of the document, then pressed his seal into the cooling wax. He leaned back in his chair to compare the plan for the conquest of Fort Ti with the realities of what had happened thus far, and a smile tugged. *By the book. General Phillips will be delighted. Delighted?* He smiled. *Perhaps satisfied, but not delighted. I doubt he knows the meaning of the word delighted.* He smiled again as the image of the cold, blue-gray eyes, the square set of the jaw, and the slight upward tilt of the prominent nose went through his mind.

From three hundred yards north of the bridge, with the smoldering ruins of the burned sawmill at their backs, Sergeant Sean Devlin looked at Corporal Evan O'Shaughnessy in his red tunic with the white belts crossing on his breast. "Where are our Indians? I haven't seen the Indians since we took the Mount Hope garrison three hours ago. Where are they?"

O'Shaughnessy pointed south, toward the bridge. "Half an hour ago they were down there by themselves."

Devlin raised up to look. "I can't see them. What the devil are they up to?"

O'Shaughnessy shook his head. "I don't know. I only know the last time I saw them they had two barrels of rum. That was before the rebels blew their magazine and burned everything. We're supposed to wait here for the other companies to get into position before we move on down over the bridge to take the French Lines, so we can surprise them. Then we move on to Fort Ti. But those Indians are beyond the bridge already. I don't know what they're doing, but I'm not going down there to find out."

"Why? Afraid?"

"With good reason. With two barrels of rum in them, I doubt those devils will even notice we're wearing British uniforms when they take our scalps. No, I'm not going."

"I will. Someone's got to keep watch on them."

O'Shaughnessy shook his head violently. "If you go, leave your musket here. Someone might need it when we take Fort Ti."

Devlin licked his lips, then wiped them nervously. "Well, someone ought to go see what they're up to."

"Not me. I'd sooner fight the whole American army than mix with that bunch. Go get an officer. Let one of them try it."

Devlin shrugged. "I'll go find Lieutenant Haughton. He'll know what to do."

Far to the south, just across the bridge, the entire Indian contingent was hidden in the heavy brush and foliage. One empty rum barrel lay smashed to splinters; the other one was on its side while the Indians dipped the last of the pungent rum with gourds. They were on their knees, trying to raise the filled gourds to their mouths, spilling more down their chins and bare chests and onto their buckskin leggings, than they were drinking. They were painted and feathered for war, with their scalping knives belted around their middles and their iron-headed tomahawks thrust through their belts. Their muskets lay where they had dropped them in their frenzy to get to the rum.

They finished the second barrel, looked for more, found none, and vented their drunken wrath by smashing the second empty barrel, as they had the first. Lacking something else to destroy, they began arguing among themselves. Heated arguments became deadly threats, and unsteady hands began fumbling for tomahawks. It was then that a wild, young, untried warrior, crazy with drink, grabbed up the nearest musket and fired it randomly into the air. For an instant all heads turned to him, and all motion and sound ceased. Seizing his opportunity to thrust himself forward as a great war leader, the drunken man threw down the smoking musket, jerked his tomahawk from his belt, pointed it south toward the French Lines, threw back his head, and screamed the high, warbling war cry of the Iroquois Wolf Clan. While the echo was still ringing in the woods, he broke into a clumsy run, repeating the blood-chilling cry again and again. With their brains lost in a drunken fog, the entire contingent mindlessly plunged after him, snatching up muskets, or ignoring the muskets altogether as they ran toward the French Lines, four hundred yards to the south.

At the sound of the single musket shot fired by the drunken young Indian, Lieutenant Thurston and his fifty advance scouts raised up far enough in the thick brush to take a clear view of the bridge. When the swarming Indians burst from the heavy cover less than one hundred yards in front of them, the startled men drew back in amazement, and Thurston shouted his first order.

"Hold your positions! Hold your positions! Wait! Cock your muskets and pick your targets, but do not fire until I give the order. Wait, wait, wait." He raised his sword, and the fifty men in his skirmish line brought their cheeks to the stocks of their muskets and sighted down the barrels at the oncoming horde. At eighty yards they could see the feathers. At sixty yards they could see the paint covering the faces and chests—white, blue, black, and the favored vermilion. At forty yards they could see the inhuman expressions on their faces as they came on.

Suddenly Thurston's head jerked forward as he watched them come, stumble-footed, some falling to rise and stagger on. "Drunk! They're drunk!" Still he held his sword high. At twenty-five yards he shouted, "FIRE!" Instantly fifty American muskets blasted, and the heavy musketballs tore smacking into the leaders. In that instant the Americans could see the absolute, wide-eyed surprise on the faces of the Indians as those in front were hurled backward to go down, finished. Those behind stopped, stunned, confused, trying to make their alcohol-fogged brains understand what had happened. The single impression burned into their befuddled brains was that the entire world had erupted in their faces, blasting musketballs from everywhere.

Thurston stood straight up and shouted his next order. "Fall back! Slow! Reload while you're moving! Pick a target and fire when reloaded! Do not run! Walk! Keep your wits about you! Slow! Walk!"

The Americans began a slow, controlled, orderly retreat, while the Indians tried to force their brains to function. The brash young leader, who had led them in their headlong charge, once again waved his tomahawk over his head and ran toward the withdrawing Americans, screaming his war cry. An American went to one knee, sighted down his musket barrel, and triggered his second shot. He heard the whack of the musketball hitting the man in the chest and saw the surprise on the face of the young Indian as he grabbed at the place where the musketball had punched in, went to his knees, then toppled sideways. The American reached for another paper cartridge in the leather case at his side, ripped it open with his teeth, and reloaded as he continued to walk backwards, slowly, controlled.

Behind Thurston, McPhee stood bolt upright on the French Line breastworks, and for ten seconds studied the battle slowly moving toward him. He turned to the men in the lines and shouted orders: "First one hundred men, follow me!" He jerked his sword from its scabbard, leaped from the breastworks to the ground, and started toward Thurston at a run. The first hundred men stormed over the breastworks and strung out in a line, voices raised in a battle cry as they surged forward. They reached Thurston in twenty seconds, knelt to fire their first volley, then joined him and his men in the slow, controlled retreat back to their lines. Behind them they heard the full-throated roar of the Americans who remained in the French Lines cheering them on. They climbed over their own breastworks and dropped into the shallow trenches, eyes bright with the flush of successful combat. They all reached for fresh cartridges and began to reload, watching the Indians coming on.

The harsh reality of battle, and of their dead, had pounded some sense of sobriety into the alcohol-muddled brains of the red men. For a moment they stopped, then rallied, then came on, jumping through the brush, bent on avenging their fallen comrades.

McPhee mounted the breastworks, took one look and shouted, "Cannon first! Fire on my command! Then muskets, on my command!" He waited while the Indians came on with their high, inhuman cries filling the air. He waited until he could see the sweat on their faces, and then cupped his hands to shout, "FIRE!"

Twelve cannon belched flame and white smoke fifteen feet, hurling more than two hundred pounds of grapeshot into the oncoming tide, ripping into the charge, shredding the brush, raising a dirt cloud twenty feet in the air. The Americans heard the heavy lead balls smack into flesh, and when the smoke cleared, there was a great hole in the center of the Indian line.

McPhee then shouted, "FIRE," and muskets all up and down the French Line laid down the first full American volley. The Indians stopped in their tracks, faltered for a moment, then turned and started to run back toward the bridge.

They rallied and came on once more, and once again the American cannon bucked and roared, and the American muskets blasted. When the smoke cleared the second time, the Indians were in full, headlong retreat, with the shouts of the victorious Americans following them.

Instantly McPhee turned to his men. "Casualty count," he ordered, and waited. Ten minutes later Thurston returned. "Sir, we lost six enlisted, one lieutenant, eleven wounded. Downing was hit in the heel, Newport in both knees, and Oxford in the thigh. The Green Mountain Boys reported five dead, seven or eight wounded."

McPhee glanced out at the Indian bodies scattered on the battlefield. "Tell the men they did well. Very well. Have them rest and drink water. We want no one weakened by heat exhaustion. We'll wait for further orders from General St. Clair."

To an experienced career military officer, there is no sound so unmistakable or so provocative as the deep boom of distant cannon. Whose guns, ours or theirs? Solid shot to destroy walls and breastworks, or grapeshot and cannister to shred incoming infantry or cavalry? Our infantry? Our cavalry? Or theirs? Who's winning? Who's losing? Invariably, for a moment, the sound provokes a moment of silence while images and remembrances of battles won and battles lost because of cannon flit through their minds and are gone.

The rolling thunder of McPhee's cannon an hour earlier had reached Fraser and had brought him up short, one eyebrow raised in question. *Cannon? Already? All our regiments aren't in place yet. No one's given the order to move south. Who's firing? At whom?*

He had risen and walked out of his tent into the sun, which was hammering down on the British camp. Nearly everyone in the camp stopped to stare south, wondering. Fraser walked to the nearest officer he could find.

"Any indication who's firing the guns?" He gestured south.

"No, sir. Wondering that myself."

"Seen General Burgoyne?"

"Not lately, sir. He was in his big tent twenty minutes ago."

"Thank you." Fraser walked back to his tent, unbuttoned his tunic, and left it open in the stifling heat. He paused at a small porcelain washbasin in the corner to splash tepid water on his face, then reached for a towel. Twenty minutes later he heard and felt the drumming of incoming horses' hooves, and a moment later his tent flap opened.

"Sir, Lieutenant Watkins just arrived with a written message from your nephew, Captain Alexander Fraser. Says you should read it at once."

In one fluid move, Fraser was off his chair and striding quickly to the open tent flap. He took the folded paper instantly. "Thank you, Lieutenant. Please wait outside in the event I need to send a reply." He unfolded the paper, as the lieutenant backed out the tent flap and forced himself to remain calm as he read the salutation, then the message.

"Contrary to the standing orders of General Burgoyne, the advance company of Indians acquired liquor from an unknown source, and in their drunkenness attacked the French Lines with disastrous results. The musket- and cannon-fire you surely heard were American, repulsing the Indian attack. Our Indian forces suffered heavy casualties, while the American losses were light. Unfortunate incident, start to finish. My first impression was that we have lost the very valuable element of surprise, however, whether we have or have not, I am now of the opinion that we

clearly maintain the superior position and still enjoy the luxury of picking time and place to begin our attack on Fort Ticonderoga. I and my
command hold a strong position on our right, fifteen hundred yards
from the French Lines. We are poised and anxious to move in toward
Fort Ti upon command. We have cannon, and superiority of numbers,
and will be coming into the Lines at an angle which will allow my entire
command to fire upon them, while only the Americans nearest us can
return the fire, since those beyond will be hitting their own men."

Relief showed in Fraser's face as he reread his nephew's message. He
walked to his table and was reaching for quill and paper when the flap
to his tent was thrown back roughly, and General William Phillips strode
into the sweltering shelter, ramrod straight, chin thrust out, nose high,
neck veins extended, face flushed with passionate anger. He paid no
attention to protocol.

"Sir, I am informed that our bloody Indians have gotten themselves
into a drunken stupor, abandoned their assigned position by the sawmill,
totally disobeyed all orders of every kind, including the standing order
to not consume alcohol, and made their own unauthorized, premature
attack on the Americans at the French Lines. To my undying satisfaction,
the American cannon and muskets have blasted a great number of them
into purgatory, where I dearly hope they will remain throughout eternity.
Were I in command, another fifty or so would be introduced into the
same place by sunset, swinging at the end of good British ropes."

He paused for one moment to catch his breath and order his words.
"It is my considered opinion that they have totally destroyed the critically important element of surprise we have so carefully nurtured. It is
gone. No one knows how many lives that will cost us, now that the
Americans have been given notice we are coming. Without doubt, they
will be waiting with grapeshot behind breastworks and stone walls, the
taking of which will now cost us dearly in both men and supplies. That
being so, it is my firm recommendation that we immediately withdraw
from our present positions, conduct a war council, and reform our plan
to accommodate the sorry place in which we now find ourselves."

He stopped, drew a deep breath, and waited for Fraser to reply.

For a moment Fraser's mind was a blank while he fumbled for a way to respond to this icon of British spit and polish. He licked dry lips, stood, and began quietly.

"General, I couldn't be more in agreement. I have had reservations about the use of Indians since I arrived from England, and what happened today confirms my worst fears. If we haven't entirely lost the element of surprise, we've lost most of it. All that remains is the fact that the initiative of when, and where, and how we commence our attack on Fort Ti is still in our hands. If we're patient and clever, isn't it still possible for us to make a feint with Breymann's Germans from across the lake, while our own regulars make a massive assault from this side?"

He paused, intently watching the expression on Phillips's face. He thought he saw the slightest softening and went on.

"I just received a written message from my nephew, Captain Alexander Fraser. Here. I would appreciate your reading it, and your opinion." He offered the message, Phillips took it, and for twenty seconds the room was silent while Phillips read. He handed it back to Fraser without comment or change of expression.

Fraser gave it his last effort. "General, it seems we owe it to the remainder of this expedition to at least go down there and see what my nephew is talking about. Maybe he's right. You'd know at a glance. May I have horses saddled for the ride?"

Forty-five minutes later Fraser pulled his sweated mount to a halt, Phillips beside him. Ahead of them rode a lieutenant with five mounted cavalry, while another five followed behind them. The lieutenant turned in his saddle and pointed ahead. "I believe Captain Fraser's position is there, sir, dead ahead."

"Excellent. Proceed."

Five minutes later the small column halted and dismounted. While the escort loosened the saddle girths on all their mounts to get air under the saddles in the oppressive heat, Fraser strode rapidly to his nephew. Captain Alexander Fraser came to a full salute. General Fraser returned it, and then turned to General Phillips.

"Sir, this is Captain Fraser. Captain, General William Phillips."

Alexander snapped his boot heels together and bowed stiffly. "I am deeply honored, sir."

Phillips bobbed his head. "My pleasure. Carry on."

Fraser spoke to his nephew. "Captain, we have read your letter. Explain to us how you see current conditions here."

"Yes, sir." He turned and pointed as he spoke. "We hold the high ground. Fifteen hundred yards down there are the French Lines. They lay generally east and west. From here, we would have the momentum in a charge, and would be coming in from the west end of the lines, which means the Americans beyond the west end would likely be unable to fire either their cannon or muskets at us without involving their own men. From here, we can send down a sizable force with orders to stay to the south of the line of fire while we use our four cannon to lay down a barrage of grapeshot and cannister. When we have substantially reduced the Americans in the trenches, the waiting infantry can storm the French Lines. I believe we can take them with only light losses, while inflicting severe casualties on the Americans."

Fraser glanced at Phillips, whose eyes were narrowed as they worked over the terrain. He was totally absorbed as he made his own keen calculations. One full minute later he pursed his mouth and turned to General Fraser decisively.

"Good. Very good. Excellent. We must hold this position. On command, our cannon can rake the American lines end to end, and then a determined infantry charge should put the finishing touches to it." Phillips face was aglow as he turned to the Captain. "My compliments, sir. Carry on."

General Fraser stifled a grin as he spoke to his nephew. "You have your orders, Captain. Is there anything you need here? Water? Food? Gunpowder?"

"No, sir. We're well situated."

"Good. We'll take our leave."

The little column was halfway back to Three Mile before Phillips broke the silence. He bobbed his head and spoke, almost as though to himself. "Good man, that Captain Fraser. Good man. I'm going to order the Twentieth Regiment to move up to give him support."

The camp drummer had sounded the long drumroll for lights out, and the camp was dark and quiet when the flap to General Fraser's tent swung open and General Burgoyne entered. Fraser was on his feet instantly.

Burgoyne's voice was soft, low. "Sit down, Simon. I heard what you did today. I had to come by personally and give you my thanks." He reached to warmly shake Fraser's hand. "Armies stand or fall on the decisions the officers must make totally on their own initiative. Today, with General Phillips, you could not have done better. I was dreading a confrontation with him when I learned of the incident with the Indians and the rum. He's a magnificent officer, and his anger was justified. Your handling of it was superb. I thank you."

Fraser fumbled for something to say. "Thank you, sir. I must say, when General Phillips saw the ground held by my nephew, he rose above himself. He set aside his grievances and saw it for what it was, which is worthy of a gifted officer. It is my great honor to be serving with him."

Burgoyne's eyes glowed with deep sincerity. "It is my honor to be serving with both of you. Good night, Simon."

Notes

Unless otherwise indicated, the following is taken from Ketchum, *Saratoga*, on the pages indicated.

American General Arthur St. Clair, commanding Fort Ticonderoga, received reports that Burgoyne was coming ever closer to Fort Ti, and that on the morning of July 2, 1777, British and German soldiers were disembarking from bateaux. To save his supplies, he issued orders to have his own bateaumen prepare to move his stores from the landing, south, down Lake George, to Fort George.

Even while his men were doing so, the British attacked the small fort at Mt. Hope, just north of Fort Ti, and drove the Americans out. Before leaving, the Americans set the fort, the sawmill, and all other buildings, on fire, then ran south to what were called the French Lines, where more Americans were positioned to resist the British. However, Burgoyne's Indians had somehow acquired barrels of rum and become drunk, then disobeyed all standing orders and proceeded south to attack the Americans. They did so, but in their drunkenness did it poorly, and the Americans stopped them. The casualty count of Americans is accurate as set forth.

Hearing of the attack by the drunken Indians, British General Simon Fraser ordered his nephew, Captain Alexander Fraser, with six hundred men to investigate. Captain Fraser did an excellent job, positioned his men and cannon at the west end of the French Lines where the Americans were stationed, and sent word back to General Fraser. General Phillips was incensed at the actions of the Indians and demanded an explanation. General Fraser took him to where Captain Fraser was waiting, and General Phillips was much encouraged. That night about ten o'clock General Burgoyne visited General Fraser and highly commended him for his actions of that day and his handling of the hot-tempered, but excellent officer, General Phillips (see pp. 165–68).

Lake Cayuga
Early July 1777

CHAPTER XVI

★ ★ ★

*T*he small, two-man canoe was running with the slow current along the west shore of Lake Cayuga, toward the place the lake narrows to drain north, forming the Seneca River. From there the Seneca turned east, then back northwest to join the Oswego River in its run to Fort Oswego, on the shores of Lake Ontario. A three-quarter moon, risen in the southeastern sky just before ten o'clock, turned the trees and the granite boulders on the shoreline into silvery sentinels and reflected off the glassy water and the backs of Billy and Eli as they silently dipped their paddles and stroked. The only sounds were the faint dripping of water from their paddles, the unending drone of night insects, and the slapping splash as pike and trout and salmon rose to take the swarming flies and mosquitoes.

The canoe glided silently past a place where rocks and pine trees jutted sixty feet into the lake, and suddenly it was among half a dozen startled loons that cackled in the moonlight and thrashed their way thirty feet closer to shore. The two men froze and held their breath, listening for the dreaded voices from the trees that would signal they had been discovered by Iroquois scouts. The only sounds were the insects and one last scolding call from a frightened, angry loon. They waited another thirty seconds, then once again began the slow, silent rhythm with their paddles.

The light birch bark craft left a "V" ripple in its wake as it moved steadily north along the gentle curve of the lake shore. The moon reached the top of its arcing course and began to settle toward the northwestern shore, while the two men continued the measured, steady dip and pull on their paddles. They peered to their right, nerves singing tight, as they studied everything they could see in the distant shadows of the eastern shoreline for any sign that might tell them they had once again found Joseph Brant and his Mohawk warriors.

Suddenly Eli straightened and raised his arm to point due north. Billy narrowed his eyes and searched for a moment before he caught the faintest gleam of a tiny point of light. Eli signaled to their left, and they cautiously, silently brought the canoe to the western shore, among a ragged heap of rotting, windfall trees. Eli raised his hand for silence, and they sat in the canoe for a time, watching, listening for any sound that was not natural to the night. In the far distance a wolf bayed at the moon; nearer, the quick squeal of something small that had been caught by something larger. Above, nighthawks darted, gathering insects they could sense but not see, while bats performed their impossible aerial maneuvers, plucking flying things from the air. There was no sound that betrayed the presence of man.

Eli turned and moved back to the cross brace in the canoe to face Billy in the dark. He hunched forward and spoke softly. "The light to the north is the council fire at the village of Cayuga. Maybe ten miles. If Brant was there, we'd see a lot more fires. If he is on the water between us and Cayuga, I think we'd see him in this moonlight." Billy could hear the frustration in Eli's voice as he continued laying out his reasoning. "We've tracked him for four days, from Unadilla across the Chenango River through the Tuscarora country while he gathered warriors. He had about twenty war canoes waiting at the south end of this lake, and he came north with about two hundred men. I think he's headed for Onondaga, and on to Ganaghsaraga to get more, but if that's true, where is he now? Did he beach his canoes on the other shore and go on foot? That doesn't make sense because it's two days faster to Onondaga on this lake and the Seneca River. Did he make camp for the night? That doesn't make sense, either. By keeping on, he could have been in Cayuga by sunset. He wouldn't make a two-hundred-man camp in the woods with the village that close."

He ceased speaking, bowed his head, and closed his eyes, fiercely concentrating, while Billy sat silent, waiting. Suddenly Eli's head came up and he hissed, "He stopped to meet someone. He's camped somewhere on the other side of the lake. Who came to meet him, and why, and how many men does he have now? We've got to know."

He raised a hand to wipe at his mouth. "The only way I can see to do it is cut straight across the lake. We're going to be out in moonlight for maybe half an hour. We'll need to keep our faces down so they won't reflect and hope they don't see us. If they do, they'll either come out in canoes to meet us, or they'll set an ambush for us when we reach shore. If they come in canoes, we turn south and outrun them. If they set an ambush, we find it before they find us."

He made gestures as he continued. "When we get to the far shore, we'll find a place with some old trees sunk in the lake. We'll tip the canoe over on its side and fill it with water, and then push it down and lock it under one of the trees. That way they can't find it, but we can if we need it again."

Eli stopped, and Billy shifted his weight, waiting. Seconds became half a minute before Eli spoke again. "If they catch us, things could get bad." In the dim moonlight Billy saw the pain in his face, and heard it in his voice as he went on. "They do things to spies. Fire. Cutting. Hours, maybe days before they die." His voice thickened. "I've seen it. If they take us, I won't let that happen to you."

For a moment Billy puzzled over his meaning, and then it struck him. He gasped and straightened. Eli did not move as he waited for him to respond.

Billy quietly asked, "Your rifle?"

"Yes."

"And you?"

"My knife."

Billy spoke. "I'll do the same for you if it goes that way."

For a few moments the two men faced each other in the moonlight, not trusting themselves to speak of the thing that had passed between them. They only knew that what tied them to each other had deepened beyond anything they had known.

Eli resumed his position in the bow of the canoe, picked up his paddle, and turned the craft eastward, while Billy dug his paddle blade deep and pulled hard. The light vessel skimmed forward, cutting through the still water with a whispered hiss. With their faces down, breathing lightly, they watched for any flicker of light, any movement in the distant trees. They passed the center of the lake and moved on slowly, creating as few ripples as they could in the reflected moonlight, watching the far shore for movement of canoes to meet them on the water. There were none. Fifty yards from the rocks and trees, they drew in their paddles and let the canoe drift forward while they searched for a tangle of dead windfall trees sunk on the shoreline. Billy whispered and pointed to their right, and they turned the canoe to glide silently toward the remains of half-submerged tree limbs and massive trunks of forest giants that had fallen into the lake centuries earlier to become gray, rotting, lifeless skeletons. They skirted the sunken snags and came in to the shore amid the frogs and crickets. The croaking quieted, and they sat motionless, waiting until it resumed again.

With their weapons laid on the bank, the two men silently eased themselves back into the water, teeth set against the cold shock, and once again the throaty call of the bullfrogs silenced. Each man seized one end of the small canoe and heaved it over onto its side and waited while it filled. Full, it settled beneath the black water with only the curl at the bow and stern showing. Eli thrust the bow beneath the surface and forced it beneath the trunk of the nearest sunken tree, while Billy drove the stern forward and down, out of sight, until the craft was locked beneath the great tree trunk. They slowly climbed onto the bank, to stand wet and shivering in the chill night air. With their weapons in hand, Eli pointed east, and five seconds later the two men had disappeared into the darkness of the forest.

They stopped in the thick foliage, where they stood in tense silence for a full two minutes, waiting, listening, to see if the interruption of the frogs had drawn a Mohawk ambush. The sound of the frogs resumed and held, and slowly the two men relaxed. Eli turned to Billy, signed a large half-circle with one hand, and Billy nodded.

Guided by instincts sharpened from earliest memory, Eli led them east more than half a mile, stopping every two minutes to stand silent, listening, before they moved on. Half an hour passed before they hunkered down, heads low, as Eli whispered, "We haven't cut their trail. If they're headed for Cayuga, we got ahead of them somehow. I think they went ashore, and we missed their canoes in the dark." He pointed. "We go south."

They worked their way noiselessly through the forest, stopping from time to time to listen to the crickets around them and to the chorus of frogs at the lake six hundred yards to their right. A stir of a breeze arose from the south, soft on their faces, and rustled the leaves over their heads. The trees thinned, and the moonlight filtered through to speckle the forest floor with silver. From far behind came the faint sound of an infant crying, and for a moment they stopped while Eli listened. "Panther," he said quietly, and they continued south, Billy startled at how a great cat could so perfectly mimic the cry of a baby. The forest opened into a clearing, and Eli stopped, eyes narrowed, doubt showing in his face. "We should have cut their trail by now. We've missed something. I don't . . ."

The strong, sweet odor of rum tainting the light breeze reached them both at once, and Eli settled to his haunches, Billy beside him. "They're somewhere up ahead," he whispered, "and whoever they met brought rum. They'll take some of it to Cayuga in the morning, and by noon they'll have about a hundred drunk warriors ready to go on with them. They'll move on to Onondaga and then Ganaghsaraga and do the same." He shook his head, and Billy saw the glint in his eye and heard the anger in his voice. "Most Indians can't resist rum, and white men use it to get them to fight their battles." He paused for a moment in thought. "The rum had to come in wagons from the north, likely around Fort Oswego, or Fort Brewerton. We need to count those wagons, and the canoes, and get an idea of how big Brant's camp is now. I doubt they know they're being followed, and they won't expect it, this deep in

Iroquois territory. With the rum, maybe they won't have scouts out. Stay close."

Crouched low, moving like a shadow, Eli crept directly into the rum-scented breeze, across the small clearing, into a neck of trees. They passed on through, and as the trees thinned on the far side the first flicker of light gleamed through. They stopped ten feet inside the tree line and each settled onto one knee, peering through the branches and trunks of pine and oak trees into a broad meadow. Eli glanced eastward. The moon had set, and the morning star shone brightly in the black sky.

Twelve scattered fires burned. On the far side of the clearing, the black, square silhouettes of wagons loomed high against the glow of the nearest fires. Hobbled among the wagons were great oxen, horns two feet long gleaming in the firelight. Standing near the wagons and seated around the closest campfires were many men with muskets, wearing tri-cornered hats, and coats. They were silent, watchful, refusing to mix with the Indians scattered throughout the clearing, feathered, painted, stripped to the waist. Four open barrels of rum were positioned among the fires nearest the center of the meadow, with Indians clustered around, unsteady on their feet, dipping, drinking, some lying in the grass unable to rise. Their voices were raised, words slurred, gestures awkward. Billy and Eli both drew out their telescopes and for two minutes studied the clearing through the trees.

Eli collapsed his telescope, gave a hand signal to Billy to follow, and turned east, working his way silently through the neck of trees, then angling south in an arcing circle. Halfway to the far end of the clearing they again stopped to crouch in the grass and ferns and begin a count of all the Indians they could see in the east half of the clearing. Finished, they silently continued south, coming in close behind the wagons to again kneel on the forest floor and count the wagons and oxen. This time they did not use their telescopes; they were too close to firelight that could reflect off the lenses.

The crimson tunics and white belts of British regulars were clear, and the shoulder epaulets of six British officers glittered. White men not in uniform were mixed among the soldiers, and Eli paused to study one man through narrowed eyes. He gestured with his head and breathed the word "Claus."

Minutes later, they once again continued their circle of the camp, coming to a stop on the west side of the clearing. With the river one hundred yards from their backs, they each dropped to one knee to make their count of the Indians in the west half of the camp. Suddenly Eli tensed, and he raised a hand to point and softly whisper, "St. Luc, and Langlade." Billy heard the acrid bite in his voice.

Moments later, Eli again raised his hand to point and utter a single word. "Brant." He drew his hand back to tap at a place just below his own throat. Billy peered intently at the cluster of Indians and caught a flash of firelight reflected from a silver plate hung around the neck of one man, just below his throat. He was taller than average, well built, and carried himself with an air of dignity not seen in the others. He was steady on his feet, and held no cup or gourd in his hand. He wore a buckskin shirt, no war paint. Light reflected off the high cheekbones and the coppery flat planes of his strong, striking face. In the darkness, Billy saw Eli finger the hammer and trigger on his rifle, then relax.

For a time the two men remained motionless, fascinated by the aura that surrounded Brant and by the near-reverent respect afforded him as he moved among his men. They watched as the Indians opened a path for him to walk to the south end of the camp where he sought out Daniel Claus. They spoke briefly, then sat down cross-legged on a blanket away from the fires to continue their parley.

Again Eli turned to look east, where the morning star was beginning to fade. Without a word he backed away from the clearing, turned, and the two worked their way back to the lake, then turned to walk south for two hundred yards. They stopped with their backs to the water and the fires of the huge Indian camp hidden by the forest. Birds broke the silence with their early morning cacophony, and on the lake, teal and loons began their movements toward the shores for early morning feeding.

Eli spoke quickly, quietly. "Brant was the one with the silver collar. King George gave it to him."

Billy remained silent, and Eli continued, revulsion plain in his face as he spoke. "St. Luc and Langlade were both there. That explains the rum. Devils, both of them. If they have their way, every white man, woman, and child between here and the Hudson will be massacred." He paused for a moment to let his anger pass, then continued. "Daniel Claus was among the whites. He's one of the British Indian commissioners and is married to the daughter of William Johnson—the man in charge of British Indian affairs. He's the one Brant went down to the wagons to talk to." Eli paused. "I didn't see John Butler there. He works among the Indians for the British, but he doesn't much like Brant, and Brant doesn't trust him. Likely he's up at Oswego bringing in more rum and gifts to stir up the Indians. I didn't recognize any of the British officers. Did you?"

"No."

"I counted eight wagons and thirty-six oxen. Maybe three hundred Indians, and one hundred British soldiers and civilians."

"That's about what I counted."

"See any cannon?"

"No."

"We've still got to find their canoes and count them, and we've got little time. It's getting light fast. They likely got guards watching them. My guess is they're a little further south—"

The slightest sound from the north froze Eli in his tracks, and Billy remained still, silent. The hair on his neck and arms instantly rose as he realized what three hundred drunken Indians would do with them if they were caught. The gray-purple of approaching dawn was charged with unbearable tension as they held their breath. Suddenly the bullfrogs bellowing to their left quieted, a hush fell over the birds flitting in the trees, and it flashed in their minds, *Too much light—can't move in this light—how many?—how far?—how soon?*

Suddenly Eli backed toward the lake, and Billy followed him, both peering north for the first flicker of movement in the trees. Then Eli was in the lake up to his chest, rifle held above his head with one hand, moving south, parallel to the bank. Billy followed, watching the telltale ripples move outward on the water as they pushed on. They had covered twenty-five yards when Eli found what he was looking for and moved directly to the shore. The bank of the lake rose five feet above the water to form a three-foot overhang with ferns and foliage dangling nearly to the surface. Ten seconds later the two men were standing in the darkness beneath the overhang in cold water up to their chests, weapons held above their heads, invisible to anyone on the lake shore. They both watched the ripples they had raised roll outward in the morning mist.

They felt, more than heard, the oncoming tread of the Mohawk, and then they heard the muffled sound of their arguing voices. Both men stared at the ripples, still moving away, dwindling in the gray of the fast approaching dawn. *Too slow—they'll see them. Unless they're still too drunk, they'll see them and know.*

At that moment both their heads jerked around at the rushing sound of a flock of teal coming from the south. The black and white fowl were two feet above the water, gliding fast, preparing to land. They veered toward the bank, and the leaders set their wings to break their speed, while their large, orange webbed feet swung forward and upward. The heels of their webs caught the water hissing, the birds beat their wings twice to stop, and the flight settled onto the smooth surface to begin feeding. Some plucked at the swarming insects, while others plunged their heads into the water, their stubby tails pointed directly upward before they disappeared, diving to the bottom to gather the growing things five feet down. They shot back to the surface like small rockets, shaking water from their oiled feathers, their short bills trailing lake-bottom vegetation rich with algae. The ripples from their landing, and their diving, spread in all directions.

Billy and Eli watched, fascinated, as the teal came ever closer to the shore. The two nearest the overhang were but four feet away when the oncoming Mohawk broke out of the trees, near the bank. The startled teal instantly set up a raucous outcry that echoed across the water, and then spun to pound their wings as they darted away from the shore, using their feet to run on the surface, then dragging them to stop thirty yards out, where they turned to squawk their anger at the Mohawk standing on the shore. Small waves and lengthy ripples reached far out on the lake.

Billy closed his eyes in relief, then opened them wide as he heard the Indians coming south, then stop. There were four of them, all standing above them on the overhang, directly over the heads of Billy and Eli. Their voices were raised in anger, their argument hot.

The two men remained motionless as they listened. Billy understood none of it, but quickly became aware that two of the voices were slurred, drunken, angry. One was reticent, quiet, apparently beginning to emerge from the stupor of too much rum from the previous night. The last one was stone sober, dominant, disgusted. In the growing light, they listened in silence, Billy watching Eli's face, reading every expression intently.

The argument above their heads raged for three minutes. Twice a smile flickered on Eli's face, then passed. Once he tapped the hammer on his rifle, and Billy laid his thumb over the hammer on his musket, waiting for the signal to cock it. Then the sober voice raised above all protests until they stopped, then barked harsh orders, and the four men divided, two going north, two south. The sounds of their leaving grew distant, and then they were gone.

Eli raised a hand, and they waited for a time before he spoke quietly. "We stay here."

Minutes became quarter of an hour. Their legs became numb in the deep cold of the lake water, and they moved their feet to avoid muscle cramps. The first arc of the sun rose in the east, behind them, and they watched it catch the tops of the trees on the far side of the lake, setting them afire for a moment, then turning them to bright emerald green. The early morning mists rose off the water and began to dissipate in the breaking of a glorious new summer day.

Ground vibrations of trotting feet reached them from the north. Once again Eli raised a hand, and they stood silent beneath the overhang, waiting. Sounds of men moving passed over their heads, faded to the south, and were gone. Eli concentrated for one more minute before he whispered, "Let's go."

He led Billy from beneath the overhang, then north in the water, to where they had entered the lake. They climbed stiff-legged onto the bank and moved into the trees, where they stopped and sat on an ancient log, soaked, water puddling around them.

Eli spoke. "The leader—with the strong voice—was one of those that ambushed us down by Albany. He recognized our tracks. He followed them from the camp to the lake, then south, and he saw where we got into the water. What he didn't know was whether we went north or south. The two drunk ones said Brant gave orders to strike camp and be in the canoes to leave just after sunrise, and they wanted to go back to camp right then. Brant's taking them north to Cayuga, just like I thought. The sober one said he'd cut out their tongues if they didn't quit their whining and act like men. They didn't believe him until he reached for his knife. He took one, and the fourth voice—the one with a head full of regret for drinking too much rum last night—took the other one. Two went north. The sober one took one of the drunk ones south. They're going half a mile both directions looking for us, then back to camp to leave with Brant and the others. The canoes are south. The British and the wagons are going north with twelve more barrels of rum and a lot of trinkets. Also some gunpowder and knives and iron tomahawks."

The chill of the cold lake water was beginning to cramp their legs. Billy shifted to break the set of his muscles, then spoke quietly. "The sober one was at that fight by Albany, and remembers our tracks?"

Eli looked at him. "He knows our tracks, and they told him about us. He knows I'm a white man raised Indian, and that you're not. He knows how tall we are, our weight, how we walk, how we move, that you're strong, and a lot of how we think. He could pick our tracks out if we walked right through the middle of their camp with four hundred other sets of tracks all over the ground."

Eli paused before he finished. "White men spend their lives studying the rules of white society and think Indians are untutored, ignorant. Indians spend their lives studying the rules of nature and can't understand how white men got so foolish. We're in that Indian's mind forever, and it's likely if he saw us right now, he'd recognize us just because he's seen our tracks. Don't ever underestimate them. In the forest, they're the king."

"What do we do next?"

"Go north and find our canoe. Then we wait for Brant's party to come past on their way to Cayuga. We'll be in the woods with our telescopes, and can get a clear count of both canoes and men. We let them pass, and then follow them at dusk. We've got to find a way to get to Brant."

Billy swallowed. "You mean walk right into his camp and talk with him?"

"If we have to."

"I doubt we'd have stayed alive for thirty seconds in that camp last night."

"Depends. If we can get them to honor a wampum belt we've got a chance."

"I'm going in with you?"

Eli shrugged. "Why not? You'll learn a lot in a hurry."

"That's what worries me. Maybe I'd just as soon not learn what they have in mind to teach."

Eli looked at him wide-eyed. "What? Your red brothers? You keep up that attitude, they might not like it. Come on. Let's go find our canoe. We've got to stop Brant somehow and then get back to St. Clair. I've got a hunch Burgoyne's going after Fort Ti soon, and our side is going to need all the help they can get. If Burgoyne gets past St. Clair, Washington could lose this revolution in a hurry. Let's move."

Notes

In preparation for the assault on Fort Stanwix, British General Barry St. Leger requested a gathering of the Indians he needed. The meeting was to take place at Oswego, where the Seneca River empties into Lake Ontario. While bringing his Indians to join the others at the proposed Oswego conference, Joseph Brant met with Daniel Claus and others on the shores of Lake Cayuga, where rum was generously distributed. Billy and Eli are fictional characters; however, the facts surrounding the meeting on the shores of Lake Cayuga are herein reported as accurately as the better historians have recorded them (see Graymont, *The Iroquois in the American Revolution*, pp. 123–25).

CHAPTER XVII

★ ★ ★

Lieutenant Colonel Heinrich Breymann approached his two sub-ordinate officers, Major von Barner, who commanded the German Jaeger riflemen, and Lieutenant Colonel Friedrich Baum, who commanded the German dragoons. The officers were dressed in the blue tunics of Hanau-Hessian soldiers, with their distinctive fifteen-inch-tall, copper-fronted hats standing high in the bright sunshine of another hot, sultry July morning. Sweat stood out on their faces as they peered at their troops.

They had one company of troops with them, with other companies of the Breymann corps spread eastward at intervals. They had given their company their midmorning twenty-minute rest and watched as the men quickly sought shade wherever they could find it in the forest lining the east bank of Lake Champlain, just over one mile north of Mt. Independence. The troops had shed their sixty-pound backpacks, removed their tall hats, sat down on anything available, and were sipping tepid water from their canteens.

Breymann, von Barner, and Baum remained standing. They drew their telescopes from their hard leather cases, extended them, and began a careful study of the troop movements across the lake. Burgoyne's Indians were moving freely in the gap between Fort Ticonderoga and the Lake George landing; effectively cutting off Fort Ti from the south. North of the fort, red-coated cannoneers were unloading General

Phillips's beloved cannon from bateaux, under Phillips's expert eye, and the Germans could hear his booming commands echo across the calm lake. To the south, forty-one bateaux unloaded more German Hessians on the east shore of the lake, below Mt. Independence.

Breymann smiled with his thoughts. *We have the Americans and their fortifications on Mt. Independence caught squarely between my command and those unloading to the south. They have no chance. They will be ours in one-half day and their fortifications along with them.*

Movement further south on the lake caught his eye, and once again he extended his telescope to study the boats crossing from west to east. *Fraser's riflemen, with Canadians and Indians to take the Hubbardton Road. Right on schedule. Burgoyne is sealing off all retreat to the south. When will St. Clair realize he is beaten and surrender?*

The three officers turned at the sound of a horse cantering in from behind and faced Lieutenant Johann Reichmann. Sweat was running from his chin, making dark spots on his blue tunic as he dismounted, came to attention, and saluted.

"Yes, Lieutenant?" Breymann said.

"Herr Colonel, I am with Captain Gottfried Strauss, one mile east. He sent me to report that East Creek is not as represented on our maps. The colonel will recall that we must cross East Creek to reach Mount Independence. The creek is not a creek, but a bog, perhaps half a mile across. My captain is doubtful men can cross it on foot, and even if it is possible, he estimates it will take two days. Either way we will be much delayed and unable to follow the schedule Herr General Burgoyne has ordered. My captain wishes further instruction."

Breymann turned narrowed eyes to von Barner and Baum. "Am I to understand that some dunderhead made these maps without scouting the territory? East Creek is shown to be nothing—a trickle that can be crossed in minutes. Now we are here facing it, only to discover it is an impassable swamp?"

Von Barner shrugged, and Baum spoke. "We are entitled to believe the British who made the maps were competent, which they obviously were not. There is little we can do now except send officers to witness the truth about East Creek, make an official document recording our findings to show Herr General Burgoyne, and then cross the bog despite their failure. It appears that once again we must show the British something about how soldiers function."

The disgust in Breymann's face was apparent as he gave his orders. "You two accompany the lieutenant back to his command. If he is correct, advise Captain Strauss that the British maps are in error and inform them we must correct their incompetence. He is to cross the bog in any way he deems best, but it must be done at once. Remind him we are German soldiers—we will meet the schedule as ordered. I am angry for the trouble the British have caused him. Am I clear?"

"Ja, Herr Colonel." Von Barner and Baum trotted to their horses, tightened the girths, mounted, and followed the young lieutenant east at a lope. They slowed as they entered the forest, working their way through on a crooked foot trail, pushing aside branches, watching as their horses stepped over and around rocks and rotting logs. Within minutes the ground became spongy and then the horses were kicking mud with every step. Five minutes later their mounts were in muck to their knees, throwing their heads, fighting the bits, battling to move ahead.

The lieutenant raised his arm to point. "My regiment is there."

The three mounted officers turned to study the swampy marsh in all directions as they slogged their way to the waiting Hessians. Mosquitoes rose in swarms to torment the nostrils and eyes of the horses. Tiny brulies formed into clouds, attracted to the scent of both the men and the horses, to attack and sting. Thousands of dragonflies, three inches long, darted and flitted, pausing to hang suspended as their four wings fanned the air in perfect synchronization. Tens of thousands of swamp insects never seen by Europeans buzzed and swarmed, stinging. Some soldiers had unbuttoned their tunics to draw them over their heads against the merciless onslaught. The tired troops were splattered with black mud to their waists, and spots and flecks showed on their tunics.

As the three officers approached the captain, he rose from the log on which he was sitting and saluted. Baum gaped. The headless bodies of four rattlesnakes and two copperheads lay draped over the log next to the captain, who came to rigid attention as he spoke. "I am Captain Gottfried Strauss. I am awaiting further orders from the colonel."

Von Barner answered. "He sent us." The major shook his head. "I believe you understated your report of this place. We are to make our appraisal of conditions, return, and make a written statement to be presented to Herr General Burgoyne." He cast his eyes over the terrain. "The British maps have led you into this impossible mess, but we are to remind you that we are German soldiers. Despite the inexcusable British blunder, you will cross this bog and continue to your objective, Mount Independence. Our forces are landed south of us on schedule and will be moving toward us, expecting us to move toward them with the mountain between us. We will take the Americans and their fortifications, on schedule. Herr Colonel Breymann instructed us to inform you that he is angry with the British incompetence that has led you into this morass. Do you understand?"

"Very good."

The captain saluted, and von Barner and Baum returned it, then turned their horses and started west, back through the thick, black ooze that sucked at their horses' legs at every stride.

General St. Clair started at the insistent rap on his door, and his aide-de-camp, Major Isaac Dunn, barged in before he could rise or speak. Dunn's tunic was open at the top, and sweat was running. He left the door standing open to cast bright July sunlight on the floor as he pointed east, across the lake.

"General, the Germans have landed both above and below Mount Independence. And it looks like some Indians and Canadians and redcoats are moving on down toward the Hubbardton Road. It appears Burgoyne intends taking our defenses on Mount Independence and cutting off any reinforcements or supplies coming in from the east."

St. Clair set his jaw and leaned back in his chair. "What about the supplies down on the Lake George landing? Did we get them back within our lines?"

Dunn shook his head. "No. Some of the oxen got frightened by the cannonfire up north and ran off. For some reason the drivers didn't go after them. They just sat there by their wagons, doing nothing. They're still sitting down there."

St. Clair jerked erect. "They did nothing? Why?"

"No one could see a reason for it. Maybe they're afraid Indians are waiting for them out in the woods."

St. Clair slammed a doubled fist down on his desktop. "Then we've lost any hope of getting those stores back up here. Send Captain Lossing and his company down there right now, with orders to get those supplies onto the bateaux, and have the bateaumen take them on down to Fort George the minute they're loaded. Tonight if they can. I won't let the British get those stores."

"Yes, sir."

"Anything else?"

A smile touched Dunn's face for a moment. "One of our pickets just reported that Seth Warner's coming in from the Grants over in New Hampshire with seven hundred men and about eighty cattle. Some sheep, too. Coming right on past the Germans to the south. Should be here sometime tonight."

St. Clair stood. "Fresh meat. Good. Has anyone told the commissary officer? He's concerned we're getting low on salt beef. Mutton will be a good change."

"I'll tell him."

"Go get Captain Lossing moving down to the landing."

Dunn turned and strode out the door, closing it behind him. St. Clair sank back onto his chair, exhausted, weary to death from days of trying to carry the entire American command on his shoulders. With Burgoyne's forces systematically moving in from all sides with a force of the world's finest soldiers four times the size of his own, what could he do? Move out to meet them? One against four on an open battlefield? Insanity. Send out what precious few men he had piecemeal, and give them away in meaningless skirmishes until he had none left? Ridiculous. With Burgoyne relentlessly tightening his stranglehold on Fort

Ticonderoga, all St. Clair could do was draw his men in slowly, bringing them back inside the fortress, where the thick walls and their own cannon would give them some sort of fighting chance to survive the final, full-scale assault.

For seven days, possessed by fears that drove him relentlessly, St. Clair had been everywhere—at the commissary, the munitions stores, the enlisted barracks, the enlisted mess, and repeatedly outside the fort in the trenches and breastworks with his men, taking the sporadic incoming musket and cannonfire along with them, patting them on the shoulder, providing generous words of encouragement and praise, assuring them, making himself a presence to his entire command. He had snatched but six hours of fitful sleep in those seven days, and eaten only sparsely. His face was lined, haggard, eyes hollow. But he had earned the respect and the love of his troops, and there was no man in his command who had failed to voice praise for their leader.

He sighed deeply, then stood in the dim light of his tiny, crude office, and reached for his tricorn. He could make the rounds once more, with the news Seth Warner was coming in from the south with seven hundred men—tough militia riflemen from the New Hampshire Grants—and enough fresh beef and mutton for nearly a month. If Warner could make it in, there was still hope. He tucked his hat under his arm and started for the door when footsteps sounded on the boardwalk outside, followed by a perfunctory rap.

He pulled the door opened to see a young private standing there. The boy was not yet eighteen years old, dressed in homespun, smooth-cheeked, awkward, embarrassed in the presence of his commanding officer. With downcast eyes he stammered, "Sir, I . . . uh . . . this was give to me, and I was ordered to get it over here right now." He thrust a folded paper toward St. Clair.

St. Clair reached for the document. "What is it?"

The boy shrugged. "I don't know, sir. Just come in with a scout."

St. Clair looked the boy in the face. "Thank you, Private. Are you all right? Getting enough to eat?"

The boy raised his eyes and spoke energetically. "Oh, yes, sir. Fine. Things is fine. Eating good."

"Glad to hear it. Go back to your company. They'll need you."

"Yes, sir. I'll do that." The boy backed away, bowing twice before turning to sprint for the big gates, grinning his relief at having completed a task that had terrified him.

St. Clair closed the door, then with trembling fingers broke the seal and read the message. His face softened, and he read it once more with a smile forming on his lips. The message was clear. General Washington had met General Howe's British regulars at Brunswick, and the British were withdrawing. It was signed by Chaplain Hitchcock.

St. Clair breathed deeply for a moment, then hung his hat back on its peg and resumed his seat behind his desk. *Seth Warner, seven hundred fresh troops, eighty cattle, mutton, and now General Washington has beaten Howe at Brunswick! How best to use all this to inspire the men.* He leaned back for a time in deep thought before he reached a conclusion. *At sunset we conduct a* feu de joie. He referred to the ancient custom of conducting a military celebration by the firing of muskets, all up and down the line, each in succession. His thoughts continued. *But we can't fire the muskets because some alert British officer will count the shots and know how many men we have. No, we'll fire the cannon. Thirteen of them, one for each of the states. That should lift our spirits. Tomorrow we'll do it again to celebrate the first anniversary of the signing of the Declaration of Independence.*

He sobered at the remembrance and forgot time while his thoughts reached back. *We hold these truths to be self evident . . . endowed by our Creator . . . life, liberty, and the pursuit of happiness.* There was a stirring in his soul, just as when the immortal document had been read to all the American troops one year earlier. The flesh on his arms tingled again at the sure knowledge that the work of breaking from British rule was not the work of man. Sitting in his small, crude office in the wilderness, his command outnumbered four to one by the greatest military power in the world, short of everything with which to conduct the hopeless defense of the fort, and so weary in body and mind that he did not know if he could get to his feet, he felt once more the transcendent force rise in his heart to fill every fiber of his being, and in that moment he knew—there was a power beyond anything mortal working its indiscernible designs all about him, and no power in heaven or on earth could stop it.

For a fleeting moment he felt a spirit fill him and the tiny, rude office with a light not of earth, and then it began to fade, and slowly withdrew, and he was left sitting at his desk once more, facing the crushing burden of his command.

A brisk knock at the door jolted him.

"Enter."

Dunn strode in, sweaty, breathless. "Three deserters from Burgoyne's army just walked through the gates. Two Germans, one British."

St. Clair came off his seat, leaning forward on stiff arms on his desk. "Sure they're deserters? Not spies?"

Dunn shook his head. "I'm convinced they're deserters. They say they want asylum, and they want to talk to you."

"Where are they now?"

"In the guardhouse."

"Bring them here."

"Yes, sir." Dunn turned to go, then stopped. "I should mention, Captain Lossing's on the way to the Lake George landing. Those stores and supplies should be loaded and gone tonight, out of British hands."

"Good. Bring those deserters."

Less than ten minutes later Dunn swung the door open and seven men entered St. Clair's small office. Between three Americans armed with muskets were two blue-coated Hessians and one red-coated British regular. The seventh man was Eric Bucholz, a Pennsylvania German with the Pennsylvania Twentieth Militia, who spoke both languages fluently. St. Clair sat stone still, eyes narrowed, watching intently as the three deserters came to his desk to stand at rigid attention, eyes locked on the wall behind him. He slowly leaned forward on his elbows and spoke to Dunn.

"I take it the Germans do not speak English."

"They do not." He gestured. "Sergeant Bucholz can translate."

St. Clair spoke to all three. "I'm told you are deserters, seeking asylum. If we discover you're actually here to spy, you'll be hanged." The redcoat did not flinch. The Germans waited while Bucholz translated and they answered. Bucholz turned to St. Clair.

"They understand. They say they are not spies." St. Clair could hear the faint German accent in Bucholz's clipped words.

St. Clair continued. "Are you willing to answer my questions about General Burgoyne's forces?"

The redcoat responded immediately. "My name is Reginald Dunphy. My commanding officer was Captain Alexander Fraser. That is all I have to say."

Bucholz translated for the Germans. "They will answer any questions."

St. Clair glared at Dunphy. "You will not answer my questions?"

"That is correct, sir."

St. Clair shrugged and turned to Dunn. "Take him back to the guardhouse. I'll talk with the Germans."

Dunn marched Dunphy out the door with one guard behind him, bayonet nearly touching his back, and the three of them angled through the hot, south breeze toward the guardhouse. The other two armed guards walked outside, took a position on either side of the door, and closed it. St. Clair gestured, and the two Germans sat on chairs facing his desk. There was no third chair, and St. Clair pointed to the one facing his small, private table in the corner. Bucholz brought it to the side of the desk and sat down facing the Germans. He pointed, they removed their tall hats, and then faced St. Clair, waiting.

St. Clair drew a sheet of paper from his desk drawer. Words and numbers were printed on it, and for a moment he glanced over them before he began.

"Did you come through Quebec and up the Richelieu River?"

"Yes."

"Was General Carleton in Quebec?"

"Yes. Governor."

"Did he remain there?"

"Yes, with a small number of his army. Most of his army came with General Burgoyne."

"How many soldiers are with Burgoyne?"

"Over eight thousand. Two thousand wives and camp followers."

"Who commands the cannon, and how many are there?"

"General William Phillips. One hundred thirty-eight."

St. Clair looked at his paper and for a time moved his finger down the column of figures. At that moment Dunn walked back into the room.

"The British regular is in the guardhouse. What are my orders?"

"Find a chair and join us. I may need a witness."

Dunn walked out the door and returned in two minutes with an empty keg. He set it beside St. Clair's desk, opposite Bucholz, and sat down. St. Clair continued.

"Who is the German officer in command of all German troops? The one who reports directly to Burgoyne?"

"Baron von Riedesel. Friedrich Adolph von Riedesel."

"What units are under his command?"

"Seven Brunswick regiments, a light infantry battalion, and four companies of dragoons."

"Dragoons? Mounted cavalry?"

"Cavalry, but not mounted. They have no horses. They expect to find horses here."

St. Clair smiled and shook his head. There weren't twenty horses fit for duty in the entire fort, nor were there enough oxen to pull five cannon. St. Clair sobered and a noticeable intensity came into his face.

"How many days of food supplies does Burgoyne have?"

"Perhaps twenty. Less than thirty."

St. Clair masked his surprise and went on. "How many wagons in his train?"

The Germans shook their heads in disgust. One of them answered, "Close to six hundred."

St. Clair reared back in his chair in total surprise. "What? He thinks he's going to move six hundred wagons in these forests? And one hundred thirty-eight cannon? He'll need close to two thousand animals—horses or oxen—to do it. And even if he had the animals, there's no way under heaven he'll get six hundred wagons through this wilderness before winter."

The Germans needed no translation. They nodded their heads.

St. Clair brought his racing thoughts under control. "If he has food for only twenty days, what does he have in six hundred wagons?"

"Fifteen wagons filled with wine and champagne. Sixteen wagons with his clothes. Delicacies for his table. Fodder for the oxen. Sacked oats for the horses."

"What horses? You said he doesn't have enough horses to mount his dragoons."

"He thinks he will get horses, either from the settlements near the lake or from this fort. He is trained for light cavalry and thinks the dragoons will be decisive when the battle comes."

St. Clair rolled his head back, unable to believe what he was hearing. "Cavalry? In this forest? What are his plans for taking this fort?"

"We do not know. We heard General Phillips persuaded him to put it under siege. Surround the fort, cut it off, and starve you out. Then we heard he had changed his mind—that he intends to surround you, cut you off, then attack from all sides at once. We do not know what he thinks now."

St. Clair moved on. "How is morale among Burgoyne's troops?"

"High. Very high. They feel that even now the trap is closing. Our Brunswickers and the Hanau-Hessians are prepared to take all troops and defenses on Mount Independence and cut off the Hubbardton Road. General Burgoyne's regulars and the Indians are ready to move against you from the west. All units will be in place within two days. They know your strength. They have no fear for the outcome. They are anxious to get it over with."

St. Clair checked his notes one more time, then turned to Dunn. "Anything you want to ask?"

"If morale is so high, why did these men desert?"

Bucholz translated, listened to the Germans, and turned back to Dunn. "They say they want to stop being soldiers. They want families. Perhaps a farm. They want to stay in America."

Dunn's eyebrows peaked for a moment in surprise before he turned to St. Clair. "I don't have anything else."

St. Clair spoke to the Germans. "You will be returned to the guard-house and later taken down to General Schuyler in Albany. A court down there will decide what to do with you. I'll send a written report on your conduct. Maybe it will help. That is all."

Bucholz translated, the Germans nodded approval, and St. Clair turned to Dunn. "Take them back, then return here."

Bucholz stood, and St. Clair nodded to him. "Thank you, Sergeant."

Bucholz followed the group out the door and closed it while St. Clair placed his elbows on the desk and lowered his face into his hands. He was still deep in thought when Dunn returned.

"Sit down, Major." He gestured to the paper, still on his desk. "Everything the Germans said was exactly what Stroud and Weems reported to us after their scout up north. I believe these men told us the truth on the things that are critical now. Burgoyne is getting ready to take this fort by surrounding it and coming at us from all sides. He's low on food. He expects to find horses and oxen here. He thinks he can mount his dragoons and do something with them in this wilderness. I think the man's right in the middle of the forest and can't see it. The notion of a light cavalry charge in this terrain is ridiculous. There are places a man can't even lead a horse, let alone ride one. But then, Burgoyne's motives often have nothing to do with military considerations."

St. Clair stood and for a moment stretched stiff muscles. "I received word that General Washington drove Howe out of Brunswick. I also received information that Seth Warner is due in tonight with seven hundred militia from the Grants, with eighty cattle and some mutton. I think we can use the information to lift spirits among the men. Just before mess, we're going to conduct a feu de joie. Have thirteen cannon loaded, one for each state, and have the men form in rank and file in the parade ground. We'll tell them the news and give three huzzahs before we fire the cannon. Have the same thirteen guns ready tomorrow before noon mess. It's the fourth of July, and we're going to commemorate the signing of the Declaration of Independence."

"Yes, sir."

Dunn had reached the door before St. Clair stopped him. "Separate the two German deserters from the redcoat. Then find Stevens at his artillery battalion and tell him to send Andrew Tracy to me. Lieutenant Andrew Hodges Tracy."

Dunn nodded and walked out the door.

The south breeze died in the late afternoon. The sweltering heat bore down in dead air. Offices inside the fort became ovens. Before evening mess, a drumroll brought the troops into rank and file on the parade ground, where they stood sweating while their officers informed them of what they thought was a victory by General Washington over General Howe at Brunswick and then promised them fresh beef and mutton and seven hundred fresh militia to bolster the defense of the fort. Led by the officers, the men gave three rousing huzzahs, then on command, the cannoneers lowered their linstocks to the touchholes, and thirteen cannon on the north wall blasted in order. Then the enlisted men took their trenchers of food out of the unbearable heat in the mess hall to find any available shade to sit in and eat their supper.

With shadows growing long, the three prisoners in the guardhouse were startled at the outbreak of loud cursing and the sounds of men in combat in the parade ground. The two Germans in one cell, and the redcoated British regular in the other, crowded around the barred openings in the thick, heavy doors to peer out.

Four American soldiers were half leading, half dragging a stocky young Irishman across the parade ground, toward the guardhouse. He was shouting curses at them, flailing at them with his feet and his hands, despite the chains that bound his wrists together, and his ankles. His old, ragged clothing was torn, one shirt sleeve ripped free at the shoulder, and covered with dust and dirt from the battle that had ensued when they chained him. His face was filthy from being thrown down in the dust, and sweat made muddy streaks through the ground-in dirt. The string that had held back his long, reddish hair was broken, dangling, and his hair was wild, dirty.

They reached the door into the cell where the British regular was being held, and he backed away from the barred opening, wide-eyed, frightened. Three of the armed guards drove the Irishman to his knees, and the fourth worked the big brass key in the lock and threw the cell door open. The guards grasped the chain that bound his wrists to jerk him to his feet, then threw him headlong through the open door. He tried to keep his feet under him, but the ankle chain was too short, and he hit the dirt floor, rolling to slam heavily into the far wall with his head and shoulder. For a moment he lay still, stunned, while the guards followed him, to grab him by the hair and jerk his head up. One American thrust his face into the Irishman's face and spat, "Six o'clock! At six o'clock in the morning you'll find out what happens to spies. But don't worry. We won't inconvenience you long. The hangin' won't take but five minutes."

The American viciously pushed the man's head down, then the three guards backed out the door, to slam it and twist the key.

Slowly the battered man rolled over, then struggled to a sitting position in the dim cell, trying to drive the cobwebs from his brain, struggling to understand where he was. Dunphy watched him test the shackles and chains, then rise to one knee, holding his ribs.

Dunphy spoke from the corner. "Anything broken?"

The young Irishman spun, fists cocked, trying to locate whoever had spoken.

Dunphy said, "Stand easy. I'm British."

The Irishman stood on unsteady legs, fists still cocked, ready. "Get out in the light where I can see you."

Dunphy stepped into what little light came through the small, square opening in the door and stopped. The Irishman saw the crimson tunic and the crossed belts and lowered his fist. "Are you a prisoner?"

"Yes."

"Captured?"

Dunphy shrugged. "What difference does it make? I'm a prisoner."

"Deserter?"

"You could call it that. I'm through soldiering. I'm going to find some ground and start a farm and a family. If that's deserting, then I'm a deserter."

"What's your name?"

"Reginald Dunphy. Yours?"

"Crawford O'Leary."

"Irish, I presume."

"County Cork."

"A spy? I heard them talking."

O'Leary sighed and slowly lowered himself to the floor, sitting down with his back to the wall, arms draped over his raised knees. Suddenly he snorted a brief, cryptic laugh. "I'm a spy until six o'clock in the morning."

"I'm sorry for you."

O'Leary shrugged. "Nothing to be done about it. I'd just like to know the name of the bloody scum who told the Americans. I'd get word out somehow, and he'd pay."

"Someone informed?"

"No other way I can figure it. One minute I was about a mile south of here walkin' this way, and the next minute six Americans from nowhere were all over me." He smiled ruefully. "Three of 'em won't forget the battle for a while."

"Coming from the south? Where?" Dunphy asked.

"Albany. I got some documents from the files of General Schuyler to deliver to General Burgoyne."

"About what?"

"The names of the officers and troops and plans for defending this fort."

"They took the papers?"

"Yes." Then, as an afterthought, O'Leary reached to pat the baggy leg of his trousers. He grinned and lowered his voice, "But they missed this." Maneuvering the chains binding his hands, he dug awkwardly into his pants to draw out a flat pewter flask. He unscrewed the cap, and the aroma of good Irish whiskey reached out. He tipped it briefly, then wiped at his mouth. "They might find the flask in the mornin', but they'll never get the whiskey." He held it out to Dunphy. "Care for a sip?"

Hungrily Dunphy reached for the flask, savored the smell for a moment, then tipped it up.

O'Leary took the flask back to hold it loosely between his spread knees. "You were with Burgoyne?"

"Yes."

"If I understood his plan, he ought to be getting ready to take this fort about now."

"Very soon."

A smile crossed O'Leary's smudged face. "Any chance he'll take it before six o'clock in the morning?"

Dunphy shook his head, and O'Leary offered him the flask again, then took it back and tipped it up himself.

"Burgoyne was coming with a lot of boats, so I heard. Gunboats? Or troop ships?" O'Leary asked.

"Both. Two big gunboats, about thirty bateaux mounted with guns, and over two hundred fifty ships and bateaux with soldiers."

"How many troops? Ten thousand?"

"Eight. Two thousand wives and camp followers."

"How did he plan to get past that big bridge and all those logs the Americans have strung across the lake?"

"Cannon. Sail right down to them and blast them with the guns on those two big men-of-war."

O'Leary bobbed his head and tipped the flask again, then handed it to Dunphy. "After he takes this fort, then what?"

Dunphy took the proffered flask, then sat down beside O'Leary and leaned back against the wall. He took another swig. "On down to Albany to meet Howe, and Joseph Brant coming in on the Mohawk River."

"Joseph Brant?"

"A Mohawk chief. That's his Christian name."

They traded the flask again.

"How's he going on to Albany? Land or water?"

"Lake George, then the Hudson River."

"Water all the way, except that little stretch just south of the lake. Maybe ten, twelve miles. Good plan," O'Leary allowed.

They sat in silence for a few moments, savoring the effect of the whiskey. When he spoke again, O'Leary's speech was slightly slurred. "How many Germans does Burgoyne have?"

"Just over three thousand."

"Good ones?"

"Who knows? Can't speak a word of English. They're near helpless in the forest."

"How many cannon?"

"One hundred thirty-eight pieces of artillery, with General Phillips to command them. Best artillery column England ever sent out. And Burgoyne won't move without them." Dunphy's speech had thickened a bit.

They drew again on the flask, and O'Leary continued. "This fort's got thick walls. How does Burgoyne think he can breach them with cannon?"

"I doubt he'll try. I think he means to set up cannon on all five sides, with infantry right behind, and start with grapeshot, then follow with an assault from all sides at once. That will divide the Americans inside the fort so no one wall will have enough men to hold it. Once he's got men over one wall and inside the fort, that should end it."

O'Leary held the flask up and shook it, listening. "Nearly empty. One last nip for each of us." He tipped the flask, then handed it to Dunphy. "You finish it."

Fifteen minutes later Dunphy had slumped over on his side and was breathing deeply, slowly. O'Leary screwed the cap back on the flask and thrust it back inside his trousers, then leaned back against the wall and drifted to sleep in a sitting position.

With the first arc of the sun catching the tops of the trees with gold, the American guards quietly twisted the brass key in the lock and swung the door partially open. Silently O'Leary studied Dunphy's face until he was certain he was in a deep sleep, then came to his feet. Stooping to hold the chain between his ankles in one hand, he quietly walked out the door. Five minutes later the guards unlocked his shackles, and O'Leary briefly rubbed his wrists and ankles, then softly crossed the boardwalk to rap gently on the office door of General St. Clair. The door opened, the guards backed away, and O'Leary walked inside the office.

A lantern burned on St. Clair's desk, casting the room in dim yellow light. St. Clair gestured, O'Leary sat down facing the desk, and St. Clair took his chair facing him. For several moments St. Clair studied O'Leary's filthy, torn clothing, and his dirty, mud-and-sweat-streaked face.

"Are you all right?"

Lieutenant Andrew Hodges Tracy answered. "Yes."

"Did he talk?"

"After we worked on the flask for a while, he told everything."

"Was he drunk when you left him just now?"

"Sleeping it off."

"You?"

"I tipped the flask, but I didn't drink. He did, all of it. He's going to wake up about ten o'clock with a terrible headache. Let him know you hung the spy, O'Leary, at six o'clock sharp."

St. Clair smiled, chuckled, then leaned forward. "All right, let's start from the top. How does Burgoyne plan to get past our bridge and chain, and how is he going to attack this fort?"

Notes

Unless otherwise indicated, the facts herein stated are taken from Ketchum, *Saratoga*, on the pages identified.

General Burgoyne's plan of attack on Fort Ticonderoga included German General von Breymann crossing Lake Champlain and moving south to take the American fortifications at Mt. Independence. To do so, Breymann crossed the lake well above Mt. Independence and marched south, where his line of march required him to cross East Creek. On the map, East Creek was identified as a small stream. In fact, it was a great marsh, or bog, at some places half a mile across. Crossing it on foot was a near impossibility, with the soldiers sometimes bogged in muck to their waists. Insects and snakes of every kind infested the swamp. Horses were in the mud to their bellies. It took Breymann's command one full day to cover just twelve hundred yards. Fearing the Germans would not reach the Hubbardton road in time to stop the Americans from escaping, Burgoyne ordered Fraser's riflemen and some Indians to cross to the east side of the lake and seize the road (p. 167).

The "brulies" referred to herein and elsewhere were extremely small, particularly vexing insects that got into clothing and hair and could sting. The soldiers called them "no-see-ums" because they were so small (p. 96).

Recognizing he could not protect his stores and supplies on the docks outside Fort Ticonderoga, St. Clair sent men down to carry them inside the fort. However, with cannonfire in the distance, the oxen became frightened and ran away. Unable to haul the supplies back to the fort, St. Clair ordered them put onto the bateaux at the docks and ferried down Lake George to Fort George at the southern tip (p. 168).

Henry Brockholst Livingston, an aide to General St. Clair, wrote to his father, giving high praise to General St. Clair, who had been tireless in preparing the fort for the British assault, inspecting, moving among the men, bolstering morale (p. 169).

Three deserters from Burgoyne's army appeared at Fort Ti and were interrogated by General St. Clair. The one British regular would give only his name and unit, while the Germans answered all questions for which they had answers. However, that night, the three prisoners were put in separate cells, and a roughly dressed Irishman was thrown in with the British prisoner. The Irishman professed to be a captured spy, sentenced to hang the next morning. He had a flask of Irish whiskey in his clothing, which he used to ply the British prisoner, cleverly getting answers St. Clair needed. After the British prisoner fell into a drunken stupor, the Irishman was released and taken to St. Clair, to whom he delivered the needed information. The Irishman was in fact Lieutenant Andrew Hodges Tracy, assigned to Steven's artillery battalion and used by St. Clair for this most clever and strategic trick (p. 168).

CHAPTER XVIII

★ ★ ★

*T*he distant boom of cannon rolled over the British camp, and Brigadier General Simon Fraser flinched, then raised his eyes from his desk. He stared at the tent wall for a few moments, until he heard the faint whump of the cannonball strikes. Five seconds later the blasting of cannon much closer sent a tremor up the canvas wall.

Fraser turned to his aide, Major Hugh Billingsley. "What's going on out there?"

Stocky, square-faced, perspiring, Billingsley answered, "I don't know, sir. I'm sure the major assault has not begun."

Fraser rose from his desk to push aside the flap and walk out into the confusion and color and noise of five thousand sweating men laboring, moving about the massive British camp. He squinted upward and then checked his watch—just past nine o'clock in another sweltering morning—and stepped to the side of Major Alexander Lindsay, sixth Earl of Balcarres, standing nearby, looking south.

"What's the shooting?" Fraser asked him.

Balcarres pointed. "Nothing important. It seems the Americans are just being certain we get no peace, and our guns are returning the favor. Nonsense, more or less."

"Anything changed since yesterday?"

"We're reinforcing our breastworks that face their French Lines. An American column got into Fort Ti a while ago—six or seven hundred militia from the Grants. Brought some cattle and sheep. The Americans made a considerable fuss over it—fired a feu de joie with cannon—but there are no changes worth mentioning. Maybe their feu de joie was in celebration of that document they produced a year ago—their Declaration of Independence." Balcarres shook his head. "They seem to think that document is going to change something." He turned toward Fraser and harumphed. "A piece of paper? Change the world?" He shook his head. "Nonsense."

From the south came another cannon volley, and both Balcarres and Fraser involuntarily ducked their heads slightly. Fraser smiled at his own actions. "Odd how the natural instinct is to duck when a cannon's fired. Even seasoned soldiers do it."

Balcarres reached with a white handkerchief to wipe at the sweat on his face. "A little embarrassing when the cannon fire is so distant, and you're not in the line of fire. I've seen a few quick-eyed soldiers who can track a cannonball in flight. If it's coming their way they simply step aside and let it pass."

Fraser's eyebrows raised in surprise. "You've seen men who can follow a cannonball in flight?"

"Yes. A few. Extremely sharp-eyed."

"I've never tried—"

At that moment an errant cannonball whistled fifteen feet over their heads to drop behind them, plowing a furrow twelve feet long in the ground and coming to a stop, smoking. Both men ducked violently, then turned to survey the damage, relieved that there was none.

Balcarres said, "That was a little too close. I trust General Burgoyne intends moving on Fort Ti in the very near future and stopping this irritating business. What do you suppose he's waiting on?"

Fraser replied, "I believe he wants all his cannon in position. Phillips is doing all he can, but there are places he has to build roads to move them across swampy ground. It won't be long."

Fraser took a moment to study the terrain surrounding their huge, sprawling camp. To the east, across the lake, Mt. Independence. West, the rolling, forested mountains and valleys. To the south, hidden from sight,

Fort Ticonderoga on its small peninsula. Behind the fort, Mt. Defiance, its peak rearing into the blue heavens. It was all familiar, unchanged. He had turned back toward his tent when a thought struck him with such force he came to an immediate stop and slowly turned back to stare south.

Balcarres considered his erratic behavior. "Is something wrong?"

For ten seconds Fraser did not speak nor move. Concerned, Balcarres walked toward him. "General, are you feeling well?"

Slowly Fraser raised his arm high, pointing. "Do you see Mount Defiance?"

Balcarres turned to look, and could see nothing remarkable—no smoke, no movement of troops, nothing. "Of course. What's your point?"

"Do I recall correctly? Isn't Fort Ticonderoga just across that narrow neck of water at the Lake George outlet, about fifteen hundred yards from Mount Defiance?"

"Correct. It's been that way for a million years. Have I missed something?"

Softly Fraser said, "What would happen if we were to get some heavy cannon up there?"

Balcarres stared, and his mouth slowly dropped open. "We'd have the bloody fort in the palm of our hand, and Mount Independence with it!"

"Exactly. The question is, can we get cannon up there?"

For ten seconds Balcarres peered at the mountain. "Probably not, at least not from this side. I don't recall what the maps say about the back side."

"Nor do I." Fraser dropped his eyes. "I'll look into it."

Eyes still locked on Mt. Defiance, Balcarres nodded. "Let me know the results."

Fraser turned and strode quickly to his tent. At the flap, he hesitated long enough to peer once more at Mt. Defiance, then ducked inside and hurried to the leather chest in which he stored his maps. With trembling fingers, he loosened the buckles, threw back the broad leather straps, and lifted the lid. Five seconds later he straightened and hurried to his desk to untie the heavy cord wrapped around a scrolled map.

Billingsley rose from his desk in the corner. "Sir, can I be of service?"

"Can you find my calipers?"

"Yes, sir." Billingsley walked to Fraser's desk and began opening drawers.

The general was scarcely breathing as he unrolled the heavy document, spread it on his worktable, shifted it to lie true with the compass, and anchored the four corners with leather pouches filled with sand. Quickly he located the five-sided figure of Fort Ticonderoga, then ran his finger southwest across the narrow neck of water that drained Lake George into Lake Champlain. Slowly he moved his finger to the top of Mt. Defiance, paused, then continued from the top of Mt. Defiance almost due east across the southern extreme of Lake Champlain, called South Bay, to the top of Mt. Independence.

He turned to Billingsley, who handed him his calipers. He spread the two needle-pointed legs of the instrument, planted one point in the center of Fort Ti, the other at the top of Mt. Defiance, then read the scale. His eyes widened. "Fourteen hundred yards." He spread the instrument once more, relocated the points on Mt. Defiance and Mt. Independence, and again read the scale. "Fifteen hundred yards."

He lowered the calipers and turned to Billingsley. "Our cannon on Mount Defiance can destroy every American defense at Fort Ti and Mount Independence in less than one day, and there isn't a single American gun that could reach us."

"It appears so, sir."

Again Fraser pored over the map, checking the contour lines to determine how steep the incline was on the face of the mountain. The map showed the lines were very close to each other, and he shook his head. "Too steep." He shifted his gaze to the back side of the mountain. In places, the contour lines were more widely spaced. Quickly he seized his quill, and without dipping it in ink, he moved the tip of it from the flat land at the foot of the mountain to the top, following only contour lines that were separated. He straightened, wide-eyed, exultant. "It can be done!" he exclaimed. "We can move cannon up the back side of Mount Defiance."

Billingsley looked at the map for five seconds before the stunning significance of Fraser's discovery struck home. "Astounding, sir. Absolutely astounding!"

Hardheaded military discipline asserted itself, and Fraser forced himself to sit down at the table and check his work, with Billingsley poring over the map in utter fascination. There was no question—it was there to be done if Fraser had men daring enough to make the attempt. He rose from his chair and walked rapidly to the flap before he turned.

"Major, do you know where I can find Captain James Craig?"

Billingsley concentrated for a moment. "I think his company is assigned to dig a powder magazine. Northwest edge of camp, sir."

"Good. Wait here for further orders."

"Yes, sir."

Officers and regulars alike paused in their work to watch General Simon Fraser as he worked his way quickly through the uproar and muddle of officers, regulars, and camp followers hustling in all directions on their assigned duties. He was sweating profusely when he slowed near a great mound of fresh, dank earth, bordering a gigantic hole thirty feet square, with men inside, stripped to the waist, sweat running as they worked with shovels, steadily sinking the hole to the desired ten-foot depth. Others stood around the top with more shovels, moving the dirt away with wheelbarrows, past a mountain of earth on the west side of the hole.

Fraser stopped at the nearest man, breathing heavily, sweat dripping. "Can you direct me to Captain James Craig?"

For a moment the man stared. He could not recall ever seeing a general move fast enough on a sweltering hot day to raise a sweat. "Yes, sir. Cap'n Craig's just past that dirt pile with some wagons."

"Thank you." Fraser rounded the great mound of fresh dirt and slowed at the sight of twenty men shoveling dirt into two huge freight wagons. Eight yoked oxen stood with their eyes closed against the mosquitoes and brulies, patiently chewing their cud while the wagons filled. Captain Craig was standing with his back to the general, giving orders to a lieutenant.

"When they're loaded, drive them down to Captain Alexander Fraser's breastworks facing the rebel French Lines. He needs the dirt for fill in front of the timbers."

"Yes, sir."

Craig turned and all but bumped into General Fraser. "Oh! Excuse me, sir. I didn't expect you."

Fraser wasted no words but drew Craig aside. "Captain, I have a critical mission for you and twenty of your men, with perhaps a few Indians."

Craig straightened, eyes narrowed in question. "Yes, sir."

"I want you to work your way up the back side of Mount Defiance and determine two things: first, can we transport cannon up there; and, if we can, is there a place up there to build gun emplacements? Then report back to me, no matter the time."

"When do you want this done, sir?"

"Now."

Craig's mouth dropped open. "You mean pick twenty men and a few Indians for advance scout and leave right now?"

Fraser bobbed his head. "Precisely."

Craig rounded his lips to blow air while his brain raced to catch up with Fraser's order. He turned on the spot and called, "Dugan, come here!"

A lean, raw-boned, bearded sergeant straightened, wiped at the sweat on his face, and rammed his shovel blade into the dirt. "Yes, sir." He walked rapidly to face Craig and saluted both officers.

"Get your men into uniform as fast as you can and wait here. I'm going to get five Indian scouts and a map. I'll be back in five minutes."

Dugan's face clouded in shocked surprise. "Exactly what does the captain have in mind?"

Craig pointed. "We're going up that mountain."

Dugan followed his point. "Now, sir?"

"Right now. Get your men into their tunics, in marching formation, with muskets."

"Yes, sir."

Fraser paced impatiently, watching Dugan bawl out his orders. Men dropped their shovels and scrambled. Minutes later Craig returned with five confused Indians and spent ten seconds inspecting Dugan's men. They were sweating in their woolen tunics, faces a blank at being ordered to throw down their shovels, grab their muskets, and fall into marching order without the slightest explanation of why. But they were ready. Craig strode to the young lieutenant in charge of loading the dirt into the freight wagons, who stood at bewildered attention while Craig curtly turned command of digging the powder magazine over to him.

Map crammed inside his tunic, Craig marched back to Dugan and called out orders. Dugan gave the cadence, and the command marched out the south end of camp, Fraser striding along beside them, keeping step. Officers, regulars, women—everyone who saw them—paused to wonder at the strange sight of a brigadier general marching an officer, a sergeant, five Indians, and twenty sweating men out of camp in full uniform, muskets over their shoulders.

One hundred yards beyond the pickets at camp's edge, Fraser stopped, watching until the red tunics of the last rank disappeared into the forest. Then he turned on his heel and strode rapidly back to his tent, mind racing as he worked with a plan. Billingsley met him at the entrance and stepped aside as Fraser entered. The general stopped and faced him directly.

"I believe the regimental engineering officer is Lieutenant William Twiss. Get him here as fast as you can. If I'm not here, have him wait."

Billingsley masked his surprise. "Yes, sir." He turned on his heel and hurried out the door. Fraser stepped to the washstand in the corner and poured water from a large, blue-figured porcelain pitcher into the matching basin. He quickly washed his hands, then the perspiration from his head and face, straightened his hair, set his tricorn squarely on his head, and walked briskly back out into the oppressive heat. Minutes later he was standing beneath the limp pennants that decorated the roofline of the great command tent, facing the picket at the flap.

"General Fraser to see General Burgoyne," he said, eyes snapping.

"One moment, sir." The picket disappeared, to return in thirty seconds and hold the flap open. Fraser entered instantly, stopped in the heat of the unventilated room, and stood at attention while his eyes adjusted to the muted color created by the sun on the canvas.

Instantly Burgoyne was on his feet, striding toward Fraser, displaying his dazzling smile—the ever-cordial, always charismatic Gentleman Johnny.

"Simon! Good to see you. What brings you here in the heat of the morning?"

Fraser spent no time playing the game of charm. "Sir, I spent part of the morning proving to myself that we can transport cannon to the top of Mount Defiance."

Fraser stopped. It took Burgoyne two seconds to grasp Fraser's drift. In an instant the bon vivant social toast of London vanished, and the brilliant, tough-minded general took over. Burgoyne's smile was gone, and his eyes bored into Fraser as he uttered one word.

"How?"

"Up the back side."

Without hesitation, Burgoyne cut straight to the stand-or-fall proposition. "Show me." In less than two minutes he had his scaled map on his worktable, corners weighted down, standing beside Fraser in silence, waiting.

Fraser shifted the map to square it with the compass, then placed a finger on Fort Ticonderoga, moving his hand as he spoke. He wasted no words.

"From Fort Ti to the top of Mount Defiance is fourteen hundred yards. From the top of Mount Defiance to the top of Mount Independence, fifteen hundred yards."

"How do you know?" Burgoyne's eyes were intense, narrowed.

"Calipers."

"Go on."

He returned his finger to Mt. Defiance. "The front is too steep, but the back is not. We can get cannon up the back side."

"On what authority?"

"The contour lines."

Instantly Burgoyne hunched forward to study the curving contour lines, and as he worked with his finger his breathing quickened, while his eyes began to shine. "Maybe. Has anyone gone to look?"

"I sent Captain James Craig with twenty men and five Indian scouts. They should be back with their report sometime after dark."

"If his report is favorable, what do you propose?"

"If Craig agrees, I'm going up there myself with our engineering officer, Lieutenant William Twiss. My aide's gone to get him now."

"When will you go?"

"Tonight, after Craig gets back. We can be far up before morning, maybe on top. If Twiss agrees, it's possible we can have guns up there by noon tomorrow."

Burgoyne's brow knitted in question. "Noon? That soon? How?"

"Start tonight. Have a company of men move them as far as they can in the dark. If Twiss and I are successful, we can signal, and they can proceed."

"How do you propose getting a two-ton gun up there without roads?"

"Block and tackle, and ropes. Build a road later."

Burgoyne's breathing accelerated to keep pace with his racing thoughts. "It might be possible. We'll have to talk with General Phillips about cannon. He has every gun assigned, and I doubt he'll be amenable to changing his mind."

"Get cannon from the ships out on the lake. The *Thunderer* can spare a few."

Burgoyne turned away from the table and began to pace, working with the thoughts that were coming in a flood. "Fifteen hundred yards? We would have total command of a field of fire, both on Ticonderoga and Mount Independence." He stopped in his tracks as the next thought impacted. His eyes grew large. "I doubt their guns could reach us."

"They could not."

"Do you mean to say that we could reduce Fort Ti and their Mount Independence defenses to rubble without a single American shot reaching our guns?"

Fraser bobbed his head emphatically. "That's *exactly* what I mean, sir."

"This could all be over in one day, then, without the loss of a single man." He caught his breath at the thought. "Unbelievable! Take Fort Ti in one day with no casualties. That would stand Whitehall and Parliament on their heads! And the king! Brilliant!"

Fraser masked his reaction at how quickly Burgoyne had jumped from the possibility of a stunning military victory, to how he was going to use it to rise to the pinnacle in British military and political circles, let alone the whirl of London's high society. While it was he, Fraser, who had recognized the staggering possibility and formed the plan to bring it to reality, it would somehow be Burgoyne who would have all England at his feet when it was finished. Fraser accepted it, and waited for Burgoyne's response.

"I'll have General Phillips brought here at once. I want his opinion on the question of our cannon reaching them, while theirs cannot reach us. Go bring Lieutenant Twiss here for the conference."

Fifteen minutes later, with all four men hunched around the table, Fraser quickly laid his conclusions and his plan before them. Phillips recoiled at the thought, then leaned forward to trace distances and locations, making silent calculations, with Twiss intently tracking. Phillips glanced at Burgoyne and asked, "Do you have calipers?" Two minutes later he stood erect, chin thrust out. "On paper, it can be done, but I will not approve the plan until a competent person has walked the ground to prove it. I cannot assign one cannon to the project, but I agree that a few guns can be spared from the *Thunderer.*"

Burgoyne turned to Twiss.

Twiss drew a deep breath. He had never been in such an intense, do-or-die war council in his life. He spoke firmly, without hesitation. "From the best information we have, Mount Defiance is just short of eight hundred feet in height. From the top, cannon should reach all defenses, including Fort Ti. The proposal to put cannon up there appears to be feasible, however, it would be a mistake to commit troops without a visual inspection of the ground. I presume that's why I was called here. If you wish, I will be happy to climb that mountain and give it my best appraisal."

Fraser interrupted. "I planned to accompany you, starting tonight, the minute Craig returns with a favorable report."

Twiss responded. "Good. I'll be ready when you are."

Fraser turned to Burgoyne. "As soon as we have reached the mountaintop, and Lieutenant Twiss has made his decision, he and I will signal to the men bringing the cannon up behind us. One pistol shot means they abandon the project. Two pistol shots means bring the guns to the top. Is that understood?"

Burgoyne nodded. "Understood. By that time I'll have a large force of men halfway to the top with the cannon."

At twenty minutes before nine o'clock, Fraser checked his watch, then settled back in the chair beside the worktable in his tent. Six lanterns cast their yellow light in the muggy air, with mosquitoes, moths, and night insects drawn buzzing to the glowing, hot glass chimneys. The curled bodies of insects that had come too close to the blistering glass littered the table and floor beneath the lanterns.

Across from Fraser, Lieutenant Twiss leaned back, one arm hooked over the back of his chair. Billingsley sat quietly at his small desk in one corner. Locked in a tense, disciplined silence, the men had not spoken in more than half an hour, as they waited for the return of Captain James Craig, to learn what would be the fate of thousands of Americans and British who were poised for the battle at Fort Ticonderoga.

Through the sounds of the gigantic camp settling for the night came the tread of a marching command. All three men came erect in their chairs as Fraser turned his head to listen. They heard muffled commands as the sounds drew near, and then the voice of Craig halting his men at the front of the tent. The picket challenged, Craig made his request, and the picket pulled aside the tent flap.

"Captain Craig has returned, sir."

All three men came to their feet, and Fraser spoke. "Bring him in."

Sweat streaked, his tunic torn by the branch of a dead tree, Craig stepped in and came to attention. "Reporting, sir."

"Yes?"

"We were on top. It can be done. Guns up there will command Fort Ticonderoga, Mount Independence, the chute from Lake George into Lake Champlain, and you can see forty miles down the lake."

In the pale silver light of a waxing moon, Fraser drew out his watch. "Twenty minutes past one o'clock," he said to Twiss. "Are you all right?"

"Let's go right on up."

"I think I can hear the guns coming up behind us. Can you?"

"When the wind's right, sir."

The moon ran its course and settled behind the western rim, and still they struggled upward, testing each footstep before continuing, looking ahead to avoid impassable trees and rocks. The first hint of the black heavens turning purple in the east found them cresting the summit and emerging out onto the slightly rounded dome of Mt. Defiance. The two weary men sat down on rocks while Twiss dropped his backpack and opened it to remove two officer's pistols. With gray creeping across the lake, he finished loading them. Ten minutes later they could define limbs on trees fifty yards distant, and five minutes later they could clearly see the broad expanse of the lake, and the thin, twisting ribbon of the two-mile-long crack in the granite that carried the water from Lake George crashing down whitewater rapids to empty into Lake Champlain, just above South Bay, at the southern end.

Carefully the men walked the perimeter of the mountaintop, judging whether there was room to construct cannon emplacements. They peered outward in all directions, awe-struck at how clearly they could see the inside of Fort Ticonderoga and the defense works on Mt. Independence, across South Bay. Satisfied, they looked at each other and nodded.

"Room, and to spare," Twiss said. "I've never seen such a commanding position for cannon."

"I agree," replied Fraser.

"On your orders, sir, do I fire the pistols?"

"You do."

Twiss walked west to the place where he and Fraser had mounted the summit. He raised both pistols at one time, and turned slightly south to avoid the balls striking their own men coming up from below. He fired the pistol in his right hand first, counted to three, then fired the one in his left, the flame leaping three feet from the muzzle in the predawn gray.

The two men backed away from the rim and sat down to reach for their canteens. They drank long, wiped their mouths, and Twiss dug into his backpack to draw out some cheese and dried beef. "Thought this might taste good about now," he said, offering some to Fraser. For a time the two men chewed and drank water in silence, with a west wind rising in their faces. They were sweated out, exhausted, bone-weary from the climb through the night, but they did not care. Inside they felt the solid, sustaining glow of having done what others thought could not be done, and with each passing moment they felt the rising conviction that what they had done would impact the affairs of the world. Cheese and dried beef never tasted better.

By eight o'clock, with the risen sun bright on their backs, they could see the heads of the men coming up from below, on the shady, west side of the mountain. The shouts and cursing of the struggling company came clear as the men tightened the two-inch hawsers to lash the block and tackle to another great rock or tree trunk, then commence the back-breaking work of throwing every ounce of strength and weight into hauling the ropes through the pulleys, at a ratio of six to one. For every six feet of rope, the two-ton cannon moved one foot upward.

At ten minutes past ten o'clock, with the west wind raising dust-devils and flying grit, the sweating, exhausted men dragged the first big gun over the crest, onto the top, and at ten-thirty, the second. The west wind shifted toward the north and became a howling gale. The five Indian scouts drew to the south, away from the regulars, to stand by

themselves. Among the soldiers, the uniform of every man was torn, either at the knees or elbows. Sweat showed on their tunics between their shoulder blades. The dirt raised by the wind caked at the corners of their eyes and mouths and in their nostrils, and stuck to their sweating faces.

They didn't care. They sprawled on their backs on the mountaintop, arms flung wide, and lay without moving for a time. Then they reached for their canteens to drink long, not caring that some of the water ran down their chins to make additional dark spots on their tunics.

After a time, Lieutenant Charles Digby wiped his chin and stood to face his men. "On your feet. We have to position and block these guns."

At ten minutes before noon on July 5, 1777, the two, twelve-pound British cannon were in position, their muzzles thrust out northeast, directly in line with Fort Ticonderoga. Their wheels were blocked against any movement forward and allowed four feet of movement to the rear to take the recoil when the heavy guns were fired. The guns in place, Digby walked to General Fraser. His face was covered with sweat and dirt, his uniform torn and filthy, but there was a look of triumph in his eye as he saluted and reported to Fraser.

"Sir, the guns are in commission. Powder in the budge barrels, cannonballs in the lockers between the trails."

Fraser nodded. "Extraordinary, Lieutenant. My compliments. I want to address your men." He walked past Digby and stood before his men.

"Remain at ease, men. I do not know what will come of this, but I do want you to know you have done what no others have dared try. I commend each of you. I will be sending a letter of commendation to General Burgoyne for this command. I am also sending orders that the entire army is to receive a ration of rum tonight, and a double ration for each of you."

Tired, sweated out, sitting on a mountaintop with a hot, high north wind shrouding them in dirt and grit, the men rose as one and gave three resounding huzzahs for their general. None of them noticed that the five Indian scouts, twenty yards south of them, had lighted a fire to signal their chiefs far below that they had reached the mountaintop. The big guns were in place. Fort Ticonderoga was theirs.

★ ★ ★ ★ ★

The hot north wind sweeping down the Lake Champlain–Hudson River corridor swirled and eddied over the walls of Fort Ticonderoga, raising clouds of dust and sending it stinging into the faces of the Americans as they hurried from their work assignments to the mess hall for their noon meal. Eyes squinted against the wind, they walked with shoulders hunched and heads lowered to stand in line, waiting to get inside the doors, away from the blow.

Colonel Jeduthan Baldwin, engineer in charge of repairs and maintenance of the old fort, marched southwest from his office across the parade ground toward the large shed used to store the tools and equipment on which his work depended. Building good breastworks required axes and shovels, and in his hand he clutched a report that there were twenty-two axes and thirty shovels with broken or split handles. If the report were true, six men were going to spend the afternoon knocking the broken handles out, and fitting new ones in. His crews were digging trenches and throwing up breastworks outside the fort at a fevered pace; he could not afford a work stoppage because of broken equipment.

He was twenty feet from the building when movement atop Mt. Defiance caught his eye. He slowed, then stopped to raise a hand as a shield against the noon sun, peering upward nearly one mile at the crest of the mountain. It appeared that a wind-whipped smudge of black smoke was blowing south. He wiped at his eyes to look upward once more and saw the smoke thicken.

Smoke? How? Lightning? There isn't a cloud in the sky. The faintest voice of alarm began in his brain. He stood rooted, staring, and suddenly there was movement in the trees and brush on the mountaintop—a flash of crimson against the emerald green. While he watched, the barrel of a heavy cannon rolled into view, stopped, and tiny red-coated figures scurried about blocking the wheels. Moments later a second cannon rolled in beside the first, and the British regulars positioned and blocked it. Sunlight glinted off the gun muzzles, and Baldwin realized they were lined squarely on the parade ground of the fort, within yards of where he was standing. For a moment he stood paralyzed by shock, then pivoted and broke into a run toward the office of General Arthur St. Clair. He pounded across the boardwalk and threw the door open, slowing to let his eyes adjust inside the dimly lit room.

St. Clair jumped the moment the door burst open and was half risen when Baldwin blurted, "The British have guns on Mount Defiance!" St. Clair jerked erect and Dunn came off his chair in an instant. For two seconds the men stared at each other before St. Clair came around his desk at a run, out into the blowing dust, Baldwin and Dunn right behind. He shaded his eyes with both hands while he stared southwest at the mountain.

Even with the gale winds and the flying dust, the redcoats could be seen moving about the big guns on the northeast rim of the mountain-top. St. Clair turned to Dunn. "Get my telescope," he barked, and in two minutes Dunn returned to jam it into St. Clair's trembling hand. With his glass extended, St. Clair studied the mountaintop for thirty seconds, then handed the instrument to Baldwin, who looked then passed it to Dunn. For long moments the three men stood looking at each other in stunned shock, faces white, eyes wide, staring.

Then St. Clair gave orders to Dunn. "Get generals Paterson, Long, de Fermoy, and Poor. No matter what they're doing, have them in my office in ten minutes."

Notes

Unless otherwise indicated, the following facts are taken from Ketchum, *Saratoga*, on the pages listed.

On the morning of 3 July 1777, General Simon Fraser was discussing the ongoing sound of the cannon with Alexander Lindsay, sixth Earl of Balcarres, commenting on the natural tendency of men to duck at the sound of cannon, even if they are not in the line of fire. A cannonball passed over both their heads, and they instinctively ducked. In this conversation Balcarres mentioned he knew men with eyes sharp enough to track a cannonball in flight. That morning the Americans did fire a feu de joie, which is a military custom of firing muskets, or cannon, in predetermined numbers to commemorate or celebrate a notable military or historical event—in this case, the one-year anniversary of the signing of the Declaration of Independence—as well as the arrival of Seth Warner with seven hundred troops, cattle, and sheep.

Immediately following the conversation, Fraser noticed Mt. Defiance, and for the first time wondered if cannon atop the mountain could reach Fort Ticonderoga. With a young engineer named Lieutenant William Twiss, Fraser climbed the mountain and saw instantly it commanded both a view and a field of fire covering both Fort Ticonderoga and Mt. Independence, across the narrows of Lake Champlain. The distances were fifteen hundred yards to Fort Ti, fourteen hundred yards to Mt. Independence.

Excited, Fraser sent a lieutenant named Craig, with men, to see if cannon could be moved up the back side of the mountain, and it was determined they could. The night of July fourth, two cannon from the ship *Thunderer* were hauled up to the top, and the morning of July fifth, they were in place and ready to fire. Indians who accompanied the men who hauled the cannon up the mountain set a fire on the mountaintop, and it was seen by the Americans (pp. 170–71).

It will be remembered that one year earlier, Lieutenant Trumbull, Benedict Arnold, and Anthony Wayne had informed generals Gates and Schuyler that it could be done; further, American cannon were fired from the fort toward the top of Mt. Independence, demonstrating that they could not reach all the way to the top. Thus, cannon atop Mt. Defiance could not be reached by American cannon in Fort Ticonderoga (p. 117).

Leckie, in his work *George Washington's War*, states that the cannon were taken to the top overnight by use of block and tackle, a very arduous undertaking (p. 387).

On 5 July 1777, Jeduthan Baldwin saw the smoke from the Indian fire atop Mt. Defiance, then saw the two cannon muzzles. He took the news to General St. Clair, who instantly saw that Fort Ticonderoga was indefensible against the British cannon. He ordered a war council that was attended that afternoon by generals Poor, Fermoy, Paterson, and Long (pp. 171–72).

CHAPTER XIX

★ ★ ★

*M*ary Flint dragged the large cotton bag full of putrid, blood-stained bandages and bed sheets from the back door of the long, low hospital building to the center of a ring of piled rocks and sprinkled a jar of alcohol on one side. She opened a small metal tinderbox, emptied the smoldering ball of shredded linen onto the bag, and watched the blue alcohol flames spread while black smoke rose into the clear, early morning sky. She wiped her hands on her apron, slipped the tinderbox back into the pocket, and walked back into the hospital. Her nose wrinkled at the stench of carbolics and alcohol, infected flesh, and too many men too closely packed and unbathed. She refilled the alcohol jar from a keg in the apothecary room, set it on the shelf, the empty tinder box beside it, then walked out into the great room of the crude log structure where cots with sick and wounded men stood end to end in rows.

Short, stout, balding, Doctor Leonard Folsom dropped his jowled chin to peer over his spectacles at Mary. "You've finished your shift. Go get some rest." He studied her for a moment, and his forehead wrinkled in concern. "I'm worried about you. You've never really gotten over that nagging pneumonia, and you're working too hard. Will you go to your quarters and rest today, or do I have to order it? Good nurses are in short supply around here."

Mary started to protest but then nodded. She drew the white scarf from her dark hair to let it fall freely and walked out the front door of the building into the heat of the oncoming day. She ran her hand through her hair and slowed to watch the great, unfolding panorama of the remaining part of the Continental army striking its sprawling Morristown winter camp. Over one thousand officers and enlisted men milled and marched in all directions. The din of human voices filled the air with shouted commands and shouted answers. Hundreds of wagons picked their way through the mass confusion, stopping, moving, going to get a load, or deliver one, with the drivers working the long leather ribbons as they bawled orders to the horses, working their way through the congestion. Men with fourteen-foot whips drove great, patient oxen with massive oaken yokes heavy on their thick necks as they plodded, splay-footed, pulling the huge Canadian carts on their two, broad, seven-foot wheels.

Teams of soldiers pulled the ridgepoles out of the officers' tents, then jerked the pegs out of the ground to throw the tieropes free while they stepped back to watch the tents slowly deflate and collapse into a heap. They swarmed onto the canvas to jerk it flat, square it, double it, double it again, and fold it into a bundle to be lifted into a wagon by a team of sweating men. With the long, hard winter behind them, and months of rest and regular meals to heal their bodies and spirits, a feeling of readiness, anticipation, a need for action, ran strongly in the men. When General Washington ordered the army to be prepared to march in two days, they had turned to the task with a will and strong, ready hands.

Weary from ten hours in the heat and the heady smell of the hospital, Mary untied her soiled apron and carried it folded in her hand as she picked her way southwest through the men and wagons and animals, watching ahead for the Massachusetts regiment. She raised a hand to shade her eyes as a feeling of nostalgic sadness rose in her heart to linger for a few moments, then recede. *They're all leaving—all the familiar faces—the morning reveille call—the noon meal—the evening mess call—the drummer sounding taps—lights out—the pickets calling out the time—all's well—the good things and the bad—the little time we've shared—gone. Tonight the camp will be deserted—deserted—*

not a sound—all gone—all gone. Will I ever again belong to a place and have a home and a family?

She set her chin and took control of the panic that surged, concentrating in the mixed mass of men to find an officer in the Massachusetts regiment, or the sharp face of Sergeant Alvin Turlock.

"Pardon, ma'am, are you looking for me?"

Mary turned to the familiar figure of Turlock coming in from her right side, swaying slightly with his bow-legged stride.

Relief flooded through Mary. "Yes, I am. I've been asked to stay here at the hospital to help for a time. No one has said how long the army will be gone. Do you know?"

Turlock shook his head. "Permanent, I think."

Mary caught her breath. "You won't be coming back?"

"Doubtful, ma'am. You worried about seeing Billy and Eli?"

"Yes."

"They might never show up here. It's likely word'll get to them we left here, and they'll come lookin' for us wherever we are. And that won't be here."

"Where are you going? Do you know?"

"Wherever General Howe goes, and right now nobody knows where that is. You see, ma'am, when General Washington took Trenton from the Germans and then snuck around Cornwallis and took Princeton from Mawhood, King George was vexed. He sent General Burgoyne to come down from Canada on the Hudson River and come in behind us and then told General Howe to send some soldiers on over to meet Burgoyne and cut the thirteen states in two, right in the middle."

Turlock shifted his feet for a moment while he ordered his thoughts, then raised his eyes once more. "Problem is, General Howe seems to have some strange ideas of his own, and nobody knows what they are. He's been sendin' out patrols like he's goin' south, then he gets ships and acts like he's headed up the Delaware, and then he sends men like he's going on to Elk's Head, and now he might be thinkin' of comin' straight on south, maybe to take Philadelphia." Turlock shrugged. "No way to know. That's why General Washington sent those regiments over to

Middlebrook a few days ago. He's got to stay close and stop Howe from gettin' over to Burgoyne, and he's got to try to protect Philadelphia if he can."

He reached to wipe his sleeve across his mouth. "An' it don't take much figgerin' to understand that General Washington can't go fight Howe on Howe's terms, because Howe's got about three times more men and cannon. So we got to play cat and mouse with him and wait for a chance to hurt him when we can. That's why General Washington's got to pull the rest of his army out of here."

He stopped for a moment, then looked inquiringly into Mary's eyes. "I hope you understand, ma'am."

Mary's face fell, and her shoulders sagged. She raised the folded apron and began to work it with both hands, not raising her eyes as she spoke. "I understand. It's just that I had been counting on . . ." Her voice caught, and she stopped for a moment before she could finish. " . . . on seeing Billy and Eli."

Turlock stared at her intently for a moment, then his three-day beard stubble moved as he spoke. "Ma'am, I know I don't have no right inquirin', but is it more Eli you're hopin' to see?" His eyes were bright beneath his shaggy brows.

Mary could not speak. She nodded her head.

"I figgered." Turlock sighed, and his grizzled old face softened at the pain of the memory of a plain, quiet girl he had loved from afar, thirty years ago. He had long held her in his heart, loved her, never speaking of it to anyone. She had kept her feelings locked inside also, until the day she lay on her deathbed with a raging smallpox fever ravaging her, stealing her life away. In a delirium she had cried out his name, called for him, and her father had sent for him. Her brother returned with Turlock that evening. She was in her bed, her father and mother by her side, and the moment Turlock saw her he knew her life was slipping away. She was calm, but her eyes were too bright, her skin too shiny. Shy, conscious of his own crude ways learned as an orphan serving as a cabin boy on a ship, he stood with his head bowed, waiting for someone to tell him what to do. The father had simply told him she had called for him, adding he did not know why. Then the father and mother had stepped aside, and hesitantly Turlock had gone to her bedside.

She stared at him for a moment before recognition came, and then she held out her hand to him. He reached to take it and held back the shock of feeling the fingers gone cold. She tried to speak, but her words were only soft whispers, and he leaned his head beside hers. She formed the words that told him she had long loved him and could not leave without telling him. He remembered the warm salt tears coming, and he did not care as he spoke low to her that he had loved her but knew she was far above him so he had remained silent. She nodded, and a smile formed for a moment before she said her last words. "It is a pity," she had said. Then her eyes closed, and she sighed, and Turlock felt the spirit leave her hand and her body. He walked away from her home, sought out the army, and never returned.

Facing Mary, he remembered the searing pain, and his heart reached out to her. "Ma'am, don't you worry. He'll either come here, or to the army. If I see him first, I'll tell him you're here and want to see him." He paused and then quietly added. "And if I'm readin' this right, he'll find you."

Mary started, then caught herself, her face flushed with having revealed her innermost feelings to the little man. "You can't tell him. He doesn't know. We've never talked about . . . I've . . . never told . . ." A tear trickled down her cheek, and she reached to wipe it away with the apron. She could not speak further, and she cleared her throat and stood silent.

Turlock looked at the ground for a moment. "There's some things don't need talk," he said. "I won't tell him, only that you're here and need to see him. Will that be all right?"

Mary nodded, and her chin quivered.

Pain showed in Turlock's face as he spoke. "Ma'am, don't—"

She raised her eyes. "Mary. Call me Mary."

He nodded. "Mary, don't trouble your heart with worry. I don't know a man more able in the woods, and in a fight, than Eli, nor a man I'd rather have along than Billy. Don't fret. They'll both be back. They're out there doin' the work of the Almighty, and He's not about to abandon 'em. Not Him."

Hope sprang in her eyes. "You're certain?"

"Mary, you'll see him again." His words were quiet, but they sank deep.

For a moment a sob stuck in her throat. "Thank you. Oh, thank you."

The little man reached to touch her hands. "You'll be fine here. Just be patient. One day soon he'll come walking in. You'll see."

Mary shook herself and by force of will took charge. "I know he will. I'll wait."

Notes

Mary Flint as portrayed herein is a fictional person, as is Sergeant Alvin Turlock.

However, General Washington did leave Morristown in the late spring of 1777, sending part of his troops to Middlebrook (also spelled Middle Brook) where he was easily capable of striking General Howe's British forces. General Howe was beginning his unpredictable game of moving his army first one place, then another, in a most confusing manner, which he later had trouble explaining to the British Parliament (see Ketchum, *Saratoga*, p. 46).

In general support, see also Leckie, *George Washington's War*, pp. 344–46.

CHAPTER XX

*T*here is mystery and magic at night on the lakes and rivers in the deep, primeval forest. Untouched and unspoiled by the hand of man, the pristine innocence of the woods draws spirits back from their unseen world to once again be near the profound pleasure and the pain of flesh and mortality. The creatures of the forest know. With instincts honed from the dawn of creation, in the quiet of the night, they sense, and sometimes see, the comings and goings of the spirits of the departed. The haunting call of an owl, or the sharp bark of a fox, or the stealthy padding of the silent feet of the panther, or the eerie laughter of a loon may mark the passage of a spirit returned to lament its mortality wasted, or to rejoice in its mortality improved. Men whose souls are awake, know, while those who have forsaken the great gift for the ways of man are left with only the troubling sense that there is a world all around them to which they are blind.

★ ★ ★ ★ ★

Sometime after midnight, heavy clouds rolled in to blot out the heavens and lock the forest in thick blackness. A great horned owl dropped from the top of a pine tree like a silent, invisible stone, wings and talons tucked, its great eyes wide as it watched a rabbit crouched eighty feet below, ears laid back, unmoving, certain of its safety in the quiet darkness. Fifteen feet from the ground the owl flared its wings wide to brake its headlong plunge and swung its legs down and forward, five-inch talons spread, ready. At the rustling sound from above, the rabbit exploded into action, too late. The owl anticipated its leap, and the black needle-sharp talons caught the terrified animal like a vise in midair. There was one quick, piercing squeal as the owl strained, wings pulling, to lift itself and the weight of the kicking rabbit back to the tree tops.

Twenty yards away, beneath a maple tree, Caleb Dunson bolted wide-eyed from a fitful sleep, knowing he had heard the squeal of something mortally struck, but not knowing what, or where, or what had done the killing. The whispered sound of wings beating the air reached him in the stillness, and he turned his head to listen to it rise to the tree tops and fade. In one motion he threw back his blanket and came to a crouch, frightened, unable even to see his hand before his face in the pitch-black. In panic he groped on the ground for something to defend himself, and there was nothing but the spongy accumulation of a thousand years of pine needles and leaves and decaying vegetation on the forest floor and his blanket, knapsack, and canteen. He grasped the heavy canteen and cocked his arm, ready to swing it like a rock. Minutes passed, and the muscles in his legs began to cramp. Slowly he sat down and eased his feet forward to stretch his legs, still grasping the canteen.

The distant belching croak of bullfrogs on a slough brought images of fearsome forest beasts, and the rustle of a ferret coming to the strange scent of man became a great serpent slithering through the undergrowth toward him. Nighthawks and bats flitting above were the ghosts of those who had been massacred in these woods in times past, returning to take their revenge.

For a moment Caleb's chin trembled, and he was afraid he would cry. Then he drew a breath, set his chin, and reached for his blanket. He backed up to the trunk of the towering maple tree, wrapped the blanket about his shoulders, and sat still, listening to the sounds of the night. He repeated over and over to himself, *Nothing to fear—nothing to fear.* Then he repeated it aloud, and felt a surge of courage from the sound of his own voice defying all the unseen demons surrounding him in the black forest. He uttered a quick, nervous laugh, then fell silent, listening, waiting, wishing fervently for the dawn. Each passing minute seemed an eternity.

Forty minutes later a light rain began to fall, softly at first, then more heavily, and it held, pelting straight down, filling the forest with a steady drumming. Rivulets formed to puddle in the low places, and the forest floor became a mass of water-soaked decaying matter and mud. Caleb pulled the blanket over his head to sit huddled beneath the dripping leaves and branches of the great tree. The chilling rain came through the blanket, then his clothes, to his skin. It soaked his hair and ran cold down his neck inside the blanket. It dripped from his eyebrows and his nose and chin, onto the place his hand gripped the blanket to close it against his chest. Uncontrollable shaking seized him, and his teeth chattered. Thoroughly miserable, the boy drew his knees to his chest and wrapped his arms around them, trying to draw warmth from them through his cold, water-soaked trousers.

Slowly his senses dulled, and he lost all sense of time. His eyes closed, his head tipped forward, and he drifted into the world of half-consciousness. He was aware of the steady sound of the rain, and of the cold, but could not understand how his mother appeared so clearly in the blackness, or how she remained dry in the soaking rain. He saw the lantern on the kitchen table, and the black stove, and the steaming coffee-pot with the baked bread nearby, and the bowl of butter and pot of honey, and he wondered how they came to be in the forest. He saw her speak, but could not hear her words above the patter of the falling rain, and then he saw her beckon to him. An overwhelming ache to be home in the kitchen, warm, safe, sharing steaming coffee with bread and honey rose in his breast, and he called out to her. His head snapped up at the sound of his own voice, and for a time he stared into the darkness while his mind came back to the forest and the cold rain. He swallowed against the lump that rose in his throat, then once again settled for the long wait through the night.

The rain slowed and stopped, and small breaks appeared in the clouds. The morning star shone brightly in the east for a time before it began to fade. The black forest began its change to purple and gray, and

Caleb watched, fascinated at how the demons of the night became chip-munks and blue jays, squirrels and rabbits, magpies and porcupines. They disappeared the moment he shrugged off the sodden blanket and rose to his feet, working with his cold, set muscles.

He dug six-day-old bread from his knapsack, and cheese, and drank cool water from his canteen, shaking in his cold, soggy clothing. For a moment the memory of steaming coffee in his mother's kitchen flashed in his mind, and the ache to be there rose again to torment him. He pushed it aside and knelt to roll his coat inside his blanket and tie the bundle. He slipped the rope loop over his head and settled it on his back, then shouldered his knapsack and canteen to dangle at his side. He had no musket, no weapon.

He trudged two miles in the mud of a narrow forest trail before the first arc of the sun turned the rainwater on every leaf into diamonds, and a misty steam began rising from the puddles. An hour later the heat of the sun had begun to dry the world, and another hour brought sweltering heat once again. He gauged time by the sun, and stopped at noon long enough to eat dried salt beef and the last of his crusted bread and to drink from his canteen. He sat on a log to pull off his muddy shoes and socks and to peer at the blisters that had formed on his heels. He dug into his knapsack for an extra pair of socks, tugged them on, then the wet ones, and then his shoes. Then he once again shouldered his bedroll and knapsack and continued southwest, watching and listening for something that would tell him he had found the New York regiments of the Continental army, moving toward Philadelphia.

The sun had touched the western tree line before he heard the distant clanging sounds of men setting up heavy iron tripods and hanging great, black cooking kettles from the center chains. Hope rose, and he began to trot, eyes bright in anticipation. *Private Caleb Dunson. A Continental soldier. Uniform. Musket. Bayonet. Danger. Battles. Friends, loyal and true.*

He sobered and a hard look came into his eyes. *A chance to repay the redcoats for my father. My brother. They'll pay. They'll pay.*

The crooked trail led him out of the forest into a broad meadow, and suddenly they were there before him. Hundreds of them—cutting wood for the fires beneath the cooking pots, some setting up tents, others skinning three deer they had shot during the day, and still others sitting on or near their bedrolls where they had dropped them in the tall grass. Muskets and swords lay carelessly dropped on bedrolls or leaned against logs.

Caleb stopped, suddenly aware he did not know how to join the army. *Who do I talk to? What do I say?* He continued forward cautiously, looking for an officer, but he could not see a uniform within one hundred yards, and he stopped with the unsettling feeling that something was very wrong. *No pickets, no uniforms, no officers, no order, no one challenging me.*

He turned to the nearest soldier. "Can you tell me where to find an officer?"

The man cocked one eye at him. "What for?"

"I came to join the army."

The man snorted. "Where's your musket? Bayonet?"

"I don't have one. I thought—"

"You thought the army had one for you. Well, it don't, at least not right now." He pointed indifferently. "That man with the beard is a captain. Talk with him."

Caleb approached the man, aware soldiers were watching him. "Sir, I've come to join the army. Can you tell me what to do?"

The tall, bearded man eyed Caleb, head to toe. "Your mother know you're here?"

"Yes, sir."

"How old are you?"

"Eighteen."

The man shook his head. "More like sixteen. Got a musket?"

"No."

"How did you expect to fight?"

"I thought the army—"

"Well, it won't. We don't have a musket to spare right now. If the French come through on their promise we might have some soon, but not now." He stopped for a moment, then continued. "If you're here for a big adventure, leave now. If you join, we expect you to stay until you're sent home. Or killed. Now decide. Do you want to stay?"

"Yes, sir."

"All right. Where you from? Boston?"

"Yes. How did you—"

"The way you talk. Why do you want to join a New York regiment?"

"You were the nearest one."

He pointed. "Go give that man your name and sign where he says. He's the quartermaster for the New York Ninth Regiment. Tell him I said you're to be assigned to the company with the Irish, because they're short of men. You got any questions, ask him. His name's McCormack. Lieutenant McCormack."

"Thank you, sir. May I know your name?"

"Captain Venables. Charles Venables."

Caleb made his way to Lieutenant Abel McCormack. "Sir, Captain Venables sent me to you. I want to join."

McCormack looked Caleb over with a shrewd eye. Nearly six feet tall, almost to his full frame, broad shouldered, big elbows, knees, and feet. He would grow into them. "What's your name?"

"Caleb Dunson, sir."

"Did Venables tell you which company?"

"Yes, sir. The Irish one that needs men."

"Third Company. Got a musket?"

"No."

"For now you'll carry a spear."

"A spear?"

"Yes. Go cut a small pine and strip the branches and sharpen the big end. A spear."

"That's what I use to fight?"

McCormack shrugged. "You can throw rocks if that suits you better. Until you get a musket, that's how you'll fight."

Caleb nodded. "Where's Third Company?"

Pointing, McCormack said, "Right over there. You go on over. Tell

Sergeant O'Malley I sent you. I'll be over in a few minutes. You've got to sign your name or you won't ever get your pay. Spell your name."

Caleb slowly spelled it while McCormack concentrated, then walked away. Caleb worked his way to Sergeant O'Malley, who was in charge of four men dicing deer meat on a plank for the Third Company stew pot. McCormack had a knife in his hand while he watched the men work.

"Excuse me, Sergeant O'Malley? Officer Venables said I'm to report to you. Third Company. I just joined."

O'Malley wheeled around. "What's your name?"

"Caleb Dunson."

"Ever cut meat?"

"Yes."

"Put down your bedroll and belongings wherever you can and get back here. We got to get this meat into the pot."

"Yes, sir."

For half an hour Caleb stood shoulder to shoulder with the four other men, using McCormack's knife to cut the fresh venison into small chunks. He worked steadily, covertly glancing about from time to time, a new feeling of pride, of belonging rising within, while his thoughts ran. *A soldier. Working with soldiers. My company. Third Company.* He glanced at their faces. They were sweaty, like his own, and bearded, while his was smooth. There was no joy in their countenances, only the dull expression of men with a job to do, and then another, and another, whatever the jobs might be. *See the pride in their faces? Comrades. Friends, good and true.*

They finished cutting the meat, piled it on the end of a plank, wiped their knives on their pant legs, then slipped them back into their sheaths, waiting for McCormack's next orders.

"Get the bones away from here. They're drawing flies."

They wrapped the bones in a piece of bloody tarp, and Caleb and another man with a four-day stubble of whiskers and a limp dragged it two hundred yards to the edge of the camp. They dumped the bones into a garbage pit swarming with flies. As they made their way back, the man spoke to Caleb.

"New?"

"Yes. Today."

"From Boston?"

"Yes."

"Watch out for the Irish."

There was an ominous tone to the man's voice, and Caleb turned to look at him before he asked, "Why?"

"They like to fight. Watch out."

Caleb fell silent for a moment, reflecting on the warning. "You been here long?"

"Since Long Island."

"You were at Trenton?"

The man nodded. "Trenton, Princeton, Morristown. Got this limp at Princeton."

"How?"

"British musketball. I got the one that shot me. Bayonet. Won't be shooting any more of us."

"Where are we going now?"

The man shrugged. "Right now, tracking Howe toward the Delaware. Maybe on to Philadelphia. I think Howe wants Philadelphia."

An hour later McCormack called Company Three to the supper line, and they waited for the cooks to ladle steaming venison and turnip gruel from the pot into their bowls or plates, thrust a thick slice of Indian cornmeal bread on top of it, and fill their cups with hot coffee. Caleb sat down on his bedroll, lost for a time in the taste of the first hot, solid meal he had had in seven days. Finished, he followed the men to a small stream fifteen yards to the north, rinsed his utensils, and returned, while other men began the cleanup of the cooking pots. He sat down on his bedroll and waited for further orders.

There were none. Men untied their bedrolls to spread them wherever they chose. Within twenty minutes the military camp of the Continental army became a mass of blankets and knapsacks, with muskets leaned or laid wherever men chose, and no hint of organization or military discipline. Trained officers turned their backs, unable to bear the sight of the disheveled camp or brook the stubborn refusal of the troops to bow to military authority.

Caleb sat astonished. *Is this soldiering? A military camp?* He studied the men for a time and saw not one salute, heard not one man say "sir." *How do I know the officers from the enlisted? And what difference does it make anyway?* For the first time a small voice of alarm sounded inside. Perhaps his expectations of military life were a tiny bit at variance with the reality.

The sun had not yet set when loud voices erupted fifteen yards to his left. Startled, Caleb leaned forward to look. A stocky, bull-shouldered young man stood near a stack of cut firewood, shaking his finger in the face of a taller, thinner man, cursing him in a rich Irish accent, so thick Caleb could hardly make out the dialect.

"Sure, an' it's you who has gone too far, desecratin' the good name of Limerick while it's there me family remains."

The taller man waved a hand. "Limerick, pshaw, it's Limerick that gets all the trash that Dublin drives out."

"Jamie, should ye withdraw those words, it's yer head you'll be savin' because if ye don't, it's yer head I'll break."

"I'll not withdraw nothin', and it's yer head that'll do the sufferin'."

"Then defend yerself."

"That I will, Conlin Murphy."

Toe-to-toe they raised their fists and began a jerky, wary circling of each other, each waiting for an opening. It came quickly, and Murphy struck hard with his left hand. Jamie's head snapped back and blood began trickling from his nose. Incensed, Jamie bored into Murphy, and for two minutes the air was filled with windmilling arms, curses, grunts, blood, and the sound of fists hitting flesh. Jamie went down but bounded back up to kick Murphy in the stomach. Murphy grunted and went over backward, gasping for breath, while Jamie stood over him, fists raised, daring him to rise. Murphy kicked Jamie's legs out from under him, and when Jamie scrambled back to his knees, Murphy caught him above his left ear with a solid right hand, and Jamie slumped back and toppled onto his side, eyes swimming in his head, unable to rise.

Murphy wiped his bloody face on his shirt sleeve and stood over him. "Now it's withdraw yer foul words about Limerick, or I'll give ye the same again when ye get up, Jamie, my friend."

The warning was wasted. Jamie did not hear it, nor could he rise.

Murphy backed away, hitched up his trousers, squared his shoulders, and boomed out to the crowd of silent onlookers, "An' there's a lesson in this fer all of ye. If ever ye speak of Limerick, the blessed place of me birth, where me sainted mother an' sister remain to this day, speak it with respect, or ye'll deal with me, Conlin Murphy."

Silence gripped the circle of men who had gathered to watch the Irish settle their differences. With Murphy's words still hanging in the air, none of them spoke or moved, except Caleb. The sudden battle had caught him by total surprise. Shocked, he had not thought to rise from his seated position to watch it. At Murphy's warning, Caleb rose to his feet and whispered to the man next to him, "Where's Limerick?"

The movement and the whispered words reached Murphy, and he turned his head to see who had defied him. For a moment he stared in disbelief, and then in three strides he was standing before Caleb, feet spread, hands on his hips. Caleb froze, and the blood drained from his face. Murphy reached with both hands to grasp his shirtfront, then jerk him out into the center of the circled men.

"So it's makin' light of me, eh?" Without another word, Murphy held Caleb's shirtfront with his left hand and slapped his face with his right— four, quick, vicious blows. Blood trickled from both corners of Caleb's mouth and down onto his chin. Caleb grabbed for Murphy's left hand and tried to break free but could not. He swung at Murphy's head, first with his right hand, then his left. His fists landed, but Murphy shrugged them off with a wicked laugh, then swung hard with his right fist. The blow caught Caleb high on his left cheek, and he went down backward, rolling, groping, trying to rise. His left eye was blurred, and he could not make his right eye focus. He got one knee under himself and was trying to stand when Murphy stepped in and swung, first his left hand to Caleb's ribs, then his right to his head. Caleb grunted and went down on his side and did not move.

Murphy reached for him, and half a dozen men stepped forward to grab Murphy, struggling and cursing, forcing him to his knees. One brought a knife blade against Murphy's throat, voice choked with rage. "That's enough! The boy meant no harm. Touch him again, and you'll fight us all."

Hate leaped from Murphy like something alive. "Cowards. Craven cowards, all of ye!" he bellowed. "Come at me one at a time, knife or no, and I'll fight the bunch of ye. I'll quit on the boy for now, but if ever he disparages me home again, I'll beat him senseless."

Captain Venables came running as the men released their hold on Murphy and stepped back, not knowing what to expect. Murphy rose to his feet, straightened his shirt, gave them one last look of contempt, and turned toward Captain Venables.

Panting from his run, Venables stopped and demanded, "All right, who started it?"

"Sure, and it was them who put upon me," Murphy said.

Half a dozen angry men drowned him out. "It was you, Murphy! You beat Jamie, and then this boy. It was you."

Venables raised both hands. "Enough! Any more of this tonight, and you'll all be in chains. Tomorrow, I'll convene a hearing. Get back to your work." He dropped to one knee to study Caleb. "I'll get the regimental surgeon over here right now. Someone see to this boy while I'm gone."

Murphy stalked away while two older men knelt beside Caleb and bent low to look closely at his face. Blood was smeared on his chin and shirt, and trickled from both sides of his mouth, his nose, and his left ear. There was a cut half an inch long on his left cheek bone, with blood running back into his hair. His left eye was turning purple and was swelled nearly closed. One reached to gingerly press Caleb's nose and shook his head. "Not broken."

The other man reached for the nearest canteen, jerked out the corn-cob plug, and raised Caleb's head to force water into his mouth. Caleb choked and coughed, then tried to open his eyes. The man poured again, and Caleb made a wild, harmless swing at him. The man caught his arm and said, "Easy. It's over. It's over."

Caleb tried to speak but choked on his own blood. He swallowed and tried again. "Where did he go?" He brought his right eye to a focus but could see nothing with his left. "Where did he go?" He struggled, but they held him.

"He's gone. We got to get you cleaned up."

"No. No. It's not over," Caleb cried, struggling to rise. "Bring him back. It's not over."

From behind both men came a voice. "I'll take care of him."

They turned to look. An average-sized man with thick, gray hair stood peering down at Caleb. His aging face was filled with compassion. There was nearly no bridge left to his nose. Scars showed through both bushy eyebrows and on his left cheekbone and his lower lip. His shoulders were square, his neck thick, forearms muscled and heavy.

"I'll tend to him," he repeated.

"Are you the regimental surgeon?"

"No, but I understand these things."

Both men rose, and the old man knelt beside Caleb. Tenderly he touched the cheek, testing to see if the bone was broken. He shifted his hand to take the bridge of Caleb's nose between thumb and forefinger and closed both eyes as he moved his hand slightly to the left, then to the right. He studied the cut on the left cheek, then forced the left eye open to study the pupil. He shifted his hands to Caleb's rib cage and carefully felt each rib, counting, from collarbone to belt.

"Son, can you hear me?"

Caleb nodded.

"You're lucky. No bones broken, except the bridge of your nose is cracked. I think it will heal without showing. I don't know about your left ear. We'll find out if it's been hurt in the next couple of days. Two cracked ribs, but none broken. I'm going to get some of my things, and I'll be right back. Don't move."

His head still fuzzy, Caleb nodded, and the man hurried away, to return with an old, small, dented metal box, a canteen, and some clean sheeting. He soaked the rag in canteen water, cleaned away the blood, then opened the metal box and began working. He washed the cut on the left cheek with alcohol, threaded a needle, and spoke.

"This will sting."

"Go ahead."

Caleb jerked when the man took one stitch to close the cut, then smeared strong, thick, foul smelling salve on it.

"Still taste blood?"

"Yes."

He uncorked a bottle, poured a small amount of a thick, dark liquid into a tiny cup, and said, "Wash your mouth with this. Don't swallow it. Spit it out."

Caleb tipped his head back and drained the cup. For a moment he thought his head was on fire. He held the foul liquid as long as he could, then spat it onto the ground. "What is it?" he choked.

"A carbolic salve and alcohol. It'll help heal the cuts in your mouth. Where's your bedroll?"

A corpulent man came puffing behind them. "I'm Major Waldron, the regimental surgeon. Is this the injured boy?"

The grayhaired man answered. "Yes, but I think he's all right."

"Let me look." For five minutes the surgeon went over Caleb, then examined the stitch in his cheek. "Seems it's all taken care of. If you need me, send word." He rose and was gone as quickly as he had arrived.

The man turned once more to Caleb. "Where's your bedroll?"

Caleb pointed.

"What's your name, son?"

Caleb spoke through swollen lips, "Caleb Dunson."

"Come on."

With Caleb's arm over his shoulder, and his box and canteen under his arm, the man walked Caleb to his bedroll and sat him down.

"Who are you?" Caleb asked.

"Name's Charles Dorman."

"Why are you doing this?"

"I've got my reasons."

"Like what?"

"We'll talk about that later. For now, we get some water from the stream and keep a cold compress on that cheek and eye. I don't think there's any permanent damage, but you'll want to get that swelling down."

With the sun below the western horizon, the world was cast in dwindling shades of bronze when the man returned. He wrung water from the rag and positioned it over the closed eye and swollen cheek. "Hold that," he said, and Caleb reached with his hand.

They sat together until dusk faded into darkness before Dorman helped Caleb spread his blanket and settle in for the night. "Your blanket's wet. Next time, spread it and let it dry after a rain. Get some sleep. We'll talk tomorrow."

In his life, Caleb had never ached as he did when the drum pounded out reveille, and he tried to rise at dawn. It took him ten minutes to put on his shoes and make his bedroll. Lieutenant McCormack came to give Third Company their work assignments for the day and stopped to study Caleb.

"I heard about it. Murphy's on report. You're off duty for today."

Caleb shook his head violently. "No, I'm not. Give me my orders."

McCormack's eyes widened. "What?"

Caleb glared at him through swollen eyes, his chin thrust out. "Give me my orders."

"All right. Fire detail. Haul wood for the cooks."

Caleb nodded. Hunched over to favor bruised ribs, he walked to the wood pile. He gathered an armload of wood and made his way to the big, black iron tripod to drop it beside the black pot, then went back for a second load. The rest of the company went about their work details, aware of him, glancing from time to time to watch as he stubbornly continued to grit his teeth, hauling load after load to the Third Company cookpots. He wolfed down his breakfast, rinsed his utensils, then grabbed an ax from the woodpile and made his way to the tree line. Ten minutes later he returned with a small pine, nine feet in length. Sweating with the pain in his ribs, he trimmed the branches, then rested the big end on a log while he used the ax to sharpen it.

Midmorning, with their bedrolls on their backs and their knapsacks and canteens hung over their shoulders, the New York regiments marched out, heading south once again. Caleb marched with Third Company, his pinetree spear over his shoulder. The left side of his face was purple and black, but the swelling had gone down enough for him to see. He held his interval in the column, hunched slightly over, chin set, eyes straight ahead.

At noon he cut and carried firewood, ate with his company, then slung his bedroll on his back, and marched out once again.

Supper was finished, and the sun was setting when Captain Venables came striding and located Caleb.

A crowd of men gathered as the captain said, "We're going to have a hearing. What charges do you want to bring against Private Murphy?"

Caleb shook his head. "None."

Venables stared for a moment. "What? After what he did to you?"

"It was a misunderstanding."

"A misunderstanding of what?! Have you seen your face?"

"No charges."

Venables turned to look, then called, "McCormack, come over here."

McCormack stopped before Venables, and Venables spoke. "McCormack, this man says he does not want to bring charges against Murphy, and I want a witness." He turned back to Caleb. "Do I understand you do not want to hold a hearing? You refuse to bring charges against Murphy for what he did to you?"

Caleb looked at McCormack, then at the faces of the other men gathered behind him. "That's right. No charges."

Venables shrugged. "Well, I can't force you. If you bring no charges, there won't be a hearing, because we have no bill of particulars to bring against Murphy. You understand that?"

"I do."

"I'll write it up just that way. All you men, go on about your business."

The crowd drifted away, and Caleb had settled onto his blanket, favoring the pain in his ribs, when he heard someone coming from behind. He tried to turn his head, but the pain stopped him.

"It's me, Dorman," came the voice, and a moment later the man was seated cross-legged facing Caleb.

Caleb spoke. "I want to thank you for all you've done."

The man nodded acknowledgment, and Caleb went on.

"You said we would talk. Why did you take the trouble with me?"

For a time the man stared at the ground. "I can't stand a bully. And I thought there must be something about you, the way you swung back at that man, and tried to get up when you knew you didn't have a chance, and then wanted them to bring him back because you didn't want it to be over. And I've noticed you today. Hauling wood. Making that spear."

Caleb asked, "You saw it yesterday?"

"No. It was over when I got there. I asked, and others told me."

Caleb remained silent, and Dorman went on. "I know something about fighting. I did it for a living for a time. I was champion in the southern half of England, many years ago."

Caleb's mouth dropped open in stunned surprise.

"I can teach you a little about it. At least enough to take care of the Conlin Murphy's of the world. If you're interested."

"I'm interested."

"It won't be easy."

"I'm interested."

"When you're able, we'll start."

"I'm ready now."

Dorman's eyes narrowed. "You can hardly raise your arms."

"Start now."

For a time Dorman studied Caleb's face, especially his eyes, then rose to his feet. "All right. Stand up."

Caleb stood.

"We'll start at the beginning." Dorman raised one hand. "Watch. This is how you make a fist." He clenched his hand, knuckles forming an even bridge, his thumb tucked tightly against his finger tips. "Keep your thumb tucked in. You can dislocate it if it is sticking out, in the way. Do it."

Carefully Caleb raised his hand and formed a fist. Dorman reached to tuck the thumb tighter. "Good. Now. Understand, you don't hit a man just with your fist. You hit him with your entire body. Every pound. Like this." He cocked his right hand, and in the instant it flicked out, his entire body shifted, bringing all his weight with it. "A good blow doesn't have to travel more than eighteen inches if it's done right. Now you do what I did, but do it slow. Always slow at first."

Caleb cocked his right fist, then slowly drove it forward while he shifted his weight into line with it.

Dorman nodded. "Good. Again."

Caleb repeated the movement.

Dorman pointed at Caleb's feet. "To hit like that, you've got to understand how to work with your feet. If you don't learn to hit from the correct foot, you'll never get your weight into the blow. Watch my feet while I do it again." Slowly Dorman cocked his right fist, then thrust it forward while sliding his left foot forward six inches. His weight remained on his right foot, planted, solid.

"Did you see it?" he asked.

Caleb nodded, then cocked his right fist again, and as he drove it forward his left foot slid forward, his right shoulder dropped slightly, and he felt his weight balanced, set solidly on his right foot.

"Very good. You do that a few times each day when you have the chance. There's a lot more to learn with your feet, but the first lesson is to learn how to hit from the correct foot."

He shifted his attention again. "Hitting a man is one thing. Hitting him where it will bring him down is another. You don't have to hit a man in the head to put him down. If you hit him hard over his heart, or on his wishbone, he'll drop. If you do hit him in the head, go for the point of his chin because there are large nerves at the place the jaw joins the skull, and if you shock those nerves, the man will go down. You can also bring a man down if you hit his forehead, or either temple, where the jolt will stun the brain. In time, we'll get to that."

Once again he shifted his attention. "There are all kinds of blows, but only three basic ones. One is when you flick your fist out to keep your opponent off balance. It won't hurt him much, but it will break his concentration. The second one is when you set your feet and hit him hard, as I just showed you. The third one is when you hook your fist in from either side. When you've learned those three basic blows, you can work on the variations."

He reached to run his hand through his gray hair. "You've got to remember, while you're doing all these things, the other man is trying to do them to you. The trick is to learn how to avoid it. Make the man miss you altogether, if you can. If you can't, at least avoid letting him hit you hard. It's called slipping a blow. Let him hit you, but not solid. Not so it can hurt you."

Dorman stopped. "It's getting dark. We've talked enough for tonight. Tomorrow we'll spend a few minutes and make a bag. Fill it with sand and leaves and hang it from a tree so you can begin getting the feel of setting your feet and hitting hard, and work on the three basic blows. Then we'll work on the rest of it when we can."

Caleb looked at him. "How do I repay you?"

A wistful look stole into Dorman's eyes. "Promise you'll use your skills only to do right. Never be a bully. There are few things so detestable as a bully."

Caleb nodded. "Tomorrow we'll make the bag."

Notes

Caleb Dunson, Charles Dorman, Conlin Murphy, and other characters herein referenced are all fictional.

However, the Irish were well known for their love of fighting, sometimes in fun, sometimes not. Hence, the fight between Caleb Dunson and Conlin Murphy described in this chapter was a scene repeated many times over in army camps where the Irish were found (see Martin, ed. by Scheer, *Private Yankee Doodle*, pp. 145–46).

CHAPTER XXI

★ ★ ★

*M*ajor Isaac Dunn swung the door open, and the hot, blustery north wind blew parade ground dust and grit into the small office of General Arthur St. Clair. Generals Mathias Alexis de Fermoy, Pierce Long, John Paterson, and Enoch Poor entered, followed by Major Dunn, who closed and bolted the door behind them. The five men stood silently in the dim light while their eyes adjusted from the bright midday July sunlight, waiting for some indication from St. Clair as to why they had been ordered to stop whatever they were doing and instantly report to him behind closed doors. The detail inside the room clarified, and St. Clair rose from the chair behind his desk.

"Be seated."

For a moment the six men did not move. Never had any of them seen St. Clair's eyes so vacant, his face so white, nor had they ever heard his voice so hollow, subdued. They stared for a split second, then averted their eyes, and took their places.

St. Clair's next statement burst like a bomb. "The British have cannon on top of Mount Defiance."

An audible gasp rose above the sound of the wind prying at the door, and all four generals facing St. Clair jerked upright. Dunn sat unmoving, eyes downcast. He had known the deadly secret since the moment the engineer Colonel Jeduthan Baldwin had barged into St. Clair's office half an hour earlier to blurt out the fact that the cannon were up there. Dunn had been with St. Clair and Baldwin when they charged out into the parade ground to stare in disbelief at the mountaintop with a telescope. Dunn's mind was still numb, fumbling, reaching to find the outer limits of the impact of their horrifying discovery. At that moment, he knew only that Fort Ticonderoga and their defenses on Mt. Independence, across the South Bay narrows of Lake Champlain, could be utterly destroyed within forty-eight hours, and that there was absolutely nothing they could do to prevent it. With no American guns capable of reaching the British cannon on top of Mt. Defiance, the enemy bombardment would be unopposed, and it could begin even as they now sat facing St. Clair. If Fort Ticonderoga and Mt. Independence should fall, the British would control the great Lake Champlain–Hudson River water corridor that gave access to the western borders of the thirteen states. And with access to the back side of the states, it would only be a matter of time until the British would be able to divide them and take them down one at a time.

The officers sat in shocked silence, stunned by the certain destruction facing them and the sickening conviction that the fall of Fort Ticonderoga could usher in the end of the Revolution and of their desperate quest for liberty. Had it all been in vain? The defiant stand at Lexington and Concord that now seemed so long ago, the terrible losses at New York, the miraculous victories at Trenton and Princeton brought off by men who were sick, freezing, starved—all for nothing? Had the Almighty turned his face from them? The men stared at St. Clair, dead, devastated inside.

St. Clair moved on. "We are here as a war council to decide what prudence requires us to do." He pushed paper and quill toward Dunn. "Major, make a record of this."

Dunn plucked up the quill, made quick entries of date and persons present, then raised his head, waiting. St. Clair continued.

"Weeks ago I discussed with General Schuyler what action I would take in the event that defending this fort became unfeasible. He agreed in principle. In my opinion, British cannon on that mountain, capable of hitting this fort and our defenses across South Bay, while we can't hit them, has brought us to that time. Do you agree?"

The four generals glanced at each other, then dropped their eyes for a moment before answering. "Yes."

"I've decided to evacuate the fort and the Mount Independence defenses immediately. I know that Congress and most of the Continental army will consider that an act very close to treason, but I have the choice of sacrificing either my character, or my men. I can become a butcher, or a coward." His face became contorted with a controlled rage at finding his entire command trapped like rabbits at the mercy of a pack of wolves.

The four generals facing him shuddered as they saw themselves on his side of the desk with the awful decision on their shoulders, and their hearts went out to him. In tormented frustration, St. Clair dropped his fist thumping. "I will not sacrifice over two thousand men for the sole purpose of satisfying public opinion. I intend saving these men to fight another day. Now I must put that decision to you. Do you support it, or not? Search your souls, for no matter what you decide, it will become fodder for debate as long as records exist."

The four generals leaned back, minds racing as the enormity of what they were doing flooded over them, swamping their minds. For two full minutes they sat in silent agony, weighing, weighing again, and a third time, deciding which purgatory they would choose: the blood of more than two thousand men on their hands, or the hatred and contempt of Congress, the Continental army, and most Americans.

They quietly answered, "Agreed."

St. Clair's shoulders slumped in relief for a moment before he continued. "You know that a retreat is probably the most difficult military maneuver to successfully make, and the odds against it are all the greater if the retreating army is inferior in number and firepower to the pursuing army. Today's report shows we have two thousand and eighty-nine men fit for duty. The British have just over eight thousand—well-armed, ready to do battle."

He paused. The only sound was the wind in the parade grounds.

"To succeed in this evacuation, there are a few things we must understand. First, time is against us. If those guns up there begin firing before nightfall, we will be in instant chaos. Second, absolutely no one is to know we're evacuating until we're ready to tell them. Some officers will guess what's going on, and we'll have to handle that when it happens. If the enlisted men find out too soon, it will spread like wildfire and start a panic. Understood?"

All nodded.

"We go about this quietly. If the British realize we're evacuating they'll be on us within minutes. We'll start immediately doing what we can and finish in the dark tonight. There's going to be only a sliver of moon tonight, which will help. After dark, there will be no fires. No lamps, no lanterns, not even a candle. Pickets are to challenge no one because men will be moving everywhere, and we can't have pickets calling out hundreds of challenges in the dark that can be heard by British patrols."

He paused for a moment. "I thought about sending runners south to get help from General Schuyler at Albany, but we don't have the time, and Schuyler doesn't have enough ammunition to do any good. Last week his men were melting their pewter utensils and ripping the lead out of the window sashes in the homes to make bullets." He stopped to clear his throat.

"Let's get down to the detail." He unfolded a large map on his desktop, squared it with the compass, and dropped an index finger on the five-sided shape of the fort.

"We're here, on the west side of the lake." He shifted his finger as he spoke. "Mount Independence is here on the east side of the lake, south across the South Bay narrows. Our Great Bridge is here, and we still hold it, so we can march to the east side of the lake and on to our defenses on Mount Independence at will. The Germans are positioned here, above those defenses, and here, a little below, ready to attack from both sides when the British begin their big assault on this side of the lake."

He straightened for a moment, then leaned back over the map, finger tracing. "Directly north of us is Three Mile, here. From Three Mile, British troops hold everything in an arc sweeping west, then south, clear down to Mount Defiance, where they've got those cannon in place."

He raised his head to look each man in the eye. "In short, gentlemen, we are almost entirely surrounded."

A sense of panic seized the four generals for a moment, then passed as they waited, and St. Clair went on. He tapped the map on the east side of the lake, very close to the foot of Mt. Independence, and an intensity stole into his face. "But with all they've done, there are two very narrow passages that remain open, at least for the next few hours."

He paused for a moment, locating the place on the map. "One is here." He placed his finger between the lake shore and East Creek on the east side of the lake, just north of Mt. Independence. "There is a strip of land that is open. The Germans haven't yet occupied it, but they will in the next day or two, and when they do we are cut off from that escape route." Again he raised his eyes, pausing again in the silence of the room.

"But if we move before they do, we can use the Great Bridge to march our men over to that strip of land, then on down to Skenesborough, here." He tapped a small dot on the western shores of South Bay, near the southern slopes of Mt. Independence. "From Mount Independence, we can take the new road our forces cut through the forest last year, east through Hubbardton, here, on south to Castle Town, here, then west again to Skenesborough, here." His finger rested on the small settlement at the southern tip of South Bay, the southern extreme of Lake Champlain.

He straightened and waited while every man in the room rose from his seat to study the route. The horrendous risks leaped out at them, overwhelmed them, and they settled back onto their chairs with a rising feeling of dark desperation.

St. Clair shifted his finger back up to Fort Ticonderoga. "South Bay is the other route that we still hold. We have our docks, and if we move right now, we can get our sick and wounded into our bateaux and move them down South Bay to Skenesborough before the British cut us off. It will have to be done at night, and I need not tell you, until the bateaux are well past Mount Defiance, they will be under the muzzles of those cannon. If this north wind holds, we'll have no trouble moving the bateaux south."

He saw the question come into their eyes and addressed it. "We would load our entire force onto bateaux right here, and take them down South Bay, if we had enough bateaux, but we don't. We have only enough for our sick and wounded. We have more bateaux tied up at Skenesborough, south of here, but with this wind coming down from the north we would never get them up here in time to be of help. So we'll carry what we can of our stores across the Great Bridge, down to Skenesborough, meet our boats there, and load them there for the trip down to Fort George. Some of our cannon will go, too. There isn't enough time to get it all down there, so we'll have to be satisfied with the best we can do. We'll spike what cannon we have to leave behind."

There was an audible murmur among the generals at the thought of spiking and abandoning their cannon, so critically needed by every command in the entire Continental army. They looked at the floor for a moment as they envisioned their own men with long, thin brass spikes, driving them into the touch holes with two-pound sledges until the spikes hit the far side of the inner cannon barrel, bent, and curled back. Once the spikes were bent back and seated inside the cannon barrel, the cannon would be useless until the spikes were dug out. Digging them out was an arduous, time-consuming task.

He stopped for half a minute while he silently went over the map again to be certain he had covered the essentials. "So, our withdrawal resolves itself to two basic routes. We sail our wounded and supplies down South Bay to Skenesborough, and march our troops over the Great Bridge, over through Castle Town, then south to Skenesborough to meet the boats."

He straightened. "Do you agree? Any questions?"

Each man in the room knew they did not have the luxury of time to debate, consider, ponder. Under the best of conditions, evacuating the entire American force with their wounded and artillery from the fort with British and German patrols swarming on three sides would be a masterstroke. Doing it at night, under impossible time constraints, would be a miracle.

Each man in turn spoke in a quiet, subdued voice. "It is agreed."

St. Clair nodded. "Then let's get down to the detail of your individual assignments. We have no time to do it twice, so I ask your undivided attention. And remember, on pain of courts-martial, not a word of this is to go beyond this room until I order it."

Fifty minutes later Dunn opened the door, and the four generals ducked their heads against the blowing grit and walked out into the parade grounds at a controlled, casual pace. As Dunn closed the door after them, St. Clair spoke to him.

"Bring Colonel Udney Hay here at once. Don't tell him why."

Dunn walked out the door to return in twenty minutes, followed by a very much puzzled Lieutenant Colonel Udney Hay, serving at that time as assistant deputy quartermaster general for St. Clair's command. Hay came to attention facing St. Clair's desk, and St. Clair gestured for him to be seated.

St. Clair raised his voice above the sound of the wind outside. "Colonel, what I am about to tell you cannot go beyond this room until I say. Do you understand?"

Wide-eyed, Hay answered, "Yes, sir."

"Twenty minutes ago the war council agreed we must evacuate this fort. They have already begun preparations. We leave tonight. The men who are fit will march across the Great Bridge, down to Skenesborough, then east to Hubbardton, and from there south, then west to Fort George. The sick will board bateaux and sail south down South Bay. All possible supplies and artillery will go with them."

St. Clair stopped. Hay gaped. "Sir, with all respect, have you received orders from General Schuyler to make this move?"

"No. Not directly."

"Then may I ask, sir, why?"

"You may. The British have cannon on top of Mount Defiance. We found out about it three hours ago. If they begin firing now, this fort and our defenses across South Bay on Mount Independence will be rubble by tomorrow morning. And once they start, there will be no way out except surrender."

Hay reared back in his chair, utterly dumbstruck, unable to find his voice for ten full seconds. "Congress . . . General Washington . . ." He could not form a complete sentence, and he stopped.

"I know about Congress and General Washington. Let me put it to you exactly as it now stands. I can fight, or I can retreat, and that reduces itself to a very simple proposition. I can save my character and lose this army, or I can lose my character and save this army. Given that choice, I will save the army. We evacuate."

For five long seconds the single sound was the rise and fall of the hot, gusty wind in the parade grounds. Dunn sat in his chair, watching the expression on Hay's face change from shock to the beginnings of comprehending the awful truth, and making calculations of the mind-destroying task that must be completed within twenty-four hours.

St. Clair moved on. "Your duties as acting quartermaster will be to move all the sick and wounded by bateaux, with as much of the medicines and stores as our boats will hold."

"Bateaux? Most of them are down at the Skenesborough landing. I doubt we can bring them here against this wind."

"I know. The sick and wounded, and some items of baggage and supplies have priority on the bateaux we have here at our own docks. Our troops will carry what they can down to the Skenesborough landing and load it onto the bateaux there. We'll have to burn what's left and spike what cannon we have to leave behind."

Hay's mind was still reeling from the shock of abandoning the fort. By force of will he brought his thoughts to focus on the assignment St. Clair had given him and forced some semblance of orderliness to what must be done. "Yes, sir. How many know about this?"

"The war council, Major Dunn, Colonel Baldwin, and yourself. I'll have to tell Major Stevens soon, so he can begin moving his artillery. Besides those I have named, no one else knows. Go about your assignment quietly so no one will suspect. I'll personally tell the men when they need to know, and not before. Evacuating overnight will be difficult enough without a panic among the men. So not a word to anyone. Can you do it?"

"Yes, sir. When do I begin?"

"The moment you walk out that door."

"Anything else, sir?"

"That's all for now."

St. Clair watched the door close behind Hay, then turned to Dunn. "Major, locate Major Stevens and bring him here."

Without a word Dunn walked out the door, and as it closed, St. Clair's shoulders sagged. Six hours of sleep in the past six days had left him with deep fatigue riding like a pall. He dug a thumb and forefinger into weary eyes, then leaned forward, forearms on his desk, fingers interlaced. For a time he stared unseeing at his hands, trying to order his thoughts by force of will.

What's keeping the British from opening up with their cannon? Wind?—Ammunition?—Waiting for all units to finish getting into position? Once they start with the cannon they won't need much else.

He ran nervous hands through his hair.

If we can march men and horses and wagons across the Great Bridge moving supplies down to Skenesborough in broad daylight—if we can start moving our cannon down to the loading docks right under their noses—if we can start withdrawing our troops from the front lines—if we can do it all without the British noticing—if none of our troops look up and see the cannon on Mt. Defiance—if none of them notice everything being moved—if—if—if—how long can we survive on if?

He slowly leaned back in his chair. *What will the troops do when they are told to abandon? They've come to fight—they believe they can hold the fort against a ground attack—maybe they can—but not against guns on Mt. Defiance—what will they say?—what will they do when they're ordered to leave under cover of dark?—what will they tell their families?—what will be said of them when they have to say they were among those who abandoned Fort Ti in the night without firing a shot in its defense?—how will they bear up under it?—what will Congress—*

St. Clair flinched at the abrupt rap on his door. "Enter."

Dunn opened the door. "Major Stevens has been ordered to his quarters by the doctor. Fever. He says he's about recovered. The doctor says you can visit him there."

St. Clair worked his way through the parade grounds at a controlled, casual pace, to rap on the door to Stevens's quarters. Stevens was seated at a small table, dressed in his trousers, heavy gray socks, with his tunic unbuttoned, his gray underwear visible.

St. Clair spoke as he entered. "Don't get up."

Stevens gestured to a chair. "Sir, have a seat."

St. Clair sat down and looked into the sick officer's face for a moment, trying to gauge the temper of the man.

Major Ebenezer Stevens had arrived at the fort in April, and since that time had been the officer in charge of artillery. Crusty, blunt, outspoken, Stevens had never minced words with any soldier, and it was a matter of profound indifference to him whether it was an enlisted man or officer he was talking to, including generals.

"Major," St. Clair said quietly, "the British have cannon on top of Mount Defiance. We are going to evacuate the fort."

Stevens head came up in shock, and he blurted, "We're going to *what?*"

"Abandon."

Stevens doubled fist came down on the tabletop. His voice was loud, hot. "Abandon this fort? Retreat again?"

"Yes. We can't defend against those guns."

"Storm the mountain!" Stevens boomed. "Send three hundred Indians up there in the night. Promise them scalps and rum. Promise them anything to take those cannon emplacements and turn the guns on the British. But don't abandon this fort! No more retreating!"

St. Clair shook his head. "Our men would never reach the top. If we don't evacuate tonight, they'll have us sealed in by tomorrow noon. We leave immediately, or not at all."

"Then let it be not at all. Abandon? That's reason to curse the day I ever put my feet into this country, there being so much retreating. Wars aren't won by retreating. They're won by standing and fighting, and attacking."

Fatigue, lack of sleep, finding himself thrust into the unbearable white heat of the cauldron, St. Clair half rose from his chair, leaning forward, arms stiff, palms flat on the table. His eyes were like flecks of flint, voice rising in anger as he bristled back at Stevens. "I know how wars are won. I know what retreating does to armies. I know what the men at this fort are going to say when they get orders to turn their backs and run in the middle of the night. I know that I will likely face a court-martial, perhaps a trial for treason. But for all that, I will not get my command butchered defending what cannot be defended! You stand to lose some cannon. I stand to lose everything. Everything! Do you understand?"

Stevens settled back onto his chair, startled, subdued by St. Clair's ferocity. "General, I. . . . It's just that we've worked hard to prepare for a fight . . ."

St. Clair brought himself under control. "I know. Now listen closely. None of what I tell you can leave this room until I give the order. This is how the evacuation will occur."

Twenty minutes later St. Clair leaned back for a moment, then continued. "While we are loading the bateaux and boats, keep one battery firing at that new cannon emplacement the British are building west of the fort. Things must appear normal to the British."

Finished, he narrowed his eyes against the blowing dust as he left Stevens's quarters to walk steadily back to his own office. Inside, he peered from one of the two small windows to watch Stevens walk out onto the parade ground, fully dressed, hunched forward, holding his tricorn on his head against the wind as he made his way to the captain in charge of the cannon on the north walls.

St. Clair turned back to his desk, suddenly weak from unutterable fatigue, unable any longer to keep the iron grip on his mind and thoughts. He sat down and buried his face in his hands as he descended into the blackness of an abyss he had never known existed. Dark despair seized his soul, and for several moments he feared his mind was disintegrating.

Gates—Adams—Congress—don't be concerned—Burgoyne will not come down the lake—he'll move down the St. Lawrence to the Atlantic to come south—no need for a large army at Fort Ti—no need for heavy defenses—no need—no need. He slowly shook his head. *But I saw it coming—I knew better—I begged them—begged them—more men, more guns—and they sent more assurances there was no need—I did it wrong—wrong—I should have demanded enough men and guns or abandoned the fort months ago—walked out—now the British are here—cannon where we can't reach them—thirty-six hours left at the most—I have to run—like a fool—a coward—I did it wrong.*

He dropped his hands flat on the desk, staring at them while scenes of battles and men ran unchecked before his eyes. *Long Island—Brooklyn Heights—White Plains—Fort Washington—Fort Lee—the Hackensack bridge—we lost them all—the banks of the Delaware in winter—scarecrow men starving, freezing—Washington in the torments of the condemned—I didn't know then what he was going through—but I know now—how did he stand it—survive it—how?*

Once again he saw the shadow of Washington, dark on the side of his tent wall on the frozen banks of the Delaware the night of December 22, 1776, pacing, pacing in the yellow lamplight. His hands were clasped behind his back as he entered the pit where all men must finally face the fires of their own acts, and there Washington stood solid as he admitted that his mistakes had cost thousands of lives, and had left him with a defeated, freezing, starving remnant of his once proud army. His body trembled in his own Gethsemane as the refiner's fire purged him, burned out the dross, left the gold.

Bright before St. Clair's eyes came the war council Washington convened the next day. He remembered the impossible decision to take what men could walk and cross the Delaware the night of December twenty-fifth; the crossing in the blizzard; the wild, hand-to-hand morning attack in a blinding snowstorm; the miracle of only four Americans wounded, none dead, the entire Hessian garrison killed or taken prisoner. The victory that stunned the world.

Slowly St. Clair straightened. A glimmer of light crept into his heart and began to swell. The hair stood on his neck, and the flesh on his outstretched arms tingled. His breath came short as the light grew to fill his mind, his soul, with a sureness he had never known before. *We didn't win the battle of Trenton the morning of the twenty-sixth! It was won the night of December twenty-second when Washington faced himself. The night he turned to the Almighty and the*

Almighty stripped him of human pride and weakness. We didn't win that battle. The Almighty did.

St. Clair sat transfixed as the certainty reached to his foundations.

This is His work! Not mine! I may fail, but He will not! We will give up Fort Ti, but somehow, in His way, in His time, it will make no difference. This battle for liberty is His, and He will turn our defeats to victory if we will only struggle on. Struggle on.

St. Clair was not conscious of the passing of time, or the sounds of the wind, or of the men on the parade ground. He sat unmoving, engulfed in the brightest inner light he had ever known. With the might of the British army on all sides, ready to descend upon him and crush him in certain defeat, he knew the British would fail. Somehow the cause of liberty would prevail.

The inner light dwindled and faded. St. Clair yearned for it to linger, but he could not hold it. He was left once more in a small, crude office in a fort that was about to be overrun, with the heartrending duty to evacuate it to save what he could of his two thousand men. But in his heart he knew. The chaos outside his office was unfolding in a design hidden to men, but known to the powers of heaven, from whence it had come. The quest for liberty was not forgotten by the Almighty.

The wind held, hot and gusting, blowing dust and fine grit through the cracks around the windows and beneath the doors. The soldiers leaned into it, moving about the fort with eyes slitted, hair and beards and eyebrows gray, and tiny balls of mud caked at the corners of their eyes.

From his window, St. Clair watched the sergeants walking up and down the lines at the enlisted men's mess, giving the first direct orders in the plan for evacuation. The sergeants knew only that their officers had given the order; they had not been told why.

"Soon as you're through with mess, go draw twenty-four rounds of ammunition each and five days' rations. After mess. Twenty-four rounds. Five days' rations. After mess."

"Why?"

"Officers didn't say. Just do it and wait for further orders."

St. Clair's eyes narrowed as he studied the men. For a moment all talk stopped, and then they turned to each other, foreheads wrinkled in puzzlement as they struggled to make sense of the order. Twenty-four rounds? The entire command? Who's attacking, us or them? At night? Five days' rations? Where are we going for five days?

With the sun touching the western treeline, the next orders were quietly given to confused, anxious troops.

"All pickets are to be doubled immediately. All other troops to stand at their alarm stations until further orders. Maintain silence at all costs. No fires, no lanterns, no lamps, no candles. Be alert but challenge no one."

"Pickets doubled? Alarm stations? No challenges? No light? What's happening?"

The sergeants shook their heads. "Ask a general. They didn't tell us. Get at it."

The troops went to their assigned posts to stand silent, wide-eyed, their minds timorously touching the unthinkable question: is an evacuation underway? Abandon Fort Ti? St. Clair? Without a fight? Never. Not St. Clair. Never.

In the windswept, fading purple of late twilight, the next order was given to all officers and every enlisted man in the fort. No officer below the rank of general had known the order was coming, save for Major Isaac Dunn, who had said nothing.

"Strike your tents and load them in the boats at the dock for transport to Skenesborough. Pack your gear, and fall into parade formation for marching. Do it now, and do it quiet. No lanterns, no lamps. No light of any kind."

Officers and enlisted men alike were stunned, their minds reeling, unable to accept what was now beyond doubt. They were abandoning Fort Ticonderoga, and they were doing it under cover of darkness, like cowards, afraid to fight, sneaking away in the night.

St. Clair walked out his office door into the darkness and started across the parade ground, holding his tricorn on his head against the wind, toward the quarters of Colonel Jeduthan Baldwin. Few noticed him in the confusion and the darkness. He watched and listened as he worked his way quietly through the men, feeling their mood, their temper.

A stoop-shouldered old man with his beard blowing raised his voice above the wind. "Been here a whole year of sweat and work and we got 'er ready for a fight and now we're walkin' out. It isn't right."

A burly corporal, hair and beard filled with blowing grit, answered. "Said come fight for liberty. That's what they said. And I figgered it was somethin' I could feel good fightin' for, maybe dyin' for, so I come. An' now what we got? Orders to run!"

A square-shouldered boy, who had never shaved, stood. "Two hundred miles we marched, some of us, and we come to finish this job. Ready to die for it if we had to. And now we get to go home and tell the folks we turned tail and run out in the night, first time the redcoats and Germans come at us."

A tall, hawkish corporal named Cogan shook his head. "Abandon Fort Ti. I can't believe it. Such a retreat was never heard of since the creation of the world."

The response was immediate. "Cogan, this isn't a retreat. A retreat means you got into a fight and was losin' so you pulled back. We never got in no fight. We're sneakin' away from one like cowards."

The rebellious rumblings were rampant in the fort. Each had been touched by a still, small voice in the core of their consciousness that quietly repeated—liberty—liberty—liberty—like a drumbeat. Over time it had reached outward to every fiber of their being, penetrated every thought, every feeling. It rose above their fear of dying, drove them to pick up their muskets and powder horns and leave hearth and home, to gather against the oppression and tyranny of those who would keep them under their heel if they could. If they had never been sure of anything else in their lives, these men were certain of this one thing. Life would not be sweet without liberty. The right of self-determination. The right to think and act according to their own best lights. For this, they had laid their lives on the altars of the Almighty.

And now, they were being denied their battle for liberty and the powers of heaven by their own commanding officer? Ugly murmurings could be heard in every quarter inside Fort Ticonderoga.

St. Clair stopped before Cogan. "Corporal, there's something I think you have a right to know."

Cogan jerked erect, squinting in the windswept darkness of the parade ground, eyes bright, defiant, jaw set stubborn. "And what might that be?" Everyone within earshot stopped dead still. Cogan had not come to attention, nor had he addressed his commanding officer as "Sir."

St. Clair glanced about at the ring of silent, accusing faces that gathered. Slowly he raised an arm to point south. "Last night the British put cannon on top of Mount Defiance. Fourteen hundred yards from here. Those guns can reach this fort, but our guns can't touch them. I believe the only reason they didn't blast this fort to pieces today was because the wind would reduce cannon accuracy. Maybe that, and they wanted to wait until all elements of their full attack are in place before they start their bombardment."

Cogan thrust his head forward. "Beggin' the general's pardon, how long has the general known about those guns up there?"

"Since a little before noon. I had a choice. Save you men for a battle you can win, or stay here and watch those guns kill most of you. I choose to save you for the battle that is yet to come."

Cogan's reply was loud, abrupt, almost a challenge: "And give up Fort Ti without a fight?"

A sergeant cut in, his voice sharp, tough. "Cogan, keep your place. You're talking to General St. Clair."

St. Clair held up his hand. "It's all right, Sergeant. I expect to be court-martialed over this, but I tell you men, we can give Fort Ti to the British now, or we can give it to them after most of you are dead. Either way, they get the fort. You have a right to know."

Without another word St. Clair pushed through the silent men. They all turned their heads south to peer into the darkness, up at the deadly cannon muzzles, while they struggled with the question of whether St. Clair was right or wrong. What had been clear to them was now clouded, muddy, obscured. They turned back to their duties, silent, with the beginnings of understanding of their commander taking root in their minds. The hot, rising mood of rebellion cooled as they walked away, pondering.

St. Clair strode to the quarters of Colonel Baldwin. He rapped on the door, then, on invitation, walked into the small, dimly lit room.

Baldwin came to attention. "Yes, sir?"

St. Clair gestured to the tiny table, with two chairs, and they sat down facing each other. St. Clair fidgeted with his hat for a moment, then locked eyes with Baldwin.

"Colonel, we're abandoning the fort tonight. You know about the guns up on Mount Defiance. We cannot survive them."

Baldwin did not move nor speak.

"Order your artificers to collect all their tools and move them down to the bateaux at the landing. There are a number of them assigned to you. Have it done by two o'clock A.M."

"Yes, sir."

St. Clair studied this square, tireless patriot for a moment, looking for any sign of regret, of resistance, of personal loss. No man had done more than Baldwin to prepare Fort Ticonderoga for the expected assault. The Great Bridge, the landing, powder magazine, redoubts, trenches, new hospital—all of them his handiwork. Tireless, dedicated to a fault, the man had spent a year poring over engineering diagrams at night, working with his artificers and crews during daylight hours, pouring his heart and soul into the endless projects. And how was it all to end? In vain. Useless. Giving a year's mind-bending, backbreaking work to the British at night, in a wind storm, without firing a shot. St. Clair searched Baldwin for evidence of acrimony, bitterness, resistance, but there was none.

Baldwin's eyes were steady, his face immobile. "I'll be ready, sir."

St. Clair felt a rise in his throat. He swallowed, started for the door, then stopped and turned back. "Colonel, I . . . your country is in your debt. It's been an honor to work with you."

"Thank you, sir, and an honor to work with you."

St. Clair opened the door and disappeared into the blowing dirt and blackness. Baldwin quickly put on his tunic, buttoned it closed, picked his tricorn from its peg by the door, and followed. With his head ducked against the northeasterly wind, he made his way to the quarters of his artisans and delivered their orders. "Have all equipment boxed and delivered to the landing by midnight."

At eleven-twenty P.M. the last crates were lifted from wagons and set on the dock south of Fort Ti, ready, and Baldwin gathered his crew. "Wait here," he shouted above the wind. "Someone will help load you when the time comes. I'm going to go help Captain Winslow with his guns and ammunition."

He wound his way through the columns of men, moving tents and equipment from all directions to the ordnance depot. Even in the darkness it was clear that not one gun, nor man, remained. He turned to go and bumped into a lieutenant.

"Pardon, sir, didn't see you," the young man said.

"Do you know where Captain Winslow has gone?"

"Yes, sir. I'm on my way to join him down at the landing. He got all the cannon loaded onto some bateaux."

"Already?" Baldwin asked.

"Yes, sir, except for a few big guns." The young lieutenant shook his head. "We had to spike 'em. A real shame."

Baldwin nodded, turned, and headed for St. Clair's office. Major Henry Brockholst Livingston answered his knock, and Baldwin quickly dodged inside before Livingston slammed the door shut against the wind and dirt. Baldwin beat at his clothes with his tricorn, knocking dust. "You acting aide for St. Clair?"

"Yes, sir, while Major Dunn is gone."

"Know where Major Dunn is? Or General St. Clair?"

"Yes, sir. Both are across the Great Bridge, somewhere on Mount Independence. Got word things aren't going well over there."

Baldwin shook his head. "I think we're headed for trouble here, too. Wind's got the lake running high and rough, and without light, nobody knows what they're doing. I'm going over to find General St. Clair."

"Very good, sir."

Despite its own weight, the Great Bridge was pitching, rising and falling, awash with the great swells and whitecapped waves kicked up by the howling wind. Drenched to the skin, Baldwin battled his way across to the base of Mt. Independence. Five minutes later he found St. Clair, hot, angry, shouting orders above the wind to a group of cowed officers.

As Baldwin approached, St. Clair pointed, and the clustered officers turned on their heels and hurried away. Baldwin came to attention. "Sir, my men have their tools on the docks below the fort. Can I help you here?"

Relief flooded through St. Clair. "When I got here, everybody was still asleep! They're not now, although I understand General de Fermoy has not yet made an appearance. Would you go up to his quarters and wake him. If he's drunk, shake him awake and get him moving. He received his orders this morning. He knows what to do. Then collect a crew—any place you can get them—and go to the stone magazine. You'll find about a hundred barrels of gunpowder. Get it all down to the docks on this side of the lake, ready to load for Skenesborough. When you're finished with that, get with Udney Hay and Lieutenant Thomas Blake from New Hampshire and try to keep things organized and moving on these docks. If things get any worse we could have a general mutiny in the middle of the night. Understand?"

"Sir, do I understand I'm to shake de Fermoy awake and see to it he's up and moving? With all respect, sir, he's a general."

The controlled rage was plain in St. Clair's voice. "If he's drunk and asleep, do it. Do you know about him at Trenton, the day before we marched around Cornwallis?"

"No, sir. I was here, not there."

"He got drunk and abandoned his command. They were ordered to slow down four thousand British until dark to save Washington's army on the banks of the Delaware."

"What happened, sir?"

"When de Fermoy abandoned, Colonel Edward Hand took over. Had two hundred of his backwoods riflemen with him. He finished the job. Saved Washington's army. If Hand hadn't stopped the British, I believe Washington would have had de Fermoy shot. So you get him up and moving. If he doesn't like it, tell him I ordered it, and that I'll bring him up on capital charges if he fails. Understand?"

"Yes, sir." Baldwin turned on his heel and started up the trail leading to de Fermoy's quarters. The hot north wind swept the north face of Mt. Independence, whistling through the brush and trees, driving dirt stinging as Baldwin ascended. He came to the plateau where he and Colonel Thaddeus Kosciuszko, the volunteer Polish engineer, had designed and built cannon emplacements and breastworks, along with quarters for officers and some enlisted men. He held his hat on as he pounded on de Fermoy's door.

There was no response from inside. He pounded again, and waited. No light showed; there was no answer. He tried the door handle and shook his head. The door was deadbolted from inside. He took one step back, and kicked hard. The pine door frame splintered, the wind drove the door open and filled the room with dust. Baldwin walked in, propped the door closed with a chair, and fumbled in the dark for a lamp on the table.

In the dim lamplight, he made out the form of de Fermoy on his bed, lying on his side, face to the wall. The room reeked of wine and alcohol. Two empty bottles stood on the nightstand, with an overturned pewter mug. Baldwin shook de Fermoy's shoulder.

"Sir, the fort is being evacuated. General St. Clair . . ."

The drunken man lay inert, making no move, no sound. Again Baldwin shook him, more roughly. "Sir, wake up! We're evacuating!" he shouted. General de Fermoy swatted at his hand, then settled back into his alcoholic stupor. For a moment Baldwin did battle with a desire to jerk the man to his feet and slap him awake. Instead, he peeled back the blanket and once again shook de Fermoy's shoulder, dropped his face a scant eight inches from de Fermoy's ear, and fairly shouted, "Sir, you've got orders to evacuate! Wake up!"

He came up with eyes clenched shut, wildly waving his hands, muttering, cursing loudly in French. He squinted in the yellow light, trying to focus, struggling to understand what was happening. "Who are you?" he blurted.

"Colonel Baldwin. Under orders from General St. Clair. We're evacuating the fort and your command . . ."

The general swayed to his feet, furious. "You dare break into my quarters—shout at me—you will be disciplined—shot—"

Something inside Baldwin snapped. His big hand clutched de Fermoy's nightshirt at the throat, and he jerked the smaller man forward, nose to nose. His voice was very close to a snarl. "You're drunk! The lives of twenty-five hundred good men hang in the balance, and you're up here drunk. You've got your orders from General St. Clair. Now you get into those clothes and you get out there. Do it, or in the name of the Almighty, I'll shoot you where you stand!"

De Fermoy backed away, bleary eyed, battling to bring his brain out of an alcohol fog. He bobbed his head once, then reached for his trousers. Baldwin watched him struggle, then steady himself with one hand on the table while he worked to get a foot started down the pants leg. Disgust and anger plain on his face, Baldwin backed out the door, slammed it shut, and started across the small plateau. The moon had risen, a thin crescent of light that did almost nothing to ease the blackness of the windswept night.

Baldwin awakened and rousted fifty confused, reluctant, sullen men from the crude log barracks near de Fermoy's quarters, pushed and shoved them into rank and file, and marched them halfway down the north face of Mt. Independence to the powder magazine built of solid stone. In the wind-driven dust he ordered them to move the powder kegs down to the docks to be loaded onto the waiting bateaux and boats. Cursing, near mutiny, the men lifted them, two men to the keg, and with Baldwin leading the column, carrying his end of a keg, they moved down the path.

The scene at the docks was utter chaos. Angry, confused men were dropping loads of tents, baggage, food, medicines, tools, muskets, and bullets in wild disorder. Officers stalked among them shouting orders above the wind, shoving, pushing the enlisted men to bring their loads to the boats. Half a dozen officers had drawn their sabers and were striking the men on their legs and backs with the flat side, threatening them with being shot on the spot if they did not obey. The lake was a mass of monstrous swells, wind-whipped to a froth, driving the huge, flat-bottomed bateaux and boats bucking, crashing against the heavy docks and pilings. Men swore as they struggled to load crates and boxes into vessels that were rising and falling six feet in the heaving swells, fearful of being crushed if they slipped on the slick, water-drenched planking and fell between the boat and dock.

From out of the blackness, Lieutenant Thomas Blake and Colonel Udney Hay approached Baldwin from opposite directions, at the same instant, hats jammed tight against the wind.

"We're never going to get it all loaded," Blake shouted, his words snatched by the wind. "There's some looting going on right now. Clothing chests broken open, shirts and trousers and shoes disappearing."

"Pass orders that looters will be shot on sight," Baldwin called back to him, and Blake hurried away.

Colonel Udney Hay leaned forward to shout, "Where's de Fermoy? Where are his men? They were supposed to be here working on the docks."

Baldwin pointed back up the trail. "Forty minutes ago he was still asleep. He should be on his way down here now, with his command."

Hay pointed back across the Great Bridge. "We got supplies in the wagons over by the fort, but no oxen. How do we get the wagons across the bridge?"

Baldwin shook his head. "Get ropes and have the men pull them. What we don't get across we'll have to leave. We've got to be out of here by daybreak."

Hay gestured to the men milling about in a state of angry mass confusion. "These men are approaching panic. They wanted to stay and fight, and now they're fast losing confidence that we can get them out of here. They know we don't have enough wagons, oxen, boats. We've got to get this thing organized—keep them busy—or we're going to have a revolt."

"I know. Move among them. Have them organize the crates and barrels. Get as many as you can on the docks, loading the boats. Anything to keep them busy. If de Fermoy doesn't come soon, I'll go back up there, and if I do, I want you along as a witness. I have St. Clair's permission to put that man in irons if I have to."

Stunned, Hay straightened, then moved away, and Baldwin heard his voice booming out orders as he went, threatening, pleading, driving the men. Baldwin turned and nearly bumped into General St. Clair. He came to attention, waiting, as Isaac Dunn came in at a run, stopping abruptly as he recognized St. Clair in the dark.

St. Clair wasted no words. "Where's de Fermoy?" he demanded of Baldwin.

Dunn broke in. "I just left him. He's up there sitting on his luggage in front of his quarters doing nothing. I think he's drunk."

Even in the darkness and howling wind, Baldwin and Dunn saw St. Clair's face cloud with fury, and they heard it thick in his voice. "I'll deal with him later. Go get Poor, Paterson, Francis, and Long and bring them here."

Within minutes all six men were gathered before St. Clair, panting from their run, wide-eyed as they waited for an explanation.

St. Clair shouted rapidly. "It's a little after one o'clock, and this is one of the shortest nights of the year. It'll be daylight by four o'clock. General Long, the minute the boats are loaded with the cannon, gunpowder, stores, the sick and invalid, and the pay chest from the fort, you take command and lead the flotilla down to Skenesborough. Wait for us there. We'll march overland to Castle Town, then west to meet you. Am I clear?"

"Yes, sir."

"This is the order of march. I give it to you now exactly as I gave it this morning at the war council." He pointed to each man as he spoke. "Poor's brigade leads. Next, Paterson's brigade. Next, de Fermoy's command. Last, Francis's command, who will be the rear guard. I have placed brigades from the Continental army in the lead, and in the rear, with the inexperienced militia in the middle. The plan is for the continentals to keep the green militia in rank and file, and moving."

He turned to face Francis. "Did you give orders to have some of your men form a line across the peninsula so they can stop any American deserters from sneaking through to tell the British what we're doing?"

"Yes, sir."

"This morning you were ordered to handpick your rear guard. Did you do it?"

"I did, sir. They're ready."

"Good. Do I have to tell you that the rear guard is the heaviest assignment in this operation? Your men have to stop, hold the British, retreat, stop, hold the British, as long as it takes. Have your men damage the bridge as much as they dare as they come across. Four of them are to man a cannon on this side to maintain fire on the British as long as they can as they try to cross the bridge. If your men fail, there will be nothing to stop the British from overrunning the entire column. It will be a massacre. Am I clear?"

"Yes, sir."

He turned back to Poor and Paterson. "Do you still have men over at the French Line? Still firing the cannon?"

"Yes, sir, three hundred handpicked men. They'll become part of Francis's rear guard. They know their orders."

"Get over and tell them to evacuate and be here at this landing ready to march not later than half past three. It will be light enough by four o'clock for the British to see what's going on. Colonels Baldwin and Dunn, stay with me."

He paused for a moment, then spoke to all of them. "Be certain you get your regimental papers to General Long down on the docks. When his boats leave, we march out. Whatever isn't loaded, leave it. Be sure to blow up what gunpowder we have to leave behind. Watch for militia. Most of them have never been in battle, and in the dark they're going to lose touch with their officers and regiments and scatter. Grab them and put them in your units as you find them. Two Massachusetts regiments have already gone—gave me notice after dark that they didn't sign on for this."

Standing there in the dark, chaos growing by the second, St. Clair tried to force a conclusion to what was to be his last war council with these men. They silently waited, nervous, anxious to get back to their commands, wanting only to get past this nightmare of trying to do the impossible in the black of night with an army of confused, angry men, coming ever closer to open rebellion.

"Remember my order of this morning. On pain of arrest and trial, no one strikes a light between now and dawn. No fires, no lanterns, not even a candle." He paused and took a great breath. "Unless you have something to say, we're finished. God bless you all."

The officers turned on their heels and disappeared in the sounds and muddle of a disintegrating army. With Baldwin and Dunn at his side, St. Clair strode to the docks and found Long.

"How close are you to being loaded?"

"Close. We've got the fort records, and the supplies and guns and powder—as much as we can take—in the boats, and most of the sick and invalid. When the pay chest gets here, I think we can leave."

"Good. We won't be far behind. How many bateaux and boats will you have?"

"Just over two hundred."

"Stay close to the west side of South Bay. Colonel Baldwin, stay here to help Long. Good luck."

Long considered for a moment. "Oh, sir, I haven't seen anything of de Fermoy's records and files. Are they lost?"

Baldwin shook his head. "I don't know. I'm going back to be certain the regiments are forming to march out as ordered, and I'll find de Fermoy. I'll send word about his records."

"Thank you, sir."

St. Clair turned to Dunn. "Find me a horse while I help start forming the column into marching order."

"Yes, sir." Dunn left at a trot.

St. Clair strode through the milling throng of men calling orders to find their regiments, stay calm, keep loading the boats, follow the orders of their officers, get ready to take their place in the column to march south. He turned at the sound of a horse coming in from behind, and in the first deep purple of morning made out the shape of Dunn leading a bay gelding.

"Your horse, sir."

St. Clair took the reins, slipped his left foot into the stirrup, seized the forward fork of the saddletree in his right hand and swung up. The gelding fought the bit, nervous, stuttering its feet in the darkness. St. Clair turned the dancing animal in a tight circle, then held a firm rein while he shouted down at Dunn.

"Has de Fermoy showed up yet?"

"No, sir. Francis told me he's still up there, sitting on his luggage. Most of his men are still with him."

"I'm going up to find him. If he's still there, I'll have him in irons. You wait here. Long's waiting for de Fermoy's regimental records, and you'll have to take him the message when I find out where Fermoy is. I won't be—"

St. Clair never finished his sentence. At that moment, whipped by the fierce wind, flames leaped high on the north face of Mt. Independence, and a column of wind-driven sparks reached five hundred feet into the dark heavens. One second later every tree, bush, rock, man, horse, and wagon on the north half of the mountain was visible in bold relief, along with the docks, boats, piles of supplies, and men desperately loading them. Instantly the howling wind fanned and spread the flames until the Great Bridge, South Bay, and Fort Ticonderoga across the water were visible. For three seconds every American stood stock-still and stared in horror, gaping, unable to believe what was so plainly true. Then their heads turned to stare west, across South Bay, holding their breath while they waited for British General Phillips's one hundred thirty-eight cannon, together with every gun in the British fleet, to blast them all into oblivion. The British cannoneers could not ask for better targets—men, horses, oxen, wagons, boats, docks—all perfect silhouettes.

It came to St. Clair—*de Fermoy has set fire to his own quarters—he's insane—if we survive this he'll face a capital court-martial.* Instantly his next thought was his command—*got to get them out!* He drove his spurs into the flanks of the horse, and it leaped to a gallop, scattering men right and left as St. Clair sprinted to reach the front of the column that had begun to form. He shouted at the militia to hold their places—get their muskets—start marching now—form as you move. Militia who had been sullen, angry, were now terrified in the knowledge they were targets for British cannon, and they pushed past St. Clair, ignored him, shouted back at him as they broke ranks and abandoned everything in their wild plunge onto the road to Hubbardton. St. Clair held his breath, desperately hoping the more seasoned continentals would hold their positions, remain with their regiments. Then one continental followed the panic-driven militia, then another, and then the continental regiments began to disintegrate as others followed.

St. Clair reached the front of the column and wheeled his horse around, sword drawn, and in the firelight his face was set like granite. "Halt where you are!" he screamed. "I'll saber the next man who tries to run!"

The continentals slowed, stopped, and turned back to their regiments.

"Form into a single file, and follow your officers. Take the Hubbardton road. Do it now! Start! Move!" He slapped the nearest soldiers on the back with the flat of his sword, and they quickly moved out, led by their officers.

St. Clair stayed for half a minute to be certain the leaders kept moving, then once more drove his spurs home, and his horse lunged back toward the great stacks and piles of crates and barrels and kegs. He reined the animal in, coming to a stiff-legged, skidding stop, facing Udney Hay.

"Get your papers—they're critical—and start your men down the Hubbardton road."

"But sir, I—"

St. Clair shouted him down. "Do it now! Forget everything but those papers. Get moving!"

Hay could not miss the restrained fear and anger in St. Clair's voice, and he answered, "Yes, sir." He quickly turned and began bellowing orders to his men, moving among them, jerking them, shoving them into a semblance of a column, and starting them south toward the Hubbardton road, following the continentals already marching out.

St. Clair licked dry lips and glanced east, where the dark purple was beginning the subtle change to deep gray. He turned his face back to the west. The yellow light of the fire that was burning de Fermoy's quarters, and the enlisted men's barracks near by, reflected off the walls of Fort Ti across the narrows of South Bay, and in helpless rage he sat his horse, teeth gritted as his thoughts ran. *They've seen us by now—why haven't they opened up with their cannon? They could kill half of us in twenty minutes, bunched the way we are. What's holding them up?* He reached to wipe a hand over his face, digging at the mud caked in the corners of his eyes. *No chance to go help those men still holding the French Lines. No chance to send orders. Can only hope the officers over there figure out something went wrong over here—disregard everything I told them— take control—break out of there and come running.*

He cantered his mount onto the docks, now vacant, then looked south down the South Bay where the last of the bateaux and boats were fast disappearing southward, riding the high, white-topped waves, running fast before the wind. He felt a surge of hope. *Long got them out—the sick and some of the supplies and guns.*

He turned back to study the Great Bridge, riding out the wrenching and pounding of the gigantic waves thrown up by the wind. *It will hold— those men over there can make it if they come now. In the name of the Almighty let them come—let them come.*

Suddenly his head jerked forward, and he narrowed his eyes, straining to see across the stormy waters, and they were there. Black dots coming at a dead run from the woods south of the fort, straight for the Great Bridge, Colonel Francis in the lead, his raised sword glittering in the fire-light. St. Clair was unaware that he stood in his stirrups and thrust his fist into the air as a shout welled from his chest, "Come on, you can make it—keep coming, keep coming!"

The leaders hit the Great Bridge and didn't slow. The bridge was rising and falling violently with the huge swells, and they kept moving, slipping on the wet planking, recovering, sprinting on. St. Clair was holding his breath, waiting for the first thunderous roar of British cannon blasting grapeshot at the men on the bridge—exposed, defenseless, virtually sitting targets in the firelight.

Inexplicably the British cannon remained silent. The men kept coming, and with each passing minute St. Clair was shouting encouragement, knowing the wind drowned out his voice, but not caring. Then the rear guard was on the bridge, pausing every twenty paces while men used huge pry-bars to tear up planking and throw it into the black waters to slow any British pursuers, while others knelt with muskets ready to stop anyone following them, but there was no one. They reached the halfway point, and then they burst from the bucking bridge onto the solid ground at the foot of Mt. Independence as St. Clair shouted a cheer and spurred his horse to a gallop to meet them.

It seemed that every man sensed that their lives hung in the balance. No one understood why British roundshot and grapeshot had not come ripping into them twenty minutes earlier. They only knew the British cannon still remained silent, and every minute, every second, was an eternity in which they could be blasted dead. St. Clair sat his horse, holding himself in, watching his officers bawl out orders, while the men obeyed instantly in desperate silence, falling into a loose marching order. They abandoned the stacks of goods as they started for the Hubbardton road, and St. Clair watched as a single-file column began taking shape, moving like a great, thin snake in the early gray light of a rapidly approaching dawn.

They might make it—keep moving, keep moving—they might make it!

He looked back over his shoulder, beyond the Great Bridge, amazed. The British cannon had still not come alive, nor could he see any red coats and crossed white belts on the far side of South Bay. He turned back to look at his own men.

Five more minutes—just give us five more minutes. It seemed every man was moving in slow motion. Ten seconds seemed an eternity as he watched the column disappear into the woods, following the narrow trail east toward Hubbardton. Under orders of Colonel Ebenezer Francis, the last four men in the rear guard fell back to the entrance to the Great Bridge and wheeled a cannon around, muzzle facing the bridge. With skilled hands they rammed the swab down the barrel to be sure it was clear, followed by the powder ladle, wadding, then sixteen pounds of grapeshot. One man blew on the linstock until it was glowing, and they all settled into their position behind the heavy gun, out of sight, waiting for the first redcoats to reach the middle of the bridge.

St. Clair drew his watch from his tunic pocket and for a moment studied the hands. It was five minutes past four o'clock in the morning of July 6, 1777. The lake, Fort Ti, the emerald green woods, were all visible in the shifting gray of approaching dawn.

It was done.

Save for the four men left at the cannon to cover the retreat as long as they could before they ran for the woods to catch up, the last American soldier had safely evacuated Fort Ticonderoga. Around him were a hundred tons of abandoned supplies and munitions and an endless scatter of clothing and blankets and equipment. But his men were out, safe. He could think of nothing that had gone as planned by the war council. The best they had in them had failed, but still, the men were out. How? How could it be?

Then, for just a fleeting moment a sharp memory cut into his brain. *He will turn our defeats to victory.* In his heart he knew, and was humbled. An unexpected sense of peace settled over him as he raised his horse to a canter following his men.

Crouched in the wind by the docks, waiting for the British infantry to come at them from across the bridge, the last four men of the rear guard held their position behind their cannon, watching, tension mounting with each passing moment. One of them wiped the grit from his eyes, blinked, and noticed one of the big wooden chests nearby belonged to an officer. The lid and two sides were splintered, smashed open.

Clothing was scattered, some tumbling south with the wind, and in the bottom he saw a small, three-gallon wooden cask marked "Madeira."

Wine? he thought. In two strides he was there, scooping up the small keg with one arm then stepping quickly back to the gun. The other three men in the crew glanced back at him, and their eyes widened.

"Wine?" one asked.

"Don't know until I knock the bung out."

He used the cannon rammer to drive the bung into the cask, then raised it to his nose. A huge smile spread. "Good Madeira wine." He raised the cask and drank from the open bung hole, then handed it to the next man.

Half an hour later, across South Bay, British Captain Henry Ottaman crouched near the entrance to the Great Bridge. Behind him a smooth-faced young lieutenant turned to a bearded, craggy-faced sergeant and ordered him to have the company drop down, out of sight, while the captain extended his telescope. For thirty seconds the captain studied the face of Mt. Independence, then the landing and the docks. Flame and smoke were still rising to stain the dawn sky, but nothing was moving except the litter on the ground, and one lone, confused Indian.

Suddenly Ottaman stood, drew his saber, shouted, "Follow me!" and sprinted onto the Great Bridge, dodging, slowing with the violent heaving of the structure and the white water that drenched him, leaping the gaps left by the torn up planking. The lieutenant set his jaw, jerked out his own sword, and plunged after the captain, shouting, "Forward, men!" The first company of British infantry rose and charged, starting their run across the Great Bridge, grimly expecting grapeshot to rake them before they reached the halfway mark.

The American gun remained silent as the British moved forward, slowed by the gaps in the planking. At the three-quarters mark they saw the muzzle of the cannon and hesitated for a moment, uncertain whether they should leap into the water to escape the blasting grapeshot that was certain to come.

At that moment they saw a lone Indian wander over to the cannon emplacement as though in a daze, reach down, and straighten up with the smoking linstock. The warrior touched the spark to the touchhole in the cannon, and before the British could move, the big gun blasted. The British all flattened on the bridge, expecting to be raked by the grapeshot, but the cannon muzzle had been tilted far too high. The entire load whistled harmlessly forty feet over their heads. They raised up to see the terrified Indian sprinting for the woods.

Captain Ottaman leaped to his feet, ran forward, cleared the end of the bridge, and with the wind at his back leaped over the low breast-works, into the cannon emplacement, sword high. He had started his downstroke at the first man he saw, when he froze, sword poised, tunic tails whipping in the wind. He gaped in stunned surprise, studying the prostrate man, then the other three, two lying on the ground, the last one slumped over the back of the cannon barrel, causing it to go down, and the muzzle up.

For a moment he stood without moving, until he understood. He threw back his head in raucous laughter as the lieutenant came pounding up. The lieutenant stopped short in wonderment at his captain, who pointed his sword at the four unmoving Americans.

"Drunk! Four of the bloody devils left behind to blast us to kingdom come, and they're all drunk! Well, they're jolly well in for a surprise when they sober up to find out they're our prisoners." He rammed his sword back into its scabbard with the realization they were standing amidst a mountain of abandoned American supplies. He shook his head in astonishment at the great stack of gunpowder kegs, with half a dozen broken open, powder spilled among the other kegs in preparation to blow the lot of them.

He faced the lieutenant. "They can't be far ahead. You go back across the bridge and find General Fraser. Tell him there isn't an American left on Mount Independence or the docks. They're running east on Hubbardton Road. They've abandoned food, luggage, blankets, cannon, muskets, and most of all, fifty or sixty kegs of gunpowder." He could not suppress a grin. "Left in a hurry, they did. Tell the general I'm after them. Tell him Fort Ticonderoga and all defenses on Mount

Independence are ours. General Burgoyne will want to know so he can tell the king." He shook his head. "He most certainly will!"

The clatter of iron-shod hooves on cobblestones rang in the street as the British major galloped his horse through Whitehall in the heart of London. People scattered ahead of him, cursing, shaking their fists in the midmorning sun as he streaked past on his horse, the crimson tails of his tunic flying behind, head low, tricorn pulled down on his head. He pulled the big, lathered mare to a sliding halt at the great palace gates, the iron shoes knocking sparks flying from the hard English stones. Two pickets stepped to face him, muskets at the ready, while he leaped to the ground before them.

One picket opened his mouth to speak, but the major cut him off, breathless, hardly able to speak.

"I'm carrying a dispatch from General John Burgoyne. Just arrived from the American colonies. To be delivered to the king instantly. Open the gates!"

One picket spoke. "Suh, no one enters these grounds without—"

The panting major's voice rose. "I know who enters these grounds! I'm telling you there is nothing more critical to the king than this dispatch. Do you know where General John Burgoyne is? What he's doing?"

"Suh. General Burgoyne is in America disciplining the rebels."

"Are you opening these gates, or do I tell the king you personally stopped delivery of this dispatch?"

For a moment the picket hesitated, then turned and inserted a great, flat key in the lock, turned it, and the gates swung open. The major thrust the reins of the horse into the startled picket's hand and sprinted up the long, broad, cobblestone approach to the castle doors, where pickets again challenged him. He pushed past them, into the entry room and stopped. He swept his tricorn from his head, awed for a moment by the luxurious splendor of the high ceilings, thick India carpets, the twelve-foot, cut crystal chandelier overhead, six-foot-tall gold and silver candelabra, spotless, shining hardwood floors.

Instantly an immaculately dressed aide approached him, indignant at the sudden, unexpected outburst. "Sir," the aide demanded, "Who are you? For what purpose have you come? Do you have leave of the king to be here?"

The major drew a thick document from his tunic and thrust it forward. "I am under orders to deliver this to the king at the earliest possible moment."

"Indeed! From whom?"

"General John Burgoyne."

The aide's jaw dropped for a moment, and his demeanor changed in an instant. "General Burgoyne? In America?"

"Precisely."

Taking the document, the aide spun and fairly ran down the luxurious hallway. He paused before a doorway long enough to straighten his uniform, then rapped lightly. The door swung open, and the man faced the king.

The aide bowed, then spoke through the open door, "I humbly beg your pardon for the intrusion, my Liege, but I have taken license to think you would want this document at earliest opportunity."

Irritated, frowning, the king growled, "All right, all right, what is it?"

"A dispatch from General John Burgoyne, my Liege."

For a split second the king's eyes widened, and he did not move. Then he snatched the document, slammed the door, and with trembling fingers ripped open the seal. For four full minutes he stood without moving, save to turn the eight pages, one at a time, while he read feverishly. He finished the document once, read portions again to be certain he had not misunderstood, then shouted, "I did it! I have taken Fort Ticonderoga! The Gibraltar of the American continent—mine, mine, mine! The United States are mine!"

He cavorted on the thick carpet for fifteen seconds, waving the dispatch high over his head, exuberant, shouting. Outside the closed door, the aide stood in shock while butlers and maids came scurrying, not knowing whether to be terrified or overjoyed. Suddenly the door burst open, and the lot of them recoiled as the king ran from his own bedroom, up the hall two doors, and without knocking, threw open the doors to the queen's bedroom and burst in, waving the dispatch, fairly dancing a jig.

The queen was dressed in nothing more than a sheer chemise, and she cried out, then grabbed a shawl to cover herself, gasping, terrified, waiting for someone to explain the king's lunacy.

He dashed toward her, waving the dispatch, and shouting, "I have beat them! I have beat all the Americans!"

Doctor Benjamin Franklin, American Ambassador to France, sat in the breakfast nook of his quarters near Versailles, intermittently nibbling at a plate of scrambled eggs and fried ham and thoughtfully gazing out the window at the rolling French countryside—drenched in mid-morning summer sunlight, splashed with color, lush, beautiful.

He was wrapped in an old, comfortable, faded wool robe, with worn felt slippers on his gout-ridden feet. He wore no wig, nor did he make any pretense at being other than what he was—a seventy-two-year-old man with an aching, aging body, who found himself in France because the Congress of the United States had sent him. Bring the French into the Revolutionary War on our side, they had said. We can't win without their help. Their tone had been nearly flippant, as though it could be done by Franklin simply showing up in the court of King Louis XVI in Paris and asking. After all, where in the civilized world was there another man so universally renowned and revered as Ben Franklin—he who had tamed lightning, written *Poor Richard's Almanac*, invented stoves and bifocals, and through his writings and wit charmed all of Europe, while proving time and again he was as shrewd, as tough, as the best Europe had to offer? Send Ben, Congress had said, and at age seventy-one the old man had risen to his last and possibly greatest call to service of his country, and the world.

Franklin forked more scrambled eggs into his mouth, then slowly chewed as he reviewed the few lines scrawled on a slip of paper beside his cup of steaming chocolate. He raised his eyes at the rap on his door.

"Do come in," he called. He did not rise.

The door opened, and Silas Deane, his associate and colleague in the impossible task of bringing France into an alliance with America to oppose the British, entered the room. Dour by nature, Deane walked with shoulders perpetually hunched, eyes furtive, as though constantly suspicious something was going wrong. Franklin brightened.

"Good morning, Silas. Have a seat. Chocolate?"

Deane sat down at the breakfast table, shaking his head. "No chocolate. Have you heard about Fort Ticonderoga?"

Franklin nodded. "Just this morning." He pointed at the slip of paper at the head of his plate.

Deane's eyebrows arched. "Where did you get that?"

Franklin shrugged. "A source."

Deane let it pass. "Vergennes is going to know we lost Fort Ti before the day is out." Deane referred to Charles Gravier, the Comte de Vergennes, French foreign minister, and clearly the most perceptive, powerful political figure in the French government. King Louis was not going to strike up an alliance with America until Vergennes said so; it was Vergennes they must persuade, not the king.

"That is likely true."

"Things between us and France are fragile right now." Deane moved, agitated, fearful. "When Vergennes finds out we couldn't even hold onto Fort Ti, he could cut us off altogether."

Franklin's head moved up and down slowly as he continued working at the eggs. "Yes, he could."

"So what do you propose we do?"

Franklin laid his fork down. "First, we think through conditions as they stand right now." He wiped at his mouth with a linen napkin.

"Do you recall the name Choiseul?"

"The one who was French Foreign Minister sometime before Vergennes? Yes."

"When France lost the Seven Years' War back in '63, they gave up all claim to America. It humiliated them, stained their honor before the whole world. Choiseul swore he would find a way to reclaim their lost territory, regain their honor. He predicted the time would come when the colonies would rise up, and when they did, France would join them in overthrowing the British. Recall?"

"Yes."

"Choiseul fell to political intrigues against him. Vergennes shared his vision, and as fate would have it, succeeded Choiseul. That simply means, Vergennes is still waiting for the time France can come into our war as our ally. He doesn't think France can conquer England alone, at least not right now, but if we show ourselves to be strong enough to make a fight of it, France will likely come in to tip the scales in our favor. Have I stated all this correctly?"

Deane's face darkened, wondering where the nimble, unpredictable mind of the old man was taking him. "Yes."

"Vergennes was grieved when Washington was defeated so badly in New York, then rejoiced when he struck down the British at Trenton and Princeton. And, his willingness to help us secretly has fluctuated up and down according to our fortunes and misfortunes. He even went so far as to turn the crew of an American ship over to the British not long ago, and those poor men are still in a Dunkirk prison."

Deane nodded.

"At this moment, if Vergennes is what I think he is, he's caught in a crosscurrent that is tugging him two directions at once. I think he's still struggling to complete the vision of Choiseul, which requires him to become our ally, and at the same time, he's afraid to become our ally until he's convinced we can either win this war, or at least bring it to some sort of standoff. Only when he believes that French forces will ensure a victory will he enter on our side. Fair? Have I stated it fairly?"

"So far as I see it."

"All right. Let's stand in his shoes for a moment. He can't yet declare an alliance with us, and at the same time, he can't sever all relationships and be rid of us. In short, he's in a very difficult place. He can't join us, nor can he afford to offend us."

Deane leaned back in his chair, waiting for something from Franklin that would bring it all to an understandable conclusion.

Franklin picked up his fork. "If you were in his place, what would motivate you more than anything else? Maybe even frighten you?"

Deane shook his head, but said nothing.

"Let me tell you what I think I'm going to do. I think I'm going to the office of the British ambassador today—Lord Stormont—and I'm going to ask for the papers to apply for a passport to visit England."

Deane jerked forward. "You're going to *what!?*"

Franklin forked a chunk of ham into his mouth. "Apply for a British passport. A mission of peace. Open talks with the British to negotiate a settlement to our unfortunate differences."

Deane's mouth dropped open. "Peace talks with the *British?*"

Franklin stopped chewing his ham and smiled. "Yes." He resumed chewing for a moment. "I'll be attending a banquet and ball tonight in honor of the birthday of Lady Julienne. She's the wife of a dignitary— the ambassador, I think—from Holland. Both Stormont and Vergennes will be there, along with emissaries from many—maybe most—other European states."

Deane was hanging on every word.

"I think a mention or two of my intention to visit London to open peace talks will reach Vergennes, and presuming that happens, I imagine it will have a salutary effect on his thinking toward us."

Deane was incredulous. Since their arrival in France in February, Franklin had studiously attended every ball, every banquet he could find, so long as heads of state or their emissaries would be in attendance. While all others had worn wigs coifed to a magnificent perfection, he had worn no wig, but had brushed his thinning hair straight back and let it hang. While they had adorned themselves with gowns and jewels that cost a fortune, he had appeared in a plain, simple, brown homespun suit with no jewelry to detract from it. While they wore head coverings and bonnets that were breathtaking, he had worn a simple round hat made from the fur of a marten.

And Europe had loved it. Ladies flocked to him, surrounded him, fawned over him, drowned him with attention, while men remained aloof in dignified envy and disgust. He could not meet all the ladies during the banquets and balls, so he had begun to receive them and their consorts in his quarters, often in the morning while he was still in his bed. Tailors all over Europe were swamped with orders. I *must* have a brown suit identical to that of Franklin. Can you duplicate that charming little fur hat? Can you create a wig that looks exactly the way Franklin wears his hair?

Casual mention by Franklin at the banquet and ball that night, that Franklin proposed a visit to London to open peace talks with the British would spread like wildfire. Every person in the building would know it within ten minutes. Dispatches by nearly every ambassador would be on their way to kings all over Europe by four o'clock A.M., carried by messengers on galloping horses.

Deane exclaimed, "That will be the end of it. If Vergennes hears you're going to treaty with the British, we'll be ordered out of this country within forty-eight hours."

Franklin sipped at his chocolate. "To the contrary. I think it's the one thing he fears most. Do you really think he's ready to give up the French dream of regaining what they lost in their surrender to England in 1763? Do you think he would dare tell King Louis that the honor and glory of France are not to be regained?" Franklin shook his head. "Regardless of how bleak it looks at this moment with the loss of Fort Ticonderoga, Vergennes needs us as much as we need him. If he thinks he is about to lose us, I think we'll hear from him soon enough. Discreetly, at a distance perhaps, but we'll hear from him, and between the lines he will be asking us to carry on for a little longer while he matures affairs in France to the point the French can ally themselves with us to drive out the British."

Deane leaned back in his chair, eyes wide, struggling to believe Franklin's audacity.

Franklin reached for a slice of bread and said, "Would you be so kind as to pass that pot of apricot jam? The French do such wonderful things with jam."

Notes

Unless otherwise indicated, the following is taken from Ketchum, *Saratoga*, on the pages identified.

The hot north wind that arose the night of 4 July continued, gusting, blowing grit and dust, hindering the men.

On 5 July 1777, having seen the British cannon atop Mt. Defiance, General St. Clair immediately called a war council including generals Poor, Fermoy, Paterson, and Long, and informed them of the catastrophic discovery. The council agreed the only rational course was to abandon Fort Ticonderoga, since to remain could only result in the total destruction of the fort, along with most of St. Clair's army. Orders to abandon were instantly given.

There were two locations yet unoccupied by the British: one was a long peninsula near East Creek, and the other was the narrows known as South Bay. The long peninsula near East Creek gave the Americans access to Hubbardton Road, and South Bay gave water access south to Skenesborough. If those avenues were taken by the British, the Americans had no way out, and Hubbardton Road was the only practical way to move out. The greater number of American bateaux were anchored at Skenesborough, leaving only enough at the Fort Ti docks to transport the wounded, infirm, and select parts of the goods and records that were of prime importance. With the strong wind coming from the north, it would not be feasible to sail the bateaux at Skenesborough up to Fort Ti, into the wind.

Each officer was to begin preparing his men and their baggage for departure, without telling them what was going on, since it was feared an announcement of the imminent danger would spark a panic. All sick, wounded, women, children, medicines, tools, cannon, muskets, the fort treasure chest, fort records, and other necessaries were taken to the docks to be loaded on the bateaux for transport down to Skenesborough, where it was intended that the army, marching overland, would rejoin them.

By afternoon some of the soldiers had figured out that they were abandoning the fort, but did not know why. They became surly, critical of being denied the battle for which they had worked so hard and were altogether willing to enter. St. Clair had two thousand eighty-nine soldiers, one hundred twenty-four unarmed workers, and nine hundred militia just arrived, who needed to leave very soon, with which to fight about eight thousand British troops. When St. Clair told his artillery officer, Major Ebenezer Stevens, of the plan to abandon, Stevens, just recovering from a severe fever, exclaimed it was "reason to curse the day I ever put my feet into the country, there being so much retreating."

In the late afternoon St. Clair told a New Hampshire soldier named Cogan the British had the guns on top of Mt. Defiance and simply informed the men he had but two choices: he could save them for a fight they could later win, or, he could sacrifice them all right then. Either way, the British would have the fort when it was finished. Cogan said, "Such a retreat was never heard of since the creation of the world." Later, St. Clair stated that he knew he was entertaining a court-martial for abandoning the fort, but said he had two choices: he could go down in history as a butcher if he stayed, or a coward if he abandoned. He chose to save his men to fight later.

The spirit that inspired the common soldiers in the fort was akin to "the search for the holy grail," so imbued were they with a lust for freedom. They were truly patriots, ready and willing to lay down their lives for liberty, respect, a voice in determining who their leaders would be, and the power to determine their own destinies.

The officers and men worked frantically into the night, trying to complete the evacuation before the British discovered them. They moved back and forth across the Great Bridge built across the narrows between Fort Ticonderoga and the Mt. Independence landing, carrying tons of goods and supplies. The wind raised high waves on South Bay, and St. Clair sent the two hundred loaded bateaux south as soon as possible to avoid damage to the boats and the docks. Leaving a few men near the fort to make a show of an American presence there, St. Clair moved nearly all the troops across the Great Bridge to the docks on the Mt. Independence side of the narrows. The marching order was supposed to be Poor's command leading in the van, Paterson's brigade next, then de Fermoy's command, and finally a rear guard of four hundred fifty men under command of Ebenezer Francis.

Then, in the middle of the night, on the north face of Mt. Independence, General de Fermoy, drunk, set his own quarters on fire for reasons never explained, and suddenly the wind-driven flames illuminated most of the area. Panic broke loose among the Americans, since the entire American evacuation became silhouetted for the British cannon across the narrows. The men began running east on Hubbardton Road. St. Clair ordered them to stop, they paid no heed, and he spurred his horse to the lead, slowed them, and forced some organization into the retreat. For reasons unknown, the British cannon never opened fire.

The men left behind, on the Fort Ticonderoga side of the narrows, left their positions just before four o'clock in the morning—with the gray of dawn showing. Leaving four men to man a cannon to stop the British when they tried to cross the Great Bridge in pursuit, the rear guard followed St. Clair's column. The four men left behind to operate the cannon found a cask of Madeira wine, drank it, and were unconscious when the British came (see pp. 172–184).

The rather comical incident wherein a lone Indian wandered up to the cannon the drunken rear guard had failed to fire, picked up the smoking linstock, and set off the gun, then ran, is factual (see p. 192).

When news of the abandonment of Fort Ticonderoga by the Americans and the occupation of it by General Burgoyne reached King George III in London, he ran down the hall to the bedroom of his wife, Queen Charlotte, threw the door open, and catching her standing embarrassed in little more than a chemise, shouted, "I have beat them! I have beat all the Americans" (see p. 206).

In general support, see Leckie, *George Washington's War*, pp. 387–88.

CHAPTER XXII

★ ★ ★

*T*he hot wind died an hour after sunrise, and the sun became a huge brass ball pounding heat into the sweltering dead air of the Hudson River valley.

The rebel soldiers came frightened, exhausted, cursing, sweating, filthy, empty-bellied, stumbling on the narrow winding trail hacked through forest so thick the only sky they could see was directly overhead. Piles of felled trees and stripped branches rose above their heads on either side. They swore at the endless ragged tree stumps and the heavy tangle of roots that caught at their feet to slow them. They struggled on, hot with gut-wrenching anger, teetering tenuously on the ragged edge of rebellion against their officers for having been ordered to pack what they could and abandon Fort Ticonderoga, like cowards in the black hours of a windswept night. The young, untried, green militiamen were sick to death of it. Singly, in pairs, threes, they bolted away from the column, into the woods, plunging headlong for home, unable longer to stomach the humiliation of the retreat or the soul-draining grind of the insufferable trail, winding toward Hubbardton, then Castle Town.

Repeatedly the soldiers turned their heads, dreading the first glimpse of red dodging through the trees behind them. Strung out for more than a mile, marching single file, they knew they were nearly defenseless. If General Simon Fraser and his British regulars engaged the rear guard, and flanked the column, the fight would be over almost before it started. It would be a massacre. The single, unanswered question that rode heavily on every American was how far behind are they? It drove them on, past exhaustion, until they knew only one thing: place one foot ahead of the other. They're coming. Keep moving. Keep moving.

The call came down the line from General St. Clair at the head of the column. Not far ahead—Lacey's Camp—north end of Lake Bomoseen—open ground—rest—food—not far ahead—not far—Hubbardton just one mile after Lacey's Camp—ten miles from Castle Town—not far—keep moving.

At five minutes past one o'clock, with the sun directly overhead hammering down like a blacksmith's sledge, few soldiers saw the farmer run to St. Clair, stop, and point ahead, exclaiming excitedly. Nor did they notice St. Clair's shoulders sag for a moment before the farmer turned and ran back up the trail, out of sight. Only General Poor knew the message the farmer had delivered to St. Clair, and Poor sucked air as it struck home.

Thomas Hubbard had received a grant to a parcel of property in 1774 and built a crude log cabin and outbuildings as the beginnings of a settlement. Eight additional families had come, the Sellecks being the most recent, and together the families had cleared the land to graze their cattle, sheep, and pigs, proudly calling their settlement Hubbardton. That was before the British advance raiding parties struck two days before, and took some of the families prisoner while the others grabbed their children, threw some cheese, dried meat, and bread into a blanket, abandoned everything else, and disappeared into the woods, running for Massachusetts from whence they had come.

The farmer had told St. Clair, with Poor listening, that a force of raiding British, mixed with Tories and Indians, still remained at the Hubbardton settlement. The Americans were walking into what could be a trap.

St. Clair sat his horse in the humid heat, sweating, forcing his mind to work. Should he stop at Lacey's Camp to rest his men, who were nearing the breakdown point? If there were British and Indians ahead at Hubbardton, did they have scouts who had discovered the American column coming? With Fraser behind and a raiding party ahead, did he dare stop, and run the risk of letting his army be caught between the two forces?

Running on grit alone, he made his decision. He reined his horse around to face the leading officers. "We will not stop at Lacey's Camp. We march straight on through to Hubbardton. If we find the enemy there we will engage them. Pass the word."

Poor wiped the sweat from his eyes and asked, "Think the men can make it?"

"No choice. We can fight what might be ahead in Hubbardton, or we can fight what is behind if we have time to prepare. But we can't fight both if we stop and they come from both sides at once. Keep moving."

Poor nodded agreement and turned his lathered horse around.

The officers rode their sweat-flecked horses on either side of the column as they came into the Lacey's Camp clearing, pushing their men on, refusing to allow any of them to falter or break away from the column to rest. They trudged up the incline, through the notch on Sargent Hill, then down the slope to Sucker Creek. They slogged through the small stream, then up a gentle hill to a stone wall, and stepped over into a field cleared of all trees. Before them was a loose cluster of crude log houses with a scatter of outbuildings.

Hubbardton.

Nothing moved in the dead, sweltering heat. The doors and windows in half the houses stood partly open, cattle pens with the gate bars down and the cattle gone, chicken coops empty, pig and sheep pens deserted, doors to most root cellars thrown open. Cautiously St. Clair led the column into the center of the clearing, every man with his musket primed, ready. There was no sound, no call, no challenge, no shifting shadows in the surrounding trees.

St. Clair halted the column and turned to Poor. "Appears deserted. See anyone?

"No, sir. Whoever was here is gone."

St. Clair drew out his watch. "Five minutes before one o'clock. Order a rest until further notice. Get the men into shade. Find food for them if you can. Pass the word."

"Some men brought a few cattle from the fort, and picked up a few more on the way."

"Slaughter them for the men. Check the root cellars and houses for anything they can find to eat."

"Yes, sir. How long will we be here?"

"I won't know until we finish a scout to find out if the British raiders and the Indians are waiting out there in ambush. If they're not, I'll wait a while for the rear guard to catch up. If they are too long, we'll have to keep moving. Find a captain and ten men who are up to it and have them make a circle one mile out, then report back. In the meantime get pickets posted and tell them to keep sharp watch."

Wearily the men in St. Clair's command shot the cattle where the hair swirled in the forehead, dressed, skinned, and quartered them. With flies swarming, they laid the hides in the grass, hair down, built fires and gathered and sharpened sticks while others cut thick chunks of meat and piled them on the hides. Ravenous men speared them on the sticks, seared them over the fires, and sat down to eat them smoking, dripping blood and grease. They wiped their fingers and their beards on their shirtsleeves, drank tepid water from their canteens, and collapsed in the shade, asleep in seconds.

At twenty minutes past two o'clock, the captain led his patrol of ten sweaty, bone-weary continentals back to General Poor.

"Sir, we've made the circle, maybe a mile and a half out. Nothing out there except some pigs rooting in the creek and two milk cows and one local farmer, hiding in a cave. He said about five hundred British and Tories and Indians left yesterday, headed on south to Castle Town."

Poor nodded. "I'll tell General St. Clair. You men go back to your units. Should be some meat left from the beef we slaughtered. When you can, go find those milk cows and pigs and bring them in to slaughter for food."

"We'll do that, sir." The captain wiped his mouth. "Can't tell you how good that beef smells cooking."

Poor watched them leave, leg-weary, shirts sweated through, then turned to find St. Clair.

"General, the captain reported no British or Indians within more than a mile. They found a local farmer hiding. He said the bunch that were here left yesterday, headed east."

St. Clair nodded. "Then we'll wait here and let the men rest until Francis and the rear guard get here. If it gets too late we'll send the main body on and leave orders for them to catch up with us. Tell the men, and keep pickets out until then." He looked at his watch again. Two-forty P.M.

At ten minutes past three, St. Clair began to pace, nervous, apprehensive, glancing constantly to the west, down the road, searching for the first sign of the rear guard. At three-thirty he walked to where Poor sat in the shade, propped against a tree.

"We can't wait longer. We don't know how many British are coming, or who's leading them. If they catch us here they could hurt us. Get Colonel Warner and meet me over in that house as soon as you can." He pointed.

Ten minutes later, seated at the table in the abandoned home of the Selleck family, St. Clair leaned forward and gave his orders to Seth Warner, commander of the one hundred fifty Green Mountain boys from New Hampshire. "Colonel, we're risking too much if we remain here any longer. I'm going to take the main body and move on to Castle Town. You remain here with your command. When Colonel Francis arrives, give his men a little time to rest and eat. You know this area better than the others, so you take command of his men, and the New Hampshire Second Regiment under Colonel Hale. Leave here in time to come within a mile and a half of Castle Town before dark, and camp there tonight. I will be in Castle Town, and I need you between my command and the British, if they get that far. Tomorrow morning have your troops fed and marching not later than four o'clock A.M. I'll be waiting for you. From Castle Town, I will lead the entire force on west to Skenesborough. We will meet Long and his command and all the supplies and guns he transported in the bateaux on the lake. From there we sail on south, eventually to Albany. Am I clear?"

"Yes, sir."

"I repeat, leave here in time to camp one and one half miles outside Castle Town tonight. I'll expect you to be there, and in my camp tomorrow morning by six o'clock A.M. Long's depending on us."

"I understand."

At ten minutes before four o'clock, St. Clair rode out, leading the main body of his command south on the road to Castle Town.

At five minutes past four o'clock, Captain John Woolcott cautiously approached the clearing from the west end, leading the first of the rear guard in at the very moment the last of St. Clair's command was leaving the east end. Weary beyond his endurance, Woolcott led his men to one side and ordered a rest while the remainder of the rear guard stumbled into the campground. He slumped down in the shade of an oak tree, and within seconds his head tipped forward, and he was asleep.

Warner stood still to watch Francis's command stagger in. They came strung out, sweated, dragging their muskets, exhausted beyond talking, with no pretense of rank and file. Officers led their men to the nearest shade where they dropped to the ground and did not move. Warner counted three hundred—five hundred—and still they came until there were one thousand. Mixed among them were some sick and invalid, and at least fifty whose only impediment was sweating out the tortures of too much rum in the night. The last man in the column was Francis, mounted on a sweating horse that showed ridges of white lather every place leather touched him—bridle, saddle, and girth. Warner walked to him as Francis dismounted and stood still for a moment, waiting for his quivering legs to take his weight.

Warner came straight to the point. "How close are they?"

Francis pulled his sweat-stained tricorn from his head. His hair was plastered to his forehead, and the hatband marks were plain. "Several hours. Had a little shooting at first, but after we got under way it stopped."

"We left you with less than five hundred men. Where did you get over a thousand?"

Francis shook his head. "Stragglers. Sick. Invalids. Drunks. All the ones who couldn't keep up with their own units and fell back. We gathered them up as we came. Slowed us down, but what else could we do? Had to leave over one hundred as it was, too sick to go another step, and we didn't have time to make litters, and no men to carry them if we did." His eyes dropped for a moment, and he shook his head again. "Hated to leave them, but there was nothing else to do."

"Got any food for your men?"

"Not much. You got any?"

"We slaughtered some beef. Might be some left if they don't mind shanks and livers and brains. Maybe something's left in the root cellars. Settle your men as soon as you can and meet me in that house over there. Bring Colonel Hale."

With their men lying prostrate in the shade, Francis and Hale walked across the clearing to the Selleck home, pushed through the front door, waited for their eyes to adjust from the glare of the five o'clock sun, and then sat on plain, rough-cut pine chairs.

Warner spoke to both of them. "How much more of this can your men take without rest and food?"

Francis had his tricorn in his hand, wiping at the sweatband with the sleeve of his shirt. "Lucky we got this far. I doubt they can go two more miles without nourishment and sleep."

Hale pursed his lips for a moment. "If my men march two more miles without sleep and something to eat, they'll be worthless for forty-eight hours. If the British caught up with us right now, my command might make a fight of it until dark. But if they go further, I doubt they'd be able to resist a British attack."

Warner's face clouded. He leaned back in his chair, staring at his hands on the table while St. Clair's orders echoed in his brain. *March on today—camp one and one half miles outside Castle Town—must have you between the main body and the British—depending on you.*

He raised his eyes and for long moments studied the two officers before him. They were as good as the Continental army had to offer. Colonel Hale, New Hampshire, political leader, then captain in the New Hampshire militia, and the one who marched his regiment from

Cambridge to Lexington when the redcoats marched out the night of April 18, 1775, to quash the revolution before it began. Fought brilliantly at Bunker's Hill, then under Washington at Long Island and in New Jersey.

Ebenezer Francis from Beverly, Massachusetts. A captain in 1775, then promoted by the Continental Congress to lead one of Massachusetts' fifteen battalions. Three brothers who were officers, he had left his home and five children to go defend Fort Ticonderoga. Tough, fair, fearless, admired and loved by his troops, despite the fact he drove them hard when he had to. His regiment was held to be one of the best in St. Clair's command, under Francis's leadership.

Warner himself, from Connecticut. It was Warner who brilliantly covered the retreat from Breed's Hill. Lately moved to Bennington, he became a skilled woodsman and was the only one of the three who knew the country they were passing through.

Flies buzzed in the silence while Warner suffered the loneliness and hot tortures of command, weighing St. Clair's clear orders to march this body of men on, against what he considered the cold, harsh reality that in his opinion these men could not make such a march and remain ready to fight. The camp was in a strong position. Good water, roads both north and south if they had to run, hedges of trees surrounding the clearing for cover, cut by the families who had abandoned the settlement. They could fight here if they had to.

He narrowed his eyes as he placed the crucial question in the avoirdupois of his mind. Can the British arrive here before morning? He watched to see which side of the scales raised and which side lowered. In the small, hot kitchen of the deserted Selleck house, he reached his decision. He turned to Warner.

"We'll camp here for the night. Tell your men. Later, when they've rested and it's cooler we'll fell some trees for breastworks to defend the clearing if we're attacked."

In the black of night, British Brigadier General Simon Fraser stood outside his command tent, feet spread slightly, staring wide-eyed across

South Bay. Minutes earlier fire had erupted on the east face of Mt. Independence, with flames shooting a hundred feet in the air, driving sparks swirling upwards into the night. A few of the British command had bounded from their tents to stand in amazement, confounded by the sight of the clean, clear silhouettes of hundreds of Americans scrambling on the mountain side. Lower, at the docks, they could make out a dim muddle of men working with horses and oxen and wagons among growing heaps of kegs and crates and boxes. The firelight caught dark figures crossing the Great Bridge carrying baggage south to the bateaux waiting at the Mt. Independence docks.

Fraser palmed his watch from its pocket and turned the face toward the fire. Ten minutes past three A.M., July sixth. He turned on his heel and narrowly avoided colliding with his aide, Major Hugh Billingsley.

"Come with me, Major," he said, and the two strode quickly back to his command tent. Hurriedly Fraser wrote a message, folded and sealed it, and thrust it to Billingsley. "Take that to General Burgoyne immediately."

"Yes, sir. May I ask, sir, what the rebels are doing over there?"

Fraser's forehead wrinkled in puzzlement. "I don't know. It has all the appearance of a general evacuation. Maybe they saw our guns on top of Mount Defiance and realized they can't hold Fort Ti. Or maybe it's an elaborate hoax to draw us into an ambush, or at least get us within range of their grapeshot. Until I know, I'm going to be cautious. The moment you've delivered that message to General Burgoyne, find Lieutenant Twiss and bring him here. I'll have the regimental colors hoisted as the gathering point. I'm taking two companies from my command over there to look."

Later, with Twiss and Billingsley beside him, Fraser led his picked men to Fort Ticonderoga, lying dark, silent, eerie in the night. He paused to order a major and one hundred men to post themselves at the fort while he continued on. He and his men halted as they came in sight of the Great Bridge. With the wind howling at their backs, they studied the structure, rising and falling on the huge swells. In the first traces of light they saw the bridge was vacant and intact. Quickly Fraser had his men

lay new planks where some of the old ones had been torn up by the fleeing rebels. They all paused at the sight of a young lieutenant working his
way to meet them at the halfway point on the bridge.

"Sir, Captain Ottaman and his company have gone on ahead, chasing
the rebels. He sent me with a message for you."

Fraser steadied himself on the pitching bridge. "What's the message?"

"The rebels have abandoned everything, sir. Fort Ti, Mount
Independence, everything."

Fraser considered, then said, "Take your message on to General
Burgoyne."

He watched the young officer pass on, then turned to Billingsley.
"Send ten men to catch Captain Ottaman and tell him to return to this
command. I don't want him engaging the rebels before I'm ready."

"Yes, sir." Billingsley turned, spat orders, and two minutes later
Fraser watched an eager captain lead ten men forward to disappear in the
darkness.

Fraser slowed and stopped as he cleared the bridge and walked
among the stacks of crates and boxes and kegs strewn all over the ground
and on the docks at the foot of Mt. Independence. Incredulous, he recognized the signs. The Americans had been panic-stricken. Besides abandoning more than a hundred tons of supplies, dozens of cannon, and a
mountain of gunpowder ready to be blown up, they had left clothing,
razors, combs, letters from home—countless personal things—thrown
down at random. Thousands of dollars in Continental paper currency
blew in the wind, tumbling along the ground to catch on broken cases
and the spokes of wagon wheels.

With the approaching sun lighting the underside of low eastern
clouds, his men could not resist the temptation. Quickly they scattered,
searching through the heaps of abandoned things for money, souvenirs,
anything of value. Infuriated, Fraser strode among them, shouting
orders, threatening, commanding his officers to take control of their men
on pain of courts-martial if they failed.

With his command once again under control, he ordered one

company to mount their bayonets and proceed up Mt. Defiance to the plateau where General de Fermoy and his command had been. If any rebels remained, destroy or capture them, raise the British Union Jack on the American flagpole, and remain there. He turned to the nearest officer.

"Get back to General Burgoyne. Tell him the rebels are in full retreat east. I'm going to follow them as long as it seems prudent to do so." Then he turned to Billingsley. "Find me a horse."

The officer left at a trot in one direction while Billingsley sprinted the other. Fraser paused for a time, setting his thoughts in order, making instant decisions while a feeling of wild exuberance rose in his breast. *We succeeded! St. Clair abandoned everything. He's running. If we catch him before he has time to set up breastworks and defenses we've got him. When we meet General Howe and Colonel St. Leger in Albany, we can move on George Washington in force. We could end the revolution before fall!*

He turned to his officers, and they caught the excited urgency in his shouted orders. "Form ranks immediately. We march in five minutes to catch the rebels."

The officers wiped at mouths and eyes covered with dust from the hot wind that was sucking the moisture out of the men. "Sir, may the men fill their canteens first? Perhaps get some rations?"

Fraser's answer was blunt. "No time. We've got to catch the rebels before they can throw up breastworks. We leave in five minutes."

The red-coated regulars set their jaws in determination and fell into their ranks. Billingsley led a black gelding to Fraser, who mounted and walked the horse to the place where the first tree stumps cluttered the entrance to the narrow trail to Hubbardton and Castle Town. He paused to peer ahead for any signs of ambush, then turned the horse and shouted, "Forward. Follow me. Keep a sharp eye for an ambush."

As the march continued, the wind died, and the narrow trail became a stifling oven. The sun turned the woolen uniforms into instruments of torture. When the trail narrowed, the column reformed into single file. Sweating men clutched their muskets at the ready, watching the felled trees and stacks of cut branches on both sides of the trail for the first movement that would tell of a rebel ambush. Mosquitoes swarmed in clouds, and insects never seen before by British soldiers came buzzing, stinging. Tiny brulies worked into their sleeves and the legs of their breeches, itching, biting. Strong men shuddered as rattlesnakes and copperheads slithered through the grass, across the trail, to coil defensively, waiting for the first unwary regular to come within striking distance. They came to rebels left behind, seated in the trail, heads down, sick, invalid, or sweating out too much alcohol, and they passed them by, left them for those who were to come behind.

Keep moving—don't stop—share canteens—chew salt beef if you have it—watch that rattler—keep your musket up—watch sharp for ambush—keep moving—keep moving—forget the sun—how far have we come?—it doesn't matter how far we've come, we keep moving until the general says stop—watch the tree roots—keep moving—I'm having sunstroke—pour water over your head and keep moving—did you hear that?— hear what?—Captain Ottaman came back with his men—says there's a clearing up ahead—some rebels there sick—the general says we stop there in five minutes—blessed stop—blessed shade.

In a small clearing with a stream meandering through, Fraser turned his lathered horse and raised his hand to the officers. "Stop the men here. Let them fill their canteens and rest for twenty minutes. Get them into some shade. We've covered nine miles, and I think we're coming up on the rebels fast. The men'll need rest if we go into battle."

Fraser called for Ottaman. "You said there are some rebels here?"

Ottaman pointed to the far side of the clearing. "There, sir. Under those trees. Something's wrong with them, but I got your orders to return before I got close enough to find out what it is."

One hundred forty yards across the clearing, twenty rebels lay in the grass or sat on logs in the shade of two giant oak trees. They were hunched forward, heads down, not knowing nor caring that the British were coming through, just one hundred forty yards distant.

Fraser raised a hand. "Hold your fire. Something's not right."

Cautiously he looked about, waiting for sound or movement of an ambush that never came. He tapped spur to his horse and moved forward, raising it to a gentle lope as he came into the huddled Americans.

They raised their heads, then lowered them again, indifferent to his approach.

He reined in facing them. "Who are you?"

A bearded man with a pasty white face spoke without raising his head. "We was with the Massachusetts militia, but not no more."

"Where are your weapons?"

"Militia took 'em."

"Where are they?"

The man raised tortured eyes and jabbed a thumb over his shoulder, but said nothing.

"What's wrong with you?"

The man only shook his head. None of the others said a word.

A laugh welled out of Fraser's chest. "You're drunk! That, or getting over being drunk. No wonder they left you. I'm General Fraser, with the army of General John Burgoyne. You are now our prisoners. Stay right where you are. A force is coming up the trail to take you into custody. If you try to run we'll send Indians after you with orders to kill and scalp."

The man only shook his head while he fought the demons inside his throbbing skull.

Fraser loped his horse back to his men, still chuckling. His story brought guffaws from those around him, while he glanced about to be certain his men were getting water and shade. Some of them were in the stream up to their knees, bowed forward, soaking their uniforms, splashing water in their faces, and pouring it over their heads. Fraser turned to his aide, Billingsley.

"Did you happen to bring quill and paper?"

"Of course, sir."

Pausing only to frame his thoughts, Fraser struck off a message to Burgoyne: "Have occupied Fort Ticonderoga and Mt. Independence. Am pursuing the retreating rebels and believe I am close behind them. Will continue pursuit and engage any of them I encounter. Send remainder of my command to catch up with me, earliest, with other reinforcements if available. Send British troops if possible."

He sealed the report and handed it to Billingsley. "When we march out, see to it Captain Campbell delivers that to General Burgoyne. Let him rest until then."

★ ★ ★ ★ ★

General Burgoyne buttoned his tunic as he quickly moved from his command tent into the clearing, eyes wide at what appeared to be Mt. Independence on fire. He saw the silhouetted rebel army in a desperate scramble as he slowed, then stopped. He turned to Fort Ticonderoga, then down to the docks, then across South Bay to the landing and the docks at the foot of Mt. Independence. For five full seconds his mind refused the only conclusion he could reach, and then the reality flooded through him like fire in his veins.

They saw the guns on Mt. Defiance! They're abandoning everything! We've got them! We've got them!

He spun on his heel and shouted to his aide, "Get generals Phillips and Fraser to my command tent!"

Ten minutes later, properly dressed in full uniform, chin thrust up and forward, General William Phillips stood rigidly at attention before Burgoyne's desk.

Burgoyne spoke to his aide. "General Fraser?"

"I could not find him, sir. He's——"

At that instant the picket at Burgoyne's tent flap interrupted. "Sir, there's an officer from General Fraser. Says he has an urgent message."

Burgoyne stood. "Send him in."

The breathless lieutenant came to rigid attention, perspiring from his run. "Sir, General Fraser sends his compliments. Fort Ti appears to be abandoned. He has taken part of his command across the Great Bridge. He sent me to tell you he intends pursuing the rebels as long as it seems prudent."

For a moment Burgoyne's forehead creased in concern. "Thank you. You're dismissed." His eyes glowed, mind leaping forward making decisions to complete his conquest of the rebels, intoxicated with the realization Fort Ticonderoga had been delivered to him without the loss of a single British soldier in an all-out attack. It ran through his brain like a chant, *We've got them, we've got them!* He seized a scrolled map and with trembling hands anchored it on his worktable with small leather pouches of sand, then motioned General Phillips to come to the table. He moved his finger on the map as he spoke.

"General, Fort Ti is ours. The rebels have abandoned it and all their defenses on Mount Independence—everything—and they're running." He tapped the Mt. Independence docks and landing. "They had about two hundred bateaux anchored here, and they're gone. That isn't enough to transport their whole force, so they've divided into two groups. One group is in the bateaux with but one place to go—Skenesborough—where they have more bateaux." He tapped the map. "The other group is apparently headed east towards Hubbardton, here." He tapped the map again. "General Fraser is in pursuit of that group right now."

He paused, his mind working furiously. "If I'm right, then it's nearly certain the group headed for Hubbardton intends turning back west at some point, to arrive at Skenesborough to meet group one. The rebels have perhaps two or three hundred more empty bateaux anchored there. Group one will load into the extra bateaux and the entire force will move on south to either Fort George, here at the southern tip of the lake, or Fort Edward, here, just a short march further south."

He raised his eyes to Phillips. "What are your thoughts?"

Prim, proper, Phillips leaned stiffly forward, quickly appraising Burgoyne's analysis. "The good sense of it is obvious. I concur."

Burgoyne thumped the table with his fist. "Then I propose the following: I will order our fleet to move south, here, through the narrows, past the Great Bridge, where you and I and most of our force will board our ships and bateaux, headed south to Skenesborough." He shifted his finger. "Fraser, over here, will likely need reinforcements. I'll send General von Riedesel with his command, along with the men in General Breymann's command, to support Fraser. When he joins Fraser, von Riedesel will take command of the entire force since he will be the ranking officer. I doubt Fraser will appreciate that, but he does understand military protocol. Von Riedesel will take over."

He moved his hand back to Mt. Independence. "The Sixty-second

Regiment will occupy and hold Mount Independence, and the Prinz Friedrich troops will occupy and hold Fort Ticonderoga." He paused for five seconds to be certain he had covered all necessary elements of the plan. Satisfied, struggling to contain his wild excitement, he again spoke to Phillips.

"Sick and wounded men can't march, so it's certain St. Clair put most of them in the bateaux, along with his money chest and records, and maybe some guns. If I'm right, those bateaux and everyone and everything on board are ours for the taking. If we get to Skenesborough before that second bunch of rebels arrive from their overland march, we can lay an ambush for the group as they come in. That could be the blow that brings down the entire rebel army. As of this moment, fate has probably delivered to us the key to ending this war. We have no time to waste."

Phillips narrowed shrewd eyes. "Possibly. However, there are a few things. If you leave the Sixty-second Regiment and the Prinz Friedrich company to occupy Mount Independence and the fort, you will have about a thousand fewer men for combat when you move south." Phillips stopped and fixed Burgoyne with a stiff stare.

"I anticipated that. I will draft a letter to General Carleton in Quebec requesting twelve hundred troops to relieve our men. They can join us as soon as Carleton sends the replacements."

"And if Carleton refuses?"

Burgoyne shook his head. "He won't. With the entire expedition depending on those replacements, he won't refuse."

Phillips remained cool. "How do you plan to get past the Great Bridge, built as it is?"

"Cannon. Blast it open, enough for our fleet to pass through. The *Thunderer* has the guns to do it."

"Destroy it? It might be very useful in the future."

"If we need it later, we'll repair it. We don't have time now for our engineers to dismantle enough of it to let our ships through."

Phillips remained stoic. "Until we have victory in our hands, it behooves us to move cautiously. Whatever their shortcomings, these rebels fight well in the woods, and our soldiers do not, and they seem to have a peculiar ability to produce surprises when forced into a corner. I am remembering Trenton, and Princeton."

Burgoyne settled down. "Well said. Do you agree with the plan I have outlined?"

"It appears to be complete, and feasible. Under present circumstances, yes, I do."

"Good. I will issue written orders to all officers at once. I recommend you get your luggage packed immediately. We leave here the moment we can."

★ ★ ★ ★ ★

Colonel Ebenezer Francis drained the last of the tepid coffee from his cup, then turned to his close friend and fellow officer, Captain Moses Greenleaf. "Going to be another hot one."

Greenleaf glanced eastward where the first arc of the rising sun cut into the clear, blue sky. Already the dead air was gathering heat. Sucker Creek ran along the west side of the campsite, with trees lining the high grass in the clearing. He nodded his head and placed his cup on the log they shared next to the small fire on which they had cooked strips of sowbelly and boiled water for their chocolate.

Francis stood and drew out his watch. Six-fifty A.M. He glanced down at Greenleaf and grunted a choppy laugh. "It's ten minutes before seven, but I can't remember what day it is."

Greenleaf smiled as he pondered. "Must be Monday. July seventh, I think. Yes, July seventh."

"I have to go meet Warner at seven. Would you parade the men and get them ready to march? I'm nervous about being here too long."

Greenleaf looked west, the direction from which the British would be coming. "So am I. Things have been too quiet. You go ahead. I'll get the men going." He rose to his feet and brushed at the seat of his breeches while Francis walked across the clearing to the Selleck house, where Warner was waiting. The door was open, and Francis walked in.

Warner pointed. "Take a seat."

With the table between them, Warner leaned forward on his elbows. "I'm uneasy about staying here longer. Are your men able to march in the next thirty minutes?"

Francis nodded. "Greenleaf's parading them right now. I'm nervous, too. So's Greenleaf."

"I'll give orders—"

The sounds of an incoming horse pounding across the clearing brought both men to their feet, and they strode quickly out the door, blinking in the brilliant sunlight. A sweating man pulled a lathered mare to a halt and remained in the saddle. He was breathless from a hard ride, agitated, unable to remain still. The mare was throwing her head, fighting the bit.

Francis and Warner both stood in silence, waiting, with a rising premonition that something was violently wrong.

"Sir," the man blurted before Warner could speak, "General St. Clair sent me back to tell you. He expected you to be just west of Castle Town, but you weren't there. He wanted you to help drive out the British, but he couldn't find you, so he sent me."

Warner felt the cut, the sting. St. Clair had been clear in his orders, and Warner had exercised his own judgment in disobeying them. He dropped his face for a moment as the messenger continued.

"So General St. Clair cleared the British out of Castle Town with his own men. There were only fifty of them, not five hundred as reported." He stopped long enough to arrange the remainder of his words, which he spoke slowly so they could not be misunderstood. "He also ordered me to tell you that General Burgoyne blasted his way through the Great Bridge. The British fleet has sailed up South Bay to Skenesborough, and they have captured all our bateaux, all our baggage, and taken General Long and his entire command prisoner."

Both Warner and Francis gaped while the man continued.

"With the British in control of Skenesborough, and Long captured, the general has changed the plan. He now orders you to follow him to Rutland. From there he'll work out a plan to move south, then back west, and meet General Schuyler on the Hudson, somewhere south of Skenesborough, then move on down the river, probably to Fort Edward."

The man paused and dropped his eyes for a moment to be certain he had said it all, and said it correctly. Then he raised his eyes back to Warner, waiting.

Warner slowly wiped his hand across his mouth, face drawn down as he labored to judge how serious the consequences were of his failure to follow St. Clair's orders, and the shock of having lost Skenesborough, General Long, and the entire American fleet of bateaux. He raised his face. "Anything else?"

"No, sir."

Instantly Francis turned to Warner, who lived in the area. "Where's Rutland?"

"Southeast of here. West of Castle Town. Almost nothing there. My command is ready to march. I'll leave now."

Francis said, "Head down the Castle Town road for a few miles, then turn east. I'll bring the rest of the men and catch you, or send a guide." He turned back to the messenger. "Water and rest that horse for a few minutes, then go back to St. Clair. Tell him we're coming as fast as we can."

"Yes, sir."

Francis turned on his heel and strode through the high grass and the clouds of mosquitoes to his own command and there found Greenleaf.

"We're marching for Rutland. I'll explain later. Get the men moving."

Greenleaf recoiled for a moment, then turned to his command, already assembled in rank and file. "We're marching," he called. "Move. Move."

Startled, concerned, feeling the beginnings of fear, the officers shouted the column into motion, moving toward the Castle Town road. The men had not gone fifteen feet when a high, shrill voice behind them came piercing the morning air.

"Redcoats! Behind us."

For a split second every man in the American camp froze where he stood, staring west at the red-coated regulars dodging through the trees, beginning to circle the clearing. Then bedlam seized them, except for the command of Francis. Without breaking step, Colonel Francis sang out his orders.

"Column, by the right flank, *march!*"

Instantly the entire column turned to their right, marching directly at the British.

"Form a battle line, *march!*"

The column broke from ranks into a long battle line, muskets primed.

Then Francis gave the order, "Forward, at double time, *march!*"

A battle cry surged from the rebels as they broke into a run straight into the face of the British, a scant forty yards distant. The red-coated regulars were the leading edge of the British regiment under the command of Major Alexander Lindsay, Sixth Earl of Balcarres. Dressed in full uniform, with knapsack, cartridge box, canteen, hatchet, and a ten-pound Brown Bess musket, they had just climbed a strong incline, worked their way through a saddle on the mountainside and found themselves winded, sweating, on the western fringes of the Selleck field at the Hubbardton clearing, facing a stone wall and felled trees and breastworks. They had seen the Americans at the moment the Americans saw them.

They took one look at the long line of screaming Americans and turned on their heels, sprinting back, over the lip of the incline, plunging back down the hill to join the full regiment behind.

Francis stopped his men just short of the incline. "Take cover behind that low stone wall and the trees and breastworks. Get ready. When the leaders come over that lip, give them twenty feet, and then fire at will!" he shouted.

The leading ranks of the British column broke over the crest of the hill onto the flat and too late realized they were staring down the barrels of what seemed an endless wall of rebel muskets. Those behind plowed into the leaders, pushing them forward, and they had gone less than ten feet when the thunder of the American muskets echoed for miles. White smoke rose in a cloud while the Americans each grabbed another cartridge, ripped out the end with their teeth, dumped the powder down the barrel, followed by the paper and the huge lead ball, jammed it home with their hickory ramrods, and leveled their muskets for the next volley.

All up and down the line, British officers and regulars staggered backward and toppled, dead, wounded, writhing, moaning in pain. The second rank hurtled over them, muskets and bayonets at the ready, charging the breastworks and the stone wall behind which the Americans were crouched.

The second American volley erupted, and great gaps and holes appeared in the British line as officers and regulars alike tumbled, finished. The third rank of redcoats saw the dead and dying in front of them, and the great cloud of white gun smoke covering the American lines, and they broke. They turned and ran, back against the ranks behind them, headlong, not caring, wanting only to be away from the slaughter up on the Hubbardton flats.

As the panic-stricken regulars came storming down the slope, General Fraser was coming up, for the first time seized with the fear he had blundered into something far too big for his command to handle. He seized a retreating officer by both shoulders and bellowed, "How many Americans up there? How many!"

The wild-eyed man stared at him for a moment before he recognized him. "Two thousand. Maybe more." The man wrenched free and was gone.

At that moment a panting, sweating officer approached Fraser. "Sir, the Twenty-fourth Foot has run into heavy opposition and are unable to move forward."

Fraser made an instant appraisal of his position. His own command was stalled in its tracks, stopped by Colonel Francis's men. They had stopped his left flank, and at the moment it was in critical danger of folding. To his right, the Twenty-fourth Infantry had slammed into Seth Warner's command, and had been stopped dead. For one moment Fraser entertained the thought of a general retreat, then stiffened in his resolve. He turned, searching for Major John Acland.

"Major, take your grenadiers and two companies of Balcarres' light troops. Move out to our right and go to the Castle Town road. Engage and stop any rebel troops moving south on that road. It is imperative. You must succeed. Move out now!"

"Yes, sir!"

He turned to Billingsley. "Find the first mounted officer you can and send him back to find General von Riedesel. Tell him we're under heavy engagement and that he's to get his men here as fast as they can come. Critically urgent."

"Yes, sir!"

Before the eyes of the officers on both sides, the battle disintegrated into half a dozen tangled fronts, each independent, disassociated from the others, following no pattern, no plan. Then, slowly, on its own terms, the sprawling battle began to take a shape of its own. The Americans formed up in a crescent-shaped line eight hundred yards long, north to south, straddling the road coming from Mt. Independence to the west, and dug in, Warner and Hale on the ends, Francis in the middle. With their long Pennsylvania rifles, the rebels had thrown back Fraser's light infantry and were advancing slowly, moving among the rocks and trees, ever closer to flanking Fraser's left, and coming in behind him. Fraser saw the danger but had no men to order into the gap.

At the other end of the long line, the redcoats under Major Acland had slung their muskets and battled their way sweating up a steep incline to high ground. Dirty, panting, they began to move down the slope that would carry them into the left flank of Warner's command. Warner saw them too late. Instantly he ordered his men to draw back and take up a position behind a log fence that bordered Pittsford Mountain and had a large, open field before it. To reach the rebels, the British would have to cross a hundred yards of open ground, with rebels at the far end, firing from behind the cover of logs.

Six miles south, General St. Clair paused and turned his head to listen to the faint, unmistakable staccato sound of muskets in the far distance. He knew only one thing. Somehow a battle had developed, and his command was engaged. He turned to Dunn and Livingston, his two aides.

"Ride to Ransomvale and tell Captain Bellows to march his militia immediately to Hubbardton to support Francis and Warner. Don't spare your horses."

Both men nodded, spun their horses, and had them at stampede gait in three jumps. St. Clair listened to the steady sound of the muskets for a time, his fears rising, then turned back to his own command. They had to move on.

Within minutes the two aides stood in the stirrups of their galloping horses, startled at what lay ahead. Captain Bellows and his entire militia command were coming toward them, away from Hubbardton, on the Castle Town road. The two majors pulled their horses to a stop, facing Bellows.

"Captain, General St. Clair sends orders. You are to turn around and return to Hubbardton. Your command will support colonels Francis and Warner, who have engaged a superior British force and are in desperate need of reinforcements."

Bellows shrugged, then turned to his men. "You will stop where you are, and turn about. We are under orders to return to Hubbardton and support the Americans there who are under British attack."

Not one man turned. Three seconds later the leaders stepped out marching, continuing due south, away from the fighting. In an instant the entire column was marching with them.

Bellows shouted, "Halt and turn around or you will all be shot."

Not a single man swerved or broke step.

Dunn and Livingston sat their horses, absolutely dumbstruck. Never had they seen an entire command simply ignore orders from a general, and never had they known Americans to so coldly and blatantly refuse to help their comrades-in-arms under attack.

Bellows shook his head. "I don't know what to do. A panic has locked their minds. It's as though they don't hear."

Dunn glanced at Livingston, who shook his head, and without a word the two aides galloped further, looking for any military unit,

Continental or militia, whom they might persuade to go to the sound of the guns.

★ ★ ★ ★ ★

With gunfire blasting continuously all around him, Colonel Francis rallied his men. "Come on, boys, we can turn their left, and once we get in behind them their line will break. They'll be ours. Follow me!"

Francis raised his saber and started forward, with his entire command right behind him, firing, reloading while they walked, firing again. Francis moved among them, shouting encouragement, heedless of the danger, leading his men on against the British. The red-coated regulars slowly began to pull back, unable to withstand the deadly rifle fire that was knocking their officers down all around them. Fraser saw it and he felt the clutch of fear in his chest as he realized that if his left folded, the Americans would be in behind the British lines. Should that occur, his command had little hope of survival. He would lose them all, either killed, or captured, and he with them. He stood stock-still, frantically racking his brain for a way out, but there was none.

Then, from the west, above the unceasing blasting of the muskets, came the faint, distant sound of a bugle floating on the midmorning air. Officers on both sides turned their heads west to stare in puzzlement, disbelief. Seconds passed, and with the piercing bugle came the unmistakable beat of snare drums, and then the high, sharp trill of fifes. Seconds became a minute, and the sound grew stronger until every man in the battle could make out the melody.

It was "The Grenadier's March." Major General Friedrich von Riedesel's column of Germans was coming in on the road from Mt. Independence, his brass band blasting out the marching tune with all their strength to give heart to the British forces who at the moment thought they had lost it all. With swords drawn, Captain von Geyso led his green-coated jaegers, with their brown leather breeches, in a frontal attack against the Americans, while his German riflemen kept up a hot, deadly fire. To his right, Captain Maximilian Christoph Ludwig von

Schottelius drove in with his blue-coated grenadiers, the sun glinting off the brass facings of their tall hats.

At that moment, victory was snatched from the hands of the Americans. Hale's New Hampshiremen could not hold against the fresh reinforcements, who were swarming in from both sides. Hale shouted orders, and his regiment began to fall back, firing as they went, trying to avoid a rout. Warner realized his command was about to be engulfed and quickly ordered his men back across Hubbardton Brook to a hedgerow where they might make a fight of it. Then Warner saw the danger. Past the hedgerow, the only thing left was Pittsford Mountain, steep and rocky. In an instant the men felt panic rise in their throats when they realized that if their only way out was up Pittsford Mountain, few of them would survive the steep climb, during which they would be clear, sitting targets for the German rifles.

Francis was the first to get his command across the open field to Hubbardton Brook, then to the hedgerow, and to commence firing on the oncoming redcoats and Germans. As the other Americans came sprinting in, the smoke became so thick that the rebels could not see the enemy. The only thing they could make out was the muzzle flashes of the British and German rifles and muskets as they continued their charge against the waiting Americans.

In the midst of it Francis realized some of the American gunfire was hitting incoming Americans, and suddenly he stood and shouted to his troops.

"Hold your fire! Hold your fire! We're hitting our own men! Wait until you can see—"

It was the last command given by Colonel Ebenezer Francis. A German bullet punched into his chest, and he crumpled, dead when he hit the ground.

For a moment the Americans stared, unable to accept his death. It was Francis who had led them through it all. They had survived on his courage, his bravery, his brilliance under fire. It had not occurred to them he could be killed. They stood in shock for a moment, and then they broke into a run in every direction, scrambling through the rocks and brush and woods, many of them trying to scale the steep hillside of Pittsford Mountain while the Germans fired at them.

The Battle of Hubbardton was over.

Slowly the Germans and British came forward to where Francis lay. In silent respect, they looked down at the man whose courage and cool leadership had nearly defeated them. They looked at him, and memorized the lines of his face, then backed away to let others take their place.

Some time later, British officers gathered to take the letters and papers from Colonel Francis's pockets and read them. Captain John Shrimpton of the Sixty-second Regiment was unfolding the documents when suddenly those nearest heard a whack and a grunt, and he went down backward, moaning, "I'm wounded badly." Then they heard the crack of a distant American rifle. All heads turned instantly to the face of the mountain. From a lone tree, part way up, they saw a trace of drifting gun smoke.

An hour later a squad of men returned to report. "We found no one. Whoever it was escaped."

The British and Germans grimly nodded in understanding. An unknown American marksman had reminded them that the loss of Colonel Ebenezer Francis would not be forgotten.

General Fraser held no illusions. He knew that his command had been saved only by the last second arrival of General von Riedesel and his Germans. Had they been one half hour later in arriving . . .

Riedesel approached Fraser and spoke in his limited English. His German accent was strong. "General Burgoyne has ordered me to assume command of all forces here."

For a moment Fraser struggled to control the instant flare of anger. But then responded, "Yes, sir."

Riedesel nodded. "Thank you." He raised his eyes to look about. Dead and wounded men, British, German, and American, were strung out from the west end of the Hubbardton clearing, past the creek, past the Castle Town road, clear to Mount Pittsford. Their moaning and crying out in pain was constant. For a moment a sense of deep sadness crossed von Riedesel's face before he spoke.

"Let us attend the casualties."

The day wore on while the living looked after the dead and the dying. Somber and silent men dug shallow graves and lowered bodies wrapped in their blankets into them, then covered them with the rich black soil. Others went to the sounds of the wounded, carrying water, bandaging when they could, carrying them to the Hubbardton cabins for amputation of limbs too shattered to mend.

They stopped for their evening meal, then returned to their grisly work until darkness forced them to stop. They sat around campfires, silent, trying not to hear the moans and cries and pleading of the wounded men still in the forest. With the rising of the moon in the southwest came snuffling sounds in the woods, and the men reached for their muskets, not knowing what was lurking in the blackness. Then they saw the yellow eyes reflecting firelight as they moved among the trees, and they knew.

A thin, eagle-faced, veteran corporal quietly said, "Wolves."

They came down from the mountains in packs, working through the timber, feasting on the dead and the dying, clawing at the graves.

John Adams reached to stifle a yawn, then stretched to ease muscles too long in one position. He had spent the morning at his desk in the chambers of the Continental Congress in heated, vituperative debate with all other representatives of the thirteen states. He could not immediately remember passions or tempers running so violently, so high, for three hours on a single issue. They had recessed for lunch, but few men had left the square, austere room, stifling in the sweltering July heat. Rather, they had gathered in small cliques and bunches while they exclaimed and gestured, and the debate went on.

Abandon Fort Ticonderoga? Preposterous! Unthinkable! What general? St. Clair? Impossible. Surely not Arthur St. Clair. Treason! When will his court-martial be heard? When will he be hanged? Who else needs a taste of good Yankee rope?

A page circulated among the men, laying copies of the newspaper, the *Massachusetts Spy*, printed in Worcester, on each desk. On the front page was an edited copy of a letter written by General St. Clair to Governor Bowdoin of Massachusetts, wherein St. Clair had taken great pains to truthfully explain his reasons for abandoning Fort Ti. It was to save the army to fight another day, in a battle they could win. It was not known if Governor Bowdoin had submitted the letter to the newspaper by accident, or on purpose, or whether it was purloined by an unethical, politicized reporter. It was only known that St. Clair's letter was published, and beside it, a lengthy, unsigned editorial that hacked St. Clair's explanations, and his reputation, and his life, to shreds.

The unnamed editor *KNEW* that St. Clair had at least four thousand healthy, able-bodied soldiers ready and anxious to defend the fort and liberty; the British had scarcely six thousand men. St. Clair had only to ask for more men if he believed his command was too small; there were ample supplies and gunpowder within the walls of the fort to sustain a lengthy defense if necessary. St. Clair's account of events *had* to be mistaken; and if not mistaken, then deliberate inaccuracies.

Adams read the letter, then the editorial. A familiar hand dropped a second newspaper over his shoulder, and without looking back, Adams picked up a copy of the *Pennsylvania Evening Post*. On the front page was the text of a letter written by a soldier under St. Clair's command at the fort, and Adams quickly scanned it.

"Had we stayed at Ticonderoga, we very certainly would have been taken, and then no troops could have stood between the enemy and the country. Now we are gathering strength and re-collecting ourselves."

Adams swung around to face Enoch Trabert, a reporter for the *Post*. "Is this your opinion on the subject? St. Clair did the right thing?"

Trabert shrugged and gestured to the article. "Opinions are for you congressmen and the generals. I only report them. That soldier was there, and he saw it the same as Alexander Scammel. Scammel's a Continental officer who was there, too."

Adams shook his head emphatically. He had informed himself of the facts. He had thought it through. He had reached his conclusion. And with typical Adams finality, he was ready to announce to the world the only right and correct view that could be taken of the humiliating, embarrassing national scandal that had erupted with the abandonment of Fort Ti. He locked eyes with Trabert and pronounced the Adams verdict.

"Schuyler and St. Clair. Two of a kind. Motivated only by self-interest and self-promotion. Incompetents who have arrived at their present stations in life by politicking, manipulation, and carefully cultivated illusion. Without substance, without a single thought beyond their own lust for power, wealth, and status. Well, we will soon enough see to them."

Trabert opened his mouth to reply, thought better of it, turned on his heel, and moved on. He had long since learned that nothing was quite so absolute and unchangeable as the Bible, and a John Adams opinion, and all too often the Adams opinion was the more weighty of the two.

Adams pushed the newspapers aside and reached for his inkwell and quill. The expression on his face, very nearly of disdain and contempt, softened as he began a brief letter to his wife, Abigail, to whom he wrote whenever occasion permitted.

> My Dearest Friend:
>
> You are undoubtedly privy to the treasonous developments regarding the abandonment of Fort Ticonderoga to the British in the past several days. Debate rages in these hallowed halls, the general tenor of which is that both generals Schuyler and St. Clair, those responsible for the scandal, should be tried for treason.
>
> I have reached my own simple and very effective conclusion. We shall never be able to defend a post until we shoot a general.

Adams paused to read what he had written. He smiled broadly, dipped his quill in the ink, and continued his letter to his beloved Abigail.

Notes

Unless otherwise indicated, the following is taken from Ketchum, *Saratoga*, on the pages identified.

It must be understood that St. Clair, and most military men, knew "that a retreat, with an inferior army, from before a superior one, is perhaps the most delicate and dangerous undertaking in the whole circle of military operations, and that it will never be effected without prudence, fortitude, and secrecy."

It must be further understood that St. Clair knew well the price he was going to pay for his decision to save the men and sacrifice the fort. Udney Hay, his acting deputy quartermaster, asked St. Clair if he had received orders from General Schuyler to abandon the fort, and St. Clair instantly knew Hay was really essentially challenging St. Clair's decision. St. Clair's response included his certainty that if he defended the fort, "he would save his character and lose the army," and on the other hand, if he retreated, "he would save the army and lose his character." He fully expected to be court-martialed over his decision.

When the Americans marched out, they left hundreds of tons of supplies on the docks of Mt. Independence, including precious gunpowder and money. Men assigned to blow up the gunpowder failed to do so, and the British got it.

The road to Hubbardton, and Castle Town beyond, was a narrow, winding trail cut through the thick forest, with tree stumps in the path and piles of slash on both sides so high the soldiers could not see over the top. The untrained militia were so angered at not being allowed to defend the fort, and by the rigors of the road, they began to desert in great numbers. American General Ebenezer Francis, with his rear guard of only four hundred fifty men, began picking up those who had become exhausted in the column ahead, and soon had one thousand men in his command. British General Simon Fraser, on his own initiative, had decided to pursue them immediately, and was but three or four miles behind.

St. Clair intended halting his men for a rest at Lacey's Camp above the swampy northern end of Lake Bomoseen, about midway between Mt. Independence and Castle Town, however, a local inhabitant appeared to warn them that British and Indians were in that area. Consequently St. Clair led his men past Lacey's Camp, across Sargent Hill and Sucker Creek, up a hill, onto the plateau where Hubbardton was built in a clearing. Hubbardton was settled in 1774 on a grant of land owned by Thomas Hubbard, and now had nine families there, all of whom had abandoned the village at the onset of hostilities.

St. Clair remained for several hours at Hubbardton, waiting for Colonel Francis's rear guard to arrive, but they did not. St. Clair ordered Seth Warner to remain with his force at Hubbardton until Colonel Francis arrived, whereupon Seth Warner was to take command of Francis's men and move the entire group on toward Castle Town and stop one and one-half miles short of the village to act as a buffer in the event the British caught up.

When Francis and his men arrived, they were so exhausted that Warner and his officers decided they could not move farther and ordered an overnight rest. In short, Warner decided to disobey St. Clair's orders to move them on to their assigned place, one and one-half miles short of Castle Town.

The following morning, while Warner's command was getting breakfast, Simon Fraser's British regulars caught them. The Battle of Hubbardton, totally unplanned, ensued. At one point the Americans had all but defeated the British, when the German General von Riedesel arrived with his troops, having been sent by General Burgoyne, who anticipated that General Simon Fraser would need them. Upon their arrival, the Americans were forced to retreat, with the British and Germans hot behind. The retreating Americans found themselves with their backs to Pittsford Mountain and quickly realized they were trapped. Colonel Ebenezer Francis, who had gallantly led his men through the harrowing battle, leaped onto a tree stump to order them to hold their fire because they were hitting their own men, and a British musketball took his life. The desperate Americans saw him fall, and without his leadership, they scattered, some trying to climb the steep Mount Pittsford, others running wherever they could to escape the onslaught.

Later, Captain John Shrimpton of the British Sixty-second Regiment searched the body of Colonel Francis and had some of the American officer's papers in hand when a lone American sharpshooter in a tree on the side of Mount Pittsford hit him with a rifle bullet.

While the Battle of Hubbardton was in progress, the British fleet on Lake Champlain approached the great boom and the Great Bridge constructed by Colonel Baldwin, which was intended to stop the British ships from reaching the lower end of the lake. With a few well placed shots from their cannon, they cut the boom and bridge and had open access to the American docks at both Fort Ti and Mt. Independence. They found the hundreds of tons of goods left there by the Americans when they made their hasty retreat. Immediately, the British set sail down South Bay in pursuit of the American bateaux that had gone on to Skenesborough (see pp. 172–206).

The night following the battle, wolves came down from the mountains in scores and were heard snapping, snuffling, fighting over the dead and wounded, digging up some graves (p. 213).

Generals St. Clair and Schuyler were both attacked by newspapers and the general populace everywhere for abandoning Fort Ticonderoga without a fight. General St. Clair wrote a letter to Governor Bowdoin of Massachusetts in which he attempted to explain the rationale of his actions. Governor Bowdoin published the letter in the Worcester newspaper, *Massachusetts Spy,* which provoked further outcry against St. Clair and Schuyler. Reverend Thomas Allen of Pittsford, Massachusetts, made a particularly vehement attack on St. Clair (pp. 218–19).

Congressman John Adams was incensed at the affair, and wrote a letter to his wife, Abigail, in which he said, "We shall never be able to defend a post until we shoot a general" (p. 219).

In general support, see Leckie, *George Washington's War,* p. 388.

CHAPTER XXIII

★ ★ ★

*I*n the glow of a golden sunset, the two men worked forward on their bellies to the rim of a granite outcropping to lay silent and still while they studied the low, sloping hills and shallow forested valleys surrounding them. On their right the Oneida River sparkled like burnished brass in the fading light as it wound its way west through the lowlands. From their left, the Seneca River flowed southeast for a distance before the earth rose to turn it back northwest, where it joined the Oneida. Their junction formed the Oswego River that flowed northwest to the great inland sea called Ontario by the Iroquois, far in the distance.

The rimrock on which Billy and Eli lay was eight hundred yards nearly due east of the place the rivers converged, and was high enough to afford a clear view of the flat, open ground on their side of the rivers, which from earliest memory was known as Three Rivers. It was a place where travelers camped and Indian councils convened.

Ten yards behind them, on the east slope of the granite rimrock, they had found a small, natural cave that reeked with the heavy stench of bears that had hibernated there through the snows of countless winters and where some had birthed their cubs with the coming of spring. Eli had crouched low to lead Billy beneath the overhang, then on through the entrance, down a sloping incline into a natural, circular room about ten feet across. The rock ceiling was a scant five feet high, and white bones of rabbits and porcupines were scattered among panther tracks on the cave's dirt floor. The two men cached their bedrolls and knapsacks against one wall with the rabbit Eli had snared that morning and together they gathered old windfall twigs and limbs for a fire in the night, before climbing to the edge of the rimrock.

With eyes narrowed against the setting sun, they scanned each of the three rivers as far as they could see, watching for movement that could be canoes bringing more men to the Three Rivers camp. There was nothing but natural riffles and snags to interrupt the flow of the waters. They shaded their eyes with their hands, and began a careful count of the lodges and tents in the crook formed by the rivers—Indian lodges on the south side, white men's tents on the north. Before the last arc of the sun dropped behind the western tree line, they tried to count the tiny moving dots, but could not. They wished they could use the telescopes slung around their necks in their stiff leather cases, but they dared not risk having sunlight reflect off the lenses to be seen by a sharp-eyed Indian half a mile away.

In early dusk they watched campfires wink on, and they counted them. Sixty-six small ones on the south among the Indian lodges, eighteen large ones on the north, where the British and German soldiers were heating their great, black cooking kettles. A smile flickered over Eli's face as he thought of the difference between the cooking fires of Indians and white soldiers. Men could gather around a small Indian fire, each to boil his own water and broil his own meat while they drew warmth. A white man's fire was large enough to drive them back while one man twisted and turned in the heat, and shielded his face while he stirred whatever was in the huge, black kettles.

The two men watched until the distant fires were points of light in full darkness before they backed away from the rim and silently made their way to the darkness of the cave. By feel Billy shaved a small pile of slivers from a dead tree limb, while Eli got his tinderbox from his knapsack. He struck sparks with flint and steel, and on hands and knees, Billy blew gently until a small finger of flame licked upward. Minutes later they had the rabbit slowly roasting on a crude spit.

Eli broke the silence. "Too many lodges, too many tents. Some sort of council is taking shape. A big one."

"Recognize anyone?"

Eli shook his head. "Too far. Bad light. There's some Iroquois down there, and some Seneca and Mohawk. If there's Mohawk, Brant's there somewhere. I think there's some British soldiers, and German, but I don't know who the other white men are."

"We'll find out tomorrow morning when we can use the telescopes."

For a time the two men sat with their backs against the rough granite walls, knees drawn up, turning the spit occasionally, watching their rabbit turn from pink to white as it cooked. They boiled water for coffee, and when the rabbit had cooled enough they pulled pieces, pinched salt onto it, and ate in silence. Finished, they rinsed their wooden cups and fingers with canteen water while the fire drove out the clammy dankness and much of the scent of bear. The light wisps of smoke worked their way up to the entrance and out into the night, unnoticed, as the two turned to their small fire.

From the dawn of time, a campfire has reached into the core of humans to irresistibly draw them near. Who knows the source of the fascination? Is it the primal instinct for warmth? Is it the everchanging, shifting undulations of flame that cut through all thoughts, all pretenses, to the foundation precept of all creation, that life is an evermoving thing, wending through time and space with a will and a direction of its own? That the whole of it is guided by a power of which man can only speak, without comprehension? Who can say? All man knows is that a campfire works its magic. Men gather around it and sit in thoughtful silence, watching the dancing flames.

The two men spread their blankets on opposite sides of the fire, then sat on them in the silence, backs against the rock walls, knees up, staring into the glowing coals and contemplating the small fingers of fire. The flickering light cast their faces in shifting shadows and reflected from their eyes. Unexpected scenes and memories from the past came jumbled and mixed, strange and unrelated, and each of the two men was soon lost in unintended reveries. Time lost meaning.

Billy sat unmoving as remembrances came. *Father—sitting on his knee— Mother setting the table for supper—the rusty hair thick on father's arms—funny I never noticed it until I was four—Mother—the large mole on her left temple that moved when she talked—never aware of it until I was six—Trudy—small, delicate—Matthew and me on the floor in his room building a kite—lost it when the wind broke the string— Matthew, serious, telling me he loved Kathleen—fourteen years old—Matthew and me in the fields south of Concord—the British redcoats—shooting—the hit—the hot lead driving through—the paralyzing bayonet—John carrying me—Matthew at my bedside—wouldn't leave—a year lost healing—leaving—Brigitte—the hazel eyes— the moment holding her—the shock of realizing she was grown—of knowing I felt something for her—Long Island—the Delaware—Trenton—Princeton—Eli—coming north on the rivers—sitting in a bear's den in the night with Indians who would mutilate us just eight hundred yards away.*

Billy reached for his knapsack, drew out the oilskin packet, and unwrapped his battered tablet and pencil. He set aside the eight letters he had written but never mailed, positioned the dog-eared tablet on his knee, and thoughtfully began to write.

Late July 1777.

My Dear Brigitte:

> I am unable to describe the conditions in which I write this letter. I can only say I am with Eli Stroud, in a bear's den, at night, with the British, Germans, and Indians camped eight hundred yards away. In the quiet I find my thoughts returning to my home, my family, and my loved ones . . .

Eli glanced at Billy, then continued staring into the coals while visions rose from his past. *Father at the door—smashed open—the screams— painted faces in the parlor—Iddy don't go!—don't go!—the brown arm sweeping me up—the nightmare of flight through the dark forest—the lodges—strange food—new language—new clothing of deerhide—slowly learning—growing—dark-skinned boys chanting ugly words, jabbing with sticks—reaching for a rock—in my hand—the solid hit—the biggest boy writhing on the ground moaning—taking my place with the warriors—the long trail—the first battle—swinging the tomahawk hard, again and again—blood flowing—battles with white men—the shock of remembering I was white—turning to the Jesuits—begging for help to learn my own history—learning English—French—the Bible—Jesus—the Americans rising to fight for freedom—George Washington—the prophecy he could not be killed—would one day be father of a great, new, free nation—something awakening inside—the agony of leaving the Iroquois—had to know more about Jesus—had to find Washington—somehow find Iddy if she was alive—join in the fight for freedom—had to be free—had to be free.*

Eli reached to thoughtfully run his thumb down the three-inch-long scar along his left jaw line.

The brown eyes of Mary Flint, filled with a sadness that reached inside—the need to reach out—comfort her—the night on the wagon box leaving Manhattan Island to move the army to Long Island—the sick man between us, the dead one behind—her head leaning against me as she sobbed—the strange need in both of us to tell our stories—the unexpected comfort in the telling—Mary coming to find me—a man named Cyrus Fielding might know where to find my sister—the wrenching inside as we parted—the thousand times her heart-shaped face and dark hair and eyes have risen before me—the yearning—the bitterness of the realization that she is a woman of wealth and breeding, while I was raised as an Indian in a world of which she knows nothing.

The glowing embers slowly blackened. For a time the men sat in the darkness still lost in their reveries, and then they silently laid down on their blankets to stare upward until they drifted into an exhausted sleep.

They wakened with the gray light preceding dawn sifting gently into the cave, and outside the raucous declaration of blue jays and ravens that sunrise was coming and that they owned the world. Both men swallowed against the sour taste in their mouths, and drank cold water from their canteens. They rose to their knees to stretch set muscles, and in the gloom of the cave, reach for tinder and flint and steel to start a fire. They drank scalding coffee and broke off pieces of hardtack to work in their mouths, rinsed their cups, and set them to dry. Billy had wrapped his pad and pencil and the eight wrinkled, worn letters and this new one in their oilcloth, when Eli spoke.

"Letter for the girl? Brigitte?"

Billy nodded as he worked the packet back into his knapsack.

Eli reached for his telescope as the thought came, *I hope he doesn't get his heart broken.*

With the first rays of the rising sun rolling westward across the vast expanse of primeval forest, Billy cautiously worked his way up the slanted entrance to stop just inside. He went to one knee and closed his eyes to listen intently. There was no break in the chortling of the birds and the chatter of the squirrels and chipmunks. With Eli following, he moved to the mouth of the cave and once again stopped while he studied everything that moved. He dropped his eyes and stopped, startled, as he saw the seven-inch marks made by the pads of a great panther. The tracks came to the entrance of the cave, paused, then retreated. The huge cat had come soundlessly sometime in the night. Striped chipmunks and gray and red squirrels stopped to stare beady-eyed, then were gone in an instant. Billy glanced back at Eli, who nodded, and Billy walked into the open, Eli following, where they straightened to full height for the first time in nine hours. For a moment they stood still, savoring the clean, clear air of a spectacular morning and a sunrise that set the tops of the emerald green trees on fire.

Eli broke the silence. "See the tracks?"

Billy nodded. "Panther. Big one."

"Male or female?"

For a moment Billy narrowed his eyes in thought. "Probably a tom."

"Good," was all Eli said.

They hunched low to approach the rimrock, then laid on their bellies to move the last twenty feet and peer over, down the slope. The entire Three Rivers valley spread before them, wisps of morning fog rising from the rivers to drift through the trees and disappear. For a moment both men lay still, struck by the power in the sweep of the great forest as far as they could see, with the rising fog and the rivers, and everything changing from moment to moment as the eternal sun once again did its work.

With the morning sun warm on their backs, they had no fear of sunlight reflecting off their telescope lenses to warn the enemy camped below. They quickly drew them from their scarred leather cases, and in a moment each was slowly working his glass back and forth, counting tents, lodges, and as far as they were able, men.

Eli spoke quietly. "Some more came in last night.

"Maybe twenty more Indian lodges, and six more tents."

"Wonder who they are."

Billy shrugged, and they continued their vigil, watching, counting, waiting while unanswered questions silently came and went. Suddenly Eli tensed, then spoke quietly.

"There he is. Brant. In the clearing off toward the lodges."

Billy shifted his telescope and twisted it to bring it into clear, sharp focus. At eight hundred yards, through a telescope, there was little to distinguish one man from another, yet instinctively Billy knew which one was Brant. He was dressed much like the others, but there was something about the way he carried himself.

Eli again broke the silence. "There's Daniel Claus. Off to the right, walking south between the tents."

Again Billy shifted his telescope until he picked up a white man among the tents. He was not wearing a uniform. Eli drew a stick of green pinewood from his belt and began cutting notches as he counted. Both men raised their telescopes as a white man came pounding into camp on a galloping horse, hauled it to a sliding stop in the open ground, and dismounted. Joseph Brant and Daniel Claus came quickly to meet him as the animated man pointed east. Brant stood still, apparently listening, while Claus moved, obviously agitated, then walked back toward his tent with Brant following. The two disappeared inside for half an hour before Brant threw back the flap and walked purposefully away, back toward the Indian lodges on the south side of the clearing. He entered a lodge, and Eli marked it well with his eye, gauging distance and direction from the trees and from the Seneca River.

Again Eli spoke. "I believe that horseman was Tice. Captain Tice. He was with St. Leger over near Fort Oswego. Whatever news he brought got Claus excited."

The sun had climbed to its zenith, then started west, when Billy pointed. From their right, approaching the campsite, nine Indians, stripped to the waist, armed and painted, broke from the forest into the open, and a column of men followed them. Mixed among them were white men, and suddenly Eli started.

"Butler! With his Indians! He was back on the Unadilla, headed north to gather warriors. There must be more coming in behind him. If he's here, this is more than just a gathering. Get a count on those Indians if you can."

Both men steadied their telescopes and began counting the moving dots when Billy stiffened and pointed north. Eli brought his glass to bear, and his breathing slowed. A column was coming in north of the Oneida River, led by a horseman in a British uniform, with gold braid sparkling on his shoulder and on the trim of his tricorn. Behind him marched an army.

"St. Leger! That must be St. Leger," Eli hissed. "That explains it. He's the one St. Clair said was sent to lead the attack on Stanwix. That's what this gathering is all about. Try to get a count, and watch for cannon."

In silent concentration they watched and counted as the column forded the river and came dripping into the camp. The leaders assembled and waited for St. Leger to halt his column in the center of the clearing and dismount. They spoke, Claus pointed, and St. Leger turned to give orders to his command. They broke ranks and gathered around him, waiting. Brant turned from the circle and walked rapidly back to his lodge, then returned one minute later carrying something wrapped in doeskin. There was a brief conference, and the leaders turned to give orders. Ten minutes later every man in the entire camp was gathered in the clearing, surrounding the leaders, who had formed a circle around Joseph Brant.

With great dignity Brant laid the doeskin on the ground before them, threw back the folds, and solemnly knelt to pick up an object partially hidden from Billy and Eli. He raised it chest high, handling it reverently.

Eli reared up in shock. "That's an Iroquois warbelt! They're going to take up the hatchet!"

Billy rolled partially on his side, staring at Eli for an explanation.

"Take up the hatchet. Declare war. If I'm right, the whole Iroquois confederation is going to be divided—ruined. We're watching the destruction of everything the Iroquois have stood for ever since Hiawatha and Deganawida buried their weapons so long ago." His eyebrows were peaked, forehead wrinkled, hands trembling. Billy had never seen him so moved, so shaken. They turned their glasses back to watch, Eli still as a statue as he gaped.

Joseph Brant raised the warbelt toward the heavens, and they watched his mouth move with words they could not hear. He lowered the warbelt, offering it to the leader next to him. The man accepted it, raised it to the heavens, and also spoke.

"That's Giengwahtoh," Eli said. "He accepts it for the Seneca."

The belt was passed to the next man, who repeated the raising and the words, then passed it on.

"Juggeta," Eli murmured. "For the Cayuga."

The belt moved on as Eli called the names. "Gahkondenoiya, for the Oneida. Shegwoieseh, for the Tuscarora."

Eli pushed his telescope away from his face and his head dropped forward, eyes closed, as the realization of what the two had just witnessed more fully drove into his heart. The mighty Iroquois, divided, split, at war with each other. The work of the greatest leaders on the continent, smashed in ten minutes. Decades of diplomacy, restraint, building, patiently building, cut down forever as they watched. A wave of sorrow swept over him, and for a moment his whole body trembled. Billy did not understand it all, only enough to realize something profound had just occurred, and that it had reached into Eli as nothing ever had before. Billy neither moved nor spoke.

In time Eli raised his head again, and peered through his telescope. The warbelt was passing among all the men, both Indian and white, with each man touching it, committing himself to fight to the death in the taking of Fort Stanwix and in the war against the Americans. In short order, Butler brought out six barrels of rum, and within minutes the camp was a scene of raucous, drunken celebration. Chests of trinkets appeared, and the Indians broke them open to seize the gaudy baubles and parade about with them like children.

Slowly Eli lowered his telescope and turned tortured eyes to Billy. "It's over. More than a hundred years of peace. Brotherhood. Compassion. Bought by white men with rum and trinkets. Bought because the white men want the Indians to fight their white man's war. Half the Indians with the British, the other half with the Americans. The peace and strength of the Iroquois confederation, all gone, forever."

Billy saw the beginnings of rage in Eli's eyes, and then Eli slowly shook his head as he took control of himself. "We better get a count."

For a long time they patiently counted before Eli reached for his pine counting stick and began cutting notches. Minutes later he spoke quietly, subdued. "I count three hundred British and Germans in uniform, about four hundred Canadians in uniform, and around seven hundred Indians and Canadian civilians. That's fourteen hundred. Maybe five, six cannon. What's your count?"

Billy turned to look at him, studying his eyes for a moment. They were flat, blank. "I'd say a few over fourteen hundred. I saw about seventy rangers in there."

"I saw them, but I didn't see St. Luc or Langlade. I wonder why they aren't here."

Billy shrugged. "Maybe they're still coming, later." He pointed west. "If they are, they better hurry. Feels like weather's coming."

The two men settled and waited. The light breeze in the trees died and an odd stillness stole over the land while the air became muggy, sweltering. Sweat ran from their foreheads into their eyebrows, then their eyes, and dripped from their noses and chins. Eli glanced west. "Storm coming off the lake. A big one."

They lay on their bellies in the sweltering heat, silent, not moving, sweating as the afternoon wore on. While the two men peered west, great thunderheads formed to billow twenty thousand feet into the heavens. They covered the sun, casting the world in a strange, premature twilight. Billy and Eli sat quietly, awed, strangely feeling their own smallness as the gigantic clouds surged and rolled. The hidden sun lined the thunderheads with silver that changed to gold, then faded to gray, and finally turned to blue and deep purple. A west wind rose, light at first, then gaining as it drove the black clouds scudding toward land, their underbellies bulging, hiding the sunset. The first fat raindrops came slanting on the wind, splatting into the pines and oaks and the rocks and rivers, followed by a steady drumming that drowned out all other sounds as the cloudburst swept over them. The sun set and was gone, leaving the world in blackness and pelted by torrential rains that made it hard to breathe.

The first lightning bolts flashed for ten miles inside the roiling clouds, and two seconds later the cracking boom shook the ground as it came rolling in. In the drenching downpour Eli tapped Billy on the shoulder. Billy leaned close and squinted to see Eli point. With lightning cracking so close they could smell the acrid aftermath, and thunder shaking the hills, and wind whipping their wet hair, the two men left their perch on the rimrock. They worked their way through the mud back to the entrance of their cave, down the slant, into the small inner chamber. They stopped for a moment, drenched, with water running from their hair, down their faces, and waited until they could distinguish between the blackness inside and the blackness outside. Then, by feel, they reached for flint and steel and tinder and dry twigs.

Five minutes later a small fire cast their shadows huge on the walls as they set water to boil and dug salt beef from their knapsacks. They used their blankets to work the dripping water from their hair, then sat down shivering near the fire, and added larger sticks for warmth.

They sat cross-legged before the fire with their wooden cups clasped in both hands while they sipped at scalding coffee and gnawed at strips of salt beef. Slowly the shivering stopped. Eli finished his cup and set it aside before he spoke.

"I'm going out," he said. "I should be back before morning. If I'm not, take the counting stick and go back to report at Fort Stanwix. There are fourteen notches. One hundred men for each notch. Three notches for the British and German soldiers, four for Canadians in uniform, and seven for Indians and Canadian civilians. Five close ones for cannon. Can you remember it?" He held out the stick and Billy accepted it.

"Yes. Where are you going?"

Eli exhaled. "Into their camp."

"For what?"

"To let Joseph Brant see me."

Billy raised his head in surprise. "With the wampum belt?"

"No. That will come later, if it comes at all. I've got to let him see me close enough for him to know I could have killed him. If we ever get to use the wampum belt, getting out alive might depend on him knowing I could have killed him, but didn't."

"You trust his sense of honor?"

Eli shrugged. "It's the best chance we've got."

"Want me to come?"

Eli shook his head. "If this goes wrong, someone's got to get to Fort Stanwix to report there's fourteen hundred enemy on their way."

"How long do I wait?"

"I should be back sometime just before dawn. If sunrise comes and I'm not here, go east along the Oneida River, past Lake Oneida, straight east until you come to the Mohawk River. Fort Stanwix is right at the place it turns to run north. You can't miss it."

Billy nodded. "You be careful."

"You, too." Eli rose to a crouch, then hesitated. "If I don't get back, will you find Mary Flint and tell her what happened? Tell her . . ." He hesitated, hunting for words that would not come. "Tell her . . . I wish her well."

Billy saw the hesitation, saw the look in Eli's eyes, and knew the words he wanted to say but could not. "I'll tell her."

Eli disappeared up the incline, and Billy settled beside the small fire, listening to the steady roar of the wind and the rain outside, working with his thoughts and the knot of fear in his chest as he pondered Eli's chances of getting into the camp of fourteen hundred men, somehow confronting Joseph Brant, and getting out alive.

★ ★ ★ ★ ★

Taking direction and judging distances during the lightning flashes, Eli worked his way down the gentle slope west of the rimrock, angling slightly to the south as he went. At five hundred yards he turned to his left through the brush and mud to the trees, until he reached the bank of the Seneca River. He followed the curve of the riverbank north, slowing as he came in behind the Indian lodges. He stopped, waiting for the next lightning to show him where they were, and how close he was to the one into which Joseph Brant had gone after his conference with Daniel Claus.

The flash came and for two seconds the entire camp was brighter than noonday while the thunder shuddered the ground. In that instant he saw the lodge he was seeking, sixty yards ahead and to his left, near the tree line. And in the same instant he saw the Indian picket just to the right of the lodge, hunkered down beside a boulder, nearly invisible.

Did he see me? Did he?

Instantly Eli broke to his left, moving quickly ten yards before he crouched beside a windfallen tree and drew his tomahawk from his belt. Silently he worked his right hand through the leather loop, took a grip on the wet handle, and waited. Seconds became a minute, then two, and he could hear no break in the sound of the wind and the rain, see no movement in the blackness. Not one campfire remained burning in the downpour. Across the campground, among the white men's tents, through the pelting cloudburst he could see a few dull smears of light where soldiers had lighted lanterns inside their canvas shelters.

Where is he? Coming?

He was rising to move when lightning broke overhead and thunder cracked, and from the corner of his eye he caught the movement. He was partially turned when the hurtling body struck him, and Eli went down to his left, onto his back in the mud, clawing upward for the hand he knew had to be grasping a raised tomahawk or knife. He missed the hand, but the outer edge of his forearm struck the wrist as the hand started its downward stroke, and he shoved outward with all his strength. The head of the tomahawk smacked into the mud eight inches from his head, and he felt the hand start to rise to strike again. He grabbed desperately for the soaked buckskin sleeve and jerked it back down, then grabbed for the tomahawk. His fingers closed on the wet handle, slid up to jam against the iron head, and he wrenched it outward, away. The man's other hand came clawing for Eli's face, fingers searching for his eyes, while the man jerked to free his tomahawk and drive it into Eli's skull.

In the instant of knowing where both of the man's hands were, Eli swung his own tomahawk in a twisting arc, and the flat of the iron blade slammed into the side of the man's head. He grunted and lost his hold on Eli's face. Eli struck once more, and the man relaxed and slumped forward, unconscious.

For a moment Eli laid still with the warrior's weight partially on him before he threw the body aside, splashing in the mud and driving rain. He rose to his feet, turned the man onto his back in the mud, and reached to feel his throat. The heartbeat was steady.

Eli shoved his own tomahawk into his belt and felt for the hand of the man before him. He pulled the weapon from the limp grasp, slipped his own hand through the thong, then bent forward to take hold of the front of the man's soaked buckskin shirt and jerk him to an upright sitting position, then stood him up and draped him over his shoulder.

Cautiously he walked, splashing through the mud to the entrance of the lodge of Joseph Brant, leaned forward, and dumped the unconscious body against the stiff deer hide that covered the low entryway. The weight shoved the covering inward, and the upper half of the body disappeared into the dim light inside the lodge, with the legs and feet remaining outside. Eli took two steps back and waited, standing loose and easy, ready to move in any direction, with the fallen man's tomahawk dangling from his wrist.

Within seconds strong hands reached to pull the limp picket inside, and then, with Eli standing less than eight feet from the lodge, Joseph Brant emerged to stand erect, head thrust forward, peering into the pelting rain and the impenetrable blackness. A moment later lightning bathed the Three Rivers campsite in shimmering light, and in the three seconds of brightness, the two men faced each other less than six feet apart, each staring at the other.

Brant did not move. Eli tossed the picket's tomahawk at Brant's feet and made no other movement while the face of each man was burned forever into the brain of the other, and then the world was once again locked in blackness while the thunder cracked over their heads like cannon. Two seconds later, lightning crackled once again, and in the light, Joseph Brant found himself standing alone. Eli had vanished without a trace. Brant stood for a moment longer in the rain, then bent to pick the tomahawk from the mud, turned, and disappeared back into his lodge.

Sometime after midnight, the lightning moved on to the northeast, to become a distant display in the clouds, and then it was gone. The thunder grumbled for a time before it, too, quieted. The rain slowed, and then stopped. By four o'clock in the morning, stars were reaching through small breaks in the clouds, and before five o'clock the heavens were alive with countless points of light.

Inside the cave, Billy listened as the rain slowed, then stopped. The sounds of water dripping from the branches and needles of the trees in the forest came quietly to him, and he listened intently, waiting for the measured tread of moccasins approaching in the puddles and mud. They came shortly before five o'clock. Hunched over, Eli entered and sat down beside the fire, soaked, dripping, mud clinging to his side and back and hair. He gestured as he spoke.

"Better get our things. We've got to go. They'll be here sometime soon. We've got to get to Fort Stanwix to warn them."

"You saw Brant?"

"Yes."

"Trouble?"

"With a picket. Not with Brant."

"You killed the picket?"

"No. Delivered him to Brant's lodge. Brant came out. He saw me."

"How close?"

"Six feet."

"Will he recognize you if he sees you again?"

"Yes. He will."

Billy nodded, then both men rolled their blankets, tied them, and reached for their knapsacks and belongings. Billy picked up his musket, Eli his rifle, and they turned toward the entrance of the cave and walked up the incline into the dripping dawn.

Notes

During the last week of July 1777, preparatory to attacking Fort Stanwix, British Colonel Barry St. Leger moved his army from Oswego to a place called Three Rivers, where the Seneca River joined the Oswego River and the Oneida River to flow into Lake Oneida. There he was met by Captain Tice, Joseph Brant, Daniel Claus, Major John Butler, and a large number of Indian leaders. The purpose was to assemble them all to give them instructions, distribute arms and ammunition, and march as a body on Fort Stanwix, just east of Lake Oneida.

While there they all participated in the Indian ritual of "taking up the hatchet," which was the Indian mode of declaring war. The ceremony was not often seen by white men. In the ceremony, each leader takes the war belt, raises it, and accepts it in behalf of those he leads. Joseph Brant was the first to do so for the Mohawk, followed by Giengwahtoh for the Seneca, Juggeta for the Cayuga, Gahkondenoiya for the Oneida, and finally, Shegwoieseh for the Tuscarora. After the chiefs had taken up the war belt, the lesser chiefs followed, and finally the warriors. At the conclusion of the ritual, large quantities of gifts were delivered, and rum.

The taking up of the hatchet at Three Rivers marked the end of one of the greatest periods of leadership and peace enjoyed by the Indians of the northeastern United States. For generations, the six Iroquoian tribes had remained unified, strong. With the taking up of the hatchet, their union was dissolved, and one tribe took up arms against another. The great work of Deganawida and Hiawatha was ended (see Graymont, *The Iroquois in the American Revolution*, pp. 125–28).

CHAPTER XXIV

★ ★ ★

*H*eavy, warm rain was falling from lead-colored clouds that locked the wilderness in a gray shroud. Major General John Burgoyne moved the delicate, handcrafted lace curtain aside to peer out the tall window in the second floor of the great stone mansion built by Philip Skene. Dressed in full uniform, service medals clustered on his left breast, Burgoyne's face was a blank, eyes reflective and thoughtful as he looked west at the devastation that surrounded the house on all sides and extended past the docks into the waters of the southern tip of Lake Champlain. In his mind he was seeing Skenesborough as he saw it that unforgettable morning nearly three weeks ago, July 6, 1777.

The Skene mansion was to be the crown jewel of Philip Skene's dream of founding a grand and glorious settlement, destined to become a great metropolis in the forest, the chosen place where all travelers on the mighty Lake Champlain–Hudson River waterway would stop to marvel, and enshrine his name forever in praise. Obsessed by his vision, Skene had importuned his former commanding officer, General Amherst, to persuade the king to give Skene a grant of land strategically selected by Skene, and Amherst had succeeded. Jubilant, Skene moved to his newly acquired treasure on the southern tip of Lake Champlain, just ten miles from the Hudson River, to begin building his dream.

With shrewd, hard, brutal dealings that left his neighbors hating him, he cleared the land for two miles, then began construction of his community. He built the wharves and docks on the lake, a blockhouse and barracks, a sawmill, guest houses for travelers, storehouses, an ironworks, dwellings for his servants, homes for farmers to feed the settlement, and finally, on a rise that dominated all else, he built his home. Two and one-half stories of stone, with a two-columned portico, and graced with luxuries previously unknown in the wilderness.

Skene knew well the singular importance of the great western waterway, and when war erupted between the mother country and the rebellious states, Skene was paralyzed with fear, for one thing was certain: the war would eventually reach Fort Ticonderoga, and when it did, Skenesborough would be sucked into the conflict by one side or the other. Calculating the British would win, he declared his loyalty to the Crown and sailed to London, where he persuaded Lord North that all it would take to kill the rebellion before it spread was to establish a British presence on his land, and then openly threaten the rebels that should they provoke war, veterans of the French and Indian wars would be marshaled to quell it by force. Lord North agreed, and Skene sailed back to the colonies with the king's appointment as lieutenant governor of Ticonderoga and Crown Point.

The rebels caught him as he passed through Philadelphia, declared him to be a threat to the cause of freedom, and threw him into prison in Connecticut, where he remained until late in the year of 1776, when he became part of an exchange of prisoners.

Again he sailed to England, learned Burgoyne was on his way to America with an army to reclaim control of the great western waterway, and instantly set out in pursuit. He intercepted Burgoyne at Crown Point, where Burgoyne immediately placed him in charge of the British commissary and granted him written authority "to assure Personal Protection and Payment for every species of Provisions &c to those who comply with the terms of his Manifesto." The manifesto was Burgoyne's order to leaders in every community within fifty miles of Skenesborough to meet with Skene at ten o'clock in the morning of the day selected by Burgoyne, to receive Burgoyne's orders regarding how local inhabitants, including the rebels, could yet escape the wrath of the British onslaught by submitting to British domination.

Then, in the early morning hours of July sixth, Skene had watched helplessly as a seemingly unending flotilla of American bateaux carrying the sick, wounded, women, and children from Fort Ticonderoga came sailing into his docks, together with tons of supplies and equipment, all under command of American General Long. Long sent the wounded, women, and children up the nearby entrance to Wood Creek, away from danger. American soldiers already at the blockhouse under command of Captain James Gray unloaded the bateaux on the Skenesborough docks, oblivious to the fact that General Burgoyne and most of his navy were hot behind them. By noon, hundreds of tons of goods and supplies were stacked on the wharves, with more than two hundred empty bateaux bobbing in the water, when one sweating American raised his head to look north. His face went white as he raised an arm to point.

It seemed that the lower end of Lake Champlain was choked with British men-of-war and bateaux bearing down on them, cannon ports open, sailors standing at their guns with smoking linstocks. The instant the British guns came within range the air was filled with smoke and thunder and cannonballs.

At the moment the first British cannon blasted, General Burgoyne and his entire staff were sitting down to their noon meal in the ward room aboard the *Royal George*, and when the guns on the deck above them erupted, Burgoyne's secretary, Sir Francis Carr Clerke, raised his glass triumphantly and toasted, "To the success of the evening." Three minutes later the entire staff was on the main deck, leaning against the rail, gleefully watching the British gunboats systematically destroy everything that floated in front of them. In minutes the American ships *Enterprise, Liberty,* and *Gates* were reduced to burning, sinking hulks. The *Trumbull* and *Revenge* struck their colors, and the flat-bottomed bateaux were exploding as fast as the British gunners could reload. Frantically the Americans put the torch to everything—their own bateaux, the supplies stacked on the wharves, every building in Skenesborogh, except the mansion. Smoke and flame leaped to catch in the surrounding forest, and the burning of

Skenesborough became a conflagration that was seen twenty miles away by men of the Forty-seventh British Regiment, marching overland to join the British fleet. To them, it appeared the entire southern quadrant of the compass was burning.

Two days later, July 8, 1777, standing amid the still-smoldering ashes of Skenesborough, Burgoyne had commandeered Philip Skene's luxurious mansion house—the only building left standing at Skenesborough—as his headquarters, and moved the base of operations for the British army inside.

Now, with more than two weeks having passed, General Burgoyne stood at the second floor window, lost in remembrance and reverie as he gazed out at the bleak, charred wreckage of Skenesborough. Masts of burned, sunken vessels thrust high out of the water surrounding the docks, and the wrecked hulls of scuttled and destroyed bateaux were scattered as far as he could see. The blockhouse, sawmill, barracks, guest and servant houses were blackened skeletons with their roofs collapsed inward, while ragged portions of the walls were still standing.

Abruptly he turned away and strode back to the desk to take his seat in the ornately carved, upholstered chair behind Skene's heavy oak desk in the huge second floor library. He selected one paper from many and leaned back to reread it, then looked at the large clock on the mantel— ten minutes before seven o'clock. His scheduled war council would convene in ten minutes. He carried the document to the large, oak conference table, laid it in front of his chair next to a stack of documents, paused to review his handwritten notes, then drew a huge breath and released it as the rap came at his door. He called, "Enter," and his aide, Major Andrew Culhane, opened the heavy door.

"The officers have arrived, sir."

Burgoyne stood, and instantly became the charismatic, theatrical Gentleman Johnny, the consummate actor. "Show them in, Major."

They filed in, General Phillips leading, followed by generals Fraser, von Riedesel, Hamilton, and von Specht. Burgoyne walked to greet them warmly, cordially, showing them to their chairs arranged about the polished conference table. He took his place at the head and drew himself to his full height. "Thank you for attending, gentlemen. I trust you all slept well." His smile was charming as he reached for the document he had laid on the table only moments earlier.

"Gentlemen, I think it appropriate to share with you the message I drafted and sent to Lord George Germain. May I read it to you." He waited for silence, read the salutation, paused for a dramatic moment, then read on:

"I have the honour to inform your Lordship that the enemy were dislodged from Ticonderoga and Mount Independence, on the sixth instant, and were driven, on the same day, beyond Skenesborough on the right, and to Hubbardton on the left, with the loss of one hundred twenty-eight pieces of cannon, all their armed vessels and bateaux, the greatest part of their baggage and ammunition, provision, and military stores."

Modest. Humble. Unassuming. He continued:

"The victory resulted from the superb performance of all officers, the exemplary obedience of all enlisted men, and the superior quality of all equipment. Indeed, the rebels fled before our troops in such manner as to leave clothing, personal effects, even chests of money behind, so desperate was their retreat."

Again he paused, then went on—the taking of Fort Ti without firing a shot or losing a man—the lightning strikes and quick, fierce battles at Hubbardton and Fort Anne—the destruction of the American fleet at Skenesborough—the terror inflicted on the surrounding countryside while loyalists came flocking to join his army—retaking the northern lakes for the British empire—establishing control of the territory between the St. Lawrence River and Fort Anne—taking the major road running from Mt. Independence eastward to Castle Town and Skenesborough.

He finished reading and lowered the document, eyes glowing at how cleverly his words conveyed becoming modesty and humility, while painting a picture of spectacular heroics beyond the wildest dreams of Germain or the king. The document was not written for Germain. It was written for publication in *The Gazette*, the most powerful newspaper in all of England. Gentleman Johnny was without peer when it came to the games played by the high and the mighty. He knew that Germain would pounce on the document, write his own brief entre in which he would very diplomatically let it be known that the unparalleled victories were the result of the rare wisdom and vision he, Germain, had shown in selecting Burgoyne to command the expedition, and it would all be delivered to the newspaper instantly. When that edition of the *Gazette* hit the streets of London, Germain would receive a strong nod of approval, while Burgoyne would be the instant toast of the town, the envy of every man who dreamed of glory, and the desire of every eligible woman in the British empire.

For a brief moment Burgoyne stood before his officers, flushed with the certain knowledge that he had succeeded, not merely in conquering the Americans, but rather, in securing a place in the annals of English history that would enshrine his name forever.

Then, casually, he laid the document on the table and turned to his notes.

"Now, gentlemen, there are a number of matters we must address. First, at eight o'clock this morning we will participate in a ceremony, which I believe will introduce a plan that will succeed in silencing all the rebels within hundreds of miles. More of that later."

The generals moved restively in their chairs, speculating on the meaning of "a plan."

Burgoyne moved on. "I have drafted letters of highest commendation for the actions taken by each of you that have so successfully brought us to our current condition of victory. Of particular note are the actions of General Fraser and General von Riedesel, however, scarcely behind them are the actions of each of you. These letters have gone on to Lord Germain, and I'm sure, the king. I deliver copies of them to you now for your own purposes."

He sorted out the documents and handed them to the men, glowing with the knowledge that they would be enthralled with the praise the letters heaped on their heads. He waited as they read them, assumed their humblest attitude and countenance, folded them, and slipped them inside their tunics, then turned their attention back to Burgoyne.

"Gentlemen, a minor problem has arisen that you should know about. I have written to General Carleton in Montreal twice, requesting enough men—about twelve hundred—to occupy and hold Fort Ticonderoga while we complete our plan to meet General William Howe and Colonel St. Leger in Albany." He raised a document for a moment. "General Carleton has answered. He states that his authority is now limited to Quebec, which prevents him from sending any of the few men he has left, south to occupy Fort Ti."

Burgoyne stopped, and every general at the table understood perfectly. More than a year before, while he was in London using every waking hour to wangle command of this expedition from Germain and the king, Burgoyne had very subtly undercut General Carleton. Carleton had been stripped of more than half his Montreal command, and those men had been given to Burgoyne. Worse, Carleton's authority had been reduced to Montreal and Quebec, and no further. While the faithful and disciplined Carleton had been supportive of Burgoyne's every wish until Burgoyne left Canada, he was absolutely not willing to further reduce his army and his local authority in order to rescue Burgoyne from his own folly. Burgoyne had been ruthless in stealing both Carleton's army and his authority over the great Lake Champlain–Hudson River waterway, now let him learn the price of his politics.

Burgoyne shrugged it off. "No matter. We will manage." He stopped to organize his thoughts. The generals diverted their eyes to glance at the table, and the clock on the mantel, but did not look at Bugoyne.

Clearing his throat, he went on. "I am aware that some of you had reservations about my decision to stop here after we drove out the Americans nearly three weeks ago. May I repeat to you my reasons: First, we were too far removed from our source of supply. And second, we did not have our cannon."

Fraser dropped his eyes. *We didn't need cannon to catch St. Clair and annihilate him, and we had enough supplies to mount a lightning strike force that could have done it in days.* He said nothing as he raised his eyes, and Burgoyne continued.

"In the three weeks we have stockpiled supplies and moved some of General Phillips's cannon from Fort Ticonderoga. In short, we are once again connected to our supply line. Remember, everything we eat, everything we wear, everything we fire at the enemy, comes from England, across the Atlantic, to Quebec, Montreal, then Fort Ti, before it comes here. No army can survive once it loses control of its support system."

He reached to wipe at his mouth before continuing.

"We have learned a valuable lesson. Moving supplies south from Fort Ticonderoga has turned out to be a serious challenge. Every bateau, every cannon, every man, and every pound of our supplies must be portaged overland at points along the route. We were promised carts and two thousand horses to handle it, but received only one third of that number. Those few carts and animals have been used so severely they are nearly broken down. They *must* be replaced, and our supply line must become more efficient if we are to complete the expedition to Albany."

He dramatically raised a hand. "For those reasons I chose to wait until we were well supplied. I will not allow momentary zeal to jeopardize the overall plan."

He glanced at his notes. "I'm aware that St. Clair and Schuyler have been active while we waited. I know they have been gathering what rebels they can from the local population, but I can assure you, when we are ready to move, there isn't the slightest possibility of them stopping us."

He glanced again at his notes, then turned to von Riedesel. "You reported that while you were engaged with the rebels in and around Hubbardton you heard rumors from some of the loyalists of abundant grain and great numbers of horses to the east, toward the Connecticut River valley. Am I correct?"

Von Riedesel nodded. "Ja. I was told many times. At Bennington is many horses. Much grain."

"I have reports of the same. I am working on a plan to send a column to get both horses and grain, and vast stores of food for our men. That will ease the strain on our supply lines. When that time comes, it is my present inclination to send Lieutenant Colonel Friedrich Baum with a column to effect the mission."

Phillips's mouth dropped open for one split second before he clacked it shut. *Baum! Baum? Sending Baum east to get horses from colonial farmers? The man doesn't speak one word of English! Precisely how is he going to ask a farmer for his horses? Shoot him first, then ask?*

For a moment a wistful look crossed Burgoyne's face. "I can only wish I had authority to move east, instead of south. With this army, we could end this war soon enough if we could move on the Connecticut River basin quickly, to the heart of the rebellion."

For a moment every general at the table stared, startled at the thought. Burgoyne read their faces and tossed it off with a flip of his hand. "But I have no such authority, so we continue south." He glanced momentarily into the face of each man. "Does anyone know where St. Clair is today?"

The generals all smiled, then chuckled. Under British cannon on Mt. Defiance, and with Mt. Independence burning, St. Clair's catastrophic stampede the night of July fifth left part of his army shot to pieces at Hubbardton, then Castle Town. He ran on toward Skenesborough to meet General Long and escape in bateaux, south, to Fort Edward. Burgoyne had read the plan perfectly and reached Skenesborough first, to lay it to utter waste on July sixth. Desperately St. Clair changed course, heading for Rutland, then discovered the British hot on his trail, and since then he had been reported in Pawlet, Dorset, Manchester, Fort Anne, and half a dozen other places, some of them not on any military map known to the British. While at Fort Anne, the British caught him again, and in a running fight he had abandoned his dead and set the place ablaze before disappearing into the forest. He had not been heard from since.

Burgoyne went on. "I do know the whereabouts of General Schuyler. He's south of us, trying to rally new recruits." Slowly he lowered his eyes, and for a calculated moment remained silent, allowing a sense of drama to creep into the room.

"Gentlemen, in my judgment we should proceed south, overland, to meet Schuyler, along with St. Clair if he joins him." He pursed his lips as he measured the surprise in the face of each man.

Fraser's eyes narrowed as his mind raced. *Overland? He's changed the plan! We were to go south on the water—Lake Champlain, Lake George, the Hudson River! Not by land. Why? What does he know now that he didn't know back in London when he laid out the master plan and Germain and the king approved it?* Slowly Fraser leaned back in his chair, waiting for the explanation.

A look of confident self-assurance passed over Burgoyne's face. "I know that will surprise some of you, but let me explain." He spread a map on the table, shifted it true to the compass, then leaned forward to lay his finger on Skenesborough. "We're here. Should we carry on with the plan to move south by water, we will have to first move backwards, to the north, recross South Bay, and march past Mount Defiance, to the Chute, where Lake George empties into Lake Champlain. There we portage everything we have two miles up to Lake George, then turn around and sail right back south on the lake, to here, on the southern tip of the lake, where we will again be forced to portage everything we have overland twelve miles to the Hudson. It will take an enormous amount of time and energy. And worse, it will appear to the men to be a retreat, a retrograde, giving up ground we have already won. The impact on them could be serious. I will not do that to them."

Fraser leaned forward. "General, may I inquire?"

This was General Simon Fraser, he who had thrown aside the book on military tactics in the chaos and howling gale of the night of July fifth, and seized the moment to go hot after St. Clair. With the north slopes of Mt. Independence ablaze, he had relentlessly pursued the fleeing Americans, giving them not one minute to slow, regroup, or prepare to do battle. When he caught them he engaged them, flanked them despite finding himself and his entire command suddenly in jeopardy. And when von Riedesel came in behind him with enough reinforcements to save him, it was Fraser who had heaped praise on von Riedesel, fairly and openly. This was Simon Fraser, favored of Burgoyne, admired, respected by every man at the table, loved by the men he commanded.

Burgoyne nodded. "Of course."

"How far south by land?"

"That depends on where we catch Schuyler and St. Clair."

"All the way to Fort Edward?"

"If necessary."

Fraser cleared his throat. "I'm sure the general is aware there are places between here and Fort Edward that will literally stop an army of this size. There is one bog three miles wide that can only be crossed on a log causeway. If Schuyler destroys that causeway, our horses will be in muck up to their bellies, and the carts past their axles. We'll be stalled for days. There are other places where half a dozen trees across our path will stop us. The rainfall this month has been heavy. Brooks are now streams, and streams are now rivers. We'll have to build bridges to cross some of them. The overland route could be a hard thing."

Burgoyne nodded. "I understand, and there's much to what you've said. However, what can be said about going south must also be said about going north, then back south on the lakes. We have to portage no matter which way we go. It's a hard decision, but I think the proposition to go on south from here is sound."

For a moment Burgoyne studied his notes, and the men seated at the table glanced out the west windows. The rain had slackened, and the steady drumming had nearly stopped. Burgoyne picked it up once more.

"Perhaps some of you know that the written orders delivered to me by Lord Germain were reviewed and specifically approved by King George."

He paused, and Fraser glanced at Phillips. *Something's coming, and he's going to lay it at the feet of Germain and the king.*

"To be specific, both referred to the use of Indians to persuade the rebels to lay down their arms. Governor Tryon of New York, as well as General Carleton have wholeheartedly endorsed the plan."

In the ensuing pause, not one officer moved or spoke. The only sound in the room was the faint pelting of the slowing rain. Von Riedesel and von Specht felt a tremor ripple through their bodies at the thought of what was coming.

"For that reason I have ordered an advance party of Indians to move into the countryside ahead of us to persuade the rebels to grant us peaceful passage south."

Every man at the table moved. Von Riedesel dropped his eyes and for several seconds refused to look up. He knew how every German soldier in the command hated, feared, detested, the very presence of Indians. Nothing in their entire lives had prepared them for the shock of fighting alongside men who painted themselves hideously to the waist, preferred to kill hand-to-hand with tomahawk and knife, hacked and dismembered their victims to eat their livers and flesh, made the quick, circular cut to the bone of the skull to jerk the scalp free, sometimes with their teeth, howled insanely, and moved in the forest with the silence of a shadow and the speed of a hawk. Von Specht turned his head far enough for the two German generals to exchange glances, and each man's face was a mirror of the sick, dead feeling that had risen in their breasts.

For three seconds Fraser let air quietly escape from his slightly rounded lips. He had seen enough of the Indians to know their allegiance was absolutely not to the British flag, nor the cause of restoring the rebellious colonies to British control. Regardless of the noble speeches made at the council fires, regardless of the promises made by men both white and red, regardless of the exchange of gifts and the rivers of rum delivered to the delighted Indians, the ultimate truth was, when the battles came, the Indians understood only three things: Kill. Take scalps. Plunder. And worse, when the bloodlust was upon them, they were blind to anything other than the color of skin of those they slaughtered. If it was white, it made little difference whether it was man, woman, or child, American, British, or German. Military discipline? The Indians did not know the meaning of the word. When orders were given, the stony-faced Indians heard what they wanted to hear, then did what they wanted to do, without the slightest deference to direct commands. The single authority that would capture their attention was the muzzle of a musket shoved in their face, with a British or German soldier on the other end, finger on the trigger, the hammer cocked.

"General," Fraser ventured, "who will command the Indians?"

Burgoyne smiled, charisma dripping as though it were palpable.

"Chevalier St. Luc de la Corne. A man who understands them and can control them."

Both Phillips and Fraser started. St. Luc! The most bloody, treacherous cutthroat in the northern regions—a sixty-six-year-old white man who had lived his adult life among the Indians and had risen to prominence and wealth by mastering and exploiting the Indian refinements of war, including eating parts of their slaughtered enemy. St. Luc had led the Indians in raids on settlements from Hudson's Bay in Canada to New York in the United States. With him was the mixed-blood renegade Charles-Michel Monet de Langlade, who stood second only to St. Luc in his mastery of the arts of killing and treachery.

Fraser swallowed hard. "Can St. Luc be controlled? Langlade?"

Burgoyne nodded deeply. "St. Luc can manage Langlade, and he has assured me his Indians will conduct themselves within the guidelines of my orders."

Fraser pushed on. "The Indians have already been forty miles out in every direction attacking everything and everyone they find who might be considered rebels. Blood, mayhem, torture—they've killed at least forty of our own loyalists by mistake, most of them while they were on their knees, unarmed, begging. They've even killed a few German soldiers. If they are given license to make a general sweep to the east to persuade the rebels to cease hostilities, I fear for the consequences."

Burgoyne shook his head. "I believe St. Luc can control them. As you know by now, all colonials, both the loyalists and rebels, have a morbid fear of the Indians. Once it becomes known we will give the Indians a free hand among the American soldiers and rebels if they don't cease resistance, they will stop soon enough." He picked up a document and turned it toward them. "Remember, the idea is not mine. It is that of Lord Germain and the king, sanctioned by General Carleton and Governor Tryon." He waited a moment, lowered the document, and for a meaningful moment locked eyes with Fraser and Phillips. Both men knew the signs. The discussion on the advisability of using the Indians was closed.

Burgoyne glanced at the mantel clock. Two minutes past eight o'clock. For a moment he leaned over the map before him and was moving his finger to point when the rattle of musketfire reached the room. Startled, all faces turned toward the west windows, when the thundering blast of cannon close by sent vibrations through the room. Every man at the table jumped and instantly turned back to Burgoyne in question.

"I believe our guests have arrived, gentlemen. That was their salute. I've arranged a formal ceremony in which I will give St. Luc and his Indians their orders with everyone present so there can be no misunderstanding. Carriages are waiting outside to take us all. If you'll go ahead, I'll be down after I clear the table."

Before any man could stand, Fraser raised a hand and all faces turned to him.

"General, what tribe?"

"Several. Ottawa, Fox, Mississauga, Ojibwa, Iroquois."

"Which Iroquois?"

Burgoyne shrugged. "All six nations."

"Mohawk?"

"Yes. Many. St. Luc has strong connections with the Mohawk."

Fraser's eyes dropped, knowing the Algonquin root of the word "Mohawk" translated into "man-eaters" or "cannibals." He could only hope against hope that Burgoyne had somehow conceived of a way to get them to rise above their heritage and subject themselves to British orders. Fraser continued.

"I've heard that St. Luc has openly stated this war must be brutalized. Has he used that word?"

Burgoyne slowly nodded. "Yes, he has. But it must be understood, his meaning was not that his Indians are to be turned into brutes who will practice murder and mayhem. He meant only that if we are to succeed in bringing the colonials scattered over the greater countryside under control, we must deal with them where they live. Defeating an army of militia on a battlefield will mean very little to families living twenty, thirty, fifty miles away. There is but one thing the families out on the farms and clearings will understand, and that is, Indians will visit them if they do not submit to us. I think the king, Germain, Tryon, and

St. Luc are correct. The Indians can do for us what we cannot do for ourselves."

Fraser refused to retreat. "No one is concerned that it will have the opposite effect? Solidify the rebels against us?"

"No. The Indian strikes against the rebels will be lightning fast and conclusive. We'll have them and St. Clair and Schuyler well in hand before they can even consider any kind of organized resistance."

A knot of fear was tightening in Fraser's stomach as he fell silent.

Burgoyne concluded. "If there's nothing else, gentlemen, the carriages are waiting. I'll be along in a moment."

Fraser rose last and followed the other officers to the door. He closed it behind them and turned back to Burgoyne. He wasted no time.

"General, a few days ago you received a message from General William Howe. I know the plan for this expedition includes meeting him at Albany. There is considerable speculation among your officers about what his message had to say. Does it have anything to do with a change of plan? Does he still intend meeting us in Albany?"

It came too suddenly. Burgoyne was not ready for the deep insights of Fraser, nor the cold nerve it took for an inferior officer to broach such a pivotal question to his commanding officer. For five full seconds Burgoyne stared at Fraser as he weighed his answer and chose his words. The rain had stopped, and the only sounds were the fading steps of boots on the staircase, then the closing of the downstairs door, and the dripping of water from the eaves. Then Burgoyne lowered his eyes and began folding the map, forcing a sense of casual unconcern.

"He mentioned Philadelphia. Either before he comes to Albany, or after he finishes at Albany, I think he intends taking Philadelphia." He stopped working with his hands, raised his head, and smiled broadly. "He was most complimentary of our success at Fort Ti. Said many warm things about your performance. And that of von Riedesel. I'll share the document with you at a more appropriate time."

For a moment Fraser stood silent, unmoving, as he read Burgoyne's eyes and expression. *He won't say it—Howe's not coming to Albany to meet us!*

He held his face deadpan as he nodded. "Thank you, sir. That would be nice." He turned on his heel and walked out the door.

As it closed, Burgoyne leaned forward, palms flat on the table. *He knows. Intelligent, intuitive, perceptive Simon. He knows, and he won't tell a soul, and he will give everything that's in him to support me. Should I have told him? Maybe. Yes. I should have. I should have. But whether I did or not, he knows.* For a time Burgoyne did not move as he struggled with his inner turmoil. *If Howe doesn't come up the Hudson to meet us . . . if somehow we can't catch and destroy St. Clair and Schuyler . . . if we get stalled at that three mile swamp . . . if the Americans cut our supply line behind us . . .* Suddenly he straightened and quickly finished folding the map, stacked the papers on top, closed them inside his portfolio, and shoved it in the table drawer.

Let Howe go on to Philadelphia. St. Leger's coming in from the west, down the Mohawk River. He'll have an army with him. With what I already have, that will be more than enough. And, there's always Clinton. He's there just outside New York. He'll come if needed. The rebels might delay us, but they'll never stop us.

He strode quickly from the room, his heels clicking on the stairs as he descended to the carriages and his officers, waiting in front of the mansion. The Ninth Regiment formed on either side of the column, and with the Union Jack fluttering proudly in the breeze, and their red coats shining in the first rays of the sun piercing the clouds, the regulars marched out smartly to escort their commander in chief away from the blackened wreckage of Skenesborough to the lush emerald green of the forest.

St. Luc's Indians—more than five hundred—stood in two lines forty feet apart, facing each other. As the British column approached, St. Luc walked out midway between the rows of Indians to face the oncoming British, and the soldiers and buggies stopped. Burgoyne, dressed immaculately in his general's uniform with the red tunic and lavish gold braid sparkling, descended from his carriage to meet St. Luc, who was dressed in a green woodsman's shirt and leggings, both fringed, and trimmed in silver.

Their greeting was a profuse demonstration of heaping words of praise on each other, shaking hands, and clapping each other on both shoulders, calculated to impress everyone. When they were certain they had achieved their show of mutual respect and solidarity, St. Luc turned and led the general forward, each walking proudly, erect, looking neither right nor left, every inch the leaders of warriors. They approached a high arbor prepared by St. Luc, with felled trees on both sides where the British officers were to be seated.

Taking his place in the center of the arbor, Burgoyne waited while St. Luc turned to give a hand signal. The eldest chief among the Indians majestically walked forward to face Burgoyne, then thrust out his hand to abide the white man's strange custom of shaking hands. Immediately the Indians in the lines produced their pipes and began the necessary smoking before anything else was said or done.

Fraser sat quietly, watching the ancient custom with great interest. Finished, the Indians knocked the burning tobacco to the ground and a moment later the long-stemmed stone pipes had disappeared. The old chief, stoop-shouldered, face lined with the weight of eighty summers and winters once again faced Burgoyne. His aged voice was high, shrill, fragile.

"When the snows of winter melted, we heard the voice of the Great General of the North, in Quebec, even General Carleton. Our great and good Father across the mighty waters said he had need for his obedient red children. He asked us to forsake wives, children, our lodges and our lands, and possessions to come to this place. He asked us to help bring his rebellious children back to his family. We did as he asked. We have walked three thousand miles to come here to join with our friends and allies who are now all of one mouth, one language, one mind, and that is to serve our king, the Great Father beyond the big water."

The old man turned to gesture grandly to his warriors. "You see us all here in front of you. Say what is your will. Speak, and we shall obey."

St. Luc was to the left of the old chief, listening intently to be certain his aging mind had not forgotten what he must say. St. Luc sighed in relief as the old man finished and stood as erect as he could before Burgoyne.

Burgoyne rose to his full height, and for a moment held a severe face as he looked up and down the two rows of painted red men, some with blankets, most with their weapons clutched at their side. He turned to St. Luc and spoke in French while St. Luc translated.

"I am Burgoyne. I am the chief chosen by King George, your good Father across the great water. He has sent me here to greet you. He sends his gratitude for all you have done—for leaving your wives, your children, your lodges and your lands, to come serve him. He will not forget your generosity."

He paused, and there was a murmur up and down the lines. It quieted, and he went on.

"The Father loves all his children. But he has many who have gone astray. They are disobedient and disloyal to all the good things the Father has done for them. They have chosen a path from which they must return. He has sent me here to bring them back. He now wishes you to help him bring these disobedient, monstrous children back to obedience."

Again he paused and waited for the murmuring to stop.

"To do this, the Father has given me permission to give you the following instructions."

The two lines of Indians became deathly quiet as they waited to learn how far Burgoyne was willing to go in removing all restraints. The only sound was the birds in the distance, and the occasional drip of rainwater working its way downward through the leaves and needles of the trees.

"His orders are these. You are to chastise his disloyal and unfaithful children. You are not to destroy them."

He stopped. The Indians looked at each other through narrowed eyes, struggling to understand.

"You may scalp those killed in battle."

Instantly the air was filled with the buzz of talk amid the smiles and gestures of the warriors.

"You may not scalp prisoners, or wounded, or women, children, or old people."

Again buzzing broke out among the Indians, and Fraser watched their faces while his heart sank. *They do not know the meaning of chastise. All they heard was that they could take scalps. May heaven help us when they go into the countryside.*

Burgoyne waited until all talk had ceased and every eye was once again on him.

"The Father has promised you a bonus—a great gift—for every prisoner you bring back to camp. If you bring back his disloyal children, they can be made to return to their rightful place among his loyal subjects."

Burgoyne stopped, then turned to St. Luc and nodded, and St. Luc nodded in return. His Indians had understood. They would obey. Then St. Luc handed his rifle to the man next to him and strode quickly to the open space between the lines, faced Burgoyne, and suddenly he began the high, warbling war song of the Mohawk. His body bent forward from the waist until he was staring at the ground, and he began to dance, slowly at first, then faster as he sang. One minute later the Indians in the lines began to join him, coming in order of rank, until they were all caught up in the dancing. Their singing drowned out all other sounds as their feet rhythmically pounded the wet, spongy floor of the forest. Within minutes every Indian had joined in, voices raised in sounds that only occasionally struck a harmonious unity.

General Phillips, brow drawn down, jaw thrust out in disgust, watched through slitted eyes. *Wolves! This pack of heathens sounds like wolves and mad dogs.*

Burgoyne gave a hand signal, and within minutes three barrels of rum were produced and the tops knocked out with tomahawks. Five minutes later what had been an Indian ceremony became a drunken, falling-down frenzy. Again Burgoyne signaled, and the Ninth Regiment marched forward to escort him and all their officers safely through the writhing, painted chaos to their carriages, and escort them back to the mansion house. The last company of men had their muskets unslung, primed, and cocked, and never quit looking back over their shoulders at the orgy behind them until they were clear of it.

All day the British and German soldiers went about their duties, packing and preparing for the oncoming day when they would march out of Skenesborough, moving south to Fort Edward. At no time did they cease listening to the inhuman shrieks and the occasional crack of a musket in the forest where the Indians continued to drink themselves senseless. As dusk settled, the soldiers doubled their pickets, with orders to use their bayonets if a drunken red man threatened them. The howling continued through the night, quieting with the approach of dawn, then stopping altogether with the rising of the sun. A company of regulars marched to the forest with their bayonets mounted and their muskets unslung, to stand in revolted silence at what was before them.

Not one red man was conscious, or standing. They were on the ground, or in the brush, or on top of each other, wherever they fell when their brains could take no more alcohol. The rum barrels were empty, smashed into splinters. Muskets, blankets, tomahawks, and knives lay where they had been dropped. Vomit spotted the ground and bodies were everywhere, mingled with the discharge of their own bowels. The soldiers breathed shallow to avoid the stench that rose to turn their stomachs. Flies and mosquitoes and insects swarmed everywhere. A few of the inert men groaned. The British looked, and then they turned to march to their own camp. They did not look back.

With St. Luc leading them, the Indians began to drift back to their camp in twos and threes throughout the day, heads bowed, moaning, dragging their muskets, not caring that they were covered with dirt and their own vomit and feces. St. Luc led them to the wharves where he forced them into the chill waters to strip, wash their clothing and their bodies before he let them come ashore to sit, dripping, heads down, eyes clenched against the hammers pounding in their heads and the thirst burning in their throats.

The Indian campfires glowed through the night as they sipped at broth and waited for the demons to work themselves out of their systems. By morning some of them were able to eat pork belly and hardtack, and walk. St. Luc declared them fit for duty, gathered them together, and with his rifle in one hand and his tomahawk in the other, gave his orders. While they had understood little of what Burgoyne had said, there was nothing in St. Luc's orders to misunderstand. They had their muskets and tomahawks, and the white rebels were all around them, waiting to be "chastised." Black eyes glittering, they disappeared into the forest.

With storm clouds gathering in the sweltering midday heat, British and Germans alike raised their heads at the sound of distant muskets. A few scattered shots from far away, then many, then silence. Four hours later all activity at Skenesborough stopped as the soldiers stared at St. Luc leading in a large company of his Mohawk. In their midst was an American militia captain with nineteen of his men, hands tied behind their backs, with a long rope reaching from one right ankle to that of the man behind. Blood covered their heads, and their faces were swollen, eyes closing from beatings.

St. Luc marched them to the mansion house and pounded on the door. While he waited, all four British and German generals came trotting, with the surgeon Julius Friedrich Wasmus among them. They slowed and stopped as the big double doors swung open and Burgoyne walked out into the sunlight on the porch. Burgoyne studied St. Luc and his painted Indians for a moment before he spoke.

"You have prisoners. That is good."

"A captain and nineteen militia."

"We'll take them now. I'll see to it the promised rewards are delivered to your men today. How many of your men were involved?"

"Forty-three. The rebels killed two of them in the fight."

"I am sorry to hear it." He turned to Fraser. "Would you take charge of these prisoners?" He spoke to Wasmus. "Surgeon, will you tend their wounds?"

Both men started to move when St. Luc raised a hand to stop them. "There's one more thing," he said. "My men want three of these prisoners."

Fraser's eyes narrowed in surprise as he waited. *Here it comes.*

Burgoyne licked suddenly dry lips. "They're prisoners of war. Why do your men want three of them?"

St. Luc's expression did not change. "They want to roast two of them and eat them while the third one watches. Then they'll turn the third one loose and let him go back to tell his people what happens if they fight."

Burgoyne froze. Fraser gaped. Wasmus turned white as a sheet and for a moment choked as his gorge rose.

Stunned, then infuriated, Burgoyne's voice rang high and loud. "Their request is denied. Do not ever say such a thing to me again." He motioned to Fraser. "Get enough men to take charge of these prisoners instantly and see to it they're guarded against all possibilities." He swung around to Wasmus. "You do all in your power to treat their wounds." He turned back to St. Luc. "I will deliver the rewards to you for distribution to your men before nightfall. Tomorrow we march out for Fort Anne. In the meantime, you will keep your men under control or I shall do it myself. Am I clear?"

A cynical, evil smile slid across St. Luc's face. *He hasn't the stomach for it. He thinks he will conquer this wilderness without brutality. Well, he'll learn, or he'll lose.* He nodded, and without a word he turned on his heel, barked guttural commands to his men, and strode away toward his own camp while they fell in loosely behind him.

Burgoyne watched them disappear, then turned to his own officers.

"Tomorrow morning we strike camp and leave for Fort Anne. From there, we proceed to Fort Edward. Prepare your men."

Rain fell at dusk, heavy at first, then lighter, and held until four o'clock in the morning when the clouds lifted and were gone. By ten o'clock A.M. the army was in rank and file, ready to march. In a humid, soggy world, Burgoyne tapped spur to his gray horse and, resplendent in a fresh uniform, led his army south from Skenesborough toward the wreckage of Fort Anne. From there, he calculated less than a two-day march near Wood Creek to Fort Edward, where St. Leger was to meet him with his army. Burgoyne's spirits were high with the thought that St. Leger should be arriving soon.

The heavy rains of July had turned the wilderness into a huge, steaming bog that made the march a nightmare of wading through streams that were not on the maps and clearing away windfallen trees that blocked their crooked, narrow, winding trail. They reached the clearing where the charred remains of Fort Anne littered the ground. Mixed in were the bodies of the dead that had been left behind during the running battle, and the stench of the rotting bodies was overpowering. The burial detail gritted their teeth and breathed shallow as they threw dirt and leaves over the corpses and moved away as quickly as they could.

They made camp in the forest at the edge of the clearing, with Burgoyne and his officers enjoying a table beneath a huge maple, set with linen, silver, crystal, wine, champagne, meats, and vegetables. The tinkle of goblets raised to toast the king and the Duke of Brunswick, went on into the night to finally end with Burgoyne seeking the company of the wife of one of his officers. No one dared speak of it, not even the officer whose fickle wife enjoyed the champagne and the attention of a British lieutenant general more than she valued her marriage vows and the company of her husband.

Dawn broke clear and calm, with the British camp bustling to their business of the day, repairing equipment damaged in their two-day march through the wilderness, resting when they could, bracing for the last leg of their march to Fort Edward. They were aware when St. Luc and Langlade led their Indians out into the forest, but paid little attention once they disappeared. Then, during the day, prisoners began arriving, along with terrified people who drifted into camp, wide-eyed in shock, sometimes incoherent, rattling on and on with stories of horror.

I was there at a breastwork one mile this side of Fort Edward when they come, hundreds of them, mostly Indians, painted, and they killed a lieutenant and nine privates. We run and got help and come back and drove them off and when we got to the breastworks our boys was there. Naked. Scalped. Hands and noses cut off, bodies all hacked up by tomahawks and knives.

Heard about the Allens? They was harvesting the wheat at John Allen's place and they come into the house for dinner at noon and the Indians burst in and killed 'em all with hatchets and knives. Scalped 'em all and cut 'em bad. I couldn't figure out what was keeping them, so I left the field to go to the house to see and they was all there, dead, cut up, house all tore up. Terrible. Terrible.

Do you know about young Van Vechten? Lieutenant in the Albany County militia.

Led a patrol out to find out what's going on out there in the forest. That Indian who killed the whole Allen family while they was harvesting their wheat—called Le Loup by some, Wyandot Panther by others—he set an ambush for Van Vechten and he got him. Killed him and two sergeants and two privates. Scalped 'em all and cut off their hands, and cut up their bodies. Never seen the like. The devil couldn't of done worse.

By late afternoon a morbid silence had seized the entire British camp. Soldiers worked at their assigned duties mechanically, edgy, jumping at every sudden sound. With the sun still high, they slowed to watch a group of Indians move into camp, two of them in a hot contest over something one had and the other wanted. As they moved into camp, British and German soldiers, including officers, stopped to stare and shudder as some of the Indians triumphantly waved fresh scalps on their way through to their own camp.

Evening mess was finished, and the sun was settling when the Indians once again ventured into the British camp. This time they paraded into the open ground around the burned flagpole to break into their war chant and begin their dance while waving their scalp sticks overhead. The regulars gasped as they recognized the raw scalps taken that day, and understood they were being proudly displayed as trophies of war.

A blocky sergeant with a bristle mustache watched the grisly sight with narrowed eyes, then shook his head. He started to turn away when the young soldier next to him suddenly gasped and lunged forward. The sergeant grasped his arm and jerked him back.

"Here, Davey, you stay away from those Indians."

Wildly the boy struck out at the sergeant while he wrenched and twisted with all his strength to be free. The sergeant held firm, taking the slamming blows before he caught both arms and pinned them, looking into the young face. The eyes were wide, wild, insane, the face contorted like that of a maniac. An inhuman whine welled out of the boy's chest, and he threw himself back with a strength of an animal while the sergeant clung to him.

"Davey, what's happened to you, boy?" the sergeant shouted. "What's—"

The boy wrenched loose and barged in among the Indians, knocking them aside until he reached the one with a raw scalp of reddish hair that was fully five feet in length. He smashed into the Indian and siezed the stick. His scream could be heard throughout the camp and into the forest as he went to his knees, clutching at the scalp, holding the long, flowing, reddish hair to his breast.

Half a dozen men from his company ran to his side, but he would not release his deathhold on the scalp. They picked him up, but his legs would not work, and they carried him away to one side, where they sat him on the ground. His sobs tore their hearts, and they recoiled as they looked into his face. They thought he had gone mad. British and German soldiers gathered around, and officers came running. Von Riedesel ordered St. Luc to get his Indians back to their own camp while other officers knelt beside the boy, trying to console him, comfort him, but they could not. The old sergeant settled to one knee beside the boy and circled his arm about his shoulder.

"Davey, it's me. Sergeant Caswell. Can you hear me?"

Slowly the boy responded. He raised his anguished face to Caswell's and nodded.

"What's happened, son?"

With tears streaming down his face, his voice cracking with unspeakable horror, the boy blurted, "It's Jane. They've killed Jane." He slowly raised the raw scalp with the long, flowing hair to the sergeant. "This was Jane's."

Pain struck into the sergeant's heart as he asked, "Your sister?"

The boy shook his head and choked out, "We were to be married."

Strong men who thought they had seen every atrocity war could present stared at the ground for a time, battling anger beyond anything they had ever felt. Caswell lowered his face and closed his eyes for a moment, then tenderly patted the boy's head. "Come on, Davey. Let's get you back to your tent. We'll find out about this."

Within minutes the story had reached every man in camp. Evening duties were forgotten as officers and regulars alike began questioning every man and woman in camp who knew anything about it. They went to the compound where the prisoners were being held and questioned each of them. In bits and pieces, a sentence here, a word there, a terrifying picture began to take form and shape. It led to a large, captive white woman, one Mrs. McNeil, who had been stripped and was loudly cursing every Indian on the continent when the British officers threw a cloak about her and began with their questions. The officers were stunned when she told them she was the cousin of General Simon Fraser. Two captains were sent to find him.

On his arrival he was speechless for a moment, then covered Mrs. McNeil with his own cloak, calmed her, and asked her what happened. In deep dusk they listened in shocked silence as she gave them the last, and most horrifying, pieces to the puzzle, to leave them sick in their souls, shaking with rage.

Jane McCrae was nineteen, tall, comely, well-mannered, gifted, beloved by all who knew her. Her reddish hair was her crowning glory; it reached her ankles, and each day she brushed and cared for it. The daughter of a Presbyterian minister, she moved to the home of her brother John near Fort Edwards when her parents died. There she met a fine boy named David Jones, and in time they fell deeply in love. With the onset of hostilities between the Americans and British, David felt a loyalty to the mother country and joined the Canadian Volunteer Corps under command of Colonel Peters. John moved his family to Albany to escape the war and invited Jane to join him, but she refused to leave until she could be reunited with David and they could be married. She moved in with Widow McNeil near Fort Edward to await the return of her beloved David. By purest chance, Mrs. McNeil was a cousin to General Simon Fraser.

After Burgoyne authorized the Indians to "chastise" the rebels earlier that day, they swept through the countryside, killing white settlers indiscriminately, including Lieutenant Van Vechten, near the McNeil log cabin. When a survivor stopped at the McNeil dwelling long enough to shout a warning that the Mohawk were coming, the two women, Jane McCrae and Widow McNeil, quickly threw aside a braided rug and lifted the trap door into the cellar. They were two minutes too late.

At that moment the door was splintered, and the Indians came whooping into the small room waving tomahawks and knives. They seized both women by the hair and dragged them kicking and screaming outside, threatening them. In the struggle Jane's hair came undone and fell to its full length. With knives at their throats, the horrified women fell silent as the Indians started back to camp, jerking them along, an Indian on either side of each of them. The warriors separated the women, and the two with Jane McCrae were quick to realize what a trophy her long, beautiful hair would be on a scalp stick. Within minutes they argued, then began to fight over whose captive she was, when one warrior turned from the other, shot Jane dead on the spot, and quickly took her scalp. He stripped the dead body, tomahawked it, then shoved it down an embankment. It stopped rolling not twenty feet from the body of Lieutenant Van Vechten. With scalp in hand, the Indian stared his companion down and continued on to camp to proudly wave the magnificent scalp on his scalp stick, until young David Jones bounded into him to knock him aside.

Appalled, sickened, Fraser made a written report to Burgoyne, who sent a written message back.

"The news I have just received of the savages having scalped a young lady, their prisoner, fills me with horror. I will visit the Indians at sunrise tomorrow. Would you assemble them? I would rather put my commission in the fire than serve a day if I could suppose government would blame me . . ."

At dawn Fraser had the Indians assembled, with a German regiment on one side, a British on the other, both with muskets primed and ready. Burgoyne arrived, rose to his full, dominant height, and turned to the Indians. His face was filled with lightning, and his voice smacked of thunder. He did not waste one second on the usual Indian formalities.

"Which man killed the woman with the red hair and brought back her scalp?"

St. Luc translated for him. Not one Indian moved. Two red-coated regulars strode in among them to seize one Indian by the shoulders and thrust him out before Burgoyne.

"Is this the man?" Burgoyne demanded.

Again St. Luc translated, and the Indian nodded.

Burgoyne's arm swung up to point like the sword of the Almighty, and he bellowed, "Hang him!"

St. Luc translated, and instantly the campsite was filled with a deafening outburst from every Indian. The officers in the two armed regiments barked out orders, and the red- and blue-coated soldiers swung their Brown Bess muskets down, bayonets leveled at the encircled Indians, and every man eared the big hammer back, ready to fire.

Fraser quickly strode to Burgoyne's side. "Sir, twenty more seconds and this could turn into a massacre. Consider it."

St. Luc arrived two steps behind Fraser, his rifle held loosely in his left hand, his tomahawk dangling from his right wrist. His face was without emotion, but his voice was not.

"You hang this man, these Indians will revolt. They'll leave here to return to their homes, and they'll likely kill every white person they find, burn every village they come to. They may even come back to raid your camp. You had better change your orders. This army might not survive if you hang this man."

He paused and for a moment locked eyes with Burgoyne. "Remember, I told you this war had to be brutalized if you were going to win. That thought was beneath you, so you and your king sent out my Indians to do it for you, and they've done it. Now you want to start hanging them. Are you ready to hang the white men who called for it? Your kindly and good king? Germain? Tryon? What about yourself, General?"

St. Luc's words were alive with sarcasm and disgust. They hit Burgoyne in the pit of his stomach like a huge fist, and he took half a step backwards. Only the fact that St. Luc had spoken at least partially in truth saved him from being thrown in irons on the spot. Burgoyne raised a hand and the campsite quieted.

"You will delay the hanging. I must consider."

Burgoyne walked away for a time, and by force of will calmed himself. He listened to Simon Fraser, then remembered St. Luc's humiliating warning. Half an hour later he returned to once more face the assembly.

"There will be no hanging. From this moment forward, no raids will be conducted by Indians except under the supervision of a British officer."

St. Luc translated, and a great murmur spread over the Indians, then quieted. St. Luc spoke to the chiefs, then turned back to Burgoyne.

"They agree." Then St. Luc lowered his face so it could not be seen, and he shook his head. *That is the most ridiculous order I ever heard! He thinks one of his officers can control a war party once the fighting starts?* Again he shook his head, turned his face back to Burgoyne, and said nothing.

The story of the murder of Jane McCrae leaped across the wilderness in hours, from settlement to settlement, family to family, growing in its hideous details with every telling. It was instantly printed to reach tens of thousands in *The New York Gazette and Weekly Mercury,* the *Pennsylvania Evening Post,* the *Massachusetts Spy,* the *Maryland Gazette,* the *New Hampshire Gazette,* the *Virginia Gazette.*

Panic seized the countryside. Wild stories sprang up everywhere. *Did you hear about the two little girls picking berries? Killed and scalped!—Have you been told about the sentries with Schuyler? Killed and scalped in the night—not a sound—right under the general's nose!—I heard thirty-four men went on scout, and only twelve came back. The others? Caught. Tomahawked. Scalped. Daniel Herd's family all gone, murdered while they were moving out to escape the Indians. Got caught. Scalped.—What happened to Captain Benjamin Warren? Got caught out in the wilderness—cost him eight dead and fifteen wounded, and two days later, another lieutenant and a sergeant.*

The Americans on the farms and in the settlements, including the militia soldiers, packed what they could in an hour and fled south with their families, terrified of being caught in the forest. In desperation General Schuyler wrote to the Albany Committee of Safety, imploring them to do all they could to dispel the awful cloud of fear and panic that was closing in on the Americans from every quarter. His letter went unheeded, and the exodus of militia and families continued unabated.

Desperately Schuyler led his men steadily southward, just hours ahead of the relentless march of the British. Twice his rear guard took cover and exchanged volleys with the redcoats, less than one hundred yards behind.

Then, like an angel sent from heaven, General Benedict Arnold appeared in Schuyler's camp.

"Reporting under orders of General Washington and the Continental Congress. I've been sent to help in any way I can. How best can I serve you, sir?"

What Arnold told Schuyler was the truth, but not all of it. Angered at a capricious Congress, which granted promotions based on favoritism or politics or prejudices or for reasons no one ever knew, both Benedict Arnold and John Stark had been passed over while men who were both younger and untried were promoted over their heads. Arnold and Stark had choked down the humiliation for the last time. Arnold wrote his letter of resignation and delivered it to Congress on July tenth, only to receive a letter from General George Washington on July eleventh, pleading with him to report immediately to the Northern Department, General Philip Schuyler, to render all possible assistance in checking Burgoyne. Arnold's letter of resignation was instantly withdrawn, and he left that day to find Schuyler near the Hudson.

Flooded with relief, Schuyler asked Arnold but one question: "How can I slow down Burgoyne?"

Arnold answered. "Give me three hundred men with muskets and axes and shovels. I'll take care of it."

Within hours the men were assembled, and Arnold moved among them, commending them, shaking hands, an arm about a shoulder here, a hand on an arm there, touching them, building them up. His voice rang strong, confident, as he gave orders. "Move north until you find Burgoyne. Start felling trees across the trails. Dam streams. Burn the wheat fields and crops. Run off the cattle and livestock. Flood roads and valleys. Tear up bridges. Block the narrow passes. Burn causeways. Force him to traverse bogs and swamps. Move big rocks where his horses and carts must go. Keep your muskets handy, and take turns keeping fifty pickets out watching for Indians or redcoats or Germans in the forest. If he sends out men to get you, don't engage them. Fade into the forest and wait. They'll go back to report you've disappeared, and when they do, go right back and continue cutting trees and tearing up the roads."

If there was one thing the American settlers understood better than any Englishman or German following them, it was how to use an ax and a shovel in the great wilderness. Clearing forests and digging stumps had honed their skills to the finest edge. Time and again Burgoyne's soldiers stood in grudging admiration at how many trees the Americans could fell in what seemed minutes, with precision deadly enough to lay them side by side, a measured nine feet apart. It seemed the American shovels had magic in them as they moved tons of dirt and rock to dam a stream well enough to back it up for miles to stop Burgoyne's advance dead in its tracks while his regulars spent hours, sometimes a day, digging out the dam.

Days later Schuyler faced Arnold. "General, your services here have been excellent, but I'm giving you new orders. Go west to Fort Stanwix. Burgoyne has sent Colonel Barry St. Leger with a force to take the fort, and then bring his army down the Mohawk Valley to gather all the Indians and loyalists he can to join Burgoyne and attack us. I can't let that happen. You are to go to Stanwix and give any help you can to Colonel Peter Gansevoort, who is in command. Do you understand?"

Arnold left that day, with Schuyler watching him until he was out of sight.

The three hundred men Arnold had sent into the woods with axes and shovels to slow the relentless march of Burgoyne's army did not let up. Reports began appearing on the table in Burgoyne's great command tent. One day had been lost clearing nine giant fir trees that lay across the trail. Two days lost finding a way around a shallow valley flooded when trees and dirt dammed the small stream. The three-mile log causeway over the tremendous bog had been burned and five days had been lost replacing it. Mosquitoes in clouds so dense they darkened the sky had swarmed all over his men. Copperhead snakes slithered into the tents at night to terrify and afflict them. Heat exhaustion and diarrhea were taking down his work force by the droves. Food was low. Men were killing and eating porcupines. The howling of wolves at night stirred up the horses, and the men.

With each delay, the British were growing weaker, while the ranks of Schuyler's fragmented army were being swelled with men arriving from the great Connecticut River valley to the east, angry at the marauding Mohawk Indians, eager to meet them in open battle, win or lose.

It became apparent to Schuyler that Burgoyne was steadily moving toward Fort Edward, and once he understood, he again changed his plans and his line of march accordingly. He issued new orders to his men.

"March past Fort Edward, on south to Saratoga. We will gather all our militia and continentals there, and we shall prepare to meet Burgoyne. Saratoga. We will gather at Saratoga."

The die was cast.

Notes

Unless otherwise indicated, the following is taken from Ketchum, *Saratoga,* on the pages identified.

Philip Skene had obtained a fifty-six thousand acre land grant from King George for property just south of the junction of Lake George and Lake Champlain, on the east side of the lakes. He built a tremendous estate consisting of many outbuildings, farms for his tenant workers, and a great stone home. The Skene landholdings became known as Skenesborough. His neighbors detested him because of his harsh business dealings. He ingratiated himself to General Burgoyne, who gave him authority "to assure Personal Protection and Payment for every species of Provisions etc, to those who comply with the terms of his Manifesto." The manifesto was a document written by Burgoyne, offering safety to all Americans who would agree to refrain from resisting the British (pp. 235–36).

When General St. Clair abandoned Fort Ticonderoga, he sent the loaded bateaux he had south on Lake George, to dock at Skenesborough, where the Americans had a great number of bateaux waiting. St. Clair intended marching his army overland to join them, then sail south with his entire command to Fort George, at the southern tip of Lake George.

General Burgoyne anticipated it perfectly. After blasting through the great boom and Great Bridge, he sent his fleet of gunboats down to Skenesborough to attack the Americans. On 6 July 1777, with General Burgoyne and his staff aboard the *Royal George* watching, the British sank, burned, and destroyed virtually the entire American flotilla of bateaux, and the Americans fled. As they left, the Americans burned nearly every building at Skenesborough. The great stone mansion was left intact. The harbor was filled with the wreckage of burned and sunken American bateaux.

General Burgoyne commandeered the Skene mansion for his headquarters. Then he held a war council, in which he read to his officers the letter he had sent to Lord Germain, informing him of their conquest of Fort Ti without firing a shot. The letter is quoted verbatim in the text of this chapter. The letter was later published in the London newspaper, *Gazette*, and it was certain Burgoyne was a candidate for the high and lofty Order of the Bath. However, in his exalted view of himself, the Order of the Bath was beneath him, and he requested his wife's nephew, the Earl of Darby, to so inform the administration. Burgoyne also wrote letters of high commendation for his officers, particular generals Fraser and von Riedesel who had pursued the Americans and successfully fought the Battle of Hubbardton.

General Burgoyne proceeded to march south from Skenesborough, twenty-three miles to Fort Edward, where he arrived with an exhausted army and decided to wait for weeks while his supplies and cannon caught up with him. His wagons were breaking down, his horses were starving and dying, and his men were reduced to eating whatever they could find in the forest. In these conditions, General von Riedesel brought news of large stores of grain and many horses in a small town to the east, named Bennington. The facts were discussed with Burgoyne, who decided he would soon send a force to Bennington to get the grain and horses he so sorely needed.

During the British march to Fort Edward, General St. Clair learned of the catastrophe at Skenesborough and changed course, marching his men to Pawlet, later St. Anne, where he fought another brief engagement with the British, who were pursuing him relentlessly. General Benedict Arnold, under orders from General Washington, arrived. Arnold had threatened to resign from the American army, feeling Congress had dealt unfairly with him, but upon receipt of the letter from General Washington, he withdrew his letter of resignation and immediately headed north to help. He quickly recognized what was needed and asked General Schuyler for three hundred men. He thereupon set about destroying bridges, corduroy roads, blocking trails, damming streams, burning crops, scattering livestock, and in general harassing and stopping General Burgoyne's army on their march to Fort Edward, until they were exhausted, weary, hating the forest and the Americans who were always present but never seen. Arnold's efforts had forced Burgoyne to use twenty-one days to cover twenty-three miles.

The weeks Burgoyne spent waiting for his supplies and cannon and resting his battered army, gave St. Clair time to gather his army, send word for reinforcements, and gather supplies.

Burgoyne carefully explained to his war council his options for pursuing the rebels further south. He could travel south from Skenesborough, on either side of Lake George, or, he could move the army north, back to Fort Ticonderoga, cross South Bay, portage everything the three and one-half miles to Lake George, then sail back down Lake George, carry everything the twelve miles from Lake George to the Hudson River, and sail on down to Albany. He had already decided he was not going to move back north, since doing so would give the army the impression they were giving up ground they had already won. The members of his war council were divided on the question, but Burgoyne would not change his mind. He was going to move south, either on the east side of the lake, or the west side.

He wrote to General Carleton in Quebec for additional men and was denied. He already suspected General Howe was not going to meet him in Albany but refused to reveal his fears to his war council. He believed that Colonel St. Leger would be bringing his forces east down the Mohawk River valley after taking Fort Stanwix, and he believed that in any event, he could reach Albany alone if he had to, seventy miles south.

Before leaving Skenesborough, Burgoyne held a great conference with St. Luc and Langlade, most of his own army, and nearly all the Indians present. There he gave his orders to the Indians, which were to "chastise" the rebellious Americans, but to scalp only those whom they had killed in battle. The orders were nearly incomprehensible to those who understood the Indians. The result was that the Indians immediately went into the forest and spread murder, mutilations, and scalpings nearly everywhere they went. The British regulars and particularly the Germans hated and feared the red men. Stories of depredations spread like wildfire.

Then came the one tragic story that marked a turning point in the attitude of the Americans. Two of Burgoyne's Mohawk murdered Jane McCrae, a beautiful colonial girl who was to marry a British soldier, David Jones. The one thing that set Jane McCrae apart from nearly any other woman on the frontier was her beautiful reddish hair, five feet long. The Mohawk who murdered and mutilated her took the scalp, and that evening paraded it on a pole in the Mohawk victory dance, attended by British soldiers. David Jones was among the soldiers, saw the scalp, recognized it instantly, and nearly collapsed, screaming in a state of shock. When Fraser informed Burgoyne of what had happened, Burgoyne ordered the Indians to assemble, called out the one who had murdered Jane McCrae, and ordered him hung. St. Luc interfered, telling Burgoyne that if he hung that Indian, the others would leave, and likely attack even the British or Germans if they ran across them in the forest. Burgoyne recanted. The Indian was not hung. Burgoyne wrote the note, stating that he was horrified by what had happened, and would rather burn his commission as a general than think anyone would believe him to have been implicated.

The Jane McCrae story was instantly published in every major newspaper in America and in England. It raised such an outcry from enraged Americans that it drew them together as nothing else in their resolve to stop Burgoyne and his Indians, and drive them from American shores.

It was then St. Clair issued orders to his army to gather at Stillwater and Saratoga, there to prepare to meet the attack of Burgoyne's army (pp. 222–284).

In support, see Leckie, *George Washington's War*, pp. 390–91; Higginbotham, *The War of American Independence*, p. 191.

CHAPTER XXV

★ ★ ★

*M*argaret Dunson paused in the kitchen to listen to the front door open, then called, "Brigitte, is that you?"

Brigitte pulled the scarf from her hair and the shawl from her shoulders and shook the rain from them before she stepped through the doorway. She stood for a moment on the woven oval rug she and her mother had made from rags, and answered, "It's me." She lifted one foot, then the other, to drop her shoes on the rug.

"Soaked?"

"Wet."

"How was work?"

"As usual. Baked sixty loaves of whole wheat. Hortense sent home some day-old bread and a tart for the children. I'll bring it." She hung the shawl and scarf on the pegs beside the door, then padded across the polished hardwood floor in her stockinged feet to set the wrapped package on the kitchen cupboard. Margaret eyed her, head to toe.

"You go change out of those wet clothes. You'll catch your death."

Brigitte drew a copy of the *Massachusetts Spy* newspaper from the great pocket of her ankle-length work skirt, which showed dustings of flour, and held it out to her mother. Margaret felt an instant tightening in her chest. "What's this? Bad news?" A chill ran through her as she waited, while her mind ran. *Please, not Matthew. Not Caleb. Not Billy.*

Brigitte shook her head. "No one we know. Just a terrible story about a girl."

Margaret's shoulders slumped in relief as she took the paper. "Who? What story?"

"Her name was Jane McCrae. The Indians got her. *British* Indians."

Margaret's eyebrows peaked. "What happened?"

"It was over near the Hudson River. Our army is still retreating. Seems like they're going to run clear off the map. The British sent a band of Mohawk Indians to frighten the settlers away, and one of them got Jane McCrae. I can hardly bear to tell you what they did to her."

Margaret gasped. "Then let me read it while you change clothes and call the children in from the root cellar. They're out getting a pitcher of milk and some cheese for supper. Tell them to be careful."

Amid the familiar aromas of carrots simmering on the black kitchen stove and a chicken baking in the oven, Margaret sat at the head of the dining table and spread the small, two-page newspaper. As she finished reading the account, she closed her eyes and raised both hands to cover her mouth and murmured, "How terrible!" Pain welled up in her heart, and she rose to peer through the kitchen, where Brigitte was holding the back door open while the children hurried through the softly falling rain toward the house. She felt a tinge of guilt with the thought, *Thank the Almighty it wasn't my Brigitte. I don't know what I'd do if . . .*

Brigitte held the door open while Adam and Prissy entered the kitchen, shoulders hunched against the rain, Adam carrying the large porcelain pitcher in both hands, Prissy a block of cheese sealed in wax and wrapped in gauze. Margaret walked into the kitchen as Brigitte took the pitcher and cheese, then spoke to the children.

"Clean off your feet on the rug."

"And get washed for supper," Margaret added. She reached a bowl from the cupboard, then motioned to Brigitte. "Get the table set. I'll get supper into the bowls."

Margaret said grace. They ate with little comment, listening to the quiet falling of the summer evening rain, each seeming to prefer their own thoughts. The women cleared the table, washed and dried the dishes, then took time to sit in the rocking chairs in the parlor to let the fatigues of the day drain and their thoughts drift. The children moved the curtains aside to watch the rain stop and the robins and jays come hopping in the yard. The brightly colored, beady-eyed birds darted quickly, to stop and turn their heads, then thrust them low until they picked up the vibrations of earthworms beneath their feet. In an instant they thrust their beaks into the wet soil to pluck out supper for their waiting young.

As dusk settled, Margaret lighted the parlor lamps and gathered Adam and Prissy around the dining table where she read them the story of David and Goliath from the book of First Samuel before the family gathered for evening prayers. She tucked them in bed with Adam asking, wide-eyed, "How big did it say Goliath was?"

Margaret pursed her mouth as she thought. "Six cubits and a span."

"How long is a cubit?"

Margaret pondered. "I don't know. Big, I suppose. Remember, and we'll ask Silas in church next Sunday." She brushed a kiss into the tousled hair, twisted the wheel on the lamp wick, and walked out the door. The last thing she heard was, "Six cubits and a span. I'll bet that's big."

She passed Brigitte in the hallway, walking toward her bedroom. "Going to bed so soon?"

Brigitte shrugged. "In a while. I'll be in my room."

A mother's intuition piqued Margaret. "What's troubling you?"

"Oh," Brigitte said wistfully, "I don't know. I just need some time to let things settle. Think about them."

"Anything special?"

"No, not really."

"That terrible thing about Jane McCrae?"

"No."

Margaret looked into her daughter's clouded, pensive face. "Call me if you need me. I'll be in the parlor."

Brigitte's lamp filled the room with pale light and shadows as she sat at the small table beside her bed, aimlessly watching the burning wick for a time. She twisted on her chair, vaguely aware of the morose, gray feeling that had ridden her most of the afternoon. She was not yet ready to force her thoughts to focus on the cause. Rather, she let her mind take her where it would.

Matthew gone on a ship—Caleb gone with the army—so young—I wonder where he is tonight—what he's doing.

She idly turned the wheel on the lantern wick and watched the flame diminish to a tiny blue line, then turned it the other way, and the flame leaped to brighten the room.

Two years—a little over—turned the family upside down—Papa gone—Tom Sievers with him in heaven—Matthew—Kathleen—Billy—Caleb—all gone. Our quiet little town gone. It will never be the same again.

Restless, she rose from her chair and walked across the room and back. Outside the rain had begun to fall again, and for a moment she stood still, listening to the quiet, steady hum. She started to sit down, then impulsively changed from her dry clothing back into her wet clothing and walked to her bedroom door and opened it.

"Brigitte, are you all right?"

She strode down the hall in her bare feet, into the parlor where Margaret sat rocking while her knitting needles clicked in a steady rhythm.

"I can't sit in my room. I'm going out in the backyard."

Margaret's hands stopped, and she dropped her head forward to peer over the top of her bifocals. "You're back in your wet clothes! What's wrong?"

"Nothing. I just want to be alone in the darkness and the rain."

Margaret started to speak, then held her tongue and settled back in her chair. She could not remember how many times in her life her intuitions and instincts had driven her to seek a quiet place to sort out the tangled web of life. She remembered long ago walking to the Boston docks at midnight in a January snowstorm. John had awakened to find her gone and spent terrified hours walking the streets looking for her. He had respected her need to be alone with her thoughts but never did understand how it could drive her out in the middle of the night, to the Boston docks, in a winter snowstorm.

She nodded to Brigitte. "Put on your scarf and shawl."

"I'll be all right. It's warm. I'll sit on the bench." She walked through the parlor into the dark kitchen to the back door.

"At least put on your shoes."

Ignoring her mother's directive, Brigitte opened the back door and walked out, closing it softly behind her. The wet grass was cool on her bare feet, and she stood for a time letting the quiet rain fall on her head and face and shoulders. She walked slowly to the great oak at the back of the yard, circled by the bench her father and Matthew had built so long ago—the bench where the Dunson children had played, and sat to dream, and to gossip, and tell horrible ghost stories after dark. The bench often shared by Matthew and Kathleen as they were growing up.

She sat and drew her knees up, and wrapped her arms around them, not caring that the bench was wet. The thick leaves on the great spreading branches slowed the rain but did not stop it from seeping through to fall on her, but she paid it no heed.

She closed her eyes, and scenes came randomly to her mind. Richard Arlen Buchanan, Captain, His Majesty's Service, was before her, smiling as he had smiled the night she first saw him at the church when the redcoats came searching for the muskets Brigitte and the other women had smuggled in. The images came quickly, and she saw him as she found him in the British hospital after the Battle of Concord of April 19, 1775. Unconscious, his left arm broken by an American musketball, head bandaged where another musketball had dug a furrow to the bone, pale, breathing slow and deep. With fierce determination that he was not going to die, she brought soup from home, cakes, fruit, and she visited him as often as the stern-faced British doctors would allow. He had lived and grown strong. She begged him to come to her home and meet her family, and she remembered his face as he appeared that evening, standing straight and tall. Strong chin, generous mouth, prominent nose, gentle eyes. And she remembered the scar that marked the brow above his left eye, a scar he had taken long ago while rescuing soldiers from a burning building filled with munitions.

In her heart she could hear his voice, deep and quiet, as he asked permission from Margaret and Matthew to spend a few moments with her in the backyard. He had led her to the bench where they sat while he placed a gift in her hands. A beautiful handkerchief, with her initials—BD—flawlessly embroidered in royal blue needlepoint at one corner. Then he rose to take her back into the house, and she felt again the exquisite tremor that ran through her as she impulsively threw her arms about his neck, and for a time his arms circled her and held her close while her heart pounded. She remembered the brief moment she had brushed a kiss on his cheek before he took her hand and led her back to the house. An overpowering longing to touch him once again, feel his arms once again, rose in her breast, and left her trembling.

The scenes in her mind moved on to the awful day, March 17, 1776, when the British marched out of Boston, moving north where they would inflict the catastrophic defeat of the Americans on Long Island, New York, and when she had stood in the narrow, cobblestone streets with five thousand other Bostonians, watching the long, red-coated column pass by. She felt once again the stab in her heart as he passed within a few feet of her, able only to look down at her from his horse as he led his company of men toward the Neck, onto the mainland.

In the darkness, with rain trickling down her face and arms and the back of her neck, the words of the letter that had been delivered by special messenger that same day to Margaret came before her eyes. It was written by his hand, addressed to Margaret, not her. She kept the letter in her bedroom, and read it silently every night for months, until it was worn and wearing thin at the folds. She could recite every word from memory.

Thursday, March 15, 1776.

Dear Mrs. Dunson:

A private courier will deliver this to you after the British military has evacuated the city of Boston. I could not leave without making my thoughts known to you, and your family, and to Brigitte.

It was my great blessing and privilege to share an

evening with your family. I have never felt nor seen bonds of love to compare with those I observed in your home that night. I will remember it always. I cannot imagine the joy I might experience, were I allowed to associate with such a family for the rest of my life, through your daughter Brigitte. I have never associated with young women before; however, in my heart I know I will have the strongest of feelings for Brigitte as long as I live.

Notwithstanding, the reality is, I am a British officer, and she is an American. I am unable to consider asking her to leave you, and your home, to live in England. While she might accept that offer now, I can see plainly that with the passage of time, she would yearn for you, and her family, and native land, which is only as it should be. My regard for her will not allow me to do that to her.

I know you can make her understand, and for that reason I address this letter to you. Please help her.

I hope I do not exceed my proper bounds when I express my love for you and your family, and for your daughter Brigitte.

Sincerely,
Captain Richard A. Buchanan.

For a moment hot tears mingled with the cool rain on her cheeks, and she did not wipe at them, nor did she care.

Where is he tonight? Was he with the British when we abandoned Fort Ticonderoga? At the Battle of Hubbardton? Was he at Skenesborough when they sank our boats and burned the town to the ground? Was he there when the Indians went into the countryside to murder the settlers? To murder Jane McCrae?

She unwrapped her arms from her knees and let her legs dangle from the bench, with her feet in the wet grass. Silently she gathered her courage, and she trembled as she allowed herself to face the three questions that had haunted her, ridden her heavily from daybreak.

Is he alive? Is he wounded? Why hasn't he answered my letters?

Oddly, the greatest pain lay in the thought that he was alive and unwounded, and that his failure to answer her letters was because with the passing of time his feeling for her had ebbed and died; he no longer loved her. His death would bring unbearable pain. Loss of his love might kill her.

Inside, something shifted, and the conflicting morass of thought and emotion clarified, settled. The gray, morose, sinking feeling that had ridden her hard all day vanished in the sudden sureness that now rose to possess her.

He's alive. He loves me. There is an explanation for his failure to write. I don't know what it is, but I will know some day.

She was aware of the lifting of the oppressive fog that had clouded her mind and emotions, but unsure of how it had happened, nor did she care. It was enough that somehow her heart and mind were once again clear and steady. She pushed aside the nagging thought that she was a woman divided. She refused to ponder the anomaly of how she could reconcile her wish to marry a British captain with the fact that her brothers might be forced to kill him in battle. It had plagued her too long. She would not allow it to raise its ugly head tonight.

With the soft rain falling on her head and shoulders, she sensed for the first time the world that awaits all women who commit themselves to love—sweetheart, husband, child—it makes no difference. To allow another into that most sacred chamber of their heart is to accept the fearful burden of knowing that forever after, each moment of life carries the possibility of the greatest of joys, and the greatest of sorrows—the inseparable, eternal companions.

Expanded, sobered, awed by her discovery, she rose and thoughtfully walked back toward the house, heedless of the rain and the wet grass that drenched her feet and ankles.

Notes

The Dunson family is fictional.

The story of the Mohawk treatment of Jane McCrae was told in the previous chapter.

It will be remembered that Brigitte Dunson fell in love with a British captain, Richard Arlen Buchanan, and he with her. His letter to her, through her mother, at the time his regiment marched out of Boston, is set forth in full, as is her remembrance of his physical appearance, including the telltale scar in his left eyebrow.

CHAPTER XXVI

*I*n the glow of two lamps on the table inside his command tent, General George Washington heaved a sigh and leaned back in his chair to dig a thumb and forefinger into weary eyes. He glanced at the clock on one corner of the table, and for a moment stared in disbelief, then quietly muttered, "Ten minutes past eleven. Where did I lose three hours?"

His forehead furrowed as he straightened, then stood to pace, struggling to hold his intense frustration from becoming anger. *Where is he? First at the Virginia Capes, then sailing north into the Atlantic, then back down at Sandy Hook, then just sitting there with his army aboard ships lying at anchor for weeks waiting for the tides! Exactly what does he have in mind? It's obvious to me he wants Philadelphia, but if that's true, why in the name of heaven doesn't he just sail his army up the Delaware and take it? Is there any human being alive who knows Howe's mind? Does Howe know it himself?*

He stopped for a moment to stare at the stack of communications sitting on the left side of his desk.

I have critical correspondence I must attend to, and all I'm getting done is playing this fool's game with Howe, following him from one place to another, wasting supplies and manpower because I have no other choice, appearing more and more like an incompetent. Now I find myself here in this gorge called Smith's Cove—not on any map—waiting for him to make a move on the Hudson. I can't simply engage him because I haven't the manpower nor the munitions to win. I have to wait to pick the time and place, and in the meantime, simply continue using up what men and supplies I have, waiting for the right time. The militia up in New Hampshire and Vermont will have to handle Burgoyne.

He glanced again at the paperwork waiting on his table. *Congress, disgruntled officers, angry militia, frightened people, suppliers who haven't been paid, food shortages, munitions, blankets, medicine—when will it ever end? How do I hold Howe in place, send men to help the militia on the Hudson, and still try to keep everyone satisfied? I have one dollar for every hundred I need, one man for every hundred I need, and only the Almighty knows whether it will ever change.*

He brought his inner rage under control, drew a great breath, and slowly let it out before he returned to the table and sat once again on the chair. He reached for the next document on the stack and quickly read it.

Schuyler, in the northern theater on the Hudson. Abandoned Fort Ti. Can't find St. Clair and his command. Congress ready to bring both of them in for an inquiry— probably courts-martial. Needs help to check Burgoyne. John Adams ready to accuse them both of treason. What John Adams needs is six months in the front lines with a musket in his hands and cannonballs whistling. I refuse to judge St. Clair or Schuyler before they've been given a fair chance to explain themselves. Henry Knox and Nathanael Green are of the same mind—give them their chance. I know St. Clair—how he fought at Long Island and Trenton and Princeton. If he abandoned Fort Ti, it was for good reason.

He laid the document down, placed his elbows on the table, and buried his face in his hands while he brought his mind to bear.

I've already sent Benedict Arnold and Ben Lincoln up there. Benedict will see that Burgoyne's greatest enemy isn't the militia, or our army. It's that wilderness. Benedict will know how to use it to slow Burgoyne, use up his supplies and men, force Burgoyne to a stand. And when the fight comes, we must win, because we cannot defend ourselves against Burgoyne on the west and Howe on the east, at the same time. We must win! Benedict will know that.

His thoughts continued. *They'll need more seasoned men for the big battle. Officers who can lead. Benedict will be invaluable, but they'll need more than just one.*

He leaned back in his chair, arms hanging loosely at his sides. *Who do we have? Who can I spare?* Thoughtfully he reviewed the officers in his Continental army command, and slowly his mind settled.

John Glover and his twelve hundred Marbleheaders are back, over at Peekskill, and heaven only knows those men are among the best. Daniel Morgan and his riflemen. Three hundred of the finest shots on this continent. With Benedict there, and Glover and Morgan beside him, they can lead the militia. And if they'll wait until the wilderness has taken its toll on Burgoyne's army, and then pick the time and the place for the fight, they'll win.

By force of an iron will that had inspired and sustained an entire army through two impossible years, Washington reached for pen and quill to write orders to two men.

John Glover. Daniel Morgan.

"O yezz, O yezz, O yezz! Hear ye one and all. The General Court of the sovereign state of New Hampshire is now in special session. John Langdon, the most reputable and honorable Speaker of the General Court, presiding."

The sweating, rotund clerk of the court mopped his brow as he took his seat beside a raw pine table that stood on the podium at the head of the square, plain room. A New Hampshire flag hung on a pole at one end of the table and an American flag at the other. The windows were all open to allow what little breeze there was to come through, and flies and mosquitoes buzzed incessantly. Outside, horses and wagons surrounded the tiny log courthouse and filled the village of Exeter. Men and women in homespun settled onto rough-finished pine benches to sit quietly, the men holding their hats in their hands, sweating in the summer heat of the Connecticut River wilderness, waiting for the court to get on with the business.

Speaker Langdon wasted no time. He cleared his throat, raised a sheet of paper, glanced over it, and spoke.

"We're here in special session at the request of Ira Allen, who represents the state of Vermont. That state has existed for only a few months now, and they have no way to defend themselves against the British army that's now over threatening the lives of just about everybody with Indians. I think you've all heard what they've been doing. Murdering, scalping—there's no end to it. I doubt any of you have forgotten what they did to Jane McCrae."

Instant murmuring broke out, rose to a crescendo, and subsided.

"I thought so. Our neighbors in Vermont are asking for us to help them. The trouble is, with what? Seth Warner's men were at the Hubbardton battle, and I doubt he has one hundred fifty men left who are fit to fight, and that's all we have right now standing between us and the British army. If we send them, we're without a militia to defend our own ground."

The room fell into silence as men pondered how to raise an army, and women pondered the fate of their children.

Landgon waited until every eye was on him before he continued. "If we don't help our Vermont neighbors, Burgoyne and his Indians can march right in on us here with nobody to stop them."

The silence held. Langdon stood.

"So let me tell you what I think. I have three thousand dollars in hard cash, and I pledge my household plate as security for a loan of another three thousand. I also have seventy hogsheads of good Tobago rum that I'm going to sell. All told, that ought to make about ten thousand dollars, and I'm lending that to a fund to pay an army of militia from New Hampshire, to go to Vermont to check Burgoyne."

There were audible gasps, and then a flood of voices.

I got seventy dollars and a sow and nine suckling pigs I can sell.

I got two mules that're for sale as of right now.

I got sixteen barrels of the best apple cider in New Hampshire—who'll buy it?

Why, I've got four quilts I been saving, ten thousand hand stitches each—should be worth ten dollars apiece.

Langdon let it run on for a time before he raised a hand to still the discussion. "The way I see it," he said, "if the British take New Hampshire, our property won't be worth anything anyway. And if we win, and they don't get our property, why, we can make a deal and Vermont can pay us back as time goes by."

Yes! Yes! Yes!

"We can raise a brigade, and our friend John Stark can lead it."

He was drowned out by a chorus of voices shouting their abundant approval. Nobody had forgotten it was their own John Stark who had fought the French in the Seven Years' War, then with Abercromby, and finally had joined the rebels to fight the British. It was he who had coolly and heroically led a New Hampshire regiment in the Battle of Bunker Hill, and been a shining hero at the Battle of Trenton, where he and John Glover had sealed up the south end of the town and held it against the frantic Hessians. No man who fought with him would ever forget him standing to his full height, sword in hand, jaw set like granite, leading them straight into the whistling musketballs and cannon and grapeshot. No soldier in New Hampshire was wiser in the ways of war in the American wilderness than John Stark.

Nor had anyone forgotten how a fickle Continental Congress had passed him over when they considered promotions, granting generalships to French officers whom they had never seen before, rather than Americans who had earned it. The proud John Stark knew that he, and Benedict Arnold, and others, had earned their promotions, and when he discovered what Congress had done to them, he sent Congress a stinging letter of resignation, handed them back his Continental army commission, and marched back to his home in New Hampshire to be with his comely wife, Elizabeth, whom everyone called Molly. At home once again, John and Molly were hailed as leading citizens among their own.

A citizen stood, and Langdon quieted the room.

"Mr. Speaker, I figger we ought to make John Stark a general of some sort, but be sure he reports to us here in New Hampshire, and not to those politicians down there in Congress."

Yes! Yes! Yes!

Langdon pursed his mouth for a moment, then turned to the other members of the General Court, who were also the New Hampshire Committee of Safety.

"If I understood that right, we need a motion, and I now make it. I move that John Stark be granted the rank of brigadier general in the New Hampshire militia, to be accountable to this Committee of Safety, and not to the Continental Congress."

"I second it."

"I call for the vote."

"All in favor?"

The room rang with the word, *"Aye!"*

Langdon concluded. "The vote was unanimous. Mr. Secretary, make a record of this for delivery to John Stark, today if possible. And write out the usual commission making him a brigadier general."

John Stark accepted the commission on the spot. Six days later, he had assembled twenty-five companies of militia—nearly fifteen hundred men. Most had volunteered the moment they heard that Stark was to be their commander. Some had walked out of church services to join. In one town, more than one-third of the adult men formed a company and marched to Exeter. In the meantime, in short order, Stark gathered food, cook kettles, axes, shovels, gunpowder, musketballs, and medicines and prepared to march, with orders in hand granting him authority to assist the militia in Vermont, or any other state, or the Continental army if in his judgment it would promote the safety of the state of New Hampshire. No militia general had ever been granted such broad authority.

On August sixth, Stark and his militia passed through Bromley, heading for Vermont. As he approached Manchester, he was informed that General Lincoln of the Continental army had ordered his command to march to Sprouts, where the Mohawk River empties into the Hudson, not far above Albany.

Stark's piercing blue eyes clouded. "Where's Lincoln?"

He found him, and his eyes drilled holes in him as Stark demanded, "Just what's going on here?"

"General Schuyler has ordered your command to—"

That's as far as Lincoln got before Stark cut him off. "Thank you, I have my orders from the state of New Hampshire, and I consider myself capable of taking command of my own men. It is my intention to march to Bennington, where I will do what my commission requires of me. Sooner or later the British will have to take Bennington, and I intend to be there to protect the citizens. Here, sir, is a copy of my orders."

Stark turned on his heel and returned to his men, marching them to the wilderness community of Bennington, consisting of one church and fourteen homes, perhaps the largest village in the state of Vermont. He did not know, nor did he care, what General Lincoln might tell General Schuyler. With insight born of his experience and knowledge of warfare in the wilderness, he understood one thing only too well.

Bennington was blessed with many horses and an abundance of grain and food supplies. Sooner or later, Burgoyne would send part of his army there to plunder the village. And when he did, John Stark and fifteen hundred angry New Hampshire rebels would be waiting.

★ ★ ★ ★ ★

Congressman Elbridge Gerry of Massachusetts laid the message on his desk, sighed, shook his head in disgust, and turned to the young, peg-legged Gouverneur Morris. "It seems that General Philip Schuyler can't even find his army, let alone stop Burgoyne. St. Clair's out there somewhere east of the Hudson, lost in the forest, while Schuyler's running around trying to save what's left."

The long, sweltering Continental Congress session had adjourned for the day, and most of the congressmen were gathering their papers and coats to leave. They slowed and fell silent to listen as Gerry, dour, cryptic, thinning gray hair, continued.

"With more than ten thousand soldiers at his command, St. Clair abandoned Fort Ti without firing a shot, retreated to Hubbardton where he lost a battle, retreated to Castle Town and just kept running to only heaven knows where, while Schuyler lost a battle at Fort Anne, then lost everything at Skenesborough, and right now is headed for someplace called Saratoga. I challenge any of you to find it on the map."

He rose and began assembling the papers on his desk, still shaking his head, face puckered. "So many unbelievable events have happened over there around Fort Ticonderoga that a committee could make a powerful case for the claim that both Schuyler and St. Clair are in league with the British. Either that or they're both monumentally incompetent. What's happened over there is catastrophic."

He stopped to face Morris and wag a finger in his face. "Right now it wouldn't take much to prompt someone to make a motion on the floor to enter a congressional order for both Schuyler and St. Clair to report to us here to account to us for their conduct. Strip them of their commands until we hear what they meant, giving away the linchpin to the defense of the whole western frontier. That's what they did, you know. Abandoned Fort Ti in the dead of night without firing a shot to defend it."

He paused for a moment while a frown crossed his face. "If the facts are as I expect them to be, I can see courts-martial coming to decide whether or not the two of them are guilty of treason. If they are, maybe they ought to be hung."

Congressman Morris of New York set his wooden leg thumping on the floor. "Interesting idea, but it leaves a heavy question unanswered. If Schuyler and St. Clair are both stripped of command, who replaces them?"

Slowly Gerry turned to face the man, eyes narrowed. "I rather think it would be Horatio Gates."

Every man who heard it stopped in his tracks, wide-eyed. Granny Gates! The general who had abandoned Washington as they were loading the boats to cross the Delaware last December twenty-fifth, and had then come to Philadelphia to solicit Congress while Washington and his tattered army stormed the streets of Trenton in the blizzard of December twenty-sixth, to take the town and the entire Hessian garrison—achieving the most spectacular victory yet in the ongoing war. It was Gates who had come wheedling to Congress every chance he could find or invent, to plead, cajole, beg, or weep if necessary, in his obsessive passion to persuade Congress that indeed he, Gates, should replace General George Washington.

Gouverneur Morris, wise in the ways of men and politics, raised one eyebrow. "Gates, you say? I'm wondering what there is in his past to recommend him for the rather, shall we say, delicate assignment of beating Gentleman Johnny out there in the forest. Oh, I have no doubt Gates would thump him soundly if he could do it from here. Write a flood of orders from here and let his soldiers do the fighting there. Extremely talented, Gates, when it comes to politics and persuasion."

"Humph," Gerry turned from Morris and busied himself with

stuffing papers into the drawer of his desk in the square, high-ceilinged Independence Hall.

Morris thumped him good-naturedly on the back as he turned away. "But then one never knows. If this august body does recall Schuyler and St. Clair, they just might finish botching the job by giving the Northern army to Gates."

Notes

General George Washington was pursuing the very complicated, nonsensical maneuvers of General William Howe on the Atlantic seaboard, when he became aware of the approaching climax to the affairs on the Hudson River. Consequently, with General Benedict Arnold already there, he pondered who he might also be able to spare to assist generals St. Clair and Schuyler. He resolved to send General John Glover and his Marblehead Regiment, and General Daniel Morgan with his incomparable riflemen (Ketchum, *Saratoga*, pp. 255, 279, 338).

Upon request of Ira Allen, representing the newly independent state of Vermont, the General Court of New Hampshire met in general session to determine how to respond to the plea for help. John Langdon, Speaker of the General Court, and a man of considerable wealth, offered three thousand dollars in cash, another three thousand from a loan, and seventy hogsheads of rum to start a fund to hire an army. Others joined in. Soon they had enough money to approach General John Stark of the New Hampshire militia. John Stark was one of the most rigid, opinionated men in the militia, and also one of the toughest, most fearless fighters in the state. It was he who walked the breastworks at Bunker Hill while British cannonballs and musketfire kicked up dirt all around him, and again at Trenton, when he and John Glover sealed off the south end of town. They approached Stark with their request, he accepted, and within days had gathered fifteen hundred men who would follow him wherever he led. He defied General Lincoln's orders to follow him, and instead marched his men straight to Bennington, knowing that sooner or later Burgoyne would arrive there to get the horses, grain, and other food stores. He could not have done better (see Ketchum, *Saratoga*, pp. 285–88).

The conversation between Congressmen Elbridge Gerry and Gouverneur Morris is fictional. However, it does convey the feeling in Congress toward generals Schuyler and St. Clair. Based upon the loss of Fort Ticonderoga, and the subsequent ongoing retreat of their army, Congress passed two resolutions, and the president of the Congress, John Hancock, issued a congressional order that was delivered to both men. A congressional inquiry was to be conducted into their conduct, and they were to report to General Washington's headquarters, ostensibly to face courts-martial (Ketchum, *Saratoga*, p. 335).

In support, see also Leckie, *George Washington's War*, pp. 400–401.

CHAPTER XXVII

★ ★ ★

*B*ritish engineers and red-coated regulars had invaded the
pristine forests in 1758 to build Fort Stanwix, at the place where the
headwaters of the Mohawk River turn from their southerly course to
wend their way one hundred ten miles west and empty into the mother
river, the Hudson. They took pride in its walls, built of a double row of
pine tree trunks sunk deep in the ground ten feet apart and thrusting
twenty-five feet into the air. The space between the walls was filled with
earth and rock. More than one hundred yards square, the tops of the
walls afforded broad walkways, with notches for cannon ports and openings for riflemen. The guns commanded a field of fire for hundreds of
yards.

Forgotten after the French surrendered to the British in 1763 at the
end of the Seven Years' War for the control of the American Northeast,
the fort became a wreck until 1776, when the American rebels suddenly
saw a need for it in their war with the British. Colonel Peter Gansevoort,
tall, well-built, strong features, fair, tough-minded, was sent with a command of six hundred men to bring the fort up to fighting condition
and prepare to hold it against any British assault. Once again men
pitted themselves against the wilderness, and nature allowed them to
reclaim their fort—a tiny, fragile, expendable in the great scheme of the
wilderness.

Gansevoort did his job well, and the British came to do theirs.

Colonel Barry St. Leger hacked a road through the forest and built breastworks a few hundred yards from the heavy walls on three sides of the fort. He left the south wall unopposed, believing an impassable swamp rendered it useless to either the Americans or the British.

Thus, with the opposing armies gathered and facing each other, the time had come for the test of arms and men.

"Right there, sir. See?" The excited young private's arm was raised, pointing over the south wall of Fort Stanwix. The nine o'clock morning sun had turned the headwaters of the Mohawk River into a bronze ribbon meandering west outside the fort's thick walls.

Lieutenant Colonel Marinus Willet, short and stocky, squinted, searching, before he saw them—three men slogging in from the swampy bog south of the fort, one in front, two behind, five hundred yards away. The lead man had no weapon. The second man carried two, the third man one. The distance was too great to know who they were, or if their weapons were rifles or muskets.

The tall, slender private suddenly jerked up his rifle and laid it over the dirt-filled wall. "That man in front's an Indian, sir, a painted red savage like the ones who's been raiding. Another hundred yards, and I can hit him from here." He eared back the hammer on his Pennsylvania rifle, settled the thin foreblade on the incoming man's chest, and waited, calculating distance and wind.

"Wait," Willet ordered, deflecting the rifle barrel. "Those two behind! Aren't they the two new scouts we sent out three days ago? I forget their names."

The private thrust his head forward, eyes narrowed as he studied the men. "Could be, sir. That second one's a white man. Looks a lot like the one from Boston."

"I think it's them, bringing in a prisoner. Keep your rifle on them until we're sure." He turned to shout at the next picket on the wall, "Hold your fire. They're friendly."

At that moment the third incoming man raised his weapon high over his head with both hands, the universal sign they were coming in peace.

"See there, sir, that third one's signaling. I think he's the white man that dresses like an Indian. I heard he was raised Iroquois."

When the men were two hundred yards out, Willet straightened. "It's them. I'll let them in." He hurried down the wide walkway, behind the trails of the two cannon with their muzzles thrust into the gun ports, and descended the stairs two at a time down to the open parade ground. He trotted to the south gates and called to the corporal, "Open them. Scouts coming in with a prisoner."

The heavy gates creaked as they swung open, and as Billy, Eli, and the third man darted through, the corporal and his three-man detail threw their shoulders against them to close them once again, then lower the heavy crossbar thumping into its four brackets.

Eli spoke in Iroquois to the Indian in front of him. The man stopped, wild-eyed, half-crouched, ready, certain that the startled, curious soldiers who came running meant to kill him. On Willet's command, the soldiers stopped in a loose circle around him as he faced the terrified Indian. Billy came to attention while Eli remained behind, his rifle pointed loosely at the small of the Indian's back. All three of them waited, dripping swamp water and mud from the waist down.

Billy spoke. "Corporal Weems and Scout Stroud reporting, sir."

Relief showed in Willet's face. "We were getting worried. I see you've brought a prisoner."

"Yes, sir."

"Follow me. Colonel Gansevoort's waiting."

The circle of soldiers opened, and Willet marched across the parade ground while men pointed and remarked at the three new arrivals—one painted Indian and two filthy, stubble-bearded white men, trailing swamp water and mud. The small detail stopped at the door to the office of Colonel Peter Gansevoort, and Willet rapped loudly. They heard, "Enter" from within, and Willet swung the door open.

Gansevoort stood behind his desk in the square, plain, rough-finished office, and his eyes swept the three men puddling swamp mud and water on the floor planking. He understood instantly what had happened.

"Glad you're back safe. Any trouble?"

Billy answered. "None, sir. We brought back a prisoner for questioning."

"I see you came in through the swamp."

"Yes, sir. It's the only place the British left open."

With his native, hardheaded Dutch practicality, Gansevoort wasted no time. He ran a critical eye over the frightened Indian. "Where did you get this man?"

Eli answered. "From St. Leger's camp."

Gansevoort turned to Eli. "What's his name?"

"Oryontyngha. Christian name's Thomas."

Gansevoort was aware that Eli had not saluted, but he ignored it. "Does he have information?"

"A sub-chief. He knows pretty much what they're planning."

"What is it?"

Eli locked eyes with Gansevoort, and the room became silent. "Siege. They're going to start with their cannon today or tomorrow."

Gansevoort pursed his mouth for a moment. "The whole force?"

"The whole force."

Gansevoort gestured to chairs and a bench, and Billy and Eli sat. The Indian backed up to the wall and refused to move. They left him standing. Gansevoort continued. "Do they know how many men we have here? Our condition?"

"Yes. Carleton told St. Leger you had sixty men and almost no cannon, and that the fort was a wreck. Claus didn't believe it. He sent his own Indians to scout you. They know you have more than six hundred men, and somewhere near fifteen cannon, and that the fort's ready for battle. They figure with your food supply you can last about a month."

Gansevoort's eyes widened. "They've scouted us? When?"

Eli shrugged. "Maybe ten days ago. While they were building their road and breastworks out there."

"How many cannon do they have?"

"Twenty, light ones."

"Only twenty, light guns! You know that for a fact?"

"Yes. We went into their camp and counted. When Carleton told St. Leger you had almost no guns, and only a handful of men, St. Leger figured he wouldn't need more than twenty light guns. It was Claus who had the sense to scout you out. Now they plan to use what guns they have and starve you out."

"How do you know all this?"

Eli pointed to the Indian.

Gansevoort continued. "Do you trust him? Is he reliable?"

Eli nodded.

Gansevoort paused to order his thoughts, then asked, "How many men do they have, and who are they?"

Eli drew a counting stick from his weapons belt, and ran his knife blade over the notches, counting. "Two hundred redcoats. Twenty men to run the cannon. Eighty Hessians. Between six hundred and eight hundred Indians. And about four hundred Canadians and loyalists. Altogether, about fourteen or fifteen hundred men."

"What tribes of Indians?"

"Iroquois. Seneca. Tuscarora. Ojibwa. Mohawk."

"Who leads them?"

"Sir John Johnson is in overall command. Brant and Sayehqueragha lead the Indians."

"I know Brant. What about the other one?"

"He's older. As smart and tough as Brant."

"Cornplanter?"

"Didn't see him."

"Ask the Indian."

Eli turned to the Indian, standing like a statue, staring at them, concerned only with how and when they were going to kill him. Eli spoke in the guttural, flowing Iroquois language. The Indian did not move as he made a three-word answer.

"No. He doesn't think Cornplanter is there. Blacksnake is."

"Blacksnake?"

"Yes. A chief. He can give us trouble."

Gansevoort accepted it and moved on. "Why did they send that man—Captain Tice—in here two days ago under a flag of truce to offer us terms of a surrender?"

Again Eli spoke to the Indian. The answer was longer, choppy.

"St. Leger knows he doesn't have enough guns for a proper siege. He hoped Tice could persuade you to surrender without a fight. That's why he's had all his men setting up log and brush breastworks out around the fort where you can see them, and why he paraded the Seneca that came in yesterday. He hoped it would frighten you. If Tice failed to persuade you to surrender, he was under orders to at least get a good look at what you have inside the fort." A smile passed over Eli's face. "When you blindfolded him coming in and going out, he didn't get one look, and it angered St. Leger."

Gansevoort's sharp blue eyes glittered. "Good. It appears I had better call my officers together to plan our defense of—"

Eli cut him off. "There's more." Gansevoort stopped and the room went silent as he waited.

"Yesterday a Mohawk woman named Gonwatsijayenni sent word from Canajoharie to St. Leger. She said Nicholas Herkimer's on his way here with a thousand militia to help defend the fort. Herkimer was in Oriskany yesterday. Could arrive here today, if it's true."

Gansevoort gaped. "General Nicholas Herkimer? Who's this Indian woman?"

"Her Christian name's Mary Brant. She's the wife of Sir William Johnson and the granddaughter of Chief Hendrick."

"Do you believe it?"

"If Mary Brant said it, I do. She stands high in Indian councils."

Gansevoort's eyebrows raised. "A woman?"

"A woman. They have their say."

Gansevoort leaned forward for a moment, mind racing, when Eli interrupted, his voice low, intense.

"If this Indian knows what Mary Brant said, so does Joseph Brant. And if Joseph Brant knows it, he's not going to let Herkimer come on through to this fort. He's going to set a trap out there somewhere and ambush him. My guess is that most of Herkimer's people will never get here unless someone goes to tell him what he's walking into."

Gansevoort stiffened, and at that moment everyone in the room flinched at the sudden banging on the door. Gansevoort called, "Enter," and a sweating, panting young lieutenant burst into the room, gasping as he blurted, "Sir, three men have just come in from the south. They say they were sent by General Nicholas Herkimer. Urgent message. What shall I do with them, sir?"

"Bring them here this instant."

"Yes, sir!" The winded young lieutenant spun on his heel and forgot to close the door as he pounded out into the parade ground. Three minutes later he returned, leading three men who were soaked from their waist down, shirts and faces splattered with mud. They came to attention and saluted Colonel Gansevoort while their leader spoke.

"Sir, I am Adam Helmer. With me are John Demuth and John Kember. We have been sent by General Herkimer to inform you that he and four companies of militia and some members of the Tryon County Committee of Safety and some friendly Oneida Indian scouts are on their way here. They left Oriskany very early this morning. They should be arriving sometime after noon."

"Do you know his route?"

"I think from the east, sir."

"You came in from the south."

"Yes, sir."

Gansevoort asked his next question and held his breath. "You're sure he won't come in from the south?"

"Quite sure, sir. His column would never make it through that swamp. I believe he'll come in on the east road. He thinks he has enough men to fight his way through if he has to. We are under orders to tell you that when we have delivered this message, he wishes you to fire three cannon as a to signal to him. Then send out a force of men to meet him and guide him in."

For ten seconds the only sound was the buzzing of flies and insects while Gansevoort battled to organize his jumbled thoughts. *If he comes in from the east, he'll have to come through St. Leger's lines.* His mind cleared and he spoke with authority.

"Very well!" He turned to Willet. "Colonel, take two hundred men of your choice and one light cannon. Pick a route that will avoid heavy contact with St. Leger's forces and go bring General Herkimer in. As you leave the gates, order the men on the east wall to fire three cannon, at ten second intervals."

"Yes, sir." Willet strode out the door and broke into a run across the parade ground.

Eli stood, rifle in hand. "I'm going."

Gansevoort raised a warning hand. "We might need you here."

"What if Willet doesn't find Herkimer, or gets there too late? There's ten places between here and Oriskany where Brant could take down Herkimer."

Gansevoort stared at him for three seconds before he nodded. "Go."

Eli glanced at Billy and moved out the door at a trot, Billy right behind.

General Nicholas Herkimer drank long from his wooden canteen, then squinted upward at the morning sun. *We'll be there mid-afternoon, if we can hold this pace. If Helmer and Demuth and Kember made it through, why haven't we heard the three cannon shots? And where's the column Gansevoort was to send out? I think we better bivouac right here until we hear those guns and—*

"The men are talkin', sir."

Herkimer started and turned to look up at Ebenezer Cox, who stood to his right, slightly behind him. It was the same Ebenezer Cox who had joined him in the council with Joseph Brant at Unadilla, short weeks ago. Cox was married to the daughter of George Klock, who months earlier had held Brant and some of his warriors at musket point to humiliate him with accusations of stealing cattle. The hatred both Klock and Cox held for Brant was legendary. It was Cox who had suddenly confronted Brant at the Unadilla council to hotly accuse him of breaking the ancient

Iroquois promise to remain neutral in conflicts between white men, and ordered him to keep his Indians out of it. In minutes Brant had his men armed, ready for battle, and it was only Herkimer's intervention that avoided a massacre on the spot. Lacking sufficient officers for the march to save Fort Stanwix, the Committee of Safety had restored to Cox his former rank of colonel in the militia.

Herkimer jammed the stopper back in his canteen and demanded, "Talking about what?"

"Sitting here. They're concerned."

"Concerned?"

"Yes, sir. Afraid we haven't got the stomach to move on."

Herkimer stood, anger rising in his chest. "You mean *me*, don't you? They think I don't have the nerve to lead them in."

A crooked smile formed on Cox's whisker-stubbled face. "Well, now, sir, I didn't exactly mean—"

Herkimer cut him off, loud, hot. "Right now we're waiting for the cannon signal from Fort Stanwix, and for a column to come lead us in. We don't have scouts out, so we don't know what's in front of us, or beside us, or behind us. Go tell your men the most ridiculous thing we can do right now is move blindly forward."

Cox was still smiling his crooked smile. "The men know all that, sir. But the way they see it, we got enough men to fight our way right on through. If we draw enough of the British and Indians into the fight, it might save Fort Stanwix. That's what the men are saying, sir."

Something inside Herkimer snapped. His voice dropped, and his eyes were points of light. "All right, tell the men to get onto their feet right now. We're ready to move."

Cox beamed. "Yes, sir!"

Major John Butler turned in the midmorning sun and raised an arm to point. "Colonel, Brant's coming up from behind with two Indians. Looks like they've been running."

Colonel Barry St. Leger pivoted to watch Brant cover the last fifteen yards and stop, facing him, two Indians on his left. The two were stripped to the waist, breathing hard, painted, sweating, tomahawks and knives in their belts, muskets in their right hands. St. Leger watched Brant's stolid face, waiting for an explanation.

"Mohawk scouts. Sent from Canajoharie by Mary Brant to tell us. Herkimer is coming from Oriskany with militia to Fort Stanwix. Many militia."

St. Leger's breath slowed. "Herkimer? How many men?"

Brant spoke to the Indians, listened, then turned to St. Leger.

"One thousand. Some Oneida scouts with them."

"*One thousand!*" St. Leger's face fell as he turned to peer at Fort Stanwix, eight hundred yards west with the sun shining brightly off its walls and flying the newly received flag of red and white bars and thirteen stars in a field of blue. "We're about to begin a siege, and we've got one thousand rebel militia coming in from behind us?"

Brant remained silent, his dark face a blank.

St. Leger threw his hands in the air. "How far behind?"

Brant spoke to the Indians, took their answers, then replied, "Two hours. Three at the most."

St. Leger shook his head. "We've got Gansevoort and six hundred men in the fort, and Herkimer and one thousand behind us. Suddenly we're caught in the middle! We don't have the men to engage both. What do we do?"

Brant's expression did not change. "I know the place to stop Herkimer. A ravine, four miles to the east. He can be trapped and destroyed. It can be done by four hundred Indians."

Hope leaped in St. Leger's eyes. "Are you sure?"

Brant nodded but remained silent.

St. Leger racked his brain for other options, but there were none. "All right." He turned to Major Butler. "Take four hundred Mohawk and twenty rangers and follow Brant. Set an ambush and destroy Herkimer's column. You can't let them flank us. You must—"

The report of cannon froze the group for a moment, then all their heads swung around to stare at Fort Stanwix, where a cloud of white smoke drifted upward from an eastwall gunport. St. Leger raised an arm to point, and his entire command came to a standstill as a second blast rolled out across the clearing, and then a third shot, timed on the same interval.

For five seconds no one moved, and then everyone moved as talk and gestures broke out all up and down the breastworks. Regulars and Indians alike pointed at the three clouds of smoke dissipating lazily into the blue sky, puzzled, a growing sense that something was wrong spreading among them.

St. Leger spoke. "I calculate that was a signal of some sort. Maybe to Herkimer." He turned instantly to Butler and Brant. "Get your men and leave. If that was a signal to Herkimer, he can't be far."

At that moment Sir John Johnson, the ranking officer, came running. "Colonel, those shots weren't to engage us. They had to be a signal."

St. Leger bobbed his head. "I just learned that General Herkimer's coming in from our rear with one thousand militia."

Johnson's eyes popped. "*What?*"

"I'm sending Brant and four hundred Indians east to meet him. Butler's taking command."

Johnson squared his shoulders. "I'm going with them." Johnson out-ranked both Butler and St. Leger, and St. Leger wasted no time. "Take command. Butler, you assume second in command."

Johnson turned to Brant. "I'll expect your Indians to be ready within ten minutes, and we will move at double time."

Brant turned and hurried to his waiting Mohawk. Within five minutes they were gathered, painted, anxious, as blood lust rose in their veins. Half a dozen sub-chiefs confronted Brant with words and gestures, and Brant listened. He shook his head and turned to go when two of them stepped forward to call angry words. Slowly Brant turned, barely in control of his disgust, and answered them. Instantly, the Indians nodded their heads and broke into loud talk and broad gestures as Brant strode quickly back to Johnson.

"My men say they were promised rum. They want it before they fight."

Johnson recoiled in disbelief. "Rum? Now? There is no time!"

Brant remained stoic. "It will take only a few minutes. They will not leave without it."

Johnson spoke through gritted teeth. "All right. Break out one barrel of rum, and see to it your men are moving east within ten minutes, double time."

In the light and shadow of the deep forest, Lieutenant Colonel Marinus Willet turned silently toward his column and raised both hands. Instantly his two hundred fifty men soundlessly dropped to their haunches and all but disappeared in the thick foliage and trees. He worked his way back among them, called his captains together, and spoke softly.

"There's a British camp up there about two hundred fifty yards, not too big. I don't think they know we're here. We're going to separate, half each direction, and move in from two sides. I'll lead the right half, Major Driscoll the left. When I'm in position, I'll count off three minutes to be sure you're in position, and then fire the first shot. That's when we all come in hard and fast."

Ten minutes later Willet wiped his hand across his mouth, cocked his pistol, took aim at the nearest tent, and pulled the trigger. The shot cracked out to echo in the forest, and two hundred fifty rebel soldiers rose from the brush as one and stormed into the British camp. The leaders had gone fifty yards before they realized something was badly wrong. As they stampeded in from both sides, one woman, and less than ten men, had thrown down whatever was in their hands and sprinted north, through the only opening left to them, to disappear instantly in the forest. Three redcoats reached for their muskets, and all three went down when the rebels fired first. Two startled Indians pushed through a tent flap with tomahawks dangling from their wrists, and toppled when the nearest rebels fired their muskets without raising them to aim. Four dumbfounded British soldiers emerged from a tent and instantly threw their hands high in surrender.

Not another living thing stirred in the camp. The rebels slowed and stopped, and their war cries quieted as they turned their heads to look every direction, suspicious, groping to understand. Willet lowered his raised sword and in near silence stood stock-still, searching for an explanation. *Have they surrounded their own camp, and set an ambush for us? No, they couldn't have. We'd have seen them when we moved in.*

He jammed his sword back into its scabbard and shouted orders. "Collect anything of value and get ready to leave. St. Leger's heard us and by now he's sent someone to engage us. Be quick!"

Fifteen minutes later he lead his column back toward the fort at a trot, carrying with them fifty brass cooking kettles and over one hundred blankets, both items badly needed inside Fort Stanwix. They had also gathered up as many muskets, tomahawks, and spears, along with as much ammunition and clothing as his men could carry. Major Badlam's men were dragging their small cannon, bouncing, jolting along on its wheels. They plunged through the dense foliage, dodging, running, and then the fort was there before them through the trees, and then they were in the open.

The cannoneers on the high walls of Fort Stanwix had heard the distant rattle of muskets and instantly swarmed to their guns. They rammed roundshot home, lighted their linstocks, and waited in silence, eyes straining to see movement in the trees. When Willet's men broke into the open at a run, a shout rolled from the throats of a hundred cannoneers, who jammed clenched fists into the air. "Come on! Come on! You can make it!"

Twenty seconds later they saw the flashes of red in the trees, and the British regulars were there led by Captain Reginald Hoyes, sprinting to catch Willet's men. The British were carrying nothing but their muskets, and steadily gaining on the Americans, who were burdened with the spoils they had raided from the British camp.

Instantly the cannoneers on the walls of the fort raised a shout, "Behind you, behind you!" They gestured wildly, pointing.

The incoming Americans heard the bedlam. They could not understand the words, but one thing Major Badlam did understand was the wildly pointing arms. He turned his head and saw the redcoats a scant two hundred yards behind. Instantly he stopped, and barked orders to his cannon crew.

"Turn the gun around, load it heavy with grape, and stop those men!"

His crew spun around, recovered from the shock, and then quickly swung the small gun around. They rammed an overload of powder down the barrel and dumped a double load of grapeshot home, then pointed it back at Hoyes's oncoming redcoats, and touched it off. The small gun roared and bucked two feet in the air, but did not explode, as the grapeshot tore into the pursuing British, and the leaders stumbled and went down. The British detachment stopped in its tracks, then backed up to recover before once again moving quickly after the Americans.

The gunners on the high walls in the fort cheered wildly, then set the elevations on their own guns, and waited. The instant the British reached the eight-hundred-yard mark, every cannon on the east wall erupted. Willet's command instinctively ducked as the cannonballs ripped whizzing over their heads, and one second later the pursuing British were in the midst of flying dirt and rocks as the roundshot hit home and exploded. At the fort, the gate detail swung the huge east gates open, and Willet and his command came on through, gasping, sweating, spent, amid the cheers of every man in the fort. They had not lost a single man.

Nor had they reached Herkimer.

With the sun not yet to its zenith, Brant held up a hand and the column stopped. They were five miles east of Fort Stanwix, standing at the head of a ravine more than a mile long, at the bottom of which ran the narrow, crooked road that connected Fort Stanwix to Oriskany. The steep sides of the ravine were choked with trees and foliage and underbrush, and sloped gradually away from the road to suddenly rise sharply. In most places, men could be ten feet apart without knowing the other was there. At fifty feet, a musket or rifle would be almost useless. A battle in this ravine would be fought with knives and tomahawks, hand-to-hand, face-to-face, and Brant's eyes gleamed. As a battleground between white men trained to fight with cannon and muskets at a distance, and his Mohawk Indians trained to fight face-to-face, this was the place for the ambush. The first volley from his hidden Indians would cut down most of the rebel officers, and from there, the combatants would be plunged into a wild, chaotic, fragmented melee. The battle would go to those who best understood how to kill quickly with close-quarter weapons: the feared tomahawk, and the knife.

Brant spoke rapidly to Johnson and St. Leger. "I will divide my men, half on each side of the road, spaced the length of the ravine. You will go back fifty yards, just across the stream. When the rebel leaders have come out of the ravine and are very close to you, fire your first volley at them. That will be the signal. Most of the rebel column will still be in the ravine. My men will instantly fire from both sides and kill as many officers as they can. Then they will attack with tomahawk and knife. We must remember, they have one thousand, we have four hundred. Surprise is our greatest weapon. If we spring the trap well, they will have little chance to recover before most of them are dead. Remember. Surprise."

Johnson looked at Butler, who nodded. Johnson took one deep breath, then said, "Proceed."

Less than fifteen minutes later, only the ravens and jays knew that Brant's men were on both slopes of the ravine, and that Butler's men were at the head—all of them sweating, listening, waiting. Minutes that seemed to be an hour, passed. Certain that the afternoon was upon them, men squinted up at the sun, wondering why it had not moved. An opossum crossed the road, with two hundred pairs of eyes watching. A large porcupine followed by two smaller balls of quills ventured onto the road, to turn back into the undergrowth and disappear.

It seemed an eternity before the first sounds of marching men reached them from the east. Brant's men instantly became part of the forest, silent, unmoving. From hidden places they watched tall, angular General Herkimer, with Ebenezer Cox just behind, lead the column forward, heads turning from side to side, searching, smelling for an ambush. Behind them came Colonel Peter Bellinger, and finally, Colonel Frederick

Visscher, leading the rear guard and wagons. Herkimer moved steadily on—two hundred yards, four hundred, eight hundred. The front of the column passed the midpoint of the ravine. Birds rose from the trees, cursing the invaders as they continued their hot, sweaty march.

The flesh between Herkimer's shoulder blades was crawling as he counted paces, judging the distance to the head of the ravine where his command would be out and away from what was clearly a perfect place for an ambush. He glanced back, but could see nothing except what eons of time had put there. He could not see the end of his column, one mile back, with the fifteen wagons and carts filled with their supplies and ammunition bringing up the rear.

With Herkimer now only three hundred yards away, moving straight toward him and his waiting command, Butler raised his right hand six inches. Muskets clicked onto full cock and slowly came to bear on the leaders, waiting, waiting. The distance closed—two hundred yards. One hundred fifty.

The blood lust, the rum, the proximity of enemies to be killed and scalps to be taken was too much to endure. Before the wagons at the rear of Herkimer's column entered the ravine, some of the Mohawk near the east end suddenly stood, fired their muskets, threw them down, and came running, leaping into the startled rebel column. Instantly the Mohawk all up and down the ravine fired and charged, bounding through the undergrowth and over rocks into the midst of the bewildered, terrified Americans, tomahawks swinging wildly, knives slashing.

At the head of the ravine, Butler screamed a curse at the Mohawk who had disobeyed orders and sprung the trap too soon, then shouted, "Fire!" He followed his first volley with a charge, into the mouth of the ravine, where he ordered a halt while his men reloaded and knelt for their second volley.

At the rear of the column, Colonel Visscher stood stock-still for five full seconds, brain frozen, unable for a time to comprehend what had happened in the ravine ahead of him. One moment it had been deserted, the next, filled with blasting muskets, screaming red men, and the heart wrenching sounds of dying men. The rear guard, under his command, took one look at the scene from his worst nightmare, turned, and sprinted back the way they had come. Too late, Visscher turned to give his commands. His men were already in blind, headlong retreat.

"Halt! Halt or I'll have you all shot as deserters!"

Not one man slowed. The abandoned wagons sat in the rutted dirt trail as they disappeared.

In the first sixty seconds, more than one hundred of Herkimer's command were down—dead or dying. Over half his officers were dead, including Ebenezer Cox. The fighting lost all sense of focus; there was no center, no breastwork or hill that could be taken to end it. The American militia had been stunned beyond their ability to rally. One moment they had been sweating their way up a ravine; the next instant the world was filled with high, terrifying Mohawk war cries as hideously painted men swept over them like an avalanche, swinging tomahawks with deadly accuracy, slashing with knives, driving lances home, giving no quarter, hacking, shouting, scalping, cutting, moving like lightning to strike hard and fast, left and right. The column fragmented, to become small groups, three, four, five men clustered together, swinging their muskets like clubs, thrusting clumsily with their bayonets, fighting with their hands, or a rock, or anything they could seize. Within minutes the floor of the ravine was covered with bodies. Blood stained the ground everywhere. Wounded men moaned, calling, but there was no one to heed or help.

Herkimer stood bolt upright and shook his head, trying to force a focus to his shattered thoughts. Then he cupped his hands to shout, "Get out of the ravine! To the left! Up the left slope! Get up onto flat land where we can form a defensive line! To the left!"

He jerked his sword from its scabbard and plunged from the trail, up the left slope, when suddenly he felt a hammer blow to his left knee, and it buckled and Herkimer went down. Militiamen nearby formed a circle around him while others lifted him, and they started the impossible climb up the left slope of the ravine. Soldiers around them saw and heard it, and began to follow. They did not know what lay at the top of the slope; they only knew that if they remained in the slaughter around them, they would be dead. Struggling to reach the top, the leaders broke over the rim, followed by those who could.

Beyond the rim the land was flat, but the trees and the undergrowth were just as thick. There was no place to form a battle line and bring some sense of military discipline or order to the running fight. With the survivors gathering around him, Herkimer ordered his men to prop him against a tree, where he dug inside his tunic to bring out his long-stemmed stone pipe, which he filled with tobacco and lit. With his back to the tree, and his shattered left leg laid out straight before him, Herkimer puffed on his pipe while he pointed with his sword and gave orders to his men, trying to rally them to a focus. Men who saw him hesitated, startled by the sight of a man smoking his pipe in the midst of the wildest massacre any of them had ever seen.

One mile away, Eli suddenly stopped and raised a hand. Billy halted beside him, breathing hard from their four-mile run. They turned their heads and held their labored breathing for a moment, listening intently to unmistakable sounds they had heard all too often. A major battle was being fought not far ahead.

Pain crossed Billy's face as Eli spoke. "We're too late. Brant's got him."

Instantly they broke into a headlong run east, dodging through the forest, hurdling fallen trees, brush, and rocks. They slowed when they saw movement in the trees ahead, then worked their way slowly forward, trying to understand the chaos ahead. With the bloody fight raging just thirty yards in front of them, they dropped to their haunches, studying the shouting, screaming men, red and white, grappling, struggling, swinging their weapons in mortal, deadly combat.

Billy's arm shot up. "There!" he exclaimed. "Herkimer's trying to rally his men over there!"

"They're not going to make it the way they're doing it," Eli shouted. "Come on!"

Both men stood and sprinted forward, dodging through the trees, shouting as they came in behind the swarming Mohawk. They tore into them headlong, firing their musket and rifle at point-blank range to knock the first two rolling, then swinging their weapons like scythes, smashing red men to either side, leaving them unconscious or dying. They did not slow as Eli swung his tomahawk left and right, and Billy used his rifle butt like a battering ram, leaving a trail of downed red men behind, moaning with broken arms and cracked skulls. The nearest warriors spun around, surprised, not knowing who or what or how many were coming in like demons from their rear. Those nearest to Billy and Eli broke clear of the fighting, pausing to peer into the trees, certain there had to be more men attacking from the rear. Those farther away saw the lull, and within seconds the Mohawk cry, "Oonah," began to spread.

Billy and Eli did not slow. They continued their headlong plunge through the startled Mohawk, slamming into and then breaking free of the melee into the place where Herkimer was seated against the tree, trying to rally his men. For a few seconds the Indians hesitated, unsure of what had happened, dumbstruck that two men had cut a path through them to reach Herkimer. In those few seconds, Eli and Billy turned back toward the Mohawk, shouting to Herkimer's men, "Rally here! Their ranks are open!"

For the first time the Americans heard an order they could understand, and they saw the slightest breach in the wall of Indians. Twenty of the militiamen came charging, more following, and Billy and Eli led them back into the breach they had opened coming in, twisting, turning, driving the wedge deeper.

"Oonah! Oonah!" The sound rose once again, and began to swell. Gradually the Indians disengaged themselves and began fading back into the forest, unsure, hesitant, waiting for someone to give them direction. Eli spun and sprinted back to Herkimer.

"General, you better order your men back to the east while you can. Three more minutes and Brant and Blacksnake will be back in full force."

Instantly Herkimer shouted his orders. "Form a battle line! Fall back to the east! Bring the wounded if you can!"

The order was passed on, and within minutes the Americans had come together in a line, and settled into a rhythm, every other man firing while every other man reloaded. Those on the west end began the retreat, and the column followed. They paused only to gather the wounded they could find, leaving their dead on the field as they worked their way east on the high, flat land, then down the slope of the ravine to the road to continue their retreat.

"Etow! Etow!" Eli heard it from the three hundred warriors as the red hoard crested the lip of the ravine and came running down to once again engage the retreating Americans. Herkimer saw them coming and shouted his orders.

"Do not break the battle line! At all costs, stay in line!"

This time the Americans were not taken by surprise. They held their line, and kept their rotation in firing, loading, firing, loading, as they worked eastward in a controlled retreat. They held their fire until their target was clear, and close enough that they could not miss, and this time it was the Indians who slowly fell back.

"Oonah. Oonah."

The shooting slowed, then became sporadic, and finally stopped. For the first time in five hours of the bloodiest fighting any man among them had ever seen, Herkimer's shattered militia dared pause to stare back at the trail of dead behind them. This day would remain in their memories forever as something unreal, a nightmare filled with screams and blood and a forest littered with men butchered and scalped and dead. Surveying the horrific scene, they drank from their canteens, wiped sweat and blood from their faces, and stared with flat eyes and expressionless faces, waiting for their next order.

Herkimer turned to Eli. "What will they do next?"

"If Brant's still alive, he'll try one more time to catch you, and kill you all. Keep moving. I'll go back. If he's coming, I'll report to you."

Herkimer reached for Eli's arm. "Who are you?"

"Private Eli Stroud. I'm a scout. This is Corporal Billy Weems. We were sent by General Washington."

"You dress like an Indian."

"That's a long story. I'll tell it later."

Back at the head of the ravine, Brant quickly sought out the war chief, Sayehqueragha. "We have them in our hands. We must follow them now, while they are beaten, and destroy them all. It will leave nothing between here and Albany to stop us."

Sayehqueragha nodded, then joined Brant as he hurried to find Claus. Claus listened, agreed, and sent a man to bring Sir John Johnson. Johnson watched Brant's eyes as the war chief unfolded his plan.

"I believe you are right," Johnson said. "When we arrive back at the fort, we'll lay it before Colonel St. Leger. If he agrees, you can rest your men for a few hours and catch them by morning."

It was late in the afternoon before the weary Johnson and Butler and their exhausted command arrived back at the breastworks surrounding Fort Stanwix. Half an hour later they were in the command tent of Colonel St. Leger, where Brant and Sayehqueragha made their statement and waited for St. Leger's response.

After listening to the Indians' proposal, St. Leger slowly shook his head. "The siege starts tomorrow. I cannot reduce my forces here to track down and finish Herkimer's command when they are already so soundly beaten they will never again be a threat. We will all remain here to storm Fort Stanwix when the time comes."

The Battle of Oriskany was over.

Notes

The first week of August 1777, Colonel Barry St. Leger and his fourteen hundred soldiers arrived at Fort Stanwix to put it under siege and take it, prior to proceeding on east down the Mohawk River valley to join General Burgoyne. St. Leger was badly surprised to discover the fort, which he had been told was in terrible condition and manned by but sixty men, was in fact in good condition and defended by six hundred fifty men under the able leadership of Colonel Peter Gansevoort.

Billy and Eli are fictional characters, hence, their arrival at the fort and their bringing a captured Indian are fictional, however, the information given by their captive Indian is accurate. The troop count of St. Leger's army, including British, Hessians, Indians, Canadians, and loyalists, and their cannon count, position, and plans, are accurate.

An Indian woman named Gonwatsijayenni, whose Christian name was Mary Brant, and who was of high standing among the Iroquois people, sent a message to St. Leger, informing him that General Nicholas Herkimer of the New Hampshire militia was proceeding from Oriskany to Fort Stanwix to join Gansevoort's men inside. Thereupon Brant proposed an ambush by four hundred of his Mohawk in a ravine. St. Leger agreed, and Sir John Johnson offered to join them, was put in command, and the force left.

Herkimer sent three men ahead to Fort Stanwix: Adam Helmer, John Demuth, and John Kember, to tell Gansevoort they were coming to his aid and asking him to fire three spaced cannon shots when he got the message and to send a force out to meet him to guide him in. The three men came into the fort from the south, through a swamp that was thought to be impassable, and delivered their message.

Thereupon Gansevoort sent out two hundred men under command of Lieutenant Colonel Marinus Willet, to meet Herkimer and bring him in. However, Willet's command never reached Herkimer. Rather, they happened onto a British camp that was nearly deserted, killed or captured the few who were there, loaded themselves with cooking kettles and blankets and other supplies that were needed back at the fort, and returned.

With his usual skill in the forest, Brant stationed the British at the head of a ravine four miles from Fort Stanwix, lined both sides with his Mohawk, and waited. Herkimer heard the three cannon shots that were the arranged signal, but wondered why the guide party never arrived.

The British also heard the three cannon shots, concluded it was some sort of a signal, and waited for Herkimer's column to walk into the trap. Herkimer led his men into the mile-long ravine and proceeded; however, the Mohawk Indians, who were rumored to have been drinking rum just before the battle, became overanxious and sprung the trap a few minutes too early, before the wagons at the rear of the column reached the ravine. The blasting muskets and screaming Indians from both sides caught the column by total surprise, and in seconds the fight was hand-to-hand, in near total chaos. Herkimer's left leg was badly injured by a musketball, and he did in fact have his men sit him with his back to a tree while he lit his pipe and continued shouting orders, directing his men. The battle raged on, then the Americans fought their way out of the ravine, up an incline to their left, onto level ground, where it ended when the Americans retreated. Herkimer lost half his men, a terrible blow to the militia. Ebenezer Cox, who had been with Herkimer at Unadilla and had insulted Joseph Brant there, was killed in the battle. Ten days later, following an unsuccessful surgery to remove his leg, General Herkimer died.

Immediately after the fight, Brant and a second war chief, Sayehqueragha, came quickly to Claus and requested permission to follow the fleeing Americans and finish killing them all. Claus took the request to St. Leger, who refused, stating he would need all his forces to begin the siege of Fort Stanwix, which was to commence in the morning (see Graymont, *The Iroquois in the American Revolution*, pp. 128–36).

In support, see also Leckie, *George Washington's War*, pp. 391–93.

The Iroquois word *oonah* connotes disapproval, negative, retreat, leave (see Graymont, *The Iroquois in the American Revolution*, p. 139). The Iroquois word *etow* connotes approval, positive, move forward, attack (see Ketchum, *Saratoga*, p. 145).

CHAPTER XXVIII

★ ★ ★

*I*n late dusk Billy and Eli found Herkimer's camp. There were no fires. Quiet men moved about cutting strips of cloth from the shirts of the dead, to bind up the wounds of the living. None spoke of the horror they had survived back at the ravine. Though many heroic deeds had been done in the fevered heat of the jumbled, chaotic battle, there were no heroes among them. None boasted. None preened. They quietly did what they could for their wounded comrades, while the officers moved about taking a silent count of the survivors. A silent General Herkimer bowed his head and said nothing as they delivered the truth to him. Half his command was missing. He could only hope that some of those toward the rear had escaped when the Mohawk sprang the trap too soon and they ran.

Billy and Eli held their weapons high as they approached camp, calling out, "Friendly," until they were past the outer pickets. They found Herkimer seated with his back against a stump, left leg splinted and bandaged. In the gloom of dusk, great black blotches of blood grew on the white cloth as Herkimer clenched his pipe in his teeth. The two men dropped to their haunches and Eli spoke.

"Brant's not coming. It's over for now. You can light small fires if you need to."

Herkimer turned to a nearby captain and gave orders, and low fires began to appear. He turned back to Eli and Billy.

"What command are you with?"

Billy answered. "General Washington sent us to help at Fort Stanwix. Eli speaks Iroquois, knows their ways.

Herkimer nodded, then shifted the pipe in his teeth. "Are you going back?"

"Yes. St. Leger's going to put the fort under siege today or tomorrow."

Eli interrupted. "It's my guess that's why Brant didn't come back to get you. St. Leger needs him at the fort."

Herkimer winced at the pain in his broken leg. "I was on my way to the fort when I walked into the ambush. My own fault—no scouts out. I have to get my wounded back to the settlement for help." He shook his head. "I've lost half my command."

Billy looked into Herkimer's face as he spoke. "Don't fault yourself too much. Your men fought well in one of the worst battles I've seen. Brant and the British lost a lot of warriors, a few regulars. St. Leger won't have as many men to take Fort Stanwix. Maybe not enough. Hard as it was, you may have saved the fort after all."

For a moment Herkimer stared, then bowed his head. The two men waited until he spoke. "I was expecting a column to come from the fort to meet me. Do you know what happened to them?"

Eli answered. "I think we heard them. There was a brief fight a little north and west of us that moved toward the fort, and then maybe ten cannon shots. I think the column you expected walked into a British camp and had to make a run for it."

Herkimer nodded. "I heard the cannon. I hoped they were coming our way, not going back to the fort." He paused for a moment, then continued thoughtfully. "It was strange, seeing our Indians fighting theirs. Strange."

Eli swallowed before he answered. "What you saw today was the end of the Iroquois Confederacy—the start of a war between the six Iroquois tribes. I saw Blatcop out there fighting like a panther against Honyery Doxtater. Blatcop was on our side, Doxtater the British. Blatcop nearly took Doxtater's hand off with his tomahawk. They're both

Oneida." A look of sadness came over Eli's face. "Oneida against Oneida. Brother against brother. The great confederacy is dead. What has been for two hundred years, is no more. The Mohawk River valley is going to be filled with war and bloodshed between the Indians, after what happened here today."

Herkimer's eyes widened as he listened. "I didn't know. I wish it weren't so."

Eli said nothing.

Herkimer sighed. "Can you tell me one thing? What were those words I heard today? Sounded like *Oonah. Etow.*"

"Mohawk. *Etow* means approval, move forward, attack. *Oonah* means disapproval, back away, retreat."

Herkimer knocked the tobacco from his pipe. "When will you be leaving?"

"Now. If we pass any of St. Leger's men coming this way, we'll get back to tell you."

"I appreciate it."

"We have to go. Gansevoort needs to hear what happened out here."

"Anything we can do for you? After what you did, we owe you."

The two men shook their heads. "Good luck with your men."

With the morning star fading in the east, Billy and Eli raised their weapons high over their heads and came dripping out of the swamp south of Fort Stanwix. The gates opened and they walked in, filthy, weary, unshaven. They stopped at a horse trough long enough to rinse the swamp muck from their clothes with buckets of water, then followed their escort to the office of Colonel Gansevoort, to stand with a puddle of water growing at their feet, spreading on the dry floor planking. Two minutes later the colonel appeared, fully dressed.

"Be seated. We've been waiting. What is your report?"

For twenty minutes they spoke, describing the battle, answering his questions, watching the concern on his face when he learned Herkimer's column was half destroyed and had turned back for the sake of his wounded. He brightened at learning the heavy losses suffered by the British forces, and his eyes narrowed as he made calculations of how many men St. Leger had remaining to assault the fort. Their report finished, Billy and Eli fell silent, waiting.

"When did you two last sleep, or eat?"

Billy shrugged. "Two days ago."

"Go to the enlisted men's quarters and clean up. Take breakfast with them, then tell them I said you were to be given a cot to sleep on. If St. Leger begins the siege today, you'll know it when the cannon begin. I commend you both for your work. Dismissed."

The deep boom and the slight ground vibrations came at the same instant, and Billy and Eli stirred, then settled. Thirty seconds later a second volley of distant cannon blasted, and the ground tremors reached their cots. The tiny voice in the center of their consciousness awakened to quietly whisper, "It's time."

The two men stirred, brushed at the flies, and swallowed sour as their eyes fluttered open and they returned from deep, dreamless sleep. For a few seconds they lay on their sides to stare at the gray, unpainted wall of the enlisted barracks, trying to understand where they were and how they had gotten there. Slowly the remembrance came to them, and they turned away from the wall to wipe at the light sweat on their faces. In muggy, humid heat they swung their legs off the cot and their bare feet hit the floor. Both turned up their toes as they looked out the west windows and realized the sun was lowering toward the horizon.

The first cannon salvo from the guns on the walls of the fort boomed, and both men flinched.

"What time is it?" Billy asked. He stretched, feeling the stiffness in the muscles of his shoulders and arms.

"I don't know. The sun's going down. I'd guess close to six o'clock."

They heard and felt a volley of eight cannonballs rip into the walls of the fort an instant before they heard the cannon blasts that fired them, and both men stood, waiting for a moment while their legs took their weight. They scratched unceremoniously, then shrugged out of borrowed trousers, picked up their own clothes from the chairs on which they had dried, and put them on.

"It's begun," Billy said quietly.

For a time the men jerked, and some involuntarily ducked, each time St. Leger's cannonballs slammed into the walls of the fort, followed quickly by the sound of the British cannon as it rolled past the fort into the forest. They jumped each time their own cannon on the walls of the fort thundered out a reply. The evening mess was quiet, subdued, as the men interrupted their meals to listen and feel as the cannonade continued.

In the early dusk they fell into rank and file while the drummer rattled the snare drums to retire the colors. For a brief moment the men raised their eyes, suddenly awed, startled, at the sight of their flag, red, white and blue. It had caught the last rays of a sun already set, to glow brightly in the sky like something alive. With a will of their own, the thoughts of the men turned to wives, children, hearth, home. In an unexpected reverie they yearned to be there, surrounded by all they treasured in life. Then a feeling came welling from within. They knew they were where they belonged, doing what must be done, and it stirred their souls. They stared in silence until the flag had been lowered and folded and the last of the sun's rays were gone. Then each man walked away in silence. Most paused to glance back for a moment, then walk on, while the cannon blasted.

The night was a confusion of big guns blasting, cannonballs slamming harmlessly into the thick, dirt-filled walls of the fort, nervous men jerking awake again and again, mumbling curses at the flashes of light and the thunder overhead as their own guns answered. Sometime after two o'clock in the morning, Gansevoort passed an order: "We must save gunpowder. Fire one salvo for every four of theirs."

Dawn came beneath purple clouds, and after morning mess the first rain came slanting into the parade grounds. The British elevated their guns, and a few cannonballs cleared the walls, to whistle overhead into the forest on the far side of the fort. By noon the British had brought two mortars into action and were dropping shells into the dirt of the parade ground, digging harmless holes. The gunners on the wall located the mortars, aligned their cannon barrels, raised the muzzle elevation slightly, and fired twelve rounds. The mortars stopped.

The routines of the day became a fixed labor of monotony. Men soon learned to sleep fitfully through the unending cannonades of night-time. Twice the big guns fell silent, and in the peculiar sound of stillness, St. Leger raised a flag of truce to send Butler and two men to offer terms of surrender. Gansevoort listened, asked for the terms in writing, then sent a stinging reply. His orders were to defend Fort Stanwix, and that is precisely what he intended to do, to the last extremity. The guns resumed their incessant pounding.

At dawn, the pickets on the wall suddenly leaned forward, pointed, and leaped down the wooden stairs calling to their commanding officers. "They've moved! Their breastworks are closer! They're tightening their circle!"

The news was brought instantly to Gansevoort, who nodded. "Of course. That is the nature of a siege. In time, they'll be one hundred yards outside our walls, and then they'll break out of their breastworks and try to take us by storm. That is when we will need our gunpowder. Keep firing one salvo to each four of theirs."

Each day became like the last and the next, and a sense of gray futility began to creep into the men. Gansevoort called a council of his officers, and they ordered the regimental cooks to prepare a ham and apple strudel supper, followed by a ration of one pint of rum for each man. Spirits lifted for a day, then settled once again into the grinding world of unending cannon fire, day and night, and six hundred fifty men confined inside the walls of Fort Stanwix. The British cannon emplacements were moving ever closer to the fort—seven hundred yards, six hundred, five hundred, and the war of nerves ate into the men. On what day will they be close enough to come out of the breastworks to storm the fort? How many will there be? Can we hold? Can we? Can we?

Then, at dawn, a man was found hunkered down outside the east gate. He was dirty, unshaven, wearing homespun and a battered tricorn. He carried a long Pennsylvania rifle and had the rangy look of a man born to the wilderness. The pickets blindfolded him, and a sergeant and two privates brought him to Gansevoort at bayonet point. Gansevoort sent for Billy and Eli.

Motioning for the blindfold to be removed, Gansevoort demanded, "Who are you?" His steel-blue eyes bored into the man.

"Corbin MacPherson."

"From where?"

"I had a farm over by Germany Flats, until I moved my family east to get away from all this. I come back to join the militia. I was sent to tell you, General Washington sent Benedict Arnold to help Schuyler, and Schuyler sent him on to you. He came in yesterday morning." He flinched at the sound of cannonballs tearing into the fort walls and of the blasts rolling past. "Looks like you might need a little help."

Every man in the room started at the name "Arnold."

"General Arnold? How many men with him?"

"None. Gen'l Washington ordered him to take command of all the Continental soldiers he could find, and as many militia as could be spared. He hopes he can get enough to help here at Stanwix."

Gansevoort's eyes narrowed in suspicion. "How did you get through the British lines?"

"Walked up a creek right past 'em. They wasn't expecting me."

"What does General Arnold want me to do?"

"Nothing. He's getting ready to come here. He wanted you to know so you wouldn't take any notions about surrender."

Gansevoort bristled. "Surrender! If we were going to surrender, we'd have done it long ago. We're here to stay. What did General Arnold have to say about matters on the Hudson, or at New York?"

"Burgoyne's got an army over on the Hudson, moving south, and they need all the men they can get over there to fight him. Herkimer lost half his command at Oriskany, and we need every man we can get to hold things at Germany Flats. Schuyler's sure he can't fight Burgoyne and St. Leger at the same time, which is why he sent Arnold over here to see to it this fort doesn't fall. He says we've got to hold this fort."

Gansevoort fell silent for a moment, weighing the message, judging whether it was a British trick to create a feeling of safety, only to discover too late it was an illusion.

Eli asked, "Could I talk to this man for a minute?"

Gansevoort nodded.

"You saw Herkimer's men come back from the battle?"

"Some of them."

"What condition?"

"Bad. Terrible."

"Herkimer?"

The man's eyes fell. "Dead."

Everyone felt the jolt, and for a moment the room was seized by silence before Eli continued. "How?"

"Got his leg—left leg—broke bad at the ambush. He hung on for a few days but they had to take it off. It killed him."

"Did Ebenezer Cox tell you what happened at the ravine?"

"Cox was killed at the ravine. And good riddance."

Eli turned back to Gansevoort. "I trust him."

"Very well. Mr. MacPherson, report to the enlisted barracks to get cleaned up and take mess. When you're rested, you're free to stay here, or go."

They watched the sergeant escort the man out the door, into the rosy glow of sunrise on the parade ground. Gansevoort leaned back in his chair, hand stroking his chin thoughtfully. "So Benedict Arnold's coming here with some men." He stood. "That will be good. You men go back to your posts. I'll make the announcement about General Arnold at the appropriate time."

Eli pondered for a moment before he spoke. "I have a notion Billy and I should go on over to Germany Flats. Arnold doesn't know we're under siege here, and he might need someone to guide him in. I'd hate to see him walk into another of Brant's ambushes."

Gansevoort considered. "I doubt he would, but then I didn't believe Herkimer would, either. Give him a message. Tell him we're under siege and that the British guns are less than three hundred yards from the fort walls. I think we can hold out, but it will be a close thing."

Both Billy and Eli nodded.

"When do you want to leave?"

"As soon as we get our weapons and a little cheese and hardtack. Maybe twenty minutes."

Fifteen minutes later the south gate to the fort opened far enough for Billy and Eli to slip through. Three minutes later they had disappeared into the swamp, working their way in a circle to the east. They ignored the smell of stagnant decay and the swarming mosquitoes and brulies while their eyes never stopped moving, waiting for the first sign of a water moccasin, copperhead, flash of red in the trees, or movement that might be an Indian waiting in ambush.

By ten o'clock the swamp was half a mile behind them, and they were standing up to their thighs in a clear, running stream, cleaning the slime and muck from their clothing. One hour later they slowed as they came to the flat land at the head of the ravine where Brant had caught Herkimer's column in the ambush, and in silence they moved through the bodies, down the slope, picking their way. The dead were all American, left behind when Herkimer retreated to save his wounded. The British and Indians had taken all their dead and wounded with them and left the corpses of the rebels to rot. The two men breathed shallow in the stench and continued on.

With the sun directly overhead they paused to wolf down cheese and chew hardtack, drink long from their canteens, grab up their weapons, and continue on east through the withering heat and humidity of the forest. They passed the settlement of Oriskany in the afternoon sun, and stopped in full darkness to make a cold camp. They finished the cheese and hardtack, drank, and lay on the forest floor to sleep. The morning star found them pushing on eastward, following the Mohawk River. The morning sun was one hour above the eastern horizon when they saw Arnold's camp, one-half mile from the junction of the Mohawk River and the West Canada Creek. They walked in with their weapons high, calling out, "Friendly," to the picket who came to meet them with lowered bayonet.

"Who are you?"

Billy answered, "Corporal Weems and Private Eli Stroud. Your man MacPherson got through to Fort Stanwix yesterday. Colonel Gansevoort sent us with a message for General Arnold."

Relief showed in the picket's face. "MacPherson got through? He's all right?"

"Tired. He'll be back in a day or two."

Eli broke in. "We need to see General Arnold, if he's here."

The picket raised his bayonet and jabbed a thumb over his shoulder. "Over there. I'll take you."

They followed the picket through the familiar clutter of an army camp, surprised as they estimated more than six hundred men, armed and ready to march. Halfway through the camp they passed the roped-off enclosure encircled with pickets, where more than sixty prisoners and enemy wounded were being held—sullen, dull-eyed, defeated. One prisoner was dressed in a heavy, tattered winter coat. His hair was long and tangled, trousers ragged, shoes falling to pieces, face and hands streaked with dirt and grime. Bits and pieces of food clung to his beard. He sat on the ground near the ropes and pickets, rocking back and forth, humming softly, holding something in one hand, stroking it gently with the other. Eli slowed as he passed, and the man looked up, face glowing, smiling, staring with the vacant eyes of one whose mind is of another world. He thrust his hand up at Eli, proudly showing his treasure, and in that instant Eli recognized that the man clutched a dead mouse.

The picket led them past the prisoners, to a plain canvas tent toward the east end of the camp. He spoke to the picket at the tent flap, who disappeared into the tent for a moment, then returned.

"General Arnold says to come on in."

They ducked through the tent flap, the private saluted, and Arnold waited.

"Sir, these two scouts was sent from Fort Stanwix. They say they've got a message from Colonel Gansevoort."

Arnold was dressed in a rumpled uniform with epaulets showing his commission of brigadier general. His command tent was unpretentious, uncomplicated, plain. His long hair was pulled back and tied with a piece of leather. His sword was lying on a table in the corner in a scarred scabbard. Thick-shouldered, square-faced, slightly hawk nosed, and thin-lipped, his entire demeanor bespoke a man who was direct, outspoken, and who had little truck with show, political nuance, or nonsense.

"When did you leave Stanwix?"

Billy answered. "Yesterday."

"MacPherson got through?"

"Yes, sir. He's all right."

"What message from Gansevoort?"

"They're under siege. The British cannon are three hundred yards from the walls, and they're moving closer. He thinks he can hold the fort, but it will be close."

"You know about General Herkimer?"

Eli answered. "We were there."

Arnold's eyes dropped for a moment. "How long does Gansevoort have? Any idea?"

"Not much time."

"I've got six hundred forty men here, and more coming. I'll have about fifteen hundred when we're ready to march, but from what you're saying, that may be too late. I'll have to go on with what I have now, and let the rest catch up."

"That might be risky," Eli said. "If you come with six hundred forty, Brant will come back to meet you in the forest like he did Herkimer. If he does, I don't know how many of your men will reach Stanwix. Brant doesn't have enough men left to ambush a full fifteen hundred, so it might be better if you wait."

"We'll have to take that risk."

Eli shrugged and remained silent. Arnold turned to his desk. "I'll be ready to march by tomorrow at noon. How long will it take to reach the fort?"

Billy pondered. "With six hundred men, about three days."

"Can Gansevoort hold out that long?"

"Maybe. Probably."

Eli interrupted. "There might be another way."

Arnold turned, eyes narrowed in question, waiting.

"You've got a prisoner out there who's mind doesn't work right. Is he insane?"

Arnold shook his head. "That's Han Yost. Not insane. Slow. Strange."

"Dangerous?"

"No. Nearly harmless."

"What's going to become of him?"

"He thinks we're going to hang him. We're not. We'll hold him until we're finished here, then let him go. As long as someone watches over him to tell him what to do, he gets by."

"Does he understand what's going on around him? Can he follow orders?"

"Generally, yes."

Eli paused to put his thoughts in order. "Let me explain something. The Iroquois believe such a man has been touched by the Great Spirit. They look at them as special, like a medicine man or a prophet. Most often they believe whatever such people say."

Arnold's eyes narrowed in puzzlement. "How do you know all this?"

"I was raised by the Iroquois."

"What are you getting at?"

"Make an agreement with Yost. If he'll go to St. Leger's camp and tell them you're right behind him with a force big enough to wipe them out in half a day, there's a chance the Indians will leave. If they do, St. Leger won't have half enough men to finish the siege. It will all be over."

Arnold was incredulous. "You mean that poor soul out there could do such a thing?"

"He might. It's worth a try. Let's bring him in here and talk to him."

Arnold spoke to the private standing behind Billy and Eli. "Bring Han Yost here. You know the one?"

"Yes, sir." The private disappeared out the tent flap to return minutes later, Han Yost in front of him. Yost still wore the vacant smile as he slouched in, hand thrust into the large pocket of the ragged, winter coat. He waited for Arnold to speak.

"Han, you know who I am?"

Yost nodded his head and laughed abruptly. "You're the one that hangs people. You're going to hang me."

Arnold assumed a stern look. "Yes, I am—unless you do what I tell you."

A second abrupt burst of laughter filled the tent for a moment. "You already told me. You're going to hang me."

Arnold raised a warning finger. "Do you want me to hang you?"

Still smiling broadly, Yost shook his head vigorously. "If you do, no one will take care of Jacob. I got to take care of Jacob." He jerked his hand out of his coat pocket and thrust it toward Arnold, palm open. Arnold stared for a moment at the dead mouse.

"Do you want to take care of Jacob?"

"He's my friend. We talk."

"Do you want to take care of him?"

"Yes."

"If you do what I say, you can take care of Jacob for a long time. Do you understand?"

Yost stroked the mouse for a moment, then carefully put his hand back in his pocket. "Yes."

"You know how many soldiers I have here?"

"Yes." A look of pride stole over Yost's face as he invented his answer. "Like the leaves on the trees."

"Yes. As many as the leaves on the trees. Can you remember that?"

"Yes."

"I want you to go to a man named Colonel St. Leger and tell him."

"Where is he?"

"A long walk from here. I will send someone to help you find him."

"Who?"

"A friendly Indian. He knows the forest, and he knows St. Leger. He will help you."

A look of deep concern came into Yost's face. "I can't go. I can't leave my mother."

"She wants you to go. I will bring her here, and she can tell you."

Arnold turned to the private once more. "Do you know his mother? She's among the prisoners."

Five minutes later a wrinkled, disheveled, round-shouldered, gray-haired woman in a long, dark skirt with a torn shawl about her shoulders was standing before Arnold. She was trembling, eyes filled with terror as she glanced repeatedly at her son.

Arnold spoke in a firm, matter-of-fact voice. "Mrs. Yost, I want to make a bargain with you. I will spare both you and your son if he will carry a message to Colonel St. Leger, who is now at Fort Stanwix. St. Leger is British. Your son wants your permission to go. I will send a friendly Indian to guide him. He will not be harmed. Will you agree?"

The woman gasped, "You won't hang him?"

"Not if you agree, and if he goes."

"Will you set us free?"

"Yes, when he returns, if he has done what I ask."

She turned to her son. "Do as this man says. He will let you go free, and you can take care of Jacob." Her eyes were pleading.

Yost rubbed a filthy sleeve across his mouth, then nodded. "If I can go free with Jacob."

She turned back to Arnold. "He'll go. He's a good boy. I do not know why God sent him this way."

"Thank you. Private, take her back." He turned back to Eli. "Is there anything else I should know about this . . . scheme?"

"Do you have some Oneida in camp that you can trust?"

"Several. One is named Ponsee. He'll know what to do."

"Does he speak English?"

"Broken."

"Bring him. I can tell him what to do. And one more thing. Yost has to make them believe he escaped. To do that, while I'm talking to the Indian, have some men take that coat of Yost's and shoot a few holes in it."

Arnold bowed his head and for a moment his shoulders shook in a silent chuckle. "This is how we fight wars now?"

Forty-five minutes later the small group stood clustered outside the command tent while Eli gave the Oneida warrior Ponsee his final words in Iroquois.

"Don't go to St. Leger. Go to Brant's Indians. They'll be in a separate camp near St. Leger's men. When they see Yost, they'll listen. It's all up to you two to make them believe. If they don't, things could go bad for you."

Ponsee nodded solemn agreement and turned to Arnold, waiting.

"Go." For a moment he hesitated, then added, "Good luck." Oddly, he thrust out his hand to the startled Ponsee, who shook it. Billy and Eli walked the two men out of camp and watched them disappear, moving west in the forest. They waited until all was silent before they returned to Arnold, waiting at his command tent.

Doubt was plain as the general spoke to Eli. "Think there's a chance this will work?"

Eli pursed his mouth for a moment. "It could. I trust Ponsee, but who knows what Yost will say with four hundred painted warriors around him?"

Arnold, practical, hardheaded, continued. "What are you two going to do?"

"Give those two about ten more minutes, and follow them."

"Concerned they won't get there?"

"Ponsee knows the way. I want to see what happens after Yost tells his story."

Arnold considered, then concluded. "I'll be marching tomorrow. With fifteen hundred men it will take two full days, maybe three, depending on the weather. Never saw a summer with so much rain. If you see Colonel Gansevoort, tell him we're on the way."

"We will."

"Stop at the commissary and get some food. Tell the captain in charge that I sent you."

The two men each drew a ration of dried fish, shriveled, raw potatoes with every eye sprouted, a handful of dried apple slices, and half a loaf of black bread from a skeptical commissary captain. They wrapped the items in cloth, filled their scarred wooden canteens with fresh water, and quietly left camp. Half an hour later Eli raised a hand in caution. Yost and Ponsee were three hundred yards ahead, moving steadily west through the trees and brush, Ponsee leading. Throughout the day Billy and Eli held their distance, moving only when they could not be seen or heard. In deep dusk they stopped four hundred yards from the tiny glow of a small Indian campfire, where Ponsee and Yost were seated. They chewed on the hard, tasteless, dried fish, ate slices of raw potato and dried apple, followed by a few chunks of the hard black bread. They drank long from their canteens, and settled in to take turns on watch.

The glow of the campfire dimmed and died at midnight. In the gray of dawn they saw movement ahead, and with the birds setting up their raucous, squawking protest, moved on westward, carefully keeping Yost and Ponsee within sight. A startled doe bounded away with her spotted fawn beside her as though her thoughts, her actions, were also his. Small things peered from hidden places at the passing of the men. A copperhead snake, more afraid of the men than they were of it, silently sought the safety of a groundhog burrow.

At midmorning Billy and Eli worked their way slightly south to avoid the settlement of Oriskany, then angled back north, once again near the Mohawk River. With the sun just past its zenith they turned directly north, following the river to where it narrowed near its head-waters. In the far distance they could see the tops of the walls of Fort Stanwix, with the flag blowing in the breeze, red and white bars, blue field of stars. They heard the timed thump of the distant cannon ringing in the forest, and they knew. The fort was still under siege. True to his word, Gansevoort had stubbornly refused to surrender.

Shortly after two o'clock Billy and Eli stopped, and Eli spoke softly. "We're going to work our way around and come in from the northeast. I don't think they'll expect it. Yost and Ponsee are going straight on in from here." He paused for a moment in thoughtful reflection. "If Yost does his job, this could be over by sunset. If he doesn't . . ."

For a moment Billy was caught up in the singular absurdity of send-ing a retarded fool into the camp of the most feared Iroquois Indian in the northeast to persuade him and four hundred hardened warriors to run from a siege that was all but completed. A wave of doubt rose inside, and he pushed it away. This was not the time to raise a protest.

Eli continued. "If this fails, there's nothing we can do for Yost and Ponsee. We go due north to the headwaters of the river, then cut a big circle to the west, and come into the fort from the south side, through the swamp. If anything happens to one of us, the other one has to get back to tell Gansevoort that Arnold's on the way."

Billy nodded understanding, and they moved on.

In the sweltering heat of mid-afternoon, Ponsee stood bolt upright and steadily walked the last five hundred yards to the fringes of Brant's camp, his demented companion following behind. He was aware that a hundred set of black eyes were watching, judging, while tomahawks began to appear. Painted warriors moved in behind the two, forming a phalanx from which there would be no escape. Ponsee did not look right or left as a path opened before him into the heart of the camp. He stopped twenty feet from the great firepit and waited.

An Indian with two blond scalps dangling from his belt walked to face him, and spoke in Iroquois. "Who are you?"

"Oneida. Ponsee. I bring a messenger."

The fierce black eyes never blinked. "He is special?"

"Yes. Taronhiawagon has touched him. He is special."

The warriors closest to them moved back from Yost, then stared at him. Open suspicion showed as the Indian continued. "Why have we not seen you before? Are you in league with the rebellious Americans?"

Ponsee could not miss seeing the Indian's hand, fingering the handle of his dangling tomahawk. "I am not with the rebels. I was in Oswego when the white British general came. I was told to gather at Oriskany to fight the rebels. I went to Ganaghsaraga to gather with warriors there. We went to Oriskany to fight, but we were too late. The white soldiers had already been trapped and slaughtered at a place to the west. We saw the defeated rebels come back toward Oriskany. There was nothing we could do. I came back to fight at the great fort. I found this man lost, seeking Joseph Brant. He is special. He says he has a message."

"What message?"

"I do not know. He will not tell me. He will tell only Joseph Brant."

For a time the Indian stared into Ponsee's eyes, testing, waiting for his instincts to tell him if he had heard the truth. Nagging suspicion was rising when suddenly Yost stepped forward, jerked his hand from his coat pocket, thrust it within four feet of the Indian's startled face, and opened his fingers. He was grinning his witless grin, eyes wide, proud to show them his friend, Jacob.

At the sight of the dead mouse, the Indian recoiled as though he had been struck in the face. The single word, "Oonah," quickly ran through the crowded warriors, and they retreated two steps to stop, unnerved, uncertain what to do next. The startled Indian facing Ponsee stepped back, his eyes never leaving the dead mouse as he gave orders. "Bring Joseph Brant."

At that moment Brant broke into the circle and stopped. His eyes took in everything in an instant. He stepped to face Ponsee, face a blank. "I heard you come into camp. Do you wish to see me?" He looked past Ponsee to Yost.

"I have brought this man. He is a messenger."

"He is special?"

"Touched by Taronhiawagon."

Yost brought his cupped hand from his pocket, shoulders hunched, and reached in to gently stroke Jacob. Brant stared, unable to see the dead mouse.

"What is in his hand?"

"His totem."

Brant took one step forward and Yost grinned at him, then thrust his hand forward as he opened his fingers. Only lifelong, disciplined restraint saved Brant from recoiling. The single changes in his expression were a tightening of the lines about his mouth and a momentary narrowing of his eyes.

Brant turned back to Ponsee. "What is his message?"

"I do not know. He will speak it only to you."

Brant braced himself, took one step toward Yost, and spoke in perfect English. "You are a white man. Are you with the American rebels?"

Yost grinned as he remembered what came next. "No. I was a prisoner, but I escaped." He reached to pull up the tails of his coat, and poked a finger through the six bullet holes, then jabbed his finger into the hole in his left sleeve, and finally the hole in the coat collar. "The Great Spirit protected me."

Brant eyed the eight bullet holes suspiciously. "What is your message?"

Yost stroked Jacob for a moment, mouth pursed in thought as he tried to remember the words. Ponsee did not move, while his eyes flitted, searching for the place with the fewest warriors. In his unexpected arrival, the Indians had not taken his knife and tomahawk as they usually did, and in his mind he went over the plan. If Yost failed, he was to instantly kill him with his knife to save him from being roasted alive and eaten, and then either break through the wall of Indians before they could move, or kill himself with the same knife. He made his calculations and waited for Yost to answer.

Yost raised his smiling eyes from Jacob to Brant and slowly recited the words. "The Great Spirit told me I must find you." He gestured broadly toward the blue sky with his free hand. "He gave me a message." He paused for a moment, his face sober as he searched for the next words. He brightened, and continued. "There is a mighty force of rebellious Americans coming here. They seek . . . revenge." He smiled at having remembered the word *revenge*.

Brant was standing like a statue, watching every expression, listening to every word. Yost continued.

"Your warriors killed many of them. Now they come to kill many of you."

Yost stopped, his bearded face a study in concentration as he went over his speech until he was certain he had remembered it all, and he burst into a relieved smile.

Brant felt rising concern and the beginnings of fear. "When will they come?"

"Before the sun sets tomorrow."

Two hundred of Brant's warriors were within earshot, and not one of them dared breathe as Brant asked the question on which it all hung.

"How many?"

The mindless smile burst onto Yost's face once more. He said nothing, but slowly tipped his head back until he was staring upward into the tops of the countless trees. Then he turned his head, his eyes moving from tree to tree, as though he were examining each of them. He raised his free hand and slowly swung it in an arc, gesturing to the millions of leaves. Triumphantly he lowered his arm and brought his grinning face back to stare at Brant.

Instantly an outcry arose among the warriors. "As many as the leaves in the trees! We cannot fight so many. Taronhiawagon has warned us. It is useless to remain. Oonah! Oonah!"

Brant turned and raised both hands, and the outcry slowed and stopped. "We do not know if this man speaks the truth. We must find it out for ourselves. I will take this message to our leader, St. Leger, and we will make a plan to see how many of the rebellious Americans are coming."

Murmuring broke out among the warriors. It was only their near-worship of Brant that held them. Slowly they agreed.

Brant spoke once more. "Return to your duties. I shall talk with St. Leger now. We will make a plan. I will tell you of it at first light of the morning." He waited until the jittery warriors dispersed before he turned back to Ponsee.

"I want to hear you speak. Do you know of yourself these things are true?"

Ponsee told the truth. "I do not know it all. I do know that the tall one with the hooked nose, named Herkimer, is dead from his wounds. Dark Horse was gathering a great force at the place they call Germany Flats." He had used the Mohawk name for General Benedict Arnold, whom they called "Dark Horse" because his skin was slightly darker than the average white man's. Ponsee continued. "Dark Horse is a great warrior. Many rose to follow him to avenge the killing of Herkimer and the slaughter of their companions at the ravine. They have more than we have here. I know they are marching this way, now. I know he means to overrun this camp, and the British. I believe he can do it. This I know because I saw it."

Ponsee met Brant's flinty stare, knowing that he could be dead within seconds if Brant did not believe him.

Despite his training in the schools of white men, his vast experience moving about in their society, learning their ways and customs, learning to speak in French and English, and his extended visit to London and the king of England, at the bottom of his soul Brant remained a Mohawk Indian. While his head told him Yost was but a demented white man, and Ponsee was part of a monstrous lie, his Indian heart screamed, "The strange one is special! Touched by the Great Spirit. Taronhiawagon has sent him with a message, which we must receive and believe, or be slaughtered by the white men who are surely coming." Brant held little fear of white men in the forest, but a message sent by Taronhiawagon struck fear into his very being! If Taronhiawagon said it, it would come to pass!

Divided against himself, Brant turned away from Ponsee and gave orders. Two of his warriors came to lead Yost and Ponsee away, to be held until it could be determined if they had told the truth. He watched as they were marched away, then turned west and strode rapidly to the British camp, to the command tent of St. Leger. One hour later St. Leger, with Brant, two officers, and and six armed regulars marched back to the Indian camp, where Brant called his men together. St. Leger waited until they quieted before he raised his voice, and Brant translated.

"I have heard that the rebellious Americans are coming. We do not know if it is true, and I myself do not believe it. I promise you, with the dawn I myself will lead an expedition to the east with the great Joseph Brant, and we shall find out if the weak-minded man who came with this message is truly a messenger from the Great Spirit, or if he and his friend were sent by the Americans to trick us. I ask you now, wait until my return before you decide."

Rumblings of rebellion passed through the Indians before they settled. Reluctantly they agreed, and a fragile, nervous mood settled over their camp as St. Leger marched back to his own tent.

True to his word, he marched out of camp half an hour before sunrise, Joseph Brant and two war chiefs beside him, leading a column of one hundred armed regulars. They moved east, along the banks of the Mohawk River, with but two purposes in mind: To determine if a column of Americans was coming west, and if it was, to find a place to lay an ambush.

Those left behind at the camp watched them go, nerves raw from the unending cannonade of the siege, jumpy in the absence of both commanders—St. Leger and Brant. They glanced from time to time at the place where four Indians were holding Yost and Ponsee. They ate their tasteless oatmeal and drank their black coffee and were moving to their duty posts for the day when an uproar erupted on the east side of the Indian camp.

Two warriors brought an Indian to the council firepit, and the ranking chief confronted him.

"Who are you?"

"Desentant."

"Why are you here?"

"I came to join you. I am followed by many enemy soldiers."

"How many?"

"Many more than I see here."

Forty minutes later, three more Indians entered camp. "There are many coming," they said. "They will be here today. The great general on the Hudson—Burgoyne—has surrendered."

One hour later St. Leger returned, his men sweated out from marching double time to get back to camp. It took less than one minute for both St. Leger and Brant to know something was terribly wrong.

"What's happened?" St. Leger demanded.

"Others have come with the same message we received from the special one. It is true. We are going to be overrun."

St. Leger exploded. "Nonsense! We have just come from the east. There is no one coming. It is a great trick of the American rebels! Gather the war chiefs this moment. I will wait here. We are going to settle this matter right now."

Reluctantly, refusing to look St. Leger in the face, the war chiefs gathered at the firepit and waited silently for St. Leger to rip into them.

"What has happened to the mighty Mohawk? General Burgoyne has not surrendered. He controls the entire Hudson River! I myself have been east of this camp, and I tell you there is no one coming. The Americans were defeated at the ravine. Herkimer is dead! We have nothing to fear! We will assault Fort Stanwix within two days and win a complete victory!"

One chief raised his head and pointed west. St. Leger stopped and turned to Brant. "What is the meaning of this?"

Brant's reply was soft, steady. "Two hundred warriors have just left. They are going back to Oswego."

St. Leger gaped. "Deserted?"

"Not in their eyes. They came to take Fort Stanwix. They did not come to fight an army from the east."

"There *is no army from the east!*" St. Leger fairly shouted.

"They believe there is."

"Are the rest of the Indians going to desert with them?"

"They are talking about it."

"Stop them!"

"They believe they have been warned by Taronhiawagon. I have no authority over him. I will talk with them."

Brant raised his hands for silence. For ten minutes he spoke to his people, listening, gesturing, exchanging hot words. Then he turned back to St. Leger.

"They want to go back to Oswego and get more heavy cannon. More men. Many more men. Then they will come back and fight."

"There is no other way?"

"None. If you do not agree they will leave now."

Desperately St. Leger looked the direction of Fort Stanwix. His cannon were a scant two hundred yards from the wall. They would be in a position to assault the fort within the next thirty-six hours. It tore his heart to be so near his tremendous victory, only to be abandoned by the very men he had to have to complete it. He closed his eyes and for long seconds battled to take control of the anger raging inside.

"All right. We will go back to Oswego. We will find more men, and we will get more heavy cannon. Then we will come back, and we will take Fort Stanwix. Do I have the solemn word of Joseph Brant and all his men on this agreement?"

Brant nodded. "If you have told the truth, you have our word."

St. Leger turned to his officers and gave orders. "Prepare the sick and wounded for evacuation. They will leave under cover of dark tonight. Have the men strike camp today, load everything into the wagons, and be ready to march out at dawn tomorrow. Each man is to have twenty rounds of ammunition and—"

An outcry at the north end of camp became an uproar, and St. Leger stood with his feet spread, waiting for an explanation. A warrior came sprinting to stop before Brant, fighting for breath as he gasped out, "Our scout came in—a great force of Americans is two miles from the landing on the river!"

St. Leger raised a hand and shouted, "We were there one hour ago. There *is no force!*"

The scout had lied on purpose. St. Leger was right, but the truth made no difference. The Indians nearest the council firepit shouted St. Leger down, and within seconds the camp was filled with the deafening roar of four hundred Indians chanting, "Oonah, Oonah!" as they ran to snatch up their weapons and blankets and sprint for the forest— a disorganized mob whose sole thought was to flee. The mindless panic swept also into the British camp. The officers and regulars alike ran to their tents to grab up their weapons, ammunition, canteens, and what little food they could find, and also run. The cannon instantly fell silent as the cannoneers watched their army in a wild, mad stampede to the west, and without a word they leaped from the breastworks and sprinted back toward camp to follow. They did not know what had caused the panic; they only knew a demented man had appeared yesterday to prophesy disaster, their leaders had been gone since daybreak, and now both camps were little more than two terrified mobs in full flight.

One mile north of the fort, crouched behind a giant fir that had fallen a hundred years earlier, Eli suddenly raised a hand to Billy. Both men closed their eyes and listened intently for half a minute before Eli spoke softly. "The cannon have stopped. Something's happened." For a time they remained crouched behind the massive, decaying tree trunk, listening. The sounds of the insects and the birds held, then began to fade as the faint sounds of an army in full, panic-driven retreat reached them over a great distance.

"It sounds like they're moving west, towards Wood Creek." Eli rose, Billy following, and set off through the woods at a run, over logs and rocks, knocking foliage aside as they moved west. Half an hour later the sounds were clear, distinct. Eli adjusted his direction to the north, and broke into a full run. Twenty minutes later he paused, sweating, while they battled for breath.

"They're going to hit Wood Creek in about half an hour. If we get there first, we can get a clear look at them when they ford the creek. Maybe get a count. You ready?"

Twenty minutes later, hair awry, sweat running, panting, they settled flat on their bellies atop a granite ledge, with Wood Creek thirty feet directly below them. Their view of the creek was unobstructed for three hundred yards to the north, four hundred to the south. They had been there for five minutes when the first of the Indians broke clear of the forest two hundred yards south, to plunge into the cold, clear water of the shallow creek, clamber up the west bank, and disappear into the forest.

In near disbelief the two men lay motionless, counting. Minutes became half an hour, then an hour, as Indians and red-coated regulars kept coming. The desperate men looked neither right nor left as they leaped into the creek, intent only on pushing their way across as fast as they could, to continue their stampede west. Among the last to cross, were both Joseph Brant and Barry St. Leger. Eli and Billy waited for ten more minutes while the stream cleared itself of the mud that had been stirred up, and then Eli turned to Billy.

"I counted close to a thousand of them, Indians and redcoats. Officers and all."

"A little over a thousand."

"That's St. Leger's whole army."

Billy nodded.

"They've abandoned their camps. They left their cannon, their tents, wagons, food, medicine—everything."

"I never saw anything like it."

"Those men are headed for Oswego. I think Han Yost and Ponsee succeeded."

"Whatever happened, they're gone."

Eli spoke with an intensity Billy had seldom heard. "Do you have the wampum belt?"

Billy patted his shirt. "Yes."

"Now is the time."

Bewilderment was plain on Billy's face as he replied. "Now? They're in full retreat. You think now's the time?"

"Yes. The best time is when they're losing. While they're winning, their confidence is up. All they can see is victory. They won't listen to someone who walks in to tell them they're going to lose. Right now, they're running away. They're scared—lost their nerve, their courage. Our best chance is to get there now, before they have time to gather themselves again. When they stop, I think we go in."

Billy remained silent, and Eli continued.

"Now listen close. I'll go in first with the wampum belt. You come behind with your musket and my rifle held high. Brant will honor the belt, and so will most of the lesser chiefs, but maybe not some of the rest. Some of them will call things at you, maybe try to touch you, or throw something, or spit on you. They'll want you to make the first move for a fight, so don't look right or left, and don't stop walking. A warrior may challenge you to a duel with tomahawks or knives. If that happens, I'll handle it. You stay close to me but don't say a word while I'm talking to Brant. I'll talk in Mohawk so the rest can understand. When I finish I'll turn and walk back out of camp the same way we came in. Some may follow us and make threats. Ignore it. Just follow me. Can you do it?"

"Yes."

There was a pause. "One more thing. This could all go wrong. If it does, there's no chance we'll come out of their camp alive. The only thing we can do is be sure they don't get the chance to torture us." He waited for a moment, pain in his eyes. "Do you understand?"

Billy nodded. "Let's go."

The fleeing army had left a trail of trampled brush and foliage four hundred yards wide through the forest. The two men followed, crouched low, moving cautiously. They had gone eight hundred yards before they came across the first body of a British regular. He had been tomahawked, scalped, stripped, and mutilated. Twenty yards farther on they found another, and then another, and then six in a tiny clearing.

Billy stopped, sickened. "Brant's Indians did this to their own army?"

"They don't see it that way. They believe they were betrayed—that the British brought them along only to do the worst of the fighting and then lied to them about Arnold's column coming in from Germany Flats. They might be right."

Cautiously they followed the trail through the forest and paused to read the tracks showing the British had now separated from the Indians. The Indians were moving slightly south, toward Lake Oneida, while the British were angling north in a direct line toward Oswego. The two men held to the left, following Brant and his Indians. Half an hour later, Eli went to one knee to study the tracks.

"They've slowed. They'll stop soon—probably on the shore of Lake Oneida, and Brant will call a council where they'll all have their say and make a plan. That's when we have to be there."

The sun was still three hours high when they saw the waters of the lake glittering four hundred yards ahead. The faint sound of human voices came through the trees, and they both peered west but could see nothing but the forest. Staying low, they moved to the sounds, and ten minutes later they saw the first movement through the trees ahead, on the shores of the lake. Eli gave a hand signal, and Billy passed him the wampum belt. For a moment Eli ran his fingers over the seashells, then raised troubled eyes to Billy, who saw his doubts, his feeling of inadequacy.

Billy smiled as he spoke. "You'll do it right. Let's go."

Eli held the belt at full arm's length, shoulder-high, and started through the trees toward the gathering on the lake shore. Billy raised both weapons above his head and followed. They were still fifty feet inside the tree line when the first sweating, painted warrior saw them. Instantly he raised his tomahawk and called a challenge, and within seconds the two men were surrounded by an angry mob, tomahawks and scalping knives in their hands. The warriors saw the wampum belt and grudgingly opened a path, threatening, shouting, crowding. Their blood lust was still running high and wild, but they would not dishonor the ancient tradition of respect for a wampum belt. Eli held a steady pace, and Billy kept his eyes riveted between Eli's shoulder blades, both weapons high over his head. They cleared the trees and moved into a small clearing deep with grass and brush, yards from the lake. Joseph Brant walked to meet them, and they stopped six feet apart.

Recognition of Eli flashed in Brant's eyes as he spoke in English. "I have seen you."

Eli answered in Iroquois, and the startled Indians quieted. "At Three Rivers, in the storm."

Brant replied in Iroquois. "You are white?"

"White, raised Iroquois."

Brant's face remained a blank. "You could have killed me that night but you did not. What was your reason?"

"You are the Great Joseph Brant. Taronhiawagon has sent you to lead your people. It would have offended Taronhiawagon if I had killed you without strong reason."

For an instant Eli saw astonishment in Brant's eyes. It passed, and Brant asked, "What is your name?"

"Eli Stroud. I am called Skuhnaksu in your tongue."

Brant nodded. "The Fox."

"Yes."

"You come under the protection of a wampum belt. What is it you want?"

Eli extended the belt to Brant with outstretched arms, and Brant accepted it. Quickly he examined it, studied the design and craftsmanship, and raised approving eyes. "What is the message in the belt?"

Eli took a moment to order his thoughts, then he said, "Joseph Brant will remember the prophecy uttered long ago in a battle far to the south. French and Iroquois ambushed the British. They killed the great British general, Braddock. Does Brant remember?"

Brant's expression did not change as he nodded, and Eli went on.

"Then Brant will remember that a young officer rode to Braddock when he took his mortal wounds. The Indian war chief saw the brave act and ordered his warriors to shoot the young officer. Eight of them got very close and shot. Their bullets struck his coat and his hat, but they could not hit him. They felt a power that shielded the officer. They returned and told their war chief, and he said he had watched."

Eli paused. Every warrior within hearing distance was listening in silence. Brant gestured, and Eli continued.

"The war chief raised his hand and made a prophecy."

The only sounds were those of the forest. Not an Indian moved or uttered a sound. Billy's eyes swept the circle, then returned to Eli.

"He said the Great Spirit had told him. The young officer who took Braddock away and led the British from the ambush could not be killed by a bullet or a cannon. He could not be killed in battle. He would live to lead a great and mighty army. He would become the father of a great and powerful nation. The prophecy spread through the land. I am certain Brant knows of it."

Brant nodded.

"I have come to tell you. The young officer was named George Washington. He lived to become commander of the army of the Americans. He leads them now. He does not wish to fight. He would treaty with the British, if they would come to the council fire, but they will not. They send many men and ships to grind the Americans under their heel. They sent Burgoyne to drive the Americans out of the great valley of the Hudson River. Burgoyne waits now for Brant and St. Leger to bring their men to help him."

For the first time, Brant narrowed his eyes, sensing Eli was approaching the heart of his message.

Eli spoke his next statement firmly. "I have fought with General Washington against the British and the Mohawk."

Tomahawks were raised as a hundred voices rose in protest. Brant raised his hand and the outburst quieted.

"I was at a place called Trenton with him. I saw him at a bridge waiting for his men to cross. Bullets and cannonballs struck all around him. Two bullets pierced his coat, but none hit him. He did not move until his men were safe. I was at a place called Princeton when he rode alone between his army and the British. He led his men very close to the British. They fired, and again bullets were all around him, but none hit him."

Billy understood none of the Iroquois words, but at that moment he was aware that an unexpected feeling was rising in his heart. In this endless wilderness, surrounded by painted warriors who would kill him if they could, a quiet sureness was crowding out all else. This war was in the hands of the Almighty. It didn't matter that he and Eli might be killed. It only mattered that they were fighting for freedom. Liberty. The right to stand as free men, to worship the Almighty according to their own consciences, to stand accountable before Him, and Him alone. He glanced at the Indians, and it was clear the same Spirit was reaching out to them.

"I have come to tell you. The prophecy of the ancient war chief is true. You cannot kill Washington. If you fight him you will lose. He will drive out the British. If you are with them, he will drive you out, too. He will form a new government. He will become the father of a great and mighty people. If the mighty Mohawk wish to see their children and their grandchildren live in freedom and peace, then they must leave the British. Do not fight the Americans. It is for Brant to lead the Mohawk away."

Eli ceased speaking. For a moment no one moved, and then Eli finished.

"I have said what the Great Spirit led me to say. I have no more words. I am going to leave, and the Mohawk will not harm me or my friend, because Brant is a man of honor and will not allow such shame to come on his people."

For a few moments time stood still while Eli and Brant each stared into the soul of the other. Then Eli turned without another word and walked to Billy, who handed him his rifle, and shoulder to shoulder they walked out of the circle of quiet Mohawk, into the forest.

The sun had set and deep dusk had settled over the wilderness before they stopped at a small stream, and Billy spoke. "Will Brant quit the war?"

Thoughtfully Eli answered. "Time will tell. We will remain here to see."

Billy cleared his throat. "Something . . . special happened back there. Did you feel it?"

Slowly Eli nodded his head. "I felt it." He raised his eyes to Billy's. "The words were not mine. My thoughts were led. It is in the hands of the Almighty."

They drank deeply from the stream, filled their canteens, and started a circle to the northwest, where they could find a place to hide and wait to see if Brant and his Mohawk warriors would quit the British and leave. They slowed for a moment and raised their eyes to peer westward, where the evening star was shining strong and bright above the horizon.

Notes

On 6 August 1777, following the battle with Herkimer's forces, now called the Battle of Oriskany, St. Leger began the siege of Fort Stanwix. It went on for days with the incessant cannon fire and the British lines slowly moving forward to tighten the grip on the fort.

It was then learned that General Schuyler had sent General Benedict Arnold to try to raise what Continental soldiers he could, and proceed to help Colonel

Gansevoort defend the fort. While raising an army in and around Fort Dayton, Arnold was informed by someone unknown that the Americans were holding a prisoner named Han Yost Schuyler and his mother. For purposes of this book, to avoid confusing Han Yost Schuyler with General Philip Schuyler (the two were cousins) the author has used only part of the name, Han Yost. Yost was mentally slow and strange. Iroquois held such persons to be special, endowed with gifts from Taronhiawagon, their highest god. Arnold struck a bargain with Yost. If Yost would go to Joseph Brant and persuade him that a great American army was following and would destroy all of St. Leger's men, Arnold would let Yost and his mother go free. Yost, and his mother, agreed. They shot holes in Yost's coat to support his story that he had escaped under fire, selected a trustworthy Indian named Ponsee, and sent the two of them to catch Brant and deliver the message.

They succeeded. When questioned by Brant, Yost informed the Indian leader of the pursuing American army. When asked how many soldiers were coming, Yost tipped his head back and, while rolling his eyes, turned his head to take in most of the trees nearby. Instantly the Indians concluded he meant the Americans were as numerous as the leaves on the trees, and they fled. They could not be stopped. St. Leger had to end the siege of Fort Stanwix to go back to Oswego for more men.

For reasons unknown, it was at this point that Joseph Brant decided to abandon the British. He did travel back to report to General Burgoyne on the Hudson River; however, he refused to stay, and from that point on, the Iroquois Indians began to leave Burgoyne, and very soon were all gone. While no one knows what caused Brant to change his mind so radically about supporting the British, for purposes of this book the author has used Eli and Billy and their wampum belt for an explanation (see Ketchum, *Saratoga*, pp. 334–35; see also Graymont, *The Iroquois in the American Revolution*, pp. 144–45).

The Iroquois named Benedict Arnold "Dark Eagle," based on his somewhat swarthy complexion (see Leckie, *George Washington's War*, p. 394).

The prophecy of the old Indian chief regarding George Washington's invincibility is recorded in Parry and Allison, *The Real George Washington*, pp. 48–49.

CHAPTER XXIX

★ ★ ★

*H*idden in thick oaks, the tall, dour, steely-eyed General John Stark silently pointed north toward the Walloomsac River. He spoke softly to his officers crouched around him. "The Tories have a redoubt there, just this side of the river. See it?"

Sweltering in the muggy late morning heat, the officers silently nodded.

"Just across the river, on that high knoll, the Hessians have built a redoubt with cannon, and off to the right, two breastworks. You can see the south wall of the redoubt from here."

Again the officers nodded.

"The commander of the enemy force is a German colonel named Friedrich Baum." Stark paused to look into the faces of his men, his face drawn into a puzzled frown. "Burgoyne sent him to get horses and oxen from the farmers, but Baum doesn't speak a word of English! He came marching up the road from Sancoick with a German brass band banging! They had a tuba you could hear for three miles!"

He shook his head at the hilarious, comical thought of a column of blue-coated German soldiers marching through the rich farms spread for miles around the small, prosperous village of Bennington to his right, with a German brass band blaring, a tuba pumping out the beat, snare drums rattling, and every horse and ox within a mile running away from the road in terror. Stark could not make his practical, commonsense, hard New Hampshire head understand the stupidity of Burgoyne in sending a commander to buy or commandeer horses and oxen from the farmers to pull the British wagons and cannon, when the man didn't have the slightest notion of local customs or temperament and couldn't speak a single word of English. Stark shook his head and continued.

"Our scouts report the roads are drying after that cloudburst yesterday and last night. By afternoon we should be able to move quickly. And this, gentlemen, is what we're going to do."

He hunkered down to clear the twigs and growth from the ground at his feet and began to draw in the dirt with a stick.

"Here's the Walloomsac River." He drew a line from the west, curving southward, then arcing back up to the east.

"Bennington's over here," he made a line pointing east, "and Sancoick's over here," he made a line pointing west.

"The Tory redoubt is right here on this side of the river, and the German redoubt and breastworks are here, and here, atop that knoll on the other side." He dug holes with his stick and glanced at his officers, then went on. "Our camp is over here to the east, just around the bend in the river. Is everyone clear?"

"Yes."

"This afternoon, as soon as the roads are dry enough, we're going to hit every one of their positions at the same time."

He waited for comments to rise and dwindle, then looked at Lieutenant Colonel Moses Nichols of New Hampshire. "You're going to take your command of men from our camp, here, and move around the bend in the river, circle up to the north, and come in on the German redoubt and breastworks from the north side, here, here, and here. Any questions?"

Nichols shook his head. "Clear."

Stark turned to Colonel Samuel Herrick of Vermont. "Your three hundred men will move across the river, here, next to our camp, and move west over to this point. From there you'll angle north to the river, cross it again, and hold your men, here, at the foot of that high knoll where the Germans have their redoubt. That will put the Germans between your force at the bottom of that little knoll, and Nichols' men, up on top. If the Germans try to retreat down the hill, you engage them. If they don't, go on up and give support to Nichols."

"Yes, sir."

He turned to colonels Thomas Stickney and David Hobard of New Hampshire. "You two will take your commands north, turn west where the river bends, cross the river, here, and take the Tory breastworks, here. Any questions?"

"None, sir."

"That will leave about three hundred men. I will lead them across the river, here, where we'll charge straight up the center, over the top of their camp, not far from Herrick's men."

He studied his drawing for a moment, then asked, "Can everyone here draw this map for their men?"

"Yes, sir."

Stark continued. "The Reverend Thomas Allen's back at camp, and he's put me on notice that if he doesn't get his Massachusetts boys into this, he'll never come to support us again. Wherever he goes, put his men where they'll get a strong taste of a good fight."

He rose to his full height, shoulders square, his face as stern as that of an eagle. "One never knows about the fortunes of battle. I doubt we'll need help, but I sent word back two days ago to Seth Warner. I'm sure the rain slowed him down yesterday, but he's due in any time. Seth will know what to do when he gets here."

Stark used his toe to scuff away his marks in the dirt. "Our scouts say Baum has about eight hundred troops: fifty British sharpshooters, a hundred German grenadiers and light infantry, three hundred Tories and Canadians and Indians, about one hundred seventy German cavalry without horses, and a handful of local loyalists."

He waited for a moment to let his officers digest the strength of their enemy.

"With the fifteen hundred that came with us, and the five hundred that Allen and the others brought from Massachusetts and Vermont, we outnumber them more than double. If we follow the plan, this shouldn't take long. Let's get back to camp. Each of you take charge of your command and give your orders. I'll want to talk with all the men just before the attack."

The officers left the oak thicket in single file, and as they emerged, Stark paused to look back across the river at the high knoll. *I wonder what that German up there is thinking by now. He's had his scouts out—knows our numbers and where we are. Has he called for reinforcements? We'll know soon.*

In his command tent, Colonel Friedrich Baum paced, pensive, nervous, hands clasped behind his back, lower lip thrust forward, perspiration shining on his forehead. His entire life had been devoted to the military. It was all he knew. He made no pretense of brilliance; his rise to the rank of colonel was built on self-discipline, tough work, and complete dedication to duty. What he lacked in sharp mental acuity he made up for in bulldog grit and determination.

Where is Breymann? He has had time to march here with two days to spare. Have the rebels engaged him? Beaten him? Is he not coming at all? The rebels have been moving in the trees for two days, taking up positions first one place and then another. They have two men for each one of mine. We cannot withstand an all-out attack.

He stopped pacing long enough to seize a cloth from his desk and wipe at his sweating face.

Major von Meibom is becoming a nervous wreck. He peeks over the wall of the redoubt and he thinks he sees hundreds of rebels sneaking to attack. He knows our Indian scouts are out looking for rebels, and they are seeing none. Only a few farmers with white bits of paper in their hatbands to show us they are friendly loyalists. He does not think they are loyalists, and that a few rebel farmers make an army, so he wants a cannon. He does not need a cannon. He needs to find a little courage, but he will not do that, so I will have to send him a cannon.

Baum jumped at the opening of his tent flap.

"Colonel, it is past noon. Shall I bring your meal?"

Baum waved the lieutenant off and continued his pacing.

They will come today. They will attack, and we will be overrun—lose all our men, killed or prisoners. Has von Riedesel forgotten us? Burgoyne? When they come, do I commit all my men to a battle we will surely lose, or do I withdraw now and retreat, or do I surrender immediately?

He stopped pacing and squared his shoulders. *I am becoming like Meibom. I must take charge of myself. I must remember discipline. I cannot lead if I cannot discipline myself. Breymann will come to support us. If we are attacked first, we will fight, and we will hold until Breymann arrives. We shall succeed. We shall win.*

By force of will he sat down at his desk, and as he reached for a document he glanced at the clock. It was twenty minutes before two o'clock.

To the south, across the river, General John Stark removed his tricorn and wiped out the sweatband with a soiled handkerchief. He held the black hat in his hand for a few minutes, waiting for the last of his men to assemble in the small clearing, shielded from the telescopes of the Germans on the knoll two miles to the northwest.

Colonel Nichols counted the last of them, then said, "They're all here, sir." Stark settled his tricorn back on his head, walked out into the center of the men, and raised his voice.

"I won't take much time. You're all here to fight for what's yours: your wives, your children, your homes. But more than that, for freedom and liberty for your children. I don't need to remind you what Burgoyne did when he turned his Indians onto us. All of you have heard of the murders and scalpings. Most of you know someone who they massacred. Some of you lost part of your family to them. You all remember what they did to Jane McCrae, and she was one of their own."

He stopped and a murmuring spread for a few moments.

"We came here to defend our land, and that's what we'll do. I'm proud to be among you. It is a privilege and an honor to lead you. I and my command will march right up the middle of their fortifications, and with you beside us, and the Almighty watching over us, we'll own that nest of Germans before we finish."

Again voices rose in support. He waited until they quieted, then turned to point to the northwest, toward the walls of the redoubt two miles distant, faintly visible in the distance.

"There they are, boys. There is the enemy, and they are ours, or Molly Stark sleeps a widow tonight."

A shout drowned him out as he dropped his arm and turned on his heel to march away, chin high, back ramrod straight. Officers Nichols, Herrick, Stickney, and Hobard followed him to his command tent. He did not enter, but stopped outside the front flap.

Nichols spoke. "General, I think my command's going to be a little thin if we have to attack the redoubt and the breastworks at the same time. Can you spare a few more men?"

Stark pondered for a moment. "I can spare one hundred men. Enough?"

"Yes, sir."

"All right. Each of you take charge of your command now. Get them into place as quickly as you can, and keep them out of sight. Colonel Nichols, we'll be waiting for your signal from up on top. Attack when you're in place, and the ground is dry enough to move fast. Remember, success is going to depend on our hitting them from three sides at once. Be ready."

"Yes, sir."

On the rim of the knoll, a blue-coated German private started, adjusted his telescope to look again, then leaped to his feet. Minutes later he careened around the corner of Colonel Baum's command tent and stopped before the picket.

"I have information about the rebel movements. Important."

Inside the tent, Baum mopped his face and listened to the excited private.

"Sir, I'm sure I saw a large column of rebels moving north from their camp. They were armed, moving fast. If they continue on their course, then turn west, they can come in behind us, from the north."

Baum leaned forward. "What's this? More stories of rebels moving around? Why have I not heard this from our Indian scouts?"

"I do not know, sir. I only know what I saw."

Baum flipped a hand and leaned back in his chair. "Go back to your post. I will send out a patrol in a few minutes."

Dejected, the private turned on his heel and left the tent. Baum glanced at the clock. Two minutes before three o'clock. He waved flies from his face and reached for the duty roster for the day, searching for a few men he could send out on a quick scout to the northeast. His finger was halfway down the first page when the first crackle of musketfire rolled through camp from the north. His head jerked up, and he sat frozen, wide-eyed, stunned, shocked. Seconds later the silence was shattered by the second sustained volley of muskets, this time from the south. The echoes had not died in the forest when the sound of two thousand American voices raised in full battle cry filled the German fortifications as the four segments of Stark's command came shouting from hiding, bayonets mounted and flashing as they reloaded on the run. They were less than fifty yards from the redoubt when they burst from the trees, and Meibom's blue-coated German scouts sprinted for the entrance with musketballs ripping into them.

The German regulars inside the walls stood fast and fired their first return volley. Americans stumbled and went down, but the charging line did not stop. In one minute Nichols's men were at the entrance, and then they surged inside, swinging their muskets, lunging with their bayonets, knocking Germans and terrified Indians backward in a wild hand-to-hand battle within the confining walls. Baum's coveted cannon were forgotten, useless in the close-quarter, face-to-face chaos. The Indians ran out the back doors, or climbed the walls, or leaped through the small windows, and then the Germans broke and followed them.

They ran pell-mell away from the redoubt, and Herrick's riflemen were waiting. Their first volley took the panic-stricken Germans by total surprise and opened great holes in the fleeing lines. Germans and Indians dropped everywhere, finished. Others threw up their hands in surrender, and still others tried for the trees, only to be cut down by the second volley from Herrick's command.

At the sound of Nichols' first volley up on the knoll, Stickney and Hobart led their men plunging into the river, muskets held high as they waded through water up to their chests, to emerge dripping five hundred yards from the breastworks where the Tories crouched, waiting. Stark jerked his sword from its scabbard and led his men forward at a run, and the charging Americans never stopped. They spread out into a battle line, and when the Tories raised from behind their breastworks to fire, the Americans fired first. They continued in their headlong charge through their own musket smoke, loading as they ran, screaming at the top of their lungs. They plowed into the breastworks, leaping over the walls, lunging with their bayonets, swinging riflebutts, firing at point-blank range. The Tories threw down their muskets, turned, and sprinted for the river, with the Americans right behind them. They leaped into the water, and when they refused to stop on command, they were shot as they scrambled up the far bank.

Up on the knoll, Nichols had cleaned every German, every Indian, out of the redoubt and the breastworks. Below, Herrick and Stark had captured or killed most of them as they tried to escape. To the south, Stickney and Hobart had captured or killed nearly every Tory who had been at their breastwork.

It was not yet half past three o'clock.

Three miles to the west, Colonel Heinrich Breymann and his command of six hundred heard the rattle of the distant muskets, and Breymann turned to shout orders.

"Colonel Baum is under fire! Forward at double-time!" Twenty minutes later he slowed his horse to stare at a man staggering toward him, bloodied, limping, sweating, dirty. Baum reached for his pistol as the man stumbled up to his horse.

"Who are you?" Breymann demanded.

The man was gasping for air as he turned and pointed back up the road. "Americans. Shooting. They've killed us all."

Breymann turned to his aide. "Give him a canteen." To his men he shouted, "Forward, at the double!" With Philip Skene at his side, followed by six light cavalrymen, he raised his horse to a canter. As he rounded the last bend in the road and came into full sight of the battlefield, he reined in his mount, unable to understand what lay before him.

The battle was over. Baum's command of eight hundred was gone, either dead or captured. Baum himself was lying in the bed of a wagon, mortally wounded. Colonial farmers with their shirtsleeves rolled up and bits of white paper in their hatbands were running toward him, shouting words in English that Breymann did not understand. He raised his hand to his men to hold their fire, certain the white bits of paper in their hatbands identified the incoming farmers as friendly loyalists. He was stunned when the leaders stopped, leveled their muskets, and blasted their first volley into his column. He shook his head to recover, then turned to call out orders.

His two cannon were wheeled around near a small log hut, and opened fire on the charging Americans, while his first two regiments ran forward and went to one knee to deliver their first volley before the Americans could recover from the grapeshot. Quickly his troops formed a solid battle line around their cannon as the cannoneers touched off their second blast of grapeshot at the Americans, who began falling back. Exhausted from two hours of close fighting, drained by the terrible heat, Stark's command was moving back, trying to gain time to recover from the unexpected cannon, rally, and get organized to meet the fresh German column that had appeared from nowhere. Stark had his sword raised, shouting, "Rally 'round me, boys, rally 'round me!"

At that moment a voice from the east rose above all other sounds to bellow, "Fix bayonets! *CHARGE!*"

Every American turned his head to see, and they raised their voices once more in a rousing shout.

Colonel Seth Warner! Long overdue, like a warrior from heaven, he was leading his regiment of Vermonters at a run, sword flashing in the blistering afternoon sun. Beside him, old Major Rand with ninety more robust men held the pace. They came streaming in, straight at Breymann's battle line, shouting, shooting, bayonets thrust forward. The Germans fired one hasty musket volley, too high, and suddenly broke to run away. Their cannoneers were only seconds from firing their next load of grapeshot when Warner's command overran them, knocked aside the gunners, grabbed the trails to turn the cannon, and touched off two loads of grapeshot into the fleeing Germans before they had covered fifty feet.

Still mounted, Breymann shouted, "Fall back! Fall back!" The German retreat became a frenzied rout as the Germans dropped their muskets to run for the woods. The Americans stormed after them, shooting, lunging with their bayonets. Breymann, fighting his rearing horse, watched in horror as more than one-third of his command was cut down while they ran. The Americans followed them a short distance into the woods, then slowed, listening as the sounds of the German stampede died. They wiped at their sweaty faces before they marched back to the road in early dusk in the peculiar quiet that settles when the guns of battle have fallen silent.

In late dusk the decimated Germans, with redcoats and Tories mixed among them, ran blindly through the trees, stopping for nothing until they came to the road back to Sancoick, within sight of an occasional cabin. Exhausted, burning with thirst, half a dozen redcoats and Tories trotted to a small log meetinghouse for water, food if they could find it, and a few moments to drop to the floor and rest.

Inside, Mrs. Ebenezer Dewey, whose patriot husband was fighting with the rebels in Bennington, listened intently, then spoke in quiet urgency to the eight women and twelve children she had led there when the battle erupted in Bennington. "Not a word! Not a sound! I'll take care of them."

She reached for the single musket they had found when they entered the old building an hour earlier. The ancient weapon was unloaded, and she had no powder or musketballs. She pulled the ramrod from its receiver and dropped it down the barrel, then jerked the door open and strode boldly out to meet the oncoming enemy. With them barely twenty yards away she began working the ramrod up and down the barrel as though driving a ball home. Suddenly she paused, then turned and shouted over her shoulder, "It's the enemy! Quick, men, load and fire!"

In an instant she whirled and ran back into the building, smashed out a window, and jammed the muzzle of the gun through it, pointing it at the leading man, now ten yards from the door.

The redcoats and Tories had seen enough of what stubborn Yankees could do with muskets from behind a wall. Without a word, they veered west and ran for the road. Inside the building, the women ran to the west window to watch, and as the last of the redcoats disappeared, they turned to cheer their savior, Mrs. Ebenezer Dewey, who was collapsed on a chair, barely clinging to the harmless musket, shaking like a leaf.

With dusk approaching, Stark issued orders, and the Americans began the work of seeking their dead, tending their wounded, counting the number of enemy who had fallen and those captured. Inside the walls of the redoubt atop the knoll, the searchers paused in surprise. Stacked beside the silent cannon were mounds of smooth stones. The Germans had run out of ammunition. They worked on into the night, searching through the woods and streams, silent, still hearing the wild shouts and screams and the unceasing din of muskets that had filled their world for three hours that seemed an eternity. The seasoned veterans, who had lived through engagements as far back as 1763, would forever remember the battle as the hottest they had ever seen.

A little past midnight the officers faced Stark with the numbers.

"Sir, it appears the Germans lost between nine hundred and one thousand men, killed or captured. We don't know how many wounded. Baum died, along with nearly every man in his command. Breymann survived, but nearly half his column did not."

Stark bobbed his head. "Very good." His bushy brows were drawn down over his piercing eyes. "It appears we have returned the enemy a proper compliment for their Hubbardton engagement."

For the fourth time in twenty minutes, General John Burgoyne looked at the clock inside his elaborate command tent. Fifteen minutes before four o'clock P.M. on the hottest day of the week. He reached for his quill, then tossed it aside. *Something's gone very wrong. Where's Breymann? Has the earth opened and swallowed him?*

Driven by the mounting conviction of a disaster, he stood and walked to the tent entrance, pivoted, and paced back. *All Baum had to do was get horses and oxen and bring them here. And what happened? He got himself wounded and captured, according to those four beaten Germans who wandered in last night, but how many of his column did he lose? Breymann got there late, but where is he? What has happened to him? Fourteen hundred men! Four cannon! Enough to hold Fort Ticonderoga! And where are they?*

He stopped his pacing long enough to take a deep breath. *I should have this command well on its way south, toward Saratoga, but I can't move without those horses! Where's that son-in-law of St. Luc? Charles-Louis Lanaudiere? He and his Indians made it back, but all he knows is that he and his Mohawk ran like a pack of cowards when the fight started.*

He stepped quickly to the entrance and spoke to the picket. "Send someone to get that son-in-law of St. Luc. Lanaudiere is his name. The one who came in from Bennington last night. Bring him here. I want to talk to him once more."

"Yes, sir."

The young lieutenant had moved only three steps when a commotion from the south end of camp stopped him. Burgoyne was halfway through the tent entrance when he heard it. Quickly, he turned and hurried into the clearing at the center of the camp, pensive, hoping. Relief flooded through him at the sight of Breymann, mounted on his horse, leading his column into camp.

Burgoyne called back to the lieutenant. "Go tell Breymann to come to my tent immediately."

"Yes, sir."

When Breymann pushed through the tent flap, Burgoyne was standing behind his large, ornate desk, facing him, face intense, drawn. He spoke but one word. "Report."

Dirty, exhausted, sweat showing through his uniform, Breymann drew himself to attention before the desk and began.

Rain delayed my march—arrived at Bennington yesterday at four o'clock—Baum's column gone—all gone—Baum wounded—we engaged the rebels—their reinforcements arrived—too many of them—we retreated—they turned cannon on us—we left the battlefield—stopped to care for our wounded in the night—came directly here.

Breymann stopped. Burgoyne's face was white.

"You stated Baum's command is gone? What do you mean, *gone?*"

"Dead or captured. All of them."

"All of them?" Burgoyne blurted. "Baum, too?"

"Wounded, lying in a wagon, probably dying."

"How many casualties in your column?"

"About half of us got back here. There are some—maybe many— who got lost in the forest and will probably make it here later."

"Your cannon?"

"Abandoned."

The signs were all too transparent to Burgoyne. He had seen too many battles not to grasp what had happened. A total, devastating, complete disaster.

His face was a blank as he spoke, and there was a bite in his words. "Very good. Make a complete written report before you do anything else."

"Sir, my men need attention. They're nearly finished."

"Leave that to your subordinate officers. I want the written report."

Breymann raised defensive eyes. "Yes, sir."

Burgoyne followed Breymann to the tent entrance and spoke brusquely to the young, wide-eyed lieutenant: "Survivors of the Bennington affair will be coming in through the rest of the day, into the night. I want them to report to me before they speak to anyone else. Arrange it."

"Yes, sir."

They came in, exhausted, dirty, sweated out, some wounded, bandaged, a few carried on litters rigged with pine branches and military coats. Their eyes were dead, flat, expressionless. They were taken directly to the command tent, where Burgoyne interrogated them while he made notes. By ten o'clock the stack of paper was an inch deep. By midnight the bits and pieces were coming together. By dawn the picture was complete.

Burgoyne leaned back in his chair. His uniform was wilted, sweatstained. He needed to shave, but he did not care. The expression on his face was that of a man who had just experienced his first taste of a fear worse than death. For Gentleman Johnny Burgoyne, the toast of London, the bon vivant of Paris, there could be no worse purgatory than failure in his conquest of the Hudson River valley. He sat slumped, head down, and he could not control his mind as it repeated over and over again the facts of the battle.

Baum, dead. Captain von Schieck left to die on the battlefield. Von Barner shot in the arm and chest. Captain von Bartling missing, presumed dead. Lieutenants Muhlenfeld, Gebhard, Meyer, d'Annieres, all dead. Hanneman shot in the neck. Spangenberg with a smashed shoulder. Breva, badly wounded, taken prisoner. Most cornets and color-bearers, killed, wounded, captured. Johann Bense, shot in the belly. Baum's soldiers, nearly all dead, captured, or missing; a few had straggled in through the night, most mumbling incoherently. Half of Breymann's column unaccounted for.

Burgoyne swallowed as his thoughts ran on. *No horses. No oxen. No grain, food, supplies. I cannot move without them—cannot go on to Saratoga as planned. Must go on with what I have. Must go on.*

A rustle at the tent entrance brought his head up.

"Sir, may I bring your breakfast?"

For ten seconds Burgoyne stared, unable to bring his mind back to his command tent and dawn approaching. He sat looking at the startled lieutenant in silence.

The young lieutenant's eyes narrowed in question. "Sir, are you all right? Sir?"

Notes

For reasons yet unknown, General Burgoyne selected Colonel Friedrich Baum to lead a column of about six hundred German soldiers southeast from Fort Edward to obtain horses, grain, and other foodstuffs from the rich countryside surrounding the small village of Bennington. Colonel Baum spoke not one word of English, and, he took a German brass band with him, which played German songs as they marched along the road that passed Sancoick, followed the Hoosic River, then the Walloomsac River toward the town. By way of comic interest, the German band did include a tuba. Higgenbotham, *The War of American Independence*, p. 191.

Baum began his march with about six hundred men, but gathered nearly another five hundred Tories as he moved along, making a total above twelve hundred soldiers. Aware the Americans were scouting him, he dug his forces in atop a rise on the north side of the Walloomsac River, with a Tory redoubt or breastwork, on the south side. Feeling uneasy, Baum sent word back to Burgoyne for reinforcements.

American General John Stark came to meet him. After his scouts reported, Stark divided his command into three sections. One was to circle to the right, climb the hill and come into the cannon redoubt from the north, another was to circle the opposite direction and come in from the left. The third was to take the Tory redoubt. At that time, Tories often put white feathers, or white pieces of paper in their hatbands as a sign they were loyal to England. On this occasion, some of the local farmers who were fighting with Stark's militia put white bits of paper in their hatbands to give the impression they were Tories, and were in among the Germans with their muskets and bayonets before the Germans understood they were not friendly.

After briefing his officers, Stark gathered his men and gave them a short but potent talk, ending with the words that have immortalized him. He concluded his speech by saying, "There are the redcoats, and they are ours, or Molly Stark sleeps a widow tonight!"

On his signal his men attacked, and the results were disastrous for the Germans. Stark's men drove them from their hilltop redoubt, overran the Tory breastworks by the river, and chased them back up the road from which they had come.

The reinforcements Baum had requested entered the battle at that moment, when General von Breymann came in from the west with his column and a few cannon. For a moment it appeared he might turn the battle, but just as the Americans were falling back, Seth Warner and his New Hampshiremen came storming in from the east, hit Breymann's command head-on, and within minutes the battle became a rout, with the Germans running through the woods to escape.

The Battle of Bennington was a rousing success for the Americans. Baum lost nearly his entire column, Breymann about half of his. Baum died of the wounds he sustained in the battle. Altogether, it cost General Burgoyne about one thousand more of his best troops, and left him shocked, stunned, unable to comprehend how it could have happened. The recital of the names of the officers he lost or who were critically wounded, is accurate (see Ketchum, *Saratoga*, pp. 291–319; Leckie, *George Washington's War,* 397–98).

The incident involving Mrs. Ebenezer Dewey and the women she hid in the small meetinghouse, and then saved by bluffing the British soldiers with a single musket, is accurate according to the records of the town of Poultney, Vermont. Elaine Child, of Utah, graciously delivered to the author a copy of the book, *A History of the Town of Poultney, Vermont, from Its Settlement to the Year 1875.* The work was published by J. Joslin, B. Frisbie, and F. Ruggles, and printed by the Poultney Journal Printing Office in 1979. See pages 17–19. The author is grateful for the interest of Mrs. Elaine Child.

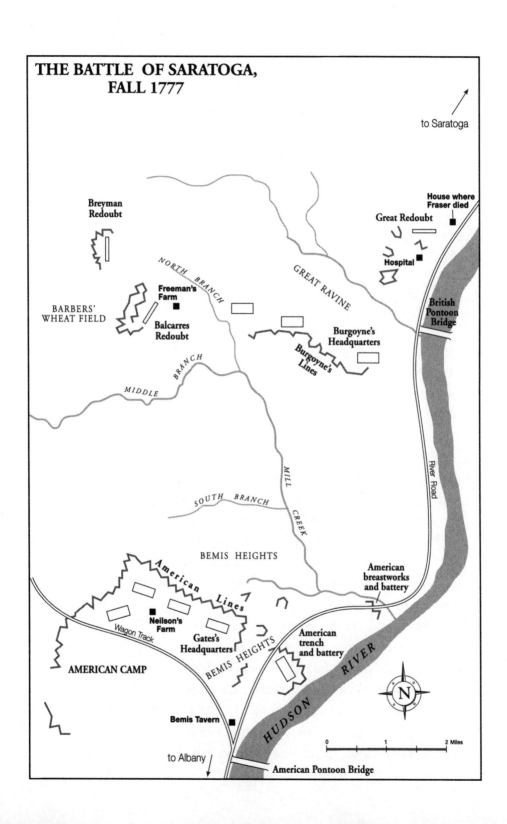

THE BATTLE OF SARATOGA, FALL 1777

to Saratoga

Breyman Redoubt

House where Fraser died

Great Redoubt

Hospital

NORTH BRANCH

GREAT RAVINE

British Pontoon Bridge

BARBERS' WHEAT FIELD

Freeman's Farm

Balcarres Redoubt

Burgoyne's Headquarters

Burgoyne's Lines

BRANCH

MIDDLE

MILL CREEK

River Road

SOUTH BRANCH

BEMIS HEIGHTS

American breastworks and battery

American Lines

Neilson's Farm

Gates's Headquarters

Wagon Track

BEMIS HEIGHTS

American trench and battery

HUDSON RIVER

N

AMERICAN CAMP

Bemis Tavern

0   1   2 Miles

to Albany

American Pontoon Bridge

CHAPTER XXX

★ ★ ★

*T*he rain stopped at noon, and by one o'clock the sun had turned the dead air in the Hudson River valley into a stifling, sultry cauldron. Wisps of steam rose from countless streams, and from the dripping leaves and branches of the forest, and from the rolling waters of the great river.

Soaked, sweating, Billy and Eli moved silently through the dense tangle of wet foliage, speckled with points of sunlight filtering through the overhead canopy of trees. The river was four hundred yards to their left, Fort Ticonderoga nearly fifty miles behind, the tiny settlement of Saratoga with its neighboring settlement of Stillwater just ahead. Suddenly Eli raised a warning hand, and the two went to one knee, peering into the thick forest in silence. Seconds ticked by, and then the sound came again, close, from their right—the sound of something large moving through the sodden woods. Slowly Eli brought his rifle to bear, and Billy brought his musket in line.

The soft sound was twenty feet away when the ferns and tangled undergrowth moved. Silently Eli raised two fingers, and Billy read them—two men coming. An instant later the shadowy shapes emerged ten feet away, hunched slightly forward, muskets clutched before them. Billy and Eli remained silent, motionless as the two passed within five feet. Their dress was homespun, their battered, dripping hats colonial.

One second later, Billy and Eli both stood and stepped out behind the two men, weapons raised.

Eli spoke quietly. "Stand easy. We're friendly."

At the sound of his voice both men pivoted, startled, thumbs reaching for the hammers on their muskets, and in the instant of their turning they saw the muzzles of the raised weapons four feet from their chests. Both men froze.

Billy spoke. "Put your muskets down."

Both men set the butts of their muskets on the ground and grasped the barrels.

"Americans?"

"Yes. You?"

"American scouts looking for General St. Clair or General Schuyler."

Relief showed in the faces of the two men as the one exclaimed, "*St. Clair! Schuyler!*" Suspicion clouded his face. "You're Americans, and don't know about what happened?"

"Tell us."

"They're gone. Called in by Congress. St. Clair gave up Fort Ti without a fight, and him and Schuyler lost about half their army wanderin' around out in the woods, so Congress called 'em in and sent out a new general to take over."

Billy broke in. "We know about Fort Ti. We were there three days ago. We've been tracking our army since. Where is it now?"

"Half an hour due south at Saratoga and Stillwater. We're out to be sure the British aren't sneakin' up on us."

"Who's the new commander? The new general?"

"Gates."

There was pain in Eli's face as he spoke. "Horatio Gates?"

"Yes. Why?"

"The Gates that was at Trenton?"

"The same. Somethin' wrong with that?"

Eli turned to look at the disgust in Billy's face and ignored the question. "We've got to talk to him. Will you take us in, or do we go alone?"

"You got somethin' to tell him?"

"Yes."

"What?"

"It's for him."

Eli and Billy started on, when the two men came hurrying after. "Hold on. We'll take you on in, but don't start tellin' about gettin' behind us."

They fell into single file and moved south through the muggy heat, watching and listening. They broke from the gently rolling, wooded hills into a clearing with a few crude log homes that formed the place known as Saratoga. A few American soldiers stopped to watch them pass as they continued on south to the tiny trading post and four cabins called Stillwater. Tents of every description, ragged, torn, patched, were scattered among the buildings and into the trees. Men and a few women slowed to look, and a few followed as the two scouts led Billy and Eli to the largest of the log buildings. The lieutenant at the door challenged, and they stopped.

The picket saluted the officer. "Two . . . uh . . . American scouts to see the general."

"About what?"

"Won't say."

The picket turned to Billy. "Who are you? Why do you want to see the general?"

"Corporal Billy Weems and Private Eli Stroud. Under orders of General Washington. Reporting a scout to Fort Stanwix."

A hush spread among those within earshot as the lieutenant's eyes widened in surprise, and he disappeared through the door, then returned. "The general will see you."

The two men entered the square room and waited a moment for their eyes to adjust to the dim light. The walls were chinked logs, the fireplace made of rocks set in mud and mortar. Behind the plain desk, Major General Horatio Gates leaned back in his chair and laced his fingers across his paunch. His round, corpulent face was a mask of cool condescension as he silently studied the two men before him, dirty, trail-stained, wet, bearded.

His jowls moved as he spoke. "Yes, what is it?"

Eli stood loose and easy while Billy saluted and spoke. "Corporal Billy Weems and Private Eli Stroud reporting, sir. General St. Clair sent us to find Joseph Brant and his Mohawk Indians, and do what we could to help defend Fort Stanwix. We've returned to report."

Gates nodded his head once. "I understand. You're aware of the current circumstances of generals St. Clair and Schuyler?"

"We were just told."

An almost undetectable smile passed over Gates's face. "Regrettable. In any event, you're back. What do you have to report?" He leaned forward casually, elbows and forearms on the desk, hands clasped as he waited.

"Colonel St. Leger and Joseph Brant placed Fort Stanwix under siege. General Nicholas Herkimer came from Oriskany to give support to Colonel Gansevoort at the fort. He was ambushed by Brant and Sir John Johnson, and the militia took heavy casualties. They retreated back to the settlement. Herkimer died of his wounds. Brant and Johnson went back to the siege. Then General Benedict Arnold arrived with a column of militia and continentals. Eli and General Arnold tricked Brant and St. Leger, and two weeks ago, St. Leger lifted the siege, then went back to Oswego to get more men and heavier guns. On the way, Brant's Mohawk went wild and murdered some of St. Leger's regulars. Eli and I followed St. Leger and Brant to Oswego. St. Leger and his army left for Montreal, and they're not coming back. Eli parlayed with Joseph Brant and his warriors to persuade them to quit the British. Most of Brant's men left him to go home. Brant gathered up what Indians he had left and came this way to get more as he came down the Mohawk Valley. Most of his men have left the British, and it looks like Brant is going to leave, too. All that comes down to the fact that almost none of the men Burgoyne expected to get from the west will be coming to join him."

Gates reached to tug at his long nose and pursed his mouth for a moment before he spoke. "Where's Arnold now?"

Billy glanced at Eli, puzzled. When one general referred to another in the presence of enlisted men, the protocol was to use the term "General." Gates had not.

"He went on to Fort Stanwix, then left to return here. He's leading a column of men. Should be here any day."

Gates brushed flies from his face. "You say he *tricked* Brant?" Amusement filled Gates's face. "What trick?"

Eli answered. "Sent a demented man with a message."

Gates looked at Eli. "A demented man?" He chuckled. "Well, we've got enough of those around. Why a demented man?"

"Indians think they're special—touched by Taronhiawagon."

Gates eyebrows arched. "Who's this Taron person?"

"The Great Spirit."

"What was the message?"

"That Dark Eagle was coming with a great army."

"Who's Dark Eagle?"

"Arnold. The Indians call him that."

Gates brows dropped. "And the Indians believed this demented person?"

"Yes. They were running west within an hour."

"Who told Arnold about this 'trick,' as you call it?"

"Me."

Gates ran his eyes over Eli's buckskin hunting shirt and breeches, and his eyes came back to the tomahawk and knife in his weapons belt, then his long rifle. "How did you know about it?"

"Raised Iroquois."

Gates quickly covered his surprise. "I see." He turned back to Billy. "Is there anything else, Corporal?"

For a moment Billy stood in silence, startled that Gates had asked not one word about conditions at Fort Stanwix, Colonel Gansevoort, his men, Oriskany, Herkimer's death, his men, or even the route by which the two of them had returned. "No, sir, not unless you have some questions."

Gates shrugged. "I have no questions. You are dismissed."

Billy blinked in surprise. "Uh, sir, do you have further orders? What regiment should we report to?"

A look of irritation flitted over Gates's face. "To the regiment you left."

"That was with General Washington."

"Then find my aide, Major James Wilkinson. Tell him I said to assign you wherever he sees fit."

"Sir, is that the Major Wilkinson that was at Trenton and Princeton?"

"Yes. It is." Suddenly Gates realized the implication, and instantly he became focused. "Were you there?"

"Yes, sir."

Both Billy and Eli saw the defensive flash in the general's eyes as he drew in his chin and thrust his chest out slightly. "Then you know Major Wilkinson. Report to him. That's all. You're dismissed."

Billy saluted, and the two had reached the door before Gates's voice stopped them. "I might mention, it is customary for enlisted personnel to salute an officer when making such a report. One of you failed to do so." His mouth smiled, but his eyes did not. "I trust that will be corrected in the future. That's all." He waved a hand and turned his attention to paperwork on his desk.

In the split second it took Eli to understand what Gates had said, Billy grasped his elbow and steered him out the door, closed it, and walked him splashing through the muddy water into the streets of the tiny hamlet. He kept his iron grip on Eli's elbow and didn't slow until they had covered ten yards. He looked at Eli's face and could see ridges along his jawline and lightning in his eyes.

"Let it go," he said. "The man has too much on his shoulders."

Billy felt Eli's arm slowly relax, and he watched the fire leave his eyes as he regained control of his anger. Eli said nothing as they continued walking through the muddy street, looking for an officer. To their left, a captain and a lieutenant ducked through the flap of a tent to stride toward Gates's office, eyes downcast as they picked their way through the muddy puddles.

Billy raised a hand. "Sir, General Gates ordered us to find Major James Wilkinson. Could you direct us?"

The captain peered at the two men for a moment, searching for recognition that would not come. "What regiment are you with?"

"Massachusetts."

The captain slowed. "There is no Massachusetts regiment here."

"Is Major Wilkinson nearby?"

The captain pointed. "At the quartermaster's tent."

"Thank you, sir."

The two men angled northward, toward a large tent with two posts driven in the ground near the entrance. A tall, black gelding was tied to one, two brown mares to the other, standing hip-shot in the mud. The mares moved as Billy and Eli approached, and the picket at the entrance flap stopped the two men.

"What's your business here?"

"Is this the quartermaster's tent?"

"Yes. Do you have orders—"

The sounds of distant voices came from their right, north of the camp, and the clamor grew with each passing moment. Every eye in camp turned to look. Within seconds militiamen came running from the forest, past the trading post and houses and tents, into the clearing. They held their muskets high, shouting as they ran into the crooked streets, mud flying.

"Gen'l Arnold's comin' in, leading a relief column! Hundreds! Thousands!"

Billy and Eli broke to their right, trotting toward the influx of jubilant militiamen. They slowed to a walk, peering into the forest north of the clearing. Minutes later they heard the first sounds of a large body of men working through the trees, and then they saw the first flashes of movement. Within seconds they made out the shape of four horsemen coming on the crooked trail, and behind them, a single file of soldiers with muskets slung, striding through the trees. Eli and Billy slowed and stopped, watching as the horsemen broke out into the sunlight, and they recognized the stocky man in the lead.

Brigadier General Benedict Arnold, riding a showy, high-blooded sorrel gelding with four stockinged feet. He held a tight rein, and the horse arched its neck against the pressure of the bit. A rousing shout erupted from hundreds of voices as Arnold paced his horse through the scattered buildings and tents into the clearing, with his aide and two officers on horseback beside him. He stopped, reined the horse around, and as his column came in, he pointed and called orders. The different companies went to the right, or the left, according to his point, stopped, and waited while the others came in, with the militiamen and a few families crowding around, gesturing, pointing, exclaiming. With his command assembled in the small hamlet, Arnold dismounted as Major James Wilkinson strode up to salute smartly.

"General Arnold! May I bid you welcome. I am Major James Wilkinson, aide to General Gates. He's in command here."

Arnold returned the salute, eyes wide in surprise. "General Gates? What happened to General Schuyler?"

"Very unfortunate, sir. Generals Schuyler and St. Clair have been ordered to report to Congress. Something about the Fort Ticonderoga incident." He turned and pointed to Gates's building. "I'm certain the general would welcome a call from you."

"Wait a moment," Arnold exclaimed. "I'm just coming in from Fort Stanwix. What happened at Fort Ti?"

"You haven't heard? General St. Clair abandoned it to the British. The entire Northern army is scattered. General Gates was sent to gather it again, and to prepare to meet Burgoyne."

Arnold was incredulous. "Abandoned it? Why?"

"His letters state the British positioned cannon on top of Mount Defiance. With their guns up there, St. Clair claimed they could reduce Fort Ti to rubble within two days, and that he abandoned it to save his men."

Arnold bit down on himself to cover the flare of anger. Schuyler and Gates had both been at the council within the walls of Fort Ticonderoga one year ago, when engineer John Trumbull warned that guns on top of Mt. Defiance could reach both Fort Ticonderoga and Mt. Independence.

They both knew Arnold and Wayne had scaled the back side of the mountain to prove guns could be moved to the top. He gritted his teeth, said nothing of the tragic failure of the American generals, and nodded to Wilkinson.

"I would appreciate visiting General Gates."

Wilkinson bowed, Arnold gave orders to his officers, handed the reins of his horse to his aide, and fell in beside Wilkinson to walk to Gates's office. Wilkinson rapped on the door, waited for the invitation, then opened it and entered while Arnold waited outside.

"Sir, General Arnold just arrived with a column of men. I suggested it would be appropriate if he made a call on you."

Gates hoisted his bulk out of his chair to stand behind his desk for a moment, face a blank. "General Benedict Arnold?"

"Yes, sir."

For an instant an unsettling feeling surged through Gates, and he fumbled for words. He steadied his thoughts and said, "By all means, bring the general in."

Wilkinson walked out the door to return instantly. "Sir, I believe you are acquainted with General Arnold."

Gates smiled warmly as Arnold saluted him. Gates returned the salute and spoke. "General! What an unexpected pleasure." He gestured to a chair.

Arnold bowed slightly. "The pleasure is mine, sir. I trust I find you in good health."

"Excellent. And you?"

"Doing well, thank you."

Gates looked at Wilkinson. "Thank you, Major. You may carry on with your other duties."

For a moment, disappointment showed in Wilkinson's face. He had learned the value of knowing everything that was going on, especially between officers of the rank of colonel or above. He had risen to the highly prized position of aide to General Gates by quickly learning the art of listening to everything, and adroitly using what he learned to skewer one officer, or patronize another. One never knew what choice tidbit could be casually dropped at the right moment to get ahead in the infighting by which too many incompetents rose to the top at the expense of their betters, who refused to play the game. This conversation between these two generals promised to be a gold mine of darts and arrows, and Wilkinson would have given a month's pay to quietly remain and absorb it all.

"Yes, sir," he said, and turned on his heel to walk smartly out and close the door.

Arnold sat down facing Gates's desk. Arnold saw no need for further banter. His voice was casual, his manner amiable. "I was ordered by General Schuyler to gather what men I could between here and Fort Stanwix and go help Colonel Gansevoort. I was just told generals Schuyler and St. Clair were relieved of duty here and you are in command. I'm glad you're here, sir. I've come to report and receive any orders you might have."

In the year since he had dealt with Arnold, Gates had forgotten that the art of overpowering a man with the politics of warmth, smiles, graciousness, and subtle compliments was totally lost on Arnold. The man was impervious to such blandishments. Gates, the paper shuffler, the major general who had not gone to the field of battle to command men for years, knew more keenly than any other man alive that Arnold was as far from him as a man could get. Arnold the pure warrior; Gates the pure politician.

Gates masked his thoughts with a smile. "Delighted to have you here. Are your men cared for?"

"Outside. My officers will see to it."

"How many men?"

"Twelve hundred."

Gates eyes widened. "You brought in twelve hundred men?"

"Yes, sir."

"Remarkable." He paused for a moment. "Less than an hour ago two men reported to me. Said their names are Billy Weems and Eli Stroud. They claimed to have had dealings with you at Stanwix. They said a battle was fought at Oriskany and that General Herkimer died of wounds. St. Leger's men and Brant's Indians were tricked into leaving for Oswego, and the whole British force has gone." He stopped to look Arnold squarely in the eye. "How much of that is true?"

Arnold's response was instant. "All of it. St. Leger and Brant won't be coming here. Brant might show up with a few Indians, but not enough to make a difference."

Gates pursed his mouth for a moment, brow pulled down in deep thought. Arnold waited in silence until Gates spoke again, smiling, congenial.

"We have a lot to talk about. Why don't you get yourself and your men settled in and take a night's rest. Then report back here. I need your talents."

The large, two-storied, ornately designed home of William Duer stood like a castle among the lesser homes that were scattered outside the walls of Fort Edward. To the west was the Hudson River; to the east a beautifully wooded hill. Fraser had set up his quarters and office inside the home when the British occupied the Fort, but the moment Gentleman Johnny saw the lush pavilions surrounding the structure, and inspected the rich interior, Fraser had deferred, and the Duer home had become Burgoyne's headquarters. The oak-paneled library, dominated by a one-ton maple wood desk and massive upholstered chair, with a monstrous fireplace on one wall, shelves on another, and grand murals on another, had become his personal office.

Simon Fraser dismounted his bay gelding, tied the reins to a stone hitching post, and walked onto the broad porch. The picket at the door nodded recognition, stepped aside, and twisted the large, polished brass door handle. The door swung inward, and Fraser entered the spacious parlor, boot heels clicking on the polished hardwood floor.

"Sir, may I help you?"

Fraser nodded to the captain behind the desk. "I need to see General Burgoyne. Urgent."

"Yes, sir."

Two minutes later the captain held the door while Fraser walked into Burgoyne's office. Burgoyne glanced up, then stood. "Simon. Good to see you." He glanced at the clock. Fifteen minutes before eight, and a look of puzzlement crossed his face. "What brings you here so early?"

Fraser took a deep breath. "Sir, I have disturbing news." He paused, then came straight to it. "Brant and his Indians are gone. All of them."

A blank look crossed Burgoyne's face, and for a moment it was as though he did not understand. Then his eyes became large, intense, and he leaned forward on stiff arms, palms planted flat on his desk top. "Repeat that."

General Simon Fraser cleared his throat. "Sir, you know Joseph Brant arrived two days ago with a handful of his Mohawk Indians, maybe eighty or a hundred. They're gone. I don't think we have an Indian left in this command."

Burgoyne's face flushed, and then he exploded. He raised one hand to slam it down on the desk, voice strained, raised too high. "When did they leave? Can we catch them? I'll have the lot of them shot for desertion."

Fraser shook his head. "They left in the night—no one knows when. And it's certain we aren't going to catch them in the forest."

With clenched fists Burgoyne strode from behind his desk, halfway to the door, then back again. The veins in his neck were extended, his chest heaving as he battled to bring his raging emotions under control. He stopped beside the large, leather-covered chair behind his desk, paced away, and whirled, jaw clamped closed, eyes blazing.

"All right! So be it! Better we find out now that the great Joseph Brant and his Mohawk are deserters, than during battle! If any of them show up, arrest them on the spot. There'll be a wholesale hanging!"

Fraser remained silent, unmoving, watching Burgoyne. Gradually he stopped pacing, his breathing slowed, and the red flush left his face. He slumped into his chair, shoulders sagging, head down, arms hanging loose. For a time he sat without moving, then raised his hands onto his desk and spoke. His voice was subdued, thoughtful.

"Our destination is Albany, forty-five miles south of here. Halfway there are two settlements, Saratoga and Stillwater. That's where the rebels are starting to gather. To reach Albany, we'll have to either go through them, or around them. To do either one, I need Indians more than ever before. Without Indian eyes and ears out in those woods to tell us where the rebels are, we're marching blind. All we've been through could be lost."

He stopped for a moment. "You already know that St. Leger has taken his command to Montreal. I have received a second letter from Carleton in Quebec. For a second time he's refused to send any men to replace those I had to leave at Fort Ti. Nearly one thousand of my fighting force is tied up back there, useless when I need them most. And now Brant and his Indians are gone."

Fraser started. "I didn't know about Carleton." He stopped for a moment, searching his memory. "Isn't Clinton just south of us? Doesn't he have men he can send to help? What about Howe?"

Burgoyne slowly shook his head. "I got a letter from Clinton. He said he knows Howe is intent on taking Philadelphia this season, and doubts Howe ever intends coming to meet us at Albany. I haven't heard from Howe since the seventeenth day of July. I have no idea where he is. Clinton's been ordered to occupy and hold the highlands north and west of New York to support Howe. He hasn't got a man to spare at this moment, but there's a chance he will have in time. I'll send him another request."

He looked Fraser in the eye. "I sent a letter to both Howe and Clinton reminding them that this expedition required that I receive support from St. Leger's command from the west, and Howe's command from the south. Had I known I was going to get neither, I would never have left England."

Burgoyne leaned back in his chair and dug a thumb and forefinger into his eyes. He sat thus for a time, forehead wrinkled in deep thought.

"My latest scouting reports say militia are coming to Saratoga and Stillwater in droves, from as far away as Massachusetts." A cynical smile stole across his face. "It seems our plan has worked out exactly backwards. I was to have additional support, the rebels less. Now it appears I will have no support at all, and they will be flooded with it."

He took a deep breath and squared his shoulders. "There's nothing to be gained by sitting here brooding. One good thing—we've stockpiled food and stores for thirty days." He smiled his standard, jaunty, Gentleman Johnny smile. "I imagine we can find a way to move from here to Albany within thirty days."

Fraser nodded.

"Simon, thank you for coming. As always, I'm in your debt. Return to your men. Give me some time to think, and we'll hold a war council. I'll send for you and the others when I'm ready."

"Good morning, General. Have a seat." A smiling Horatio Gates sat at his desk and waited for Benedict Arnold to take a seat opposite him.

"Good morning, sir."

"I trust your men are settled."

"They are."

"Had breakfast?"

"Yes, with my officers."

"Good." Gates sobered. "There are a number of matters needing attention. The first one is a proposal regarding yourself." Gates paused for a moment. "I propose that you should take command of a division of the army. Included will be Major Dearborn's light infantry, and two brigades of New Hampshiremen under Ebenezer Learned and Enoch Poor. Those two regiments are composed largely of veterans in the regiments of Joseph Cilley and Alexander Scammel. If we get the New York and Connecticut militia I've been promised, they'll also be assigned with those regiments." Again Gates paused, and a slight smile formed. "You'll also be getting Daniel Morgan and his company of riflemen."

No company of soldiers in the American cause stood higher than Morgan's riflemen. They were gathered from the forest, where they had mastered their long Pennsylvania rifles and the art of surviving and thriving indefinitely in the wilderness. They wore buckskins and long hair, trusted the man next to them with their lives, shared the good and the bad, and revered Daniel Morgan. They would follow their intrepid leader wherever he led.

Arnold eased back in his chair with his thoughts running. *A strong corps. Good leaders.* "Thank you, sir."

Gates nodded. "I take it you'll accept command of the division?"

"Of course."

"Do you have your staff picked?"

"I've asked Henry Brockholst Livingston and Matthew Clarkson to join me. I'll have others as soon as we get organized."

A cloud passed over Gates's face. "Wasn't Livingston on Schuyler's staff? Isn't he going to be leaving soon to join Schuyler in Albany?"

"Yes. I've asked him to join my staff until he goes. Good man."

"Isn't Clarkson, Livingston's cousin?"

Arnold's eyes widened. "I hadn't thought of it, but you're right. He is."

Gates's eyes narrowed for a moment while he slowly nodded his head. "I see." He continued, and a coolness crept into his voice. "General Schuyler has been relieved of command, for good reason. He surrendered Fort Ti, and his army was all but annihilated. I have no use for his policies, and I have deep reservations about having someone from his staff close to anyone on my war council. Would you reconsider those two? Livingston and Clarkson?"

Gates's signal to Arnold was wide open, clear, blunt. Two years of relentless acrimony between Schuyler and Gates had left each man detesting the other. With Schuyler fallen from grace, Gates found himself with the unbelievable, incredible gift of replacing him at precisely the time when the tides of war had subtly shifted in favor of the Americans. No man was going to stand between himself and his one golden chance to humiliate Schuyler, and put himself within striking distance of the one goal that had come to dominate his mind, his heart, his life. Whatever it took, he would find a way to replace George Washington. The name Horatio Gates, and not George Washington, would be forever enshrined in American history.

Arnold shrugged. "They're both good men. I'll look around, but until I find someone as capable, I think I'll have to use them."

Gates's mind snapped shut. *He's a Schuyler spy—calling in Schuyler men to assist—they'll make trouble—can't trust them.*

Arnold, the pure warrior, direct, unsophisticated, hating politics and politicians, had almost totally failed to grasp what Gates had so plainly laid before him. The distancing that instantly began between himself and Gates went unnoticed by him, as did the chill that now quietly settled between them.

Gates continued. "Before leaving Philadelphia, I petitioned Congress for seven thousand seven hundred fifty men. Congress consented. Most of them have arrived. I have Enoch Poor with a brigade five miles up the Mohawk River. They were waiting for St. Leger, but with him now gone they're on their way here. More than half the command is on Van Schaick's Island. With your twelve hundred, and General Morgan's riflemen, we're close to eight thousand. When the militia arrives from New York and Pennsylvania we should have ten thousand."

Arnold bobbed his head. "Good. What condition are these men in? Clothing, food, morale?"

"Excellent. I demanded fresh vegetables and meat and substantial shoes and clothing for my men. Congress obliged. On my orders, the camp and hospital were cleaned up. We began holding inspections every morning, drilling every day, and started conducting courts-martial for the laggards. It took some doing, but discipline is high, morale is excellent, the men are in good health, with good clothing. I believe we're ready."

Arnold sensed the well-deserved pride in Gates's voice. "Do you know the condition of Burgoyne's command?"

"Not entirely. We know their uniforms are in poor condition, and they were running low on food. They were eating roots and porcupines and raccoons for a time, but Burgoyne stopped long enough to stockpile supplies at Fort Edward. Perhaps enough for a month. His men are approaching exhaustion from clearing trees to unblock roads, digging out dams, replacing bridges, rebuilding burned causeways."

Arnold interrupted. "That's Schuyler's work. Even when he was retreating, he was doing everything he could to eat away at Burgoyne's army—slowing them, wearing them down, using up their food, their oxen, their horses. He provided us time to gather our forces. He set the stage for what's now happening."

For an instant hostility flared in Gates's face at the suggestion that Schuyler was in any way responsible for depleting Burgoyne's army. The truth of it was lost in the abhorrence Gates felt for the man. He brought himself under control and went on.

"The critical fact is, it is becoming obvious that the condition of his army is such that he must make a choice. He can no longer sit where he is. He must retreat back to Quebec, or he must move on to Albany. I've known Burgoyne since we were lieutenants together years ago. My personal judgment is that his pride will not let him retreat. That means he must go on to Albany, and to do that he must first get past my command, here, at Stillwater and Saratoga."

The truth of it seized Arnold. "What is the plan?"

Gates spread a large map on his desk and anchored the corners. He scanned it for a moment, then tapped a finger and moved it as he spoke. "We're here. Burgoyne's here, at Fort Edward. We don't know how he intends getting past us, but we do know he has but two choices. Either he crosses the river at Fort Edward and comes down this side to Albany, or, he comes down the far side of the river, the east side, and crosses just above Albany, here, near Half Moon. His problem is, the river is fairly narrow at Fort Edward, but not at Albany. At Half Moon and Albany it's wide."

Arnold was totally absorbed in the map.

"He can cross at Fort Edward quickly, and under cover of his own cannon. But if he tries to cross at Half Moon, where it's wide, his men will be on the river for a much longer time. With very little preparation, we can place our cannon out of range of his, and sink most of his bateaux and boats before they even come close to the western banks of the river, without so much as a single British cannonball to stop us."

Arnold raised his eyes. "Burgoyne won't commit his army to a river crossing he can't control. He'll cross at Fort Edward and come down our side of the river."

Gates's eyes were glowing. "I'm sure of it. That brings us to the question, where is the best place for us to prepare to meet him?"

Arnold's response was instant. "Not here. This whole area is too flat, too open. Perfect for the way the British fight. We need to meet them in the hills and woods, where our men are at their best, and his are at their worst."

"Precisely. I've asked some of the locals about it. They say there's such a place three or four miles north, near the river. Owned by a man named Jotham Bemis. Called Bemis Heights. There's a tavern where the road forks, and a farm there, and another close by, some fields, hills, wooded areas."

"Has anyone gone to look?"

"Not yet. I plan to send Major Wilkinson and Udney Hay in the next day or so. Perhaps the engineer, Thaddeus Kosciuszko."

"Good. The sooner the better."

General Simon Fraser used the iron cleat on the doorstep to scrape mud from his boots, rubbed both boot soles briskly on the heavy bristle of the doormat, shook rain from his hat, then stepped into the parlor of the elegant, two-storied Duer house. He followed Burgoyne's aide to the large, glass library doors, waited until he was announced and invited, then walked into the library. Burgoyne rose from behind the great maple desk. Seated on his left were generals Phillips and von Riedesel, to his right, General Breymann.

"General, thank you for coming."

Fraser nodded. "Sorry to be late. We had a disturbance. I had to stay for a few minutes."

Burgoyne asked, "A disturbance?"

"Two enlisted men. One drew a knife."

"Anyone hurt?"

"No. Nothing serious. Tempers flared. It's settled."

"What was the disturbance about?"

Fraser hesitated for a moment, then grunted a laugh. "An argument over a pair of socks. But that wasn't the real problem. The men are becoming alarmed. Frightened. They know the rebels are gathering all around us by the thousands, and the forces we were promised haven't come. They're starting to think they've been lied to. It boiled over half an hour ago. It's taken care of."

"Good. Be seated, there, by General Breymann."

As Fraser sat, Burgoyne spoke. His face was a mask of discipline, his voice steady, devoid of emotion. The men at the table quieted, sensing something had reached deep inside Burgoyne, far past the charismatic Gentleman Johnny.

"As some of you might know, Colonel St. Leger is not coming. Brant was here only long enough to inform me that he and his Mohawk Indians are returning to their home grounds on the Mohawk River. They believe George Washington cannot be defeated." He paused. No one stirred in the silence. "It has become clear to me that General Howe does not intend coming to meet us in Albany. He wants Philadelphia. General Carleton has refused to send men to relieve the one thousand I left to occupy Fort Ti. We lost another one thousand at Bennington. We lost more at Hubbardton and Fort Anne, and sickness and desertions are serious, and ongoing. This morning's duty roster shows less than four thousand effectives."

He paused long enough to draw and slowly release a huge breath. "Without Indians to act as scouts and advance skirmishers, we are blind. We don't know where the enemy is, or their numbers. If we march, it is without eyes and ears ahead of us, or beside us, or behind us. The moment the enemy discovers we've lost our Indians, we are vulnerable."

A murmur arose around the table and died.

"At this moment the militia from nearly every state to the east of us is gathering like a great, dark cloud on our left flank, and behind us. Ahead of us, the rebels have gathered about eight thousand men, with more coming every hour."

He selected a map and began unfolding it. "It is clear to me we cannot remain here. Our choice is simple. We retreat back to Quebec, or we push on to Albany alone."

He stopped, and his eyes flicked from man to man. The next moment he stunned them. "I've decided we march on to Albany."

Fraser stiffened. *No questions—no discussion—no suggestions—simply decided it without us and that's the end of it! Something's wrong!* He glanced at the other generals at the table. They all sat staring, faces a blank.

Burgoyne flattened the map on the desk and droned on, indicating with his finger as he spoke. "Here we are, at Fort Edward. Gates is gathering his forces down here, in and around Saratoga. To reach Albany, here, we have to get past Gates's forces." He raised his head. "We can do that by going down this side of the river and crossing the Hudson just above Albany, or we can cross the river here, and go down the west side."

Again he paused while the generals methodically put the building blocks in place in their minds.

"If we cross the river here, at Fort Edward, we will not be on the water very long, we'll be in control, and they will have no cannon to sink our bateaux and boats. If we cross down here, at Albany, we'll be on the water much longer, and if they place their guns right, they'll be able to reach our bateaux and boats, while we won't have a gun that can reach them. In short, it will be a massacre."

Once again he raised his head, asked no questions, and delivered his decision. "We cross the river here, at Fort Edward."

Phillips leaned back in his chair, brain approaching deadlock. *Precisely what does he think he's doing? War council? This is no war council! This is a case of pure dictatorship!*

Burgoyne went on. "When we conclude here, order your men to pack their baggage at once, and load all tents, munitions, food—everything—into shipping crates for the crossing. We leave nothing—absolutely nothing—here."

Riedesel reached to wipe at a dry mouth. *He intends breaking all connections with our supply base. When we leave here, there is no returning! We succeed in getting past the rebels at Saratoga, or we are defeated!* Von Riedesel turned to look at Breymann and read the identical thoughts in his startled eyes.

Burgoyne spoke with cold finality as he folded the map. "Thank you for coming. Take charge of your troops for the river crossing and march to the south. You are dismissed."

★ ★ ★ ★ ★

The picket pushed aside the flap at the entrance of the command tent of General Benedict Arnold. "Sir, the two men you sent for are here. Weems and Stroud."

Arnold finished pulling on his boot, then stood and stamped his foot hard to settle his foot inside. "Good. Send them in."

A minute later Billy and Eli stood facing Arnold. Billy saluted. "Reporting as ordered, sir."

Arnold smiled. "Glad to see you two again. I heard some things about Brant and his Mohawk. After that trick with that deranged man—what was his name—Han Yost—I wanted to hear from you two what happened over at Oswego, after Yost scared the Indians into running away from Stanwix. Were you at Oswego?"

Billy nodded. "Yes, sir."

"What happened?"

"Eli walked into Brant's camp with a wampum belt and told him the British were going to lose the war. If Brant was with them, he'd lose, too."

Arnold's eyebrows raised in surprise. "Just walked into his camp and told Brant he's going to lose?"

Billy turned to Eli, and Eli spoke.

"Indians respect a wampum belt. Billy and I made one, and it got us into their camp. Brant's an honorable man. I reminded him of a story—sort of a prophecy—made by an old Indian a long time ago. The old chief tried to kill Washington in a battle and found out his men couldn't hit him with their muskets. He prophesied Washington could not be killed in battle, and would live to become the father of a great nation. Brant knew about that prophecy. What he didn't know about was the times I saw Washington in battle. Washington should have been killed at least six times, but wasn't. I told Brant. He believed it. We left."

"You persuaded Brant and his Indians to quit the war?"

Eli shrugged. "It appears so."

Arnold shook his head in amazement. "That's the most remarkable thing I ever heard." He stopped for a few moments, his thoughts running. "With both St. Leger and Brant gone, Burgoyne's going to have about three thousand fewer men than he planned on." He stopped for a moment to consider, then raised startled eyes. "You've crippled the British army! Remarkable. I thought that trick with Han Yost was unbelieveable, but what you did at Oswego is far beyond that. I owe you. This country owes you."

Eli shrugged. "We were lucky."

Arnold shook his head. "That wasn't luck." He turned to pick up his tricorn from his desk. "I was on my way to General Gates's quarters. Some business that won't wait. I'll see if I can get a full report of what you've just told me into the army records." He stopped, then suddenly thrust out his hand. "It was my privilege to work with you over there at Fort Stanwix. I want you to know that." He shook their hands, then led them to the door. "I wish we had a little more time, but General Gates won't wait. Come on. I'll walk part way with you."

The three stepped out of the tent into the heat of the day, and half a dozen soldiers slowed at the sight of a general striding through camp with enlisted men. Arnold said his thanks, nodded, and angled away, toward the small building with Gates's name on the sign above the door. On his approach the picket opened the door, spoke to General Gates, and waited for Arnold to enter before he closed it.

For a moment Arnold stood still, waiting for his eyes to adjust from the bright sunlight. Gates laid down his quill, leaned back in his chair, and interlaced his fingers across his paunch. "Be seated, General. There's something you wanted to discuss?"

Arnold sat facing Gates across the desk. "I understood I was to be assigned three New York companies. I found out late yesterday that Major Wilkinson assigned them to General Glover's regiment. Did Wilkinson make a mistake?" Arnold's manner was direct as always.

Gates looked at him steadily. "No, Wilkinson did not make a mistake. The error was mine. I shall correct it."

For several moments Arnold stared at Gates, struggling to believe that a general whose entire military career had been an example of office work could make such a monumental blunder. Gates the paper shuffler. That he could misplace three companies of New York militia was unthinkable. A question rose nagging in Arnold's thoughts. *Is he trying to hurt me because I didn't replace Livingston and Clarkson as my aides?*

A voice of alarm sounded in the back of his head, and he moved past it. "I thought those men were under my command, and I gave them orders. They ignored me. It was humiliating when they said I wasn't their commanding officer."

"I'll take care of it. By the way, have you found anyone to replace your two aides? Livingston and Clarkson?"

At that moment a disquieting assurance took root in Arnold's brain. *It is Livingston and Clarkson. He's punishing me!* An almost indiscernible edge crept into his voice. "Not yet." He took a breath and moved on.

"There's another matter. I understand John Brown is now a lieutenant colonel in Benjamin Lincoln's command. John Brown has spread vicious lies about me and others. Totally unreliable. I take it as a personal affront that he's been lately coming to war councils, when I haven't been notified to attend. He's a colonel, I'm a general. I don't understand it."

Gates's answer was casual. "He's been called in regarding matters on which he has certain knowledge. Nothing more than that."

"The other generals were invited."

Gates shrugged. "If you were not notified, I was unaware of it. I sent my aides."

"Wilkinson?"

"And others. I'll see to it they make certain you're notified in the future. My apologies for the error."

"There's one more thing. I understand today is the day Wilkinson and Udney Hay, and maybe Colonel Kosciuszko, are going north to look for a better place to meet Burgoyne."

"They are. They're going to the place the locals mentioned. Bemis Heights, three miles north of here."

"I'd like to go along."

"For what purpose?"

"If we pick the right place, we can take down Burgoyne's whole army."

Gates shrugged. "As you wish." He fixed Arnold with a dead stare, waiting.

Arnold rose. "That's all I had. If there's nothing else, I'll take my leave."

"Report back when you return from your tour with Major Wilkinson."

Arnold turned to leave, and as he closed the door, the thought struck him: *Is he trying to provoke me into an act of insubordination? This matter of John Brown—Wilkinson assigning three companies of my men to Glover's division—failing to notify me of war councils? Would he do that to provoke me?* Slowly, thoughtfully, he walked through the morning sun to his own command tent and ordered his tall, black horse, Warren, to be saddled for his ride north.

With Arnold leading, the four men cantered their horses from Stillwater, north on the River Road that followed the meander of the Hudson River, flowing south one hundred yards to their right. They were sweating beneath a fierce sun, moving slowly, critically studying the rise and fall of the hills and valleys to their left, seeking a place where the build of the land would give them the high ground, with little chance the British could reach their flanks. The sun was three hours high before Arnold pulled in his mount, wiping sweat from his eyes as he peered at a rise just ahead, to his left.

"That might be the place." They spurred their horses left, from the River Road onto a dim wagon track skirting the base of the hill. They passed the Bemis Tavern, in the fork of the road, and minutes later left the wagon track to circle to their right, upward, until they crested out on top. With an eye made wise by the successes and mistakes of countless battles, Arnold turned his horse facing north and sat still, going over every inch of the ground, from the east where the River Road skirted the Hudson River, to the west, where thick, dense woods covered the hills and sharp ravines. The other three men fanned out beside him, each sitting his horse in the sun, sweating, also studying the lay of the land.

Several minutes passed before Arnold broke the silence. "This will do." For a moment he sat in sober reflection, pondering his strained relations with Gates. He turned to Wilkinson and Hay. "You better get General Gates to come inspect it. I'll stay here with Colonel Kosciuszko to ride further north to be sure what's there."

It was past four o'clock in the afternoon before Gates and his staff sat their horses on the top of Bemis Heights, listening intently as Arnold laid out the field as he saw it, Kosciuszko beside him.

"If Burgoyne is going to succeed, he'll have to take this hilltop. So, here, on this high ground, is where we build our strongest breastworks. This is where our headquarters should be." He pointed to his right, toward the Hudson. "There, down between the River Road and the river we'll put a battery of cannon with breastworks to stop anything coming down the river." He shifted his point to his left, where steep ravines broke the land nearly a mile distant, with maple, pine, and oak so thick it was nearly impassable. "The British will not want to come through those ravines. They know our woodsmen will pick them apart in those trees." He changed his point once again, due north. "Directly ahead is Mill Creek. It runs nearly due south, and has three branches, all coming in from the west. Near the headwaters of Mill Creek is a farm owned by a man named Freeman. He's gone, but a man named Leggett has taken over the farm. Leggett left when he found out we were coming."

He paused, then again raised his pointing hand. "About a mile past Freeman's farm is a big ravine. Steep, rocky sides, with a creek in the bottom. Burgoyne's going to have trouble crossing it if he comes that way, but it can be done."

He stopped to consider, then went on. "The building west of us is a barn. It sits on a small farm owned by John Neilson. Neilson's joined us. We can reinforce the barn and use it as part of our breastworks." He dropped his hand and turned toward the group of men. "If we build solid breastworks here, and dig in with cannon, they'll have trouble dislodging us."

He pointed again. "With the river to the right, and that broken ground to the left, that leaves but one place the British can come. Straight at us, across that open ground in the middle. My guess is Burgoyne will come somewhere close to Freeman's farm. There's some rolling ground there, away from the trees, and it's not as exposed as the ground a little further east, directly ahead of us. If he does, we can meet him right around Freeman's farm. There are patches of woods there, and some fences that can hide our men. We should be able to either stop him, or slow him down. If he gets past Freeman's farm, he'll come on to this place, and we'll be waiting with cannon and our reserves."

There was no man among them, including Gates, competent to dispute a thing Arnold had said. Gates turned to Wilkinson. "Draft orders for me to sign." He turned to Kosciuszko. "Can you see to it the proper fortifications are built?"

"Yes, sir."

In the lamplight of Burgoyne's command tent, no one spoke or moved as Burgoyne finished giving orders. "Our scouts tell us the rebels are entrenched on Bemis Heights. To defeat them, we'll have to push them off. I remind you again, their strength is now reported to be above nine thousand. We have less than six thousand, so there is no room for error."

He paused for a moment while his war council accepted the fact that Burgoyne's decision to sit for four weeks at Fort Edward collecting supplies had allowed the Americans to regroup, send out messengers, and gather militia and continentals from nearly every New England state. None had dreamed they would come flocking, outraged at the horrors inflicted by Burgoyne's Indians, waiting for the day they could avenge the brutal killing of Jane McCrae. Now they outnumbered the British, who were only too keenly aware that the entire rebel army could hardly wait to tear into their red-coated ranks, win, lose, or draw.

Burgoyne continued. "You all understand? General Fraser, you take our right wing, with cannon. You will turn their flank and push them east toward the river. I will be with Brigadier Hamilton and General von

Breymann in the center, moving straight south toward Bemis Heights. General von Riedesel will command our left wing, over by the river. Once General Fraser turns their flank, we drive them to the river where we trap them and destroy them."

Each of his generals nodded their head. "Yes, sir."

Burgoyne glanced at the clock on the worktable. Ten minutes past ten o'clock P.M. "It's late. Go back to your troops and get some rest. We march south in the morning as soon as the weather permits. Good luck to each of you."

Dawn was little more than a change of color in the thick, wet fog that lay heavy on the Hudson River valley. It collected on the brows and hair and beards of the men to leave their faces glistening, their clothing damp. They sat shivering at their battle stations, eating cold, sliced mutton and cheese, and gnawing on hardtack. They lifted the frizzens on their muskets to check the gunpowder in the pans again and again.

From far to the north the ghostly clanking of moving cannon reached them queerly in the drifting gloom. They closed their eyes to listen, and tried to count, but could not. They wiped at their beards and brows, checked their gunpowder once more, and waited. In their breasts smoldered a need for the battle they had been denied at Fort Ticonderoga, and they were counting minutes, anxious to finally come face-to-face with those who had sent Indians into their farms and settlements to commit their unthinkable atrocities.

At the west end of the American breastworks, under command of General Benedict Arnold, Billy and Eli sat with their backs against the thick, two-mile long, dirt-filled log wall that Kosciuzsko had designed and the Americans had built at the crest of Bemis Heights, facing north. Gates had established his battlefield headquarters inside the three-sided fortress, and with cannon batteries covering all approaches, Gates was certain of one thing: all he had to do was wait for Burgoyne to throw his army against the breastworks. The rebel cannon crews would leave half of the British dead on the open ground stretching before the foot of the hill, and the remainder of them on the slope beneath the cannon muzzles. Gates had his entire command inside the walls, waiting to see how Burgoyne would proceed to attack, for one thing was certain: Burgoyne had to attack. He had to take the American breastworks on the ridge of Bemis Heights or forever be denied reaching Albany.

Odd thoughts arise in the minds of men while waiting for a battle. The probability of killing, and the possibility of being killed, lurk continuously in the far, dark recesses of their consciousness to color every thought, while a source beyond their control feeds common things to their brain, disconnected, unrelated. *Is Sarah all right?—with the baby six months along—did the calf get over the colic?—did Jeremy fix the leak in the well bucket?—the pigs are going to be ready by fall—ham and bacon for the winter—got to find a way to keep the rats out of the corncrib—wish I could write to Martha and the children—must learn to write.*

Billy shifted his musket and moved his legs. "Fog's bad for this time of morning."

Eli spoke without moving. "Makes people edgy."

Billy rested his head back against the log wall. "Thought much lately about your sister?"

"When this is over, I'm going to talk to some of the people from up there. Vermont, New Hampshire. Maybe someone will know."

"I hope you—"

A voice came calling in the fog. "Weems and Stroud! If you're there call out. Weems and Stroud!"

"Here!" Billy called, and both men stood, waiting.

Two soldiers appeared, shrouded in the fog. "You Weems and Stroud?"

"Yes."

"Come on. Gen'l Arnold wants to see you."

They followed the two dark forms more than a hundred yards before they came to Arnold's command tent. One man pushed the flap aside, entered, and returned immediately. "Go on in. Gen'l's waiting."

A lamp cast the room in yellow gloom. Arnold stood beside his desk, impatient, anxious. He wasted no words.

"Stroud, you ever scout in the fog?"

Eli nodded.

"Can you go find those redcoats and report back to me?"

"I think so."

"How do you keep from getting lost in fog this heavy?"

"Walk in straight lines and count steps. Helps if you know the country. The landmarks, like rivers and mountains."

"You know this country well enough to do it?"

"Yes, after working on these breastworks for a week, I know the country."

"You go alone, or does Weems go with you?"

"That's up to Billy."

"I'm going."

Arnold nodded. "Burgoyne's no fool, and I have a feeling he's trying to flank us. I have to know. Any reason you can't leave from here, right now?"

Eli shrugged. "No."

"Get back here as soon as you can."

At twenty-five minutes past nine o'clock, Arnold stopped pacing when his aide pulled back the tent flap. "Weems and Stroud are back, sir."

"Get them in here!"

Eli spoke. "You were right. There's a strong force off to our left, about four miles north, moving this way. Redcoats, Germans, some Indians, Canadians, and a few Tories. They have cannon. If they come on in the direction they're moving now, they'll be out there on our left."

Arnold's chin thrust forward. "Go on."

"There's another big force directly in front of us, coming right up the middle. Mostly British. Some cannon."

"And the east? Anyone coming from the east?"

"They're Germans, but I don't know about cannon, or how many, because we ran out of time. Somebody better pay attention to that bunch coming in from our left. If they get in behind us with a cannon, we could have trouble."

Arnold bobbed his head once. "Just as I thought. Stay here." He grabbed his tricorn off his worktable and hurried out into the fog. Three minutes later, without knocking, he barged through the door into General Gates's small office. Gates jerked upright in his chair, startled.

"What's the meaning of this?"

"This couldn't wait on all the formalities. There's a strong column of British working their way around our left. They have cannon. If they flank us, we're going to have trouble."

Gates asked, "How do you know all this? We have no scouts out in this fog."

"I sent two out."

"Without notifying me?"

"I didn't think I had to notify you. The question is, what do we do about it?"

Gates still had his feathered quill in his hand. "Nothing. We wait. The fog will lift soon. We can attend to them after that."

Arnold took an iron grip on himself. "Sir, when the fog lifts, may I recommend we send out some of my command to find that column coming on our left?" He paused to weigh his words, threw caution aside, and plunged on, voice rising. "Battles are won by those who take the initiative. Strike first. If we let Burgoyne pick the time and place to attack, we'll be giving away some of our advantage."

Gates's eyes sharpened and he shook his head decisively. "This breastwork was designed to withstand any attack. I'm not going to waste time or men, out trying to engage a small part of Burgoyne's army, when all we have to do is wait for him to attack."

Arnold's answer came hot. "Don't underestimate Burgoyne. He's vain and pompous, but in a fight like this one, he's shrewd and tough. If he flanks us with enough good men, he can hurt us. Bad."

Gates abruptly stood and tossed his quill on his desk, tenuously clinging to his temper. "All right. Send out some men from Morgan's command, and from Dearborn's, and remember, what comes of it is on your head, not mine. Morgan's and Dearborn's, and none others. Not one more man in this . . . futility."

For a moment the two men stood still, facing each other, eyes blazing, nearly trembling. In a single stroke what had been festering between them for weeks was laid wide open, raw, ugly. Arnold, the warrior, knew in his soul that the battle that would likely turn the entire revolution was but hours away, and he knew just as surely that Gates, the politician, was incapable of fighting it. And he knew with deadly certainty that at this moment it would shatter the American army if he forced an open, bitter split with Gates. Divided within itself, the army would fail, and above all else, Arnold would not let that happen if he could avoid it. Shaking, with every fiber of his being crying to strike out at Gates, Arnold clamped his jaw tight, turned on his heel, and strode from the tent. He did not slow as he stalked through the fog back to his own command tent and turned to his aide. Billy and Eli stood quietly to one side.

"Get Morgan and Dearborn over here."

Arnold selected a map, unfolded it, anchored the corners, and was studying it when the aide opened the door. "They're here, sir."

General Daniel Morgan entered first, Dearborn following, Billy and Eli right behind. Six feet tall, thick-shouldered and necked, strong face, Morgan had run his own freight wagons before he joined the British army in their war against France. Strong, agile, a born rifleman, leader, and forest fighter, it was Morgan who had defied ridiculous orders from a pompous young British captain. The captain made the mistake of reaching for his sword, and with one blow of his fist Morgan knocked him rolling into a corner, unconscious. When the officer regained his senses he ordered Morgan punished with five hundred strokes of the lash. Forever after, Morgan claimed he only got four hundred ninety-nine strokes—that they still owed him one—and he had joined the rebels when they rose against the British. Dearborn was average in build, round-faced, tended to be quiet.

Morgan faced Arnold. "You wanted to see me?"

"Yes." Arnold looked at Dearborn, and behind him at Billy and Eli. "Come on over to the table. Daniel, Henry, this is Eli Stroud and Billy Weems. Stroud's white, but was raised Iroquois. Weems is from Boston. They work together."

Morgan turned critical eyes on both men, and they met his gaze evenly.

With the four of them gathered, Arnold wasted no time.

"Burgoyne's sent a column of men over toward our left. These two men located them this morning. They're a strong force, and have cannon. I don't know what they're up to, but it could mean trouble if Burgoyne sent them to circle clear in around our left and flank us. I intend engaging them before they ever get that far."

Morgan spoke. "Located them in this fog?"

"Yes."

Morgan looked at Billy and Eli again, then turned to the map. "Where are they?"

Arnold turned to Eli. "Show them."

Eli pointed. "About four miles due north is a farm house, marked Freeman's farm on this map, here. Just north, there's a column of mixed redcoats, Germans, Canadians, Tories, a few Indians. They have cannon. They're working this way, staying close to the woods off to the left. If they continue, they're going to come out in a position to flank us."

"Sure?"

"Sure."

Morgan turned to Arnold. "What does Gates say?"

"Send you and Dearborn."

Dearborn's eyebrows raised. "I thought we were going to sit here and let Burgoyne come to us."

"Gates changed his mind."

Dearborn grinned. "How long did it take you to persuade him?"

Arnold ignored the question. "Get your company ready to move. The minute the fog raises, you two go find that column. In your judgment, either engage them, or report back here. Morgan, use your riflemen as skirmishers. Dearborn, you wait in reserve if anything goes wrong."

Morgan and Dearborn glanced at each other, then turned back to Arnold. "Anything else?"

"No."

They both nodded to Billy and Eli and walked out the tent entrance.

Arnold spoke. "You two go on back to your company with Dearborn. You'll be in action soon enough."

Without a word they started for the door, when Arnold's voice stopped them.

"Thank you."

Notes

To make what history now calls the Battle of Saratoga manageable, the author has somewhat compressed the time element, since the events surrounding this pivotal battle began in August of 1777 and the final surrender of Burgoyne and his army occurred 17 October 1777. Thus, in this chapter few dates have been given, in an effort to maintain the flow, and reduce hundreds of pages of factual material to an acceptable number, and still maintain the integrity and authenticity of this event.

Congress recalled generals Schuyler and St. Clair, for a congressional inquiry into their failure to defend Fort Ticonderoga on 6 July 1777 and an explanation of their continual retreat for weeks thereafter. They were also to report to General Washington, likely to face courts-martial for their conduct. Most officers, including most generals, who were wise to the ways of the battlefield, understood what St. Clair had done, and why, and found his actions acceptable, even praiseworthy in saving his army to fight another day. It was the men St. Clair saved who became the core of the army that finally met General Burgoyne at Saratoga. Further, General Schuyler, even while retreating, was steadily wearing down Burgoyne's army by blocking their roads, damming streams to stop them with floods, burning the crops to starve them, and constantly harassing them with snipers. Men who were there knew it was these actions of Schuyler that reduced Burgoyne's effectiveness when the final battles were fought. General Nathanael Green, one of Washington's best generals, commented, "The foundation of all the Northern success was laid long before Gates's arrival there . . . he appeared just in time to reap the laurels and rewards."

To replace General Schuyler, Congress commissioned General Horatio Gates to take command of all American forces on the Hudson River. On 19 August 1777, General Horatio Gates arrived at Albany to take command. He found morale terrible, men sick with smallpox and with what was called "camp disorder"—fever, and ague. August had been an extremely hot month, with unusually heavy rains. Because of their prior years of animosity and rancor toward each other, Gates refused to consult with Schuyler on any matters whatsoever, especially what Schuyler had done despite his weeks-long retreat, and this although Schuyler had extremely valuable personal knowledge of the countryside and the inhabitants that would have been immensely helpful to Gates. The Americans continued gathering at Stillwater and Saratoga, as Schuyler had previously ordered.

By the end of August, however, something had shifted. With the tremendous victory at Bennington, and the total collapse of the British effort at Fort Stanwix, and the disappearance of Colonel St. Leger's forces and Brant's Indians, the Americans sensed something was changing, as did Burgoyne and the British. Without Indians to serve as his scouts—eyes and ears in the forest—Burgoyne was marching almost totally blind as he proceeded south.

Albany was but forty-five miles south of Fort Edward; however, Fort Edward, where Burgoyne was located, was on the east side of the Hudson, and Albany on the west. Thus, Burgoyne had two choices: to cross the river at Fort Miller where it was narrow, just south of Fort Edward, where his cannon could cover the crossing, and march south on the west side of the river, or, march south on the east side of the river, and cross at Saratoga, or Albany, which is just south of Saratoga. However, if he crossed at Saratoga or Albany, where the river was wider, his bateaux and fleet would be under the muzzles of American cannon for a long period of time, and his cannon on the east bank could not reach the American guns. Hence, his bateaux and fleet would likely be nearly destroyed on the water. He chose to cross at Fort Miller and march down the west side of the river, despite the fact he would have to fight his way through the Americans now gathering at Stillwater and Saratoga. Once the decision was made, there was no turning back.

On 28 August, a troop of Connecticut cavalry arrived at Stillwater, and another on 1 September. On 30 August, Daniel Morgan and his riflemen arrived. On 31 August, Benedict Arnold and General Learned arrived from Stanwix. The gathering of a formidable American army continued.

In near despair, Burgoyne began to realize his true circumstances. Howe was not coming to meet him at Albany. St. Leger had abandoned him and was on his way to Montreal. General Carleton refused to send him any reinforcements. His men were exhausted, dispirited, hungry, and clearly showing the strain of their march through the sweltering, snake- and insect-ridden forest.

Before leaving Philadelphia to take command of the Northern army, Gates, the "darling of Congress," had requested seven thousand seven hundred fifty men, and they began arriving. With those already present, including the twelve hundred Arnold brought back from Stanwix, and Morgan's riflemen, the American army gathering for the great and final battle outnumbered the British.

Shortly after Arnold's arrival, Gates appointed him commander of one division of his army, but Arnold soon discovered a very cool attitude from Gates, and quickly understood it was because two men he had on his staff, Livingston and Clarkson, were distant relatives of General Philip Schuyler, whom Gates detested. Gates suggested Arnold remove them from his staff, but Arnold, insensitive to such nuance, did not do it. As a result, Gates began distancing Arnold from himself, eventually not even notifying him of staff meetings, while bringing other men of inferior rank to such meetings, which was an open insult to Arnold. Arnold quickly realized that trouble lay ahead between himself and Gates.

Stillwater was not the place to force the next battle. It lay on flat, cleared land, which would accommodate the European style of fighting and favor Burgoyne. So Gates directed Udney Hay and Major James Wilkinson to go north three miles to a place owned by a citizen, Jotham Bemis, which reportedly was an ideal place to bring the battle. Arnold asked permission to accompany them and did so.

There, on a hill to the west of the Hudson River and River Road, Arnold found the ideal place, called Bemis Heights. To the left were heavily forested ravines where Americans could fight well and the British could not, and to the right was the Hudson River. Straight ahead was rolling country, fairly open. By entrenching strongly on the top of the hill at Bemis Heights, American cannon could cover all the ground directly north, and, if the British survived the American cannon fire, they would be forced to climb Bemis Heights under tremendous musket and grapeshot fire. On the hilltop was a barn owned by a man named Neilson. About three miles due north, on another rise, was a second farm owned by a man named Freeman.

The Americans built a great, strong breastwork on Bemis Heights, where Gates established his headquarters and waited.

Burgoyne had to attack. The season was late, he could not turn back, and he either had to reach Albany or face the oncoming winter and certain annihilation (see Ketchum, *Saratoga*, pp. 336–448; Leckie, *George Washington's War*, pp. 389–426; Mackesy, *The War for America*, pp. 130–41; Higginbotham, *The War of American Independence*, pp. 193–97).

CHAPTER XXXI

★ ★ ★

*T*he fog lifted shortly after ten o'clock A.M., and Morgan and his riflemen headed west, into the forest, then turned north, rapidly working their way through the trees, moving like silent shadows. Dearborn's command followed, Billy and Eli with them. At twenty minutes before one o'clock, with the sun directly overhead, Captain Van Swearingen, leading the company at the head of Morgan's command, suddenly dropped to one knee, out of sight, on the southern edge of the clearing surrounding Freeman's farmhouse. Instantly all three hundred men in the company disappeared while they waited for Swearingen's order. Slowly he raised his head high enough to study the far northern edge of the field where a flash of red in the trees had caught his eye.

Quickly he counted, believed he was looking at the advance skirmishers of a British column coming into the open field, and gave a silent hand signal. The entire command worked forward, invisible in the high grass and trees, and within minutes some had reached an old log hut while others crouched behind a rail fence and the balance were hidden in the tall grass or were perched in oak and maple trees. They cocked their long Pennsylvania rifles and through slitted eyes started picking out the oncoming British, the ones wearing gold epaulets on their shoulders gleaming in the sun.

With patience borne of many battles, Van Swearingen calmly judged the distance from where he was to the dead branches of a gnarled old oak tree in the clearing. *Sixty yards. Close enough.* He settled his cheek against the smooth stalk of his rifle, partially closed his left eye, and lined the sights on a British major coming straight at him. The British officer was walking hunched forward, head swinging from side to side, sensing something he could not see. Cautiously he paused behind the bare limbs of an old oak snag standing in the field, then pushed on past.

Van Swearingen took up the last one-eighth inch of the trigger pull on his rifle, and the long barrel recoiled as it blasted flame three feet out the muzzle. The .60-caliber rifleball drilled through the place where the white belts crossed on the officer's chest, and he went over backwards. At the crack of Van Swearingen's rifle, three hundred more of the deadly long rifles cut loose, and a cloud of gun smoke two hundred yards long blossomed in front of the terrified British column. In the opening volley, more than two hundred British officers and regulars went down in the hail of deadly American rifleballs. Few of them moved after they hit the ground.

In shocked chaos the redcoats turned and ran in disorganized terror, wanting only to be away from those accursed Pennsylvania long rifles. Instantly Van Swearingen broke from his cover, shouting, "Follow me, boys, go get 'em!" The riflemen appeared as if by magic, from behind trees and fences, out of the tall grass—and they sprinted after the panic-stricken British, reloading as they ran.

The shouting Americans reached the center of the open field when suddenly, from their left, a volley of British musketfire came whistling. Startled, Van Swearingen slowed while he tried to grasp what was happening, and then came the blast of a cannon, and a hail of grapeshot tore into the Americans. Van Swearingen's left leg buckled, and he grabbed his left shoulder and went down, shouting, "Fall back! Fall back!"

At the south end of the clearing, General Daniel Morgan watched, horrified when he finally understood. He had thought the oncoming British were but the point skirmishers, but they were not. He had committed his corps of riflemen against the entire center of Burgoyne's army of three thousand crack British troops! The British skirmishers he had expected to meet were to his left, part of Fraser's command, and had come to the sound of his rifles to catch his men by total surprise. It nearly broke his heart to see his beloved riflemen taking the unending roar of musketfire, and the thunder of cannon blasting grapeshot. With tears in his eyes, he cupped his hands around his mouth and sent out his call to his men to fall back, reassemble—the high, peculiar sound of a wild turkey gobble.

The battle in the open field of Freeman's farm should never have happened. Neither side had planned for it, intended it to occur. It had been triggered by purest chance. As with many battles, perhaps most, it occurred on its own terms, with both sides committing brilliance and blunders so rapidly it was impossible for anyone to form a plan or give it shape and direction.

Within seconds British and American soldiers alike were running in all directions, sometimes into enemy gunfire, sometimes away from it. A British support company ran from the forest into the clearing and opened fire, only to find they were killing their own troops. Another British officer screamed, "Cease-fire!" and it stopped. Four redcoats seized the wounded Captain Van Swearingen and hauled him away to General Fraser, who remained on his horse to question the prisoner while musket and cannonfire erupted all around. With drawn sword he shouted at Van Swearingen.

"Who is leading the rebels?"

Van Swearingen calmly answered, "Generals Gates and Arnold."

"What is their plan?"

Van Swearingen looked Fraser in the eye. "Generals Gates and Arnold are our commanders. I have nothing more to say."

"Answer, or I'll have you hung where we stand."

Van Swearingen didn't blink an eye. "You may, if you please." Fraser shook his head in grudging admiration as he turned his horse back toward the battle. He paused to give orders to an artillery lieutenant.

"Take charge of that man, and see to it he is treated well."

At the south edge of the clearing, Arnold shouted to Dearborn. "Get more men in to help Morgan!"

Dearborn bawled out instant orders. "Cilley, Scammel, get out to support Morgan."

Three seconds later Cilley and Scammel were running north, out into the clearing, leading their commands into the hottest fighting. Clubs, swords, bayonets, rocks, muskets, rifles—hand-to-hand, face-to-face in the boiling sun, the armies clashed. The Americans pushed the British back and took possession of the British cannon, only to find the horses dead, strewn helter-skelter on the ground, and without them the Americans could not move the cannon. The incensed British rallied, turned, and came back shouting, shooting, and the Americans fell back, yielding up the prized cannon.

General Benedict Arnold could no longer restrain himself. He jammed his spurs home, and the big black horse lunged north, out onto the battlefield. With sword drawn, shouting like a man possessed, far above anything resembling fear, Arnold charged first one place, then another, shouting orders, sending one company to help another. Musketballs sang past his ears, nicked his clothing, cut hair from his horse's mane, ricocheted off his sword, but none hit him. The Americans watching him held their breath, certain this wild man would draw enough British fire to kill him, but he did not go down. They drew courage from him, stopped, dug in, then moved forward.

At the north end of the field, General John Burgoyne came galloping on his tall gray horse, resplendent in his tailored uniform, sword flashing, shouting orders to his men. American musketballs cut his cape, his collar, but he rode on, unharmed, rallying his men, shouting them to a stand-still, then turning them to face the Americans.

Four miles south, General Horatio Gates sat in his headquarters, drinking coffee, listening intently to the unending roar of musket- and cannonfire. Not once did he leave his chair, or his quarters.

Then, with no signal from either side, and no reason anyone could define, the gunfire slackened and slowed, and then stopped. It was as though the mindless panic that had seized both sides had ebbed and dis-appeared, and each was groping to recover, take stock, bring some sense of order to their thoughts and their scattered army. For two hours the only sounds were the pitiful groans and cries of wounded and dying men in the field, begging for help, for a surgeon, for water. Strong men on both ends of the field turned their backs and bowed their heads, and wept, under orders not to go into the field to help. Too many good soldiers had been shot trying to reach their wounded and dying comrades.

In the undeclared lull, Burgoyne received the disheartening news with a somber face. Those accursed Pennsylvania long rifles had cut his officers to pieces. Most of those who had led his army on the open battlefield were dead, along with a catastrophic number of his regulars. He accepted it, considered, and gave orders to his aide. "Get over to Riedesel on our left, by the river. Tell him to keep enough men at the river to hold his position, but send all those he can spare to come reinforce our middle."

"Yes, sir."

The young major mounted his horse, wheeled it around to the east, and was gone in a pounding of hooves.

Two minutes later an American lieutenant stopped before Arnold, fighting for breath from a run. "Sir, Burgoyne just sent a messenger east, toward the river. General von Riedesel and his Germans are over there!"

Arnold's eyes opened wide. "Riedesel! He's calling in reinforcements. We've hurt him worse than I thought." He leaped on his horse and drove his spurs home. The sweated mount hit stampede gait in three jumps as Arnold reined him through the woods and fields, headed south. He hauled the lathered animal to a stiff-legged, sliding stop before Gates's cabin headquarters, dismounted, and barged through the door, sweating, face streaked with stains from gunsmoke.

Gates recoiled like he had been struck, voice high, angry. "What do you think you're doing?"

Breathing hard, Arnold paid no heed. "We've got Burgoyne's whole army in trouble. He's sent for reinforcements. If we can hit him quick, on his left flank, we can get in behind his Germans that are coming to reinforce him, and he's finished. We can end this thing now."

Gates stood silent, bewildered. Arnold plowed on.

"I know where to hit him. I'm offering to lead Learned's brigade. They're waiting in the woods, fresh, and there's enough of them. Burgoyne can't fight what's in front of him, and at the same time fight Learned's men coming up behind. There's no time to waste."

Gates licked dry lips, hating the fact that Arnold had been on the field of battle when he had not, hating the fact that he must now listen to a man he thoroughly detested, hating the fact that if Arnold's request succeeded, it would be Arnold, and not Gates, who would receive the laurels.

Gates straightened and raised his chin. "Very good. I shall order General Learned and his men to take the field immediately."

Stunned, Arnold stared for three full seconds. His voice was venomous as he nearly shouted, "To go where? He doesn't know where Burgoyne is, or how to get in behind him!"

Gates's chin was still high, domineering. "He can find Burgoyne, and he can use his own judgment in how to flank him."

Arnold's finger shot up, pointing, accusing. "You send him out there to engage Burgoyne, he'll fail!"

"Nonsense." Gates strode to the door, threw it open, and stalked to the tent beside the cabin. He threw the flap aside and called to Major James Wilkinson inside. Wilkinson bolted from his chair and charged outside, facing Gates.

"Yes, sir?"

"Major, go tell General Learned I'm ordering him to proceed north immediately. He's to locate General Burgoyne, and move immediately on Burgoyne's left flank. Stop the Germans coming to reinforce Burgoyne. Stay with the general and report back to me when he makes contact. Am I clear?"

Wilkinson looked into Gate's defiant eyes, and then at Arnold's face, livid, red, ready to explode, and he understood.

"Yes, sir." Three minutes later Wilkinson left camp with his horse at a gallop, headed west toward the distant trees.

Arnold threw up his arms in despair and strode to his mount. He had his foot in the stirrup when Gates's voice came from behind.

"General, you will remain here at headquarters."

Arnold dropped his foot to the ground and turned, incredulous. "The battle's four miles north. I'm going."

Gates's voice was cool, level. "I am ordering you to remain here. You may be needed here. Are you going to disobey a direct order?"

A quiet voice reached through Arnold's boiling anger. *He's baiting you. He wants a reason to put you in irons—report you to Congress—revoke your commission.* Slowly Arnold brought his outrage under control. He said nothing. He reached for the cinch on his saddle, to remove it to get air to his sweated horse.

Seldom had Arnold suffered the agonies he now endured. The crackle of musketfire and an occasional cannon drifted over the walls of the American headquarters, and Arnold closed his eyes to listen intently. *That's not from Burgoyne in the center. That's off to the west. Learned! He's in trouble!* Arnold lost track of time as minutes became half an hour, then an hour. He saddled his horse once again, then tried to read the battle by the shifting of the sound. Learned was locked in a death struggle. Arnold's hands were trembling when the sound of a galloping horse turned him, and he watched Major Wilkinson coming from the west, his horse lathered, laboring. Wilkinson pulled his mount to a stop before Gates's quarters, leaped down, and pounded on the door.

"Enter."

Wilkinson pushed through the door, Arnold right behind, standing in the door frame.

"Sir," Wilkinson cried, panting, "General Learned sent me to report. He got lost in the woods and was caught by light infantry, probably under command of General Fraser. He's there now, sir, fighting his way out. He never did reach Burgoyne. He wanted you to know."

Behind him Arnold's face filled with lightning. He could take no more. His voice filled the room like thunder. "By the Almighty, I'll soon put an end to it." He ran to his horse, swung up, and left Gates waving his arms in his doorway as he disappeared at a gallop, heading west.

Gates grasped Wilkinson's arm and bellowed, "Catch that man and tell him I've ordered him to return here at once."

One mile west of the big wall surrounding the American headquarters, Wilkinson shouted Arnold to a stop.

"General Gates sent me with a direct order. You are to return to his headquarters at once." He paused while his winded horse fought for air, throwing its head, stuttering its feet, and Arnold once more brought his wrath under control. Without a word he reined his horse around and started back to headquarters.

Four miles north, on a battlefield now strewn with the bodies of dead and dying men from both armies, in the silence of the lull that had lasted nearly two hours, the British once more loaded their cannon, and in the heat of the waning afternoon blasted round and grapeshot into the woods where the Americans had taken cover, regrouping, bracing for another attack. The Americans answered, and once again brave men from both ends of the field charged into the open, dodging as they came, firing, loading, firing.

Within minutes the air was filled with the continuous concussion and blasts of cannon and the rattle of musketfire, so thick and heavy it was as an unending roll of thunder. General John Glover and his Marblehead Regiment drove straight north to meet the center thrust of Burgoyne's army. The roar of the guns overrode all commands shouted by the officers, and the men were left to decide from moment to moment the direction and heat of the battle.

Dearborn saw Glover's regiment stop Burgoyne's attack in its tracks, and instantly swung his command to his right, to support Glover. General Poor sensed they were about to turn Burgoyne's center, flank them, trap them, and end the battle, and led his command in a headlong charge to their right, hot on Glover's flank, and the Americans surged forward.

In the leading company of Dearborn's command, Billy and Eli were in the second rank when it closed with the red-coated British regulars, and they plunged into the midst of them, hand-to-hand, knocking aside bayonets, Eli swinging his tomahawk like a wild man, Billy using his musket like a scythe to clear men out before him. Billy scooped up the sword of a fallen British officer and with a battle cry surging from his throat, swung it like an avenging angel. The Americans behind the two men leaped to follow, cutting a hole in the British line, widening it, and Dearborn's command poured through, then angled right to rip into the side of Burgoyne's center command.

From the American's left came the sound of cannon, then the first volley from Brown Bess muskets, and the patriots paused for one second to peer to their left. From the woods, a company of redcoats was charging straight at them, cannon blasting, the British firing in volleys, one rank at a time. They were just over one hundred yards distant—too far for accuracy with their muskets, but they did not care. They came shooting, and the random musketballs reached the Americans to knock some stumbling.

Billy saw the British officer leading them, astride a tall, brown gelding. He was young, taller than usual, sword drawn and waving above his head as he led his men forward, shouting them on, uniform showing battle stains, with the epaulets of a captain bright on his shoulders. With their leader five yards in front of them, lifting them, inspiring them, the regulars drove on, coming in like a horde to break the American charge.

With grapeshot and musketballs whistling from every quarter, Billy's arm shot up and he shouted, "Eli!" as he pointed.

Eli was already slamming his ramrod down his rifle barrel against a rifle ball seated on a linen patch when Billy shouted. He had seen the young British captain leading his men, and in the wild chaos of the battle, he went to one knee. He tapped powder from his powder horn into the pan of the rifle, slapped the frizzen closed, and settled his left elbow onto his knee as he brought the thin blade of his foresight squarely into the center of the notch of the rear sight. He eared the hammer back and brought the sights to bear on the incoming British officer. He gauged the distance—ninety yards—and in the instant the gunsights lined perfectly he squeezed off his shot in the dead air. He moved his head to the left to avoid the white cloud of rifle smoke, and he saw the hit, squarely through the cross made by the two white belts on the officer's chest. The impact of the .60-caliber rifle ball jolted the young captain in the saddle, sent him reeling, grasping for the horse's mane to stay mounted. He lost his reins, tried to regain them while keeping his sword high, and turned to shout his men onward. Then, slowly, his arm lowered, his sword fell from his hand, his head bowed, and he went slack in the saddle. He rolled from his horse to land heavily on his head and shoulder, and lay motionless on the ground.

Even in the tumult of the battle, in an instant his men were around him, straightening his legs and his right arm, and his crooked left one— the one that had been broken by a rebel musketball in the retreat from Concord two years before. They wiped the sweat and smoke stains from his face and closed his vacant eyes. They retrieved his sword and slipped it into his scabbard, straightened his tunic, and covered the bullet hole directly over his heart. Some wiped at their eyes while others stopped to take their last look at the young face of their fallen leader. They studied the prominent nose, the square jaw, the build of a face that was at once plain and handsome. But most of all, they looked for the last time at the deep scar that divided his left eyebrow. The scar he had taken years ago in his desperate attempt to save some of his beloved comrades from a burning warehouse filled with munitions.

The relentless heat of battle gives no time to mourn the fallen. The charge of the company led by the fallen British captain came to a standstill, and with the threat of his attack gone, Billy and Eli had not one second to ponder who he was. They turned their faces back toward Burgoyne's stalled army, and they ran on with Dearborn's command, reloading, firing, knocking redcoats back with tomahawk and sword.

The American officers caught it like a scent in the air. *We can win! We've got Burgoyne's center turned! We can beat him!* It lifted them above themselves, and they raised their voices in a shout that caught among their men, and they raised their voices as one. They were no longer an army. They were a horde, surging forward like a tide, rolling over everything in front of them.

Three hundred yards—two hundred—just two hundred more yards and they are ours!

At one hundred yards, the first blast of grapeshot ripped into the right side of the screaming mass of rebels, knocking men down, rolling, stumbling. An instant later the second blast, and grapeshot opened a hole in the American right. They faltered, stunned, looking east, unable to grasp what had happened. They saw the white smoke from the cannon and in the same instant saw the blue-coated Germans under General von Riedesel surge out of the forest, bayonets gleaming. On command, the first rank of Germans went to one knee, aimed, and fired. They rose and reloaded while the second rank moved in front of them and went to one knee to deliver the second volley. Both volleys tore into the American right, and the startled rebels broke to their left, away from the timed firing. Instantly the Germans sprinted forward, raising a battle cry, and the surprised Americans fell back. They were fifty yards from flanking Burgoyne, folding his command in on top of itself, beating him, when the howling charge of von Riedesel's crack German troops broke their forward momentum, turned them west, slowed them, stopped them. In the chaos, the Americans fell back, gave ground, retreated, stumbling over the bodies of those who had fallen, both British and American. Within minutes the tremendous victory that had been within their grasp was turned into a rout as they pulled back across the open field. Far to the west, in the woods, General Learned was still locked in a running fight, trying to escape the advance skirmishers of Fraser's command.

Only a few ever understood that had Gates granted Arnold his request to lead the regiment to trap Burgoyne, Arnold would have intercepted von Riedesel, spoiled his surprise, blunted his attack, and taken down Burgoyne's entire command. Burgoyne's expedition to take the Hudson River corridor would have ended in the afternoon of that day.

But Gates, the politician, had allowed his animosity toward Arnold, the warrior, to blind him, and he had sent Learned instead—Learned, who had become lost in the woods and never did reach von Riedesel, the man he had been sent to stop.

Their charge and momentum broken, the Americans fell steadily back, and the British and Germans surged forward. Sweating, smoke-stained, bloodied, the two armies struggled desperately on, giving ground, regaining it, the blasting of cannon and muskets making a rolling thunder that reached Gates's headquarters four miles to the south, and Burgoyne's headquarters to the north. The sun touched the western trees, and then it was gone. In the purple of dusk the cannon and muskets blasted their last volleys of the day, with flame and smoke leaping from their muzzles, and then they stopped.

In the eerie silence the Americans withdrew from the battlefield with what wounded they could carry, leaving their dead, and in late dusk the British gathered their wounded and backed away. Baroness Frederika von Riedesel, petite, beautiful, caring, the wife of General von Riedesel, opened her quarters for the wounded. She put her three small children beyond harm, then spent the night tirelessly gathering bandages, persuading other wives to come, nursing, tending the wounded.

In full darkness Burgoyne's officers came to report their losses, and Burgoyne took the figures in dead silence. More than six hundred of his best troops, dead, wounded, missing. One general forced a grin, tried to put a bold face on the battle. "But we won, sir. We drove them from the field."

Burgoyne nodded, said nothing, and waved the general on. In his heart he knew. They had not driven the Americans from the field. The Americans had simply left the field first. As for the casualty count, it was clear that the Americans had lost far fewer men than Burgoyne. And one thing he sensed from every officer who reported to him: the Americans, without uniforms, understanding nearly nothing of military protocol, dressed in homespun, carrying the rifles and muskets they had used for years to feed their families and survive in the wooded frontier, had met the best the British army had to offer. Met them in a fair fight, in the forest, and in the open fields, and had given the British better than they got. For the first time the British army sensed that this rabble, who came from farms and forges and shops, with no pretense of military training or skills, had something inside of them that rose above all else to drive them on. The red-coated officers shook their heads in wonder. With king and God and right clearly on their side, what was it these rebels had?

Few understood that they were not fighting men. They were

fighting an idea, a feeling. Freedom. Liberty. And no cannon, no musket, had yet been invented that could kill the idea once it had taken root in the heart of a free man.

In the American camp Billy and Eli stripped to the waist, and one poured water from a bucket while the other washed away the battle stains of the day. With the stars and a quarter moon overhead, they sat on their blankets, gnawing on crisped sowbelly and brown bread and raw turnips. They tried not to hear the sound of hundreds of wolves in the forest, and on the open battlefield, prowling among the dead and wounded, howling, snarling, fighting as they attacked the bodies.

Billy spoke. "We were close. We could have ended it if the Germans hadn't come in."

Eli nodded. "Did you get a feeling out there today?"

Billy looked at him, waiting.

"Something happened to our side. I think they started to believe they could really beat Burgoyne. A strange feeling."

"I felt it. And I think the British caught the notion we could do it."

"They did."

Billy reached for his pouch and took out the packet of letters, his pencil stub, and the few badly wrinkled sheets of paper that were left.

Surprised, Eli asked, "Going to write home?"

"No. Just wanted to be sure I hadn't lost them."

With the campfire casting its flickering yellow glow, the two men laid down on their blankets, weapons at hand, staring into the flames while their thoughts drifted.

Inside his small, austere office, Gates laid down his quill and reread his written report of the battle. The battle he had not seen. The carefully worded document smacked of confidence, was replete with incidents of American genius and bravery, painted a picture of smashing the British attacks in open battle. He smiled broadly in the lantern glow, knowing that when Congress received it, there would be crowing and back-slapping, and his name would become the word of the day. He folded the document and laid it on his desk. He would send it by messenger at first light. He began unbuttoning his tunic, and again the broad smile split his jowled face. The name Benedict Arnold did not appear once in his official report.

It was well past midnight when the picket at the flap of Burgoyne's command tent pushed the flap aside. Burgoyne was inside, sitting alone in the stillness, staring at the glowing wick of the lantern on his desk.

"What is it?"

"Sir, a messenger. Says he's from General Clinton."

Burgoyne started. Clinton! Could it be? Burgoyne lunged from his chair. "Send him in."

The young major, exhausted, dirty, stepped into the dim lantern glow and saluted. "Sir, General Clinton sends this written message." He thrust a sealed document forward.

Burgoyne snatched it and with trembling hands broke the wax seal, opened the paper, and held it toward the lantern, scarcely breathing while he read it. It was a full paragraph, rambling, nearly meaningless. Quickly Burgoyne snatched up his quill, and drew the hourglass figure through the central part of the writing, according to the code he had worked out with Clinton months earlier. Within the hourglass the message emerged, and Burgoyne read every word.

"You know my good will and are not ignorant of my poverty of troops. If you think two thousand men can assist you effectually, I will make a push at Fort Montgomery in about ten days. But ever jealous of my flanks if they make a move in force on either of them I must return to save this very important post. I expect reinforcement every day. Let me know what you would wish."

Never had Burgoyne felt the rush of relief that surged through his being. Clinton! Coming up the Hudson! Reinforcements! Two thousand fresh troops! Relief! Blessed relief! His shoulders sagged, and for a moment his breathing constricted. He walked back to his desk and sat down, once again reading the words.

The young major cleared his throat. "Sir, are you all right?"

Burgoyne raised his face. "Yes. Thank you. You need food and rest. Let me take you to my aide."

He walked the young major to the tent next to his quarters, gave orders, and returned to his own desk. For long minutes he reflected on the message, and his mind settled.

We will not engage the rebels again until Clinton and his two thousand men arrive. We will entrench ourselves here where we are, and we will wait. With time to regroup and rest our men, and build defenses, and with two thousand fresh troops, we will overrun the Americans and end this thing.

We wait for Clinton.

"Be seated, gentlemen." Burgoyne waited while generals von Riedesel, Phillips, and Fraser took their chairs at his council table. Four lanterns burned, casting huge, distorted shadows on the tent walls. Outside, the pickets tied the officers' three saddled mounts to hitching posts, then resumed their position at the tent entrance. For a moment the horses moved, nervous in the darkness, eyes glowing wine-red in the dull light of the tent walls.

Inside, Burgoyne wasted no time on protocol. "Gentlemen, it has been fifteen days since I received General Clinton's message. I do not believe he is coming." He paused and pursed his mouth for a moment. "We've had frost. Cold weather will close in on us within days. As you know, the Americans have given us no rest, no peace, day or night. Those long rifles have driven in our pickets, killed our scouts, killed our officers, without letup. Our men have not slept three hours a night in fifteen days. They've lived on sowbelly and flour too long. They need fresh meat, vegetables, fruit. They're starving, exhausted, fearful of venturing twenty yards from camp because of American patrols and rifles. We cannot remain here."

He paused. Every word he had spoken was but an echo of what each of the three generals had said to themselves over and over again in the past forty-eight hours.

Burgoyne continued. "We've completed our defenses here. The

Breymann redoubt at the northwest end of our defenses is in place. It's well-positioned, strong, big, able to withstand anything the Americans care to try. South of it is the Balcarres redoubt, and it is also unassailable. The breastworks just south of headquarters are finished, and they will hold against any attack. We've finished the floating bridge across the river, and can move back and forth."

He paused, cleared his throat, and went on. "The Americans have built their bridge south of ours. They too can cross the river at will. They remain as they were two weeks ago, behind their breastworks five miles south of us. Their forces have been vastly expanded by militia and continentals coming in every day over the past two weeks. Their strength now is above fourteen thousand."

Silence settled around the table as each general accepted what they had already silently calculated over the past fifteen days. Burgoyne's decision to wait for Clinton had given them time to build strong defenses, but it had also allowed the Americans to gather men from all over the northeastern section of the continent. Numerically, the Americans now outnumbered them four to one, and with the catastrophic imbalance in their favor, the Americans were waiting for one of two things: winter to arrive and starve Burgoyne out, or, Burgoyne to mount an attack and try to break out. The sole question they had not been able to answer was how long would Burgoyne wait before he faced the terrible decision.

Burgoyne went on. "I am ordering a full reconnaissance to move south—three thousand five hundred men. It is my intent to attack the American left and break their defenses. Once that has occurred, we will move on down to Albany."

Von Riedesel jerked erect, shock plain on his face. "That will leave less than eight hundred to defend our headquarters if the Americans counterattack. Our supplies, munitions, medicines, food, all at risk. If our attack fails, we could fall into a trap of our own making."

Fraser watched Burgoyne's face intently. *He's not thinking right! He's in trouble!*

Burgoyne sat down on his chair, and for long minutes they could hear the mosquitoes buzzing around the lamp chimneys, and see the moths being drawn to the flame. Burgoyne stood once more.

"I think you are right. I will send fifteen hundred south, the balance of our force to remain here to protect our stores and defenses. The fifteen hundred will be divided into three equal commands, under generals Fraser and von Riedesel, and Major Acland. They will proceed west from here, then turn south to cross a wheat field not far from the house on Freeman's farm. They will proceed directly south to engage and defeat the American left."

Fraser interrupted. "Sir, sending out a reconnaissance of that size will give the appearance of an all-out attack. If Gates sees it that way, he may send out half his forces to stop it. If that occurs, we will have no chance in an open battle."

Burgoyne shook his head. "I do not think Gates will send out a sizable force. I think he will send out a small one, to feel out our strength. When they realize what's happening it will be too late."

He drew a deep breath and slowly let it out. "The reconnaissance will leave tomorrow morning."

The first purple of dawn approached in the spectacular beauty of the reds and yellows of leaves that had been nipped by October frost. As far as the eye could see, the forest was a rolling carpet of breathtaking colors that brought men to a standstill, staring, awed by the incomparable power and glories of nature.

In the gray preceding sunrise, a young lieutenant rode clattering through camp to halt his laboring horse before Gates's office. He rapped on the door and waited, breathing hard. The door swung open and Gates stood before him barefooted, wrapped in a royal blue robe. His hair was awry, and he was squinting in the light.

"What is it?"

"There's movement to the north. A force of British is coming this way."

Gates pointed to the tent next to his hut. "Get Major Wilkinson. Tell him to report here, now."

Three minutes later, still buttoning his tunic, Wilkinson stood before Gates's desk. Gates spoke from his chair. "A scout just reported that the British are moving this way. Go find out what they're up to and report back here."

"Yes, sir."

Five minutes later Wilkinson reined his horse west and galloped out of camp. The young lieutenant who had made the report looked at Gates's closed door, then at Wilkinson disappearing to the west, shrugged, and started toward the officers' mess, leading his horse.

In the officers' section of the camp, General Daniel Morgan swung his feet from his cot inside his command tent. For a time he sat, elbows on knees, square face buried in his big, callused, scarred hands. Never had he been part of an army camp in which every enlisted man, every officer, was cowed, quiet, withdrawn, divided.

Fourteen days earlier, Gates had sent to Congress his written report of the battle at Freeman's farm, but had dealt General George Washington, his commander in chief, the highest insult anyone had ever heard of when he did not send a copy to him. Inevitably it became known that the written report not only failed to include the name of Benedict Arnold, but did not even mention the companies that Arnold had commanded in the battle at Freeman's farm, nor the fact that it was Arnold's men who had led the American army into battle, and very nearly taken Burgoyne down. And there was no mention of the fact that had Gates granted Arnold his request to go cut off von Riedesel to prevent the German attack that turned victory into a retreat, the vaunted Gentleman Johnny and his entire army would now be American prisoners.

The despicable report burst like a bombshell when it became known in the American camp. For a time Arnold stood in disbelieving shock, then stormed into Gates's office and left the door wide open. Never had any man in the American army heard anything faintly comparable to the shouting, cursing, accusatory acrimony that flooded out of the door into the open compound. Men stopped in their tracks, staring wide-eyed, silently asking each other for anything that would explain the ferocity of the confrontation in the office of their commanding officer. And when Arnold came storming out, face white with anger, lightning leaping from his eyes, men backed up to give him free passage as he stalked back to his own command tent.

Two hours later Arnold marched back to Gates's office and once more burst through the door, strode to his desk, and slammed down a four-page letter. On those four pages was a truthful, accurate recital of every slight, every rotten thing Gates had done to Arnold since his arrival. The last paragraph included the ultimate insult Gates had heaped on Arnold only that morning when they had their monumental, head-on collision. Gates had reassigned Arnold's men, including Daniel Morgan's riflemen, to General Lincoln. Arnold was a general with no command!

The closing sentence was clear, direct, the strongest words Arnold could find.

"I therefore request permission to return to General Washington with my aides, where I might serve my country, since I am unable to do so here."

Arnold stormed back to his quarters to wait for Gates's reply. When it came, it was a copy of a brief, casual note sent by Gates, not to Arnold, but to John Hancock, president of the Congress, in which Gates professed total surprise at Arnold's outburst and gave him permission to leave. Again Arnold wrote to Gates, demanding he address a letter to himself, Arnold, giving him permission to leave. This time Gates responded with a brief written statement of total innocence, stating he had no idea what Arnold was excited about and granting Arnold what Gates called a "common pass" to go to Philadelphia. No one ever knew what was meant by "a common pass."

News of the unbelievable, vitriolic confrontation went through the entire camp instantly. Every enlisted man and every soldier knew what had happened in the battle. It was Arnold, and Arnold alone, who had swept through the cannonfire and musketballs time and again to lead the

Americans on, inspire them, lift them above themselves. Insensible of danger, his reckless leadership and courage and his innate sense of where to be and what to do had been their guiding star. And every man knew that while Arnold was becoming the greatest warrior in the battle, Gates had sat behind closed doors, drinking coffee, and never leaving his office.

Incensed, fearful that Arnold was going to leave, every officer in the American camp, except for Gates himself and Lincoln, drafted a petition, signed it, and delivered it to Arnold. In it they begged him, pleaded with him, to stay. They knew what he meant to the American army. If he were to leave, the spirit they had fought so hard to gain, would go with him.

Gates learned of the petition, and in his political mind he sensed that if he pushed his corps of officers too far, they might mutiny. Should that happen, it would be aired out in Congress, and Gates had no stomach for having men of the quality of Morgan, Dearborn, Poor, and Learned all standing before that body, all repeating the truth. He had no choice. He relented. Arnold could remain, but he would have no command.

Morgan dropped his hands from his face and heaved his body onto his feet. Soldiering had taken its toll on joints and muscles, and he stood for a moment, letting his frame take his two-hundred-pound weight, while his thoughts ran.

Burgoyne's going to have to make a move. Winter will lock him in soon if he doesn't either go back to Canada or try to come past us. He shook his head. *If he comes past us, we'll have a battle, and if that happens, what will Gates do without Arnold?*

He could not force a conclusion in his mind, and he reached for his buckskin breeches, feeling a rising sense of frustration, nearly anger. He was on his way to the officers' mess when the crackle of distant musket-fire from the north reached him. He slowed for a moment to consider. *The pickets and scouts are under fire.* His pace quickened as he turned toward Gates's command hut. As he approached, eight other officers came striding, including Learned and Poor. They all slowed when they saw Benedict

Arnold hurrying toward them, and they stopped to wait. With Arnold among them, Morgan rapped on Gates's door. Gates opened it and stood facing them, fully dressed except for the top few buttons on his tunic.

"Yes?" he said.

Morgan spoke. "Sir, we all heard musketfire from the north. Sounds like the beginning of an engagement."

The sound of a horse coming in at stampede gait turned all their heads, and they watched Wilkinson come charging through camp like the devil himself was nipping at his hocks. He brought his mount to a sliding halt and hit the ground in the cloud of dust, ten feet from Gates.

"Sir," he panted, "there's a major British force coming down toward our left. I'd guess close to two thousand regulars and Germans."

Gates's eyes widened. "You saw them?"

"Yes, sir." His report tumbled out, one word on top of another. "They're up in that field—the Barber wheat field—next to the Freeman farm. They've got troops out cutting grain for the horses. Burgoyne and two other officers climbed onto the roof of a barn up there and used a telescope to locate our scouts and pickets. They know we don't have any force up there. I think this is the attack we've expected."

Gates replied, almost casually, "Well then, let General Morgan begin the game."

Arnold broke in, and every man among them fell into instant silence, eyes wide, bracing for what could become an historic confrontation.

"I request permission to go see what's happening."

Hope leaped in the heart of every man present, except Gates, Lincoln, and Wilkinson. Every man turned his eyes to Gates, hard, cold, flat, waiting for his reply.

He sensed the ugliness in their mood, and he fumbled for words. "I am afraid to trust you, Arnold."

Arnold's reply was instant. "I give you my word. I will go, look, return, and report. Nothing more."

Gates dared not impugn Arnold's promise in front of his officers. "Then do so." He turned to Lincoln to deliver his blow. "Go with him. See that he does as ordered."

A dead silence among the officers hung heavy for a moment before Lincoln answered. "Yes, sir."

Arnold took the monumental insult, turned, and ran to get his horse.

One half hour later he galloped back into camp, Lincoln following, and the officers came quickly out of their mess hall to join him for his report to Gates.

"There's a large force coming this way. They'll hit our left flank hard, and unless we meet them, they'll roll our left into our center, and likely take us all down."

Lincoln interrupted. "General Arnold is right. It will take a large force to stop what we saw coming. If we fail, our left will fold, and we'll be in danger of total collapse."

Gates's response was immediate. "I'll send Morgan and Dearborn out to our left. They can get west of the British and hit them from the side."

Arnold shook his head violently. His eyes were cold flecks of flint, his words sharp, ugly. "Not enough. This will take a major force."

Gates lost control. His face flushed, and the veins in his neck extended, red. With eight of his officers standing within ten feet of him, he nearly shouted at Arnold. "I have nothing for you to do! You have no business here! Go to your tent, and don't come out until I send for you!" His arm shot up, pointing toward Arnold's distant command tent.

For a moment Arnold stood, shaking with rage. Then, fearing he would lose control and throttle Gates, Arnold turned on his heel, and the generals opened a path for him to march away, still trembling.

Gates brought himself under tenuous control and faced his officers. "General Morgan and Major Dearborn, prepare your men to march. Report to me when you're ready."

"Sir."

Gates turned to look at Lincoln. "Respectfully, sir, if just those two companies go to engage what I saw, we're going to suffer terrible casualties. I highly recommend at least three regiments will be required."

Gates's voice came loud in the silence that followed Lincoln's bold request. "Very well. Three regiments. General Poor, you accompany

General Morgan and Major Dearborn. General Learned, you follow for support where needed."

In his tent Arnold listened to the three regiments march out. By force of will he sat on his cot, sweating, calculating time and geography. He was still sitting when the first sound of distant cannon reached his tent. Instantly he was on his feet, pacing, listening, trying to read the battle from the sounds. Musketfire became a continuous rattle, mixed with the sharp crack of Morgan's rifles. He jerked aside the flap of his tent and strode out into the compound, facing north. A low, white cloud of gun smoke rose to hover above the tree tops, and then the black smoke of something burning. The firing became hot, heavy, and it did not let up. In his mind he was seeing the Americans, charging, falling back, advancing once again, caught up in the chaos of a battle being fought hand-to-hand.

Take the redoubts! The Balcarres redoubt and the big Breymann redoubt. Once you've taken the redoubts you are in behind Burgoyne's headquarters and those breastworks will do him no good because they'll be on the wrong side.

Time became meaningless as Arnold listened, watching the clouds of white gun smoke and black smoke reach higher into the clear blue heavens, but the center of the battle was not moving. It was being fought in Barber's wheat field, where the two opposing armies had collided nearly two hours earlier.

Arnold turned to look at Gates, sitting at a table outside his office door, with messengers coming and going while Gates casually issued orders. Arnold turned once more toward the smoke, and the thought came welling up inside. *He's killing them! Those good men out there, and Gates is killing them! Three more hours of this, and they'll all be gone!*

Something inside Arnold gave way. He ran to Warren, his tall black horse, vaulted into the saddle, and spun the animal around to face Gates, still sitting at his table. Gates raised his head and stared full into Arnold's face. In that instant each man knew what was in the mind of the other: Arnold was going to the sound of the guns, and Gates could strangle on it; Gates would have Arnold in chains if he could catch him.

Arnold sunk his blunted spurs into Warren's flanks, and the horse lunged forward. Gates stood, shouting, as Arnold disappeared in a cloud of dust. Frantic, Gates turned to the nearest officer he could see, Major Armstrong. "Major, catch that man and bring him back! Use whatever force necessary, but bring him back!"

For a split second Major Armstrong stared in disbelief, then leaped on his horse and kicked it to a high gallop after General Arnold, who was out of sight.

Arnold followed a faint, old wagon track that wound through the tall trees, scarcely slowing in his headlong run. The horse, Warren, held the pace, quick, sure-footed. One mile from camp, Arnold came on a cluster of men from Learned's command, separated, lost, drinking from a brook. "Come on, good men, follow me!"

For an instant they hesitated. They had heard what Gates had done to Arnold, and for a moment they were confused, knowing he had been stripped of all command. But there he was, General Arnold at his best, sword drawn, urging them on, leading them to the sounds of the battle. As one man, they grabbed up their muskets and broke into a run behind him, shouting as they reloaded. Arnold cantered his horse onward, shouting to others who had become separated from their units, and they melded into the growing command behind him. The men broke from the trees into the open wheat field, and for the first time Arnold saw the entire field of battle. In twenty seconds he knew where the Americans had to strike, and he drove his spurs home. The big black horse lunged forward once again, headed straight for an entrenched and determined German line. As he swept past the command led by General Learned, Arnold shouted, "Follow me!"

No one, including Learned, paid heed to the tremendous breach of military protocol as Arnold spontaneously took over Learned's column. Stunned at the sight of Arnold charging past, shouting them on, it took two seconds for Learned's men to decide, and they sprinted from cover to follow him, shouting, straight into the middle of the Germans. The Hessians were among the best in the world, and with their tall, copper-fronted hats they doggedly stood their ground, firing, reloading, watching the Americans drop before their cannon and muskets.

To Arnold's left, Morgan and Dearborn suddenly jerked erect, startled at the sight of the big black horse leading the charge, and in an instant their commands were on their feet, shouting, rising above themselves, charging into the side of troops led by the German general, Balcarres, to overwhelm them, scatter them. With the Balcarres company gone, the flank of the Hessians facing Arnold was exposed, and Morgan did not hesitate. With Dearborn beside him, he tore into the blue-coated troops, flanked them, divided them, turned them.

Ahead, Burgoyne, dressed in a scarlet coat with gold epaulets, conspicuous above all other men, rode his horse back and forth, shouting orders. To Burgoyne's left, Simon Fraser spurred his tall gray horse onward, leading the light infantry and the Twenty-fourth Regiment in a desperate drive to check Morgan's surging command and save the Hessian line.

Through the confusion of the battle, Arnold saw Fraser, one hundred fifty yards ahead and to the right, and knew the man had the bravery and leadership to crack the American attack. Instantly Arnold raised his sword, pointing at Fraser, and shouted, "That man is a host unto himself! He must go!"

Morgan heard the shout, saw the point, and in a heartbeat turned and raised his old wagonmaster's bellowing voice. "Tim!"

Three hundred yards to Morgan's left, Private Timothy Murphy, frontiersman, seasoned Indian fighter, and the best shot in Morgan's select riflemen, heard the shout of his leader and froze, searching. In one second he picked out Morgan, waved, and Morgan waved back, then turned to point with his sword.

With understanding born of years together, and battles unnumbered, Timothy Murphy understood. In three seconds he was perched on the limb of an oak tree, his long Pennsylvania rifle resting over a branch before him. From his position he had a clear field of vision above the heads of the two clashing armies. He calmly cocked his rifle, studied the movement of the cannon smoke in the faint breeze, judged the distance at four hundred sixty yards, and lined the sights. At that distance, Fraser was but a speck on the back of a gray horse when Tim squeezed off his

first shot. At the crack of the rifle he moved his head to peer past the smoke to watch. Half a second later the rifle ball grazed the sleeve of Fraser's coat and clipped hair from his horse's mane.

Instantly Fraser's aides shouted, "General, get back! Get out of range! A marksman is trying to kill you!"

Fraser shook his head. "I'm needed here."

Twenty seconds later Murphy shoved the ramrod into its receiver, laid the long barrel over the branch once again, made the tiniest adjustment for the soft crosswind, and squeezed off his second shot. With the queer knowledge of a born rifleman, he knew at the crack of the rifle that the second shot was going to hit. He set his teeth and half a second later involuntarily grunted as the slug punched into Fraser, dead center in his stomach.

The whack of the slug and the gasping grunt from Fraser came just before the general buckled forward. His sword fell from his hand, and his head drooped forward onto the neck of his horse. Immediately, his aides were on either side of him, grasping his arms, holding him in the saddle while they turned and retreated through their own men to get the general out of range, away from the battle.

For a few seconds the British in Fraser's command stood stock-still, mindless of the raging battle. Fraser was down! Simon Fraser, their leader! He who had won their hearts and their loyalty with his selflessness, bravery, courage, and his unending devotion to his beloved army and England! They watched the two aides working back through the lines, Fraser between them, limp, head slumped forward, feet dangling outside his stirrups. They saw it and they faltered. Their inspiration, their reason for going on, was down, dying, gone.

Five hundred yards distant, Burgoyne saw Fraser rock in his saddle and slump forward. Simon, his confidant, his best friend, his trusted right arm, down! He closed his eyes and his head rolled back with the unbearable pain in his heart. With the instincts of a field general he knew that his army was done. Finished. Quickly he sent runners to both Phillips and Riedesel to cover the retreat, and then he shouted his orders.

"Back! Back! Return to headquarters!"

The red-coated British and blue-coated Germans began their retreat, backing away from the Americans, giving ground more rapidly with each passing minute. They came streaming in behind the fortifications and breastworks on the south side of Burgoyne's headquarters, bringing the wounded they could carry, leaving their dead behind on a battlefield littered with the bodies of those who had fallen.

They flocked around the two aides who guided Fraser's horse in, and they didn't stop until they came to the hut where Baroness Fredericka von Riedesel had set up her tiny hospital. Strong, gentle hands lifted the general down and carried him inside. A table was thrown out to make way for a bed, and they tenderly laid the general down. Moments later they had his clothing stripped to the waist and their faces fell. None spoke, but they all knew. The general was dying.

The Baroness took charge. Get water. Get bandages. Get carbolics. Get his boots off—cut them off if you have to. She did all she could for Fraser, but no one could remedy the pain of a .60-caliber rifleball in the middle of his stomach.

Back on the battlefield, Arnold did not waste one minute celebrating the monumental victory over Burgoyne's regulars. He shouted orders to the gathered Americans.

"Follow me, boys!" He stood tall in his stirrups and pointed with his sword. "We're going to take those two redoubts. With the Breymann redoubt in our hands, we control the path in behind Burgoyne's headquarters, and by the Almighty, before the sun sets this day, they will be ours!"

He set his spurs and once more Warren lunged forward, straight toward the nearest redoubt, held by a regiment commanded by Major Alexander Lindsay, Sixth Earl of Balcarres.

Far behind Arnold, Major Armstrong sat his horse, hidden in a clump of oak trees, peering at Arnold as he led the charge against the entrenched Germans. He had watched Arnold make his wild plunge into the middle of Burgoyne's army, and he had gaped when the Americans followed Arnold, shouting like wild men, to turn Burgoyne, drive him from the field. Now he was watching Arnold again leading an attack against entrenched cannon and muskets. *The man's insane! If Gates thinks I'm going in there to tell Arnold to return to headquarters, then General Gates is mightily mistaken!* Armstrong held a tight rein on his horse and remained hidden.

With Arnold leading, parts of General John Glover's command, along with men from Paterson's command, fell in behind him to run straight at the Balcarres redoubt. The Germans inside gritted their teeth and stayed to their guns, firing as fast as they could load. The grapeshot was taking its toll, and the American attack slowed while the men ducked behind trees and rocks to escape the flying lead balls. Arnold looked eight hundred yards to his left, to where Morgan's riflemen were crouched behind anything that would give cover, maintaining a deadly fire at anything that moved in the Breymann redoubt.

The Breymann redoubt! The fortification that controlled access to the back side of Burgoyne's headquarters! Morgan was already there! Then, from out of the trees, Arnold saw Learned's command surge out of the forest, running toward the north end of the redoubt.

Mindless of his own safety, Arnold reined his horse left and kicked him to a stampede gait. The black horse responded, and the crouched rider flashed in front of the entire length of the Balcarres redoubt, with half the Germans inside shooting at him. No one understood how he survived, but survive he did! He held his horse to a high gallop across the open space to the south end of the Breymann redoubt, past Morgan's men, to the north end of the redoubt. Hauling Warren to a sweaty halt before Learned's men, he shouted, "Follow me, boys! We can take this redoubt!"

Among Learned's command were parts of other commands, including Billy and Eli. They stormed into the first cabins where Canadians had taken cover, and cleaned them out. With the Germans concentrating on their battle with Morgan's men, Arnold's charge from their far right caught them by complete surprise. Too late they turned to face him. With Billy and Eli in the leading ranks, Learned's men swept into them like demons. For ten minutes the fighting was brutal, hot, chaotic, face-to-face inside the redoubt. The Germans tried to back their cannon away from the ramps and turn them to fire at the incoming Americans, but there was no time. With his high, warbling Iroquois battle cry Eli cut a swath with his tomahawk. To his right Billy was swinging his musket like an ax handle, knocking the Germans right and left as he plunged forward. A German officer appeared in front of him, loading a pistol. Billy swept a German musket from the ground, cocked it, and fired it point-blank a split second before the pistol fired. The officer threw his hands high and went over backward, finished. When he fell, the Germans turned and ran for any way they could find to get out of the slaughter within the walls of the redoubt. Shouting, Arnold led his men after them.

He had reached the south end of the redoubt when he heard the whack and felt his horse shudder as Warren took a .75-caliber musketball through the neck. The mortally stricken horse stuck its nose into the ground and went down. At the instant the heavy ball slammed into Warren, a second musketball bored into Arnold's left leg, midway between his knee and his hip, and with the numbing shock he felt the bone break. He tried to throw himself clear of the falling horse, but he could not, and they went down in a heap. He did not know how long he lay dazed before he shook his head and tried to rise. It took him ten seconds to understand his broken right leg was pinned beneath the dead horse.

Men came swarming. They lifted the horse, and as gently as they could, they moved Arnold's broken, twisted leg, while he groaned through gritted teeth and clenched eyes. With sweat running in a stream, he opened his eyes to peer up at Learned, who spoke.

"Don't you move. You let us move you. Hear?"

Arnold grasped Learned's arm. "Ebenezer, the redoubt. Did we get it?"

"We got it. We're in behind Burgoyne's headquarters, and they haven't got enough men left to move us. It's over."

Arnold tried to rise, and a great paw of a hand settled onto his shoulder. He turned to look up into the big, square face of Daniel Morgan. "General, you stay still. We've got men rigging a stretcher right now. We'll get you back home. You'll be all right."

Billy and Eli, with four other men, lifted Arnold high enough to slip a stretcher fashioned of pine limbs and a blanket beneath him. They slipped a belt between his teeth when they straightened his leg, and then they lifted him. Two hours later they settled him onto a table in the hospital, and the surgeons ordered them to leave. Generals Learned, Morgan, Glover, and Poor quietly told the surgeons they would remain there until they knew Arnold would be all right.

Major Armstrong walked into the room, and all eyes turned to him. He swallowed, and approached Arnold. "Sir, General Gates has sent a direct order. You are to return to headquarters at once."

Half unconscious with pain, bleeding from a shattered right leg, weakening from loss of blood, Arnold gaped at Armstrong. Then he laid his head back on the operating table, and he laughed.

Armstrong glanced around, embarrassed, and without a word he quietly turned and walked out.

The chief surgeon slit the pant leg wide open and washed the wound before he spoke to Arnold. "Sir, I'm afraid the leg is too badly damaged. It will have to come off."

Arnold looked him in the eye. "It stays on. See to it."

In somber silence Burgoyne waited behind the desk in his command tent. He did not want to endure the agony of repeating his message twice; every officer to the rank of major was coming to attend a solemn council of war. They came in groups, quiet, subdued, to stand inside the log structure, waiting. By ten o'clock those still alive were present, and Burgoyne rose and motioned.

"Be seated, gentlemen."

They took their proper places, and for a moment Burgoyne glanced at the empty chairs, among them those belonging to Fraser and Breymann. He raised his chin, took a deep breath, and began.

"I will not keep you long. Our position is indefensible. We have lost some officers who are irreplaceable. You know about Fraser and Breymann, and there are others. We have no more food. No more horses.

I have just received word that General John Stark—the militia general who led the Americans at the Bennington catastrophe—has marched in north of us with more than one thousand of his men from New Hampshire and Vermont. We are sealed off, both north and south. We cannot return to Fort Ticonderoga, nor can we fight our way through to Albany."

He cleared his throat. "We can fight on, but at the cost of most of the men we have left. I will not sacrifice them in such a futile way." He paused for a moment, fighting to maintain control, and could not. He bowed his head and for a time his shoulders shook in silent sobs. Then he straightened, wiped at his eyes, swallowed, and continued. "I have resolved that the only honorable course left is to seek terms of surrender from General Gates. I sent him a message. He has sent me a proposal."

Dawn broke cool and foggy. The formalities of the surrender were to be conducted at ten o'clock in the morning, on the banks of Fish Creek, at Saratoga. Gates had issued firm orders that only those Americans directly involved were to be present at the surrender, in an effort to avoid further humiliation for Burgoyne and his army.

At a little past nine, the fog lifted, and in bright sunshine, dressed in the immaculate, crimson, tailored uniform he had brought from England to be worn at his triumphant entry into Albany, Burgoyne rode at the head of his army. A great feathered plume attached to his tricorn fell over one shoulder. Behind came his men in their tattered, faded uniforms, pieced together the best they could. Heads high, chins set, with battle-torn colors flying, drums rolling, and pipes playing, the remnants of the Ninth, Twentieth, Twenty-first, Twenty-fourth, and Sixty-second regiments marched to the surrender ceremony. The Royal Artillery under General Phillips followed, and behind came the chaplains, surgeons, quartermasters, adjutants, and engineers. General von Riedesel led the blue-coated Germans, with the wagons and women and children in the van.

The artillerymen parked their cannon and turned and walked away, and did not look back. Infantrymen emptied their cartridge boxes, then laid their muskets on the growing stacks. A few smashed the stocks of their own muskets before flinging them on the pile, and four of the drummers stomped the heads out of their drums before throwing them onto the growing stack.

The American army gathered at the Saratoga church meetinghouse and slowly walked to line the road to Dovegat and beyond. Following the surrender, Burgoyne's army would march down that road, and the Americans wished to see them as they passed.

Burgoyne abided the formalities. He handed his sword to Gates, who accepted it, then returned it. The articles of surrender were signed. Burgoyne remounted his horse and led his men forward onto the Dovegat road, stretching ahead for miles. The British marched with chins high, at first ignoring the Americans. The Germans marched with arms swinging, anger and disgust on their faces. An American band struck up "Yankee Doodle Dandy," and the impudent little English folk song with American words floated out over the valley as the somber procession moved on.

Then, an unexpected feeling crept into both armies. The Americans remained silent. There was not a smile, nor a grin, nor a catcall among them. It seemed they had gathered to pay their respect to an enemy who had fought well. They nodded from time to time at someone as they made eye contact. Some removed their hats.

The British and Germans looked at the Americans for the first time, not as an enemy, but as men, and they were startled. Their clothing was tattered, torn, shoes nearly nonexistent. Their weapons were whatever they had brought with them. The men were generally taller than average, sinewy, hardy. And they had fought like demons. They had brought down eight thousand of the finest fighting men in the world. The defeated British and Germans looked at them, and they wondered.

Burgoyne commented to Gates, "I commend your men for their discipline. It almost seems they are here to honor us. I congratulate you."

The long column continued south, moving down the rutted road leading to Boston, where they would be held pending transportation to their homelands across the Atlantic, all according to the terms of surrender. The Americans watched, and when the column had passed and disappeared in the dust, they left the road in small groups to make their way slowly back to their camp.

As they walked back toward their own camp, Billy spoke. "Want to go find General Stark's camp and ask about your sister? He's camped just north of here. Might be your last chance for a while."

The two shouldered their weapons and walked along the twisting wagon track leading north. The afternoon sun was warm on their shoulders as they wound through the spectacular colors in the trees. For a time they walked in silence, each working with his own thoughts, trying to comprehend what the Americans had done. They struggled, then put it away in their minds to be brought out another day, when they would better understand how far-reaching the defeat of General John Burgoyne would be.

It was midafternoon before they came upon the camp of the New Hampshiremen, who were dressed in fringed buckskin breeches and hunting shirts, with moccasins made from the leather of the neck of a bull moose. The men were subdued, thoughtful, reflective, pondering how it could be that the great John Burgoyne had fallen—beaten by farmers and fishermen and blacksmiths and storekeepers.

Billy and Eli walked among them, asking. Does anyone know of a man named Cyrus Fielding? Might be a reverend, or a preacher? Has anyone heard of him? Or of a blue-eyed girl that was given to his family a long time ago?

The day wore on with heads shaking no. With the sun dropping low in the west, the two men reached the far end of the camp, and Billy walked to a small group of men setting a tripod and cooking kettle for their supper.

"Anyone heard of a man named Cyrus Fielding? An older man, might have been a preacher?" Billy asked.

A sergeant with a graying stubble beard turned to him. "Who wants to know?"

"We're looking for him. He might know of a girl, an orphan, who was given to his family eighteen years ago."

The sergeant pursed his mouth for a moment. "I don't know a Cyrus Fielding, but you might ask Cap'n Ben. He stands yonder." He raised a hand to point to a man ten yards away. He was taller than Billy, dressed in buckskins and moccasins, wearing a battered tricorn. He was broad in the shoulders and moved with the grace of one raised in the forest. His features were regular, hair dark, brows heavy over cavernous eyes.

"Captain Ben who? What's his last name?"

"Cap'n Ben Fielding."

Billy's heart leaped as he strode to the man. "Are you Ben Fielding? Captain Ben Fielding?"

The man turned and raised steady eyes to Billy. "I am. New Hampshire militia. Might I know who you are?"

"Billy Weems. Massachusetts regiment. I'm here looking for anyone who might know of a man named Cyrus Fielding. An older man. Might be a minister, or a reverend."

The man stared hard into Billy's eyes, searching, and then spoke evenly. "Cyrus Fielding was my father. He passed on eight years ago."

Billy's breath came short for a moment. "Eighteen years ago, was a four-year-old girl brought to your father's home? Blue eyes, light hair? An orphan named Stroud?"

"Yes."

Billy turned and called to Eli. "Come here."

Eli heard the urgent ring in Billy's voice and came running.

"Eli, this is Captain Ben Fielding, New Hampshire militia. His Father was Cyrus Fielding. I believe your sister was brought to his home."

Eli started. He stared into Ben Fielding's face, afraid to believe, afraid to ask. He licked dry lips and said, "Her name was Stroud? Iddi Stroud?"

Fielding's eyes narrowed for a split second, and then widened in shock as understanding broke clear in his mind. "Iddi? Did you say Iddi?"

"Yes."

"Are you Eli?"

"I am! Eli Stroud."

"Her name is Lydia, not Iddi. But her infant brother couldn't say Lydia. He called her Iddi!"

Eli choked it out. "Is she alive?"

"Alive? My family raised her. I married her four years ago. She's my wife! She's at our place now, three days march north and east of here. She's the mother of our two children, our daughter, Hannah, and our son, Samuel."

Eli tried to speak, and could not, nor could Billy. Fielding went on.

"She's never given up on you. We've asked everywhere we could—travelers, hunters, Indians—anyone who might know. She's prayed every day for eighteen years, waiting for this."

Eli found his voice. "Is she all right? Healthy? Strong?"

"A handsome, strong, good woman. A blessing in our home." Fielding paused only long enough to see that Eli could not speak, and he continued. "We're breaking camp in the morning, heading for home. You'll come, won't you? You've got to come see her."

"Yes. We'll come. We have to go report back to our company, and then we'll come back here at dawn."

"I'll be waiting."

For several seconds the two men looked at each other, lost in the moment, only beginning to believe that the search and the pain and the waiting for eighteen years had come to an end. Eli bobbed his head and turned, and Billy followed as they walked back south to find Dearborn's regiment and request permission to leave for a time. Eli stopped once to look back, and Fielding was standing still, feet slightly apart, watching him.

Billy walked beside him in silence, giving him time to get hold of what had happened. Ten minutes passed before Eli quietly said, "Lydia. I remembered the minute he said it. Lydia. Two children. Hannah, and Samuel. I have a niece, and a nephew. A good woman, he said. Healthy. Strong. A blessing. My sister. Lydia."

He shook his head, and there was a radiance in his face.

In deep dusk they found Dearborn's regiment gathered within the walls of the fortifications on Bemis Heights, along with Morgan's rifle-men, and Learned's command, and most of the others. They ate warm mutton stew with dark bread and drank cool water from a bucket, then moved among the men, looking for General Dearborn. Strangely, talk was light among the men. It had happened too suddenly. The grinding, soul-destroying weeks and months of running, retreating, and then the bloody, frantic battle, and then it was over. The men were quiet, groping to comprehend what they had done. Hundreds of them sat cross-legged near campfires, paper and pencil in hand, writing, pondering, writing again, to wives, mothers, fathers, loved ones.

Billy walked past Private Oliver Boardman, a young soldier with a Connecticut regiment, who had camped next to Billy, who had befriended him. Boardman raised his head from his writing to speak.

"Billy, what is the date today?"

Billy reflected. "October 17, 1777."

"How do you spell 'providence'?"

Billy dropped to his haunches and carefully spelled it while Boardman laboriously wrote it. Billy asked, "Writing home?"

"To mother. How does this sound? 'It was a glorious sight to see the haughty Brittons march out and surrender their arms to an army, which but a little before they despised and called paltroons.'"

Men slowed and stopped, listening in the firelight as Boardman read on.

"Surely the hand of Providence work'd wonderfully in favour of America."

More than fifty men had gathered to listen as Boardman concluded.

"I hope every heart will be affected by the wonderful goodness of God in delivering so many of our enemy into our hands, with so little loss on our side."

Boardman raised his eyes back to Billy, and for the first time realized he was surrounded. The men peered down at him, sitting beside his campfire. They wiped at their eyes, then nodded to him as they moved on.

Boardman watched them go, and turned back to Billy. "Was it too much? Did I say it too strong?"

Billy stared at the fire for a moment. "No, it wasn't too strong. It was fine. It was fitting. The hand of Providence was with us."

Billy and Eli found General Dearborn at the hospital. He came outside to talk with them, and Billy made their brief report.

"Sir, we were sent here by General Washington. General Arnold assigned us to your regiment. We finished what General Washington sent us to do, and we've got to return to report to him. We can't talk to General Arnold, so we thought we better tell you."

"I understand. I'll tell Arnold."

"We're going to move north for a few days with a New Hampshire militia regiment. Eli has found his sister after eighteen years. He needs to see her."

Dearborn turned to Eli. "Lost her?"

"Our parents were killed. I was taken by the Indians. She was given to a family to raise. I've been looking for a long time."

A smile crossed Dearborn's face. "Well, it's nice to know things work out sometimes. Go see her. Get back down to Washington when you can, and tell him what a job we did here."

Billy answered. "We will, sir." He turned to go when Dearborn stopped him. "Say, I think you're the one I've been looking for. Were you two there when we stormed the Breymann redoubt?"

"Yes, sir. With your regiment."

"Aren't you the one that picked up a German musket and shot an officer who was about to kill you with a pistol. Someone—a sergeant—described a man like you."

"I remember that. Yes, sir."

"Do you know who that officer was?"

"No, sir."

"General Heinrich von Breymann. When he went down, his men ran. I wanted you to know that."

"When he came up in front of me I didn't know who he was, sir."

"Doesn't matter how it happened. The redoubt was ours the minute he went down."

"I didn't know, sir."

Eli interrupted. "Is Arnold inside? Were you here to see him?"

"Yes."

"Is he going to be all right? We saw what he did at that last battle. Hard to believe."

"His leg is bad, but I think he'll recover."

Eli hesitated for a moment. "Has Gates made out his report on that battle? We heard what he did to Arnold in his other report."

Disgust showed in Dearborn's face. "He's finished with the latest report. Gates never left his quarters during the battle. Morgan and Learned and a few of us helped him get his facts straight this time. General Arnold's name is in every paragraph of this report. We all helped, but it was Arnold who beat Burgoyne finally. Like it or not, Congress is going to have to give Arnold his due this time. If they don't, a few of us will pay John Hancock a visit."

"Thank you."

Dearborn turned and disappeared back into the hospital.

Billy turned to Eli. A deep weariness had settled on both of them.

"Come on. We better get our things and get some sleep. We have to be in the New Hampshire camp by dawn tomorrow."

Horace Walpole stood in his tiny, cluttered office, squinting one eye as he raised a steaming mug of coffee to blow, then gingerly sip. He sat down on the worn chair facing his desk in one corner, and raised the cup once more before he set it down on a month-old newspaper that showed a dozen coffee rings and stains. Slight of build, hunch-shouldered, hawk-faced, thinning gray hair, and the most famous and powerful sage and newspaper writer in London, Walpole reached for a copy of a dog-eared, well-worn article he had written weeks earlier, and he scowled as he scanned it again.

"Humph," he grumbled to himself. "Ah yes, Burgoyne the pompous.

Our premiere general was delivered his first lesson in September, and not a word from him since. Either he has subdued the colonies altogether, or they have swallowed him up." Walpole tossed the document back onto his desk. "With the world scarcely breathing while it waits for war news, we must deal with the wilderness and three thousand miles of the Atlantic for it to get here." He reached for his coffee cup. "It is so inconvenient to have all letters come by the post of the ocean. People should never go to war above ten miles off, as the Grecian states used to do."

He was sipping at the steaming cup again when an urgent banging on his office door brought him up short. He set the cup down too hard, and it spilled on his finger and the newspaper. He licked his finger as he hurried to throw the door open.

Robert Lawrence, wrapped in a heavy woolen coat with a scarf piled high under his chin, pushed past him and turned, breathless. "Horace, this just arrived from Quebec. Carleton. He reports that Burgoyne and his entire army are now prisoners of the rebels!"

Walpole gaped, then seized the document. With the skilled eye of one whose long life had been spent putting thoughts into words, Walpole scanned the writing in five seconds, then snatched his coat off its peg on the back of the door. He reached to thrust two coins into Robert's hand, exclaimed, "Wait for me," clapped his tall, stovepipe hat onto his head, and was buttoning his coat and wrapping his scarf as he hurried out into the morning traffic in the raw salt air of London's streets. He fairly trotted the two blocks to the palace gates where the two stiff, uniformed guards swung the gates open to his familiar figure, and he hurried up the cobblestones to the palace door. The guard at the door said, "Good morning, Mr. Walpole," and opened the door to him without question.

Inside the sumptuous room, Walpole paused to remove his hat as a man wearing an impeccable uniform with the epaulets of a major in the British army strode across the shining, polished floor, boot heels clicking. Faint, muted sounds of a human being in deep agony reached the two of them from down a long, broad corridor to Walpole's left. Walpole had been down that richly decorated hall many times, visiting the king in both his conference room and his private quarters.

"Mr. Walpole. A pleasure as always. I presume you've heard the news."

"Ten minutes ago. The world is waiting. Might the king have a statement?"

The officer raised a manicured hand to thoughtfully stroke his chin. "I believe it would be prudent to wait. Perhaps this afternoon."

The groaning and wailing from down the corridor increased, and Walpole turned a knowing eye for a moment to look. He pondered for a time, then brought his face back to the major standing before him. He spoke not a word, but his eyes asked the question.

The major said nothing, but slowly nodded.

Walpole bowed. "I thank you, sir, for the brief but most penetrating interview."

The major returned the bow. "My pleasure, sir."

Robert lunged from his chair the moment Walpole rattled the doorknob and walked in.

"Well?"

Walpole quickly hung his hat on its peg, unwound his scarf, and was working with the buttons on his greatcoat before he spoke.

"The king got the news."

Robert's eyes were wide. "And?"

"I was not allowed to see him. I interviewed Major Alexanderson. Most poignant." He sat down at his desk, drew his inkwell from its corner, seized the worn quill, and turned to Robert.

"If you want to learn this questionable business, draw up a chair and watch."

Walpole's face drew into a pucker as he searched for the words that matched his thoughts. He bobbed his head once, dipped the quill, and began scratching, while Robert leaned forward, watching in rapt silence.

"At long last we are privileged to receive enlightenment concerning the fortunes of our expeditionary forces in our wilderness colonies across the ocean. However, not from General John Burgoyne, whose presence has lately deafened us with silence, but from General Sir Guy Carleton. You will recall that General Carleton once commanded the Northern army of His Majesty, with General Burgoyne as his second in command. That arrangement was reversed after General Burgoyne's five-month visit to London, and several trips to the local steam baths and social events with Lord Germain.

"With some sense of ironic justice, I'm sure, General Guy has informed us this morning that General Burgoyne himself, along with his entire army, are now prisoners of our rebellious family in North America. A hasty visit to the king's palace, and a brief but penetrating interview resulted in two observations:

"The king has received the news. And, upon receiving it, the king fell into agonies."

Walpole straightened in his chair and tossed his quill beside the scrawled words. He studied them in silence for five full minutes, while Robert watched his every expression. Then Walpole picked up his quill once more, to begin the scratching out of a word here, a thought there, adding, refining the flow, the adjectives, until it all fit together to create the impression he wanted.

One line remained unchanged. "The king fell into agonies."

The clatter of horses' hooves and iron rims on buggy wheels against the cobblestones brought Ben Franklin to the window of his home in Passy, a small, beautiful, quaint village within easy distance of both Paris and Versailles. Franklin pushed aside the curtain and watched the driver come back on the reins to the two horses. The buggy slowed and stopped with the horses stamping their feet, blowing vapor from their nostrils.

The carriage door burst open, and Silas Deane stepped to the street. He dug coins from a leather purse, paid the driver, and turned to hurry up the brick walk to Franklin's door. At his rapid knock, Franklin called, "Come in, Silas."

Deane pushed the door open and was unbuttoning his heavy overcoat while he spoke.

"You've heard the news?"

"About Burgoyne?"

"We defeated his whole army! They're all our prisoners, he with them."

"So I'm informed."

Deane tossed his overcoat over the back of a chair. "All of France is celebrating. You'd think it was their victory, not ours."

"In a way, it is."

"This changes everything! The question is, how do we best use it?"

Franklin nodded. "Well said. Any suggestions?"

"Somehow we've got to see King Louis. I doubt he can find a way to avoid joining us now."

Franklin gestured. "Take a seat. Coffee? Chocolate?"

Deane shook his head.

Franklin went on. "We'll see the king, but all in good time. First we've got to persuade Vergennes to put this before the king on exactly the right footing. France has to recognize us as an independent nation, with rights and powers to treaty. Then they'll have to agree to declare war on England, not just assist us with men and equipment. And finally, they'll have to sign an open alliance with us with mutual guarantees. They'll provide sufficient men and ships to defeat England. Getting all that done in the right order will take some thought."

"Have you heard from Vergennes?"

"Nothing significant. I'll arrange an audience with him as soon as we've done a few things."

"Like what?"

Franklin gestured to his desk in the corner. "I received a letter from Lord Stormont in London. Apparently he heard about the loss of Burgoyne's army several days ago. His letter openly asks us to meet with him at once, to discuss what we must have to put aside our differences and return to the English empire."

"Have you answered it?"

"No. At the time, I didn't know what to say. I do now."

"What?"

"At the moment, nothing at all. I think Vergennes ought to see that letter. The quicker the better. If anything will bring him into line instantly, it ought to be the thought that we might be making arrangements with England to rejoin them. We can't forget that Vergennes's one great dream in life is to avenge the humiliation France suffered when they surrendered to England to end the Seven Years' War. That was 1763. For fourteen years they've waited, and it's my judgment they see us as their last great hope to give England what England gave them back then."

"Then let's get the letter copied and delivered."

"We will. But with it will be two other documents. I received the news about Burgoyne from Jonathan Austin. You've met him. He's a ship owner who has substantial trade with France. His report is far too long to set in print, so I've already drafted a twenty-two-line statement for Vergennes. The other document we'll need is nearly finished. It's a detailed summary of what Britain lost when we defeated Burgoyne."

Franklin paused to take a deep breath. "It's impressive. Did you know they lost nine thousand two hundred and three soldiers—British, German, Canadian, and loyalists—killed, wounded, or captured? Plus deserters? They gave up more than one hundred forty cannon, and close to ten thousand muskets. Gunpowder also, and tents, uniforms, food supplies, shoes, boots, money." Again he paused and a faint smile showed. "Among the prisoners were four members of their parliament!"

Deane reared back in his chair. "We got four of their parliament?"

Franklin chuckled and nodded. "A tragedy, wouldn't you say? I'll have that document finished by two o'clock. Would you care to accompany me to Versailles to deliver all three documents to Vergennes today?"

In the cold midafternoon sunlight, Deane waited while Franklin laboriously lowered his seventy-two-year-old body from the carriage to the cobblestones, then turned to tell the driver to wait. They walked to the front door of the building housing the foreign ministry offices of Comte de Vergennes, and five minutes later were seated across the ornate desk from the slender, immaculate Vergennes.

Franklin nodded graciously. "My thanks for allowing us to visit on such short notice."

"It is my pleasure. Was there something pressing?"

Franklin glanced above Vergennes's head at the huge oil painting of

King Louis XVI, then back to Vergennes. "Not pressing, but significant. I'm sure you've heard of the downfall of General Burgoyne?"

Vergennes's expression remained calm, controlled. "Yes. A few days ago."

"It seems his defeat has shifted the affairs of the world somewhat. I didn't know if you were aware what his surrender cost the British, so I took the privilege of making a somewhat detailed list." He chuckled. "It seems we are now holding captive four members of the British parliament. I doubt any of them expected that outcome when they joined that august body."

He leaned forward to lay the document on the near edge of the polished desk. "In addition, I've prepared a brief extract of the message I received from America, outlining the details of Burgoyne's surrender." He laid that document on top of the first one.

"And, I thought you might take an interest in this letter received lately from Lord Stormont in his official position as England's ambassador to France." He also laid that letter on the desk.

Vergennes caught himself in time to retain control. He did not reach for the Stormont letter. He smiled mechanically. "The letter concerns France?"

Franklin shook his head. "No. Not directly. It simply asks what we Americans want, short of total freedom, to come back to the British empire. I haven't answered it because I didn't know what to say. I'm still not certain."

Vergennes straightened in his chair. "I very much appreciate your consideration in sharing all this with me. May I have time to study this matter out?"

"Of course. I will be delighted to hear from you when you are ready."

Back in the carriage, Franklin leaned out the window to call orders to the driver. "Would you drive down a short distance and stop?"

"Where?"

"It doesn't matter. Near a tavern, if you can find one. You can drink some hot rum while we wait."

Forty minutes later, with Silas Deane becoming increasingly nervous, Franklin suddenly leaned forward, peering out the carriage window. The unmistakable, slender figure of Vergennes hurried from his building to a waiting carriage. Franklin adjusted his bifocals as Vergennes slammed the carriage door, and the horses lunged into their collars to set the carriage in motion, rocking as it sped up the street.

Franklin turned to Deane. "You can go inside and get the driver now. Vergennes has left for Paris to show our handiwork to the king. It shouldn't take long."

At noon two days later, a messenger appeared at Franklin's door, hat in hand. "The Comte de Vergennes, foreign minister of France, inquires would it be possible for you to visit his office?"

Franklin raised his eyebrows. "When?"

"At your earliest convenience. Hopefully today."

At half past two o'clock, Franklin and Deane took their places opposite Vergennes in his office. Vergennes leaned forward, forearms on the desk, fingers interlaced.

"The king received your documents most favorably. He has authorized me to deliver the following message. He is determined to acknowledge the independence of the United States, and to enter into a treaty of amity and commerce, as well as any others that are appropriate. He committed France to support your rise to independence with every means and power available."

Deane gaped. Franklin smiled. *They're ready. They'll go to war with England, and they'll give us the men and the ships we need.* "It is most humbling. I presume that proper documents will be prepared to make this arrangement known to the world?"

"The king requests the honor of your presence at an official signing. Six days from today at eleven o'clock in the morning, in this office. The king will appear personally to attach his signature and the official seal of France."

On the sixth day, the street in front of the French foreign ministry offices was jammed by ten-thirty A.M. Soldiers of the King's Guard lined the walkway from the street to the door, and political figures of every nationality crowded the streets for fifty yards in both directions. Franklin's coach was delayed ten minutes covering the last one hundred yards.

Inside, Vergennes's office was crowded with dignitaries from most European countries, each dressed in finery intended to outshine that of the man next to him. Powdered wigs abounded. King Louis was cloaked in a mink-lined, bejeweled robe that cost the people of France most dearly. The room quieted when Franklin walked in. He was dressed in a simple homespun brown suit, white stockings, square-toed leather shoes. His long, thinning hair was brushed back, hanging loose, and his bifocals were perched on the end of his nose. No one in the room presented a more striking figure.

Vergennes brokered the meeting. Formalities behind them, copies of the documents were laid before Franklin and the king at the same time. The king knew every word. Franklin took but thirty seconds to scan them, then raised his face, smiling.

King Louis spoke first. "Firmly assure your Congress of my friendship. I hope that this will be for the good of the two countries."

Franklin bowed his head deeply. "Your Majesty may count on the gratitude of Congress and its faithful observance of the pledges it now makes."

Each took a quill in hand, dipped it, and carefully affixed their signatures to the documents before them. They exchanged the copies, and again dipped their quills to execute their names.

They raised their heads, and it was done.

France had joined with America in the war against England.

Notes

The morning of 19 September 1777 broke chill and extremely foggy. Burgoyne sent his army south, across the rolling hills straight toward the American fortifications on Bemis Heights. By about ten o'clock the fog lifted and the American scouts noticed activity that told them Burgoyne was coming. The news was sent on to Gates. And Gates did nothing! Arnold pleaded with him to take the initiative, since battles are not won by those who sit and wait for the enemy to take the offensive, but by those who seize the moment and attack. Gates refused, but finally relented, informing Arnold he could send Morgan's riflemen out to scout. Arnold did so. Morgan's corp reached Freeman's farm before they met the oncoming British, and being the crack frontiersmen they were, disappeared instantly behind trees and bushes, and into an old barn. With their long Pennsylvania rifles, they caught the first company of British in the open, and in less than three seconds had more than two hundred of them on the ground.

However, Morgan had unknowingly blundered right into the heart of Burgoyne's army, and within minutes the center of the British army was charging him. Morgan's corp took many casualties, but did not break. Morgan is reported to have had tears in his eyes at seeing his beloved riflemen going down.

Thus began the Battle of Freeman's Farm. It continued through most of the day, with the two opposing sides locked in an unending seesaw fight, first one taking the ground, then the other. General Arnold spent the day riding through the thickest parts of the battlefield, encouraging his men, directing them, ignoring the constant threat of being shot dead. Toward evening the Americans under Arnold were at the point of flanking Burgoyne's army and defeating them, when a courageous charge by von Riedesel broke the American attack, and the battle ended with neither side clearly the victor. At the end of the day both sides withdrew to try to regroup for what was surely to come. In the four hours of intense, hand-to-hand combat, Burgoyne's army had learned one great lesson: the Americans, for whom they had previously held no regard as fighting men, had stood up to the best troops the British and Germans had, and they had given them better than they'd got, and come within minutes of beating them before von Riedesel saved the day for the British. In the four hours of the Battle of Freeman's Farm, something went out of Burgoyne's army.

It was generally conceded that if Arnold had not insisted on sending out Morgan's corp of riflemen to make contact with the British, and then take the fight to the British, the outcome of the day's battle would have been vastly different. It was noted that General Burgoyne was riding among his troops, ignoring the obvious danger, inspiring and directing them. Gates, however, never left his headquarters. When Gates wrote his report of the battle for Congress, he did not mention the name of Benedict Arnold. That fact became known to many, who could not believe Gates would do such a thing. It was becoming clear that Arnold, the warrior, was going to have difficulty with Gates, the politician.

Baroness Frederika von Riedesel, beautiful and courageous wife of General von Riedesel, opened her dwelling to the wounded and spent the night tending them, as she did many times later. The men called her "Red Hazel" because of her beautiful, long red hair, and they came to nearly worship this great woman.

Burgoyne planned another assault the next morning, 20 September 1777, but in the night received a message that led him to believe General Clinton might be coming up from Albany to reinforce him. The pertinent language of the message is set forth verbatim in this chapter. Burgoyne decided to wait about ten days, in the vain hope Clinton would arrive.

While Burgoyne waited, his army built two great redoubts on the ground surrounding Freeman's farm, about four miles north of Gates's headquarters on Bemis Heights. The redoubts were named the Breymann Redoubt, which was the largest and the cornerstone of the British defenses, and the Balcarres Redoubt, smaller. They were named after the generals who were to command them. About two miles to the east, Burgoyne built strong breastworks where he established his headquarters.

Clinton never came. Burgoyne could wait no longer. Either he would fight his way through to Albany, or he and his army would perish in the oncoming winter, since their condition and lack of supplies would not let them retreat.

The morning of 7 October 1777, the British attack began.

Again Gates ordered the Americans to simply sit in their fortifications on Bemis Heights and let the British try to take them; however, he did send out Major Wilkinson to find the British and report their movements. Wilkinson did so, watching the British forces infiltrate a wheat field owned by a farmer named Barber. He saw General Burgoyne and other officers climb onto the roof of a barn and use their telescopes to study the American positions. Wilkinson reported back to Gates, who decided to continue waiting. Arnold instantly requested to be allowed to go look. Gates feared it, saying, "I am afraid to trust you, Arnold." But Gates finally allowed him to go.

Arnold returned in half an hour, advising that a large force of British was marching around the American left flank to take the headquarters fortifications. Gates said he would send Morgan and Dearborn to swing around the British. Arnold told Gates that was "nothing, you must send a strong force." Gates became furious and told Arnold "I have nothing for you to do. You have no business here." With that, Gates stripped Arnold of all command and confined him to his tent until further notice.

The battle at Barber's wheat field was under way. It raged back and forth as had the previous battle at Freeman's farm. Sitting in his quarters, Arnold could hear the guns, and it tore at him. Finally he could take no more. Against orders, he strode from his tent and mounted his horse. Gates saw him and stood trans-fixed as Arnold looked him in the eye, said nothing, wheeled his horse, and left for the battle at a gallop. Gates sent Major Armstrong to bring him back, but for understandable reasons Armstrong did not follow Arnold as he rode into the hottest part of the battle. At Arnold's arrival on the battlefield, suddenly everything became electric. He was riding first here, then there, assuming com-mand of any who would follow him. And follow him they did! He rallied the Americans and charged the Balcarres Redoubt. The battle mired down, and when Arnold saw Morgan's men further north attacking the Breymann Redoubt, which was the cornerstone of Burgoyne's defenses, Arnold turned his horse and rode at stampede gait for half a mile past the British lines with half the British army firing at him. They hit his clothing, but not the man. He swept up before the Americans, shouting for them to follow him, and they did.

To his left, General Simon Fraser was rallying the British to come to the rescue of the Breymann Redoubt when Arnold saw him. Pointing, he declared the Americans must stop that man, meaning Fraser. Morgan turned and shouted to Timothy Murphy, the finest shot among his riflemen. Murphy climbed a tree, and from his perch shot Fraser, mortally wounding him. Burgoyne saw Fraser fall, and at that moment something went out of Burgoyne. Baroness Frederika von Riedesel received the stricken Fraser into her quarters and nursed him overnight, but he died at eight o'clock the next morning.

Arnold led the Americans around the left end of the Breymann Redoubt where desperate hand-to-hand fighting ensued. While leading them in, Arnold's horse was shot out from under him, and his left leg was badly broken by a mus-ketball between the knee and the thigh. The men he had led to the brink of suc-cess at the redoubt went ahead and captured the redoubt, which gave the Americans easy access in behind Burgoyne's headquarters. The Battle of Barber's Wheat Field was essentially over.

Then Burgoyne learned that General John Stark, with more than a thou-sand men from New Hampshire, had sealed off all roads to the north. It was obvious to Burgoyne that he had no chance of victory. He exchanged negotia-tions with Gates, terms of surrender were agreed upon, and on 17 October 1777, in formal proceedings at Fish Creek, near Saratoga, Burgoyne surrendered his sword, and what remained of his tattered army, to General Gates.

This time, when Gates wrote his report to Congress, he had no choice but to give Benedict Arnold his due. Too many other generals, such as Dearborn, Learned, and Morgan, knew what had happened. The report was glowing with Arnold's bravery and courage.

The surrender of Burgoyne's army was reported to King George on

2 December 1777, and Horace Walpole, famed London sage and newspaper writer, reported that "the king fell into agonies."

When the news reached Benjamin Franklin in Passy, the small town where he lived, near Versailles, he used it effectively in a meeting on 12 December 1777 with Comte de Vergennes, the French foreign minister, to persuade Vergennes, and then King Louis, to enter the war on the side of the Americans. On 6 February 1778, the long awaited treaty between the United States and France was signed, bringing France into the war with a promise of men and ships to fight the British. On 13 March 1778, France declared war on England, and on 13 June 1778, open shooting warfare occurred between a French ship and two British ships near Ushant, a small island off the Brittany coast.

France had become America's ally in America's quest for liberty (see Ketchum, *Saratoga*, pp. 336–448; Leckie, *George Washington's War*, pp. 389–426; Mackesy, *The War for America*, pp. 130–41; Higginbotham, *The War of American Independence*, pp. 193–97).

The reader will recall the incident after the battle was over wherein Billy spoke with young Oliver Boardman. Oliver Boardman was an American soldier who did write the letter to his mother. The letter as it appears in this book is quoted verbatim from that actual letter. The American soldiers believed with all their hearts that "the Hand of Providence" had "work'd wonderfully in Favour of America" (see Ketchum, *Saratoga*, pp. 436–37).

Northern Vermont

October, 1777

CHAPTER XXXII

*T*he three men rolled their blankets while the morning star faded in the east. They built a low fire and ate cold strips of mutton with hard bread while they sipped steaming coffee from wooden cups. At dawn Eli shot a spike buck deer at a salt lick. He poured water over the head and quietly thanked the deer for its sacrifice, assured it that it had honorably filled its purpose on earth and that its spirit would dwell forever in heaven. They cleaned the carcass at a small stream, washed the liver and heart and put them in the chest cavity, then tied the forelegs together, followed by the hind legs. They cut and stripped a ten foot pine, slipped it through the tied legs, and Billy and Eli shouldered the pole as they continued north with Ben Fielding leading through the forest on trails he knew.

At midmorning they stopped to drink cold water from a stream and to peer for a moment at the astounding beauty of a forest caught in the resplendent kaleidoscope of colors that mark the midpoint in its change from summer to winter. Fat squirrels and chipmunks were everywhere, chattering, cheeks bulging with acorns and pinenuts, hair growing for the long, cold months ahead. A badger waddled across the trail, heavy from gorging on the nuts and berries ripened in the fall. It stopped and thrust its nose into the air, testing the scent of the men that its weak eyes could only see as a blur, then disappeared in the foliage.

"One more hour," Ben said. He wiped his sleeve across his mouth and picked up his rifle. His face was a study of anticipation and concern. It had been six weeks since the reverend from Hennings and two men from the church knocked on his door with the heart-wrenching stories of the murders and scalpings done by the Indians with Burgoyne's command. He had looked at Lydia, and she had handed him his rifle and a small sack of food. She had three-year-old Hannah on one arm, and one-year-old Samuel on the other as she watched the men leave the clearing.

Were they all right? Had anyone come to harm them? Indians? The British? Sickness? Accident? Had she gotten some of the crops in? Were the cow and the calf all right? Would the weaner pigs be big enough for winter meat?

He remembered the feel of Lydia close to him, and the clinging of Hannah's small arms tight around his neck. In his mind he saw Samuel with his thatch of stubborn brown hair, asleep in his arms as he sat at night before the fireplace. He was unaware that he had picked up the pace.

Fifty minutes later he said, "Just around the bend," and then they were there. The square log cabin stood at the head of the clearing, with outbuildings on either side. The cowshed and pen were there, with the pigpen adjoining. Trenches were in place for adding a room to the cabin. Smoke rose from the stone chimney, and clothes hung on a line moved in the soft breeze.

Ben cupped a hand and called, "Hello in the house!"

A moment later later Lydia rounded the corner of the cabin. She was tall for a woman, square-shouldered, her long, honey-colored hair pulled behind her head with a leather thong. Her face was striking. She carried a woven reed basket on one hip, partially filled with string beans. Beside her, leaning against the corner of the cabin, was a Pennsylvania rifle. A sturdy three-year-old girl with one long French braid peeked from behind her skirts. Lydia shaded her eyes with one hand, then dropped the basket and came running. Ben ran to meet her, and Billy and Eli slowed to give them their time together. They threw their arms about each other, and stood thus for a time, saying nothing, lost in the feel and the wonder.

Hannah jerked at Lydia's skirt, and Lydia broke from Ben to sweep her up. "Your father's home."

Hannah took one look at him and buried her face in Lydia's shoulder. Lydia laughed. "It's been too long. She'll remember soon."

Ben turned, eyes alive with anticipation. "Lydia, I don't know how to tell you. I've brought someone home."

Billy and Eli lowered the pole to the ground and stood waiting. Lydia looked at them, saw the tomahawk in Eli's belt, the Iroquois beadwork in his moccasins. She turned inquiring eyes to Ben.

Ben gestured. "This is Eli. Your brother."

Lydia gasped. For several moments she stared at him without moving, not daring to hope, to believe. Her forehead furrowed, and she murmured, "Eli?"

Eli had not taken his eyes from his sister since she appeared from behind the cabin. Billy took his rifle.

Eli said, "Iddi?"

In that instant Lydia saw in Eli's face the stout little two-year-old she had lost eighteen years before. She rushed to him and threw her arms about his neck and the dam burst. She sobbed, tears flooding as she held him, and Eli wrapped his arms about her and he held her close for a long time.

Hannah stood looking up at three men she could not remember or didn't know, with her mother sobbing as she clung to one of them, and suddenly her lower lip began to tremble, and then she also burst into tears. Ben reached for her, and she pushed at his hands and sat down on the ground, howling. Lydia pushed away from Eli and picked her up and suddenly began to laugh through her own tears.

"She's frightened. And here I stand, crying, and I don't know why—I'm so happy, I don't know what to do. Oh, Eli! I've waited so long." She reached to touch his face with her free hand, then suddenly pulled her brother to her again, nearly smothering Hannah between them.

After a time, she released him, and drying her eyes with her apron, said, "Goodness, where's my manners? You men are tired and thirsty. Come on to the house. I've got apple cider in the well and ham in the root cellar."

Eli gestured toward Billy, who had stood without speaking, watching the reunion. "Lydia, this is my friend Billy Weems."

Lydia put Hannah back down and reached to shake Billy's hand. "Welcome, Billy," she said, then with her arm around Eli's waist and with Ben's arm around her shoulder, they walked toward the house, Billy following, carrying the weapons.

"Is Samuel asleep?" Ben asked.

Lydia's chin dropped, and she clapped a hand over her mouth. "I forgot! He's in the back, by the garden."

They hurried around the house, where Samuel sat in the dirt. A fifteen-foot cord was tied, one end to the house, the other to the back of his overalls. His hair moved slightly in the breeze as he looked up at them, mud covering his chin. He had been eating a dirt clod.

Lydia snatched him up and instantly wiped at his chin, then thrust her little finger into his mouth, probing for stones. "This child loves dirt." Ben's eyes glowed as he reached for his son and held him close while Lydia untied the tether. Then they all walked to the back door.

Lydia cleaned up the children. Billy and Eli went back for the deer, and hung the carcass in the barn while Ben went to the well to pull up the jug of apple cider. Lydia set it on the table with half a ham, and bread and butter, and fresh tomatoes. Talk and laughter and exclamations and stories flowed. Time was forgotten.

Ben heaved a sigh. "It's getting on. I better go look at the animals." He stood, and offering to help Billy followed him out the door. Lydia sat down at the table facing Eli.

The sun was low in the western sky when Ben and Billy returned, and Ben spoke to Lydia. "You did fine. Half the grain's in, the calf's grown, and most of the pigs will be ready for winter meat. Chickens are good, most of them laying. We still have to make soap, but we can do that after harvest." He dropped his eyes for a moment. "I wish I could have brought you and the children something—a gift—but there was no time, no place to get one."

"Oh, Ben, you brought me a gift. You couldn't have done better." She looked at Eli.

The men did the evening chores. Supper was a time of unending chatter. Lydia insisted she wash the dishes alone, Ben shook his head, and while she washed, he dried, with her telling him the whole time it was woman's work. In the late evening, Ben opened the family Bible and gathered them all around the dining table. Ben turned the pages to Proverbs, chapter 31, and began to read:

"Who can find a virtuous woman? for her price is far above rubies. The heart of her husband doth safely trust in her, so that he shall have no need of spoil. She will do him good and not evil all the days of her life. She seeketh wool, and flax, and worketh willingly with her hands. . . . she bringeth her food from afar. . . . with the fruit of her hands she planteth a vineyard. . . . she reacheth forth her hands to the needy."

Lydia was still, holding Samuel while she stared quietly at the tabletop. Eli never took his eyes from his sister as he listened. In his mind, Billy was seeing the hazel eyes and the face of Brigitte. Ben read on:

"She maketh herself coverings of tapestry; . . . She openeth her mouth with wisdom; and in her tongue is the law of kindness. She looketh well to the ways of her household, and eateth not the bread of idleness. Her children arise up, and call her blessed; her husband also, and he praiseth her. . . . beauty is vain: but a woman that feareth the Lord, she shall be praised. Give her of the fruit of her hands; and let her own works praise her in the gates."

Ben quietly closed the book. For a time they sat in silence, aware that they were sharing something rare and powerful and good. Samuel moved, and Lydia kissed his hair. Ben looked at her, and when he did, Eli saw something in his eyes akin to worship. Eli glanced again, then looked away.

Ben spoke quietly. "It's late." He looked at Eli and Billy. "We have prayer at night. Would you join us?"

They knelt beside their chairs, and Ben bowed his head. "Almighty God, for thy great goodness we thank thee. For all thy blessings on this household we acknowledge thy hand . . ."

Billy and Eli took their blankets to the bedding straw inside the small barn. In the quiet darkness, Eli turned to him.

"I never dared to hope my sister could have what she's got."

Billy thought for a time. "I wish I knew why men can't spend their lives that way. Family. Home. Building something." A deep sadness crept into his voice. "How many men have you and I seen crippled and killed? Five thousand? Ten? And for what? Sometimes it seems like all they really want is what Ben and Lydia have right here. Why can't they see it?"

"I wish I knew. One thing I do know, Ben and Lydia understand what peace means, and where it comes from."

They laid back on their blankets and drifted into a weary, dreamless sleep.

The piercing crow of the bantam rooster woke them. They washed and took their places at the dining table for hot oatmeal, fried eggs, fresh white bread, honey, and buttermilk, and the men ate in reverent silence while Lydia watched them, glowing.

They finished, each of them paid their respects to Lydia, and they moved out to do the morning chores. At noon they gathered back at the cabin for the midday meal.

Billy turned to Ben and Eli. "I think I had better go on back to find General Washington. Eli, you should stay for a while. "

Eli reflected for a moment. "I think I will, if it's all right with Ben and Lydia."

Ben brightened. "Of course!"

Lydia spoke from the stove. "As long as you will."

"Winter's coming on. I can help get the rest of the grain in, and the potatoes and squash. Maybe we can finish the extra room. The trenches are dug. All we have to do is cut and notch the logs. There's pigs to get ready for winter meat. Maybe I can help with that. Earn my keep."

Ben bobbed his head. "It's settled."

With the noon meal finished, Billy rolled his blanket, gathered his bullet pouch and powder horn, shouldered his musket, and walked back to the house. They met him at the door. He shook Ben's hand.

"It's been special here with your family. I won't forget."

He turned to Lydia, and she spoke. "You'll come back, won't you? Sometime?"

"I promise I'll try."

He turned to Eli. What lay between the two men required no handshake, no embrace.

"I will see you later."

"I'll come when we finish getting ready for winter. Tell Mary if you see her."

"I will. Be careful."

"Follow the lake on south, then the Hudson."

Billy smiled. "I know. I can live in the forest."

"I know you can. Watch yourself."

Billy nodded his head once, then turned and strode across the clearing. He turned at the far end to look back, and they were there. Eli was beside Lydia, who held Samuel in her arms. Ben was on her other side, holding Hannah. For just a moment Billy stood still, memorizing the clearing, the cabin, the people.

Then he turned and walked into the splendor of the autumn forest, musket in his right hand, the sun warm on his shoulders.

Notes

Billy and Eli and Eli's sister and her husband and family are fictional.

BIBLIOGRAPHY

Earle, Alice Morse. *Home Life in Colonial Days.* Stockbridge, Mass.: Berkshire House Publishers, 1898. Republished as an American Classics edition, 1993.

Flint, Edward F. Jr. and Gwendolyn S. Flint. *Flint Family History of the Adventuresome Seven.* Baltimore: Gateway Press, Inc., 1984.

Joslin, J., B. Frisbie, and F. Rugles. *A History of the Town of Poultney, Vermont, from Its Settlement to the Year 1875.* New Hampshire: J. Joslin, B. Frisbie, and F. Ruggles, printed by the Poultney Journal Printing Office, 1979.

Graymont, Barbara. *The Iroquois.* New York: Chelsea House, 1988.

_____. *The Iroquois in the American Revolution.* Syracuse: Syracuse University Press, 1972.

Hale, Horatio. *The Iroquois Book of Rites.* New York: AMS Press, 1883. Reprinted in 1969.

Higginbotham, Don. *The War of American Independence.* Boston: Northeastern University Press, 1983.

Leckie, Robert. *George Washington's War.* New York: Harper Perennial, a division of Harper Collins, 1992.

Mackesy, Piers. *The War for America, 1775–1783.* Lincoln, Neb. and London: 1964.

Martin, Joseph Plumb, ed. George F. Scheer. *Private Yankee Doodle.* New Stratford, New Hampshire: Ayer Company Publishers, Inc., 1998.

Morgan, Lewis H. *League of the Ho-de-no-sau-nee or Iroquois,* Vol. I. New York: Dodd, Mead & Co., 1901. Reprinted by Human Relations Area Files, New Haven, Connecticut, 1954.

Parry, Jay A. and Andrew M. Allison. *The Real George Washington.* Washington, D.C.: National Center for Constitutional Studies, 1990.

Riedesel, Frederika von Riedesel, tr. Marvin L. Brown Jr. *Baroness von Riedesel and the American Revolution.* Chapel Hill: University of North Carolina Press, 1965.

Trigger, Bruce G. *Children of the Aataentsic.* Montreal: McGill-Queens University Press, 1987.

Ulrich, Laurel Thatcher. *Good Wives.* New York: Vintage Books, 1991.

Wilbur, C. Keith. *The Revolutionary Soldier, 1775–1783.* Old Saybrook, Conn.: The Globe Pequot Press, 1993.

ACKNOWLEDGMENTS

Richard B. Bernstein, Esq., noted Revolutionary War authority, continued his excellent guidance of the historical accuracy of this work, for which the writer remains most grateful. The staff of the publisher, most notably Richard Peterson, associate editor, and Richard Erickson, art director, and Jana Erickson spent many hours in the detail of preparing the manuscript, jacket, composition, and artwork. Harriette Abels, longtime consultant, mentor, and good friend, again shared her wisdom and encouragement. The author depended in large part on the monumental work of Richard M. Ketchum, *Saratoga*, for much of the detail in this volume. Mr. Ketchum has blessed this country greatly with his outstanding research and his writing about our beginnings.

Without question, the most powerful contributors to this work are those heroes of so long ago, whose spirit continues to reach across time to touch the words as they take shape on the page. The author knows he is but the scribe.